IN SIEGE OF DAYLIGHT

BOOK ONE IN THE COMPENDIUM OF LIGHT, DARK & SHADOW

GREGORY S. CLOSE

In Siege of Daylight is a work of fiction. Names, characters, places and incidents either are the product of the author's imagination or are used fictitiously. Any resemblance to actual persons, living or dead, events, locales or rituals of sorcerous destruction is entirely coincidental.

❋

Copyright © 2013 Gregory S. Close
Cover design, art and logo copyright © 2012 Mike Nash
Editor: Thomas Weaver
First publication: April 2013
First edition

❋

All rights reserved, including the right to reproduce this book, or portions thereof, in any form.
IN SIEGE of DAYLIGHT

ISBN: 0988852012
ISBN-13: 978-0-9888520-1-3

Library of Congress Control Number: 2013903439
Gregory S Close, San Carlos, CA

❋

Gregory S. Close

www.lightdarkandshadow.com

@gsclose

Mike Nash

www.mike-nash.com

@MikeNash

Thomas Weaver

www.northofandover.wordpress.com

@Weaver2392

In Memory of Maxwell L. Close
My Obi-Wan,
My Gandalf,
My Friend and My Father.
1941 – 1997

Prelude

The old man navigated the maze of tables in small, practiced steps. His arms were pressed close to his sides, hands clasped before him, avoiding the precarious array of hand-blown glass vessels that he'd spent his lifetime arranging. He passed them without a glance, ignoring the bubbling multicolored contents, his watery blue eyes focused on the small open window at the other end of the room. The pale, pure light of Illuné shone in through the weathered stone opening, while the Dead Moon, Ghaest, secreted itself in her flowing cloak of clouds. He stepped into the moonlight, the brisk breath of winter on his face, and looked down from his high tower toward the frost-dusted ground below.

They were there, just as he'd seen in his vision, gathering about his door with broadswords and short curved bows. Their eyes burned yellow in the night, their breath hot wisps of steam between sharpened teeth and narrow lips.

Dirty beasts, the hrumm, he thought. *Brutish creatures.*

It had been decades since he'd seen their kind at his doorstep. But the old man's eyes passed over them without interest or fear. They could not harm him in any way that mattered. The Pale Man was with them, at the front, his dark cloak snapping in the wind and the ashen blade of his vile sword bare and hungry in his hand. As it was in the dream, so the Pale Man spoke.

"Gai! Open the door. You know why we come."

The lines of the wizened face in the window wrinkled into a grimace. Gai knew the sword-bearer from a time long past and a life already lived and buried. Esmaedi Elidiaeol. Exile. Oath-breaker. And a wizard of the Tenth Order, at the very least – even without the bonesword.

Gaious Altuorus was not short on titles and honors himself, though such accolades lay under the grave dirt of his previous life. Still, he had seen worse in his day.

"Open it thyself, Esmaedi," he growled. "Or have your pets beat it down for you."

The pallid face of the man at the door looked up toward Gai. The smile crossing his delicate features almost concealed the intent in his almond-shaped eyes. "Ah, there you are." The voice was measured and polite, if a bit dismissive. "*You* locked in a tower, and me beating down the door? How times change, Gaious."

"How indeed," answered Gai. "Once, you warred with legions under your care, Esmaedi. Now, you hold the leashes of filthy animals, and are but held on a leash yourself."

The Pale Man laughed. It was nothing more than a conversational chuckle, as if two friends were bantering to and fro over morning sweetmeats. "I am called *Dieavaul* now – Esmaedi is as dead as the Empire we served. There is such power in a name, don't you think, Gaious? Or is it simply Gai…" His voice lilted over the words playfully. "No matter. I hold a new leash, over new filthy beasts, but I see little difference. One must have means to one's ends, yes?"

"If you mean to have my end, I welcome it. Don't think fear of death will serve you here."

Dieavaul shrugged. "You have made your life irrelevant, Gai. I seek your end no more than I would seek that of a toothless old lion hiding in the back of his cave. Spare your life, if you wish, or forsake your oath and make your grand last stand. Either way, I tire of this discourse. Open the door." The Pale Man gestured, and without pause, his hrummish soldiers hefted a felled pine trunk and heaved it on their shoulders. "I've not built a reputation as a patient man."

"Indeed," responded Gai, "and I'm not known as an accommodating man. If you are intent on murdering me, I will not help the dagger along on its course. Good night."

With that, Gai slammed the shutters on the night and his unwanted guests. He turned and sighed, placing a trembling hand to his chest to alleviate the dreadful weight gathering there. He stumbled to his highbacked oaken chair and sat down on the threadbare cushion even as the relentless pounding began below. Agrylon had strengthened the timbers with a Word of Binding when last he visited, but it would not delay their entrance long.

Gai had not recognized the Pale Man's current incarnation in his dream, when first it came upon him. But in the flesh, those mocking black eyes stared up at him and sparked his memory. Once, he had known Esmaedi as a War Mage of the Third Legion, apprentice to the Archmage Dmylriani herself, and High Blade of the Lymiruia. Even then Dieavaul had been a man of great power. But it was not the man that worried Gaious.

No, it was the sword – *ilnymhorrim*. A weapon of legend, few even believed it existed outside the metered verse of the *Song of Andulin*.

Osrith had believed, he remembered. The recently departed mercenary's own experience with the Pale Man attested that the Hellforged had chosen well for its dark purposes.

Prelude

And now it had come for him.

What saddened Gai most was leaving his work. He had come so far in his research at this secluded retreat, it was a shame it might all soon be in ashes. The trespassers entered below with a splintering crash, followed soon after by dreadful screams.

Gai frowned. He'd told Osrith not to delay himself by setting any traps before he left. Valuable time had been wasted.

Gai closed his eyes, muttering a soft incantation. He whimpered as his *iiyir* coalesced at his command; he gathered and channeled it only to turn it back inward, against itself. His life energy was reluctant to facilitate such a self-destructive act, but his iron will forced it to obey.

I won't die by that blade, he resolved, and not for the first time. He couldn't risk revealing his knowledge to the likes of the Pale Man or the Undying King he served. Gai found it ironic that the first offensive spell he'd cast since burning his Black Robes and coming to the mountains, he cast against himself.

Gai's heart slowed.

He wondered if killing himself actually violated the oath he had taken that day, as the flames consumed his raiment of death. *Does violence against oneself to save others fall under the mien of offense or defense?* He supposed once he was in the greylands, he might have time to contemplate that. In his stead, Agrylon would likely blast the lot to flinders with angry magic, devoid of any such philosophical worry. Gai himself might once have done so, before forsaking the ways of war. He had certainly seen, and dealt, enough death and devastation in his lifetime.

But the Pale Man would not fall so easily. Esmaedi would not prove easy prey even without *ilnymhorrim*. With it, depending on how much myth and legend had exaggerated its powers, Esmaedi might be more than a match for both him and Agrylon.

Gai's breath grew shallow.

He drew some small comfort from the fact that Osrith and the dreamstone were already away. He had done what he could to warn them. If there was anything to be done about the evil across the mountains, it would be for Guillaume and Agrylon to determine.

Gai convulsed quietly.

It wasn't painful. He had removed all feeling of pain with Saint Aerylan's Wort in his morning tea, but his body still fought for life despite its own best interest, struggling against the increasing stranglehold his own powerful *iiyir* had clamped onto his feeble physical self.

He wheezed one last time, and then his lungs succumbed to his deadly magic and were still.

There was a commotion from the hallway beyond his chamber, then a gurgled scream and crash of bodies down the long spiral stair, accented by angry cursing. Gai's lips curled slightly as the gentle light in his eyes grew dim. With the last issue of sound from his throat, his heart's tired beating stopped, and he felt his body drifting away.

His last thoughts were of his messenger.

Osrith. It's all in his hands now...

Chapter One

Mylyr Gaeal

GREY. It swallowed the world in its uncompromising maw, reaching down from the sullen skies to the snow-blanketed hills below with no concern for what lay in between. Not long ago the snow had been brilliant and white, a mantle of purest silver aglisten in the crisp awareness of day. Now, in the soft but unyielding grip of twilight, only grey.

The slopes of the Crehr ne Og were gentle here, the dwindling swells of a great undulation of limestone and weathered marble that lapped at the shores of the grassy plains leagues below. Trees, naked of leaf in the seasonal chill, huddled in scattered thickets, growing denser and less passable the further into the highlands they reached. Small rivulets of water ran recklessly through narrow gullies, feeding into the crashing roar of the Vlue Moignan as the mighty river continued its own long journey to the crystal blue waters of the Ceil Maer.

A ruined castle clung to a ragged promontory of bare stone, splitting the edges of the wilds. The aged foundations of the fortress clawed for purchase on the sheer weathered rock even as nature worked to strip its tenuous grip away. The dark hand-cut stone melted into the natural substance of the earth, each year more memory than testament to the dead hands that wrought it.

Within the remains of the keep, smoke drifted into the sky from a low sputtering fire nestled in the half-shelter of a buckled archway where two figures bent over a game board. For but a moment, the light of the great moon Illuné shot down through the clouds, her pale lance finding a chink in the armor of the storm, and in that heartbeat their ghostly shadows danced on the granite walls of the empty fortress before vanishing again into the advancing night.

Calvraign looked upon the somber landscape, lost in thought. Brohan often brought him to these ruins for the impromptu lessons that comprised his education. The displaced stones of the castle lay scattered about them, their glory long since surrendered to time and nature in all but legend. As a boy, Calvraign had eagerly awaited the long trip into the foothills. Then it had been an enchanted playground, a place where he did battle with honorless barbarians, matched wits with andu'ai and dragons and vanquished the unliving minions of Ewanbheir. Now, it was a study in history, warfare and politics. Those innocent games of his childhood seemed so far away now, buried by the layers of knowledge and experience that commonly smothered youth.

Brohan still watched him, his sparkling green eyes hinting silent laughter. Not the mocking laughter all too common for those with his intellect and bearing, but rather a reflection of genuine mirth. His face was beautiful, skin smooth and black, body slender but strong. He had the long manicured fingers of a bard, as agile in the art of his instruments as in the weaving of his minor magics. He was dressed modestly in green and tan leathers, his winter cape pulled around his shoulders and the hood over his long, silken dark hair. It was rumored that his mother, a princess from one of the far lands to the west, had enjoyed a tryst with an aulden that left her Brohan as the unwelcome result. He had never asked Brohan if the rumors were true, but he suspected that the answer would only be his laugh of liquid silver in any case.

Calvraign turned his thoughts back to the dark expanse of snow, ice and rock wherein he sat. *Bad enough to gossip,* he thought, *but gossiping to myself?* He cleared his mind with a shake of his head, struggling to remember what consternation had led to his distracted musings. One glance at the circular, five-tiered game board reminded him of his dilemma.

Mylyr Gaeal was a game of kings and scholars. On its five translucent tiers were stylized monarchs, faerie, knights and other beasts of fact and legend, arrayed for battle. Though most versions of *Mylyr Gaeal* were based upon the Blood Wars, pitting the fae and their allies against the slaoithe, Brohan often spoke of other, more exotic boards on which the game could be played, with alternate rules and pieces. He had promised that if Calvraign ever defeated him in the standard version that they would move next to the *scylithwr* board, which reenacted the ancient conflict of the giants, when the Duath Andai and the Neva Seough battled across the lands of Wyn, in the Time of Mists. For a good year now he had been losing to Brohan, though the last few games had brought him a small amount of grace in defeat. He was, even now, searching for that elusive bit of grace, but very little seemed evident.

"Feeling sorry for yourself shall do little for victory, lad. A less forgiving opponent would already have claimed forfeit for your delay."

Calvraign frowned at Brohan in response. "Ach, be still! I'll be about it in a moment."

"Temper, Cal," chided Brohan. "*Mylyr Gaeal* is a game for civilized opponents. You must temper your anger with a sense of style and a sharp wit. By snapping at me, you have lost face. Had this game been played in the venue of the king's court, even if somehow you managed a victory, you would have lost the respect of your peers."

"And how *should* I respond if so insulted?" challenged Calvraign defiantly.

"Well, since you beg the answer...." Brohan tapped a slender finger against his cheek. "Ah! Perhaps this: *Please excuse my delay, sir, but you have left me so many options that I find myself distracted.* Or maybe this: *a thousand apologies, milord, but it seems your strategy, much like your company, has lulled me into a pleasant stupor.* Better still –"

"No need, Brohan. You've driven your wit home. I mustn't forget the game within the game, if I take your meaning."

"Indeed. The sharper and more damaging the wit, the more entertainment the game provides the audience, many of whom are little interested in the strategy of the game itself. There is no insult too great for your opponent, so long as it is delivered during the game and with a smile. "Well," he reconsidered, "assuming you are not playing too far above your station. Then it might be best to hold back your most poisonous barbs."

"After these many years, why tell me this *now*?" asked Calvraign. "We're in the midst of the game, not my lecture."

"Why indeed?"

Calvraign stared blankly at Brohan for a moment, then at the board. There must be something there that he had missed. Brohan had taught him a twofold lesson. Not only the art of insulting his opponent under the veil of grace, but perhaps the more relevant art of distraction as well. The threat must be real, if not obvious.

Then he saw it. Amidst the chaotic clutter of the middle board, *Rahn*, Brohan's reaver threatened Calvraign's unicorn. He could ill afford to lose the unicorn at this stage of the game. Only this piece, bearing the legendary magic of the horn, could fell the slaoithe lord with one fatal attack. It must be protected at all costs.

He examined and re-examined his avenues of attack and defense on the checkered battlefield and then made his move. He grabbed the ivory figure of a running archer, his *wilhorwhyr*, and challenged the ebony hrummish shaman that occupied the defensive position he sought. The dice roll was but a formality. Calvraign's *wilhorwhyr* had the advantage, attacking from a green-tinted forest square, and moments later, Brohan's piece was his and the unicorn was under the protective watch of its real-life woodland ally.

"Well played, lad," praised Brohan. "We shall see if you can sustain your advantage."

"I have confidence you shall sustain your disadvantage without much help from me," Calvraign said smoothly, his crystal blue eyes shining with the taste of victory.

Brohan laughed and tipped an imaginary hat. "Touché, sir! You learn quickly enough!" He moved a hrummish hunter threateningly close to the *wilhorwhyr*, but held his distance. "Unfortunately for you, I already know what I'm doing."

Without so much as blinking, Calvraign sprang his trap, moving his lord high marshal from the back of his ranks to the nexus in the center of the tier. The color of the tier changed immediately from its neutral hue to a soft white luminescence, signaling that Light claimed this tier and thus the advantage on subsequent challenges.

"I sincerely hope I haven't inconvenienced your strategy, sir." Calvraign sat back with a smile, leaning against the remnants of a weather-eaten wall behind him.

"Not at all, young lad. If you'll notice, your *wilhorwhyr* is but a dice throw away from being paralyzed by my shadowyn. Roll."

Calvraign's smugness evaporated in an instant. He shot upright and bent over the board, looking in amazement at the pieces below him. By moving his lord high marshal, he had exposed a square on the lower tier of Shadow from which the shadowyn could launch its spell. The paralysis would last only three Turns, but this could mean disaster for Calvraign's strategy. He picked up his carved bone dice and rolled them between his palms. He still had a chance to resist the effects of the creature's foul magic.

"A pity," said Brohan as the dice settled to seal the *wilhorwhyr*'s fate. "He shall be no help to you now. And you were doing so well."

Calvraign refrained from cursing at the top of his lungs. His unicorn was once again at the mercy of Brohan's menacing reaver. He could stave off the attack, if he was lucky, but would almost certainly be left weakened and vulnerable. With a sigh, Calvraign made his decision. He must go on the offensive and use his control of the nexus to his advantage. If he was successful, the unicorn and the *wilhorwhyr* might both survive. If he was not, he concluded that the situation couldn't get much worse anyway.

"Unicorn challenges reaver," stated Calvraign formally, moving the rampant equine figurine within the shadow of Brohan's twisted ebony piece.

"You are taking a grave risk, Cal. Care to reconsider?"

"Don't insult me, Brohan. You'd not afford such luxury to any serious opponent. Roll the bones." Cal was oblivious to the falling snow, the whipping winds, even the bitter winter cold that moments ago had been stinging his extremities. All he saw were the game board, the pieces, and the dice as they tumbled recklessly from Brohan's hands, carrying the balance of his young pride with their result.

"A draw," said Brohan, almost masking his surprise. "Your gambit has not spelled disaster yet."

"Blood and ruin!" spat Calvraign, his rage written on his reddened face.

Brohan fixed his pupil with a disapproving stare. "You cannot expect to win every gamble, Cal. With every victory comes sacrifice. You did quite well, considering the odds were stacked against you. Of all pieces, the reaver poses the greatest risk to the unicorn. Even *with* the nexus, you had but a small chance to survive, and that you have done."

Calvraign shook his head slowly, slumping against the old wall in defeat. "Little good that does me! My unicorn's but a meal for your beasts, now. The game is yours, Brohan, lest Oghran Herself comes to blow on my dice. Though She's done precious little for me thus far."

Brohan laughed and reached over to pat Cal's arm. "Putting one's faith in Lady Luck will do little for winning a game of strategy, lad. She is a fickle Mistress, indeed. How many great generals carried Her banners into battle before them? Symbus? Celian? Saint Kaissus? Not a one, my boy, not a one. Look to Irdik for tactics, Illuné for honor, even Kazdann for might, but look to Oghran for naught you truly need, only what you might like to have. Now, are you conceding defeat so early, or shall we continue?"

"Ah yes, the proverbial *wisdom, honor and valor* of the Three Swords," sighed Calvraign with a rueful shake of his head. "I appear to be short a blade or two, then. Proceed with the slaughter."

"You disappoint me, lad. Do you give in to defeat so readily that you find no insight in the process? Look to the legends you love so dearly and count the times that victory was snatched away from the careless by brave hearts and keen minds. Might you not do the same?"

"You argue as if the whole of Providayne were being overrun by Shadow, and I was the lone flame to dispel it. And, at any rate, I'm no Andulin to do the deed."

"True enough, but nor am I a dark god for you to vanquish. Take hold of what you have and fight with it. Don't dwell on the prices you've already paid. Concentrate on the task at hand."

Calvraign threw his hands in the air, grinning despite himself. "Enough of your lecture, Brohan. Move before we freeze here and join the spectacle of these ruins."

"As you wish. I was simply trying to bolster your spirits so you could more adequately deal with *this*." Brohan challenged the unicorn, and a tick later his dice claimed the piece as his. "Remember, focus on what you still have, not on what you've lost."

"You are joking, of course," mumbled Calvraign.

"Please don't start complaining again," pleaded Brohan. "You'll distract me from rubbing your nose in my victory."

Calvraign tightened his jaws. Perhaps Brohan was right. Even if a quick, glorious victory was now out of the question, he could still make victory for his opponent a difficult and costly one. With that determination firmly in mind, he settled down for a long, hard fight.

⁓

The midwinter snows outside the small village of Craignuuwn had not yet reached Calvraign's waist, but at the rate the large fluffy flakes were falling now, he knew that by morning they certainly would. The shepherds were finishing with their work, securing the livestock within the town pen and stirring the glowing embers of the fire pits. Only the longhaired sheep were left to fend for themselves in the growing cold of night. Their fleece was thick enough to dispel all but the deadliest chill, and their tendency to bleat alarm at the sight or smell of anything unfamiliar made them ideal animals to stand watch. Several of the Cythe tribes relied on the sheep as their first line of defense, much to the amusement of their former allies and conquerors alike. Despite its proven effectiveness, the thought of the highland sheep playing any tactical role in the high art of defense or warfare did not fit into the strict rules of honorable combat that the aristocracy held so dear.

According to Brohan, the people of Providayne, and especially the noble houses, still regarded the Cythe and other tribes in the Crehr ne Og to be little more than half-tamed barbarians. Their ways and their culture, as ancient and proud as they were, still held no place for respect outside these rugged hills.

Of course, that didn't stop the king's army from gathering soldiers from Cythe villages. Calvraign's father Ibhraign had been one of those recruits. He had fought and died in the War of Thorns when Calvraign was still learning to string words together. He had died proud, a hero in the eyes of both his fellow Cythe and his Providaynian lords, giving his life to save King Guillaume in battle. His reward had been a royal pension for his widow and her son, including Brohan's tutelage, which Calvraign knew was no paltry sum. Yet still his father was a barbarian, as was he, as were his people: not worthy of land or title, only blood money. These thoughts gnawed at his heart as he waded through the snow toward the center of town and his mother's modest house.

"I can smell that mutton from here!" exclaimed Brohan, breaking the silence that had descended with the setting suns. "We may use the path now. My hunger trumps your training tonight."

Calvraign found it interesting that Brohan chose the word *we*, since the bard had been on the path the entire journey. For whatever reason, trudging through the snow had suddenly assumed paramount importance as a part of the increasingly broad description of things that Brohan called Calvraign's *training*. Training for what, he wasn't exactly sure. Whatever the end goal, the sensation of his legs falling stiff and frozen from his body apparently led to it somehow.

Calvraign didn't want to give Brohan the satisfaction of seeing him give up now. "I've come this far, I'll go twelve steps further. You go on ahead and warn my mother that you've crippled me," he said with a wry smile.

"As you wish, lad. She'll be happy as naught to cuff me for having you out so long in this weather, anyhow."

Calvraign watched as Brohan trotted ahead toward the squat stone cottage and entered its warmth with a swift knock of warning. His mother's cries of outrage and worry were cut off along with Brohan's laughter as the thick door shut behind him. His mother would be busy chastising Brohan for a bit yet, so Calvraign made little haste to follow. As engrossing as his sessions with the famous bard were, Cal often as not found himself unusually drained by them. Brohan taxed every whit of his being, from his mind to his heart to his soul, tiring each in their fashion, and after dinner there would be more lessons still. There was nothing he loved more, really, than hearing Brohan tell the histories of Rahn and its people. But the sheer volumes of knowledge that Brohan imparted were so vast that he found it rather intimidating.

What was he to do with such knowledge, after all? He could join the king's army in the south to fight the Maccs, and perhaps die as his father had. He could become a bard, like Brohan, and wander the forgotten kingdoms and wilderness of the west, seeing sights that most preferred to leave safe in the yellowed parchment of their lore books. But he was not yet ready for such adventures, said Brohan, and doubtless his mother would agree. In fact, it was not likely that she would *ever* agree. No amount of argument had gained her assent for tutelage in fencing. Even now she refused to allow it. Only through begging and subterfuge had he managed to convince Brohan to secretly teach him. With some pride he remembered Brohan's praise for his ability with a blade.

Without warning, the pride and wind were both knocked out of Calvraign as he was tackled from behind. He landed in the snow with a wet thud, gasping for breath and wincing in pain, a bony arm planted at the base of his neck.

"Well met, Lord Askewneheur," said a soft, lilting voice in his ear. "'Tis a fine night for a walk. Care for company?"

Calvraign recognized the voice instantly and attempted to right himself. He met with little initial resistance, but made no more progress than to rest on his back rather than his face. His reddened, tired eyes looked up into the dark chestnut eyes of Callagh Breigh, her short brown hair tangled in front of her flushed face. He could feel the warmth of her breath, and her lean body pressed against him, holding him down with apparent ease. They had been friends and sparring partners as long as he could recall; but as she assumed some of the more prominent characteristics of womanhood, he found this physical aspect of their relationship awkward, at best. She was only recently sixteen years of age, almost two years his junior, and he wasn't entirely sure what or how he should feel about her now. Unfortunately, she suffered from no such confusion.

"Callagh, please, I'm very tired, and mother's waiting."

"Let her wait, then!" she quipped, moving her lips close to his, her eyes half closing in anticipation.

In a panic Calvraign found his strength and rolled away from her, gaining his feet a moment later. "Callagh! You bold girl, what are you doing?"

"Ach, Cal, if ye dunna know… ," she teased.

He did know, of course. But he had no desire *talk* about it. He was much too confused by this change in her to respond in any sort of intelligent fashion. He only knew his instinctual reaction, which was to run away from the moment and then dwell on it later. He was a little old to feel so awkward around the fairer sex, a fact that he was all too aware of but powerless to change. Perhaps he spent too much of his time practicing with his gwythir, or reading Brohan's precious books, or fencing with sticks out in the hills while he watched his family's flock. Regardless, he little wanted to explore the reasons or their ramifications right at this moment, despite the girl who'd rather literally pressed the matter on top of him.

"'Tis a bit late for a snow frolic," he said, brushing the wet snow from his tunic and trying to make his expression as reproachful as his words. "You'd best get yourself home. What if your father comes back and you're not there? You don't want a beating, do you?"

Callagh sat up and shrugged, her legs crossed in the snow in front of her. She wore huntsman's leathers, lined with fox and rabbit fur, and didn't appear even mildly concerned by the cold. "Da's already home," she said, tracing a line in the snow with her index finger. "He never goes hunting on Lorday, you know that. He's all full of piss and drink by now anyway."

"Aye," Calvraign said, the sternness of his tone dissolving into a sort of resigned understanding. Callagh's mother had died three years ago when the pox had struck Craignuuwn. Her father hadn't taken her death well, to say the least. He was still the most accomplished and valuable huntsman in the village, but Ewbhan Breigh was a powerful man and an angry drunk. Callagh had suffered the brunt of his temper on more than one occasion. He often wondered at the whim of fate that allowed a man like Ewbhan to live on while those like his father and her mother met such untimely ends. He offered her his hand. "C'mon, you can stay here again tonight."

Callagh accepted his hand and pulled herself to her feet. "I'll bring ye a hare tomorrow," she promised.

"Calvraign! Get your wee *óinse* in here straight away!" Oona Askewneheur yelled from the doorway of the cottage. "You'll freeze to th' bones, you will!"

Calvraign made haste toward the open door, relieved by his mother's stern command. He would rather face his mother's rage than fend off Callagh's advances or face his inability to protect her from Ewbhan's ire. Oona knew better how to talk to Callagh about these matters, anyway.

"Callagh, is that you, girl?" his mother yelled again. "Ye best be in too, lass – there's plenty to go 'round!"

Calvraign stopped in the doorway and gave his mother a quick appreciative smile. He took a moment to kiss her on the cheek and then proceeded down the short flight of steps into the cottage, followed shortly thereafter by Callagh.

There was only one room in the modest home. The stone walls were bare save for a multitude of wooden pegs and the implements that hung from them. There was one chair with an oft-mended leg, pushed under the chipped table Calvraign used to mend it. The straw sleeping pallets and the woolen bedclothes were off to one side, stacked neatly and out of the way. The three family dogs, longhaired highland wolfhounds with lean frames and long legs, were curled in a bunch on their own pallet, staring wistfully at the iron pot of mutton they would be lucky to taste. They charged Calvraign happily as he entered, and then Callagh behind him. Brohan sat by the fire, his cloak and boots shed, his grin widening as he winked at Cal.

After appeasing the hounds, Calvraign removed his own outer garments and spread them out on the flat drying rock near the fire pit in the center of the great room. Aromatic smoke drifted lazily from the flames and lingered by the thatched roof, eventually finding its way outside through the vents built into the uppermost outside edge of the stone walls. It was quite warm inside. Half of the structure was buried underground for insulation, trapping the heat in winter but retaining a pleasant coolness in summer. It was sturdy and functional, even comfortable in its own fashion.

Calvraign sat by the fire next to Brohan, spreading his fingers out to absorb its warmth, and watched as his mother ladled large portions of mutton stew into worn walnut bowls. She served Brohan first, then Callagh, and finally Calvraign. He wondered how long she had waited before eating, herself. The evening was lengthening toward the silent bell of highmoons, long past the gloaming bell when Brohan promised they would return. Brohan sometimes spoke of time in *ticks*, *clicks* or *hours*, but there was no Imperial clock-tower in Craignuuwn to count it, and no dignitaries rushing to and fro on king's business to care. The sheep seemed content with bells. Regardless, he could see his mother was not happy with the bard by the frown on her generally pleasant face.

"When the Hand of Death comes for my soul, Oona, I most certainly hope something this delicious awaits me in the greylands," Brohan said smoothly, the warming tone of his voice already thawing his mother's disposition.

"You are a *devil*, Brohan Madrharigal!" she exclaimed as if only now discovering some new facet of his personality. She stroked her callused hands through her blonde hair, its once beautiful strands now greying and losing their luster. Her puffy red cheeks lifted up toward the corner of her eyes in a bashful smile. "How is Cal coming along with your game, then?"

"Quite well, Oona," Brohan responded, returning her smile. "He comes closer to besting me every time. Almost a draw today."

"Aye, but he hasn't no patience," said Callagh in an offhand tone, and then, as if just realizing she had spoken aloud, turned to her untouched stew.

Brohan and Calvraign both started in their seats, turning in surprise to the young girl. Brohan spoke first. "How do you mean, lass?" he asked.

Callagh looked sidelong at Brohan, carefully avoiding meeting anyone's eyes directly. "Well, he moved his unicorn into danger when he needn't."

"What would you know of it?" blurted Cal, slamming his wooden dish down next to him. " I –"

Brohan held up a hand, motioning Calvraign to be silent. "How much of the game did you see?"

Callagh continued scrutinizing her meal. "All of it. I followed you this morning."

"Really?" whispered the bard, smiling at the girl. "Was this the first time?"

"No," she admitted, "almost since the beginning. I've always loved the stories you told, and then when you started playing the game, that was even better. I was going to tell you, but then I thought you mightn't want me to come along, and I certainly didna' want that to happen." She looked up from her bowl, then, and her face was defiant. "And why *shouldn't* I come? I'm just as clever as Cal, and I've never so much as disturbed you. Why is it always –"

Brohan laughed away her burgeoning indignation. "Easy lass, I'm not *upset* with you. I'm quite honestly amazed. You've been following us for years, then?"

"Aye."

"You've no right!" cried Calvraign. He was being selfish, and he knew it, but he didn't care. Brohan's teachings were a gift for him, paid in full by the blood of his father. It didn't seem right that she had made a place for herself in what was rightfully his. "You can't just..."

Brohan held up his silencing hand once more. "Be still, young Askewneheur. There's no harm done, save perhaps to your pride – and *mine*, I shouldn't wonder. Anyone who can sneak up on me deserves whatever knowledge they can get away with. It certainly doesn't diminish the quality of your learning that someone else has benefited from it."

Callagh relaxed and sent a triumphant grin in Calvraign's direction. He did his best to ignore her completely, shifting all of his attention to consuming his meal. He tried not to notice the amused glances exchanged by Oona and Brohan.

Calvraign bent over his bowl, enjoying the treat of fresh mutton that Brohan's visit had brought for him. His mother always did whatever she could to make his stay comfortable in their plain surroundings. The master bard seemed strangely at home here for a man who had supped with kings and nobles from Mazod to Tiriel. Calvraign risked a quick glance up at his tutor and immediately regretted it. Brohan acknowledged him with a grin and turned once more to Callagh Breigh.

"What would you have done, Callagh? Did you see a different tack?"

The girl first confronted Calvraign's hard stare until he looked away and then met Brohan's friendly green eyes with a small flush of ruby in her cheeks. "I wouldn't take the nexus so quickly," she started tentatively, but with a gentle nod from the bard, she continued with more confidence. "Calvraign's gryphon knight could've protected the unicorn from above, then his marshal could move close enough to threaten the nexus. Then Master Brohan would have moved in to protect the nexus and the *wilhorwhyr* could challenge the reaver. That way, even if the *wilhorwhyr* lost, the lord high marshal could still take the reaver, or the nexus, or maybe both?"

"The whole point of taking the nexus was surprise," said Calvraign, shaking his head and wondering how she'd remembered so much of the game in detail. He attempted to mask his amazement with irritation. "You have to take the advantage while you have it."

Callagh snickered and brushed the hair out of her eyes with a finger. "Surprise is only good if you can win, Cal," she taunted playfully.

Calvraign's jaw clenched. He felt his mother pat him on the shoulder, in part to comfort him, in part to warn him away from anger. This was only a game to Callagh, another diversion to pass her day. But it was his pride and skill that she mocked, though innocently, and he only swallowed his hot rage with an effort.

"That's interesting, Callagh," mused Brohan, "but how are you so certain that I would scamper to the nexus so quickly?"

"I can't say." She shrugged. "I've watched you both play so much I just *knew* you would. Ach, I'm prob'ly wrong."

"No, dear girl, you are quite perceptive. Sometimes a quiet observer can see more than those absorbed in the game. Perhaps Cal and I have both learned our lesson for today. Tomorrow," he paused, pointing at each of them in turn with his wooden spoon, "we'll see how well you play against each other."

Callagh's face burst into a broad smile. "I would like that!"

"But only, of course, if Calvraign is willing to accept the challenge."

Cal looked up, his ego still injured but his temper subdued. It was next to impossible for him to remain angry with his friend when she smiled that way. At least this was a chance for vindication. "Tomorrow it is, then," he agreed.

"Good," said Brohan. "Then let's clean up this mess for your mother and finish your history lesson before I fall asleep sitting up."

Chapter Two

The Messenger

OSRITH Turlun crouched close to the small mound of warm, smokeless embers, his aging muscles sending a dull, throbbing ache throughout his body. His breath lingered about his lips in a wispy cloud, reluctant to leave the warmth of his body, but eventually drifting over his shoulder into the night sky. The frigid mountain air had begun to penetrate his fur-lined garments. It crept in slowly, stealthily, as persistent as Death Herself, until its chill seeped into his very bones and nibbled at his soul. Once there, it would stay; stay until he could set himself before a blazing hearth inside the thick stone walls of Castle Vae, a cup of mulled wine cradled in his hands and a basin of steaming water to soothe his tired feet.

So vivid and appealing was the thought, Osrith nearly drifted from the nightmare that surrounded him. Away from the makeshift camp, away from the biting wind and the snow-darkened sky, away from Dieavaul, away most of all from the accursed rock that hung like an anvil in the pouch around his neck. Its very weight dragged him from his respite, forcing his thoughts back into the unwelcome fetters of reality.

He reached for it absently, his right hand fondling the soft leather pouch. The stone was but a thumb's width across, perfectly smooth and unblemished. The words of Gai came un-summoned to his mind. *"Speak naught. Tarry naught. Speed this to the king and surrender it to none but he! The eyes of darkness are upon you even now. Make haste!"*

"Eyes of darkness," mumbled Osrith through his numb lips, "seers and bards – all the same breed."

And now, sixty leagues later, here he sat – the stone still safe, but his body worn by fatigue and his destination still half a day before him. His tired brown eyes watered at a fresh and vigorous onslaught of wind, the tears freezing into his beard. Indeed, his resolve might have faltered already were it not for the sealed parchment buried safely in his bundle. The writ guaranteed him a handsome payment for his troubles. More than handsome – princely. Yes, that was indeed worth the bother of a few days' hard travel. That, and a memory.

A screeching howl echoed off the granite walls around Osrith. He lurched into motion, instinct driving him before conscious thought. The bestial cry rang with the urgency of a predator closing on its kill, and Osrith had no illusions regarding who was the prey.

Damn nightwolves, he thought, sliding more than running down the steep, rocky slope of the mountain. The fir trees towering above him were heavy with snow, and the *wilhorwhyr* path beneath his feet icy and treacherous. The air pounded into his lungs, cold enough to strike like a solid block in his chest with every breath.

He guessed that the war party following him was composed mostly of dringli. They were numerous in this part of the Ridge and it was their custom to hunt with nightwolves. They would make fast and expendable scouts for the Hrummish Host. And leading *them*, of course, would be Dieavaul. In a dark corner of his mind, Osrith could still see the merciless coal-black eyes shining against the assassin's porcelain skin, mocking him even as they delighted in the blood on that cursed sword. It had been many years, but the image of his failure was etched with the acid of guilt on his memory. He could only assume that Gai also lay slain and rotting by the hand of his nemesis, and knew well what his own fate would be if they overtook him.

At the base of the slope was Ingar's Way, a wide commercial road that ran between Ten Man Pass and Castle Vae. He was closer than he thought. Undoubtedly there was another hrumm or dringli contingent closing in on him from the direction of the pass, and Dieavaul would try to cut him off further up the road. The highway promised safety if he happened upon a squad of the Border Knights, but it would be pure folly to count on such an unlikely bit of providence.

Without further thought, he plunged into the trees on the far side of the road. He had lost the *wilhorwhyr* trail that had taken him the last few leagues, but considered himself lucky enough to have stumbled upon it for any length at all. Legend had it that Nighthawk himself blazed the paths through the wilderness for the benefit of his disciples. But Osrith held little stock in legend. Legends were good for campfires, not so good for marking and maintaining hidden trails.

The howl assailed the silence of night once more, louder and closer than before. They would be upon him soon. His keen ears discerned the cries of several scouts and the snort of a nightwolf. He pushed himself forward with renewed vigor. He didn't fear the dringli. They were dangerous enough to the inexperienced, or in waves of hundreds sweeping across the field of battle, but to a seasoned warrior such as himself, a dringli out of its lair was little cause for worry. If he tarried to deal with the scouts, however, it would be a short time before his neck was within range of Dieavaul's damned blade.

Osrith soon found himself at the icy bank of the River Daemeyr. The nearest bridge was more than half a league upstream, where the highway met the river. He didn't have the time to reach it. He extended his foot over the Daemeyr's silvery surface and tapped the ice. It was solid enough to the touch, but Osrith knew full well that this was merely the wintry river's tempting deceit.

It might hold his weight; it might not.

He delayed only a moment before edging out onto the river's surface, flat on his stomach to spread out his weight, using his hands to propel him to the middle of the frozen waterway. He spun around to face the shore he had just left and removed his great axe from its traveling harness on his pack. The axe was a heavy instrument, made of sturdy blackthorn oak and cold-smelted kinsteel. The haft was just more than three feet in length, the dark blade's cutting edge slightly less than a foot. It was at home in the winter night, grey and cold as its surroundings.

Osrith turned the axe in his hands and drove the haft cap of the mighty weapon into the ice. He used great care not to crack the ice through and through, using only enough force to fracture the surface in thin silvery spider webs. When he felt the ice sufficiently weakened, he made his way slowly to the opposite bank, cracking the ice as he slid backward across the captive rapids of the river. He covered the marred ice as best he could with the thin layer of snow on the river. With any luck, it would serve to attract their attention to his trail without garnering careful examination. He crawled to the safety of solid ground, thankful his attempt to thwart pursuit hadn't backfired and sent him into the deadly cold waters.

He stayed in sight until the nightwolves burst into view. They padded up and down the riverbank, their thick, bristling black fur raised on their hackles. Their white-masked snouts lifted from the ground at the riverbank with a snort. They had his scent, and soon after their light blue eyes looked across at him hungrily. There were two of them, both stepping on the ice and then retreating, cautious of the frozen expanse before them. Splintering howls sang their discontent.

Osrith watched patiently as five hideous creatures armed with broadswords appeared from the tree line to join the wolves. They were roughly the same height as a human, but thicker in torso and limb. Their heads were larger as well, with sloping foreheads and small unobtrusive noses level with their deep-set eye sockets. Coarse black hair was pulled back from their faces, tied in topknots that allowed the excess hair to fall about their necks. Their lower lips protruded distinctively, accentuating their powerful, jutting jaws. A web of criss-crossing scar tissue snaked around their grey, chiseled features, dyed black as night. In the flickering light of their torches, it seemed as if the tattoos leapt from their eyes like ebon lightning.

Osrith's perception of his situation changed within the beat of a heart. These were not dringli, but their larger cousins, the hrumm. And, if he read their tattooed markings correctly, not simply hrumm, but elite hunters of the Host – *graomwrnokk*. This, then, was why the pursuit had been so swift, so persistent. This was why Gai had urged him to accept no delay in his journey. He turned and sprinted through the thinning trees, not bothering to wait and see if his trap would snare any or all of the scouts.

He had underestimated his foe. Not drastically, but enough to cause him some worry. A scouting party of dringli or hrumm he could handle; a party of *graomwrnokk* was another matter entirely. He gripped his axe tightly as he ran, his feet pounding the snowy fir bedding of the forest floor with the steady rhythm of his long stride.

Then he heard it: the sound of splitting ice and the surprised squeal of its victims. If nothing else, it had bought him some time.

Emerging from the trees, he found the countryside familiar. The High Ridge formed a mountainous wall to the north and west, but only a brief expanse of rocky hills and small farm plots lay between him and the castle. A low stone wall sat atop the next incline, delineating the border of one of the outlying properties. A small trail of black smoke drifted skyward from somewhere beyond. Osrith took his bearings once more: the copse of trees to his right, the bald limestone crest of the hill on his left, the overgrown horse trail winding its way down to the river behind him. *He knew this place!* The Eavely's farm lay on the other side of that wall, the smoke rising beyond evidence of a sizzling breakfast on their hearth.

Osrith almost felt relief as the morning's light slowly pushed away the black curtain of night with the soft amber glow of dawn. Even the grey clouds above looked less threatening with their edges painted in gold. His legs pushed hard against the snowy slope as he struggled up toward the wall. The Eavely's farm might be a pleasant memory, but it offered little in the way of escape from his pursuers. Thomas was a man beyond the years of battle now, and his surviving son crippled by a cruel twisting of bones, if he still lived at all.

A sharp twang preceded the hail of arrows. Osrith dove into the snow, his axe out to his side, and covered his head with his free arm. One arrow stabbed into his left leg, just above the back of his knee, another into his right shoulder. Osrith pulled them from his flesh and, with a grunt, started again for the wall. They weren't broad heads, and the thin, light points hadn't penetrated far through his furs and leather armor. Another discordant strum of bowstrings sent a barbed shaft into his lower left calf. He cursed, but continued doggedly toward his goal, ignoring the pain. It was clear these arrows hadn't been intended to kill, and he wondered for a moment why they bothered loosing the shafts at all – until the burning of poison slowly spread from his wounds, followed by creeping numbness.

They want me alive, Osrith thought. Another volley fell around him, two arrows snapping harmlessly on the fur-covered iron shield strapped to his back. *Or he does.*

Osrith chanced a quick look behind. Six hrumm made up a row of archers; six more climbed after him. He didn't see Dieavaul among them, but a growing pain in an old wound assured him he was near. The nightwolves were nowhere to be seen, evidently sucked into the chilling current of the Daemeyr or, at the very least, scared off. He couldn't tell if the scouts from the riverbank were among his pursuers, and didn't particularly care. A dozen would be enough to finish him handily even if five were frozen to the bone.

Osrith dove for safety over the four-foot wall, blinking away a brief ripple of dizziness. A hail of arrows clacked harmlessly against the granite as Osrith pulled his shield loose from the bindings holding it on his back and discarded it. Even as he found the balance of the axe in his hands, he heard the heavy tread of the hrumm warriors closing in.

No more arrows, at least. The hrumm were vicious opponents, but they wouldn't needlessly risk their own.

Osrith breathed in the still morning air. He savored the breath before battle. His fingers unraveled the knot securing the hilt of his broadsword to his scabbard, tapped each of his throwing knives, and then his long knife, before settling back on his axe.

Poisoned.

Injured.

Outnumbered.

Graomwrnokk leading the pursuit.

He exhaled.

Survive first, he told himself. *There is nothing else. Survive.*

Osrith stood and turned, steadying himself for the coming onslaught.

The first of the hrumm jumped the wall with little effort, its blade scything down at Osrith. It was too fast, too strong and far too eager. Osrith stepped inside the swing and pivoted, cleaving its back with his axe as it stumbled past and sending it crashing to the turf with a wail. Two of its fellows cleared the wall, and Osrith rushed them as they were in mid-air, barreling one creature into the next. As they flinched, he pressed the attack on the closest hrumm with a blow to the chest. The hrumm fell back against the wall, the crunch of its splintering ribcage louder even than its cry of pain. Osrith pulled his axe out of the beast with an effort and stumbled backward, out of the spray of its heartblood. Numbness tickled his extremities, and he dug his fingers into the haft of his axe.

Survive first.

Osrith stepped back as the survivor regained its footing, even as three more hrumm warriors hurdled the wall. Two of the three were *graomwrnokk*. Osrith kept a careful distance, staying just close enough that they feared to sheath their close-quarter weapons, but distancing himself from the wall. If they hemmed him in and pinned him against the wall, the rest of the Host would join them and the fight would be over.

Osrith backed away toward the farmhouse, but the hrumm moved quickly to cut him off and surround him. They started in slowly, taunting him and probing his defenses, but Osrith merely turned in circles, watching them intently. They drew in closer, tightening their ranks, then closer still. They understood the reach of his long axe, and though time and numbers were on their side, the advantage of fighting distance was distinctly his. He looked in their eyes and met their vicious stares with his own contempt. Then with a powerful battle cry he lunged forward.

The hrumm before him braced for an attack that never came, fooled by the feint, and Osrith attacked his left flank. With a swift stroke, he sliced through the neck of the nearest hrumm. It crumpled, clutching the open wound at its neck with a thick gurgle.

Osrith wasted no time on the dying, turning immediately toward the other hrumm and singling out the nearest *graomwrnokk*. He closed the distance between them as it raised its weapon back to strike, checking the sword stroke with the head of his axe before it had any force behind it. He rammed his helm into the hrumm's face, and it gagged on its teeth as they shattered down its gullet. Reeling back from the blow, the hrumm created space for Osrith to swing his axe, and he hewed into the *graomwrnokk's* shield arm. The kinsteel blade cleft through its shoulder and into the meat of its chest.

Osrith tried to pull his axe free, but the force of the mortal blow had wedged the weapon in his victim's breastbone. He released the axe handle without wasting effort to free it. Instead, he spun toward the last two hrumm, his broadsword whistling from its scabbard to point unsteadily at his assailants.

They held their distance. Osrith was losing his fight against the poison, and he could see that they sensed it. He swayed, panting, staring them down and hoping to bluff through his faltering stamina by intimidation. The remaining *graomwrnokk* snorted and moved toward Osrith's left, barking an order at its last surviving soldier. Osrith was fluent in hrummish, but his basic sense of tactics would have deciphered the guttural command just as well.

Let him fall, it had said. They would contain him until the poison brought him down. He would do the same in their place: take the most certain course with the least amount of risk.

Osrith's head swam, and he stumbled down to one knee. There was a ringing in his ears, like distant horns, and a wave of nausea almost overtook him. The *graomwrnokk* was now almost directly behind him, and Osrith knew time was short. If he couldn't draw them in, somehow engage and kill them before he collapsed, he would be at Dieavaul's feet before mid-morning.

Osrith dropped his sword into the snow, his numb fingers shaking over the hilt. The hrumm in front of him snarled and edged closer. A disciplinary bark from the *graomwrnokk* stopped it in its place.

No matter, thought Osrith. He didn't need this one too close, just off guard. His hand flashed to his belt of throwing knives and let one fly. The blunt end struck the hrumm's helm with a loud clang and Osrith gritted his teeth. "Damn it," he spat under his breath, and fell face first into the snow.

He welcomed the cold wet touch on his brow. It was an ally against the easy surrender of sleep. He heard horns again, this time closer, and felt a tremor through the earth. Horses.

No, not just horses... *Cavalry.*

The *graomwrnokk* snarled.

Osrith's fingers searched for his dropped sword, wrapping around the hilt under the stillness of his fallen body. He waited, drawing shallow breaths and conserving his strength. They would come to him. Their hand was forced now if they wanted him alive – if only just barely.

A moment later hrummish claws grabbed at the fur-lined leather at Osrith's neck, dragging him upward. He braced his arms at the elbow, letting the momentum of the hrumm's action carry his sword into its gut. It howled and staggered backward. Osrith removed the blade with a twist and the hrumm slipped from the steel.

He tried to turn before the *graomwrnokk* reached him, but his leaden feet were too sluggish, and it tackled him to the frozen turf. Its full weight drove him hard to the ground, pinning him and driving the air from his lungs.

Osrith looked into the yellowed eyes of the predator, an inch from his own, and breathed in the stench of its hot breath as it twisted the sword from his hand. The *graomwrnokk's* own blade made one thrust, penetrating Osrith's armor and stabbing into his gut. The warmth of his own blood spread over his half-numb skin, but Osrith knew it was not an immediately fatal wound. It had been a calculated strike, to immobilize its prey, to make further struggle as dangerous to the wounded as to the hunter. He would likely die from blood loss or infection over time, but not before the hrumm delivered its prize to Dieavaul.

The ground trembled with the thunder of horses' hooves. The *graomwrnokk* rose, pulling Osrith's limp body over its shoulder as it turned toward the low stone wall. Osrith saw the colors of Castle Vae fluttering from cavalry lances. The hrumm stutter-stepped, trying to evade the mounted pursuit, and Osrith gritted his teeth against dizziness as the hrumm spun left and right, seeking escape.

One of the knights was bearing down on them, charging a few scant feet in parallel to the wall, the morning sun catching the blurring flash of his armor in an orange gleam. The knight drew his arm back, a short javelin in his grip. The hrumm mounted the wall and made a powerful leap. The javelin whistled through the air and cracked the hrumm's skull before its feet touched the downward slope. The *graomwrnokk* fell, and Osrith tumbled with the corpse through the snow for several feet before another hrumm carcass brought him to a jarring halt.

Armored forms swam in and out of his vision, their voices in and out of his head, and the blackness threatened to take him once more. He coughed and tried to lift himself from the ground.

"More... down the slope," he sputtered, trying to focus on the nothingness around him.

"Calm thyself," a voice said from somewhere nearby. A steel gauntlet pressed him back onto the sod. "You have done well to survive, Sir Osrith. Now you must lie still."

"Prentis?" The voice sounded familiar. Osrith could almost picture the gangly young squire who had borne the colors in the ranks of his House Guard, but the image refused to coalesce in his mind. Of course the voice was much deeper now, the quaver of youth long since shrugged off by the resonance of adulthood.

It had been eight years...

Drifting down the long tunnel of sleep toward the longer, darker tunnel beyond, Osrith couldn't help but approve that the young man had become a knight, but something kept him from the comfort of oblivion. Something was still wrong. There was a greater danger near at hand. He was certain of it. The thin scar of an old wound awoke with a searing pain, and his eyes opened with an alertness borne of terror and fear.

"Dieavaul.... More following.... Get to the castle."

"All is well in hand," comforted the voice. "Rest yourself, you are safe."

And with a deep-throated moan, Osrith was still.

Chapter Three

Past and Present

In a village the size of Craignuuwn there was but one inn, a two-story building with a few sparse accommodations on its upper level and a tavern below. Not much trade came through this region of the Crehr ne Og, so close to the wilderness, but the occasional party of hunters or travelers did happen by. Two stone chimneys piped black smoke into the air from the thick-woven thatched roof. A simple sign hung above the door, depicting a mug filled with foaming ale. Normally, the sounds of drunken laughter and merriment would pour from within, but today there was but one melodious voice raised above the hushed silence. The word had spread quickly that a bard had come, and the entire village nestled now inside, anxious for news, stories and song. All of these Brohan Madrharigal happily delivered.

Calvraign sat in a smoky corner of the inn with his mother and Callagh Breigh, a contented smile on his young face. He was handsome, his skin smooth and unblemished, his eyes a refreshing deep blue. The blue eyes, along with his blonde hair, were odd for the Cythe people, and marked him easily amongst the other youth of his village.

Still flushed with his early morning triumph over Callagh in their first game of *Mylyr Gaeal*, Calvraign felt vibrant and sure of himself. His hard-won victory had restored his self-confidence and his somewhat injured pride. Callagh had been excited enough at the chance simply to play the game she had watched so long in secret, it hadn't seemed to concern her at all that she lost – or not much, at any rate. Currently, at least, she seemed more interested in Brohan's storytelling than in reliving their hard fought contest.

Calvraign watched in blatant admiration as Brohan's fingers danced fluidly across the strings of his intricately crafted lap harp. The clear notes sang from the instrument, rising and falling in both volume and tempo under Brohan's flawless execution. Calvraign had long ago memorized this piece; it was a favorite of the locals here – *The Lament of Celian*. Though a general in the fledgling Dacadian Empire, Celian had befriended and fought with the Cythe in the ancient wars against Maccalah in these very hills. Brohan had already recounted his deeds of valor, and after this instrumental interlude, he would shift to a minor mode and sing of his final betrayal. As with every listener, Calvraign wanted desperately for the story to end cheerfully at each performance, but as always, it was not to be.

Brohan's perfect voice flowed evenly into the chord transition as he sang the final bars.

"This day is ours, the battle won!
Let all the praise of bards be sung!
Put swords in sheath for peace is ours,
enemies were we – now friends avow!"

So Celian spoke, and held his council;
in triumph he was kind and merciful.
But with victory, life and hope secure,
Celian, by misplaced trust was lured.

His vanquished foes, penitent false,
dined within his gracious halls.
And Celian's fate was sealed by vagary,
House Malminnion's blackest treachery!

For the food he supped and wine he drank,
with Shadow's blood and poison stank.
It felled him low amidst his throng,
his assassin named but in this song.

*No heir had he or wife to sire,
and so with him his line expired."*

Now the entire tavern shook as the patrons raised their voices in the final chorus of the lament, some with tears in their eyes, others with sobs in their voice, and all with an ache in their hearts. And no voice held more emotion or sorrow than the ringing tone of Brohan.

*"No more to ride the hills in Spring,
no more, oh more, oh Celian!
No more to dance and epics sing,
no more, oh more, our Celian!*

*The Sword of the North has been called to rest,
in Oa's Halls of the True and Bless'd,
with Cyhlt, Cuaihln and the Duath Andai,
forever at peace, in the Palace of the Sky"*

The tavern was silent for a moment as listeners of all ages said a silent prayer in honor of their long-dead hero. Brohan sat on the edge of his table and set his harp next to him, taking a reflective sip of his steaming spiced wine. Calvraign waved and smiled, wanting nothing more than to be the center of such unquestioned respect.

Someday, he thought. *If ever this place is behind me.*

After the brief pause, the room erupted into a din of hand clapping and fist pounding. Old Pek waddled from his place behind the bar and patted his meaty hands on the bard's back, his puffy face glowing with pleasure and, no doubt, some of his best stock of ale.

"Oh, Brohan me lad!" he exclaimed. "If that don't sound better every time you sing it, I don't know me ale from me cider!"

Brohan raised his clay goblet in salute to the barkeep. "Well, sir, that is fine praise, indeed – for you certainly seemed to know both tonight!"

Old Pek joined his patrons in another round of laughter as he bustled about the inn refilling mugs and tankards. The arrival of a bard did more than just entertain; it filled the inn's coffers more than weeks of normal business. As the general merriment died down, someone called out from the back of the room.

"Tell us another! Tell us another!"

Brohan shrugged in mock indifference and looked about the room. "Shall I? Does anyone else wish to hear another tale? I don't want to bore you all with my prattle."

There was a loud and emphatic shout of "More! More!"

Brohan held his hand aloft in a conciliatory gesture. "So, the people of Craignuuwn have spoken! More it shall be! What, then, would you hear? Something short, I prithee. I'll not make it through *The Litany of Swords* tonight, for that I'll give the gods' own guarantee!"

The entire inn seemed to confer before an anonymous voice yelled out, "We've heard some tales of old. Let's hear something from recent memory. Tell us again of *Ibhraign and the King*! He's one of ours. Tell us of the Dragonheart!"

Brohan turned to Calvraign and his mother. His eyes asked an unspoken question. Oona nodded her assent, and Calvraign as well. It was easier for him, Calvraign guessed, since the memories of his father were just a few scattered images and broken phrases. Calvraign knew him better through the local stories and his mother's own accounts than his own memory. She put up a strong face, he knew, and she mourned his passing quietly with every telling of the tale. But, as Brohan often told him, it was better to remember the greatness of a man in life rather than dwell on the circumstances of his death.

"So be it!" proclaimed Brohan, his smile returning. "Then I shall tell the tale of a great man and an honored warrior, not of noble house, nor great wealth, nor at the time even a king's knight, but a fearsome *madhwrrwn* of the Cythe and one of your own – Ibhraign Askewneheur."

At this point, a few of the older patrons, and even Old Pek himself, raised a salute to the widow and her son. Brohan continued, drawing himself up to full height and projecting his voice clearly and cleanly throughout the room.

"It was nigh on fifteen long winters gone that the men of Providayne marched to war in the Southlands. Messengers from King Guillaume rode forth to all his vassals, urging them to send what men they could to join in the defense of his realm, for his allies in Paerytm were heavily beset by the warlords of Callah Tur. There were many who balked at these words, and asked what concern it was of the Cythe to fight the battles of a foreign prince. But from within these voices of dissent there was one man who spoke for the king, and his name was Ibhraign.

"*I speak for no other here, but I for one will go and fight,* he said. *For if Paerytm falls, then Mneyril or Providayne will surely be next. Then do the Cythe march? Or do we hide still behind the lances of our allies, waiting as the Calahyr come closer, hewing away stone by stone the wall of friends that stands between us and our foe? Then, when they are all gone, and the fiends are upon our homes with torches in their hands and lust in their eyes, you may argue when to fight them with your heads at the top of their spears!*

" All who heard this plea rallied to Ibhraign and the cause of the king, and so the War of Thorns was joined. Many battles were fought, and many great and brave men died on the hills and plains of Paerytm before the southerners were driven back to their own lands. But it was in this last battle that the Cythe were given their greatest honor and dealt their saddest loss. The king and his Knights Royal, cut off after a failed charge, were trapped between their foes and the swift merciless waters of the Vlue Macc. The Knights Lancer had been outflanked – the knight captain general himself captured by mercenaries from the Iron Coast! There was no relief in sight. None but the Cythe.

"Ibhraign, seeing the plight of his king, leapt upon the horse of a fallen comrade." At this, Brohan jumped on the table, brandishing an imaginary sword. *"To the king! To the king!* he yelled. Marshaling what stalwarts he could to the king's aid, he blasted through the enemy lines by sheer force of courage. Mightily he hewed at the barbarians, and they fell back from him like corn before the reaper! He joined the king and his knights, and they held the Calahyr at bay.

"But, alas, of their foe there were many and of themselves but a few, and one by one the great knights of Providayne fell dead or wounded around their king. Sir Halen of Bridmark, Sir Vanelorn the Grey and the mighty Sir Gruswold would wake not for days; while Sir Oulds the Stout, Sir Pyrtwin and Sir Qurisin were but a few of those who would wake not at all! Of all these and many more, the only left standing were Ibhraign and the good king himself! On they fought, pressed against the foaming rapids, when finally the last of the Calahyr came at them. Adhrig Red-Axe, the Macc adh Calha, led the charge himself, flanked on either side by his fearsome skull-bearers, who carried no less than fifty gilded heads between them."

Brohan looked sadly across the room. "Now Ibhraign knew his time had come. His blood lay mostly at his feet, and his wounds were deep and many, for any stroke meant for Guillaume he had taken himself. Pheydryr held out Her pale hand to take him, but he swatted it aside with his sword, for he would not leave his king even at the summons of Death Herself.

"And so he stayed on the bright side of Shadow, raining blow after blow upon the frightful enemy, slaying such multitudes that the Grey Lady could spare no time to pry his own life from him! It mattered not who challenged him, knight or squire or skull-bearer of the clan, one by one, each fell in turn. When Ibhraign finally laid himself down, there were no more foes to fell and but one king left standing. Guillaume's army was victorious. The Battle of Vlue Macc was won!"

There was a subdued cheer from the crowd, and some scattered toasts to Ibhraign's courage, but the gathering quieted as Brohan held up his hands.

"The king was filled with sorrow and admiration for this man and took up the fallen warrior's sword, and asked of him his name. Then, before his assembled knights, soldiers and lords, King Guillaume knighted him *Sir Ibhraign Dragonheart*.

"Knowing at last his duty was done, Sir Ibhraign took his final breath on this mortal world, and answered the beckons of the Grey Lady. It is said that as he passed through the Veil there was thunder but no lightning and a great moving of the earth, for not in recent memory had such a warrior been welcomed home to Irdik's Hold. And though his body perished, his honor and his spirit live on even today in the hearts of those he loved. In the king's heart, in the realm's heart, and in *our* hearts!"

The crowd let loose a rousing cheer. Oona blinked away tears, and Calvraign reached for his mother's hand, squeezing it gently. The village remembered its warrior hero. Oona dwelled on the love of her life, her husband, and father to her son. Even after these many years, he saw the long lines in her face, the hurt, the loneliness.

Calvraign closed his eyes. He remembered a sly wink from an all-too-serious brow; laughter, the scent of smoke and sheepskin and winter ale; strong arms throwing him into the Spring-kissed air and catching him without fail. All bright, brief flashes from the very edges of his recollection. And yet, for all that, Calvraign could not recall Ibhraign's face. A hero's face, a husband's face, his father's face – it was an empty hole in his memory that filled his heart.

"Care to dance with the vanquished?"

Calvraign looked up to find Callagh holding out her hand, the orange glow of the hearth reflected like suns-rise in her wide eyes, her mouth upended in her quirky smile. Old Pek's son Dendwr had begun playing a jig, and the townsfolk all about him were taking to their feet as Brohan played the spoons.

"Go on with you," Oona said, placing his hand in Callagh's. "Leave an old woman to herself and dance a leg off, for me."

Callagh led him to an open space on the floor, and Calvraign slipped his free hand around her waist as they danced. This time, he did not shrink away from her. Whether it was the song, or the drink, or the rawness in his heart, he held her close. He smelled the rose oil in her hair, and when she kissed him, he tasted the salt on her lips and the wine on her tongue and whirled her about merrily.

For the rest of that night there were music and dancing aplenty in the tavern of Craignuuwn. Gone were worries of the winter. Gone were concerns for the herds or the crops or the trading prospects of the morrow. This night, they celebrated. They knew it would be the last such night for a long, long while.

With dawn came more snow. It seemed apparent to Brohan that winter would show no respite this year. He stretched again, the last of his weariness dissolving quickly in the brisk wind from the west. The soft murmur of sheep drifted to his ears from their pen-yards. Soon, even these hardy creatures would need to be sheltered from this onslaught or risk being buried in it. He walked over to their enclosure and leaned against the low stone wall that kept the animals from wandering aimlessly about the village.

The largest of the ewes trudged over to him through the gathering snow and stared at him with wide brown eyes devoid of worry. He reached out a hand to stroke its chin, but the ewe insisted on sniffing his palm. On discovering it empty, the sheep gave a disappointed snort and turned its back to rejoin the huddled flock. Brohan chuckled softly. Though royalty and ancient houses might be happily satisfied with his company, to some he was evidently just another man without a carrot.

The bard looked up into the bruised clouds above him with more than a small amount of worry. If he was to reach the capital in time for the Winter Festival he must leave soon. He harbored little hope now that the unseasonably early snows would abate to ease his journey. If anything, he had dallied here too long. He tended to enjoy his time with Calvraign a little too much, he reflected.

But he holds such promise.

"Master Madrharigal?"

Brohan turned quickly at the sound of Oona's voice and fixed her with a frown of mock annoyance. "Oona, how long have I pleaded with you to address me as Brohan and not Master Madrharigal? I have little liking for pretense and certainly no need of it here. This is the last time I'll tell you, henceforth I am Brohan, or I'm deaf and dumb!"

Oona shuffled her feet in the snow. No one had yet stirred in the village, leaving them undisturbed. She pulled her thick woolen coat tighter around her neck and took a step closer.

"Brohan," she began again, but allowed the wind to eat her words.

"Oona, what is it?" He leaned in close, examining the creases of worry in her forehead. Her eyes flickered from one spot to the next, but never settled on his. "It's just me, after all," he prodded.

"I know, but I feel so foolish."

"Oona," Brohan pleaded. "Out with your words or you'll choke on them!"

"Yes, yes, you're right, of course." She took a deep breath and swallowed hard, then continued, "It's just that, I've, well, I've had a dream, Brohan. More of a nightmare it was, truth be told, and it's shaken me to me bones."

"A nightmare?" said the bard, not naïve enough to discount a powerful vision outright. "What about?"

"That's just it, Brohan, I don't rightly understand it. There was a man – I'd never seen him before – a dark man, but pale, cold as death and laughing." She shivered, her eyes pleading with Brohan for comfort. "There was blood all over him, covering him, dripping from his sword – and that sword, Brohan, it was, well, it wasn't like anything I've ever seen. It wasn't steel, or bronze. No, more like polished *bone*, it was. And, and… . Oh, Brohan, it was Cal's blood, I know it was, he'd killed me Cal! He'd killed him!"

Brohan reached out and folded the sobbing woman into his arms. "Now, Oona, it was just a dream. An *awful* dream. You know I would never let anything like that happen to Cal."

Oona pulled herself away from Brohan and grabbed his shoulders, her eyes wide. "But when you go, Brohan, who'll protect my boy then? We have no warriors of note here, and those we did are away in service to the king. What am I to do?"

Brohan gently stroked her cheek. "Oona, it was only a dream. You're a worried mother, not a seer. You mustn't take such things seriously." He hoped she was more convinced in hearing his words than he had been in speaking them, but her expression did nothing to show it.

"When my father died, I dreamt of it. When my husband died, I dreamt of it. Is the same fate to befall my only son? No! I'll not have it! You must stay here with us, Brohan, stay and protect my Cal. If ever you loved him as you claim you do, you must do this thing!"

Brohan stood in silence. Her words rang true. In his heart, he felt an echo of the dread she carried. By itself, the description she gave troubled him enough, giving life to ancient text and verse that would best have stayed just that. The fact that she had experienced other premonitions, accurate ones, only made matters worse. But if what he suspected were true, this village would not be safe with himself and the whole of the King's Guard standing watch. But to tell Oona of this…

No, not now; but he had to do something.

"Listen to me, Oona. If what you say is true, then Cal could indeed be in grave danger. But I cannot stay here, and nor can he for that matter. We must be away to the capital in all haste. I will take him with me to Dwynleigsh, and there he will be safe, with many powerful and watchful eyes to look after him. If your dream was a vision, it only shows you what might be, not what will be. For whatever reason, the gods have given you warning, and we must take advantage of their courtesy, so rarely does it guide us."

"Yes, of course," said Oona, though more to herself than to Brohan. "Dwynleigsh. Guillaume will protect him. He owes us that much."

"Everything will be fine, Oona, you have my word. Whatever this mysterious man wants with your son, he'll have to hack his way through all the knights in Providayne to get it. And then he'll have to deal with me!"

"Aye."

Oona at last seemed comforted by the casual bravado of his words. Apparently she didn't notice the troubled flicker in his eyes, or his fingers fidgeting where he normally slung his longsword. That, at least, he was thankful for.

"I'll wake Cal. We have things to discuss before we go. You can prepare his pack in the meantime. We should be off before highsuns today."

⁂

Calvraign fell back with a clang of steel on steel and caught his balance just in time to parry low. Brohan pressed into him tirelessly, pinning his sword to the ground and driving his shoulder into Cal's chest. Calvraign tumbled down the slight incline, plowing a trail through the wet clinging snow. Brohan stomped down toward him with an uncharacteristic lack of grace, holding both swords.

"I believe in our initial fencing lessons I told you that the first rule of swordplay was *don't lose your sword*. Without it you're just another target." He threw the sword at Calvraign's feet. "That's three times you've died in ten clicks. Try not to make it four."

Calvraign snatched up the weapon and scrambled to his feet. Though such words often left Brohan's lips, he'd never heard this tone before: deadly earnest, almost bitter or angry. He wasn't sure what he had done to earn Brohan's ire, but he regretted it, whatever it was.

"On your guard!"

Within a moment of Brohan's warning, Calvraign found himself on the defensive yet again, attempting to stave off the swift and furious attack of the glowering bard. His arms ached from the repeated jarring impact of blade on blade, and he wondered exactly how long Brohan intended to keep this up. He needed to catch his breath and clear his mind. He scanned his surroundings quickly and found what he needed only a few feet away. He sidestepped to his left and put a leaf-bare tree between himself and Brohan.

They circled, exchanging feints and thrusts, until Calvraign, sensing his moment, locked swords with Brohan and pivoted out and away from the tree. Before their swords untangled, he stepped back in close enough to wrap a leg around one of Brohan's, hoping to take him off balance.

"Good," grunted Brohan. "I see you're finally taking this seriously."

"Not that you're giving me much choice," he retorted breathlessly, trying to force Brohan's leg out from under him. "I don't understand."

Brohan released his sword without warning, and Cal found himself falling forward as the momentum of his sword arm suddenly met with no resistance. For one moment he was off balance, and in that time Brohan pushed off from the tree and used Cal's leg lock against him, knocking him to the ground. Brohan landed squarely on top of him.

"Of course you don't," said the bard, his knee pinning Calvraign's sword arm uselessly to the ground, "but if you're going to Dwynleigsh with me, you'd best be able to defend yourself in case we meet with trouble."

"Dwynleigsh? What are you talking about?"

"Your mother and I have decided it's time you saw some of the world. The king always mentioned he would someday like to see the result of all the time I've spent with you, not to mention his gold, so we're going to King's Keep and showing him. You've heard of his Winter Festival, of course?"

"The king?" Calvraign hoped his voice didn't sound as much like a squeal as he thought. "But I don't understand."

Finally, Brohan's grin returned. "So much you've said, already. Now let's get ready to go. Your mother should have us both packed by now, I suppose."

"Now?" Calvraign was fairly certain *that* sounded like a squeal.

Brohan stood and extended a hand for him. "We'd best hurry before your mother changes her mind. I had a hard enough time convincing her to let you go."

Cal sprang from the ground with renewed vigor, sheathing his father's sword. Calvraign frowned as Brohan recovered his own. "What about the first rule of swordplay?" he said. "Never losing your sword, and all that?"

"Ah, Calvraign!" Brohan laughed as he headed up the slope back toward the village and Cal's waiting mother. "Always know when to break the rules!"

Chapter Four

Homecoming

CASTLE Vae had watched over the foothills of the High Ridge for centuries, standing in bleak defiance of the terrain and its less-than-friendly inhabitants since humans dared settle these lands. First constructed as a border fortress by the legendary general Kiev Vae of the long vanished Dacadian Empire, the castle's original structure had expanded greatly through the years.

The outer curtain walls were merely seventy-five years old, reaching fifty feet into the sky with the same triple crenellations commonly found in recent Providaynian architecture. Around this wall was a moat twenty feet in width and fifteen in depth, its bottom covered with spikes of rusty iron. Although drained during the winter months, it still served as an effective first line of defense. Through the drawbridge was the lower bailey, an open courtyard covered in plush grazing grass and compost heaps. Livestock were forbidden here save in the instance of siege, and so it served now as a practice range for a dozen archers.

The secondary wall was built on the crest of a sharp incline in the hill's slope, its parapets graceful and decorative as well as defensible. The well-wrought carvings and intricate designs of the crenellations dated this portion of the fortress at near three hundred years in age. Beyond this was the upper bailey and the dateless central keep, a monolith of granite that had borne the brunt of both war and nature for centuries on end.

Within the twenty-foot thickness of the keep's walls lay a man not far from the gates of death. Wrapped in bandages and covered by a quilt, Osrith Turlun rested on a thick down mattress next to a subdued peat fire. A scattering of torches lit the small room in a dim but sufficient fashion, revealing it to be bare of decoration. The sole, tightly shuttered window trapped the thick aromatic smoke from the hearth inside the room.

The heavy oaken door creaked outward, and a brighter stream of light shone into the room from the hallway beyond. A shadow fell across Osrith's sleeping form, stemming from a monstrous silhouette that nearly encompassed the entire doorway. The figure was close to seven feet tall, with elongated, muscular arms and an oddly oval head. It made little noise as it approached Osrith, and as its frame bent down toward him, he was engulfed completely by its girth.

Osrith's eyes flicked open in shock, and with all his will he urged his sore body upward. One scaly, three-fingered hand held him down easily as a reptilian snout, hellishly lit by the red flames of the fire, leered down at him.

"Lie still," chided a throaty voice that hinted of restrained thunder. "You've done yourself enough harm already. Don't be in such a rush to undue my work."

Osrith stared in disbelief at the huge creature before him. Dark green scales ran from the thickly corded neck up the back of its oblong head, lightening to a softer emerald down the snout, with small brown mottling speckling the flattened space between its eyes. The eyes themselves were an opalescent blue-green, set toward the sides of the head, and stared from beneath a bony, protective brow. Its huge torso was covered in a sleeveless purple garment belted at the waist by a thick corded rope, its legs bare save for the sandals on its feet.

"You," sputtered the mercenary.

"Yes," replied the lizard. "Obviously the lessons of time have not improved your eloquence."

Osrith relaxed, the pain returning quickly without the comforting numb panic of adrenaline. His gut burned from within, his left leg and right shoulder throbbed mercilessly, and he found it impossible to breathe normally through his swollen nose. "Yours was never a face I enjoyed waking up to, Kassakan, but this once I'll make an exception."

With a grunt bordering on growl, Kassakan knelt down by the wounded man's bedside. "Practice your wit as you may, Osrith my dear, but your wounds have troubled both of us most grievously. You have tested my talents this time."

Osrith snorted and turned his head to stare in the opposite direction.

"Had it not been for the hze-te poison slowing your heart and the cold thickening your blood," continued Kassakan in what was unmistakably a tone of irritation, "you would now be staring contemptuously from the wrong side of a burial mound."

"I've been through worse," Osrith grumbled back.

"Indeed. When you were a ten-year younger." Kassakan's voice trailed off into a hissing snicker.

Osrith whipped his head around to face his old friend, an action he immediately regretted, and spat defensively. "I'm strong as an ox!"

"Aye, yet no longer spry as a fox," quipped Kassakan.

Osrith simmered quietly as Kassakan moved in and out of the chamber, bringing in fresh bandages, a small chest, and a covered iron pot that nestled cozily into the glowing embers of the fire. Watching the imposing figure of his old companion moving about before him awakened images in his memory faded from disuse. The reckless adventures of his youth, and those who shared it with him, flashed before his eyes. Remnants of past glory fluttered like pennants in his mind for a moment, then ripped and tore like ragged pieces of sackcloth in the unforgiving wind of his own inner shadows.

Osrith forced himself into the present, concentrating on the pain. Ignoring all but the pain. That was how he lived, now. That was his instrument of day-to-day survival. It didn't bring respect, or glory, or friendship, but it was effective. He watched as Kassakan stirred the concoction in the pot, wondering what chance had brought them both to remote Castle Vae. He knew as much about the hosskan as any human, perhaps more than most. After all, he had considered Kassakan Vril his closest friend for years, even after they had parted ways. Inexplicable as their friendship was, he still felt the immediacy of their bond. Deeper than blood or nationality, it had become a part of their very beings. Yet he understood little of Kassakan's motivations.

"What brought *you* here?" he said, dredging up what force he could manage.

Kassakan chuckled, producing a noise to which Osrith realized he'd have to become re-accustomed, and began pouring the steaming liquid from the pot into a wooden bowl. "You did, of course."

Osrith sighed and twisted his lips into a scowl. "And how did I do that?"

Kassakan lowered her eyes and soaked the fresh bandages in the bowl. The aroma was pungent, and Osrith found his scowl lingering naturally as the scent reached his nostrils. Kassakan set the hot cloth on Osrith's healing wounds, pressing it against his skin and smoothing it over with an expert touch. "You are my *j'iitai*. You are a part of my soul, and I of yours. I heard you call though you yourself did not."

Osrith closed his eyes and exhaled as noisily as he could manage. "Don't set in with your spirit talk, Kassakan. I haven't the strength to run or the patience to listen. You're here by Oghran's whims – let's leave it at that!"

"As you wish." Kassakan pulled the quilt back up over Osrith's freshly bandaged chest and sat near the hearth. For the space of a few long clicks the fire chattered to itself. "Was the dreamstone the cause of all this?"

Osrith's eyes narrowed. "What do you know of it?"

"Don't trouble yourself. I discovered it in your neck pouch, but I have not disturbed it."

"Good," he said tersely. "It's no business of yours."

Kassakan recognized his tone. "Please, Osrith, my kind have strict rules about murdering our *j'iitai*. It is considered… bad. But I *will* kill you if you refuse my help."

Osrith smiled very faintly. "Have at me, then, woman. I've no intention of splitting my reward with anyone or any*thing*."

Kassakan smiled her unnerving, toothy smile. "Would you prefer to pay my standing rate for healing, perhaps?"

"I think not," said Osrith, his tone softening to one of friendly surrender. "I'll tell you, then; not to please your damnable whims, but to preserve my silver from your greedy claws.

"A seer named Gai sent word into the Deeps that he needed help. Ruuhigan dispatched me to investigate, and the old man promptly hired me to see the stone into the hands of King Guillaume. Apparently it holds a vision or some such thing. I don't know or care, but it attracted enough attention whatever it is. I was tracked through the mountains by several parties of hrumm – I think they were Dieavaul's."

"Dieavaul?" Kassakan's tail swished from underneath her tunic, sketching nervous patterns on the stone floor. "What makes you think it was he?"

"Gai had a vision the day I left him. He saw a pale man whom he described in great detail. A bringer of death, he said, and he mentioned the sword. By virtue of reputation, I suspected Dieavaul. And, in the mountains, the old wound began to ache."

Kassakan lowered her head and spoke softly. "Yes, I noticed the scar seemed agitated. I knew this day would come. Life is ever a circle."

"Right." Osrith closed his eyes and lay his throbbing head back on his pillow. Kassakan always felt the need to insert her philosophical diatribes into otherwise practical conversation. She was right to some degree, he supposed. It did seem odd that here, of all places in the Eastern Realms, he once again faced Dieavaul. Here, where the darkest stains on his memory clung indelibly to his every waking thought, where every stone, every tapestry, and every face was likely as not a disturbing reminder of why he had left in the first place. He recognized that the thickness in his chest and throat was not merely from his wounds and medications, and clenched his teeth against the distraction of nostalgia. He cleared his throat to speak, intent on changing the subject, but Kassakan interrupted him.

"You will be travel-worthy within a ten-day – maybe two. Until then you should rest. You will need all of your strength."

At that point Osrith realized he had no idea how much time had passed since his collapse near the Eavely's farm. "How long has it been?"

"Four days," replied Kassakan. "I wondered at first if you would ever awaken."

"Four! Gods Below!" *So much time lost.* Osrith wanted to jump from his bed and be on with his journey, but his pragmatic center knew this was impossible. It would be best to take the lizard's advice and rest. The sooner he recuperated, the faster he would be done with this mess and intent on nothing more complicated than spending his reward. His body had lain dormant and inactive for so long that he was both exhausted and bed-weary. His muscles twitched with a desire to stretch, yet ached when he moved. Despite it all, it was his restlessness that decided him.

Osrith sat up slowly, holding the bed sheets to his naked body, his face frozen in an expression determined to hide his pain. Kassakan eyed his movement warily from the hearth. Osrith felt a strange headiness as blood flowed with renewed energy through his limbs. His arms and legs didn't feel completely fallow. Kassakan's experience as a healer was extensive enough that she knew to exercise them while he was indisposed. But there was still a great deal of pain.

"A ten-day and no more," he said gruffly. "We have to make the capital before Guillaume returns to the front."

Kassakan nodded her huge head. "We will leave when you are ready."

Osrith had long ago ceased to marvel at her ability to agree without agreeing and so barely acknowledged her statement. "Meanwhile, I need to occupy myself with *something* while I'm yet awake."

Kassakan turned toward the fire, keeping Osrith in focus with one eye, and poked at the embers with a blackened stick. "There are those who would like to see you, if you are well enough to receive visitors." She paused, watching him fidget with his bandages. "Lady Evynine has been impatient for news of you."

Osrith looked away.

"She is your hostess, here. Perhaps it would be wise to-"

"The wounds are still too fresh," cut in Osrith sharply.

"Your wounds should have healed enough by now."

"They pain me even as we speak." Osrith glared at Kassakan's back, increasingly hostile. "As you should well know, lizard."

"Yes," conceded Kassakan, but her tone quickly turned to one of scolding impatience. "Your pain *is* great. So great it threatens to swallow you because you refuse to share its burden with anyone. Worse, you refuse to allow others to share theirs with you."

"I've refused no such thing!" he returned vehemently.

"Indeed?" Kassakan fixed Osrith with an unblinking stare. "You have refused Evynine for eight years. Or did you expect her to follow you into the Deeps and share your self-imposed exile?"

Osrith's jaw clenched, and his lips tightened into a thin uncompromising line. He lay back down on the bed, breaking Kassakan's gaze and staring instead at the cold stone ceiling. "Leave me. I need to rest."

"No."

"It's not your concern."

"You *are* my concern, Osrith," insisted Kassakan. "Watching you dwell in your past to hide in the present is my concern. If you can't shake yourself of this nonsense, then I shall shake you from it myself!"

"Is it really so hard to understand?" he growled, pressing his fingers against his temple.

"You did what you did, my friend. That you couldn't do more is lamentable, but it's no cause to lay blame at your feet."

Osrith scowled, unconvinced. "Then at whose feet would I lay it? I betrayed her trust. I was careless and arrogant."

"You did all you could," said Kassakan softly.

Sometimes Osrith wondered if he had done even that. Wasn't there a part of him that had wanted nothing more? Hestan had been his friend, the father of his charge, and the husband of his liege-lady. Husband to Evynine.

"Obviously, that wasn't enough," he muttered.

"If you will not speak with her for your benefit, at least think on what I have said, and do it for her sake. Don't waste any more of your life, or hers, bearing this alone."

"I'll think on it."

"Good. Now sleep. I will wake you soon for a meal."

Osrith closed his eyes and was surprised to find he drifted off to sleep easily. Whatever Kassakan's poultice had contained, it spread a slow, numbing calm throughout his body and limbs that he only hoped would spread to his conscience.

༄

The landscape that unfurled from the castle walls was covered in a crisp white blanket of snow. The wind howled through the nooks and crevices of the stone fortress like a beast alive and hungry, but the ancient towers stood resolute and unyielding. Osrith felt the slap of frozen air across his face and breathed deeply. He found the fresh air invigorating despite its numbing chill. He was clothed only in wool breeches, for his midsection still needed the frequent attention of Kassakan's skilled hands. His shoulder and leg were healed and without pain, though plagued with a persistent stiffness.

He left the shutters open and walked back to his bed in slow, measured, steps. For all his time in recovery, his gut still pained him greatly. He could not recall any time in recent memory when he had sustained such a stubborn wound, and surmised that Kassakan had not exaggerated her worry yesterday after all. The scar was impressive, at any rate.

He settled into the bed, propping himself up on the pillows he had been provided, just close enough to the fire to allow some small amount of warmth. The stars winked at him from behind the cloud-strewn sky, and the noises of night blew in faintly through the window. The whistling chatter of a spinnet, mixed with distant lupine howls and the lonely query of an owl, provided a musical score as enchanting as any bard's lyric tale, punctuated for a moment of drama by the harsh shriek of a nightwing.

"Osrith?"

The quiet melodic voice cut into Osrith like a razor. He looked up at the doorway and found her there, almost as he'd remembered her. Her hair fell to her shoulders, framing her dove-white face in a flaxen waterfall, her slender frame accentuated by the curve of her modest bosom and a slight flare at her hips. He could see the dark liquid blue of her eyes in the torchlight from the hallway, the glimmer of the flames lost in their depth. She walked to his side without a sound and sat next to him on the bed. She was clothed in a thick wool nightdress, lined with soft cotton but plain of decoration and flattering in its trim fit.

"Osrith?" she repeated, her skin rustling against the fabric. "Did I wake you?"

"No," he said, more gruffly than he'd intended. "I couldn't sleep."

"I hadn't expected you to be awake. Usually at this hour you are well asleep." Her lips spread into a smile warmer than the fire beside them. "I was worried. Your wounds... ."

She reached for his left hand, but Osrith moved it aside, his eyes darting away from hers. Evynine's smile flickered for a moment, then resumed, only slightly hampered by concern. "It's been so long," she said simply, but with a slight tremor. "Whatever ill fortune brought you here, I find myself thankful for it."

Osrith's hardened visage melted a moment at the edges. His lower lip held a slight quiver and his cheek twitched. His eyes searched for any place to rest where they wouldn't find her. "I-"

Evynine sensed what he struggled to say, and silenced him by placing a delicate finger to his lips. Osrith closed his eyes, relishing the soft tingle left by the touch of her skin.

"Not now. Let it lie in the past, where it belongs," she whispered. "Let it lie."

Osrith forced his features into a semblance of control. He disliked his lack of composure with her. Anger was his primary defense, but Evynine's presence disarmed that readily. "I can't," he said.

"By the Grace of Illuné, Osrith!" Evynine's tone was edged with temper and frustration. "If I may do so, why is there yet any reason for you not to do the same? Others say what they will. *I* believe in you – I have always believed in you."

Osrith looked up into her eyes, into her unflinching sincerity, and almost believed her. Even if she believed herself, he knew that somewhere inside something less pleasant, less forgiving, was waiting. It had to be. "As you wish, milady," he acceded.

Lady Evynine's smile returned once more, pleasantly deceived by his lie. "Mistress Kassakan tells me you will not be long here. I wish to know everything that has happened to you, when you feel you are ready. She says you fought alongside the underkin in the Deeping Wars. I must hear every word!"

Osrith had a brief vision of Kassakan's neck between his hands. *Never trust a lizard with a secret,* he thought, clearing his throat. "It isn't much to tell, really. A minor skirmish with the hrumm."

"Minor skirmish, indeed!" she chided. "I am told you felled *Pakh Ma Goiilus* yourself. This is certainly no small deed!"

"With all due respect, milady, there was after all a contingent of five hundred battle-frenzied kin in my support. And Kassakan is known to have the gift of a bard when it comes to storytelling. Five hundred may as well be five or five thousand the next time she tells it."

Evynine's laugh echoed across the cold emptiness of the room. "You speak not far from the truth," she admitted.

Osrith was content to watch her, as always, enjoying her quiet mannerisms: the tilt of her head, her hand brushing loose strands of hair from her eyes, the relaxed yet graceful way she sat next to him. Guiltily, he shook his head of such thoughts.

"How fares the Western March?" he said, fearing he knew already.

Osrith watched Evynine's subtle transformation from caretaker to baroness. Her back straightened, as did her brow, and her smile turned to a slight frown before she answered. "The war has taken many of my people from their homes and their families. It has also taken our grains and fruits, our livestock, and our steel. Few will venture west of Ingar's Way. The Border Knights are hard pressed to police this territory with so many of their number in service to the royal army." She paused, the very depths of her fathomless eyes filling with dread and compassion. "I fear that our peace here is over. My very spirit aches with this knowledge. I only hope that I am wrong."

"Everywhere it's the same. Even in the Deeps we heard news of the surface world's troubles. It seems the scourge of war and famine reaches far. But you are strong, and your people are brave."

"I tire of being strong, Osrith." She reached out and brushed his cheek with the back of her hand. "I wish to rest, just one night, without the weight of my own strength to hamper me. Just one night."

"You've always been your own worst enemy," said Osrith with a frown. "And what of Kiev? Isn't he old enough to share these burdens? He's certainly bright enough... ." Osrith stumbled over his last word as he saw Evynine drop her head. "What is it? What have I said?" he asked, suspecting and dreading the answer. He had seen her face like this before.

Evynine's tone softened to a whisper. "The sleeping sickness took him two years ago. There is only Aeolil now, and she is away in Dwynleigsh."

Gods Above, Below and Between! he swore silently. *Damn the lot of them. Useless.*

Hestan had been a good husband to Evynine. He'd been a soldier first and foremost, a knight of the House adh Boighn, and an able enough assistant in the governing of the Marches. Even if he'd thought Evynine was a bit *out of hand*, a bit *too close to the common folk*, he supported her. Though Hestan had been baron in name, it was only by right of marriage, and Evynine had never even hinted at giving up what was hers, by right. He'd given her two strong sons and a daughter stronger and smarter still. Together, they had ruled in strength and governed in wisdom. Now, as Kassakan had so recently reminded him, she bore the brunt of that power alone.

"I'm sorry," he said quietly. There were no other words, no other way to express his grief. He knew Kiev as a young boy, but never again. Like so many others – now just a memory.

"He never understood why you left."

Osrith was taken aback by her words. It never occurred to him that someone would not understand. Between the gossip and the facts, he thought everyone had understood. "I had no choice."

Evynine stood then, and half turned toward the door. It was obvious to Osrith that her mood had paled like the cold light from the window. "You made a choice, captal. It was not made for you."

He saw the anger rise and blossom on her cheeks. He knew too that it had been there all along. Despite her attempt to forget, to leave the past where it was, it had festered in her all these years, awaiting its release, starving itself for that one moment when it could feast on her rage and consume her in the process. He knew this, because he knew anger and hatred all too well. They had made a meal of him long ago.

"I must rise early on the morrow," said Evynine, regaining her composure to some extent. Osrith could already see the regret on her face, shortly replaced by fatigue and lingering concern. "Rest now. The journey ahead is a long one."

"That it is," he replied as she exited his chambers. "It is indeed."

&

Chaos swirled in vivid tendrils of magenta and black behind Osrith's eyes, rushing into the ravenous, open mouth of the whirlpool at the nexus of his dream. Their touch was cold, almost real, but not chilling enough to wake him from his slumber. He felt dizzy and ill at ease, as if staring down from the edge of a towering precipice. An ethereal voice called to him softly from somewhere, gentle but insistent. He turned, seeking it out, and stumbled into the maelstrom.

Osrith fought his way deeper into the wind of colors, shirking aside their freezing touch to find the source of the haunting cry. In a rush of terrible sound, he stumbled through into silence, and within was Evynine, clad in her funeral gown. Her face was long and solemn. Her hands cradled a small, withered bouquet of flowers, their dry petals drifting to the ground. Osrith tried to avert his eyes, but was unable. He was familiar with this dream.

Or so he thought.

The Pale Man stepped between Osrith and Evynine, his dark smile facing Osrith's shock. "I missed your company in the mountains, Captal Turlun. You rushed away too soon, I think."

The flame of his old wound burned in his gut.

"Dieavaul," spat Osrith. To him it was more curse than name.

"In the flesh, more or less." The Pale Man's chuckle was dark as his smile, and echoed wildly around them. "Don't make the same mistake twice, captal, lest you be an island in a sea of death," he paused for a lingering moment, "again."

"Your wit is dull, Dieavaul, even for an apparition in a bad dream."

The sword appeared like a cloud at midnight from the folds of the Pale Man's swirling cloak. Osrith's eyes could not move from its flat, unreflective surface.

"Ah, but you know I am more than a dream, Osrith. I am worse than your pathetic guilt. I have come to *warn* you. To allow you an escape from the cruel, repetitious whims of destiny."

Osrith readied his great axe, tensed for battle. "And why would you do that? Turned over a new leaf, have you?"

"It's quite simple, Captal Turlun," replied the Pale Man smugly, his coal black eyes glistening. "I *pity* you. You cannot defeat me now any more than you could have eight years gone. But now, you see, more is at stake. More than just a few lives will slip through your clumsy fingers this time, captal. And I will begin with *her.*"

The Pale Man struck out with his blade toward Evynine's silent, motionless form, but stopped short at the sound of Osrith's shout.

"No!" He watched the blade, poised above her defenseless flesh, and clenched his jaws.

"Send out the dreamstone, captal. You will know where to find me. Send it out and forget you ever saw it. Return to skulk in the Deeps with the underkin, away from this graveyard and its resentful caretakers. It is in your power to save them or damn them. I leave it to you."

Osrith shifted his grip on the weapon in his hands. "Bugger off," he replied dryly.

"That choice is yours, captal," returned Dieavaul smugly, "but remember it is just that. Your *choice*."

In a flash of blood and midnight, Evynine fell backward, and the Pale Man vanished into a thin vapor of soft contemptuous laughter. Osrith willed himself to awaken, but lingered in the thrall of his gruesome vision, fixated by the spectacle sprawled bleeding at his feet. He could feel his sleeping body refuse his command to rise, his numb lips ignore his desire to yell. He clawed at consciousness, but his eyelids were sealed by a will of their own, latched down over eyes that strained to see once more into the waking world.

But his struggles and desire were for naught. He was trapped and helpless.

Helpless again.

Chapter Five

Raogmyztsanogg

DIEAVAUL shook in a violent spasm as he awakened from his trance, his dark eyes quivering and a cold sweat beading on his skin. The surge of *iiyir* brought about by his communion with Shadow threatened to burst the dam of his will, but he diffused it slowly with the composure of countless years of experience. The remnants of the flood trickled impatiently back from whence it came, to the powerful ethereal flow of the *ur'iiyir*, the World Tides.

With a deep breath, he welcomed the familiar surroundings his tent provided: the touch of the Maccalite wool he rested on, softened by the delicate texture of a layer of fine silks; the amber flame of a solitary candle; the bundle of garments and supplies near the entrance; and the comforting non-gleam of *ilnymhorrim* resting in his lap. Even the faint stench of his hrummish bodyguards did not offend his sensitive nostrils. He gathered it all in and focused on it, centering himself back in the realm of the real. To be lost in the nether-realms was a prospect that held a small amount of fear even for him.

Dieavaul stood on shaky legs and strode into the waiting night. His guards fell in behind him, their awe and fear barely cloaked by their discipline. He inhaled deeply and sheathed the sword, resting his left hand on its pommel.

The camp was active but silent. Hrumm warriors made their way purposefully here and there while the smaller dringli scurried about underfoot. In the distance, the walls of Kirith Vae stood defiantly on the landscape. What his army was preparing to undertake was a formidable task. This same fortress had countless times protected the borders of Providayne from westerly invasion, and the Dacadian Empire before that. That his army was so near and as yet undiscovered was miracle enough, but to accomplish what he had been ordered still seemed daunting.

Too soon, Dieavaul thought, frowning. *Malagch's patience is ever a thing in motion, but this game must be played with a steady hand.*

The Pale Man looked over his small force, tucked discretely behind the trees that dotted the edge of the gentle sloping hills where they were encamped. They bore no banners, wore no colors; indeed, they would appear no more than a wild band of marauders if discovered.

Excepting for his own presence, of course, and that of his three *urghuar*. Dieavaul eyed the masked hrummish shamans as they began their guttural chant. The three humans were bound to the trunk of a fallen oak, their eyes wide and their cheeks streaked with tears. Normally they would have screamed, and normally this would only have added to the spectacle of the sacrifice, but circumstances dictated some caution, and so they were gagged. The shamans' curved knives opened their bellies; steel slicing cleanly through naked flesh.

Their chant continued through the muffled shriek of death wails. Thick hrummish claws moved with surprising deftness, removing their organs whole, each in turn, lifting them in offering to Shaa, and then committing them to the cold, smokeless fire that smoldered at their feet. The bodies twisted in their bindings, muscles jerking first in defiance, and then in the spasms of last breath. Their captives' eyes stared dull and glassy at their murderers by the time their hearts were taken and shared in the grisly blood meal that concluded the sacrifice. It was a poor offering. Two old men and a barren woman offered little in the way of *iiyir* to feed their spell, but in the end it would be little *enough*, he supposed.

You once warred with legions under your care. The truth of Gai's taunt echoed in his thoughts. *Urghuar* were no Black Robes, no matter if he had taught them to join and cast some magics in communion. And these feral warriors were no Third Legion, even if he'd taught them to march straight and hold their lines in battle.

True enough, he admitted to himself. *But it is not the sword alone that makes a swordsman dangerous; it is his control of the blade.* The *urghuar* did not serve the Magistry, and the hrumm did not serve the Imperial Crown. *They serve me, even before Malagch. And* that *is my power.*

Dieavaul turned away from the blood ritual to look once more upon the flickering watch fires of Kirith Vae. There was yet a great deal of open ground between them and the castle. Even if his stratagem was successful and the spell of concealment worked as planned, the advantage of surprise would not last long. He knew better than to underestimate these humans who lived on the frontier. They were a rugged breed, resourceful and tenacious.

But Dieavaul knew he could not turn back now. Taking the castle was out of the question, of course – even Malagch did not intend or hope for that. But if Osrith was not foolish enough to bring him the dreamstone, then he would lay siege to Kirith Vae and lay waste to the lands surrounding it until those within were desperate for a quick solution. Osrith and the stone would be his ransom, and for the price of one man, the baroness would certainly spare her people the ravages of war. She would remember the sting of his sword. She would give him up.

Dieavaul spotted his hrummish war-chieftain supervising the assembly of a light ballista fifty feet deep in the woods. He covered the distance in a few ticks, though none could see any evidence of hurriedness in his manner.

"*Pakh Ma* Thatt, report," he commanded.

The seven-foot hrumm turned and bowed deeply at the waist, its topknot spilling wiry black hair over its tattooed cheekbones. Where most hrumm were marked with at least a bolt or two of their lightnings, Thatt's face was a veritable storm of black blood-ink. "We waits your command, *Gal Pakh*," it said proudly through a thick accent. Dieavaul rarely spoke their guttural language, and their attempts to master his native aulden tongue merely aggravated him. Human speech provided the easiest compromise. "Whens the shamans call fog to hide us, whens is time we ride."

Dieavaul nodded his approval. "Shaa will feast on the blood we spill. This offering will be a rich one."

Thatt smiled broadly, exposing its yellowed, needle-sharp teeth in a carnivorous grin. "Leave trees whens fog come. Whens suns awake, attack swift and take humans with many great surprises."

Many great surprises, Dieavaul thought, suppressing a grin. *The bards would be sore tasked to fit that into one of their great ballads. Small wonder the hrumm preferred howling to song.*

Despite its simple speech and brutish manner, Dieavaul had great confidence in his *pakh ma*. Humans, underkin, and even his own disowned race had undersold the hrumm on intelligence for centuries. While they had little grasp of architecture or invention, they were quick learners and cunning warriors. His troops lacked the good manners of the Knights Lancer, but they were not wanting for martial expertise. Aside from this, of course, they were even easier to manipulate with religion than humans.

Where the humans were simple enough to maneuver through creative use of their fears and superstitions, they had many disparate gods and beliefs, and no one common bit to rein the lot of them where he would. The hrumm's single-minded devotion to Shaa proved most convenient, however.

Then, with a great deal of surprise, Dieavaul fell backward from the jarring impact of an arrow striking him squarely in the temple. The feathered shaft splintered from the blow, and the razor-sharp broad-tip careened wildly into the air. Though his protective enchantments had saved his life, they failed to save his balance. With a grimace, he toppled to the ground.

The shrieking of arrows filled the camp as hrumm and dringli bodies began dropping to the earth. Thatt helped Dieavaul up from the ground, and they sprinted deeper into the mass of swirling bodies. Thatt barked orders as it ran, and the soldiers obeyed without question, taking cover and searching the trees for their ambushers, but not before a score of their number lay dead and several more bleeding.

Dieavaul crouched next to Thatt behind an overturned wain, waiting for the attack to renew, but there was only a disquieting silence. He surveyed the camp and noted all three of the *urghuar* amongst the dead, each well-feathered with arrows. There would be little obscuring fog now unless he reached into his own reserves. A large-scale conjuration would leave him distracted, drained and vulnerable, and that he wouldn't do.

The damning accuracy of the attack arose his suspicions. The assailants had been very precise, very quiet, and knew enough about the hrumm to spot the garishly masked shamans and know what they were attempting. The Border Knights did not excel at such stealthy attacks; they were more for thundering charges. The local garrison was accounted for elsewhere by Thatt's scouts, and the farmers who populated these lands simply did not possess the skill.

They had watched the innocents' deaths, he thought, with growing realization. *They allowed the* urghuar *to butcher them and siphon their iiyir, and only then did they act.*

"Wilhorwhyr," he whispered to Thatt, with no attempt to hide his contempt.

Hatred and fear mingled in *Pakh Ma* Thatt's expression. "Raogmyztsanogg," it muttered in reply.

The Dread Forest Watchers, Dieavaul translated. *Perhaps the hrummish word is more descriptive, after all.*

Foolish chivalry, short-sighted heroism, or ignorance of the intricacies in blood ritual would have moved most humans to act prematurely in an attempt to save the captives from their plight. But letting them die and *then* killing the *urghuar*, along with all of the newly harvested *iiyir*, making waste of the blood ritual at the expense of innocent life. That restraint, precision and cold calculation could only be the work of *wilhorwhyr*.

"Send a picket line of your best scouts into the woods. We cannot allow them to destroy all we have worked for here – to taint our great sacrifice." He turned to look directly into the hrumm's yellow-red eyes and smiled the smile that made even *Pakh Ma* Thatt's blood run cold. "*Algiil ma hil*," he whispered. It was one of the few phrases he deigned speak in the hrummish tongue.

We hunt.

༄

Bloodhawk watched the hrummish scouts enter the edge of the forest with his keen half-blood eyes. *Clumsy enough, though not so loud and careless as the average human soldier.* The hrumm were, after all, predators in the wild. Even this domesticated army of Malakuur still carried the most basic instincts of their race.

Brushing a strand of jet-black hair from his weathered face, Bloodhawk weighed the situation. He and his companions numbered only five, and the army gathered here nearly five hundred. The death of the *urghuar*, worth perhaps ten times their number in simple warriors, had accomplished much. And the Pale Man, protected by powerful magic and surrounded by fanatical bodyguards, was not easy prey.

Enough, then, for now. We have more pressing matters to deal with at the castle. With the sharp whistle of a nightwing, he signaled retreat.

Bloodhawk waited patiently for his companions to reach his position. They arrived swift and silent, moving like wind through the leaves, their passing murmur indistinguishable from the chorus of forest voices around them. First Two-Moons and then Symmlrey appeared. Two-Moons had the leather face of a veteran outdoorsman, his brown eyes watching his young aulden student carefully from within their wrinkled burrows of flesh. Symmlrey, her fine features still flushed from battle, stood tall beside her human mentor. Her devotion was common to the newly initiated. The bond with a Guide was an intense one, forged in the fires of their dangerous training and cooled in the chill of an even harsher reality. Only two short years ago, Bloodhawk had felt the same for Singing Arrow. How long ago and far away that time, yet the feeling still lingered.

Two-Moons wove his hands through the air in elaborate gesticulations. *What of Khyri and Jasper?*

Bloodhawk frowned and responded in the silent tongue of weaving fingers. *Should be near. I look now. Wait.*

Two-Moons and Symmlrey took watch in the lower limbs of the trees as Bloodhawk shouldered his recurve bow and melted into the foliage. Jasper was young and newly bonded; he could have fallen to misfortune. Khyri would doubtless lend aid, but it was odd that she sent out no call for help. This troubled him. If it was Khyri who by some circumstance had suffered misadventure, Jasper may have panicked and not signaled distress.

Or they could both be dead.

Bloodhawk blinked away his speculation. He had no time for such conveniences. He would need to make a small hole in hrumm perimeter to infiltrate their lines and clear a path for retreat. It did little good to sneak in if the path to escape was blocked. With most of the wildlife scared away by the siege-craft construction, it was not difficult for the *wilhorwhyr* to detect the group of hrumm patrolling this area. It was a small party, numbering only six. He paced them, examining their deployment and judging which of the warriors posed the most risk. When he was satisfied with his appraisal, he allowed them to pass his position and fell in behind, unnoticed.

The rear guard had an iron necklet about its throat. This made a silent attempt at its jugular difficult. There were other alternatives, of course. Bloodhawk withdrew a long, thin dagger from its sheath at his waist and matched his victim's pace for a few yards. Then, as the hrumm was in mid-stride, he deftly kicked its supporting leg at the knee joint and pulled the off-balance scout backward onto him, cushioning its fall even as he plunged the stiletto through the unprotected eye socket and into the brain. Its death was quick and without even a gurgle.

The next was much easier prey. With no protection on its neck, a deep slice to the throat rendered it lifeless in moments, the warning of its gurgling lifeblood drowned out by the soft steps of its companions. Bloodhawk moved on to the third and smallest of the hrumm, breaking its neck like a rotten branch and lowering the corpse to the ground.

The point guard stopped and held up its hand to halt their march. The hrumm stopped and looked around suspiciously as Bloodhawk felled another hrumm with a dagger thrust between the two plates of armor protecting its back, severing its spinal column. By the time the last two hrumm had turned around to face him, Bloodhawk pressed the attack with longsword and dagger in hand. He swung his sword in a high arc aimed at its head, but the hrumm reached up and blocked it easily with its own blade. Less than a heartbeat later, Bloodhawk's dagger plunged into the exposed armpit of its outstretched limb. The hrumm fell dead with cold steel in its heart.

Bloodhawk ducked the crossbow bolt that shot toward him and tackled the last hrumm, its hand locked helplessly on the now-empty weapon.

It tried to scream, but as they landed on the frozen turf, Bloodhawk's knee was planted firmly in its belly. The only sound it made was the whoosh of air from its lungs. Bloodhawk rose and drove his sword into the hrumm's chest, pinning it lifeless to the earth.

Bloodhawk withdrew his longsword, wiped it clean and returned it to its scabbard. After retrieving his dagger from the neighboring corpse, he set off again toward the hrummish camp, to the area Khyri and Jasper had marked as theirs. It was not long before he heard the noise of battle. From the sound of it, things boded ill for his friends. Hrummish war cries, unabashedly exultant, echoed along with the clash of steel on steel. He doubled his pace, no longer worried about the threat of sound. With the battle raging so near, there was little chance of his soft tread attracting any notice.

The scene he discovered weighed heavily on his heart. His companions were in a small gully not twenty-five feet below him, surrounded by tens of jeering hrumm. It was considered a point of pride, even a coming of age, for the hrumm to taunt a *wilhorwhyr* in the wild and escape with its life. It was a dangerous tradition, a test of courage and skill, and one that often met with failure. Outnumbered to this extent, however, there was little for the beasts to fear, and their scurrilous yells were many.

Jasper stood over Khyri's unconscious form. An arrow pierced his right leg just below the knee, speckling the snow around him with blood. The young man held his longsword out in an unwavering challenge, slowly shifting on his good leg. His face was drawn and pale, his lips tight with pain, but his eyes gleamed with a courage and defiance that would make Khyri proud. In his mind, Bloodhawk could see her risking all to save her wounded Initiate, running back into danger to bring him out safely. But things had gone awry, and now, unless he could stop this, they would both die. He almost called for Two-Moons, but realized the risk was too great. Someone had to reach the castle. Bloodhawk was willing to sacrifice his life, but he could not sacrifice their mission. With some resignation, he let loose the cry of the desert kess. The hrumm hardly noticed the wispy call, but Two-Moons and Symmlrey would understand just as surely as Jasper. To his credit, the boy did not betray the realization to his foes with so much as a twitch.

A frontal assault would be a wasted effort; even a well-executed ambush would meet with dubious success. There were simply too many of the blasted creatures for his one quiver of arrows to eliminate. Even bending light offered no advantage. The Pale Man was both sorcerer and full-blooded aulden. He would meet Bloodhawk there in the halfway world of the Veil and end him and the rescue without pause. He had searched the forest for allies before their ambush on the shamans, but to no avail. The wolf packs had all fled from the great commotion of the enemy encampment, as had the birds of prey and the mountain cats. The grey bears would not have strayed far, but they yet slept their winter sleep, deep in the caves that scattered these foothills.

The caves, he exulted silently. *Always the little things.*

Singing Arrow always preached that the little things made victory certain. Whether in the wild or on the plains of battle, it was attention to detail that made the difference. Those who overlooked or discounted the insignificant often fell prey to it. Confusion would be his ally, not brute force. But he had little time to act.

Bloodhawk sat with his back against a tree, set his bow on his lap and his quiver at his side, making one arrow ready should a hasty draw be necessary. He closed his eyes and shut out the sound of the hrumm below him, focusing inward past the cage of his physical awareness. He felt the rush of nature flow through him and into him like a torrent of white water, his own petty being washed away like a mote in the deafening roar of life around him. Every tree, every insect, every rodent and reptile formed into this maddening cyclone of screams and whispers. He narrowed his focus, sifting through the countless voices until he found what he searched for, beneath the rock, clinging by the hundreds to the dank shallow caves all around him. Bloodhawk summoned his will and directed it toward the sleeping creatures, shaping it into a powerful *call*, more in images than in words, a vision that would drive them out of their holes in unquestioning panic.

An eloth will do. An eloth, coiling to strike.

Within moments, the ground at the feet of the hrummish left flank erupted in a cloud of thundering leathery wings. Streams of bats fled skyward, instinctually avoiding the constricting grasp of the cave serpent whose image filled their minds. The hrumm broke formation in surprise as great pillars of blackness darkened the starlit sky throughout the forest, and the maddened, panic-stricken creatures fluttered about them.

Bloodhawk raced through the startled hrumm. He could just make out Jasper's limping form dragging Khyri up the opposite side of the shallow embankment. Bloodhawk shifted direction to intersect their path. He knew that the confusion of the bats would not last much longer. If nothing else, that dark, writhing column might be visible for leagues, alerting the castle that something was amiss in the forest.

As Bloodhawk neared his comrades, he saw Jasper's pain in every line of his face, every plane of his straining muscles, every drop of blood that oozed from his injured leg. A cold emptiness spread in the pit of his stomach, and with the suddenness of his disturbing revelation, Bloodhawk halted in his tracks.

This is not Jasper.

The dark red ichor that so convincingly pumped from his wound left no trail in the snow. The desperate panting image before him was merely illusion, the lure at the center of a complex snare. The bats had fortunately caused sincere confusion amongst the hrumm. Bloodhawk little doubted his fate otherwise.

Escape must be immediate, before they recovered in full. The way he had come was out of the question. Doubtless the woods would be teeming with more hrumm than even he could deal with alone. Only the river offered safety. With a small enchantment he could ward off its biting chill, if but for a short while.

But Khyri – what if *she* were not illusion? She was like a sister to him; he couldn't leave her here, even if it meant his death. He could also not risk close quarters combat with whomever or whatever pretended to be her doubtless deceased pupil. And he had a good enough idea just who that might be. Whatever he was to do, it must be done with haste, before he betrayed himself to his would-be captors.

"Jasper!" he yelled, "Drop her and run! Make haste, she burdens your escape!"

The pretender's face seemed genuinely startled. "But, I can't leave her –"

"*Now*, Jasper! I will take her!"

Jasper's lips curved into a knowing smile, and then, with a ripple of light, he dissolved into the form of the Pale Man, his blade at Khyri's back. "No more games, then. Surrender to me now or watch her die."

"No surrender," Bloodhawk stated, hiding the regret of his failed bluff. "Take me in battle if you feel Oghran's luck, but call off your beasts."

Dieavaul laughed. "I think not! Why waste such willing rabble by matching blades with you myself? Bards and storybooks have killed common sense in this age. Lay down your sword and come away as my prisoner or stand against my army and fall. Only the former will save the life of your friend."

The hrumm were attempting to regroup below him. Bloodhawk felt his options slipping away with every moment he wasted in indecision. His mouth dried, and his throat tightened – he knew what must be done. He could not let Khyri fall prey to that damnable sword. He raised his bow and sighted a path along the arrow straight to one of Dieavaul's soulless black eyes.

"Waste the arrow, if you wish. It will change nothing," taunted the Pale Man.

The hrumm made their way up the slope behind their master, their remaining confusion quickly distilling into rage. There was little honor for hrummish warriors fleeing from a bat. A few of the archers reached for their quivers.

Forgive me, my friend, thought Bloodhawk in resignation, then let his arrow fly.

It struck true, burying itself in Khyri's breast and knocking Dieavaul back a step, his face agape in shock and what may have been a kind of warped admiration. Hrummish arrows whistled into the snow where moments before Bloodhawk had stood, but within two ticks the *wilhor-whyr* had disappeared out of their sight on the other side of the ridge.

He ran to the riverbank, sick in body and spirit over what he had done. *May Ingryst speed your soul*, he prayed silently as he broke through a thin patch in the ice. Better simple death than the unholy suffering Dieavaul's sword promised. With a soft-spoken word of invocation, he dove into icy waters that could still a beating heart in the space between breaths. His minor spell would preserve his warmth for a short time. With luck, it would be enough. When the hrumm arrived at this spot, they would find only a jagged hole in the ice, and none would dare follow him here – not even their dreaded master.

Chapter Six

Bad News Gets Worse

Two-Moons and Symmlrey sprinted over the broken expanse of land between them and Castle Vae, carried on legs seasoned by leagues of hard travel. The exodus of bats told Two-Moons enough to guess that his friends were most likely in dire peril, but he could do nothing for them now. Far more people would die if they did not reach the castle with their news, and none of his stranded companions would want him to sacrifice innocent lives for their rescue. Still, it did not sit well with him.

"Why did we leave in such haste? We could have felled *dozens* more!" cried Symmlrey from just behind him.

He could hear the eagerness in her tone, the reckless abandon of youth. For her, all things were possible, except death or defeat. *Was I ever so foolish?* He knew in his heart that he must have been, but he could not recall it. He looked ahead at the granite walls of their destination as it loomed ever closer on the horizon and pointedly ignored his student's question.

She persisted. "Two-Moons! Why don't you answer?"

He knew her mood would be less curious if she suspected that none of her companions might emerge from the forest alive. He reached out and touched the panicked minds of the bats for an instant and surmised that Bloodhawk had *called* them, probably as a diversion. He could only hope it helped affect the escape of one or all of his friends.

"*Two-Moons?*"

The elder *wilhorwhyr* looked back at Symmlrey for a moment, sucking her into the depth and calm of his learned gaze. "Child, why ask questions whose answers you already know?"

Symmlrey seemed to ponder this for a moment. "Surely with five of us, we could-"

"Child." Two-Moons sighed the word, speaking volumes with but one syllable, simultaneously chastising and sympathetic, impatient and tolerant. "One of us to every hundred hrumm is only fair odds in bard reckoning."

"Of course," she agreed, "but we could have killed tens more in our retreat. I have seen you do no less time and again. And Bloodhawk and Khyri, *they* are –"

"Dead for all we know," cut in Two-Moons, his tone taking on the slightest edge. Slight, but razor sharp. "Have you forgotten our purpose in your excitement?"

"No," she replied, defeated by his reason, "we must warn the castle at all cost."

"Aye, and let us hope that cost grows no greater."

Symmlrey's subsequent silence was a relief for Two-Moons' tired ears. Though the aulden had a reputation as dark and brooding, his student was of vanneahym stock, by far the most free spirited of the Seven Tribes, and even they considered her wild and reckless. She was atypical in many other respects as well. Not many aulden deigned to travel with mere humans, let alone be instructed by them. The *wilhorwhyr*, though friendly with the elder races, were still primarily of human or mixed lineage, and Symmlrey was an oddity in either group. Truth be told, Two-Moons suspected it was only as a *wilhorwhyr* that she would ever find any sense of belonging. She was not understood by her own people or welcomed by any others.

As the castle drew nearer, the drawbridge lowered, the portcullis cranked open, and a band of twenty knights issued forth from the gates at a full gallop, their armor ruddied by the glow of torches. It took less than half a span for the party to arrive, kicking up stunted clouds of snow as they came to a hasty stop in front of the *wilhorwhyr*.

The knights were lightly armored, in surcoats of azure emblazoned with the bold argent moon of Illuné. Their shields also bore the lunar device, some with a small eye staring out from four intersecting halos of light, in sinister chief. Border Knights. Their leader, set apart by his plume of glowing silver, raised his lance in salute.

"Good greetings to you both from Castle Vae," he proclaimed. "I am Sir Prentis, Captal of the Watch. We must make haste within the walls. There is a war party not long behind you."

Two-Moons raised his eyebrows, a gesture of great surprise against his placid features. "Your eyes are sharp in Castle Vae," he said quizzically, "and your hearts very trusting to offer solace for two strangers in the night."

Sir Prentis brought forward two bare back, bridle-less, mounts from the rear of his column. "Trust is not easily won in these times, milord, but by the grace of Illuné you were recognized by someone within the castle. The Lady ordered us make haste and deliver you within safely."

"Did she?" mused Two-Moons as he gently mounted the offered horse, comforting the animal with a gentle caress. Symmlrey mounted the other beside him. "I don't recall ever meeting her. No matter, let's be off. As you said, time is short."

"Yes, milord. So it seems for anyone with business at Castle Vae of late."

Two-Moons didn't bother to inquire further; there would be time enough for that inside. They set off again at a full gallop, and not long after the gates shut behind them with a solid clang of steel on stone. Torches were ablaze all along the inner courtyard, and soldiers scurried about purposefully, preparing the lower bailey and gatehouse for battle. Ballistae and catapults were cranked into firing ready, and pots of boiling oil and tar already awaited any who dared breach the walls. They had apparently been preparing for quite some time. Could the bats have been visible this far away in the dark of night?

Sharp eyes, indeed.

The immensity of the stone walls surrounding them made Two-Moons slightly uneasy. He didn't care for closed environs. He had visited several such places: Tiriel, Mychah, Khalamahr, even once the vast sprawl of Moot Khy, but never by choice, and never for long. He was at home in the sweeping plains and dense forests of his home, comfortable enough in the mountains, tolerant of the Great Desert and the formidable Ice Reach, but definitely ill at ease when within these walls, within *any* walls. Necessity was an uncaring master, however, and he resigned himself to make the best of it. He would not stay long.

After dismounting, Sir Prentis led them through the outer defenses and then inside the central keep itself. Two-Moons noticed that Symmlrey kept quiet, her hood pulled low over her face. *Just as well*, he thought. *Best not to attract any unwanted attention to her race.*

Humans had little love for the fae, and he had no desire to test the hospitality of these people. Tales of aulden folk making away with good human stock for their mysterious purposes were still alive and well and sometimes even true. The fae were an enigmatic bunch, even to their allies, and speculation about them was not uncommon even within the ranks of the *wilhorwhyr*.

The interior of the keep was dark, lit by sputtering torches at intervals just regular enough to keep the passageways on the lighter side of dim. Thick, colorful, tapestries lined the walls, woven with epic images of battle and romance. Two-Moons recognized some of them as scenes from the *Stands of Kiev Vae*, others from immortalized tales of the Border Knights. The smaller hangings depicted various coats-of-arms of distinguished nobles. He guessed that such workmanship must have been quite expensive.

As they rounded the final bend in a flight of spiral stairs, many of Two-Moons' questions answered themselves as he spied the imposing reptilian form of an old friend. "Kassakan! A blessing amidst curses! I wondered what eyes had seen so much where so little was to be seen."

"Welcome," said Kassakan, putting one of her scaly hands on his shoulder. "And thank you, Captal Prentis. I know you are anxious to return to your post, you need delay no more."

"Yes milady. Thank you."

As their escort left the way they had come, Two-Moons introduced Symmlrey to his friend. Kassakan bowed her neck slightly toward the hooded young woman, her nostrils flaring as she sniffed the air. "Welcome, child of the Vanneahym. This is a rare pleasure. Destiny's call has reached the ears of many in gathering us to this place."

"Thank you," replied Symmlrey.

"Come, the Lady Evynine awaits us." Kassakan swung open a door of belwood at least two feet thick with no apparent effort and then led them into the large brightly lit room beyond.

Within the chamber was a collection of paintings, tapestries and sculpture that shamed the articles lining the entry halls, and that was no mean feat in itself. Two-Moons looked upon portraits that seemed ready to walk forth from their burnished frames, creatures of fact and legend held only in cages of oil and canvas; and landscapes, some exotic locales where he himself had tread, like windows looking out on all corners of the world from within the confines of this one room. The thick, yielding rug on which they walked depicted the journeys of Goron Lionshield, one image flowing to the next as it led the viewer along on his ancient quest of exploration and discovery. Two-Moons had little use for material wealth that he could not carry on his person, but for him the wealth in this room far outweighed that of kings who filled their coffers with bits of shiny metal and jewels, thinking themselves rich beyond compare. This was treasure rich in spirit as well as gold.

Three large hearths lit and heated the room, one on each wall save that housing the main door, with a long obsidian oak table set before each.

The tables were beautifully wrought, the legs rendered in the form of two entwined dragons, wings outstretched to support their polished surfaces. The tables on either side of them were empty, but the head table opposite the door was set with chairs and victuals.

A tall woman sat before them, gowned in a woolen garment of deepest blue. Her golden hair was pulled back from her face in a single braid, revealing features at once striking and welcoming. On her right was a bearded man, his bloodshot brown eyes staring from dark sockets, dressed only in a thin coverlet that clung to his moist, sweat-soaked skin. He had a warrior's girth, slighted by his stooped posture and the tight look of pain on his pallid face.

Kassakan strode before them and bowed slightly to the table. "May I present Lady Evynine, Mistress of Castle Vae and Baroness of the Western March; and her friend and ally, Sir Osrith Turlun." Kassakan then pivoted to indicate the guests. "And this is Two-Moons of the Ebuouki and his young charge Symmlrey, *wilhorwhyr* both, and friends to all that is good."

"Welcome," said Evynine. "Please accept our hospitality." She waved at the empty chairs across from her. "Your journey has not been an easy one, I'll wager. Eat and drink your fill, and we shall share news."

Two-Moons eyed the plates set with aromatic cheeses, fresh-baked breads, pots of honey and fruit preserves, and several flasks of wine, ale and milk. A worthy meal for such short notice, and very politic to the strict dietary requirements of the *wilhorwhyr*. "Forgive my manners, but I am a man short on small graces. My news is best delivered straight away."

Evynine tilted her head quizzically. "Do you not bring news of the hrumm? This we now know, with all thanks to you and to Kassakan's discerning sight. We are well defended here, and well provisioned, not to mention extremely stubborn. Take a moment to rest, and we may yet discuss the details at length."

"Alas, Lady Evynine, I regret that there is more afoot than what awaits you in the woods. We no more expected to stumble upon these hrumm at your doorstep than you expected them there. Your peril is greater than siege or ambush alone."

"Indeed?" Evynine sat back in her chair, frowning. "This is troubling news. Please explain, but rest yourselves while you may."

Two-Moons nodded, and he and Symmlrey took their seats, for which even his seasoned limbs were thankful. He poured himself a goblet of the clear wine before beginning his story, relishing its sweet caress as it washed away the dryness in his throat. He closed his eyes for a moment, loathe to deliver such tidings, but finally spoke.

"I will come right to it. The force here is but a vanguard. Malakuur has an army at Ten Man Pass, and they prepare even now to march against you. Worse, this is not like any army yet assembled by the thars. They have gathered hrumm, dringli and humans, as before – but leading them are at least a half dozen andu'ai. We do not know if any of their number are *qals*, but they are certainly making ready for war alongside the Malakuuri."

There was silence.

Two-Moons waited as the impact of his words sunk in. The Lady Vae's face paled as she bit her lower lip. Kassakan nodded her snout, as if the revelation made some sort of sense to her. Osrith furrowed his brow and sneered back at Two-Moons, reaching for his wine goblet.

"Andu'ai?" he scoffed, taking a large drink and wiping his mouth with his sleeve. "Not bloody likely."

Symmlrey leaned forward, her voice icy. "Do you really think we would be here if we weren't sure it was the Old Foe, and not some clever subterfuge?"

Osrith rolled his eyes, but didn't answer.

"I understand your reluctance," Two-Moons said with a nod. "When Raefnir came to us from Malakuur, we too were skeptical. She was one of the most honored of our Order, but her body was twisted and half-eaten by plague and her brain wracked by feverish visions. We couldn't know if what she told us was real or her illness eating away her reason."

Two-Moons paused to quench his dry throat with more wine before going on, the corners of his mouth turning downward at the memory. "In truth, though we'd been fighting this wasting sickness since Goldenmoon, I had not yet seen the affliction so advanced. Her tongue was so swollen she could barely speak. By all rights she should have been long dead, but Raefnir was, well…." He sighed, unable to find the words he sought.

"Tenacious of will," interjected Kassakan. "She was a strong ally and a good friend. She will be remembered well."

"So how do you know she wasn't crazy?" pressed Osrith.

"My companions and I infiltrated Malakuur to see what could be seen for ourselves. To our dismay, we found the andu'ai just as Raefnir had described, amongst the massed troops and clearly in charge."

"Goddess Above," whispered Evynine, her head shaking ever so slightly from side to side. "Andu'ai? But –"

"How? Why?" Two-Moons finished the question for her. "We do not know. We have been preoccupied with the wasting sickness, perhaps to a fault, but until this news plague seemed our greatest worry. Regardless, it is now more a question of what we may do to stop them. They do not come to the Malakuuri empty-handed. We believe they have tapped an *iiyir* well."

Only Kassakan's reaction betrayed any hint of what that simple statement implied.

Osrith straightened in his chair, focusing on the white haired *wilhorwhyr*. "What in the pits is an *ear well*?" he grunted skeptically. "I'm as well-traveled as any man, more than most, and I've not heard scream or whisper of one before now."

"*Iiyr* wells are known by many different names; they are called *feain iiyir* by the Seven Tribes, *muachmii* by the underkin, and *y'rtai* by the hosskan. To humankind, they are more readily recognized by given names, such as the Riven Tree or the Starless Pool. Regardless, they are all the same, links to our world from a place of infinite energy. They are great and inexhaustible sources of magic."

"The Starless Pool," Osrith sighed, though decidedly not in relief. "*That* is a name I recognize."

"But Andulin destroyed the Starless Pool, or so the legends say," added Evynine. "Can we not do the same to this other *iiyir* well?"

"I'm afraid it won't be an easy matter, milady," said Kassakan, her eye slits contracting. "Andulin was forced to destroy the Eye of Miithrak to close that Well. Such an artifact is not available to us. At least not to my knowledge."

"Nor mine," said Two-Moons, "but the good sage Gaious resides not far from here. He may have help for us."

"Gai? I'm afraid he'll be of help to no one," said Osrith, pulling a crust of bread from one of the loaves on the table. "Dieavaul's first visit was to his retreat. That's where I came from. I doubt he still lives."

Silence again.

The fires crackled and spat in an attempt to heat the room, but for Two-Moons it grew only colder. Gaious should have been no simple meal, even for the Pale Man. He had worn the black robes once. He could cast the greater spells, *had* cast them in the past, before his oath. This was indeed a loss.

Two-Moons rubbed his cheek with his index finger. Reaching Castle Vae had only been a short-term goal. He and Bloodhawk had believed they could best find their way from here, like surveying the land from the tallest peak to choose the clearest path. Instead, Two-Moons found fog and mist clinging to the valleys below his vantage point, obscuring his sight and the road before him. Perhaps he simply needed sleep. Perhaps, but there was no time for that now.

"I am leaving for Dwynleigsh in the morning," said Osrith, interrupting the stillness. "I'll carry your news there along with mine. I never trusted the likes of Agrylon much, but Gai spoke highly of him. Maybe he can be of some help."

Evynine turned on the man to her right, eyes wide and face flushed. "You are not yet well, I forbid you travel anywhere! You agreed to stay until you were whole again."

Osrith laughed, but Two-Moons detected no mirth in the hollow sound. "That, milady, is not likely to happen soon. At any rate, my presence here has brought evil to your gates. If I leave, perhaps it will follow."

"Kassakan," pleaded Evynine. "Dissuade him from this foolishness."

"It is foolish but necessary, milady. Perhaps the errand that Gai set for Osrith shall provide us with the answers we seek. And, as he says, his presence here is dangerous for you and your people. We will have to risk the journey as soon as possible."

The baroness set her jaw squarely and bent her eyes downward. "Very well, I shall have my castellan supply you with all you need. Horses, provisions, men-at-arms if you'll have them." She looked across the table at the *wilhorwhyr*. "What of your plans, Two-Moons? You are welcome here as long as you'll suffer our limited hospitality."

Two-Moons shook his head. "I will bring your friends to Dwynleigsh unharmed, through paths hard traveled and little known. Then we shall see. Agrylon is known to me only in name, but he is wise among men. He may offer a plan to destroy the *iiyir* well, or defeat the andu'ai. If he has naught for us, then we shall make our own way."

"I suppose I shall wait here for siege or fever, whichever comes first," sighed Evynine. "I offer you whatever you may need, as well as my prayers and good wishes. I hope they suffice."

"Gods!" spat Osrith as he rose and made for the door. "The war will be fought before you finish with your pleasantries. The Empire was won and lost in the time it takes you to say goodbye. I must make ready."

Two-Moons watched as the door slammed behind the disheveled mercenary and stood, laying a hand on Symmlrey's deceptively delicate shoulder. "Gruffly put, but true enough. Thank you for your kindness, Lady Evynine, but we must away."

"The thanks will be mine to give if you bring that dour man to Dwynleigsh alive," said Evynine, waving the back of her hand at the door. "He's not yet ready for the task himself."

Two-Moons offered what comfort he could in the steady confidence of his voice. "No steel shall touch him while under my protection," he promised, his gentle tone contrasting the boldness of his words. "You must concern yourself with far more than one man, no matter how dear a friend, so I shall concern myself with him."

"As will I, milady," Kassakan assured her. "He will be well guarded from Dieavaul and his beasts."

Evynine drew herself up and smiled on her guests, the worried lines about her eyes and mouth melting away into her soft milky skin. Two-Moons was almost fooled by her show of relaxed acceptance, but years of experience allowed him to peek beneath the well-oiled armor of her court etiquette and see the anxiety that dwelled within. He admired her show of strength, and he had no illusions for whose benefit it was displayed.

"I shall summon my castellan," she said as she walked from the room. Pausing at the door, she added, "Good speed to you all, and good luck."

As her footsteps echoed down the hallway beyond, Two-Moons exchanged a glance with his silent companion. They both knew they would need whatever luck was left to offer them.

And all too soon, he feared.

Chapter Seven

Storms and Wards

CALVRAIGN sat on the crooked tree stump with a grunt, leaning the heavy iron woodsman's axe against the oaken remnant and flexing the stiffness from his fingers. He wiped his leather gloves on his thighs and brushed bits of dirt and bark to the half-frozen ground. Dawn was breaking, a pale gleam stealing across the horizon like a stealthy knife in the dark. He inhaled deeply and stretched his arms out over his head. A slow burn smoldered in his muscles. Four stacks of wood, nearly half a cord, were piled next to the back door of the Wayside Inn.

The work was hard, but along with the ache in his shoulders came familiar comfort. Calvraign had scarce left Craignuuwn, and this passing moment of the mundane was a welcome peace. For all his thoughts of adventure, he'd not much occasion for travel save an odd trip or two to Eahnswod or Brinishire to trade, and once, to Draenuuwn for a woodsmote with Ewbhan Breigh. He was beyond it all now, in the windswept in-between of the plains where his father had once tread on his way to war.

This road led him to the greylands, he thought.

Calvraign closed his eyes. He could still see the column of soldiers, winding like a steel snake through the hills, with colors flying bright against the suns-set from spears and halberds and staves of oak and ash. Marshal Bowen's return brought tales of triumph, glory, and the return of the King's Peace to the plains of Paerytm. But the old Marshal also brought with him the cost of that victory, in dead and dying flesh.

Ibhraign had been wrapped from head to toe in linen and then dressed in his mail and leather cuirass and greaves. His helm had been split but secured to his head with wires, and fitted with fresh plumage of eagle and hawk feathers. Ibhraign had marched out of Craignuuwn side by side with Bowen and the other war captains of the Cythe, the *madhwr-rwn*, Faille and Gabhougn, but only the Marshal had returned on his feet. They'd left Faille in Dwynleigsh with a death of fever; Gabhougn had fallen at Haight Hollow; and Ibhraign had come home on his shield.

Bowen had fed Calvraign's father to the barrow mound with all the honors due a fallen hero and knight of the realm. There had been feasting and drinking and tales of his valor and his victories and finally a dirge of his death. Ibhraign was buried with spear and bow, but Calvraign had received his father's sword. For his mother, the king had sent a pensioner's purse and a sealed writ she'd burned after reading.

Calvraign couldn't recall his father's face, not truly, nor but a hint of his voice. His legend, he had committed to memory. His sword, he wore at his hip. But of the man himself, his remembrance was but a shadow on a breeze.

The scent of sizzling bacon tickled at his nostrils, and his thoughts fled as his empty belly grumbled. Calvraign rose to seek out the matron. She'd promised him a full breakfast in exchange for his labor, as was the custom at the Wayside Inns that dotted the king's highways. Brohan had chosen to pay in coin, but Calvraign neither wished to skip a meal or take the bard's generosity for granted. He'd mucked the stables and repaired a faulty hinge the night before, and then risen well before dawn to milk the cows and split logs for firewood. It had been more than he was asked, but he hoped to earn either a few copper talons or some extra biscuits for the trail.

Calvraign pushed open the rear door of the inn, leaving behind the frosty morning for the warmth of the kitchen's cooking fires. Pots and utensils hung from the walls, and foods in various states of preparation were laid out on the oaken worktables at either end of the room. It was not a large kitchen, but it was well provisioned with several varieties of colored squash, meats, potatoes, cheeses, eggs, bread and dried fruits.

The matron was not difficult to find. She was a robust woman and not a soft speaker. Currently, she stood at the farthest of the hearths, sweating over a pot of porridge. She wore the same plain black homespun garb as all the servants of the Wayside, her thinning gray hair pulled back into a bun. She directed her two sons with the help of an oat-caked wooden spoon, the loose skin of her arm flapping with each gesticulation.

Calvraign caught her eye, and the glistening flesh of her cheeks rippled into a smile that revealed too few teeth to be attractive. "You're a busy lad about this morning," she said. "No stranger to work, I can tell. Go sit b'the fire, and my Hedwin will bring you a bite."

"Perhaps two bites, if I'm lucky," Calvraign said, eyeing the abundant fare with a smile and a wink.

Calvraign retreated to the common room. The pre-dawn glow seeped through the windows, illuminating half a dozen long oak tables with benches, one doublewide hearth, and a pair of young boys playing timbo sticks in the corner near the stairs. The Inn did not offer many comforts, but it was clean and warm, and this alone was great improvement over the last two nights wrapped in a blanket on the side of the trail. The tables sat vacant, and though the fire was still young in the hearth, Calvraign waded through the thick layer of fresh rushes to claim a seat with his back to the warmth of the awakening flames.

Hedwin was not long behind him, and delivered oat porridge and thick-cut bacon on a trencher of rye, with a cup of thin ale to smooth its passage. The matron's daughter was only a ten-year, if that, but she had wide beautiful eyes of chestnut brown that reminded him of Callagh Breigh. He was surprised how much he missed her already. How much he remembered the feel of her against him at the dance, how he could but just recall the wispy memory of her kiss. He wished he could have at least bid her a fare-thee-well before leaving Craignuuwn, but Brohan had practically chased him down the road that morning they'd set out for the capital.

"Thank you," he said, as if showing her courtesy might assuage his guilt, or soothe his unsettled loneliness. "Many thanks, indeed."

Hedwin nodded, biting down on her smile as she backed away to the kitchen.

Calvraign made short work of the meal. The porridge was not remarkable, but bacon at breakfast, save during the Feast of Oa, was an exceptional and welcome treat. By the time he spotted Brohan descending the steps at the far end of the room, only a bit of trencher remained.

"Shall I get you a bite to eat?" offered Calvraign.

Brohan smiled. "Did you leave any? No matter. I've done my damage to the stores this morning already, with Sister Aidhen. Fried apples with spiced sausage and light, crusty bread slathered in a thick cream of butter. Delightful." Brohan paused for a moment, taking a seat across from Calvraign. "Ah, and how was your porridge?"

"It seems you had better company and better fare than I managed," Calvraign said, with a perturbed shake of his head. "I hope she was worth whatever coin you lavished upon her. A real lady from the House of Flowers is not without price, or so they say."

"Sister Aidhen and I are old friends. Or, at least, I'm old and she's friendly. She finds me companionable enough, and she knows how best to entertain the likes of me."

Calvraign laughed aloud at that. "What? She plays *Mylyr Gaeal* with you all night, and lets you win?"

Brohan only grinned, changing the subject with a nod at the door. "We should go. The suns are waking, and we've more long days ahead of us."

Calvraign nodded. "I'll get the packs," he said, rising.

Brohan waved him down with a roll of his eyes. "Sit, sit. They'll bring our packs, lad. You've done all but mend the thatching around here. The custom is to trade a chore for a hot meal and lodging, not to indenture yourself, by the Gods Between. Had they any horse in the stable, I'd take them too, in trade for the work you've done."

"A horse *would* be nice," Calvraign agreed, resuming his seat. "Even a pack mule."

"Only the busiest of the waysides are stocked with anything but some basic foodstuffs, these days," lamented Brohan. "We're still a bit off the beaten path, here – at least for king's business."

"But, by Oghran's luck, you manage to find a pretty flower and spiced sausage where I find a straw pallet and a bowl of porridge," Calvraign observed.

"I make my own luck, lad. My comings and goings are not so much of a secret this close to the Winter Festival, and the flowers know from whom to mine coin in hard times. Aidhen... ."

Further explanation died on Brohan's lips as the heavy main door flew open with a creak and a thud. Calvraign shifted his attention to the doorway as well, and the three men who walked in stiff and cold as the morning breeze.

Thick winter cloaks of dark forest green were draped over their mail byrnies, half-helms cradled in the crook of their arms, their free hands but a thought away from the long swords sheathed in black leather scabbards at their sides. The steel of their mail and helms was dulled, oiled but not shiny, almost black in the faint light of morning. Calvraign could just make out a small badge sewn into their cloaks, a blue shield bearing a black wolf's head, with a bar of silvered lightning, sinister.

House Malminnion, thought Calvraign. *That's the baron's own seal.* They were lightly armored, so likely not part of a main battle party or the formal Baronial Guard, but only those in the direct service of the baron bore that device.

"Keeper!" shouted the shortest, and oldest, of the three men. The sweat from his bald scalp still steamed from the chill air outside. Two wide scars sprang from the upper left of his face, one splitting his iron grey brow, the other his leathery cheek, flanking his eye and continuing in thick rills of white puckered tissue across his angular features. Although the higher of the two scars ended just short of the bridge of his nose, the lower scar terminated at the corner of his mouth, where the taut skin tugged his expression into a perpetual, and most unnatural, one-sided grin.

Calvraign guessed he must be their leader, both from his bearing and from the telltale black wolf-fur trim on his cloak and the silver brooch that fastened it. The symbol on the broach was an old one, the eternally entwined First Tree, whose roots and limbs reached up and down and toward each other, connecting to form a delicately filigreed circle surrounding the trunk. He recognized the heraldry, and placed the man in the Macc adh Tremaign – or rather, what *used* to be the Macc adh Tremaign. The family name had shifted, with the family loyalties, from the Cythe and their tongue to the Dacadians and theirs, centuries ago. Now, the family was known as Tremayne, and some things less reputable, in private company.

Calvraign swallowed and took a tentative breath, intimidated despite himself. It was not the first time he'd seen a soldier, nor even one with a nasty scar; but, as for a man descended from the oldest lines of Cythe royalty, scarred and steaming and apparently in a foul mood – this was a first. Brohan nudged Calvraign's boot gently, and then cast his eyes downward, hiding his face by resting it on his opened palm and staring into the fire.

"Keeper!" the man repeated, throwing his gloves onto the other unoccupied table next to the fire, but as yet, paying Calvraign and Brohan no mind. The ease and force of his baritone voice only affirmed Calvraign's guess that he was a man accustomed to command. "Provisions!"

Even as his men shrugged off their cloaks and took seats on the bench at the adjacent table, the matron and her daughter were through the kitchen door, the former balancing a tray of fresh bread, butter and jam, her bluster tamed at least for the moment. Hedwin carried a clay flagon of steaming spiced wine, and three matching cups, and served the men without a word. When she finished, she took her place behind her mother's skirts.

"Milord," the matron deferred with bent head. "I pray the Swords have kept you safe on your travels. I'll have Hedwin bring some sausages and bacon, and we have porridge if you'd like it. Is there ought else?"

"I've a score more men down the road. They'll be hungry, but we'll not need lodging. His Grace and his host will be but a day or so after, so be ready. He shall stay a night, maybe two if the weather turns foul."

The matron paled. "Hi… His Grace? Here? Tomorrow?"

"Aye," he affirmed, taking a goblet and sipping carefully from the corner of his mouth opposite his disfigurement. He was not looking at the matron as he spoke, however; his gaze had landed and fixed on Brohan.

"I did na' think His Grace would be ready for a wintry road, so soon." She paused, her voice pinched. "So soon after the red pox, that is."

"Mmmm," mused the ever-grinning man, still staring at the master bard. "His Grace, Baron Haoil, made a colder journey. The pox claimed him last Lucenday. However, Ezriel has assumed his father's title, and now rides to the capital in order to meet with the king and consecrate his birthright."

The matron moaned and held her hand to her mouth. "Blasted pox," she lamented. "He was better a man than deserved to die abed. We shall all mourn him, just as we shall welcome Lord Ezriel, um, Lord *Malminnion* to –"

"That will do," dismissed the man, nodding at her briefly. "Go and prepare and waste no pleasantries on me. I shall be gone as soon as I've supped. My thanks for the food."

No sooner had she gone than the unnerving grin turned back to Brohan. "Well, if it isn't the Black Bard," he said flatly. "I waste a year of my life looking for you without any luck, and now that it makes no matter, here you are."

Brohan shifted his head in his hand to meet the man's gaze. "I do apologize, Lord Tremayne. Your ill luck was my good fortune, I suppose." He wiggled his fingers. "I'm rather fond of these. I would have hated to have you part them from me."

Lord *Tremayne*, Calvraign marveled. *Not simply* of *the Macc adh Tremaign. This is* the Macc adh Tremaign! *In another age, this man might have been my king.*

"In hindsight, we are both better off, I'm sure." Tremayne sat across from them, took another sip of wine, and pointed at Calvraign. "Who's this lad? I see he wears a sword, but I see no badge."

"Lord Ashgar Treymane, Warden of the Crehr ne Og and Captain of Ezriel's Outriders, may I present my apprentice, Calvraign Askewneheur of Craignuuwn," answered Brohan.

"Ibhraign's son?" Tremayne said without pause. He raised his brow, and consequently the entire left side of his face. He cocked his head. "I suppose you have his look about you."

Calvraign had heard that his whole life. No one could ever seem to pinpoint exactly how, what feature or mannerism triggered the recognition, but there it was: *he had his look.*

"My lord, I am honored to meet you," Calvraign said, though in fact, he was mostly puzzled. He felt he should rise and then ask for leave to sit again, but Brohan made no move, so he merely fidgeted.

"Be still," chastised Tremayne, deciphering his discomfort. "We're not at court, and we don't need to play at Imperial manners, here. I'll be in the thick of *thees* and *thous* and bowing and scraping soon enough without help from you."

"Yes, and that's an interesting business," interjected Brohan. "Poor Haoil. I'll miss His Grace. I half-expected Ezriel to play the righteous lancer and defer the title and lands to Garath."

"Don't bait me, I'm too tired," demurred Tremayne.

The sausages and bacon appeared then, as quickly as Hedwin vanished, and Tremayne turned his attention to the food. "I suppose you're off to the festival, then?" he inquired between mouthfuls.

"Aye," Brohan agreed. "I would offer to share the road with you, and perhaps more news, but I'm sure you wouldn't care for the distraction. Be sure to give our regards to His Grace, when you see him. Perhaps we will have occasion to break bread at the festival."

"Hmmm," Tremayne commented. "Safe journey."

&

Calvraign stared at Brohan's back. His weary eyes squinted against the glare of the snow about him, his legs moving mechanically, attempting to match the bard's steady rhythm. For leagues about them he saw only a smooth expanse of glaring white. The rolling hills of Craignuuwn had vanished days ago behind them, and he imagined it would be at least another two or three before the legendary spires of Dwynleigsh rose from the plains to greet them. Though sore, cold, and exhausted, Calvraign carried himself on behind Brohan without comment. At last, the life he had long dreamed and hoped for now lay before him – colder perhaps than he would prefer, but before him nonetheless.

The wind was a chill reminder of the season, but brought with it only straggling flakes of snow today. The sky was dark and threatening, but docile enough as yet, for which he overheard even implacable Brohan muttering thanks under his breath. Out on the plains, with only the occasional defiant copse of trees to break the wind, there was little in the way of shelter, and any respite from the storm was appreciated.

They had spoken little since their departure from the Wayside Inn. The first day, when Calvraign had attempted to broach the subject of Lord Tremayne, Brohan's response had been a rather terse, *Practice your scales.* That had set the mood for the day, and the next was no better, when his curt answer had been, *Recite the Lays of the Maernwold.* Calvraign knew the *Lays*, of course – it was a classic pre-Imperial piece – and it was a revered example of the ancient forms and diction as difficult as it was long. The day after, he was commanded to translate it from Old Dacadh to Middle Imperial. All the while, the master bard marched on, frowning into the snow without comment.

What bothered Brohan specifically about his encounter with Tremayne, Calvraign did not know. Although he didn't know it was Tremayne who had chased him, he had certainly known that Brohan was the infamous Black Bard that House Malminnion had despised to the point of sanction. There weren't enough black-skinned men, let alone minstrels, in the Crehr ne Og for there to be any confusion over his identity. The death of Haoil Malminnion surely shouldn't bring on such a sour mood, since it had been Haoil who outlawed him in the first place. What then?

Calvraign decided that finding out was worth whatever interminable task Brohan might have in store to keep him quiet for another day, and picked up his pace to draw alongside him.

"You can at least tell me who'll be at court," he began, only to be silenced almost immediately by Brohan's dry chuckle.

"Really? Seems to me the *least* I could do is say nothing at all."

"Well, you don't want the king to think my worst is your best, do you? You've had how many years to –" Calvraign paused, swallowing his pent up anger and defensiveness. He held up a hand to still the bard's tongue. "My knowledge of history and verse is good, but of the modern court and its intricacies… ." He shrugged. "Mostly we talk of theories and practices of politics, or ancient histories, but seldom the court intrigues of the day. I don't want to embarrass you, myself, or the king."

"Better," conceded Brohan with a nod. "An explanation is more persuasive than a declaration, at least in intelligent company."

"Does this mean we're on speaking terms again?" prodded Calvraign.

"I don't see that I have the luxury of continued silence, Cal. You aren't wrong. Had I known a year gone that we'd be making this journey we'd have delved into that mess for you and made some sense of it. Even so, you'd not be entirely ready for court. Many an aristocrat has lived out his life and gone to his grave with still less a clue than you might have. But, I'll do what I may while I can."

Brohan took a moment to gather his thoughts and continued, throwing his arm about Calvraign's shoulder as they trudged on together. "The easiest guide through politicking is to live by these three words: *watch your back.*" He poked Calvraign between the shoulder blades with his index finger to emphasize each syllable, and then dropped his arm back to his side. "Those who appear friendly are often not your friends, just as those who appear villainous are not always your enemy. You must never make a snap judgment based on appearances alone. Look beneath the facades, around the corners and behind the curtains. Choose your friends and your words wisely."

"That makes for a nice speech, but I was hoping for some more practical advice."

"Advice is always a tricky thing. It's only practical if you practice it, and even then it's not always effective. Still, sometimes there is naught else to say."

"Well, I'm not planning on engaging in any political maneuvers. I mean, what enemies could *I* possibly have at court?" scoffed Calvraign. "I've nothing to offer nor offend. Surely, if they even know who I am, then they know my father saved the king's life at Vlue Macc?"

"Indeed they do, Calvraign. Acutely. I do not expect your arrival to go unnoticed, in fact – this is what worries me. Your father's deeds do not make for you as many allies as you might think."

Calvraign stopped in his tracks, then shuffled forward again to catch up with Brohan. "What?" His voice was pitched somewhere between incredulity and disbelief. "Would they rather see the king dead? I thought Guillaume was well liked, well respected?"

"Ah, my boy, you are still a bit naïve, I'm afraid. There are many with much to gain from Guillaume's death, then as now, and they might not look favorably upon those taking great pains to extend his life. Though not actively seeking its end, neither would they shed more than a diplomatic tear should the time come sooner rather than later. Remember, when your father saved the king, the princes were just young lads, and Vingeaux was barely of an age to rule. Many a peer would have sought to fill the role of regent and thus extend the influence of their respective House. You might serve as an unpleasant reminder of lost opportunity, or even an embarrassment."

"An *embarrassment?*" Calvraign seethed. "I will not hide who I am, or what my father did, to placate anyone."

"Yes, well, I'm not asking you to hide anything. Hiding won't help you. You can't very well hide from a pit, can you? You just need to avoid falling into it."

"Might you illuminate my steps, then?"

Brohan looked away, but Calvraign spotted an odd flicker of uncertainty in his eyes that only added an awkward gravitas to the brief silence that hung between them. "Calvraign," he started, then pinched his lips in a frown. "Cal," he started again, in what seemed a forced familiarity, "have you ever thought it odd that I was dispatched to be your tutor? That your mother's pension was so generous?"

"No," Calvraign answered. "My father saved the life of the king. He is a hero many times over. I expect that Guillaume is merely grateful and generous."

"Very generous, Cal," the bard agreed. "But not questioning such generosity is one sure way to fall into that pit we're trying to keep you out of. Think on it. Find the truth here, and you understand not only the ties that bind you to the throne, but those who might be disadvantaged by such a bond. And those who might benefit most from severing it."

"He saved the king's life," Calvraign repeated, flustered.

"Stop thinking like a boy," chided Brohan, and not gently. "It's my own fault, I suppose. I always found your quaint affect refreshing and enjoyable; I think I rather encouraged it. I should have been beating it out of you. I may have misread things. I may have done you disservice."

"What?"

"Your father was a good man and a good soldier. But Calvraign – giving his life to protect the king, in the eyes of the nobility it was no more than his *duty*. For certain, he executed that duty in dramatic and heroic fashion, and a reward would be expected. Coin and some small parcel of land, perhaps even squire you out to a House of some repute and make a knight of you. Your mother could have been taken into any number of households and lived a comfortable life. It's not that rewards are uncommon, and Guillaume is – *was*, at least – a generous king in this way.

"But Calvraign," he pursed his lips again. "I am a *master* bard. I record histories, I advise kings… ."

Calvraign's stomach rolled as he finished the unspoken words in his own thoughts, *This is beneath me.* "Yet you accepted the task," he said quietly. "You didn't turn him down."

"I *did*, in fact. Several times. But he was very persistent and very nearly dead, and so I relented. We were closer then." Brohan squeezed Calvraign's shoulder firmly. "I don't regret the decision, Cal. Not at all. But you must be wary. If the king has chosen to be so charitable with you, it is not without reason. And that reason could be both your boon and your bane, so we must not ignore it. We must dissect it until we discover the entrails of truth."

"The entrails of truth?" Calvraign repeated, as if he'd tasted something sour. "Not your better turn of phrase, Master Madrharigal."

"I'm cold," explained Brohan, lightly. "We'll re-write it into something more fitting in the histories."

"You think *this* conversation will be in the histories?" laughed Calvraign.

"That depends on who is writing the histories, of course. My point is that until now you have rested a little too comfortably on some simple pillars of truth, ignoring the catacombs of hidden motivations and complex realities that honeycomb the foundations. We must know what ground this is all built upon, to shore up the walls and withstand a siege."

Calvraign smiled. "The words have scarcely left your lips, and you've already begun editing them. But, I think you have your new analogy. I much prefer the truth as sturdy chunks of stone and mortar to messy innards."

"Even a master bard has to adjust his tune, now and again."

"I'm glad to see that wasting your time with me can still have its uses."

Brohan's easy humor evaporated. "Never wasted," he said. "Don't think for a moment that I feel it's wasted. There's no jest in that."

Calvraign nodded and turned his attention to the crunching snow beneath his boots. There was a fundamental truth to Brohan's words. It was so fundamental, so basic; he wondered that he'd never thought to ponder it before. It seeped into him like the cold. It had always been there, but while distracted he'd paid it no notice. Once the chill took hold, however, dispelling it was no simple matter.

The king wants something from me, he speculated. *He expects something. His kindness is not the end itself; it is the means to an end.*

Calvraign remembered something General Vae had said, after being elevated to the peerage by Empress Émariel. "Some gifts are more dear to accept than bequest," he quoted aloud.

"Yes!" Brohan approved, his bright eyes intense. "You see? I told you my time was not wasted. On with it and out with it."

Calvraign's lips were only a moment behind his thoughts. "He saved the Empire. Émariel raised him to Baron of the Western March as reward for his heroism. He was awarded the very lands he'd done battle on, but it was more than simple generosity. It was a fitting prize, but one weighted by the Empress' charge to maintain its defense."

"Yes," Brohan said slowly. "But you examine only the mixed nature of the prize itself, not the subtlety of intent behind it. You think in only two dimensions – let that only be the start. Émariel had yet to birth an heir, Dmylriani had sailed away, Celian was murdered, and here returns a strong, intelligent and resourceful general fresh from legendary victories over an invading hrummish Host."

"Did she see him as a *threat*?" Calvraign struggled with the notion. Perhaps any other general – but Kiev Vae? Not only had he secured the Western March, he'd revolutionized the concept of military tactics and honor. Betrayal seemed unlikely from him, if any of his lessons were true.

"A precaution, perhaps," mused Brohan, sensing Calvraign's disquiet. "You must always keep your generals busy – especially the good ones. I'm not quite old enough to remember that first hand, I'm afraid. But then again, perhaps the threat she perceived was not so much *to* her or *from* him. Could it be she sent him away to protect him from elements at court threatened by his new standing? Might not the great Council of Lords be put off by a baker's son in ermine, even after proving he's not lost his skill at pulling buns from the fire?"

"Even after saving their empire, they saw him as a commoner?"

"Even after saving their empire, Cal." Brohan's look was hard, but sincere. "Even had he saved their king."

Calvraign's throat knotted, and his eyes burned.

"For many, it is bloodline that dictates one's limits, not deeds. You must not be quick to judge, but neither quick to trust. Merely being who are you are may make you enemies, and vehement ones."

"That brings us back to where we started, but I'm afraid you've terrified more than enlightened me," Calvraign said.

"Then you're all the better prepared for our little visit. Sometimes an enlightened man may miss the shadows around him; a terrified man rarely does."

Calvraign's appetite for excitement took on a slight taste of apprehension, and even a hint of fear. "Have you any enemies at court, Brohan?" he asked, to distract himself from his own nerves.

"Certainly," he answered with a dismissive shrug. "Sing a song glorifying one knight's deeds, and his rival is always put off. But I have the king's favor, which still counts for a good deal, so few will speak against me in the open. I try not to bother too much with the politics of the noble houses. They are, for the most part, far too absorbed in their own shortsighted dealings."

"Even now? But we're at war! Surely the maneuvering can wait until the Maccs are dealt with?"

Brohan gave Calvraign a truly startled look, his eyebrows arching above his wide eyes. "Such common sense is beneath the trained intellect of the noble houses, my boy. The war could be won a year gone if they could put aside their bickering, but poor Guillaume has lost the strength or the will to bind them together as he once did in the War of Thorns. And Prince Hiruld, I'm afraid, is a better huntsman than statesman."

"A greater pity about Vingeaux, then. He would have made a strong king."

"Hmm," considered Brohan. "Strong yes, but not necessarily wise. He was a warrior, first and last. And last, it seems, won out."

"Did he die well?"

"Gods, Calvraign! What a question!" said Brohan, shaking his head. "What difference does *that* make? He is dead. Gone. Bled to grey with his guts in his lap. He died in battle, if I take your meaning, but to me at least, that means nothing."

Calvraign's face grew dark as he spoke. "My father died-"

Brohan, realizing the boy's affront, was quick to abate it. "Your father is a hero because he sacrificed himself for the good of others, not because he fell in battle. Had he lived, still he would be a great man. How he died is not what made him so."

"I suppose," replied Calvraign, not entirely convinced.

"Take, for example, King Eamperiun. Was he a great man for consolidating the old Kingdom of Dachadaie, for turning back the hrumm at Mychah, or for cracking his head open when a cranky horse got the better of him?"

"But that's not the same thing, Brohan!" he protested, batting ever-larger snowflakes away from his face.

"But it *is* the same thing!" emphasized the bard. "Would you love the memory of your father less if after Vlue Macc he died of fever or snakebite? Of course not! Your head is lost in the heights of fancy and legends. Get it back down here where the air is cold but not so rare!"

Resigned to once more losing a debate to Brohan, Calvraign trudged on through the thickening snowfall. The weather had been bad with spells of miserable, and there was a hint of consternation in the bard's keen eyes as he looked around them.

"Well, if this isn't a sour turn," he muttered, hands on hips.

"What?" Calvraign shouted, finding it difficult to hear through the growing keening of the wind.

"I've lost the river, I'm afraid. I was so busy talking that I forgot to pay attention to where I was going. Either we've drifted a little too far north, or the snow has capped the riverbed completely. In any event, we'd best find it again soon."

Calvraign could hardly tell the sky from the horizon. Everything seemed to blur together into one mass of silver. He squinted into the distance, shielding his eyes from the glare, then shrugged. "I can't make anything out," he confessed.

"Nor can I!" Brohan shouted back. The storm seemed to be coalescing, snow and wind conspiring to drown them out.

"What should we do now?" yelled Calvraign, but the words were ripped from his throat and tossed away by another, fiercer gust of wind, and he found himself staggering backward from the sudden gale. "It seems Father Oa has released his falcons!" he exclaimed, blinking away tiny bits of snow and ice that whipped into his eyes.

"Aye," agreed Brohan, bracing against the wind and holding back a hand to Calvraign. "More like the Chariot of Winter. Take my hand, lad!"

Calvraign reached out but once again found the wind holding him back while gnawing his flesh with its icy bite. He tried to focus on the shadow ahead of him that moments before had been Brohan. He thought he heard the bard call his name, but amidst the wind's angry howl he couldn't be sure.

Calvraign struggled against the unreasoning elements, sheltering his eyes with a wool-covered hand. He kept Brohan's dwindling figure in sight only briefly before it disappeared and left him alone in the swirling, shifting snows. The wind lulled for an instant and then blasted him from behind, throwing him headlong into a man-sized drift. He struggled against the cold hands that sought to hold him down and entomb him here, struggling first to his knees and then to his unsteady feet. Whatever he had done to arouse winter's fury, he found himself regretting it.

Calvraign's face stung. Amidst the unceasing attack of the wind and snow, he felt his skin was too thin a shell between himself and the forces of nature that beset him. He stumbled and righted himself again, though he had no idea where he was going. He shuffled on, dazed, occasionally making a sound from his cold-clumsy lips that he hoped still sounded like Brohan's name.

He was here just a moment ago. Panic grabbed the pit of his stomach even as the cold clutched at his heart. Calvraign had been in storms before. Winter was not new to him. He'd weathered many a snow squall in the hills, tucked under a rock, behind a dolmen, or nestled in the hollow of a tree. But here, in the flat and featureless expanse of the plains, he was without benefit of experience. And this cold. *So cold. It wasn't this cold a moment ago.*

Calvraign bit into his tongue until the warm metallic tang of blood wet his mouth. Blinking frozen tears from his eyes, he squinted once more into the blizzard. Against the never-ending white of the invisible horizon, a shadow glimmered briefly to his right. He turned, swaying on his unsteady feet, then drove toward the tempting silhouette. Be it real or illusion, it was a goal, a single point on which to pin his hope, and Calvraign grabbed at it with the enthusiasm of a drowning man for a branch.

His occasional glimpse at the elusive apparition suggested it was a man in grey and black armor, a tattered cloak hanging limply from his broad shoulders even in the whipping winds of the storm. The face seemed unnaturally pale, but he could not make out its expression. He held something in his gauntleted hand, the sharp edges of its shadowy outline suggesting a long sword. As Calvraign finally drew near, the figure raised the blade before him. Calvraign fell back, a chill deeper than any bite of winter in his heart, and would have run were he able. Instead, he lay helpless at its feet, his body and defiance spent.

An instant later the phantom was replaced by a blinding flash of blue light and the deafening retort of a thunderclap. Lights danced on a dark sky before Calvraign's eyes, but he heard a crackle, spit and hiss nearby and then felt an odd sensation licking at his limbs. He crawled with what energy he could closer to the sound and the alien warmth that tempted him to hope again, striving to find the source of the flames, but unconsciousness found him first.

Chapter Eight

Passages

OSRITH ducked his head to avoid another low hanging mist of cobwebs and choked back another sneeze. The back of his throat was thick with dust and phlegm, and his breath crawled from his gullet with a rattle as he walked. Prentis led the way through the narrow corridors, followed closely by Osrith, Kassakan and the two silent *wilhorwhyr*.

Cramped, dank, underground tunnels didn't bother Osrith – but he was less fond of the eight legged crawlies that occasionally dropped on their silken strands to tickle the back of his neck. He shrugged off a shiver and followed the trail of oily smoke that loitered in the wake of Prentis' torch. It hurt to move, hurt more to crouch, but he knew what fate awaited him if he stayed, and it was easy to push through the pain. This old sortie tunnel would bring them out far to the north and a little to the west of the castle perimeter. It would buy them some time, at least.

"How much farther?" he grunted.

"Still a bit to go, captal," replied Prentis.

"It's a bit longer stretch than I remembered."

"And bigger spiders," added Kassakan.

"Big enough," Osrith agreed. "I was content leaving this patrol to Bleys."

Prentis chuckled, swiping more stringy webs from his path. "I'm not sure he much appreciated the honor, captal."

"It wasn't for *his* sake I sent him. And stop calling me captal – that's your standard to bear, now. Though I'll wager Bleys didn't much care for that appointment, come to think of it."

"No. He didn't think *Osrith's little runt* was fit for duty. Old Trandt was captal when you left, but after he passed and I was named, Bleys called me out to settle his complaint on the field of honor."

"Did he?" Osrith tried to keep the surprise out of his voice. Surprise both that Bleys, as resentful and self-important as he was, would dare such presumption; and surprise that a young Prentis lived through the challenge. Trandt still had wits about him; but even when Osrith knew him, he was a frail man whose glories were past him. Bleys was the most deadly of the men in the House Guard. Prentis was younger, smarter perhaps, but blade to blade... .

"It didn't come to blows," Prentis continued, as if sensing his line of thought. "Her Ladyship did not take kindly to the impertinence. She sent him off to Dwynleigsh to watch over Aeolil. His honor is intact, and he may keep his title as an honorarium, if naught else, and Lady Evynine may count on his loyalty without so much worry for his judgment."

"Demons take Bleys." Osrith spat a stray cobweb from his mouth. "If I don't get a chance, first."

"Maybe you'll get your chance in Dwynleigsh, captal."

"I told you to stop calling me that."

"I beg your pardon," Prentis apologized. "Was that an order?"

Osrith shook his head and glared at the young knight. "I can't give you orders anymore, Prentis."

"Yes, captal."

"You can't blame him, Osrith," said Kassakan, "he didn't have the best mentor."

"That's true enough." Osrith grinned. "Lady Evynine chose you well, nonetheless."

Prentis didn't respond. Osrith didn't expect him to. He'd said what needed saying, and Prentis had heard what needed hearing. That was enough for both of them. He glanced back at Symmlrey and Two-Moons, but the *wilhorwhyr* seemed unaware or uninterested in his exchange with Prentis. Their very lack of attention reminded him that any pride in the boy's elevation was of minimal importance compared to what lay ahead.

"What are you going to do about the siege?" he prompted.

"I'll lead a contingent of men across the Daemyr. If the Pale Man chooses to siege Castle Vae, then we will lay siege to his lines of communication and supply. I will make the traverse between the Daemeyr and Ten Man Pass a killing zone."

"Did you run that plan by Evynine? It's damn risky."

"Run it by her?" Prentis responded with a chuckle. "It's *her* plan, sir."

"Well, why should that surprise me?" Osrith struck Prentis' shoulder. "But you're supposed to talk her out of that rubbish. A good captal brings some common sense to the high born so they don't get themselves into too much trouble with their chivalric nonsense."

"So you were always fond of saying," agreed Prentis. "I don't recall that working very well for you either, in practice, sir."

"For a boy who'd speak once a fortnight, you seem to have found your tongue," groused Osrith. "When'd that happen?"

Prentis shrugged and kept his eyes forward, picking his way carefully over the rough ground of the passage. Osrith noted his tightened jaw and averted eyes. And his silence.

It was Kassakan's voice that answered. "Captal Trandt and Bleys exchanged words about you often, and about the Pale Man. Trandt believed you were honorable but outmatched. Bleys, well, as you know – he felt you were complicit. He lobbied more than once to have your head on the walls and he volunteered to separate it from your shoulders himself."

That was hardly a revelation. Bleys Malade had always resented Osrith's favor with House Vae, his friendship with the baroness and her husband, and most especially his appointment as captal. There would never be getting around that.

"And?" Osrith prompted.

"And one day Bleys took it too far. He questioned not just your loyalty, but Evynine's fidelity to Hestan. Certainly nothing that hadn't been whispered before, but he said it outright, in front of the men, and in front of young Kiev. Trandt was taken aback, and he faltered. That was the day Prentis found his tongue, and likely the day Evynine found her new captal."

Osrith clenched his jaw and sucked in a breath of damp chill air through his nose. Blood pounded in his ears, throbbed against the taut bandages in his abdomen and leg. He pressed on behind Prentis, no longer through the pain, but *with* it. Osrith marched in time with every angry pulse of blood, and every fresh moment of pain brought him one step closer to the end of the tunnel, to the mountains, to Dwynleigsh, to the king and a purse of silver and gold.

And to Bleys.

The suns rose above the towering spine of the High Ridge, high into the cloudless sky, the golden princess Ilieam followed by her diminutive silver Handmaiden, Nymria. Their heat was tempered by the cold wind, but there was nothing to dim the divine sisters' light. Dieavaul studied his scant shadow absently, tracing its outline with a squinted eye down the tip of *ilnymhorrim*.

There is no shadow without light, he reflected. It was the subtitle of the eighth passage of the Fourth Arcanum, *The Delicate Balance*. Reading it had transformed him. Elevated the young boy Esmaedi from a competent but disaffected pupil of the arcane into the hand-chosen pupil of the greatest mage in the Magistry. For a time, he had channeled his impulses as he'd thought Dmylriani would approve, but eventually the ruse ended. Dieavaul was born. *To remove one thing necessitates replacing with another.* It seemed only just that if he murdered himself he must also be reborn – Esmaedi dies and Dieavaul lives. *If there is no balance, there is only Void. Oblivion.*

Dieavaul brought *ilnymhorrim's* tip and his gaze up from the ground and aimed instead at the stark granite of Kirith Vae. He needed to find his own delicate balance, now. Osrith had somehow fled the castle without alerting his patrols, which would not be impossible, considering how thinly they were spread. But how he'd slipped the unliving and unwavering notice of *ilnymhorrim*, he could not ascertain. Regardless, it was done, and he had finite resources at his disposal to deal with both this fortress and his escaped quarry. To apply force here, another force would have to be redirected from one of the armies in Malakuur. To *not* apply force could be even more disastrous. And there was the matter of tracking down the dreamstone, again.

Dieavaul shook his head and brought his sword down, turning to *Pakh Ma* Thatt. "We must keep them engaged, but we cannot rely on traditional siege. Once our numbers are apparent, they will send sorties to whittle us down."

Thatt snarled, shaking his head in the hrummish equivalent of assent. "This *hruthwaor* not fall without many thousands blood spilling."

And therein, the problem, he agreed to himself. The hrumm were a mighty force, but they fought wars in a different way than the children of men. An army of human knights and all their retainers and camp followers could entrench for months or tens of months, lay siege, and still be fit for battle in some fashion when the time came. Where they might be a lake, wide and deep, the hrumm were a river, fast and strong. If they did not keep moving, hunting, conquering, then the stillness would drive them mad and erode their discipline. They could not sit and stare at these walls for a ten-moon; he would lose them.

"This is the Host of the *Gal Pakh*," Dieavaul stated, even as his stratagem took shape. "We do not sit and wait, pissing into the wind. We *hunt*."

Thatt pounded his chest.

"You will stay here, my *pakh ma*. You will lead the Host, but you will not sit idle. Raid the farmsteads, burn the crops, break the ploughs, douse the forge-fires. Kill every man, woman and child; every pig, cow and dog. Lay it all to waste. They will come to you, then. Bit by bit, they will sortie forth to loose your stranglehold. This is the game you will play – strike them and vanish, then strike them and vanish again. You must not be caught in open battle or tricked into ambush. You will not siege the castle, you will siege the land it defends."

"Yes, *Gal Pakh*," Thatt agreed. "We spill their blood 'till no blood left to spill. We wash their land with blood."

"I will hunt the dreamstone. I will take but a score or two with me, and half the *graomwrnokk*. It may be many moons before I can rejoin you, here. Do not relent."

"Until they are dead, or we dead first, we staying to be here."

"Shaa will honor us both with victory," proclaimed Dieavaul. Even as he said it, the creeping pain seeped from *ilnymhorrim*, little white-hot pinpricks that walked under his skin across the back of his neck to smolder in his scalp behind his eyes.

Ah, he thought. *There you are.*

꙰

Callagh Breigh sent a shower of burnt orange and yellow-green leaves scattering in chaotic eddies behind her as she cleared a path in the undergrowth with angry swings of her knotted ironwood cudgel. She swatted branches aside, her careful hunter's step lost in her rage. She knew these woods and its secrets as well as any man or woman, save her father, but caution was not her worry today. Craignuuwn was a half-day behind her, as was Oona and her unwelcome but half-expected revelation.

The old man was right, after all, damn him.

Even with his cryptic forewarning, Callagh had merely stood and stared at Oona, her hands clutched into fists at her sides, her well-chewed nails biting into her rough palms. There was a lump in her throat, of sentiment, or bile, or some combination of both, as her stomach twisted sour in her belly.

"What?" she'd repeated, when finally words came.

"He wanted to see you before he left," Oona explained, her eyes plaintive, "But Master Madrharigal took him straight away that morning. You'd already risen and gone off, and we didn't know when you might return. We couldn't risk it."

Callagh frowned at the memory. *Risk? Risk what?* It made no sense at all. Finally Cal had seen her, responded to her as a woman and not a silly girl; kissed her, danced with her and held her close. *Finally.* And now, she returns from the hunt only to find he'd struck out for Dwynleigsh the morning after things were settling in as they should?

She'd always feared this day. She knew that Calvraign was not likely to remain in Craignuuwn. He was meant for more than shepherding; his was a proud line and he was a leader born even if he didn't realize it, yet. One day he'd be off to receive his own mantle from the Bard College, or join the king's army, or gods-knew-what.

But why now, and so suddenly?

"You cannot run from the day you fear," the old man had said. *"The day will always find you. You must not avoid it, but prepare for it. No one can escape fear. What will you do when it finds you? That's the question, ahn cranaoght."*

"Why d'you call me that?"

"Not for who you are, but what you'll be."

Another branch shuddered aside from her insistent bludgeoning. *Calvraign, you stupid boy. What've you done?* she raged to herself. He'd noticed her. She was sure of that. She'd felt as much when he'd embraced her at the inn. *There was no hiding that,* she remembered with a flush. So, why abandon her so quickly?

"We'll all die," she'd laughed at the old sack of bones, there on his fallen log by his dying fire. "We'll all be ghosts."

"That's not what I meant," he croaked, his blind white eyes staring just past her shoulder. *"You'll just be a little dead. A little ghost."*

Callagh kicked a stone from the game trail into the gorse, and spat after it. Oona was bothered by something – bothered and busy looking *not* to be bothered by it. Was Calvraign in danger? It seemed unlikely, unless one of his sheep had finally objected to his gwythir playing. But what else could it be?

"Funny, comin' from you," she'd laughed at the hermit, he but a jumble of bones with skin thrown over him. *"You look mostly dead, yerself."*

"Ha! Yes!" he'd responded, his air squeaking from tired lungs. *"Looks can be deceiving. You flatter me, little ghost."*

Callagh hadn't known if the old man had lost his senses to age or if he was just crazy. He looked older than the dead tree on which he always sat, and not much better for wear. But he was not completely witless. Somehow, he lived out in the deepest thickets of the Crehr, the Ad Craign Uhl, where even she tread with great caution, lest she wake the old trees or disturb less savory spirits from their sleep. He lived here, unafraid and undisturbed, and no matter how hard she looked she could never find him unless he first sought her.

"But I'll find you today," she muttered to no one, lashing out at another tree branch. "You said's much, yerself."

Some of his stories told of Duath Andai who would take on mortal guise. When she was younger, she'd thought he might be of the Duath, or perhaps a draough or an aulden; but when he referenced either it seemed he spoke as if he was not of their kind. And yet, not of *her* kind either, she'd noticed. But she loved his tales as much as she did Brohan's, and he'd never caused her harm. His occasional meanderings into his *ahn cranaoght* nonsense had always seemed harmless enough. From what she could tell, he was something less than the Duath but something more than a gypsy fortuneteller.

Now, as she crested the small ridge that looked down into the bramble and thistle of the unkempt highlands, where the Ad Craign Uhl marked its boundary with prickly thorn and beautiful bloom, she reconsidered.

"I've to get on, now," she'd said, "but I've a bit to spare, if you're hungry." She nodded to the hares and spotted greykierks slung across her shoulders.

He'd refused, as always, waving her away with a sly smile, "*You are kind, but I've eaten already.*"

The encounter had ended as countless others before, and she'd turned to climb down to Craignuuwn with a hard day's hunt balanced on her back and a new story to pass along to Cal and her Da'. But when he spoke again it changed everything.

"*When next we meet do not shirk. You will know what must be done. But you must hurry. Your swain has fled his cage, and you must be there and back before the moontide ebbs, or he will be forever beyond your help, and you beyond mine. Keep to the old ways, ahn cranaoght, and the old ways will keep you.*"

She'd stood frozen in mid-step, unable to move or even breathe, a chill sinking deeper with each word he spoke. She whirled about when his last word died, only to find the tree trunk empty, the clearing still and silent. He was gone, and vanished without a single blade of grass bent to his passing.

Callagh picked her steps more carefully as the shadows of the Ad Craign Uhl enveloped her. The old growth forced her to closer attention. She'd no wish to rouse anything more than had bestirred already. There had been more than enough surprises for one day, and she doubted not at all that the old man would have one more waiting for her in his clearing by the brook.

That knowledge did little to prepare her for what she found.

The clearing was there, as always: a stream, a cushion of purple heather spotted with the golden red blooms of highland wildflowers, and a log in the grass more moss and ants than wood. She'd found it a tenyear or more gone, and little had changed over the years. Sometimes the old man was there, sometimes not, but she always looked when she happened this way.

At first, she just assumed that the man was leaning against the log, asleep. He'd never been asleep before, and something in her gut told her that she never should or would find him asleep, but she could not leap to the most obvious conclusion without first pausing here.

"I'm back, just as you-" but her voice caught in the back of her throat as she drew nearer.

The skeleton lay in repose against the mottled green tree trunk, clad in tatters and rotted down to polished bone. The mouth gaped, the lower jaw cracked and hanging in an eternal sneer. Rose vines crawled and flowers blossomed through his teeth, nose and eye sockets, curling around his arms and legs and through his ribs and hips down to his leg bones and toes.

Dead. Years dead. Perhaps a lifetime or two dead. Yet it was him, there was no doubting that. His cloak, the glistening silver brooch that fastened it, his staff with its carved bird's head handle – it was her old man, her odd hermit, and she realized with a strangled sob, *her friend*. She took a settling breath.

When next we meet do not shirk. You will know what must be done. His words were hollow echoes in the confused buzz of Callagh's thoughts. *Keep to the old ways, ahn cranaoght, and the old ways will keep you.*

"Why didn't I ask your name?" she wondered aloud, even as she began to make her preparations. It wouldn't be a deep grave, but she would dig it. She looked through her pack for the small spade she used mostly for trapping, and began to break up earth.

It seemed to her that he'd chosen his spot – here by the log where he'd sat, or she'd *thought* he sat, for all those visits. She wasn't sure how the otherworld worked, exactly – had it all been an illusion? Had she been talking to a skeleton and a log all these years, merely thinking him a man? Or had it been real? Did his ghost rise and take a form to speak with the living? It was long hard work, but she had no more answer when she'd finished than when she started.

"Still, I should have asked yer name," she panted, gently cradling the remains and laying them in her trench. "I can't make a marker with your name if I dunna know it. Old Bones," she murmured, "that's all I know to call you, now."

Rising from the freshly dug gravesite, Callagh walked into the woods to gather some wood for a fire. Aside from the kindling, she returned with willow branches, pennyroyal and a handful of juniper berries. It would take some more time, but the old ways were more stringent than the new – he couldn't just be covered with dirt and be done with.

The willow branches she laid on either side of him, lining his resting place and both protecting him from meddlesome spirits and securing him in otherworld, safe from further interference by the living. She took a few moments to straighten his cloak, and she put some dried meat in his jaw so he would not have to search for his first meal on the other side. He had no weapon, so she placed the thin dagger Brohan had once gifted her in his delicate hands, so he would not be defenseless. As her token, she took his brooch and slid it into a small bait pocket in her pack, so he would recognize her as a friend if ever he did return.

The fire was slow to take, but Callagh coaxed a few stubborn flames and warmed a small palm-full of water from her drinking skin in her tin cup. She watched it smolder in the coals and listened to the wet wood hiss and whisper at her. Using a rock as a pestle, Callagh crushed the juniper berries and the pennyroyal into a muddy paste with the water and some ash from the fire.

Whoever he had been in life, in death his spirit had lost its way in the greylands once before, languishing between worlds with only a girl for occasional comfort. She didn't want to take any chance that he would have such difficulty again. Callagh dipped her thumb in the fragrant paste – pennyroyal to speed his passage and juniper to guard it – and marked his skull with the blessings of the dead. She recited the oldest rite for the dead that she knew, one that the old man had probably taught her himself, years ago.

> *"May the mountains stoop before you,*
> *may the flowing air bestir you.*
> *May the deep waves part around you,*
> *may the quiet earth support you.*
> *May the suns fire warm you,*
> *may the stars in heaven guide you.*
> *May you find the infinite peace,*
> *to the Light,*
> *through Dark,*
> *through Shadow,*
> *where the Shining Ones await."*

Callagh shoveled the dirt over his remains until the rich soil formed a small barrow mound. With no name to make a suitable marker, she pounded his bird-staff into the soil to mark the head of the grave. She spread the remainder of the pungent minty paste on the eyes of the carved crow headpiece.

No sooner had she stepped back from her work, than a large raven alighted on its wooden likeness. Callagh jumped backward with a shriek and fell into the fresh dirt. The enormous black bird didn't make a sound, but continued to watch her intently.

They call the ravens that ferry souls the roibhe ahn cranaoght, she remembered. *Is that what he meant?*

"Be on your way, old spirit," Callagh said gently.

The raven cocked its head, and with a swift beat of its wings sailed into the night. She looked out to the horizon, now dark and moonless, getting her bearings. Dwynleigsh would be roughly southwest, and several days of hard travel. "Now I must be on mine."

Chapter Nine

Walking in Rainbows

Bloodhawk sniffed the breeze but detected no hint of the distinctive hrummish scent lingering in the fresh air. He nodded, satisfied. Doubling back and setting the false trail to the north had evidently thrown them off. With any luck, they would be well on their way into the demesnes of House Vespurial. Between the Border Knights, the Vespurial's notorious Foresters, and perhaps even the rare aulden or two, the hrumm would soon cease being hunters and start being quarry. They would not carry on the chase much longer, if at all.

Then again, they were natural hunters, and *wilhorwhyr* their most valued prey. And what reward offered their heartless master for failure?

He scowled away his satisfaction and moved forward.

Bloodhawk was surprised that Dieavaul had spared so many of his war party to chase down one man. His plans of siege disrupted, perhaps he wanted vengeance or another soul for his collection? The thought of that siege still troubled Bloodhawk. With such secret armies as they had hidden in Malakuur, why risk alerting Providayne with such an underpowered attempt on Castle Vae? If they planned invasions, why not come through in force? A few hundred hrumm against that ancient fortress was like throwing a handful of leaves at a wall. Dieavaul was more assassin than general, to be sure, but he was not stupid.

A feint, perhaps? A mere distraction with the Pale Man at its head to lend it credence?

Bloodhawk harvested a handful of snow from a low hanging tree branch and rubbed it into his eyes. *All in the past*, he reminded himself. Whatever its purpose, it was either fulfilled or foiled, and he was no longer in a position to affect it.

After his escape, as he stood dripping and shivering on the banks of the Daemeyr downstream of the Pale Man and his minions, Bloodhawk knew what he must do. Two-Moons had surely warned the castle, so it was left to him to warn the aulden. The Ceeaemyltu had surpassed the Old Foe before; they had *led* the Seven Tribes against Anduoun. The aulden might provide some strategy to turn them back again. If not, they still deserved as much warning as the human kingdoms on their border. They too would be subject to the steel of Thar Malagch and his hrumm; they too would be put under heel of the andu'ai when the war came.

Yes. To the aulden, if he could find them, and from there he knew not – but first to them.

Bloodhawk's abdomen stirred, and not for the first time since sunsrise. He'd been ignoring the inconvenient need gathering in his gut for the better part of the day. The pursuit had been too close. Now, however, he resigned himself to making a stop to relieve himself. Defying nature too long never yielded good results. He eyed a sheltered spot under a maple, the approach tangled with nettles and the waxy green and white leaves of poison star weed. It was the worst possible place to attend such business, so it would serve him well. He picked his way carefully through the unwelcoming flora, melting into the underbrush.

Bloodhawk set his bow and long sword within easy reach, and plucked two arrows from the quiver at his shoulder, spiking them into the dirt. He dug a hole with his worn trench knife, deep enough to hide any telltale scent from his trackers, but not so deep as to prevent natural decay. He unfastened his breeches and settled in to do what needed doing.

Bloodhawk was not pleased to be immobile and indisposed. It allowed his thoughts to drift, and the reasons for his flight were still too painful. The loss of Khyri, too close to the surface of his memory. Her death, by his own steady hand, still haunted him. His arrow had penetrated her breast and stolen her life with unerring precision, sending her from the world with the passionless cold kiss of steel.

I'm a fool not to rejoice in that shot, Bloodhawk admonished himself. *She runs with Ingryst now, rather than bound to the hellforged. At least I spared her that.*

Bloodhawk missed her, ached with the very absence of her. No emotion, neither fiercest love nor most furious hate, could ever fill that space. When his spirit sped from the mortal realms, he would join her. He drew some comfort from this.

Unless there is no one left to spare me in turn, he reconsidered, peeling back the top layer of moss from the forest floor. *Cheerful thought.*

Bloodhawk ripped the coarse green film of fuzz into smaller pieces and cleaned himself dutifully, discarding the soiled moss in the small latrine ditch. The fading suns-light cast long shadows across the ripple of leaves and swaying branches, and as the amber glamour washed over his eyes, his skin pricked into gooseflesh. He paused, halting his last toss in mid throw. He sensed in the ripples of *iiyir* what he could not see, hear, or smell. The smaller prey animals had gone quiet, and in the stillness it was as if the trees themselves had drawn and held their breath.

Bloodhawk froze and let the forest speak to him.

The footfalls were silent, but he felt them through the roots, stones and soil of the Caerwood. A dozen hrumm surrounded him, cordoning him in, pulling the noose tight.

Bloodhawk had been sure his clever backtracking and skillful misdirections, his careful, subtle marks in the foliage and turf, had fooled them. But whether they had seen through his masking, or lost his trail completely and just stumbled on, they had found him. Through fate or fortune, here he was, crouched over his own offal, his pants about his ankles.

Twelve, counted Bloodhawk, trying to swallow his alarm. He pivoted his head without moving his body, looking for any visible sign of his pursuit emerging from the closest line of trees. *Not yet,* he almost sighed audibly. *They know I'm here, but they haven't seen me yet. But twelve... .*

Striking from ambush, with the advantage of terrain and the convenience of planning, Bloodhawk could deal with twelve hrumm. But not like this. Exposed, surrounded, and bone weary – he would die before even half his hunters hit the ground.

But there *was* a way.

Singing Arrow had never liked what the *wilhorwhyr* called *bending light*. *Aulden magic was best left to the aulden*, she often said. She thought it a crutch, at best – *walking in rainbows* – and an unreliable one at that. Since the time of the Sundering the lands of Faerie were a dangerous place to linger even for the fae who once called it home. Their once bright realm was now haunted by treacherous storms of *iiyir* and hungry shadows of the Dark. If he ventured too deep without a tether to the mortal world, he might never return, and he had no talisman or wilderwine to bring him safely home. But even Singing Arrow had acknowledged that sometimes the worst option could end up being the last best hope.

Bloodhawk closed his eyes.

*A' widdershins we go,
to Faerieland, beyond the Veil.
A' widdershins we bend the light,
to skip behind the shadows.*

The rhyme held no magic in itself, but it served to center him. It had been that rhyme tripping from his lips when he'd first walked widdershins and found his way into the Veil as a child. It had been easier then, when his aulden blood guided him, before age and human reason clouded the way. It had been years since his last venture into Faerie. But, with some effort, it could still be done, at least for a short time.

Bloodhawk opened his eyes, focused on a leaf, solely that leaf, and moved it moonwise in his mind. He let his eyes lose focus on all else, but the leaf remained crisp in his vision, crisp and green and haloed in the waning light.

One heartbeat.
A snowflake's tear sparkled on its surface.
Two heartbeats.
Each vein throbbed in sharp relief on the blade.
Three... .
The leaf twitched, shivering within itself, then split into two identical selves. Bloodhawk followed the leftward leaf as it shimmered widdershins. Then the light moved, flickering, and the mortal world dissolved.

Looking at the world from within the Veil was both the same and different. Everything was in its proper place, but nothing looked the same. Shadows twisted around their sources instead of falling from them. The light that shone down was pale, like the moons, not warm and gold like the suns. And here, on the doorstep to the otherworld, there were advantages beyond a change in scenery.

Shifting back and forth from Faerie had once allowed the aulden fantastic power. They had come and gone as they pleased, traveled leagues as if footsteps, appeared and disappeared at will, done battle as half-seen and unassailable wraiths, and the other races had bowed or cowered to them. But the andu'ai had shattered the Veil on their arrival, and when they mended it – blocked the way to Faerie. The aulden had been trapped in the mortal realms, and this brief flirtatious bending of light to trip within the shadow of Shadow was all that was now allowed to them.

Bloodhawk hoped it would prove enough for him.

Time moved differently within the Veil. The mortal world turned slowly, dreamlike, while Bloodhawk moved like lightning. He had never felt more in tune with the *ur'iiyir*; the ebb and flow of the world tides surrounded him in streams of muted silver. The thoughts of the forest, such as they were, flowed through him. For but a fleeting moment, Bloodhawk *was* the Caerwood, and like a heartbeat, leagues away, he sensed the forest heart. The Sacred Grove. The aulden.

Bloodhawk blinked away the distraction. Closer, like a weed, the intrusion of the hrumm invaded his vision. His mouth soured at their taint.

The first hrumm broke through the tree line to his right, running at its most furious pace, though from Bloodhawk's side of the Veil, the creature appeared to flail upstream against a powerful current, slow and clumsy. Bloodhawk availed himself of the first weapon at hand, flinging soiled moss at the hrumm's startled face. The filthy missile struck true, and the hrumm halted, gagging, and tried to clear its eyes.

Bloodhawk grabbed the bow and arrows he'd left at the ready and swung to his left, loosing both shafts at the next two hrumm. He watched as each broad-headed arrow gleamed on its way to hrummish flesh, kicking his loosened breeches off of his legs as he moved forward. The first strike took the hrumm off its feet to tumble in the brush, dead. The other hrumm spun, clutching the feathered dart that suddenly poked from its side, and fell squirming in the dirt.

Bloodhawk rose, discarding his bow and unsheathing his long sword to meet their advance. An arrow flew into the thicket, striking the maple as he dodged the sluggish missile. He felt the pain of the old tree through the *ur'iiyir* and grimaced. Two more shafts whistled toward him, but he shifted on his feet and slipped between them. The world outside was moving faster now.

Bloodhawk sprinted half-naked from the foliage to his right, cutting down the hrumm he had inconvenienced with his well-aimed waste, and flanked the hrumm who were charging his position straight on. He tracked the quick darting glances under their furrowed brows as they searched the trees, unable to fix his position. He was still but a ghost flitting through the trees, and so long as they looked for him directly he would elude them. Wild hrumm might have looked askance, trying to catch his true form where it was most vulnerable to detection, out of the corner of the eye. But these trained hrumm of the thars had the edges of their hunting instincts whittled away, so that they might march in straight lines and wield steel and die for Malakuur above all else. And fortunately so, for him, mused Bloodhawk.

Bloodhawk slipped in behind and left the two hrumm dead in as many sword strokes. The blade, striking from within the Veil, passed through mortal flesh with uncanny ease. *Seven more*, he thought, weaving through the trees, moving ever moonward as he followed his remaining prey.

A' widdershins we slip,
to otherworld, of moonkiss'd shadows.
A' widdershins we weave the light,
to dance in faerie hollows.

The hrumm were throwing down their bows and drawing curved blades of fire-blacked Malakuuri steel, hunting the twilight for any hint of movement. Three were bunched close together, poking in the undergrowth by the maple with their sword tips.

Bloodhawk had *called* plants to his aid many times, just as he had animals. But never here, from the Veil, and it was not so much *calling* out to the natural *iiyir* of the starweed as it was *calling in* – like twitching his own fingers to snake up the legs of the advancing hrumm, binding them in root and leaf and dragging them down in a helpless jumble amidst the nettles and soiled dirt of his latrine ditch.

Screams of terror were rare in the hrumm, and so Bloodhawk heard a rare thing. "Ul raog ha'uhiir!" barked one of the hrumm, trying to free its tethered sword arm. "Aald'naogh! Aald'naogh!" it rasped, even as the vines constricted the breath from its lungs and choked the sound from its throat.

Yes, the forest is alive, Bloodhawk agreed, the fading pulse of the tangled hrumm throbbing against phantom fingers. "Nòg aald'naogh," he corrected, his voice floating from nowhere, "ma raogmyztsanogg!"

Whether they thought he was aulden or *wilhorwhyr* really mattered little to Bloodhawk, save for any additional terror a lightbending *wilhorwhyr* might bring them. Without *urghuar* or Dieavaul to intercede and pull him from the Veil, either would be dangerous enough to the hrumm. And indeed, they shuffled nervously, one of them eyeing escape over its shoulder.

But Bloodhawk's tenuous bond to the shores of otherworld was fading – the Veil folding in behind him, pushing him back and out to the mortal world. He pushed himself forward, straining to retain his advantage for one more span of heartbeats.

A' widdershins we glide,
through tides of glimmer-life.
A' widdershins we drink the light,
to join in faerie glamour.

The hrumm pointed their blades, shouting, a fierce light kindling in their eyes as they finally picked their phantom from the twilight. Bloodhawk charged, his sword high, and braced for a scything swing. The turf pounded beneath his feet, more solid with every step, the shock of steel through bone and flesh traveling up his arms to his shoulders – almost normal. Two hrumm died from that last fae blow, their swords still aloft and pointing, their own viscera spooling into their laps as they fell. The light of purplish dusk was suddenly warmer, and the breeze whistled colder around his exposed legs and privates. His thigh muscles seized, hardening and cramping as if he'd run twenty leagues with no respite, and he fell in the steaming blood of his victims.

And so ends the rhyme, he thought, head swimming.

A' widdershins, we tarry,
as the fair folk make us merry.
A' widdershins, they bid us stay,
before the suns call us home,
before the suns call us home.

A' widdershins, they bid us stay,
before the suns call us home.

Bloodhawk tumbled through the mess of worming innards, rising with a weak parry that saved his life but lost him the grip on his sword hilt. Without thought to the lost sword, he grabbed the swinging arm of his assailant, his instinct and battle training acting through his delirium. The hrumm spun off, slipping in the bloody mire and, in a stroke of unplanned providence, impaled itself through the side as it fell.

The last hrumm was in mid-swing, and Bloodhawk slipped his arm inside the arc of the sword in a defensive parry that sliced him from wrist to shoulder blade but spared him the intended heart-stroke. Face to face with the hrumm, he crushed its sturdy larynx with a sharp punch, grappled its neck in an iron hold, then pivoted and broke its spine with a thunderous crack.

Bloodhawk collapsed. His arm burned, and the shorn sleeve of his quilted undershirt was soaked in blood. He examined the wound and found it a nice long slice, not deep, and certainly within his skill to mend. But the flesh already stank.

Barrowshade. He grimaced, recognizing the strong moldering odor.

Barrowshade was rare, and fatal – to humans, at least. Aulden were more resistant, and at worst might fall terribly ill. Bloodhawk wasn't sure what effect the barrowshade would have on his mixed blood, so he sat down to clean and dress the wound as best he could before moving on. At best, the poison would have little or no effect on him. At worst, between his aulden blood and healing lore, he would be manageably ill.

In years to come this encounter might prove an amusing anecdote. The story could serve to illustrate the folly of overconfidence to wide-eyed Initiates equal parts eager and foolish. For now, he had to mend his arm, and continue to the heart of the forest, to the Sacred Grove.

Find the aulden, he thought, his purpose unclouded by grief or self-doubt, or even his short-lived self-pity. *Find the Ceearmyltu.*

But first, he reminded himself, *my breeches.*

Chapter Ten

Dwynleigsh

Calvraign struggled to wake, swimming in a murky lake of unconsciousness but failing to break the surface. He felt some degree of comfort in hearing Brohan's disembodied voice floating to his ears. He concentrated on his words as he rose into the shallow waters of half-sleep.

The master bard was conversing with a man whose voice he didn't recognize, "…would never have found him had it not been for the lightning strike. That was a double stroke of fortune for your friend. The burning tree guided me to him even as the flames kept him warm."

"Aye, the same fortune brought me. I'd begun to think I would never lay eyes on the poor lad again," responded Brohan's familiar voice. "I had occasion to weather such a storm once, in the Iron Peaks. Never here, where the winters are comparatively mild. Very curious."

Calvraign heard someone stirring the coals of a fire, and then a pop and hiss as fresh wood took flame. Though he was, for all he could tell, warmed through and through, he still felt a lingering chill not related to the snow or the wind, but tied to the dark apparition he had seen just before passing out. He wanted to ask Brohan or this stranger if they had seen the phantasmal figure as well, but he could not break through the last thin layer of sleep. Instead, he continued to drift just beneath the surface of consciousness, listening.

"Whither or whether, we are fortunate you happened by, sir knight," continued Brohan. "Not many care to travel the winter moons lightly."

"I was meant to be in Dwynleigsh a ride gone, but my duties delayed me, and my mount was lost to the winter. My Lord Elvaeir has granted me leave to joust in the festival."

"Ah yes, I know Lord Elvaeir quite well. Why, I was in Tiriel just last Goldenmoon to sing for him. What news from the north?"

Calvraign heard the strange knight speak for quite some time and struggled to concentrate on his words. Evidently the early storms had beset Tiriel with more anger than they had yet seen in the Crehr ne Og or Providayne. The snow on the windward side of the city walls had climbed halfway to the parapets, and similar drifts had buried shepherds and livestock alike in the fields. Baeden Maer had frozen before the full stock of winter supplies had arrived, trapping the great river barges on the wrong side of a massive ice jam. And the inclement weather had brought in its wake andu'ai from deep in the Ridge that walked about without care or concern in gales that would freeze human blood solid in the vein. The Old Ones had not been seen for a thousand years in such numbers. Some, he claimed, feared this was merely the beginning of *arachaemyyhl*, the ancient aulden legend of Eternal Winter, and that there was no hope to fight against it.

Brohan must have been disturbed by mention of this, for he stopped the knight in mid-sentence. "Surely Elvaeir can't believe such nonsense? One can't yell *arachaemyyhl* every time an andu'ai is seen, regardless of the weather!"

"Master Madrharigal, do not make light of this, I prithee. We have lost many good knights in battle already, and not to solitary andu'ai but to bands of three and five. Even the Qeyniir have sent us aid. And, before I departed, we had just received word that andu'ai were seen in the Bryr Moill on the border with Symbus. If this is not cause for concern... ."

Calvraign finally managed to open his eyes and took in his surroundings through his first tentative blinks. He was in a small shepherd's hut, which apparently had been abandoned for the season. Roughly hewn timbers sealed with tar and sap made up the ceiling and walls, sheltering the dirt floor from the elements. A fire lit the hearth, next to which sat Brohan and a tall man in a thick but well-worn traveling cloak fastened at the neck. There was a faint glimmer of steel at his wrist and collar, betraying the armor he wore beneath. He could not make out the stranger's features in the dim flickering light of the fire, but he could see that Brohan wore a deep frown over his ever-present smirk.

"Concerned, yes, Sir Artygalle, but not with the end of the world, only with the uprising of an ancient and powerful race. The andu'ai's stranglehold on Rahn was broken once before when they were more than just scattered bands in the wilderness. They can be dealt with again. *This* is why Lord Elvaeir sent you to the festival, then? Not merely to joust in the tourney, but to gain allies."

"Didn't you always say that the andu'ai defeated themselves, Brohan?" interrupted Calvraign from his straw mat, propping himself up on one elbow. "I mean, wasn't that the whole point of the *Litany of Swords*?"

Brohan glanced in Calvraign's direction, at once surprised and annoyed. "What?"

"You always said it was their internal struggle that toppled them. What if they are united again?"

"Welcome back to the waking world, young sir," said Artygalle, turning to face the boy with a nod, "and thank you for your kind words of agreement."

Calvraign returned a brief nod and examined the knight. He seemed young, not many years past his own age, and his eyes were bright and alert with the wonder of the newly traveled. Artygalle was not a handsome man, yet not homely, with nondescript dark blond hair and unassuming brown eyes.

"Cal," rebuked Brohan, kneeling by the straw mat and laying the back of his hand on Calvraign's forehead. He nodded to himself, satisfied, and continued. "What you speak of and to what Sir Artygalle refers are entirely different. The Empire of Anduoun was a vast kingdom of kingdoms, and the andu'ai ruled it *millions* strong. To throw off their yoke was a much different thing. Of course their own strife helped sow the seeds of their destruction. But these attacks are not some grand revenge of the Old Foe! More likely it's a restless remnant that's been hiding in the mountains, enjoying the brief opportunity this weather has provided to make mischief. It should hardly require a monumental alliance to drive them from whence they came."

"The Qeyniir evidently disagree," responded Calvraign with a quiet shrug.

Brohan halted his retort before the words even passed his lips.

The Qeyniir, of all the Seven Tribes, had perhaps the most dangerous reputation. Known as dark and brooding even amongst the dark and brooding aulden, they had never shown mercy to any uninvited human who dared trespass within Bael Naerth. If they had been drawn outside their groves to lend aid to humans, even those of Tiriel, whom they trusted only slightly more than other human folk, perhaps the situation was a dire one. And Brohan knew all of this, for it was he who had taught the very same to Calvraign.

"Regardless," Calvraign continued, taking advantage of Brohan's momentary pause, "what concern of ours should it be if this is *arachaemyyhl* or not, if it serves the purpose of uniting our people against a common foe? You yourself said that the nobles lack the common sense to do so of their own accord. Perhaps this will give King Guillaume what he needs to bring them together again."

Brohan's mouth opened and closed once or twice, but still he did not speak. His frown deepened. This was the first time Calvraign had ever seen the bard literally speechless. He stared into his mentor's eyes and with a sudden realization he understood. *It's the semantics.*

"Brohan, forget about Eternal Winter and the end of the world. You're so concerned that people might be misinterpreting the myth, you're neglecting the facts at hand. Tiriel needs help, Providayne needs unity, and if fear of aracha*myyhl* and the return of the andu'ai will help supply both, then that makes your task of convincing Guillaume to lend aid to Tiriel that much easier. Leave the academics for later."

"*My* task?" said Brohan, equal parts bemused and surprised. "How has this become *my* task, Calvraign?"

"Well... ." Calvraign wondered at that answer himself. He took a deep breath, trying to ignore the pointed stares of the bard and the knight, and spoke past his embarrassment as best he could. "Someone must lend credence to Sir Artygalle's words and whatever request he brings from his lord in Tiriel. And *I* certainly have no influence in the matter."

"Your apprentice speaks convincingly, Master Madrharigal. You have taught him well," remarked Artygalle. "And he is correct. Although I carry with me messages to Guillaume and the archbishop from Elvaeir, I will need a second to make my case effectively, even if I win the tourney and the King's Lance. I would be indebted to you for any help you might offer."

Brohan did not look away from Calvraign even as he answered the knight. "I wasn't aware I had taught him all *that*. But he is right. You are both right, of course. Sometimes I am too busy singing of a rock to see the mountain before me. Thus I am no general or leader of men. I will do what I can to sway the king."

Brohan examined Calvraign, his smirk returning, and spoke to him quietly. "There is wisdom in you, Calvraign – wisdom and strength. Perhaps there is more of your father in you than you realize." He patted the boy's head with affection. "Rest yourself now, for tomorrow we will be nearly at the walls of Dwynleigsh, and I have much more to teach you before we arrive. I think the king will be well pleased with you."

Sir Artygalle was a pleasant traveling companion for Calvraign. He was unassuming in nature, quiet and reserved, but quick to laugh and always ready with a kind word. He spoke readily of the battles he had seen, but not fondly, and never with praise for his own deeds. Unlike the sagas that Brohan had related over the years, Artygalle's stories lacked the glorified drama of war, focusing instead on the great losses faced by nobles and peasants alike. He was not at all like the dashing knights of Calvraign's imagination, whose swords were quick as their tongues, and whose brave deeds and handsome faces won the hearts of swooning maidens. But he was intriguing in his own right, a man of real depth and, aside from Brohan, the only person of wider experience with whom Calvraign had conversed.

They stopped to rest at the crest of Vaelyhn's Drop, where the Vlue Moignan met the Ciel Vlue, both plummeting a hundred feet to a cragstrewn foaming roar where the ancient lovelorn lady had met her self-inflicted doom. During the more agreeable moons, this was a favored picnic ground for lovers old and young alike. Despite its sad history, it commanded a wonderful view of the capital and the Ciel Maer, with fields of golden grains and wildflowers laying a carpet all the way to the city's grand North Gate. On a clear day, it was even possible to spot far away King's Keep on its solitary isle. This, unfortunately, was not a clear day at all. The view this vantage point afforded them was of cloud, mist and fog, and so Calvraign was robbed of his first glimpse of Dwynleigsh.

"A shame," remarked Brohan from behind Calvraign, "but you will see it soon enough. We are only a few hours' ride from here. Even on foot we should reach the city by nightfall."

A faint smile crossed Artygalle's lips as he looked into the haze before them. "There were times I doubted this day would come," he said, almost to himself. "Now that it's here, all the weariness of my journey comes upon me at once. Still, I offer thanks. Thanks to you, Illuné, for guiding me to new friends, for leading me when I had lost my way, and for bolstering me when I had no more strength. In Your wisdom I trust, and in Your way I follow." He made the circular sign of the moon over his breast. "Amen."

Calvraign and Brohan nodded their heads in affirmation of Artygalle's brief prayer. Calvraign had not adopted any particular patron, though he did have a penchant to blame Oghran for any ill fortune that fell in his path. Most of the Cythe worshipped Father Oa, for they were a people of the wilderness and respected the whims of Old Man Nature. Some of his people still paid tribute to the Old Ones: Ghaest, God of the Dead; Pheydryr, Death Herself; and the Three Sisters, Kahtriae, Muirea, and Sehmbet, Goddesses of the Forbidden, the Arcane, and the Arts, respectively. But Calvraign had no special place in his heart for any of them. It seemed Oa did as he wished regardless of the prayers of man, and that was doubly so for Ghaest and Pheydryr. He had no knowledge of the Forbidden Arts or of Arcana, and so of the Three Sisters, the only one he considered relevant was Sehmbet, to whom he heard Brohan offer an occasional word. But still, though he recognized their place in the universe, he felt no call in his heart to truly worship any of these gods.

Instead, it was two of the Dacadian gods who captured his interest: Illuné, to whom combat meant little without honor, and Irdik, whose sharp eyes saw strategies out of necessity rather than love of war. Though these were not the gods of his people, something in the songs and myths of old spoke to his heart. Around them, it seemed, the old struggle of good against evil always rallied. It was the Three Swords that had triumphed in the legend of the First Battle and freed the humans from the yoke of Anduoun. It was their names that struck fear into the hrumm and dringli, that routed the armies of countless would-be invaders, that had unified the largest human empire the continent had ever seen. Even now, the last remnants of the once-mighty Dacadians still revered their names here in Providayne.

But when Calvraign looked into Artygalle's eyes and saw the depth of devotion within, it was clear enough that he lacked the sincerity of the knight's reverence. Where he might be intrigued by the more dramatic aspects of religion, Artygalle felt and acted upon a strength of belief that was foreign to him.

"We should be off now if we're to spend the night with a down coverlet and a roaring hearth," mused Brohan with a quiet insistence. "I've had enough of the outdoors for one journey!"

Calvraign and Artygalle agreed with broad smiles, and once again the small group set their tired legs in motion. They crossed the solitary bridge that arced over the Ciel Vlue just after its marriage to the Vlue Moignan, its solid timbers treacherous with a thin film of ice. Come the warmer moons, a King's Warden would stand guard here at this bridge built by the aulden centuries long past. Below them, the half-frozen river rushed over the embankment, offering disconsolate souls the option that bards had rather dramatically dubbed *Vaelyhn's Choice*.

Once across the bridge, they descended the steep incline along an ancient switchback trail, the stones well worn from hundreds of thousands of footfalls. A similar trail mirrored this one on the opposite side of the bridge, which led off to Mneyril, Aeyrdyn and other points east and north. Their own path led south down to the broad causeway of Rivers' Run, which paralleled the Ciel Vlue as it broadened and eventually emptied into Ciel Maer, where in ages forgotten by humankind the aulden had built their beloved Dwynleigsh.

Sir Artygalle met with the most difficulty on the short but steep descent, for what armor he did not wear he had stowed in his oversized pack, and the weight of it made him ungainly on the slippery track. After noting his difficulty, accentuated in no small part by his fatigue, Brohan suggested that Artygalle walk in the middle of their group rather than as rear guard. And so, with Brohan to provide a shoulder to balance on and Calvraign to help support him should he falter, they arrived at the base of the cliff without incident.

Calvraign drew in his breath sharply, paying no notice to the bite of the cold in his wonder and excitement. Before them, hidden by the mists from above, lay Rivers' Run. The roadway itself was impressive enough, even partially covered in snow. The paving stones were smooth as sanded wood, almost imperceptibly slanting from the center down to drainage gullies that ran on either side of the road. Calvraign estimated that its immense width could hold five to six carriages side by side.

More incredible than the highway itself were the trees and statues lining either side. The Crehr ne Og contained forests that were by no means young growth, and within them there was a great variety of woods. But these trees, with fifteen-foot girth and heights he could only guess were close to sixty feet – their branches gnarled masses that tangled in and around each other like the confused, directionless talons of some gigantic bird of prey – these were like nothing he had ever seen. More amazing still to his young eyes, they were all covered in healthy, thick leaves of varying shades of green and red, waxy and glistening and all but free of ice and snow. Here and there a lush golden blossom poked from the foliage.

Next to these, the twenty-foot-tall, slate-grey statues of aulden warriors on guard were almost unobtrusive. They apparently served as league markers of some sort, for at regular intervals they stood watching from the trees, little pieces of some crystal flashing from inside their winged stone helmets, giving the unnerving impression that they were, in some respect, alive – and watching. The crests carved into their shields were unfamiliar to him, no doubt representing long-forgotten aulden houses; and the armor, graceful even in granite, was far more smoothly articulated and decorative than any he had seen. Not, he reminded himself, that this was saying very much. Aside from the knights of House Malminnion that rarely occasioned through the vicinity of Craignuuwn, and now Sir Artygalle, he had not seen anyone in full plated armor.

Calvraign wasn't sure how long he walked with his mouth agape before Brohan interrupted his gawking with his soft, knowing chuckle. "Impressed, are you?"

"It's... incredible. How could you have mentioned Rivers' Run to me so many times without telling me how magnificent it is?"

"Ah, Cal, I'm afraid you will find that there are many things I have mentioned all too briefly. Had I tried to describe this to you, could you possibly have pictured what you see now?"

Calvraign shook his head, face still blank and eyes still staring. "How long does it go on like this?"

"How long? Why, right up to the North Gate!" said Brohan with a triumphant bellow. Clearly, he was enjoying this.

Calvraign thought about that for a moment. It seemed odd to him that anyone would want such a nice, wide highway leading thirty leagues right up to the front gate of their city. It seemed like an open invitation to invaders, intimidating statues or not.

He frowned at Brohan. "Isn't that rather foolish? Militarily, I mean? The trees are beautiful, and the statues are magnificent, but, well, perhaps in a time of peace… ." Calvraign halted when he noticed the smirks of his two companions. They knew something they had not yet shared, and he had learned to read the look on Brohan's face years ago. With a sigh he prepared himself for the coming lecture.

"From what you know of the aulden," began Brohan in his tutorial tone, "do you consider them a very inviting and open race?"

"No," said Calvraign slowly, wary of an embarrassing verbal miss-step, "but the Ceearmyltu built Dwynleigsh, and presumably this highway, and they dealt with humans for a time, didn't they? After their war with the Maccs? Perhaps this was a gesture of some kind?"

"An interesting justification, but what if I told you that the Run was built during the Blood Wars with the slaoithe?"

Calvraign was taken aback. The Blood Wars didn't seem a logical time to build a causeway that led right to the gates of a major citadel. Such a smooth surface as this road provided would be ideally suited to siege engines and the like. The aulden must have engineered some sort of failsafe. He looked up at the flashing eyes of a towering statue as they put another league behind them. Of course! The aulden had once been privy to great magic. The statues must be the key to their defense. Still, it didn't sit well with him.

"During the Blood Wars the slaoithe and their allies numbered in the thousands of thousands," Calvraign said. "How could less than a hundred of these put the merest dent in such a force?"

Brohan's eyes followed Calvraign's finger as it pointed to one of the granite knights, then returned to rest on the boy. "The Sentinels are not to be underestimated when unleashed, but still, you are correct. They could not turn back such an army as you describe. Not alone."

"You forget, perhaps, from whence the aulden draw forth their power, my friend," said Artygalle gently.

"The Sacred Groves," Calvraign muttered, looking at the immense trees surrounding him. "Well, I suppose that makes sense. They channel their magic through these trees and the, uh, Sentinels, and they have a trap several leagues long."

"Yes, that would be it, more or less," agreed Brohan. "These trees are oft used in the wild by the Seven Tribes as guardians of their forests. They are called *ylohim*, which translates roughly to-"

"Bloodroot," answered Calvraign.

"Yes, good," beamed Brohan, noting Artygalle's surprise with some amount of pride. "The point being that while the *ylohim* can exist with a standard diet of water and rich soil," he paused, lowering his voice for added drama, a bard trick with which Calvraign had become well acquainted, "they *thrive* on blood."

Artygalle looked up into the swaying tangle of branches sheltering them. "And these trees have certainly fed well over the years."

Calvraign swallowed nervously. "So why are we so unconcerned right now? What if they're hungry?"

"Don't worry, these *ylohim* are relatively friendly and only half awake. If we don't molest them, they won't reach down and pull us apart at our joints. If you come across one in the wild, however, run very fast in the opposite direction. Most aren't particularly vicious, but you never want to take the chance that it's a bad seed, if you'll pardon the pun. If you come across a *grove* of them in the wild, run faster, because you are most likely about to trespass on a group of fae. And that, I think, begs no further explanation."

"No," agreed Calvraign. Innumerable stories leapt unbidden into his thoughts, making any detailed description wholly redundant. But this new information only left him with more questions. "So how did the Maccs overrun the Ceearmyltu? They certainly didn't have magics of this ilk."

"Certainly not!" confirmed Brohan with great conviction. "But the human tribes had not spent the last thousand years at war against the hrumm or the slaoithe or even the andu'ai before them. The Maccs were battle-hungry and fearless. The aulden, well, they were tired, weakened and disillusioned."

Brohan cleared his throat and continued in a brief melodious verse from an old ballad that was only half familiar to Calvraign:

"Sore of arm, sore of mind, and sore of heart,
the aulden without a blow from Dwynleigsh didst depart.
Away from their constructs of stone and of steel.
Away to their woods and their flowers and fields.
And though its shadows still flicker on the glassy Ciel Maer,
Dwynleigsh is but reflection of what once stood there.

"The Ceearmyltu were tired of war, and left their cities and their castles, including Dwynleigsh, in the hands of High King Cachaillan without so much as a skirmish. I suppose they thought this would secure them from further wars. A pity for them they were so wrong."

Calvraign nodded. "I remember the story, now. It just seems so senseless. To spend centuries building this city, and then simply to walk away."

"The fruits of war are seldom sweet," said Artygalle.

"Aye," agreed Brohan, "but more dangerous still when the fruit *is* sweet, for it tempts you to take larger and larger bites. And then, when you are consumed by your desire for its sweet ambrosia" – Brohan made a painful cracking sound with his knuckles – "you break your tooth on the pit."

Calvraign chuckled, and a hesitant, uncertain smile crossed Artygalle's lips, but no more was said of the matter. Instead, Brohan concentrated on briefing his companions on the current state of affairs at court. Calvraign listened with a focused intensity, and didn't even notice that Artygalle, evidently disgusted by the machinations of House politics, dropped out of the discussion entirely. And so they progressed until, as night fell, they found themselves at the very gates of the fabled Fae City.

Calvraign had thought he would see none of its splendor due to their late arrival and the darkness of this moonless winter night, but as Brohan had promised, even now the city was a sight to behold.

In front of them was the North Gate, an entryway every bit as grand in width as Rivers' Run and thirty or more feet tall, with a final pair of Sentinels standing guard. Its timbers were of polished golden oak, bound with reinforcing steel bands. On each of the double doors, the crest of the city was set in a carefully laid filigree of silver and gold. The emblem itself was a tower rising from azure waves, with the larger, golden sun, Ilieam, on one side, and the smaller, argent sun, Nymria the Handmaiden, on the other.

The outer wall that surrounded the city reached outward from the gate in a protective embrace, watch fires set at regular intervals along its battlements. Calvraign wondered how long it had taken to build this monstrous wall alone, never mind the city that lay behind it. Brohan had taken him within sight of Kirith Celian once, when he was younger, and until now that had seemed the most impenetrable place in the realms. He quickly revised his opinion.

Because the city was built on a series of small hills, Calvraign could make out quite a bit of the architecture beyond the walls. Dozens of delicate, fluted spires reached into the sky, lit by uncountable torches, braziers and multi-colored lamps. Beneath these towers was a vast cityscape of stone that seemed to flow seamlessly from one building to the next. Domes, arches, manses and cathedrals, each beautiful in its own right, together formed a spectacular whole that flickered gently in the varying hues of lamplight. Along the paved roadways, Calvraign could see statues and monuments, fountains and courtyards and, most incredibly, a small forest of trees throughout the city itself. In daylight, he could only imagine how the emerald would offset the alabaster, marble and granite of the ancient buildings.

His attention was brought back to the gate by the sentry's challenge. "Who comes hither? None may pass the gates after suns-set."

Brohan adopted a pathetic, quivering tone. "Can you not make an exception for three weary travelers out in the cold?"

"Nay, I cannot," was the firm reply.

"Perhaps a token of our appreciation would sway you?" Brohan persisted, winking at Calvraign with a smile.

"Nay, I tell you," came the irritated and overly formal response. "Now get thee hence!"

Brohan hung his head forlornly, but spoke clearly in his full voice. "Well then, good sir, you leave me no choice but to compose a lyric regarding our sorrowful treatment at the city gates. If you'll but surrender your name, I shall immortalize you for all time. Then, at the very least, your family will have something to remember you by while you're rotting to your death in the gaol for delaying the King's Bard to the festival!"

There was a brief commotion above them as the sentries fumbled for a bulls-eye lantern amidst an exchange of accusation, blame and disbelief. A moment later, a light shone down from their post and illuminated Brohan's grinning visage, his hood thrown back to reveal his features.

"The King's Bard! The King's Bard!" yelled a voice in almost restrained panic, starting a chain reaction of shouts and footsteps. "Open the gate! Open the gate at once! A hundred-score apologies, Master Madrharigal!"

The sentry continued to stutter nervous supplications, but Brohan laughed it off in good humor. Calvraign knew the bard could never resist a harmless prank, but evidently the guard didn't feel as secure about his good nature. He paused as his companions walked through the opening maw of the North Gate, turning to look behind him with a start. He felt a familiar chill spread through his bones. Had one of the Sentinels moved? Or had it been a trick of the torchlight and the shadows of the night? Or something else?

With a deep breath, Calvraign followed Brohan and Artygalle over the threshold of the city and into whatever destiny lay before him, the after-image of a deathly, cloaked figure burned into the back of his head.

Chapter Eleven

Under the Spur

OSRITH looked over the edge of the cliff down into the impenetrable pool of darkness below. He dislodged a small rock with his foot and watched as it careened down the mountain's edge. It was a considerable time before he heard it strike bottom. He didn't remember how he had come to be at this place, alone, nor for what reason he had done so, yet it seemed familiar to him. No wind stirred, and above him only the stars illuminated the night. He turned when he heard Evynine's soft voice behind him.

"Osrith," she called, her long legs carrying her over the roughened expanse of rock between them gracefully, effortlessly. A thin, translucent coverlet clung to her skin, wrapping around the supple curves of her form without entirely concealing her nakedness.

Osrith's heart clenched in his chest. She had never come to him like this before, even in his most fervent dreams.

"Milady?" he whispered.

She smiled at his puzzled tone, her eyes shining brighter than the stars above them, and reached out to stroke his cheek. The warmth of her touch was soothing and exhilarating all at once. He felt himself drawing away, attempting to check the feelings that burned inside, as he had done so many times before. But his will was sluggish, distracted by the sight of her flesh, the scent of her hair, the promise of her gaze.

"Osrith," she said again, an edge of sorrow in her voice, "it must *end* here. You know we cannot continue as we have, nor can we be together now. There is too much between us."

Osrith knew what she meant, somehow. He turned back to the cliff and peered over once more, the persistent pull of the darkness tugging at his resolve. She pressed against him, the warmth of her breasts against his back, her arms reaching around to hug his chest, her lips brushing against his ear as she spoke.

"Perhaps then we can be together," she prodded.

Osrith took a step closer to the edge. How many times had this very thought crossed his mind? The blackness below invited him again silently, but he did not jump. Something held his limbs in place, planted solidly on the rock beneath his feet.

"It is your time, Osrith." The voice was a hollow sound with a coarse edge and, like everything else here, familiar and distant. It had been several years since last he'd heard it, but he knew it still, and it clawed at every nerve in his spine as it spoke again.

"Hestan," he said as he spun on his heels, the name catching in his throat as he saw the bloodied, limping form that approached him. Evynine stepped back.

The man he had once called friend and lord hobbled toward him slowly, his left leg dragging limp and useless beside him, his mail rent from his neck to his loins and his curdled flesh ripped open to expose the yellowed bone beneath. His gaunt, bearded face was contorted in pain left over from the last bitter moments of his life, his eyes dim but penetrating.

"Come back with me, Osrith. You don't belong here. You were not meant to suffer like this." Hestan reached out his hands, offering to take him over the edge and into oblivion. "End your pain."

"No," whispered Osrith. "There are things afoot I must finish."

Anger twisted Hestan's face. "You are destroying *everything* as you once destroyed me!" The corpse rushed Osrith, grappling at him wildly. "I *will* take you back!"

Osrith parried the clumsy blow, pivoting and throwing Hestan forward – and into the black gap of empty air behind him. Evynine screamed, collapsing to her knees. Osrith's stomach knotted, and his muscles tensed as familiarity slowly dissolved into recognition.

"A tempting alternative, captal." Dieavaul's tone was sympathetic over Evynine's wailing ululation. "This could be your escape. Ultimately, perhaps even your victory, if you choose."

Osrith remained silent and still. His eyes focused on the dark pit calling to him from below. He wondered how much of his desire to jump was Dieavaul's doing, or if he only wished it were.

"It would save them all, of course," continued Dieavaul. "I have no reason to harm any of your friends if you are gone. Evynine, Kassakan…. Both could live out their lives in peace. This could be your gift to them."

Osrith turned to face Dieavaul, biting off his words in anger. "Your master's designs reach far past me."

"I have no *master*, Turlun," replied Dieavaul shortly, his ashen lips thinning into a tight line. "But if their fate does not concern you, then consider this – by destroying the dreamstone, you rob me of victory. You could go to the greylands tasting my defeat."

Osrith frowned. "I'd just as soon not taste any part of you, given the choice," he responded dryly.

Dieavaul gazed at the mercenary with no trace of amusement. "This is your last chance, captal. I suggest you take it. My pity moves me only so far."

Osrith glanced past the Pale Man at the weeping figure of Evynine behind him. It was a hollow illusion without his own desires to give it depth. He looked back into the merciless orbs from which Dieavaul viewed the world, knowing from bitter experience that there was no way to harm this dark reflection of his enemy here in his own nightmare.

"Your pity's not worth the dung on my boot. If it's the dreamstone's end you seek even above my own, then *that* I'll protect above all else."

Dieavaul answered his defiance with more mocking laughter. "I shall have to ask him to be sure, but I believe you once made a similar oath to protect the life of Hestan neVae." In a blur he drew the bonesword, bringing its razor tip to Osrith's chin. "And we both remember how well you kept that promise."

Osrith doubled over, his fingers clawing at the sudden pain in his gut. Blood ran cold over his fingers, dribbling from the old wound down his tunic and onto the grey rock at his feet. He closed his eyes against the visions that the pain rekindled. But there was no place he could hide from this, no place to run, for this torment was not wholly of Dieavaul's making; it was partly his own. In all these years, he'd found nowhere to run that his guilt could not follow.

The wind caressed his brow, and with a tired fascination Osrith realized he was no longer asleep. He sat upright on his sleeping roll, shivering and still holding his side. He did not know how long he'd been awake, or how long Symmlrey had been watching him there. He returned the curious gaze of her sapphire-violet eyes with a hard stare. He had never liked the aulden much, and only marginally cared for *wilhorwhyr*, who he considered a self-righteous lot. In his eyes, she had very little going for her.

"If you're standing watch, little girl, I think you'd be better served looking someplace else."

His derision, though purposeful, apparently had little effect. "You are injured," she replied with a soothing calm. "Your sleep is troubled."

"Is it, now?" growled Osrith, rising from his mat and girding himself in his studded leather harness. He grimaced when he cinched the straps about his tender midriff.

"I mean no offense," she said, her tone more informative than apologetic.

Osrith stroked his beard, trying to awaken his numbed face, and broke her gaze. Kassakan sat, presumably sleeping, next to him. It was hard to be certain with the hosskan, because the thin membrane that covered their eyes during repose was transparent, serving to ward off dust and insects rather than light. He saw no sign of Two-Moons in the sheltering cave they had discovered the night before. Though he judged it was still a handspan before daylight, he wished to be on their way immediately.

"Where's Two-Moons off to?"

"He is on watch outside," replied Symmlrey. "He's troubled."

"And well he should be," he muttered. "Call him in."

Symmlrey nodded and then mimicked the bark of a small mountain cat. Two-Moons appeared in the tiny cave entrance, his silhouette only slightly darker than the night beyond.

"How close are they?" asked Osrith in a tone that displayed he knew or suspected the answer.

"They are traveling straight through the night. We have only a few spans before they reach us here."

Symmlrey shook her head in consternation. "How can that be? We've been so careful."

"Yes," mused the old man. "I have seldom been tracked at all, let alone with such ease." He paused, examining Osrith's face. "What know you of this, Osrith?"

"It's Dieavaul," he answered, spitting the word like venom. "He walks in my dreams and follows in my footsteps. There is a piece of me yet in his damnable blade."

Two-Moons stepped back and sat heavily on a boulder beside his student. "You were wounded by the hellforged? *Ilnymhorrim*?"

"Call it what you will, he stuck me with it."

"Not many live to tell that tale," said Two-Moons. "You should count yourself in the gods' good graces."

"Fortune or fate allowed me to heal him, I don't know which," said Kassakan from her reclined position, her protective membrane still eerily in place, "but the wound still troubles him."

"The pain grows when he's near. No doubt it draws him to me."

"Yes," Two-Moons agreed, "you are an unfinished meal. Once that sword has tasted of your flesh, it does not forget. I see now why your nature is taciturn."

"Don't be so easily fooled," Kassakan added lightly. "He was surly enough long before that sad day."

"In any event, we have to swift-leg it out of here. If we can't elude them, then we'll have to outrun them." Osrith began packing away his bedroll and gear as he spoke. "Once we reach the plains, they'll retreat. Even with Dieavaul at their head, they won't be anxious to follow us into the open."

"Are you fit for such travel?" asked Symmlrey. "You are still weak, and if this other wound now troubles you... ."

Osrith answered with a dry chuckle. "Our options are limited, girl."

The young aulden shrugged. "There is always ambush."

"Don't be a fool!" snapped Osrith. "He would sense me before we could spring any trap!"

Symmlrey's face betrayed only the glimmer of a smile. "That," she said, "is why *you* will be our bait."

Osrith was without answer to her folly, so taken aback was he by her suggestion. Strategically it was a bold move, perhaps even an intelligent one, but practically he knew it too dangerous. She did not understand the power that Dieavaul possessed. Even above the magic of his unholy sword, he was a sorcerer and assassin of great measure. When *ilnymhorrim* chose its wielder to be the Pale Man, one of the Walking Gods, he was sure it made the choice carefully. Perhaps if an army were at their side, or a great wizard, but not these few, tired companions. And not with the dreamstone at stake.

"I believe Osrith's choice more prudent, child," said Two-Moons diplomatically, "but we will certainly make their pursuit a memorable one."

Symmlrey shrugged, nonplused but obviously disappointed. Osrith could see her battle lust brimming beneath the surface of her resigned expression. The same feeling had rushed hotly through his blood when he had first taken up the sword, a day now so many years in the past that it seemed like another lifetime. It had not taken many battles, many wounds, or many dead friends to cure him of that youthful affliction. He suspected the same curative would find its way to her heart before long, and soon, if their circumstances did not improve. All too soon.

Osrith moved past Kassakan as she stood and stretched, extending and retracting her claws with a yawn, her eyes once more bright and alert. He walked to the cave entrance and peered outside. A light breeze blew from the west, stirring the fallen snow but bringing no fresh powder to the mountain slopes. Huge overhangs of ice and snow threatened them from the upper reaches of the mountainside. In the spring, when the great thaws began, the slightest of noises, echoing and reverberating from cliff to cliff, could release these frozen masses in a slope-scouring avalanche. Many a caravan had been buried in a misguided attempt to be the first through the passes. Some believed this was the wrath of disgruntled mountain spirits who saw fit to demonstrate their displeasure on the heads of hapless travelers. Though he gave the supposition little credence, he noted that there had been enough early snowfall to arm the mountain should it be provoked into striking. The kin possessed many ways of encouraging such an avalanche to strike on their behalf. He had heard some stories in the Deeps claiming... .

"Two-Moons," he said over his shoulder, scanning the peaks around them intently, his eyes searching to validate his scant hope, "is there any other way through the pass save this trail?"

The old man joined him on the ledge. "Not for many leagues. We use this trail because it is inaccessible and isolated. We cannot turn back now."

"But if we blocked this trail, they would have no way to follow us?"

"Not without sorcery." Two-Moons eyed the higher slopes, then shook his head. "But if you're thinking what I suspect, it's far too dangerous. We'd bring the mountain down upon ourselves as well as our pursuit."

"Yes." Osrith's lips spread into a broad smile across his face. "Exactly!"

"I'm not certain how to respond to that," said Two-Moons, "but I assume you don't mean to kill us all."

"I wouldn't give him the satisfaction," Osrith said. He heard the soft footstep of Symmlrey behind him, and Kassakan loomed like a shadow out of the corner of his eye. Two-Moons watched him, awaiting explanation. Osrith knew he would have to make it quick. "This trail – it's pretty old, right?"

Two-Moons nodded. "Aye, as old as anyone can remember."

"I thought as much. Let's march. I'll explain as we go."

The four companions were away in short order, without further comment about Osrith's mysterious plan. He assumed this was because they all knew staying at the cave and arguing would be more dangerous than arguing on the move. Conventional wisdom suggested whatever they decided to do would best be done as far from Dieavaul as possible. Though his idea would be seen as reasonable enough in some circles, he doubted his present company would consider it conventional.

"This trail – and the caves spaced out for shelter – these aren't *wilhorwhyr* doing. They're older. Probably dates back to when Birijohr ruled the Deeps. This small arm of the Ridge was once a part of the Underkingdom of Raetchensgraab called Brecholt's Spur. From here they traded with the Ceearmyltu and the surface world."

"How does this help us?" asked Symmlrey from just behind him.

"It helps us because there are still some kin stationed here. They maintain several outposts out here for border defense and security. If we can find the right cave, we should be able to gain entrance to their stronghold. They'll grant us safe passage under the mountain."

Symmlrey's skepticism was unabated. "How can you be certain? Have you had dealings with them before?"

Kassakan answered before Osrith could open his mouth. "If there are any underkin in this mountain, rest assured he will be welcomed, and us along with him. He is somewhat of a hero to their people."

Osrith cringed. It annoyed him that Kassakan brought that up at any available opportunity. He decided to change the subject before Symmlrey's curiosity really got the lizard talking. "More importantly, they can help us be rid of Dieavaul for the time being."

"What number is their force?" called Two-Moons from the rear. "How long do you think they can hold them off?"

"Their number?" yelled back Osrith. Evidently Two-Moons hadn't yet guessed what he had in mind. "Probably no more than a dozen, but that will be enough."

"A dozen! By what reckoning is that enough?" laughed Symmlrey. "Anyway, I thought you said fighting would be foolish."

"Aye, it would," he conceded, "and I don't intend to fight. Once we gain entrance through the cave, we bring the mountain down on them. By the time the survivors dig their way out, we should be well on our way."

"I told you he could be useful," Kassakan chided Two-Moons quietly.

Osrith smiled as he concentrated on navigating the narrow trail. He wished he'd been privy to that conversation. He could guess most of it.

I'm not much for first impressions.

They continued on in silence, saving their breath for the travail of the steep climb. The air was thin here, and each breath was precious. The gradient was increasingly unforgiving, eschewing the luxury of switchbacks for a direct ascent to the summit. The trail was a loose tumble of scree that lined the bottom of a narrow gulley. The footing would have been poor even in temperate weather; now, with knee-deep snow covering the slick sheen of ice on the rocks, each step was more treacherous than the last.

Osrith marked off time by the rasps of their labored breathing and grunts of pain. Two-Moons occasionally confirmed that they were remaining a safe distance ahead of their dogged pursuit but losing ground slowly. Osrith knew his own injuries encumbered their movement, and without him escape would be a less tricky situation. The wounds he received at his last encounter with Dieavaul's hrumm, though healed in most part, still fatigued him, and the fire that burned inside the long jagged scar on his belly delivered him constant torment. Thanks to Kassakan's careful ministrations, however, he endured.

As the sky began its subtle transformation into the purple haze of twilight, they approached the tree line, where only the most tenacious and gnarled vegetation clung stubbornly to the barren rocks. Up beyond this point would be the old entrance, where it could command a good view of the trail. If the watch-kin were alert, they might already have been spotted, although most likely the kin were not keeping an active lookout on such a seldom-used track.

The wind picked up as the trees thinned, blowing a chill into their bones. Osrith could make out the dark shadow of the cave coming into view ahead. He jumped when Two-Moons appeared, as if from nowhere, at his left. Osrith swallowed a curse, trying to hide his surprise.

"They are very near, now," Two-Moons said, catching his breath. "Their scouts are almost in bow shot. You take the others into the cave and make your arrangements. I'll follow shortly."

Or not at all, noted Osrith silently. If Two-Moons tarried too long, he would be cut down in short order by the main battle group, no matter how cunning a warrior he might be. There was one thing he'd decided for certain about Two-Moons, however – the old man knew what he was doing. Despite his air of superiority and pseudo-mystical tongue waggling, he knew how to keep himself alive.

As did Osrith. He didn't delay his own escape to argue.

"Kassakan, Symmlrey, come with me," Osrith said. "Oghran's luck, Two-Moons. We'll wait for you inside."

They tarried only long enough for Two-Moons to assuage the automatic protest of Symmlrey, who, as always, wanted only to stay and fight. But she turned from the promise of battle with a strained look of obedience and helped Kassakan with Osrith as they struggled up the last thirty feet of the slope.

The cave loomed nearer, its mouth swallowing the scant light of burgeoning night. Osrith halted his escort and removed the glove from his right hand. He took two steps toward the opening, raising both hands, palms outward. If kin were indeed watching, they would understand the gesture, and they would see the mark on his forge-hand.

"*Mishtigge! Ahi benm Shaddach Chi!*" he yelled in fluent kinspeak.

"*Osrith behnett-kinne Dulghazz, schlaggar ven Pakh Ma Goiilus, denndar ta -*"

"Shut up and get inside!"

Osrith grinned at the sound of the deep, resonant voice. This was why he liked life with the kin, he remembered. They were a people decidedly short on pointless ceremony. He stumbled forward, followed closely by Symmlrey and Kassakan, entering the darkness with an inaudible sigh. His eyes adjusted quickly, and soon the shadow that wavered before him took on a firmer outline.

The guard standing in the cave was little more than four feet in height and covered from head to foot in protective steel. In his left hand was a short broad blade of the ruddy iron their race was famous for forging, on his right arm a stout shield bearing the crossed hammer crest of the Watch, and on his face the frown of a man who would rather be sleeping.

"*Mishtigge*, friend," said the sentry, reaching up to pound Osrith firmly on the chest with his fist. "I am Vaujn. What in the Pits is going on?"

Osrith returned the greeting with his own fist, leaning down but not kneeling to reach Vaujn's chest. For a human to kneel on one or both knees when speaking to a kin was considered a sign of belittlement and disrespect. He had learned that lesson himself the first time he had met Duragun Two-swords. The painful way. "Shelter," he answered. "We're being hunted by a small army of hrumm."

"Really?" said the kin, his tone reflecting the deep respect his race held for sarcasm. "I hadn't noticed. Every nook and cranny of my mountain's been echoing with hrummish footfalls for a day now, and I haven't slept two winks. Bring in your damn friends and let's be done with the brutes."

Vaujn indicated the grey outline of a doorway behind him, and they darted inside to a smooth-hewn passageway lit by a series of glowing wall sconces. Osrith breathed in the familiar smells of oil, coal and sweat that thickened the air in the tunnels of his adopted people. Already he felt the pain in his old scar diminishing, fading with every step he took into the mountain. Vaujn turned an iron wheel set into the wall, lowering several tons of granite slab that served as the door with little noise or effort.

"Osrith!" yelled Symmlrey, clutching his shoulder from behind. "Two-Moons is still-"

"I know. I know." Osrith held up a conciliatory hand. "Vaujn, there's a *wilhorwhyr* out there at rear guard."

Vaujn stood in the half closed doorway peering out into the cave. "Is he a lanky old man with silver hair who runs pretty damn fast?"

"That would be him," confirmed Osrith.

"Hurry up, old man!" yelled the guard. "You're about to be part of this mountain!"

Not a breath later, the door almost slammed down on Two-Moons' ankles. Symmlrey went to him, supporting him as he caught his breath. His leathers were slashed open in at least two visible places, and his winter cloak was missing altogether. His hair hung limp and wet about his face. He still clutched his bow in his right hand, and Osrith couldn't help but notice there was not an arrow to be found in his quiver, although a rather large throwing axe was embedded in its cracked shell.

"You met with resistance, I see," Osrith said dryly, but couldn't see the *wilhorwhyr's* face to know if his jest was appreciated. Somehow, he doubted it.

Vaujn ignored the injured man and turned to a metal pipe sticking from the polished stone wall. "Bhakkash!" he yelled into it, striking it three times with his sword to produce three loud ringing tones. He turned around to his guests and shrugged. "Well, that should about do it. In a click, half the west slope is going to be knocking all those noisy hrummish feet on their asses."

Vaujn lit a torch from the nearest wall sconce, further illuminating his bearded face. His hair was black and wiry, falling just to his shoulders, and his beard had less than half a dozen war braids. He was young, perhaps only fifty years by human reckoning, but seemed confident despite his relative youth. He brushed past the two *wilhorwhyr* and the hosskan to walk next to Osrith as he led the way deeper into the mountain.

Osrith recalled his amazement the first time he laid eyes on the artistry of kin engineering: the smoothness of the stone, the doors fitted with nearly invisible joints, the pulleys, the levers, the intricate systems of pipes and bells and gongs. Machines that heated, cooled, circulated and filtered the air, somehow powered by the boiling waters of cauldrons or hot springs. It was all rather incredible to the eyes of a common man such as he, and far beyond the mechanical prowess of any other race he'd seen.

Such things bordered on heresy in the upper world. *Physience*. The Forbidden Art. He remembered when, as a boy, he had seen Balduoun of Lot burn fifty alchemists at the stake for treading too close to this forbidden ground. And such acts were ignored, if not supported, by the waning powers of the Collegiate Arcana and the growing influence of the Church.

But Lord Balduoun had never warmed his feet at a vent in the wall that reached, through leagues of hand-carved stone, down to the bowels of Wyn for its heat; or but turned a crank in the wall to pour already heated water into his bath; or laid waste to the castles of his enemies with a kin-worked siege engine. At that last thought, he decided that it might be best that such ambitious human physients were not given free reign.

Osrith looked back at Symmlrey. She was hovering next to Two-Moons, confirming that he was not too seriously hurt. She looked about, taking in her environment with wide, wary eyes. This was far from her natural element. Two-Moons seemed nonplussed. Judging from his age and breadth of experience, that wasn't surprising.

Osrith nudged Vaujn and jerked his thumb back at the aulden. They exchanged a wry grin at about the same time the deep rumbling began. As they walked, the sound took on a physical presence, shaking the walls and the floor beneath their feet as the bone-jarring rhythm grew in speed and intensity. Two-Moons pitched forward and hit the ground, and Symmlrey was thrown against the wall, her breath shooting out of her lungs in a loud rush rendered silent by the deafening cacophony all about them. She slid down slowly, eyes wide, until she sat on the floor next to her shaken Guide. Kassakan stood with legs spread out and claws dug into the ceiling, her tail held out for added balance. Osrith and Vaujn rode out the rumblings with a loose, well-balanced stance.

Then it was over, leaving only faint echoes of the mountain's thunder to rattle in their ears. Osrith looked over again at Vaujn, who was now beaming with pride.

"Well, thank you for that!" the kin chortled. "It's not often we get to do that anymore out here!"

"Don't worry, you'll probably be getting more chances than you'd want soon enough if Dieavaul has his way." Osrith sighed. He felt safer with the comforting weight of the mountain above his head, his pain only a distant ache. "With any luck, we caught him by surprise. I'd love to have him buried out there for eternity and a day."

"Who's Dieavaul?" asked Vaujn as they set off again, leaving the others to help themselves to their feet.

Osrith considered a moment. The kin were not, as a people, overly fond of the supernatural. In fact, they had a downright mistrust for most magic not linked to their mountains. And although he didn't want to panic them or raise their ire, it would be more dangerous for them if they didn't know the truth. Still, he didn't want the news coming from his lips.

"Kassakan, you know your history. Tell Vaujn about Dieavaul."

"As you wish." The lizard's voice was soft, but reverberated in the passageway. Osrith knew she relished such opportunities to speak as much as he despised them. "He is called the Pale Man in legend, as were his predecessors. He is the wielder of what the humans call *Deathbringer*, a weapon forged from a piece of Ewanbheir's twisted soul in his attempt to unmake reality hundreds of years ago. As such, the Pale Man can control and channel energies that would burn the life out of any mortal man and-"

"Stop!" barked Vaujn, halting in his tracks and holding up his hand. He turned and looked up at Osrith with a disturbing glare. "This is a joke, right?"

"No," replied Osrith. "She could continue, but I suppose there's no point. I'll summarize. You would call him one of the Guhddan-kinne. He was the reason I came to the Deeps eight years ago, and the reason I've returned."

Osrith could see Vaujn's jaw clenching even beneath his thick beard, and his black and gold eyes held no sign of amusement. "Well piss on my head! I don't even *want* to know what you did to invoke the wrath of this whatever-he-is."

"I'm sorry for bringing my trouble under the mountain," said Osrith, "but we had nowhere else to go."

Vaujn shook his head and pounded his fist on Osrith's chest to accentuate his words. "No! Don't be sorry! You are *Shaddach Chi*. It's an honor to face death for you if that's what it comes to." He tugged on Osrith's beard to emphasize his sincerity, then smiled ever so slightly. "But in case you're curious, it's *this* kind of mess that convinced us to cut off the surface world in the first place."

Osrith didn't doubt it. Without further comment, they moved on.

⁂

Osrith awoke from a dreamless sleep. He peered into the darkness around him, lit only by the purplish incandescence of the nightmoss that grew near the short arched doorway. He felt rested for the first time in months, his mind untroubled by Dieavaul's ceaseless intrusions. The dreamstone still hung around his neck, cold and unnaturally weighty, but no longer burdensome. His companions lay sleeping around him. They all welcomed this respite.

Osrith's thoughts drifted for a moment back to the Hall of the High King and the life he had lived for those many years with Duragun and Härgrimn and the others of the *Shaddach Chi*. Their victories were just short of modern legend, their friendship as true as any he had known. Why then, was he here, in the midst of a mission for a foolish old seer? Why had he not left well enough alone and stayed where he belonged, beneath the earth with the kin?

He didn't know the answer to that question any better now than when King Ruuhigan had put it to him. He only remembered the immediate and certain desire he had felt to be Gai's messenger. Perhaps it was practicality. In these times, the human world was not receptive to the fae, and any kin who accepted the charge would be unlikely to succeed. And old Fellhammer wasn't about to let his good friend Gai's request for aid go unanswered. The high king always repaid his debts and honored his alliances. So shouldn't Osrith have been the natural choice? Still, his eagerness to take up the journey had surprised even him.

No matter now, he told himself. He wasn't the type to sit and endlessly muddle over the choices he had made. It was enough that he'd made them, and here he was. A fool on a fool's errand. But hopefully, in the end, a rich fool.

"Excuse me, sir."

Osrith turned to the voice of the kinsman who stood in the doorway, visible only from the tinge of the nightmoss light. "What?"

"Captain Vaujn would like to brief you now."

Osrith slid from bed and slipped a pair of soft-soled boots onto his feet. He threw a plain tunic over his head and belted it. He rummaged through his pack for a moment and pulled out a pair of rounded spectacles. The rim was of kinsteel, and the lenses were a polished amethyst glass. He set the finely crafted glasses on the bridge of his nose, and the room around him jumped into view with the crispness and clarity of a sunlit day. One of Ruuhigan's most treasured gifts, the magical spectacles gave him the unhindered eyesight of the kin in the dark.

You'd be a fine and tempting target as the only member of my battle company with a torch, Old Ruh had said with a laugh. Osrith smiled at the memory.

"Let's go, then," he said to the kinsman.

It wasn't far to the briefing hall. Vaujn had given them quarters in the reserve barracks just down the hall. With only a token complement left here in the outskirts of the Underkingdom, finding space for the unexpected visitors hadn't been a concern. He had offered Osrith his own personal quarters, as any good kinsman would have done for one of the King's Own. Osrith had turned him down. He'd have welcomed the softer bed and the privacy, but a small company stayed together. Eat, sleep, fight, die. Together. Old habits died hard.

Vaujn waited inside the room, sitting alone at a table that could seat at least twenty, a stack of parchments spread out before him. He stood and motioned to one of the empty seats beside him. "Sit. If matters are as urgent as you say, you'll need to make up some time."

"The faster we reach Dwynleigsh the better, I say," said Osrith, taking the offered seat. "What have you got there?"

"Maps," replied Vaujn, "lots of 'em. I can get you there any number of ways. Depends on the risks you want to take in the process."

Osrith looked at the pile of papers, all marked with the faintly luminescent ink the kin manufactured from crushed nightmoss. Each had detailed routes planned out to a dark smudge with *Duinlesh* spelled out boldly beneath in the blocky, efficient letters of kinspeak. From other markings on the map, it was clear it had been drawn up at a time before Providayne was even a border province, let alone a sovereign realm. Most telling was the enormous size of the forests, complete with their ancient aulden names.

"What do you suggest, Captain?"

"I'd *suggest* you stay here, but I know that's not about to happen. The surface is buried in snow, and most of the tunnels have been out of use for a couple of centuries – at least. Ktharn's Gouge is probably serviceable, and Buingarr's Passage is mostly clear."

"How long?" asked Osrith.

"In surface reckoning, hmm, that'd be a halfmoon or more, if I had to guess – either way."

"Too long. What else?"

Vaujn was tapping a quill pen against his nose, inadvertently leaving a luminescent indigo dot behind. He pulled a map from the bottom of the pile and shoved it in front of Osrith. "That's the quickest way. I don't recommend it, but if you're in that much of a damned rush... ."

Osrith read the ancient script at the bottom of the map. "Mordigul's Plunge. Why does that sound familiar?"

Vaujn got up and walked to a sideboard at the far end of the room. He poured two drinks from a stone jar and returned, setting one in front of Osrith. The strong hops scent sang to Osrith's nose, and he took a deep drink of the rich ale. None could compete with the underkin when it came to the art of brewing. Of that, there was no dispute.

"You've probably heard the story before. It's a popular one in the Deeps," said Vaujn, taking his seat once more. "You know, the quest for the Eggs of Ohrme. Mordigul and Merridel and the *duaurnhuun*. It's practically the king's favorite."

"That was here?" Osrith took another drink from his chilled stone mug. "I always thought that was out west in Dyrkensgraab somewhere?"

"Nope. The river Dolset runs east from here." He jabbed his finger at the map. "East, but mostly *down*. You'll drop several thousand feet before it levels off completely, and you'll drop pretty fast, too. The rapids are some of the meanest and longest I've ever seen, and I grew up in Rockflow, so you can guess what that means. That way will cut your time in half if you don't drown. But there are other complications."

"Other complications? That's usually where I tell prospective employers to forget it."

"Yes, well, that's probably a good policy. You see, some parts of Mordigul's legend don't want to die and fade into memory."

Osrith didn't like what he was hearing. Vaujn was being deliberately evasive. It was obvious he didn't even like broaching the subject. "*What* part, exactly?"

Vaujn shrugged apologetically. "The part about Oszmagoth."

Oszmagoth. The Sunken City. In kin legend, it was one of the most mysterious and dangerous of places. A once-proud andu'ai metropolis that was struck down by cataclysmic magics, falling through the center of Mount Tanigis to rest in the Deeps, where it became the haunt of every unspeakable creature in the whole of creation.

It was a good story, when told well, but Osrith didn't put too much stock in it. He had seen more of Rahn than any handful of men, and of the hundreds of tales he had heard, there were only two or three that seemed close to reality. Certainly there was once an andu'ai city on Mount Tanigis, and certainly it had plummeted down the throat of the still smoking volcano, but of the rest he was less sure. Shadowborn and *srhrilakiin* and misshapen creatures from beyond the Veil: these were not at all uncommon in the embellished world of myth and adventure. But where Osrith dwelled, in the cold grind of day-to-day reality, they were a rare bunch. Of the ancient legends, it seemed only the hrumm and dringli were found in any real numbers.

Then again, he reconsidered; he *was* being tirelessly hunted by the Pale Man himself. He'd once thought those stories were but legend, too. He decided to treat the idea of Oszmagoth with a little more caution, at the very least.

"So," he finally managed to say, "what sorts of *obstacles* should we expect to find there, then?"

"Well," said Vaujn, very business-like, "we're pretty sure the dragon's gone now. Has been for a couple of years, if we hear the signs correctly. It's a very distinctive sound they make, you know."

Osrith paled. As most sane men, he had no desire to seek out a dragon for any reason. He would as soon turn around and go dig Dieavaul out of the snow and then jump on his unholy sword. "Is that the *same* dragon?" he asked, trying in vain to remember how many hundreds or thousands of years ago the kin heroes had gone on their adventure.

Vaujn shrugged. "Does it matter?"

"I suppose not."

"Anyway, it's gone now. But we think that the *srhrilakiin* are still thereabouts, and there are some wild dringli tribes down further deep from up here – possibly some hrumm. And there's *always* the occasional cave-mantis or eloth ready to drop on your head. Oh, and stay on the south bank. The blood mites generally tend to avoid it down that end because of the rockfishers. At least you can *see* the rockfishers, right? Before it's too late, I mean."

"Was there anything else?"

"Aside from the curse, no. Not that we know of."

Osrith returned the look of irritation and exasperation that the captain had lent him when Kassakan revealed who and what had been buried in the kin avalanche. "And I should probably know what that is?"

"Oh, no," dismissed Vaujn, "nobody *knows* what the curse is. That's the problem, you see."

"Because nobody comes back?"

"I told you I didn't recommend it," said Vaujn. "We've avoided it like the grey plague ever since Merridel dragged her husband out by his hair. But there's always some kin with delusions of grandeur. You know the type."

Osrith put his face into his hands and pressed his fingers against his eyelids. There was no getting around it. He was an idiot. Though it went against every mercenary adage he had ever learned, he could feel in his heart what his decision was going to be. And it was a stupid one.

"Give me some more ale," he muttered, and tried not to think about it.

Chapter Twelve

Old Bones

THE night closed in, enfolding the edges of the Crehr ne Og in an embrace of moonless dark. Callagh was nestled in the thick mid-limbs of an oak, bundled in her cloak and sheltered from the numbing wind, her lidded eyes keeping watch in the stillness. She had come far in a few days, and they were days dimmed early by the constancy of bruised skies and sporadic gusts of obscuring snow.

A distant baying floated on the wind, and Callagh closed her eyes. *The Wolves of Winter*, she thought. *That was the legend. The wolves of Arag Ghûol. When they came, so did the iron season.*

The beasts were seldom seen but often heard as they embarked each year on their eternal, and seemingly futile, hunt. Their barks and howls floated across the heaths and highlands in counterpoint to their silent master, Ghûol. He quested in their wake for the dreaded *rhiad-bannon*, the Hound of Souls, so that he might wrest the spirit of his beloved daughter Lleuwyn from its charge. The same daughter he'd doomed to that fate, wagering with the gods.

The Old Gods do love a bargain, she thought.

Ghûol drove his wolves hard after their quarry this year. Deepingmoon and Darkmoon brought snow, and deep snow on occasion, but storms did not usually threaten in earnest until the aptly named Stormmoon.

Callagh shivered, but not from the cold. Cold alone didn't bother her. She'd weathered worse, and dwelling on discomfort didn't help. No, it wasn't the cold or the snow or the early onset of winter that made her wary – it was thoughts of Arag Ghûol and his wolves and the tracks that she'd followed for the past two days.

Legends such as that of Ghûol and the Chariot of Winter, and the dreaded beast of *rhiad-bannon* that he hunted: these were stories that once had thrilled her. She'd believed them, at least in a distant sort of way, but her experience in the Ad Craign Uhl had changed that. There was a frightening depth to every legend now, that even in sincere belief she had previously not devoted much thought.

Is Ghûol really hunting the rhiad-bannon? *she wondered. Does it really hold the secret of his sweet Lleuwyn? Or was Da' right – just a bunch of damn geese makin' grief for skittish hunters?*

The tracks.

Geese did'na make those tracks, she thought, as if she needed the reassurance. *Nothing should make those tracks.*

She had followed them out of curiosity and convenience. The imprints were roughly the size of a bear's, but with distinctly canine pads, and spacing and depth that revealed a long loping gait. She'd never seen anything like it. It headed in roughly the same direction as she, so she stalked the beast, whatever it was.

It was that first night that the baying began, but only several spans later did she make the connection with the legend of the *rhiad-bannon*.

What else would make those tracks? And what else, but the wolves of Arag Ghûol, give it chase?

The beast of legend was the size of a bear, a giant wolfhound with scraggly mottled coat and eyes that burned green. In some stories, it was winged; in most, it was not. But in one thing all legends agreed – it had eaten Roald adh Rhiad, the Lord of the Hunt, and only spit him out again at the behest of the divine hunter's sister, Roaìl. But not before first digesting his arm, and with it, all of his forest lore.

Callagh brushed her thumb over the brooch in her pocket. *Keep to the old ways, ahn cranaoght, and the old ways will keep you.* Those words echoed in her head, a constant toll and a persistent reminder that the life she had known was somehow changed forever. *Old things are waking.*

Callagh pulled the cloak's cowl down over her face and settled her thoughts. *I don't need to know what river I'm on to know I'm floating downstream,* she told herself, and eased into a wary sleep.

✦

Callagh blinked, wondering if she'd slept through the night, but the darkness that greeted her told her it had not been long. Perhaps a half-span, at most. She glimpsed the ruddy light of Ghaest through the clouds as the restless wind briefly exposed the Dead Moon to the night, but it was a few spans to suns-rise, of that she was sure.

Chased off the big bright girl, did ya'? she thought. A grin may have played about the corners of her mouth, but no sooner had she started to relax than her spine stiffened.

Callagh sensed it, before she even looked – something watching her. It was the feeling of *being prey*. Once, after a fruitless morning running far afield to track a mighty buck, she'd had the same feeling. She'd turned back only to find the tracks of a mountain cat trailing hers from the edge of the brush. The cat had apparently decided she was not worth the effort, or found better game, and Callagh hoped she might have similar luck this time.

But when she peered down, it was not a mountain cat that watched her. A pair of lambent green eyes sparkled from a translucent shadow, a giant hound sitting on its haunches, staring back up at her.

The *rhiad-bannon*.

Those eyes lead to undernland itself, she thought, and then in horror, looked away. *I looked into its eyes! Right into them like a damned half-wit stupid girl in a bardsong.*

She didn't die, however; and the *rhiad-bannon* didn't threaten her. Nor did it move away. As she examined its shadowy bulk from her perch, it watched and waited, its eyes never blinking.

"What?" she asked aloud, fear swallowing any intended insolence into a harsh whisper as her throat tightened around the words. "What do ye want of me?"

It cocked its big shaggy head, just as one of Calvraign's hounds might startle at an odd noise. Then it rose and lumbered a few yards away. It looked back at her and sat, staring to the southeast.

That bloody beast is bigger *than most bears,* she thought.

Callagh dropped to the ground, her heart racing, but she knew what it wanted of her, and she couldn't imagine refusing it. Her bow was strung, but she didn't bother to nock an arrow. She didn't think for a moment that she could outrun it or slay it. The Hound of Souls did not appear to a mortal without reason, and foolish was any mortal who might take such an omen for granted.

She stopped next to it, fighting an urge to reach out and run her fingers through the ruff at its neck. Instead, she followed its gaze. There was a faint glimmer off in the woods, an orange-red flicker barely bright enough to cast a shadow, tucked in the hollow of a shallow hillock.

"A camp?" she asked, this time her whisper intentional.

A distant baying lilted through the wood, and the rhiad-bannon's ears lay flat against its head. A low growl brewed in its throat.

"I'll do what ye want," Callagh said. "But I've no clue what-"

The Hound leaped, and a cold strong wind blew through the trees after it, rustling the leaves with a keening insistence. The baying sounded more distant than ever, yet felt somehow as if it was just over her shoulder, out of sight.

Then silence and emptiness.

Callagh looked to the light of the nearby fire and frowned. "Ah, hang me!" she cursed under her breath, and crept forward.

Callagh's footfalls were soft, and her pace that of a patient hunter all too aware of the price paid for haste. She had an arrow at the string, but lowered it after a careful examination of the clearing.

The hillock was long and narrow, covered in mossy rocks and comparatively young growth. Callagh judged it might be an old barrow mound and, considering the company she'd been keeping of late, it seemed an appropriate place for the Hound to point her. But, aside from the low, hot, almost smokeless fire, there was no movement here, and no life. Not so much as a curious tree-nape.

But the smell told her there was more to know, here. The stink of copper and sweet perfume and acrid charcoal was thick in her nostrils. It was the smell of flesh and blood and organs as they burned, not cleaned and dressed for the cook fire, or wrapped for a funeral pyre – a body burned whole.

Callagh found a plethora of prints in the dirt and snow about the fire. Boots, mostly heavy tread, possibly armored. They had come in from the southeast and exited the same way. Nothing had been dragged, but she did notice one delicate set of prints entering the clearing. A child, or a very petite woman, had accompanied perhaps a dozen men. But there was no sign of her exit. More puzzling, there was no indication of a struggle.

Callagh stared back into the flames again, and the dark blotch of a body on which the fire still fed. Hesitant but determined, she approached the dwindling blaze. The flames were low, and white, and hotter than she thought was quite normal. She grabbed a thin branch from the ground and poked at the remains.

She jumped back with a scream when the blackened husk moaned, tripping on her heels and falling on her backside.

"*Ahn cranaoght,*" the corpse intoned in a familiar voice, flames licking from the jaw as it spoke. Its empty eyes and nasal opening glowed eerily from within. "*Do not fear me, little ghost.*"

Shaking, Callagh crawled to her knees, dizzy. She found no words, staring mute and pale into the fire.

"*My thanks for your attention to my bones. It has been years since I have felt kindness. It is dark where I dwell.*"

"Why aren't you at your rest?" Callagh managed to say. "I thought.... I thought I helped you."

"*Ah, but you did help. No longer to my mortal husk am I tied. And I am here because of that. Here to help you.*"

"Why?" Callagh's gaze was transfixed on the delicate skull. *So small.* There was no doubt that this was a child, and less than a ten-year if she guessed right. She fought to swallow her bile. "Am I dead?"

"*Not yet. Not even a little.*"

"Then who are you? And why help *me*?"

"*I am a friend to you, and a servant to a power that you also serve, by action if not word. I can say no more. The Wards of the Dead prevent me from speaking plain, or I'll bring greater doom on us both. That, alas, is how it must be between us.*"

Callagh had always been puzzled by the old man in the Ad Craign Uhl, but also amused, and never threatened. Now, suspicion ate at her gut. "And what's it I'm doin' that needs helping? There's too much chance droppin' in my lap all at once to think it coincidence."

Callagh planted her fists on her hip. "The old man I talk to for years on end just *happens* to be some kind spirit to help me, and he speaks from a lil' girl burnin' up in a fire that just *happens* to be on my way, that just *happens* to be past the Hound of Souls and to the left, eh? It's bloody odd, I think."

"*Not so odd, and no coincidence. Our conversations over the years were no more happenstance than the Black Bard's with your young beloved. You were both crafted to a purpose.*"

Callagh snorted. "What am I, then? Some pawn to be played."

"*A pawn? Certainly not. A game piece of sorts? Well, yes. We all are, by someone else's hand. You have played* Mylyr Gaeal *– you know the truth of it. It's easier to put your piece into play with your opponent than it is to set up the strike. Positioning the pieces several moves in advance. Anticipating your opponent without tipping your own strategy. Tricky. But here we are, and for several players of the game, including the hand that guides both of us, pieces held in reserve for years are nearing conflict.*"

"And what if I'd rather have a scone and a nice cup o' hotblack, eh?" Callagh challenged. "What then?"

"I won't make decisions for you. I will only give you choices. How you choose will determine how the game is played out. And how the other pieces may fare."

Callagh felt some of her defiance drifting away. "Calvraign," she said, nibbling on her upper lip. "Does he serve the same power? I can help him?"

"No, a different hand moves his destiny; and yes, you may indeed help to save him. But we have little time left. The door to your world is loose on its hinges, but even so – when this flame dies, this door closes."

"And what about her?" Callagh asked, pointing at the charred skeleton. "Did she have a choice?"

"She was not one of us, and nor was her choice – but she gave herself to the flame, and she is consumed to the purpose. In so doing, she left the door ajar for me. It was an unexpected courtesy.

"The flame she served is growing hungry, little ghost, and this flame burns with more heat than light."

"You want me to go put this fire out for you, is that it?"

"Oh no," he said. "Follow these tracks. Find the men who made them. They are going where you need to be, and they can help you for a time, if you can gain their trust. As it happens, they are short one young servant girl in their camp.

"No, I don't want you to extinguish this fire. Not yet. Sometimes it is the heat of a wildfire that brings life to a dormant seed from which a mighty tree might grow. For now, I want you to tend it."

The flames were dimming, the heat fading, the skeleton crumbling to ash. The voice was thinner as it continued, "You will be far from our source of power. I do not know when or how we may help you once beyond our boundary, but look for our signs and you will find them. If you do not look, they will not appear."

"All very bloody mysterious," complained Callagh. "And how am I to know that I've found the right men? Or what this fire is, and how to tend it? Can you not start me off a bit with another damn riddle or some such?"

Darkness was reclaiming the dying fire, and the skull cracked, shifted, as it spoke again, so faint that Callagh leaned as close to the fire as she dared.

"The Lord of Winter is not the only one with wolves prowling hereabout. Find these others, their mortal kin, and you will find the immortal fire."

The final word lingered on the wind even after the last desperate tongues of flame consumed the remains. The fire extinguished, leaving only a dark stain on the grass and a circle of melted snow to show it had ever burned. There was nothing left of the girl on which it had fed.

A raven alighted on a branch overlooking the tracks that marred the snow. It spread its ebon wings and cawed.

"Ach," grunted Callagh as she stood. "I suppose that'll have to do." She set off to the southeast, following the tracks with a frustrated grimace as she passed beneath the crow. "But a unicorn would have been nice."

Chapter Thirteen

Roses in Winter

AEOLIL Vae sat alone in the small courtyard, her legs curled beneath her, sinking into the voluminous azure dress that flowed out and around her like a pool of liquid sky. Her auburn hair fell loose about her face, hanging down in curly tendrils only recently freed from tight formal braids. Her eyes, like her mother's, were a deep royal blue that stunned with but a glance. Her skin was fair, her freckles betraying her love of the outdoors without blemishing her delicate appearance.

This was a quiet place, generally forgotten by the courtesans and sycophants that peopled King's Keep. Her only company were the pearly marble statues of aulden children at play, the dual rows of redberry trees, and her own sullen likeness which stared back at her from the still waters of the rectangular reflecting pool. The solitude of this place made it her favorite retreat from the court and its bickering politics. The trees remained in bloom all year round, their trunks and limbs embraced by the tangled curls and red-blossom kisses of rose-vines and the weepy white clouds of fragrant dragonmist. Like many of the trees throughout the city, they were nurtured by some unknown enchantments the aulden had left behind. Here she could find peace with her thoughts, if but for a short time.

Aeolil knew it would not be long before Bleys or her suitors discovered her, and neither prospect held much joy for her.

Bleys rarely let her out of his sight, watching over her like a horned eagle even within the king's stronghold where such attention seemed unnecessary. If an assassin could manage the feat of reaching this fortified retreat and breaching its formidable defenses, she doubted her name would be high on the list of intended targets. But Bleys had always been over-protective, even back at home, and here it was much worse. Perhaps it was understandable, considering her family's more recent history. She could elude him for a short while, occasionally, but times such as this were rare. She was not overly fond of him. He was ill-humored and serious, stern, and not gifted at conversation. But he had served her family, and served them well, for as long as she could remember, so she had learned to tolerate his behavior.

He would find her soon enough.

She hoped to Illuné that she could avoid her suitors more successfully. She knew she must take a husband, and her mother refused to arrange a marriage for her yet, hoping that she could wed for love rather than position or title. Aeolil smiled at the thought. It was a nice gesture her mother made, but impractical. In these times of growing instability, it was more important than ever to cement or create alliances, and marriage was an expedient and successful way to accomplish both. She knew her duty, even if her mother would spare her from it.

Her parents' marriage had been one of political beginnings. They had loved each other as two close friends might, but she knew there had not been real passion between them. Regardless of love, as a result of their union the Houses of adh Boighn and Vae were both strengthened. She must now do the same and find a man whose lineage and standing would offer something to the Western Marches.

She had little doubt what the suitors felt *she* offered. Aside from the obvious political advantages, she was a beautiful young woman. Because her legs were long and lean, her skin fair and her breasts and hips well-formed – because of this she was less a person and more a prize. Since her years of bloom, countless men of rank had pursued her. Their eyes picked over every inch of her skin, slipping their slithering gazes under her garments to take in all that they imagined was there. A shudder ran from the base of her neck down her spine and ended somewhere in the pit of her stomach, leaving a cold emptiness there. She wondered if men knew or cared how obvious were their wandering eyes.

No matter. She was guilty of similar, if not entirely equal, offenses. Often she saw people in terms of their potential usefulness or how they might represent political advantage. How sad, she thought, that people must be a web of possibilities rather than human beings to her. Sad, perhaps, but there was no helping it. It was simply how she was, and how she had always been.

A shaft of suns-light escaped the clouds and slanted through the water to shine with redoubled brilliance on the golden stones at the bottom of the reflecting pool. It was the moment she had waited and hoped for. In that instant the courtyard erupted in a dazzling shimmer of light that danced from the water and across the small statues, bringing them to life in a scintillating illusion of motion. Aeolil could almost hear the children at play as they ran without a care beneath the rose-vines and redberry boughs, their hair flowing about them as their voices rose and fell like the notes of a song on the wind. She could feel the *iiyir* crackle silently about her, within her and through her. Then, a heartbeat later, the shadow of a cloud silenced the imaginary music and laughter as it smothered the suns-light. The pool was dark and still, the stones dull and lifeless, and once more she was alone.

"There she is, Your Highness! I should have known!"

Bleys did not sound pleased. She heard his hard-shod boots patter against the stones of the stairway behind her but didn't bother to turn. His Highness would certainly be Prince Hiruld, one of her more interested admirers, and one of her better prospects. He was attractive, no more than ten years her senior, and the king's only living heir.

"Well, young Lady Vae, you had us on a merry chase!" The voice was resonant and powerful. "I believe Captal Malade was on the brink of panic."

Yes, definitely Hiruld, she told herself. Aeolil rose, turned and curtsied in one motion. She came face to face with the tight sneer of Bleys' disapproval. He towered over her, standing near six feet and two inches, his hulking frame attired in formal mail and tunic. A bead of sweat trickled down from where his polished iron helm met his brow, traversing the angular terrain of his hard features to dangle precipitously on his scarred chin. Smaller droplets were caught in the thick black mustache that dropped from above his lips down past the corners of his mouth and to the very edge of his face.

"Your mother shall hear of this," he rasped quietly, his eyes locking with hers.

Aeolil stepped past her bodyguard and repeated her curtsy for Hiruld's benefit. "My Prince," she said. "To what do I owe the pleasure of your visit?"

Hiruld's face was considerably more pleasant to look upon than that of Bleys. He had long, curling blonde hair that was well combed and scented, and features brightened by his rakish smile. In height he was even a finger's breadth taller than Bleys, and his equal in girth as well. His gold and blue robes were fitted exquisitely and adorned with a variety of gemstones.

"Good news, this day," he answered, offering his arm in escort. "Sometime between last night and this morning, Father's favorite bard returned from his meanderings. He's brought some barbarian curiosity with him from the Crehr ne Og. His understudy, I gather, and this *really* got Father's attention. He's quite anxious to hear them entertain, and he's called a special luncheon for this afternoon. And I would have you at my table, if you please."

She took his arm and nodded politely. She knew, in truth, she could refuse his arm no more than his invitation. "I would be honored, Your Highness. Why such urgency? My breakfast has yet had time to settle."

"Yes, well, with the festival upon us in a day or two, who will notice one extra feast? It has been a long while since last Brohan sang for us, and you know how his presence brightens the court, and Father especially."

Aeolil nodded. The court had become a somber place. For every year that the war dragged on, every son who returned scarred and ragged or failed to return home at all, for every House that pulled its purse strings tighter and tighter as the financial burdens of conflict overtook their coffers' gains, there was less and less to be mirthful or joyous about. Less of everything except tears. Since Vingeaux had fallen last spring, the king's heavy heart was at the center of this depression. Now they needed the glow of Brohan's voice and the wonder of his stories more than ever they had in years before.

"Yes," she agreed, but withheld further comment as the prince led her back up the staircase and into the warm interior of the castle. Bleys came behind them at a respectful distance. She knew that Hiruld missed his older brother, and worried for his father's health, but she also knew that he had neither the intent nor the ability to step into the power vacuum and assert the full measure of the House Royal's influence on the splintering factions of the kingdom.

Of course, were she to marry him, she could help steer him in the right direction. She would make a good Queen. Agrylon never lost the opportunity to plant that thought in her fertile mind, the meddling bastard, but she knew it was true regardless. She was more than a match for Hiruld mentally, and had the common sense and practically that had been the hallmark of her line since Kiev won his land and title centuries ago. Not to mention the potential their children would have. Yes, there was much to say for such a union.

"Is my company tiring you?"

Aeolil looked up at the prince with a wide smile that washed away any concern from his face. "On the contrary, Your Highness, I was reflecting on the truth of your words."

Comforted, the prince led their conversation into the small talk and irrelevant niceties with which he was accustomed when speaking with ladies. Aeolil paid him the appropriate respect and responded when necessary. In her heart, she longed for the stillness and silence of the glittering pool in the courtyard. In her mind, she prepared for entrance into the realm of the king's court, where words could prove more deadly than steel. With but one misstep, she could lose her hard-fought standing with the House Royal, and worse even than that, betray her mother's implicit trust. Her late father and brothers had once been expected to share this burden, but as the only surviving child, it was now hers alone, and she thrived on its inherent challenge as she hated its ever-looming presence.

Hiruld led them around a corner, still chatting away contentedly to himself, and Aeolil felt a warm burst of air rushing down the corridor to greet her face. They were nearing the Eastern Audience Hall, where the king entertained only the most favored of the aristocracy. Unlike the Grand Hall, where most of the king's parties would be held during the festival, the smaller size of this venue allowed for a more intimate setting. The bards would sit at fireside with the nobility arranged before them in a semi-circle of finely appointed tables. The low stone ceiling, trimmed with ornately carved rafters, trapped in the heat and sound instead of letting them flit away aimlessly as in the vaulted heights of the larger chamber.

She stopped in mid-step as the gilded doors drew nearer. Bleys almost walked over her, so sudden was her halt, and Hiruld turned with a confused blink. The prince's query dropped short when he saw her hands reach for her hair. He knew as well as she that though attractive enough, such a casual hair style was not befitting a lady of her station on the arm of the crown prince. Such a sight would prove fertile soil for gossip; and where gossip thrived, scandal soon grew with a healthy bloom.

"Your pardon, Lady Aeolil. I shall await you within," he said, excusing himself with a gentleman's nod. A moment later he had passed through the doors.

Bleys sent a smug, almost malicious smirk in her direction. She realized that Hiruld considered his departure a mark of politeness, leaving her to finish her womanly business in peace, but it was more a mark of stupid neglect. He, of course, had already seen her hair in disarray. What matter if he was present as she remedied the situation? Meanwhile, he had left no one but Bleys to guard the corridor from intruding eyes or inopportune approach. Then again, how was Hiruld to know that Bleys would choose inaction as his method of revenge for her temporary escape?

Aeolil worked her hair around her fingers and tried her best to approximate the intricate work it had taken her handmaidens an hour to perfect. Without a looking glass, she found it that much more challenging. She should not have let her hair, or her guard, down at all. Her visits to the secluded garden were a selfish indulgence – an attempt to live a life of her own instead of the life chosen for her. She must not show such weakness again. But, even as she pledged this to herself, she knew it was a distraction she could not give up.

She heard footsteps approaching from behind, somewhere around the corner as yet, and felt her heart race in apprehension. With her luck it would be Garath or Derrigin, young rakes on the prowl for any hapless victims on whom they could unsheathe their barbed tongues.

Bleys' smile widened.

Bastard! she thought. *He's relishing this. Men and their damned court niceties.*

Aeolil gritted her teeth, wondering again at the ridiculous pomp of life at court. In the more casual protocol of House Vae, a ponytail would have sufficed. But here… . Anything out of place was fodder for the political wolves and the rumormongers.

As if seeing my hair undone actually reflects upon anything of importance!

By all accounts, it seemed men actually preferred a lady's hair wild and free, and yet took great measures to ensure they would rarely see it so. Aeolil had determined that all this foolishness was a product of their fear. Fear of awakening their own desires, fear of the self-control that would slip away and, worst of all, fear of rejection. She knew all this, and had spent her time at court harnessing their fear and forging it with her own wit and looks until she could wield the knowledge like a weapon. Unfortunately, the keener the edge became, the easier it was turned back upon her, and the deeper the wounds would be. This coming wound would not be severe, she realized, but it would be painful and bothersome all the same.

Or perhaps you've just become too proud, Aeolil, she chastised herself. *Perhaps, at long last, vanity has conquered your common sense.*

The footfalls grew ever closer, and a bright laugh reached her ear – they were right around the corner. She had no more time. The ridiculous situation enraged her so that her fingers fumbled with the final braid and sent it falling from her hands and over the horrified expression on her face.

To keep up appearances, Bleys stepped belatedly in front of her as the two men strode into view. The first, a tall beautiful man with dark skin and almond eyes of shining green, was wrapped in fine emerald and brown garments of elegant cut, a long cape fluttering behind him. The other was a boy recently become man, blond with pale blue eyes and handsome features lit by a flush of excitement. His garb was the same, absent the long cape that marked a master bard.

"Well met, Lady Aeolil!" exclaimed the first, his rich voice soothing and commanding. His eyes darted to her tangled coiff. "It appears you are a few strands shy of a proper braid. May I?"

"Master Brohan, you would honor me greatly!" she replied, returning Bleys' smirk tenfold as relief washed over her. "Oghran has taken pity on me, it seems."

The master bard came up behind her and began his work.

"Not much time, I'm afraid," said Brohan casually as his fingers danced through her auburn tresses. "The young Lords Vespurial and Malminnion are but scant steps behind. Oghran's pity, you know – rather fickle."

Aeolil's pulse quickened.

"No worry, though," continued Brohan, popping his head around her left shoulder for a quick wink. "When young Calvraign here stops staring he's apt to do something chivalrous."

The young apprentice started at the mention of his name, blinking and averting his eyes as scarlet shaded his cheeks. "Yes, yes," he stuttered. "At your service, milady!" He tripped on his feet as he rushed to turn around and then bounced off of Bleys with a grunt.

Aeolil could see Brohan's grin out of the corner of her eye as his apprentice sprinted around the corner. Soon after there was a great crash of bodies to the floor and an indignant yell that was unmistakably Calamyr Vespurial's.

"Oaf! You'd best watch where your leaden legs carry you!"

Aeolil could almost see the arrogant young lord's furious expression as Brohan's apprentice stuttered nonsense in response.

"Almost done," whispered Brohan.

"Will he be all right?" she asked. "My pride is not worth so much as that."

Brohan was silent for a moment as Garath Malminnion's voice joined in scolding Calvraign, then answered, "If he keeps his head, he'll keep his head. From the sound of it, they just want to remind him of his place. Besides, the great Captal Malade would not allow harm to a boy who just saved his charge from undue embarrassment. That would be a great dishonor, indeed."

Bleys grunted, and his expression soured. "Ah, yes, I forgot myself," he muttered with a decided lack of conviction. "I'll see to him."

"There," said Brohan with a flourish. "I should have been a hairdresser."

With a quick dip into his vest pocket, the bard withdrew a palm-sized silvered mirror and held it up for Aeolil to see. She gasped and smiled. Not only was her hair once again braided to perfection, but interlaced with her hair were several filaments of reflective silver silk which accented her deep blue gown in keeping with her House colors. She was impressed, and not only with the end result. Her time spent in Agrylon's tower allowed her to identify a subtle use of the Craft in his effort, and that intrigued her most of all.

"Absolutely beautiful, Master Brohan. I owe you no small debt for your kindness."

"My pleasure, milady." He replaced the mirror in his pocket. "Ah, here they come."

Calamyr and Garath were the first to round the corner, straightening their slightly ruffled appearance as they walked. Soon after came a cowed Calvraign in the protective shadow of Bleys. The young noblemen stopped and bowed slightly at the waist toward Aeolil.

The two men were physically quite different. Though roughly the same size and muscular build, Calamyr possessed a fine-featured face and elegant manner. He carried himself with obvious pride, his hand at rest on his sword pommel. Garath, whose face was not blessed with Calamyr's symmetrical good looks, hid his rough features behind a well-trimmed black beard. His eyes held the same defiant pride as his friend's, but lacked his unwavering gaze of self-confidence.

"You outshine yourself this morning, Lady Aeolil," said Calamyr, a sly smile creeping across his face. "Why, you look like a *princess*!"

"Thank you," she responded curtly. It would do no good to acknowledge his thinly veiled inference.

Garath directed his attention to the master bard, his tight jaw betraying a lingering ill will. "I should have known this dog belonged to you." He flashed an angry glance back at Calvraign.

"Where are your manners, sir?" Aeolil said, irritated.

Garath ignored her. "I have half a mind to cut him down where he stands!"

Brohan raised an eyebrow as Malminnion fingered his sword hilt. "Half a mind? Well – I'll not quibble percentages." Garath's nostrils flared, and his eyes glared from their sockets, but Brohan pressed on. "And though you are doubtless a skilled dog-slayer, you will have to abate your practice until some other time. Unless you would keep the king waiting?"

"You dare!" Garath's voice was a hot whisper. He shrugged off Calamyr's hand from his shoulder. His grip tightened around his sword hilt.

Aeolil stepped between them. "Lord Garath, stand back. It was you who hurled the first barb! If you cannot win a battle, whether with wits or steel, I suggest you do not join it."

"She speaks the truth, my friend," soothed Calamyr. "Temper's tongue is quicker than reason's. Let's forget the matter and make our entrance."

Garath stood, his eyes locked intently with Brohan's, waiting for provocation. Aeolil glanced between the two, her heart racing. If blood was shed to protect the honor of her hair, she would never forgive herself. But Brohan was far too clever to deliver himself into such harm. He stood, calmly returning Garath's glare, smiling amicably all the while. If only

Hiruld possessed an ounce of Brohan's composure, she thought, the kingdom would be in competent hands.

Finally Garath turned, snapping his cape behind him, and strode towards the doors at the end of the hall. He turned at the midpoint. "I will go, but I will *not* forget!" he stated icily. The guards opened the doors, releasing another warm waft of air and the growing sounds of merriment, and young Lord Malminnion made his entrance.

Calamyr smiled. "Good day to you, Lady Aeolil. Master Madrharigal." He nodded in their direction, and then paused for a moment, assessing Calvraign. "And to you, sir. The company you keep speaks more for your character than your dexterity, it seems."

"And good day to you, sir," responded Aeolil with a curtsy.

"You are most gracious, milord." Calvraign bowed deeply, though his face showed that this did not come easily for him.

"Indeed you are," added Brohan with a less awkward bow of his own, "but your friend has a high sense of drama. A dangerous trait for those not trained in its complexities."

"Yes," he agreed, "so I keep reminding him. Fortunately, drama is your business, Master Bard." And with that, he withdrew.

"I had best go ahead of you," said Aeolil. "Thank you both once more for your assistance. If there is anything I may do for you, you have only to let me know, and it shall be done."

"Your gratitude is thanks enough," said Calvraign, his eyes as wide as his smile.

"Yes, well," said Brohan, giving Aeolil a knowing look. "Your gratitude and perhaps a small favor."

"Of course, Master Madrharigal. What is your need?"

"There's no urgency to it," said Brohan, with a casual toss of his hand. "Perhaps we may speak later?"

"Your convenience would be my pleasure, sir," she replied. "For now I had best take my leave."

Aeolil left them behind with another brief nod of courtesy. The guards watched as she passed, alert for mischief but unconcerned with political or personal squabbles. The rank and file of the King's Guard were commoners with no links to any of the major Houses. Their loyalty and their purses belonged solely to the king.

The herald tapped his staff of office on the floor once, twice, then three times. His voice was clear and strong as he presented her to the assemblage of her peers. "Her Ladyship Aeolil Vae of the Western March."

She entered with the slow, deliberate gait and fluid elegance that she had learned in her childhood. Bleys discretely stepped off to the side with the other personal retainers. The eyes of the court were on her, following each perfect step toward the King's Table and her empty seat at Hiruld's side. She ignored the stares, presenting herself with a deep curtsy to the crown prince. He accepted her hand and guided her to the chair to the right of his own, one place removed from where his father would soon grace them all with his presence.

Aeolil caught the golden gaze of Agrylon from the shadows behind the king's chair, his eerie eyes reflecting the torchlight like miniature stars. He seemed but a cloaked wraith, his short silver beard and steeply slanted brows dulled into a stark grey by the shroud of his hood. Though she knew Agrylon well, possibly better than any here save the king himself, she did not wholly trust him. This was common enough. Wizards, who wielded powers that most could not understand, demanded a combination of fear and respect that made a casualty out of easy trust. She knew enough of these powers herself, thanks to her secret tutelage at Agrylon's own hand, but it was his mind she feared more than his magic. He was a great manipulator, one of the most dangerous at court, and she had no wish to be his witless pawn. As she broke the lord high chamberlain's expectant gaze, she wondered if she already was.

Aeolil took a moment to assess the rest of the High Table, her eyes sweeping across the assembled personages with a nonchalant turn of her head. To her right, at the end of the table, was her cousin, the youngest of Michael adh Boighn's red-haired sons, Stuart. He was a great friend of Hiruld, due mostly to Stuart's skill as a gryphon trainer and rider. The king and Hiruld both shared a fascination with revitalizing the airborne gryphon knights that Dacadia had once used to fearsome efficiency. He was pleasant enough, if a trifle obsessed with his creatures. The red and gold of his doublet accentuated the thin beard that outlined his youthful face.

To her far left, at the other end of the table, was Grumwyr son of Gruswold, heir to House Bruhwn. He was often referred to as *the Bear* outside of proper circles, and from his appearance it was obvious why. He was just shallow of seven feet in height, and must have weighed near three hundred pounds. He was not obese by any measure, but rather a hardened man of sinew and muscle. He had dark eyes and darker hair, the latter of which covered his exposed arms like a coarse-woven carpet, making the delineation between his black and green shirt and his arm itself hard to determine. He was quick to humor, but his temper was ferocious and quicker still. She had once seen him at work on a delinquent member of his House Guard.

A bear, indeed. He was one of the favorites to win the King's Lance this year. Again.

Then there was Sir Vanelorn, lord high marshal and hero of countless battles. He was showing his age now, his iron-grey hair still long but receding from his brow. His eyes, too, were grey, and his austere garments. He was a grave man, and a noble one, with a dignity all his own.

He had been a friend of her father's once. Noticing her gaze, he nodded and smiled briefly, in his eyes a certain melancholy. Whether for himself or for her, she was not sure. She smiled in response, wondering what worried him so. Of course, there always seemed to be something.

Finally, sitting to the left of the still-absent king was Lady Myrtma. Poor Tianel, who had lost not only her father but her two brothers in the war. Aeolil knew the pain that resided in her heart, forced into responsibility too young, with all that she ever loved taken violently away from her. She still wore the plain black garb of mourning instead of her House colors. She had earned her exalted place at Guillaume's side from his pity and in no small part from his guilt. For her, attendance at the festival was no more than a responsibility this year, and a bitter burden to bear.

"A fine turnout, this," remarked Hiruld in little less than his normal speaking voice. "Father will be pleased."

"Yes," agreed Aeolil.

Scattered about the rest of the tables in the small audience hall were the most respected and powerful of the peerage of Providayne, Garath and Calamyr among them. Although both were from powerful and respected Houses, neither was the eldest child or court ambassador, and had reprieve from paying respects under the scrutiny of the High Table. Aeolil almost envied them that, but the general mood of the chamber seemed festive and abnormally relaxed. A performance by Master Madrharigal was a rare treat for many of those here regardless of where they sat.

"Aye! But where in shadow *is* your father, My Prince?" said Stuart in mock impatience. His thick accent reminded her acutely of Brohan's new apprentice. "At this rate, the rats are liable to eat our dinner a'fore we do."

"Hah!" spat Hiruld with feigned arrogance. "If His Majesty wishes the royal rats to dine first, then so they shall, and who are you to question it? You're lucky he lets you join us at all, wearing that silly dress!"

"A *dress*, is it?" Stuart's voice rose at least an octave. He leaned around Aeolil, pointing at her gown, "Nay, My Prince, *that's* a dress. This here's a kilt. Two different things, a kilt and a dress. Room enough for a man in a kilt, if you'll pardon me saying so, Lady Aeolil."

Aeolil blushed slightly at the jest, but just slightly, and spoke no reproach. She took no offense at the joke, and though it was improper not to at least feign shock or disgust, she felt no need for such pointless deception in present company. The blush would do just as well. At any rate, it seemed Stuart had been at his mead goblet early this day.

Hiruld seemed relieved at her good graces, beaming boyishly like a child playing in the yard with a wooden sword. "My apologies, sir. A kilt it is, then. I'll have to look into commissioning one for my royal personage."

The herald's staff tamped the flagstones thrice more, and the room fell silent with a hurried hush. "All rise for His Most August Majesty, Rightful Heir to the Imperial Throne of Dachadaie and King of Providayne, Guillaume II of the Royal House Jiraud, Regent of the Western Demesnes, Master of the North, the Lord Protector of Paerytm and Defender of the Holy Mother Church."

The nobility rose as one and proclaimed, "All hail King Guillaume! All hail House Jiraud!"

They repeated the cheer as the aged king entered the hall and ascended to his place at the head of the High Table, followed closely by His Holiness, the Archbishop Elgin Renarre, who stood behind the king and to his right. Aeolil could sense the charge of tension between the feral glare of the chamberlain and the laughing not-so-innocence of the high priest. Theirs was a battle for the ear and favor of the king that would end only in turmoil for the whole of Providayne. Though their ideologies were diametrically opposed, their personalities were disturbingly similar. She hoped, with a brief thought to her earlier misgivings, that she had made the right alliance for her, for Vae, and for the kingdom at large.

The king bade them silent and waved them to sit. The broad smile betwixt his wrinkled cheeks was an oddity after this past year of grim and mirthless expression. The distant dreaminess of his faded blue eyes to which the court had been accustomed was also vanished, replaced by a vigorous twinkle.

This is the Guillaume of old come back to visit us. Aeolil smiled to herself at the notion as she resumed her seat. Even the shining crown of gold and platinum seemed to sit straighter on his grey-coifed head. Hiruld had not exaggerated his father's improved mood.

Already the change had been noticed. "Long live the king!" came an enthusiastic shout.

"Yes, long live *me!*" joked the monarch, his smile turning to an infectious chuckle. "*This is a good day!*" he proclaimed with heartfelt certainty.

Aeolil noticed that the archbishop's feet shuffled behind her and she chanced a quick glance in his direction. His face, though still plastered with his superior smile, seemed detached, worried – even annoyed. It was something in his eyes, a furtiveness to his quick glances – glances in the direction of Agrylon.

Then she noted the wizard's face, also nearly unreadable, but with the slightest of smiles at the corners of his mouth. Renarre was squirming silently, in good grace, and Agrylon was enjoying his discomfiture in the same unobtrusive manner. Something was afoot, clearly. She would have to put the question to the plotting mage when next they met.

"Many of you may not remember the War of Thorns," said Guillaume, his facial expression fading from jolly to composed in a seamless transition. Sir Vanelorn stiffened noticeably. The scar that bisected his face from temple to chin served him as a constant reminder. Many others in this room bore similar scars. There was a general murmur of assent. That had been another bitter war. One of many.

"And some may not remember the Battle of Vlue Macc!" he continued, again receiving affirmative but indecipherable grunts in response. "But on that fateful day, on that battlefield that served to end that horrid war, on that very ground did I almost breathe my last!"

The gathered nobility rushed to express their confidence that he would not have fallen, but he cut them off impatiently. "I remember the day, and *it was so!*" The king looked at Vanelorn, who nodded his clenched jaw in agreement. "The Calahyr had sprung a trap on me and my host, and we were alone and disheartened, cut off by the river! My Guard fought bravely, but one by one they fell dead or wounded to the turf, and who do you think came out to risk their lives for the king?" His eyes were on fire now, boring holes of accusation into the silent rank and file of his subjects. "Each and all, I watched the ranks of the Great Houses hesitate to aid us in our plight! Each and all of those not already by my side."

The silence was thick now with shock and mounting dread. Had the king regained his stamina and his will as well as his youthful vengeance? Many faces were pale as his speech drew on, but there was a collective look of relief at his next statement. "I blame none for this. It was as it was, and battles are a confusing affair. For whatever reason, the peers of the Realm were delayed in relief of my force by fatigue, despair and mounting casualties of their own. So I ask you again, who was it that came to my aid?" There was a slight pause, as if beckoning comment, but none there gathered were so foolish. "A commoner!" he yelled, as if in exasperation. "A foot soldier! A *barbarian* from the hills!"

Guillaume's voice was gaining volume even as his speech gathered momentum. "I heard him scream for a rally to arms: *to the king!*, he yelled. I remember it as if it were yesterday, and I saw him – an infantryman, mind you, in leathers with but a buckler on his arm, a spear and a blade his only means of battle – I saw him grab a steed from under the startled behind of a Calahyr knight and charge across the river!"

Aeolil was alarmed at his passion, but inspired as well. *He was a king in his day*, she thought. His intensity was like her father had once described to her. Fearful and motivating, confident but not quite haughty.

"And so he came, braving the water and the foe to fight at my side. Vanelorn himself says he's never seen a finer warrior – and I think he's fought side by side with all of *you*. Yes?" His eyes roamed the hall, landing occasionally on those of a flinching aristocrat.

"But soon enough, even the mighty Vanelorn succumbed to their numbers, and it was but the barbarian and I. Ibhraign was his name, a Cythe warrior from some backwater village. But I didn't know that then. I only knew that he alone of all my armies stood next to me for those fateful clicks that dragged on like hours before help finally came. And though I live to tell the tale, this man lay before me dying, with grievous wounds in his flesh that had been meant for mine. I asked his name then, and knighted him before he died, so he would leave this world with greater honor than he had entered it. Ibhraign of the Cythe, who came to me when my knights could or would not. Dragonheart, I named him."

The king was looking down at his hands, spread out on the table, and Aeolil saw he was struggling to maintain himself. From anger or sadness, she wasn't sure. Not an eye wandered from his face as he stood there in a quiet all to himself. When he spoke again, his voice was calm and steady, like his gaze, and the anger was gone from him.

"I remind you all of this because, though Sir Ibhraign can never come before us and claim the laud that is due him, his son may. My bard has come as pleases us for the Winter Festival, but this year he brings with him an apprentice, a lad called Calvraign – *son* of Ibhraign Dragonheart. And as is my wish and privilege, I bestow upon him his father's honorary but sadly posthumous rank. Treat *Sir* Calvraign like a Cythe commoner, and you will be mocking the man who saved mine own life! And that would be like unto mocking *me*." The threat in his voice was more telling than a drawn sword.

Aeolil stared wide-eyed at the king. As, she noticed, did most of the assembled lords and ladies. All except Vanelorn and Grumwyr, who squared their jaws and nodded their approval. They both had as much reason to respect the son of Ibhraign as did the king. Vanelorn surely would have perished were it not for his timely aid, as well as the father of the Bear. She also noticed the arched eyebrows of Calamyr and the pale, nervous look of Garath – who had just finished threatening the life of *Sir* Calvraign not a quarter of an hour before. She did not know what lay between the master bard and the younger heir of House Malminnion, and for the latter at least, it was no trifling affair. But, she considered, it couldn't be worth so much as the trouble in which he'd just ensnared himself. She didn't much care for Garath, but she pitied his poor timing.

The king signaled the herald, and the doors opened. As the master bard and apprentice made their entrance, they were met with a unanimous roar that deafened only slightly less than surprised them.

"All hail Sir Calvraign, Son of Dragonheart!" they roared, and then again. All save Renarre and Agrylon, who instead only shared a look of mutual contempt. Then the wizard's eye flickered for but a moment to her own with a faint smile that made her shiver.

Yes, thought Aeolil, *something is most definitely afoot*.

Chapter Fourteen

Songs for a King

For one not accustomed to large surprises, Calvraign thought he handled this one very well. Brohan had said there might be some mention of his father when they were introduced, but from the dumbfounded bard's own wide and unblinking eyes, Calvraign surmised that this was not what he had expected. The entire hall of gathered nobility was on their collective feet, with their goblets held high as they shouted out the toast one final time. The chamber itself – with its ebonwood rafters and trim; tables set with bronze, silver and gold; wall length tapestries and glowing aulden candelabra – it all faded into the back of his mind.

"Welcome, Sir Calvraign!" roared an old man with a lustrous crown on his brow. "Welcome to King's Keep!"

The king! The reality of it hit Calvraign in the gut like a mule's hoof. He reacted by what must have been instinct, for in truth he was in a state somewhere between the realization of dreams and abject terror. In a quick motion, Calvraign knelt on his right knee and bent his head in a bow of respect. "You do me a great honor, Your Majesty. I hope to follow in my father's footsteps, though none could fill his boots, and prove myself worthy of your grace. I am yours to command."

Calvraign could feel the very weight of the air above his head, and the multiple stings of querious eyes upon him, assessing him, ascertaining his worth and his character through this first vital introduction into their midst. Brohan was silent beside him, his own graceful homage ignored. Everyone knew the master bard possessed eloquence and composure; it was his apprentice they were interested in.

The king smiled at him in what Calvraign approximated was genuine affection or approval. He relaxed inwardly, but held his outward poise. *No sense leaving the gate open after the flock is in the pen*, his mother would say.

"Well said, boy, well said indeed!" boomed the king merrily. "Now up off your knees, and don't so much as bend them again to any man but me!" Calvraign noticed the scrutiny of the peerage shifted from him to their liege in astonishment, though he wasn't sure why. Perhaps that was unusual. The king went on, "Now, the last Brohan spoke of you, he said a fluent harp you played. Don't make a liar of the King's Bard, now!"

"Please!" agreed Brohan, taking the opportunity to step to the fore. Calvraign could see the temperament of the audience wasn't to Master Madrharigal's liking, and he quickly set about brightening their mood with some light jokes as they prepared the stage.

Brohan had made all the arrangements earlier with the steward and castellan, and the servants brought all the needed instruments and chairs within the semi-circle of tables with capable haste. They had conferred and decided upon the program over the course of their travels, choosing first instrumental pieces that would showcase Calvraign's young, dexterous fingers and his natural feel for a melody. Brohan also considered this more appropriate for background music. Those who could appreciate such artistry would do it while they ate, and those too banal for the subtler things in life would not be tired by it. Then, after the repast was served, they would begin with the story and song.

They had decided against telling *Ibhraign and the King*, for it would seem self-aggrandizing. *The Lament of Celian*, though a favorite of them both, was far too controversial in such company, especially for a debut performance. And they would under no circumstance, save royal decree, render *The Song of Andulin*. In Brohan's opinion, it was much overdone already, and he suspected he would be forced into its utterance a score and a half times by festival's end. And so they had decided on ballads that were not special in and of themselves but would yet display the talents of the gifted apprentice – *The Tors of Traleagh*, *The Farmer and the Fae*, and *Good Sir Gullimer's Pies*. The sheer inanity of this last one Brohan insisted the king would enjoy, and the length of the three together was enough without being too much.

In truth, Calvraign found the performance relaxing. He felt at home with his fingers on the bone frets of his gwythir and lyre, or dancing along the strings of his field harp. He buried himself in his melodies, Brohan effortlessly strumming chords in his support, adjusting to Calvraign's instinctive style of play. Somehow, he did not worry that he played for the king, or notice that the clamor of the gathering was quelled to a subdued hush. Somehow, he didn't see the eyes of the ladies take full notice of his young face, his clear blue eyes, and his deft, articulate fingers on his instruments; or the added attention that brought from their lords.

He did realize, however, when he set down his gwythir after completing Jeunjar's masterwork, *Spring Suite*, that before the hum of its sixteen strings had faded he was enveloped in applause. The applause of the nobles, of the king, of Brohan, and of Lady Aeolil. He blushed despite himself at her frank scrutiny and looked abruptly away. He had never known a woman so beautiful, and feared he had already made himself a complete fool in her eyes earlier in the day. Now he felt he had confirmed it, blushing like a farm boy. He nodded his head in deference to their courtesy, hiding his clenching jaw, and made an effort to smile again when he raised his head.

"Brilliantly done, boy! Brilliant, indeed!" the king praised. "Brohan has not done you justice."

"You are very generous, Majesty," replied Calvraign. He found it ironic that it was easier to focus on the monarch rather than the young lady of House Vae. But one glance from her and his heart had jumped up his throat to beat madly between his ears. *Idiot*, he chastised himself.

"You are too modest!" insisted Guillaume with a gentle admonishment. "You play as well as any I've seen."

"Begging Your Majesty's pardon," said an affable Brohan. "I may take offense if my pupil further pleases the royal ear. Perhaps we should withdraw while my reputation is still intact!"

The master bard's remarks elicited the intended chuckles and smiles. The king merely waved his hands at them. "Play on, play on! I'll not worry you with any more praise for your apprentice. What have you in store for us today?"

"Some light and capricious fare, Your Majesty, as befits your rather remarkable mood. We shall have enough morally weighted discourse during the festival."

Calvraign took a deep breath and tried to return to whatever place he had been before that had provided him such penetrating calm and confidence. Brohan began the lilting tune of *The Tors* and Calvraign waited for his cue. They would sing the first chorus in rounds and then join in the second verse in two-part harmony. He concentrated on keeping pitch as he joined in the floating, happy melody. His talent was not in song. His voice was clear enough, and tone rich enough, but it was not his purview. Still, he sank into the task with grateful ease, once again removed from his surroundings by the rapture of the muses.

Soon enough they were in the last verse of *Good Sir Gullimer*, and Brohan and Calvraign sang away with unbridled frolic at the traditional tempo that so rankled most minstrels. But they delivered the well-rehearsed piece with crafty and fluid adroitness. Even Vanelorn, ever the stern implacable warrior, was laughing heartily by its end.

And so good Sir Gullimer, Gullimer Sir,
was stuffed in dough and baked today.
Oh, good Sir, good, good, Gullimer Sir,
with gooseberries and a goose, they say.
In good Sir Gullimer's Pie, they say,
good, good Sir Gullimer's Pie!
Good sir, good, good, good, Sir Gullimer,
good Gullimer Sir, good Gullimer, Gullimer,
good Sir Gullimer's Pie!

On past the day and into the evening the festivities lingered, and master bard and apprentice alike were afforded the luxury of dining with the host of the king. Dancing there was, even for the venerable king, and stories and tales told by all. It harkened back to the times between the wars when blood was shed seldom, and angry words were rare. The torches burned late into the night, and there was laughter in King's Keep. Laughter, song and mead in equally generous portions. Laughter enough to stave away the endless queries that normally welcomed those newly in favor to the throne. Laughter enough even for the likes of dour Agrylon, who indeed seemed to enjoy the occasion with rare levity.

But, even as he heard it, Calvraign was reminded of Brohan's oft-delivered warning against complacency for the traveling bard, even in the face of success: *one night's laughter is but a memory on the morrow.*

And the morrow was halfway here already.

Chapter Fifteen

The Nyrul Cayl

BLOODHAWK stirred. First one eye, then the other, opened upon the painful world. It was dark, and the air cold and musty. The scents of rotting leaves and carrion and his own infected wound filled nostrils he was too tired to cover. He tried to stretch for a moment before he remembered where he was, and succeeded only in bruising his elbow.

What's another bruise, he thought, too tired to be bitter.

One bruise upon another upon another: they all faded into one small, dim flash of lightning within a greater storm of pain. Adjusting to the light, his eyes helped his feverish mind remember where he had stuck himself.

Once, this bed of leaves, fir needles, feathers and soft, white down had made the hollow in the bole of the tree trunk a fit home for a family of tree-napes. He'd always liked tree-napes. He and Khyri had adopted a small colony of them in Oam, where such protection was needed from the relentless furriers who trolled the forests for their prized coats. He didn't know the derivation of the common usage *nape*, but he thought the Ebuouki name was more suited to them, anyway: *eti nu'm*, cat-monkeys. Now, the napes had moved on and it was the *wilhorwhyr* settled here in their place.

The old oak, hanging bent and tired over the riverbank, reminded him of the rhyme his mother used to sing:

Old Man Oak, not quite dead,
lingering by the river.
Low hang his brittle branches,
low to scrape the ground

Beaten down by the weight of centuries,
beaten down, he waits for time.

Hundreds of summers' growth, he knows,
rich with leaves and flowing sap.
Hundreds of autumns' chill, he knows,
and hundreds of tiny deaths

Hundreds of deepest winter snows,
through which the old oak slept.
And hundreds of shining springs, he knows,
and breathes another years' breath

Old Man Oak, not quite dead,
lingering by the river.

Bloodhawk blinked away returning sleep. *Not quite dead, just like the man who's sought refuge within the hollow of your trunk. Lingering... .*

His limbs were frozen in place, stiff and unresponsive. He coughed, and the pain of the spasms was an unwelcome ally to his resolve, feeding his mind with unwanted alertness, forcing him further from tempting sleep.

Just a little sleep.

"No," he said to himself. The sound of his voice startled him. He chuckled. Not mirthfully, but a dry, self-incriminating sound of disgust. "Talking to myself or Old Man Oak?"

Bloodhawk forced his stiff body out of his shelter and into the snow and leaves of the forest floor. He wanted to stay there, prone, for the scavengers to feed upon. He wanted no more of anything. His will, as always, acted in contempt of, and despite, his despair. He struggled to his feet. He stumbled, balancing himself on the tree, feeling a faint glow of warmth at his fingertips.

No, he thought sadly, moved and ashamed, *no more. You've given me more than I deserve already, Old Man. Keep some for yourself. The winter is young.*

The wind rustled in the empty branches, and the warmth in his fingers grew almost hot to the touch as he felt fresh life flow into his bones. He looked up at the gnarly ancient and reproached himself. Who was he, a surly man-child, to lecture this Old One? This tree that had outlived him by tens of scores of years and persevered through more wars and plots and swinging axes than he was ever likely to see? Foolish, indeed. He carried on forward, limping from the stiffness in his limbs, and he could almost hear the tree singing the song in his ears with mocking humor.

Old Man Oak, not quite dead.

After a day or two of travel south into the Caerwood, Bloodhawk had come upon less tamed corridors of leaf and limb. The trails of the foresters were gone, surrendering to the close-crowded vegetation around him. The marks of hunters and trappers progressed a league or two further in, but they soon melted away as well.

Many of the trees had shed their leaves for the winter, naked arms reaching into the sky in mute supplication. Their leafy ornaments now lay cracked and frozen beneath the snow and ice, once a canopy for birds and forest animals, now only a decorative ceiling for worms and mites and movers of soil. The straight-backed discipline of the tall northern firs was challenged by the sag of branches under the weight of winter's frozen tears. Some of the trees succumbed to their burden, their tired, bent boughs dipping in a lowly ground-scraping bow. The shallow tracks of a fox and the deep indentation of a rabbit's quick leap for life were the only blemish on the smooth tableau of shining white beneath the trees.

Bloodhawk leaned against a lightning-shattered husk of silver-barked sannegrin, shivering more from fever than cold. He had exhausted his supply of poultice, and though capable, he was not the equal of Two-Moons in the art of healing. His condition was worsening, and only careful rest and a moderate pace kept it manageable. Had his father's aulden blood not beat in his heart, he would already have surrendered his husk to the worms. Even so, the barrowshade that smeared the hrummish steel was stubbornly about its work. Normally the hrumm used more straightforward poisons. Barrowshade was nearly as dangerous to the handler as it was to the intended victim. Apparently, the death of a few hrumm was a cost Dieavaul was not reticent to risk or pay.

Bloodhawk ended his brief respite and picked his way silently forward. He walked on the balls of his feet, pressing in with the tips of his split-toed boots. It was an old *wilhorwhyr* trick, one of the first he'd learned as a young Initiate, and came as naturally as a leisurely walk. In his wake he left a trail of deer-like imprints in the snow. There was many an experienced tracker in the Realms who, recognizing the odd markings were not what they seemed, attributed them to the wanderings of Buerhoune the unicorn. Quaint tavern talk, that, he thought. As if Buerhoune, or any other of his majestic kind, would leave *any* tracks at all.

The aulden should be near, judging from the increasing age and snarl of the woods. His greatest worry now was that they would not deign to show themselves at all. He had gone through their midst many a time without so much as a whisper to acknowledge his passing. He had known they were there, like watchful eyes in the dark, but they had neglected to appear for his benefit. He would have to hope for better luck this time – possibly insist on it.

~

Bloodhawk opened his eyes slowly from his mid-day nap. The small clearing was still. A hurn chirped over his head as it preened the feathers of one rosy-gold wing. There was no sign of anyone near, but the hair on the back of his neck was alive and bristling. He sensed more than saw them, a presence shifting in the background of the forest. He sat up, his back against an aged maple, and waited.

In the distance, to his right, three faint globes of pearly luminescence shimmered into existence. He averted his eyes, afraid that in his weakened state the charm would draw him away. A common trick of the fae – sometimes meant simply to divert unwanted guests, sometimes serving a more sinister purpose as they led the way to a bog or mire. The balls of light danced expectantly, hypnotically, at the edge of his vision, but Bloodhawk waited patiently where he was.

The voices were next, and for all his experience, he almost fled. The whispers were in the ancient aulden tongue, speaking beautiful words more fluid than running water but with such wicked intonation that his skin prickled on his arms. The bodiless voices haunted first one ear, then the other, and then both, spoken as if by the whirling wind that sprang so suddenly around him. He relaxed the tension that had wound up the fiber of his muscles with a deep breath. He knew this enchantment as well, for all that it remained unnerving, and he allowed it to rage about him in quiet relentless tones as he sat unmoving against the maple.

He'd not dealt with the tribes this far east, and it was clear that they were a cautious bunch. He was welcomed, though often as not with tepid hospitality, by the western tribes, and so was no stranger to the aulden in general. He was especially familiar with the Elyrmirea, to whom he was blooded, but each of the Seven Tribes was distinct.

He waited.

When it was clear he would not be led away by deception, the unseen watchers changed their tack. An arrow plunged into the powdery snow beside him, then another, and then one more sank into the leather of the pack by his side. Bloodhawk did not so much as flinch. He knew this would be coming, and even at their worst the aulden rarely murdered the unarmed and wounded. Then again, he wasn't interested in testing their forbearance.

"*Ieylulki*," he said in fluent auldenish. "*Y oeleiad ley -*"

"Stop! I won't suffer our tongue butchered by your lips." The frosty female voice bit off his words, leaving the rest unspoken in his mouth. "Your kind is not welcome here."

Bloodhawk eyed the arrows about his person. That much, he had deduced already. "Peace, then," he began again, in the trade tongue. "I seek parlay."

An aulden woman emerged from the dark recess between trees at the other side of the clearing, next to a small spring. She was tall, cloaked in brown and white over the hint of a mail shirt, a recurve bow in her hands with arrow half-drawn. Her face was shrouded by a large shadowed hood, one wisp of blue-black hair waving in the breeze before her face. Of that face, he could make out little save the gentle curve of her nose above a delicate chin and the thin line of her lips. She was beautiful, by mortal standards, as were all of the aulden. His own heritage immunized him from the disarming glamour that ensnared many human men with its false promises. From somewhere within her dark cowl he felt her watching him.

Rising slowly, for he had no desire to test his weary reflexes against their arrows, Bloodhawk held out his hands with fingers splayed empty before him. He could still detect her companions in the trees, and knew that their bows were also drawn and nocked.

"I am Bloodhawk Moonstone," he said. "I have news of import for the Ceearmyltu."

"Any news of yours does not concern us, half-man." Her tone was distilled contempt. "Begone."

Bloodhawk's brow lifted in surprise. He was rarely referred to as *half-man*. To the humans he was half-aulden, or a *faelle*, or sometimes even a changeling. The few aulden counted among his acquaintance avoided reference to his mixed lineage unless they wished to do him injury. Then they would call him just that – half-*man*. To the aulden, this referenced the disgraceful, ignorant, barbaric side of his lineage. Emphasizing that part of him, in their minds, discounted their shared blood as if it were mere technicality.

If she had intended that simple insult to dissuade him, she would be disappointed. He had thicker skin than that. "Malakuur has tapped an *iiyir* well. I know more, if you think my words now worthy of your ear."

There was a stillness to her then, a change in attitude more sensed than seen. Perhaps her lips tightened, or her cheek twitched, or maybe nothing. She was silent for only a short time, during which Bloodhawk got the distinct impression that she was relieved in some odd way by his news. An explanation found where none was sought or expected, perhaps? An answer to a question unasked? Or she could simply have been quiet. It mattered little when she spoke what her reason had been.

"It's not for me to judge your worth, half-man, or that of your words. I'll bring you before the *nyrul cayl*. They'll decide both." Her tone had lost none of its ire. She turned back into the wood, a shadow returning to the dark.

Bloodhawk stood with determined silence. His pain had diminished little with his short rest, and he still felt the lightheaded touch of infection in the cloudiness of his thoughts. But it wouldn't do to show any weakness now. He followed after her and out of the forest three other aulden warriors appeared, bracketing him in their midst. The women were indistinguishable from each other, gliding through the forest with bows at the ready, an unspoken warning at the tips of their gleaming arrows.

They offered no comment on their journey, nor did Bloodhawk. He felt clumsy in their presence. The woodland skills in which he so prided himself, that he had practiced since he could walk and still practiced to this day, were natural to the fair folk. Where he must decide on which leaf or twig to tread, however quickly and unconsciously, they knew immediately and instinctively how to move. Normally his footfalls were like the softest of woodland voices. Now, he felt like a shrill cry in a council of whispers.

They traveled without rest as the suns made their own journey across the sky, and then continued as the great silver orb of Illuné began her own nightly ascent. Only when the smaller, darker orb of the Dead Moon emerged in the stillness between night and morning did they make camp.

Bloodhawk knew he had pushed himself too hard. At his own pace, he had been able to stay within his limits and provide his body with adequate rest. At the grueling pace the aulden had set today, he was afforded no such luxury. He was resolute about hiding his injury and his fatigue, and curled into his cloak. He was now losing his struggle against the infection, and his skin was clammy with feverish sweat. On the far side of the clearing, the aulden also made ready for sleep. When he drifted from consciousness, it felt more like a dead faint than slumber.

A hand pressed against Bloodhawk's mouth, and he awoke with a start. His eyes flickered open, and he immediately relaxed. An aulden woman's face, smooth and pale, bent down over his own, long silky strands of hair the color of wheat and berries touching his skin. Her almond eyes of pale silver begged his silence. She removed her hand from his mouth and began lifting up his shirt and jerkin, her eyes darting furtively to her sleeping companions.

She pulled his wounded arm from its sleeve and removed his makeshift bandage. She took one look at the hastily stitched gash down his arm, raised and swollen and flaming red, then back into Bloodhawk's eyes as if to scold him. She removed the old dressing and cleaned the wound with a damp cloth. Bloodhawk clenched his jaws and swallowed a scream. The inflamed skin was white and frothy now from her ministration. Still without a word, she re-wrapped the wound with leaf-lined cloth and fastened it with a silver brooch from her cloak. Bloodhawk's trembling arm reached out to touch hers in thanks.

"*leylulki*," she whispered into his ear. "You must eat this. For strength."

She produced a fruit that was the size of an apple but with the irregular whiskered skin of an oversized, purple strawberry. She cut small mouthfuls of the fruit with a slender dagger and fed them to him one by one. At every bite, Bloodhawk felt the crisp, sweet fruit dissolve into relief in his mouth. It was jujoehbe fruit. Prized for its healing qualities, this was a rare and precious gift. Already he felt its effect, along with a welcome, peaceful, drowsiness.

"Your name?" he whispered.

"Jylkir," she said. "Now sleep."

Then she was gone, and Bloodhawk slept.

❦

Just before daybreak, as the birds of the wood began their sweet song to woo the dawn, a soft-soled boot nudged Bloodhawk in the ribs. To his surprise, there was little pain.

"Get up, half-man." The voice of the aulden captain was familiar and cold. "You've slowed us down enough."

Bloodhawk got to his feet and made a wordless response by readying his pack as she stalked away. The fever had broken, and he felt rested and whole, as he hadn't since parting company with Two-Moons. He tried to determine which of his escort was Jylkir, but found it impossible to tell with their hoods pulled forward to hide their faces. Without even the pretext of a morning meal, they were off again.

The pace quickened, whether because the aulden were in a hurry or because they realized he had strength enough to keep up, he did not know. Their long strides put league upon league behind them. The day grew long and their shadows grew longer, the half-tame outskirts of human settlement were left further behind for the thicker growth of the ancient wood. Few but the aulden tread here in peace.

Though the vegetation was different from the southern coastlands of the Elyrmirea, the signs of Faerie grew more and more abundant. Winter, though not abated, was mollified. Trees flowered and bloomed out of season, and foliage danced from limb to limb to form a sheltering canopy of emerald overhead. The aulden ways did not work against nature, but with it, denying no season its time, softening the harsh edges into smoother, gentler lines. Death, like winter, was not denied, but even when Her cold hand came to enforce Ghaest's will, an aulden grove remained a place of life above all else.

Just after suns-set, when finally the intertwined branches of towering bloodroots laced before them like webs of a giant wood-spinning spider, Bloodhawk knew they had reached the gateway to the Sacred Grove of the Ceearmyltu. He noted the deeper bronze coloring of the thorny bark and the golden petal starbursts that hung from the leaves, marking them apart from the trees of their like in Edgewood and even Oam. As he considered it, he remembered Symmlrey describing the bloodroot of her own tribe, the Vanneahym, and they too were different. He wondered absently if there were seven types of bloodroot for the seven tribes of aulden.

"Wait here, half-man," said the aulden captain, breaking her day-long silence. "I will send for you when the time for council is nigh."

As the aulden passed through the wall of tangled bloodroot, the figure that had been the rear guard caught her captain's sleeve. There was a quick whispered exchange, and then she turned back toward Bloodhawk as the others continued on. She sat with her back against a birch, in a hollow almost clear of snow, and motioned Bloodhawk to join her.

"It may be awhile, and though I doubt that you need a guard, I thought perhaps you might desire some company."

Bloodhawk smiled when she pulled back her hood. As he'd suspected, it was Jylkir, who had shown him such kindness the night before.

"Thank you," he said. "I am in your debt."

"No," she returned with a dismissive tone. "I simply don't share the opinion of Du'uwneyyl and the others."

"About half-men in general, or me in particular?" prompted Bloodhawk.

"Both," she replied, but elaborated no further.

Bloodhawk brushed the snow from a shelf of rock that protruded from the turf between two towering trees and sat. The diffuse orange-red light of the suns was now retreating somewhere beneath the invisible horizon, and the glimmer of the brighter stars could be seen infiltrating the purple twilight. Always in the vanguard like its namesake Irdik came the North Star, bright and true; then the Three Sisters, a triangle of diamonds only slightly less bright, low to the tops of the swaying trees. Then, as the darkness coalesced around them, the other stars and constellations peeked out from the night.

Some, like the Dragon Meet, or the Great Tree, were known by peoples all across the continent of Rahn. But others, through the eyes of disparate peoples and experience, were seen differently or not at all. The Archer, to his people, was Nighthawk – first of the *wilhorwhyr*. In the East the same bowman was known as Buoain, for a Macc hero. The Lovers and the Chariot, both favorite constellations east of the Inner Sea, were not known to the West, nor was the bright sword Juut, with Irdik in its pommel, known to the East. But the stars, whatever their name, were good and faithful guides, and Bloodhawk was steeped in the science of their dances across the sky.

It was Jylkir who broke the silence. "I haven't the skill, but I'm told the stars are a script for those versed in their language, and that they chronicle time, but backwards, so that our future is written clearly in their passages."

Bloodhawk pulled his thick cloak tight. This night, so clear and beautiful, was thus unforgiving in its cold recompense. "I put little stock in such talk. I don't believe the future is written anywhere but in the present, and each day unfolds as a fresh page, blank until we write upon it with our actions. But, I am no philosopher or mage. I suppose it's possible that the gods know what will be before it is, and they have hidden the truth for those clever enough to find it.

"But *I* am not so clever as all that," he confessed, his lip turning up slightly into what passed for a smile on his stern face, "so I'll use them to steer by, and I'll gaze on their silent peace and thank Father Oa for their comfort. That is enough for me."

Jylkir nodded, an expression of understanding, if not necessarily agreement, on her face. "I hope what you say is true. Those who claim to know such things read only doom in the stars."

Bloodhawk stared in silence, watching the moonlight on the snow at his feet. With all he had seen the past twelve-moon, he knew doom was an imminent possibility. Malakuur was strong; the East was divided and weak. The wasting sickness reached its rotting fingers into fragile human flesh, and the Pale Man once again walked openly in the Realms. Dire tidings, these – perhaps reflected in the stars if not predicted by them.

"What is the state of the Ceearmyltu?" he asked without looking up. "Are you ready for war, if need be?"

"We are stronger than in recent years," she said, a faint tremor of doubt in her words. "Yet there are few with the heart to fight for causes or people not our own. Word reaches us that the Qeyniir fight alongside humans in the north, and the Milfuiltea in Symbus as well, against the Old Foe. But there is no such common enemy here. Some might even suffer the presence of the Old Foe rather than the humans on our borders."

Bloodhawk looked up, eyes narrow. "That is foolishness," he said in acid tone.

"I would agree. But my belief is not a popular one. We have endured much at the hands of the human nations."

"Malakuur would make a harsher neighbor still," breathed Bloodhawk. He found anger welling up but choked it down like bitter bile. "Such would be the price for inaction."

Jylkir stood and paused, looking into the branches of the trees that surrounded them for curious eyes and ears, then crossed the distance to Bloodhawk in a few quick strides. She brought her lips close to his ear. "Inaction is not the worst of councils I have heard. Be on your guard."

She moved back to her original place of rest, staring away into the forest beyond the bloodroot. Bloodhawk felt his heart still clutching at the back of his constricted throat at her words. The unimaginable possibility that any of the Seven Tribes would ally with the evil beyond the mountains was something even cynical Raefnir would not have considered before her untimely death. Their intolerance of humans he could in part understand, but to ignore their most ancient enmities and align themselves with the forces of the Priest Kings was assuming a hatred he had never guessed at. Perhaps in the centuries since winning their freedom, the aulden had forgotten the fifteen hundred years they suffered under the yoke of Anduoun? Or the despair that fell on Rahn like a dark rain when the ancestors of the Priest Kings last tried their hand at usurpation?

Bloodhawk sank into deeper contemplation as the stars continued to trace their inexorable patterns above him. *Ingryst help me*, he thought, trying to calm the swirling whirlpool of fears in his gut. Fear of his own death, a minor thing; fear of war and pestilence, something greater; fear of the ultimate wasteland Malakuur would make of beautiful creation, like a raging torrent. And another fear, small but insistent, that it was all written in the sky above his head, and that there was nothing in the whole of the world he could do to change what would be.

It was handspans later that Du'uwneyyl's scalding tone melted through the chill silence. "It is your time to speak, half-man, if you still wish. But be quick about it."

Bloodhawk looked up to see the aulden captain, her cloak discarded completely, standing in a mail shirt and helm of shining silver-green, each scale like a shifting wave on a rippling ocean. Her arms were crossed over her chest, the gloved fingers of her left hand dangling close to the hilt of her slim long sword. The errant strand of hair that had once fluttered from underneath her cowl now spilled from her helmet across her high cheekbones like a rivulet of jet-black water on alabaster banks. Her eyes were unusually dark for an aulden, shining black orbs with flecks of deep purple and lavender near the pupil.

He rose and shouldered his pack. Du'uwneyyl led him through the imposing bloodroot barrier and past the night-shrouded dwellings of her people. Bloodhawk could see in the posture of her walk that she was a deadly warrior. Balanced and poised, she looked to him like a predatory bird or a great cat of the plains, all sharp eye and honed muscle and deadly instinct, so fluid in her lethal movements that it was mesmerizing, even as she circled for the kill.

His attention was then drawn to a large, blazing fire about which hundreds of Ceearmyltu were gathered. Most present were female, as they attended to most matters of government and war, but the occasional male sat among them, just as fae and beautiful. Sitting on a wooden throne, under a pavilion of branches adorned with a rainbow of wreaths, leaves and flowers, was the Ceearmyltu *lyaeyni*. A queen by human reckoning, she held ultimate authority over her tribe. Three chairs flanked her on the right and left, and in somewhat less beautiful adornments, sat the other six members of the *nyrul cayl*, her closest councilors. They were all fair-haired and light-eyed, but their lips were turned downward into frowns that had almost fully matured into scowls. The flickering firelight played across their angular features, and for a moment Bloodhawk thought he was looking on an assortment of wicked lifeless statues, but the light shining back from their eyes belied their origins of flesh – if not quite dispelling their baneful aura.

Du'uwneyyl took him to the center of the ringed aulden, within a few feet of the seated rulers of the tribe, and pitched her voice for all those assembled to hear. "This is the half-man *wilhorwhyr* I came across in the thinwood. He calls himself Bloodhawk Moonstone."

With no further words of introduction, she stepped to the side, still watching him with stolid resolution. Bloodhawk stood patiently. He knew better than to speak before the *lyaeyni* addressed him. He was once again thankful for his experience with the Elyrmirea.

When it was clear he would not be baited, the *lyaeyni* spoke, her voice soft but strong like steel wrapped in silk. "Speak, Bloodhawk Moonstone."

And so he did.

He related the tale of the *iiyir* well and the vast horde that awaited release by the Priest Kings. He made certain to describe the andu'ai that lurked in the ranks of the army, and the purposes that the Priest Kings ultimately served. If there were any who sympathized with the destruction of the Eastern Realms, he hoped to remind them that the price, once paid, would be unbearable. When he had finished, there was disquiet in the attending crowd and a lingering silence on the lips of the *nyrul cayl*.

"Go to your rest, half-man," said the *lyaeyni*, "and we shall ponder what you have said. Do not attempt departing without our leave. High Blade Du'uwneyyl will show you your way."

Bloodhawk made a perfunctory bow and left the flame-lit circle in the company of Jylkir and Du'uwneyyl. The dour captain left them at the door of his accommodations, heading back toward the council, and Jylkir led him into the upper reaches of the hollow *ilyela* tree. At sixty feet in height and twenty in width, it was roughly the same dimensions as a small round tower. Not a large specimen by the standards of aulden treesingers, but Bloodhawk recognized it as sufficient for its purpose.

Jylkir's eyes did not meet his as she shut the door of the tower room, leaving him alone in its stark, windowless confines. She sang a sad note, and there was a sucking sound as the door melded seamlessly into the wood surrounding it. "I'm sorry," she whispered, and then the sound of her footsteps receded down the long stair.

Bloodhawk stood for a moment and stared into the darkness, then lay down for a nap. He had eaten nothing of real substance save the jujoehbe fruit of the night before, and he needed rest. He could hope they would be sensible and that sane voices would prevail. If not, he would need most of his strength and all of his wits to escape.

Especially if he had to fight past the likes of Du'uwneyyl.

⁓

Jylkir Leafingblade stood in the shadows outside the Great Tree where the *nyrul cayl* had retired to consider the half-blood's testimony. The guards hadn't yet noticed her huddling against the yielding bark of the ancient *ilyela*, listening with growing apprehension to the arguments within. The great fire was now only a collection of smoking embers, the common folk having left the opening caucus after their *lyaeyni* and her six *caylaeni* had retreated within for their private consultations. The Ceearmyltu slept as their fate was decided by the angry voices inside.

Lyaeyni Meimniyl, as always, led the majority, which was undecided but not disposed to kindness on the cause of humankind. She wanted nothing to do with the human world, and favored keeping to their quiet isolation. If the humans weakened themselves in the process of their foolish war, she argued, all the better for the Seven Tribes. This point of view was very popular with the three *caylaeni* of Meimniyl's own older generation.

Ililysiun, who despite her youth was considered a wise and prudent councilor, argued alone for lending aid to the human realms. Though her reasons were sound, her soft-spoken manner began to falter against the glare of hatred from those who would crush the humans in their time of weakness. Soon she was merely struggling on the defensive, attempting to stave off their persuasive and impassioned oratory and preserve at the very least a neutral aspect.

But Ryaleyr and Hlemyrae, the proponents for war and possibly even a brief alliance with Malakuur, were carefully playing upon the existing hatred and resentment of the older *caylaeni* and fanning the flames of their latent rage into open aggression. Jylkir could hear them turn one by one as the tempting fruits of victory were laid out on the table.

"... there's Dwynleigsh. How long have we suffered its occupation?" Jylkir recognized the voice as Feylobhar's, elder even than Meimniyl. "Perhaps we *should* march again."

"Yes!" The venom in that voice definitely marked it as Ryaleyr's. "Every year the thinwood grows thinner under the human axe, and we hide deeper and deeper to avoid their notice. These Priest Kings are no better and no worse than the rest of their ilk. We can deal with them after this war."

"Do you hear yourself, Ryaleyr?" pleaded the desperate voice of Ililysiun. "The Aelfeniir fight off the Malakuuri from their borders even now. Do we ally against our own to mete out your vengeance? Do we fight side by side with the Old Foe? And what of the *iiyir* well?"

"Do be still, Ililysiun!" snapped Hlemyrae's high, harsh, voice. "You are making much of nothing. Of course we will not fight our own. We will choose our battles, and they will be against the humans and the humans only. The *iiyir* well explains this abhorrent, unnatural winter, but the humans don't begin to understand its power and its uses. It will devour them before they are any threat to us.

"As for the andu'ai, *pfagh!*" Her tone had disintegrated into complete disgust. "That half-man lies to gain our alliance. Who here thinks the Old Foe would ever do the bidding of *humans*, by the First Tree."

That last statement seemed to garner Hlemyrae and Ryaleyr even more support. Eleulii even broke her silence to agree. Jylkir had to admit that it sounded very far-fetched that those of such powerful and arcane heritage would do the biddings of mortal humans. But Bloodhawk had not asked for aid, for himself or any other, he had only warned them of their peril. And she had seen in his eyes honesty, and gravity, and purpose. No, he did not lie. But the *nyrul cayl* did not share her opinion.

"Silence," hushed the *lyaeyni*. "I have heard all your council I can hear, and the final decision is mine." She paused, and Jylkir held her breath. "First, I thank Ililysiun for her kind advice. But, though she intends well, this is not the time to show kindness. We have skulked about in the shadows while humans glory in the suns-light for too many long years. Now is the time to take back our birthright, and though I will not be one to ally with one enemy to defeat another, neither will we hinder the course of their plans. That is my judgment. How finds the *nyrul cayl*?"

Jylkir did not wait to hear their verdict. It was mere formality. The *lyaeyni* rarely judged against the *nyrul cayl's* popular support, and they in return rarely challenged her ruling. It would be near unanimous, this time, with perhaps an abstention from neutral Niealihu and Ililysiun's objection. She ran at frantic pace toward the tower tree where the half-blood was imprisoned. They would do one of two things with him now, and she considered neither fair nor honorable. Death or imprisonment were their only options, for he would surely warn the human realms if he were allowed safe passage from the Caerwood.

Jylkir ascended the steep slope in a succession of short leaps, putting every fraction of her energy into the final sprint to the tree's solitary door. It could take them another span or more to decide his fate, but she intended to take no chances. She reached the door and sang the opening chime. A thin black line materialized from the smooth bark, and the door rocked open on its hinges with a sighing hiss of air. As she started up the tight spiral of the staircase, she heard the sound of soft footfalls behind her and turned just in time to see a gauntlet shoot out like silver-green lightning and grab her collar.

Jylkir tried to twist out of the grip and slip up the stairs, but with a powerful tug she was off balance and out of control. She fell against the edge of the stair and scarcely held in her cry of pain. Her back throbbed, and her head swam as she looked up into the dark eyes of her captor and cursed.

"Leave me be," she hissed with unbridled vehemence. "Let me up!"

But the grip was unrelenting.

"You're lucky it was I who spotted you eavesdropping and not Caethys or Duybhir." Du'uwneyyl shot back, dragging Jylkir to her feet but retaining her merciless hold. "Are you mad? You didn't really intend to *release* him, did you?"

"What if I did?"

"Treason," spat the High Blade. "Treason and stupidity. I'll not let you kill yourself over some childish infatuation."

Jylkir's jaw dropped. "Is *that* what you think?" She struggled anew, but still was helpless in the stronger woman's grip. "Do you take me for a suckling infant? Or some dreamy-eyed human girl?"

"What, then?"

Jylkir enunciated her words slowly and carefully for emphasis. "He has done us no wrong!" She was close to tears in her desperation. "If you truly love me, you must let me free him before it's too late. You must!"

"No," Du'uwneyyl forcibly removed her from the interior of the tower tree and released her with a gentle shove away from the door. "I would kill him before I let you ruin yourself on his account."

Jylkir channeled her rage and frustration into words. Loud, hateful, words that she no longer cared who overheard. "Die a thousand bloody deaths, Du'uwneyyl. I curse the day Mother bore you!"

Jylkir fled without a glance back in her hated sister's direction. She didn't see the cold, passionless stare that followed her, or the clenched jaw or narrowed slits of her black eyes. Nor did she see the momentary tightness that clenched at her sibling's throat at her last furious execration.

Without remark, Du'uwneyyl stepped within the windowless tower tree and sealed the door on the feeble rays of dawn.

Chapter Sixteen

Oszmagoth

OSRITH had spent so much time worrying over what they might discover in the ruins of the Sunken City that he nearly forgot what little regard he held for boats. The river craft supplied by Vaujn's people was long and slim, with a shallow keel and prominent steel-shod prow. It was styled in the shape of a *duaurnhuun* head, which a surface dweller might easily mistake for that of a wolfhound, its level snout pointing the way before them. There were several dents on the metal plating of both the prow and the gunwales, not unusual for a boat that plied the meandering rocky channels of these underground rivers. But it was not this boat that worried him; the kin were talented and reliable shipwrights.

No, it was not *this* boat; it was any boat, the principle of boats in general, which disturbed him. Rivers were for fishing and fording, maybe washing, when the need arose, but why anyone wanted to sit in a hollowed-out log to shoot down these twisting waterways was beyond him.

But for the kin, it was more than a simple matter of *wants*. They relied extensively on both the natural rivers and their own kin-made canals for trade, transport and communication. Before his own journeys in the Deeps, he had assumed they were a landlocked people, but this was another example of common myth not stacking up well against actual fact. The kin were, for all intents, masters of the underground lakes and rivers of their realms. He had even heard rumor of an air-filled hollow ball some kin inventor had used to plumb the depths of the Great Deeping Sea. Duragun had seemed to believe it, but Osrith refused to accept the possibility. Traveling on top of the water was bad enough; he couldn't imagine anyone going under it on purpose.

Two-Moons and Symmlrey shared none of his concerns and, in fact, agreed to the idea of taking to the Dolset at once. In an otherwise alien environment, this was relatively comfortable and familiar for them. Osrith gathered they were of the type that *liked* boats. He had no qualms letting them take charge of the journey at this point. He was content to sit in the middle of the craft, leaning against the stowed gear and complaining about Two-Moons' reckless steering. Symmlrey kept watch in the prow, her superior vision picking out the jutting rocks and shallows, which appeared with alarming rapidity at their breakneck speed, dipping in her paddle when necessary.

Kassakan had no need of the boat at all. She was at home in the water, and scouted ahead for potential threats that might escape even Symmlrey's keen sight. Though she insisted on calling this work, Osrith knew it was more like pure frolic as he watched her glistening scales slice through the water with casual flicks of her muscular tail. In the dim purplish light of the nightmoss planted on either side of the river passage, she was a fluid shadow dancing in and out of darkness.

He still remembered, and with great enjoyment, the surprised looks that had flashed across the faces of those riverwardens in Hzieak Hzed not that long ago. *A smooth bit of work that was*, he thought. They had slipped in and lightened the city coffers, then slipped out again before anyone was the wiser. Except those poor wide-eyed riverwardens, left to splash in the waters of the Miielor as Kassakan made good her escape.

Osrith chuckled. Then, with a grunt, brow furrowed and grin buried, he realized it had not been such a short time ago, at all. *Almost fifteen years.* He rubbed his eyes with the back of his hand as if to dispel the now irksome memory. It bothered him to consider too much that his past might now be longer than his future.

With a creak of steel scraping against rock and then the louder, jarring thunder of full impact, the ship halted against a large boulder on the south bank. The stern began to drift back toward the middle of the Dolset under the sway of the river's pull, and Two-Moons barked something in what Osrith guessed was his native tongue. Symmlrey yelled back something equally incomprehensible. The waters rushed against the sides of the boat, pressing hard in an all-out effort to capsize the floundering vessel. But the two *wilhorwhyr* maneuvered the boat in a dizzying circle, using the current to their advantage until at last they were pointing straight down the Dolset's underground gullet once more.

"Gods Between!" Osrith rumbled, twisting in his crouch to face Two-Moons. The lantern at the steersman's feet lit his face from below like a carved gourd on Undernday. "It's a boat, not a battering-ram, old man."

Two-Moons only laughed. Odd enough in itself – but with his face aglow in the orange flicker of lamplight, he looked for all the world like a maddened river-spirit guiding them all gaily along to the greylands. Not far enough from the truth, as far as Osrith was concerned.

The rest of their first day on the river was uneventful. The river was fast, but not unmanageable, and the passage was wide and well maintained. Aside from the occasional bat, or a school of white, sightless fish that slid through the dark water beneath them, they were alone. They made camp at an old kin post that Vaujn had marked on their map, the last such the kin even pretended to maintain in the hinterlands of their empire. The roar of the water here was louder and angrier as it began its steeper descent to the lower river.

The others unpacked their gear and dragged the boat fully ashore, and Osrith, with his kin spectacles balanced delicately on the bridge of his oft-broken nose, set off to examine what was left of the stores at their campsite. Not a half score yards from the bank he found the door. It opened with a reluctant creak under Osrith's determined pull, revealing a chamber that could house ten fully equipped kin in reasonable comfort. The fondness of the kin for vaulted ceilings made maneuvering only slightly unpleasant for a person of Osrith's girth and height, though he imagined Kassakan would be less at ease.

There was no food in the pantry, save for three jugs of beer, temptingly chilled by a small stream of water channeled from the river outside to cascade in a miniature waterfall down the back wall. It ran into the wide basin holding the jugs with a muted trickle and splash, and then drained back to its source through the same invisible handiwork that had brought it here.

Trust the kin not to spare expenses just to keep their beer cold, he thought. It would make a handy wash sink as well, he supposed, but that was probably an architectural afterthought. The kin weren't nearly as fond of bathing as they were of drinking. There was still a good supply of dry wood and sticks stacked neatly against one wall, supplemented by a larger pile of sooty coal, and Osrith busied himself preparing the small hearth for a fire.

His joints were stiff after the long ride in the kin's oversized canoe. Mumbling profanities that could wilt the hairs in the most grizzled sailor's ears, he sat heavily on the floor and massaged his right knee gingerly. This, unfortunately, only served to further aggravate his already aching back. Groaning, Osrith twisted around until he heard a muffled pop, then rested his sweaty forehead against the cool stone of the wall.

"Two-Moons has herbs that can soothe your joints," said Symmlrey from over his shoulder.

Osrith started at the sound and twisted his neck around to put a face to the disembodied voice. She stood behind him, a large pack slung over her shoulder, her eyes almost luminescent through the amethyst lenses of his spectacles. "Damn it, girl, don't sneak around like that. Like as not you'll find an axe in your head before I know who you are."

"I wasn't sneaking –"

"And I don't need any of the old man's weeds and berries, either," he grumbled, fishing in his own gear. "Just a cramp, is all."

Symmlrey stared at him a moment, shrugged, and walked to the other side of the room to stow her burden. Osrith rummaged for another moment and then produced the object of his search with the glimmer of a grin. It was a rounded piece of flint, attached in the center to a steel arm about three inches long and half an inch in width, with a clip-like handle. Upon squeezing the clip, the tiny mechanism dragged a sharpened edge of steel against the flint wheel, immediately issuing a spark into the prepared kindling. Osrith nursed the barest hint of a fire into a comfortable blaze. He sat back, secured his glasses in their padded leather case, and let the warmth seep into his bones and while away the stubborn aches that still nestled there.

The door opened again, and Two-Moons entered with Kassakan a step behind. As Two-Moons and Symmlrey spread out their bedrolls next to Osrith's place of silent repose, Kassakan brought out the rations hastily provided by Vaujn's portly quartermaster, Ouwd, and distributed the hunks of bread and cheese to her companions. With a look of disdain, she handed a slab of some salted meat to Osrith and then washed her hands thoroughly in the basin before touching her own food.

Osrith's beard crinkled in a smile as he watched Kassakan nibble at her bread as daintily as a court dandy at King's Keep. Her rounded teeth were not those of a hunter, and she had never been able to tolerate meat of any sort. He had never figured out how she got so big eating plants, fruits and breads. He'd heard more lectures on the subject than he cared to in his lifetime. As if it wasn't bad enough she'd convinced herself not to eat meat, she often felt it her task to convince him of the same.

Osrith ripped off a large section of what his nose told him was dried beef, from the squat underkingdom equivalent of a steer, and offered the remaining slab to Two-Moons. He was met with a disdainful frown and a shake of the head. Before he could repeat the gesture for Symmlrey, the aulden had turned to face the fire with a more severe expression of her own.

"What?" muttered the mercenary in mid-mouthful. "Are your palettes too delicate for dried beef? Or is it my company?"

Two-Moons' reply was cut off by Symmlrey's quicker tongue. "*Wilhorwhyr* don't eat of animal flesh. You're worldly enough to have heard this."

Osrith rolled his eyes. "I also heard you spit acid and bugger unicorns, but I never believed that either," he answered. "Maybe I should rethink all that, too."

"*Rethink?*" she scoffed. "That would imply twice in a day's span."

Osrith saluted her with his half-eaten beef. "Spoken like the self-righteous leaf eater you are. Damned unnatural anyhow."

Symmlrey's jaw clenched, and her anger painted her cheeks dull rouge. She made ready what was surely to be a caustic reply, but a thick tail of shiny green scales brushed against her thigh. She looked over at the reclining Kassakan, her delicate mouth still half-open in belayed speech.

"A wise fish doesn't rise to the bait, friend," the hosskan said. Her opaline eyes stared sagely at the greasy-bearded man and then back to the aulden. "I know from experience."

"You stay out of this, lizard," complained Osrith.

"He's not happy unless he can grouse about something," continued Kassakan, "and he'll never agree with you, no matter how much sense you make. That's what passes for principle with him. He can defeat the most intelligent of arguments with sheer vulgarity and rudeness of wit. He'll get worse once he starts on the beer."

Symmlrey's mouth hung open for a moment more and then closed with a nod of understanding. She leaned back against the far wall from Osrith and made what passed as an effort to peel back the skin from his face with her poisonous gaze. "I understand," she said, her soft voice camouflaging her restrained temper.

"Don't condescend to *me*, little girl!" Osrith said in a tone that bordered on a growl. He dragged himself to his feet and stomped purposefully to the water basin, removing one of the ceramic jugs with a splash. "I need a good drink just to put up with your damn company!" He popped the cork off with his free hand and sent it flying into the fire, which flared in answer to his offering.

"At the risk of interrupting this valuable discussion," said Two-Moons as Osrith resumed his seat, jug in hand, "I'd suggest we discuss tomorrow."

Osrith took a long swallow of smooth amber beer. "By all means," he said with a satisfied wipe of his mouth. "What needs discussing, exactly?"

"I'm not well versed in kin lore," Two-Moons explained, "and Oszmagoth means little to me save in name. I know what it *was*, but little of what it is. I gathered you and Vaujn think it dangerous."

"Hard to tell. No one comes back, so they say. Either it's dangerous or just real comfortable."

"My people have told stories of the dragon. Brighteye, I think," Symmlrey added. "She was most dangerous. Vaujn is certain she's gone?"

Osrith detected a slight tinge of fear to her words. That reassured him. At least it proved she had *some* sense. He took another pull on his jug. "Girl, I might be the biggest fool you ever met, but I'm not *that* big a fool! Of course she's gone." As if to punctuate, he belched. "But chances are there's a lot still down there with no love for any of us."

"Assuming the depth recorded on the map is accurate," yawned Kassakan in an impressive display of her cavernous maw, "which doubtless it is to the *etahr*, knowing our kin friends, expect dringli in the greatest numbers. More worrisome, however, would be the *srhrilakiin*. The kin speak of hundreds in the tale of Mordigul and Merridel. That, I would think, is an exaggeration, but even a few are dangerous."

Osrith offered the beer to Two-Moons, who accepted with a smile, restoring some of his faith in the old *wilhorwhyr's* character as well. "Look, we're not planning on staying in Oszmagoth. We're just going to float right on through and out the other side. No *srhrilakiin'*ll cross running water – *can't*, they're at least half Shadow from what the kin say. As for the dringli, well, we'll just have to take our chances."

Two-Moons nodded, wiping his chin with his sleeve as he passed the jug to Symmlrey. "Aye, that would seem the wisest course. Through and through and done."

"What of the curse?"

Osrith looked at Symmlrey as if her question had been a dagger thrust. "Not much we can do about that, is there? If it even exists."

"Oh, I would think it does," said Kassakan in a matter-of-fact manner, now stretched out like a great, scaled cat on the floor. "Oszmagoth was a place of great power even before King Gulgazamoun sat on the Ivory Throne. When it was cast down, it was no small matter. The rebel magi who called that city home were sure to cast fearsome wards on their untimely grave before departing this life. And barring that, possibly after."

Osrith pulled his cloak tightly about his neck and shoulders, as if chasing away an unwelcome chill. "That's fine talk right before sleep."

After that, no one had much to say, and each drifted into quiet thoughts. All save Osrith, who wished to spare himself further thought at all with a second trip to the chilly basin.

The next morning came much earlier than Osrith would have preferred. There was no light filtering in through the windows, no birdsong to soothe tired eyes from sleep, just the insistent nagging of an old longhaired *wilhorwhyr* who claimed he knew that somewhere the suns were rising. Somewhere, no doubt, they were, but Osrith questioned how Two-Moons arrived at the conclusion it was *here*. Arguing proved fruitless, however, so he settled for the time-honored kin tradition of being generally unpleasant in the morning.

The party broke camp and floated the boat with the expedient ease of veteran wayfarers, pausing only to determine their best choice for illumination now that the nightmoss had all but disappeared. The kin had provided them with crystal globes containing their own supply of the luminescent fungus, and these fit tightly into the jaws of the carved prow.

"Don't mistake this for anything more than a guide light," Osrith explained as the moss globe clicked into place. "These are used more like warning beacons in the busier trade routes. They're useful enough instead of a torch if you're on foot, making way steady but slow. But here... ?"

"The lanterns will not do, either," commented Symmlrey.

Osrith agreed. The range of the lantern light was relatively feeble. In the broader, slower expanses they had already traveled, it had been sufficient, but with the quickening rapids and the narrowing confines of the passages ahead, its inconsistent flicker cast misleading and dangerous shadows in the rushing waters. The torches were useless for those and other reasons: open flames were best avoided on a wooden craft, and in the Deeps strange and volatile gasses could be vented unexpectedly, with explosive results.

"Perhaps the lantern and the globes together," Two-Moons mused, not sounding at all convinced.

"What of your lenses, Osrith?" asked Symmlrey. "I can manage somewhat in the dark. If Two-Moons could also see... ."

"No," said Osrith after a moment of consideration. "From what Vaujn says, this'll get pretty rough. All well and good if they stay on his face, but if they fly off when we're in the middle of those rapids... ." He shook his head firmly. "No, they'd best stay in my pack."

Kassakan cleared her throat. That sound never failed to get their attention. "I shall make light," she said with a resigned sigh.

Both Two-Moons and Symmlrey seemed somewhat surprised as the lizard summoned forth a ball of colorless fire into the palm of her hand with a whisper and a muted gesture. It sat there a moment, between her thumb and three fingers, and then sailed off to hover patiently above the boat.

"I was beginning to think you'd retired," Osrith said; though he knew she'd always been reluctant to use the Craft, save for healing. Hosskan ethics regarding magic were odd, but it was well appreciated by those of Osrith's own opinion: *the less of it, the better*. Not that he would ever begrudge her its use, especially the curative aspects, but neither did he normally encourage it.

"Yes, that will do nicely," approved Two-Moons, regarding Kassakan with a bewildered smile. "I never knew you were a N'skil'ah."

"No longer," she said, her manner casual but her tone haunted by the ghost of something more. "Now I am just Kassakan."

Osrith saw concern or doubt in Two-Moons' face, but the old man said no more. Symmlrey seemed ready to pursue the matter further, but a quick gesture from her Guide stayed her questions. Osrith met his eyes for an instant, and knew that this man understood the hosskan as well or better than he. A hosskan did not, *could not*, simply retire from the sacred order. Their silent rapport lasted only an eye blink, and then they were both picking their way down the last few feet of rocky shore to the boat.

Under the wan light of the fire globe, they could see that the rapids just ahead were white with angry foam as the water lashed viscously against any rock that dared obstruct its course. A sharp bend cut off their view twenty yards ahead, but the roaring discontent that echoed back to their ears warned that from here they would be working at increasing odds against the river.

"You'll have to join us in the boat, I think," said Symmlrey to Kassakan, frowning from the rapids to the lizard. "This seems dangerous even for you."

"Yes, I think you're right," she agreed. "But I'm afraid I'll lower your draft considerably."

This proved to be true, but the craft held up under the additional weight and still responded reasonably well to Two-Moons' steady hand. Osrith could no longer lean without a care against their supplies. The river now demanded the concentration of all hands to ensure their safe passage through the twisting narrow channels worn by centuries through the rock of the mountains. The river dropped suddenly and often, sometimes lifting them out of their seats with the force of their rapid descent. Without a sure purchase on some solid portion of their boat, they risked being thrown out altogether.

Symmlrey and Osrith dug their paddles into the violent froth, shouting and straining to master the river. Two-Moons, grim and focused as always, sent them through the narrow channels with less frequent but well-chosen strokes. It was decided early that Kassakan best served their needs by staying low and still so as not to upset their delicate balance. She disliked this, arguing that she wished to be of more use, but the others assured her that her light was the best help she could provide.

Each night as they lay in camp, amidst the ruins of once-frequented kin waypoints, new aches were visited upon Osrith's already beleaguered muscles and joints. By their second encampment, he no longer fought off Symmlrey's persistent offers of help. Her nimble fingers probed his tender flesh, digging in with brutal precision on the knots that tightened his shoulders, arms and back. At first, he thought she meant to torture him for his contentious nature, as his old pains were replaced with new and harsher sensations. But the pain had faded, like clouds in a slow but powerful wind, making way for the sweet relief his much-abused body so desperately needed.

It also became clear, as they dropped further and further into the Deeps, that Vaujn had not underestimated the multitude of threats and nuisances that would beset them. No less than three eloths had dropped from the dagger-like stalactites above them; one, at twenty feet in length, had nearly taken Osrith out of the boat before Two-Moons and Symmlrey had beaten it off with their paddles. Only Kassakan escaped the festering bites of the blood mites. For the others, the tiny vermin that crawled into every unwelcome orifice became a constant nuisance. Every night she pored over the naked bodies of her less fortunate companions to remove the tiny leeching insects before they gained enough purchase to become a real danger. Unmolested, a blood mite could reach adulthood at alarming speed and an even more worrisome rate of blood loss. Toward the end of their third day, it became more a challenge to simultaneously scratch and paddle than anything else.

The rockfishers grew more and more numerous as they fell deeper and deeper into the earth. At three feet in length, not including the added reach of their whiplash tails and questing proboscises, they were of a size none of the inveterate travelers had ever seen before, nor would wish to see again. That third night the campsite was so overrun with the chitinous creatures that they had moored to a stalagmite rather than make landfall. The night was punctuated with the sickening crunch of the rockfishers' victims as they were split open and devoured by the ravenous beasts.

The next afternoon Osrith plied at the river with his paddle, thankful to be away from that place and leaning all of his weight into each powerful stroke. It was hard to see the significance of the effort. At this point the Dolset's raging moods were barely tolerant of their unwelcome presence. Kassakan's globe of light danced luminously through the shadows, chasing them away just as the prow sliced through the water ahead of them. The passage was widening, but the river no less swift, and despite Two-Moons' considerable skill and effort, they were adding several new dents to their already pitted *duaurnhuun* figurehead.

"There!" screamed Symmlrey against the increasing roar around them. She pointed with her paddle at a point on the wall to their port side. "There's a path!"

"If that's the beginning of the Great Stair," Osrith yelled back at Two-Moons, "then we must be close!"

"Paddle hard on starboard!" answered Two-Moons. "If we don't cut across the current now, we never will!"

The river lent them no time to waste on further discussion. Osrith and Symmlrey shifted to starboard, stabbing into the rapids with their paddles. The river forced them toward its swift center with gathering strength. At first it seemed their efforts would make no difference. But then, ever so slightly, the bow of the boat began a slow turn to port and the beckoning safety of the shore. Osrith didn't let up for an instant. The sound of the falls ahead was now a hammering rage in his ears, and their escape from the pull of the spitting white water looked narrow enough for his liking. So focused was he on driving them onto dry land and away from the hostile intent of the Dolset, he almost didn't hear Symmlrey's shout of warning.

"Dringli!" she yelled, pausing in mid-stroke. "Dringli on shore!"

As if in punctuation, six arrows flew from the shadows on the nearing shoreline. Four sailed past to land with a splash in the river, one broke on the metal prow, and one stuck in the wood just between Osrith and Symmlrey. A chorus of loud whoops and jeers followed next, and another volley of arrows fell around them.

"Further down! Land further down!" Osrith yelled over his shoulder. He knew as well as anyone else on the boat that they couldn't fight and paddle. They had to make landfall before they engaged the dringli. He could almost make out their short, stubby shadows, but he paid them no mind.

Two-Moons adjusted their angle of approach, but even as it became apparent that they would avoid the hostile archers, it became equally clear that they would not reach shore in time. The same rapids that took them so swiftly away from their enemies now delivered them back into their original peril. Osrith and Symmlrey channeled all their remaining strength into their paddles, and Two-Moons grunted with the strain of fighting the willful current, but in the end it was to no avail. With its fingers securely fastened about its long elusive prey, the Dolset hurried them on to their fate.

When at last Mordigul's Plunge rushed away into darkness, Osrith was almost relieved. Now, at the very least, they were *here*, and for one moment all decisions were out of their hands. There was nothing to fight, nothing to decide, and nothing he could do. Any such satisfaction was dispelled a heartbeat later as he sailed into the yawning space of air, mist, and spitting foam that plummeted away beneath him.

They fell end over end, unsecured goods and paddles flying into the dark. Osrith wrapped his arm around a crossbeam and wedged his knees against the side of the boat. He felt an odd mix of nausea and weightlessness as the world tumbled around him. There was a strangled cry and then a flurry of motion as Two-Moons flew away from the boat and out of sight. Then some timeless span later, they crashed into the volatile churning waters at the waterfall's base. Kassakan was next, tossed like a rag doll to the starboard side in the roiling fury about them, and then she was gone. She disappeared into a green dot downstream, her little globe of light trailing after.

Osrith felt the crossbeam he was clutching give way with a mournful crunch as the boat was thrown down by the last violent whim of the seething cauldron, and a moment later he was underwater, flailing and helpless and straining to hold his air. In the absence of Kassakan's magic, the darkness was absolute, and it was only by luck that he kicked blindly to the surface. He gasped a lung-full of air, and then struck a rock with his shoulder as the current carried him relentlessly downstream. Something cold and fleshy touched his hand, and he flinched away. He grunted as he struck another rock solidly with the middle of his back.

The touch again, but this time with a voice: Symmlrey's. "Feet," she gasped, trying to turn him around. "First."

Osrith floundered and managed to do as she asked, and found the frequent impact with rock and stalactite much less painful when absorbed by his legs. Still, he was more or less out of control, and utterly convinced that he was going to die. The water was so cold he could already feel his limbs stiffening, slowing, dragging him down to rest at the bottom. Symmlrey's grip tightened, and his forward momentum slowed and then stopped. She'd found something to hold onto, evidently, but in the pitch black around them he couldn't see what.

"Osrith!" screamed Symmlrey over the rushing torrent. "Climb up my arm! Hurry!"

Osrith's freezing fingers reached clumsily up her arm, shivering and numb, but still responsive. He could hear her grunting as he pulled against her arm, knowing from the give in her joint that it must be dislocated. He grabbed at her shoulder and then her back, holding on to her with all his dwindling strength.

"Climb around me," she whispered. "Hurry."

With a final effort he heaved himself around her back and found purchase hugging the opposite side of the same smooth, rounded stalactite as she. He folded his fist into her shirt, in case she lost her own grip, and tried to catch his breath. This would only bring temporary salvation. Soon enough they would still die from exposure or be swept away as their numb fingers lost their hold. They had, at best, a few clicks.

"Now what?" he yelled, his voice barely distinguishable over the mad turmoil of the river.

"One moment." Her breath was short and labored. "Think I see... Yes! The boat!"

"In one piece?" Osrith had assumed it was now sodden flinders and tinder wood, or far downstream, at best. "Where?"

"Hard to see, even for me. Hold onto my ankles."

She climbed over him, and Osrith shifted his hand to grab her ankle as she stretched invisibly before him. He could hear her curse in frustration, straining against his grip to reach wherever she thought she saw the boat, and then finally she made a subdued sound of triumph.

"Pull me back. I've got the tether. The current will take it as soon as it's free. Be ready."

Osrith inhaled deeply and gathered his remaining strength. If this met with failure, he knew the river's chilling, determined hands would pull him under and away from breath and life. He gripped the rock with his legs, pressing back against it as he pulled on her body, placing one hand above the other as he dragged her in by inches. As he reached her upper thigh, he felt her body tighten and pull against him. The boat was in the current, dragging them both back into the main channel.

"The rope!" she screamed back at him, and he clutched up her body until he found it, wrapping its end around his wrist even as Symmlrey pulled herself up its length to the backward-facing prow.

The boat dragged him behind, limp and gasping for air, and then he was being pulled aboard. He lay on the bottom of the boat, shivering and thankful for her aulden-sight, listening to the still raging river and their ragged breathing. Their packs, still secure to the crossbeam, were nonetheless half open and disordered; whatever contents remained were thoroughly water-logged. Osrith felt his way through them until at last he felt the warm touch of a moss-globe against his fingers.

He brought it out, revealing his hand, the boat, and the battered form of Symmlrey in its faint lavender light. From what little he could tell, it seemed that the waterway had widened and stilled somewhat, though the current remained strong. Symmlrey knelt down before him where he rested his head against a sodden canvass bag, and panted with no attempt to conceal her exhaustion.

"I didn't... think we would... make it," she said between breaths.

Then, out of the black behind her, a hand twice again the size of her entire body emerged, the immensity of its outstretched grip dwarfing her slender silhouette. Osrith's eyes widened, and his trembling finger pointed, but no words escaped his blue lips, only a low moaning cry. Symmlrey blinked, turned, and was knocked soundly on the head by the oversized appendage. She fell on top of Osrith, unconscious, blood streaming from her temple.

Osrith cringed as the boat floated under the outstretched hand, but it made no further move toward him. As he looked closer, he realized the hand, and the arm it was attached to, were merely parts of a much larger whole. The body attached to the arm was thick, the head atop the shoulders long and severely featured. He had never seen one of the Old Ones, except perhaps in his imaginings, but he had no doubt that was exactly what stared down at him. Then, just as the fear had grasped him, it eased its hold. The andu'ai remained unmoving, expressionless, smiling blankly and unseeing as they drifted past.

A statue, by Oghran's Chance, he thought, *only a statue.*

In his relief, Osrith almost let the possibility slip away, but for all his fatigue his first reaction was to survive. Sometimes his body acted before waiting for the convenience of his thoughts to guide them. Often enough, that led to trouble; but this day, as many previous, it likely saved his life. Stumbling on his knees, Osrith lurched to the prow, which still gazed serenely back the way they had come, and wrapped the tether line around one alabaster finger before the beckoning arm could leave them again for the concealing dark.

Osrith stared up the girth of the thing, wondering what type of precious stones caused those narrow, almondine eyes to glitter like fire in the moss-light; what animal's bones supplied the gleaming ivory of that needle-toothed smile? The construct's base and legs were underwater, the river reaching up just beyond its belt, but the statue seemed unconcerned. Even in stone, the andu'ai had a wicked, knowing look about it. He thanked his luck he was born well after their time.

"Damn it all," he cursed with an accustomed bitterness.

They had reached Oszmagoth.

Chapter Seventeen

Lights in the Dark

Only the steady lapping of the river against the boat and Symmlrey's shallow breathing marked the passage of time. Osrith found another moss globe intact and affixed it in the waiting duaurnhuun's metal jaws. The other globe he kept near Symmlrey, for it provided a small amount of warmth with its light. She would live, but not without the affliction of a truly awful headache. He wrapped her head in damp cloth to stop the bleeding. She stirred but did not regain consciousness.

Osrith rubbed the dark stains of blood from her cheek, noticing the smooth and gentle lines of her face. Symmetrical. Precise. But soft. Her beauty was so perfect that she seemed inhuman. She was, of course, inhuman, he reminded himself. She was a child of the fae. According to common myth, he should be ravaging her unconscious body even now, under the sway of her faerie glamour. He almost laughed, but he lacked the energy even to scoff. Maybe he was just too old or too bitter for her magic.

Or too tired.

Osrith realized then that one thing he wasn't, to his amazement, was cold. The water had been like fluid ice over his skin not long ago, but he sat here, a mild wind ruffling his beard, without so much as a shiver. It took a moment for him to recognize that the breeze was warm, its scent tinged with sulfur.

Naturally, he chided himself. Oszmagoth was in the bowels of Mount Tanigis, and Mount Tanigis was a volcano. Not so volatile as once it had been, but its heart was still of fire.

That was good. He wouldn't worry about dying of exposure, at least.

Osrith saw no sign of Kassakan or Two-Moons within his small expanse of light. The lizard yet lived. He knew that somehow, somewhere, deep inside of him. He supposed she would have some meaningful explanation for that, being her *j'iitai* or some such nonsense. Relief though that was, there was enough else to worry him that it provided little in the way of lasting comfort. And there was no telling what had become of the old man.

He looked across the wide rushing waters toward the nearest shore, trying to judge if distance or strength of current would preclude a swim to dry land. Both did, he concluded, at least for his less than impressive swimming skill – certainly not with Symmlrey to drag behind him and a moss globe in one hand. And there was still the matter of the dringli. They had passed beyond the party laying in wait at the top of the falls, but it was quite possible there were more of them in the ruins of the city. Aside from the grey outline of the shore itself, it was impossible to make out any detail of the ruins.

And the srhrilakiin, he thought dryly, *and the cave-manti, and gods know what else is down in this pit.*

A flickering light caught his eye from downstream, and Osrith threw a sack over the moss globe on the prow to veil its light. He picked through their weapons, and though most of them had survived intact under their protective wrappings of oiled cloth, his crossbow had suffered a splintering blow, possibly from the shifting weight of the axe next to it, and lay cracked and useless at his feet. His belt of throwing knives had fared better, and he slung it over his left shoulder. Even as a well-balanced hilt fell into his waiting palm, he knew it would be unnecessary, for as the light drew nearer it became clear the source was Kassakan.

"Is that you, lizard?" Osrith asked, more as a greeting than a question.

Her scaly head sliced through the water up-current with enviable ease, her ball of dweomer-light following above like a trained and loyal bird. Her eyes looked like deep, reflective marbles in the strange light, locked on Osrith and the boat as she swam steadily closer. She didn't acknowledge his comment until one of her three-fingered hands reached up to steady herself next to the battered riverboat.

"How is Symmlrey?" she asked, only slightly short of breath from her swim "I smell her blood."

Osrith shook his head, pinching a grin out of the left corner of his mouth. "She's fine. Took a slap to the head."

Kassakan nodded, and an unspoken question hung between them for a moment. "He could have washed up on the far shore," she said at last, "but I didn't see him on the near side."

"He could be dead," said Osrith.

"Yes," mused Kassakan, taking her time with the word. She looked out past her floating light into the cowed but lingering dark and made a throaty noise roughly equivalent to a sigh. "Yes, he could be dead."

Osrith felt a small tug in his gut. Despite his lingering suspicion of the *wilhorwhyr* as a whole, he couldn't fault the old man or the girl for much aside from stilted talk and dramatic speeches. He might not care for their dogma, but when it came right down to a fight, he would put his back against theirs without a second thought. Two-Moons was a good companion, a good man; it was a shame to lose him like this. But he was only one amongst many in Osrith's memory.

"Well, we're in no shape to find him right now, alive or dead," he muttered. "Can you tow us in to shore? We can look for him after we set up camp."

Kassakan lowered her eyes and nodded her serpentine head. "I think I can manage it. Hold on to Symmlrey."

Osrith balanced his weight on his knees and bent over the young Vanneahym to hold her in place at the shoulder. Kassakan took the tether rope between her rounded teeth and set off toward the near shore with a combination of powerful arm and tail strokes. She didn't move with her normal undulating grace, but she still sliced through the water with considerable power and enviable ease. She reached the rocky shoreline soon enough, and after an additional moment of searching for a suitable landing, she heaved the riverboat onto dry land.

Osrith stepped out of the boat, but instead of finding dirt or rough, natural rock, his feet fell on the cracked but solid surface of ancient pavement. He bent down to examine it more closely in the light of his moss globe and discovered it was some type of turquoise-streaked marble. A somewhat expensive and elaborate choice, if it covered the entire city floor, but then the andu'ai had taste that was nothing if not excessive. The rest of his surroundings were too dim to make out properly, but the shadows of crumbling ruins and towering columns lurked in every direction.

"We'd best find shelter," he suggested, pulling one of the reassembled packs from the boat. "I'd feel a lot better with a wall against my back."

Kassakan already had the remains of the other two packs over her shoulder and was removing Symmlrey from the boat like a newly hatched child. "I won't argue with that, old friend," she agreed, "but we shouldn't go too far right away. Not if we have any hope of finding Two-Moons before sleep."

"Do you smell anything helpful?"

"Strange scents. Old scents." She raised her snout into the air, nostrils twitching. "The air is so thick with sulfur," she paused again, then looked down at Osrith. "There is an unfamiliar scent close by – raw flesh and sweet musk. Acid. And something else, more distant, a *wrong* smell. But I can't be sure."

"Wrong," mimicked Osrith. "Shadowborn, maybe?"

"Possibly. Something of Shadow, in any event. According to Vaujn, *srhrilakiin* would seem a likely assumption."

Osrith made a rumbling noise deep in his barrel chest and looked around with a wary glint in his eyes. "Well, that first scent sounds like cave-mantis, so be sure to sniff us away from any of them. I'd rather not end up as dinner for the local horde. And let's just hope the wrong smell stays a distant smell."

❦

Two-Moons coughed up another lung-full of water and then slumped forward, shivering on hands and knees in the total darkness. He was not cold so much as exhausted and somewhat bruised from his narrow victory over the river. He refused to embrace his hard fought success immediately, for he recognized that he was not yet out of peril. He remained alone, effectively blind, armed only with his long knife and a lifetime of experience, in a city legendary for its less than friendly denizens and cursed by the gods besides. Now was certainly no time to sit idly admiring his luck.

Two-Moons forced his breathing to a normal, steady rhythm, and he listened. Past the hammering beat of his heart, through the rushing of the river behind him, into the stillness. A drip of condensation found a new home in a puddle not far away; a hiss of steam escaped from some volcanic vent in the ground to his left; and the nearly inaudible caress of wind kissed the rock. He almost crept forward then, but his instinct held him back, freezing his muscles even as they started to move.

He furrowed his brow. Something about the wind, he realized, something about the wind was not right. He ignored the competing sounds that filled his keen ears, concentrating only on the wind. The wind that sighed like a breath against stone, perhaps fueled by the stirrings of the steam mixing with the cooler air of the cavern, perhaps from the falls. But the smell was not right for that. *Perhaps.... .*

And then he knew, for the wind had done what no natural breeze could ever do – it stopped. It didn't fade and go, it simply ceased, and Two-Moons gripped the hilt of his long curved knife tightly. This wind was nothing more than the feeble evidence of a creature in passing, a solid body displacing the air it moved through.

Two-Moons reached inward to focus and then looked out with a perception more discerning than any physical sense, opening his mind's eye to the intricacies of life and nature around him. He swallowed an audible gasp at what he saw. There *was* no life around him. Nothing, not even the fleeting echo of life existed here. Worse and still more unnatural than that absence alone were the holes that drifted about on the edge of his perception: holes in the fabric of creation that moved in silence toward him, stalking. Holes in life itself. *Srhrilakiin* or their ilk, and far too many of them. Over a dozen, at least, but his sense of them was nebulous beyond a few yards.

He was not far from the river, and he knew that was his best, if not only, avenue of escape. These were beings of Shadow, shades of unlife who sucked at the marrow of the living world. To them, water was anathema, the very opposite of all they were – alive and flowing with life. Even in these times when the ancient magics seemed all but lost, the water-spirits still had power enough to halt all but the most powerful of the shadowborn.

He might very well drown, and though he had no wish to die, neither did the concept terrify him. His wife had made the journey before him, as had one of his sons, and he knew that they would await him in the greylands. To all living things came death, and if there were no other recourse, he would accept his fate. Rather that than the horror awaiting him at the claws of the shadowborn. They would rip him to shreds, body and soul, and that fate he would *not* accept.

Two-Moons knew he was no more than ten feet from the water, but in the few moments it would take to cover it, at least one of the beasts would have opportunity to attack. And where one saw opportunity, others would descend in haste. He would have to kill quickly if he was to avoid taking them on in numbers, and with just his knife to fight with, that would be difficult. Like all *wilhorwhyr* weapons, there was silver in the blade, but that would only allow the edge to penetrate their shadow; he would need much more to mortally wound them.

Ingryst, lend me Your strength and Your light, he prayed, and coaxed the life force in his own being out along his fingers and into the knife beyond. With so little to spare, the effort was painful, but in the midst of the dark a thin sliver of light appeared, like a phantom blade floating suspended in midair. Its light was not bright enough to illumine even the hand that wielded it, but seeing any breach in the curtain of blackness around him lifted Two-Moons' heart.

And the *srhrilakiin* flew at him, their keening howls echoing in the lofty recesses of the Sunken City.

Even blind, Two-Moons knew precisely where the river lay in relation to him, and he made for it directly. The closest of the *srhrilakiin* was on him less than a breath later, but Two-Moons could feel the creature's unnatural presence, and his knife slid home more accurately than his mortal sight could ever have guided it. He felt the blade penetrate and focused his extended life force through the cutting edge. There was a momentary flash of white fire and an explosion of awful, thunderous pain – and then the shadowborn beast was gone.

The effort had taken more of him, literally, than he had hoped. Two-Moons staggered and fell, still a few short feet from the water's edge, as the others came to feed. He didn't have enough life or *iiyir* left in him to fight them all off, but even knowing that, he could not give in. He struck out again and again with his long knife, and the *srhrilakiin* fell about him as the life in his mortal soul dwindled and drained with every blow. He felt their claws in his flesh, and their phantom claws digging deeper, as one after the other took a share of their meal.

There was but a glimmer of Two-Moons left, little enough that many would already have fled their shells and been devoured by the *srhrilakiin*. But for the *wilhorwhyr*, there was just enough remaining to land one more blow before oblivion erased his soul. He drew a shaky breath, and screamed the name of his beloved wife that she might at least hear him before the nothingness robbed them of their long-awaited reunion.

"*Waeuu ne N'Iuk!*"

The cry rang out, smothering the gleeful shriek of the *srhrilakiin* for an instant before it was stifled by another, more powerful sound, a deep crack of thunder that shook the ground beneath Two-Moons as if the earth itself trembled in fear. Then the air burst into flame all around him and light poured into the darkness, filling it like an empty vessel, and the *srhrilakiin* scattered back to the shadows.

Two-Moons held on to that last vestige of his being and nurtured it, too weak to move anything more than his head. A ball of blue-white fire three feet in circumference radiated cleansing light from above him, and he felt the hairs on his neck and arms stirring against his skin.

"Kassakan?" he managed weakly, though doubtfully.

"Ah, Kassakan," answered an unfamiliar voice, its tone an unnerving harmony of bass and tenor. "*Blessed wind*, if my *hosskanae* is still accurate. But no, I am not."

There was a pause, and Two-Moons strained to discern the figure standing behind the light. The features were impossible to make out through the glare, but the overall size was apparent enough. The stranger stood at close to fifteen feet in height. Two-Moons felt an uneasy tremble in his gut as the voice continued.

"A human, I see," it stated, moving still closer, "and old by your standards. You fought quite bravely. Most of your ilk freezes stiff at the mere touch of those pesky brutes, but you…. Ah, you *impressed* me."

Two-Moons began to reply, but the other voice continued as if not noticing the attempt at all.

"I am not easily impressed, you see. But then, with humans, anything more than utter failure is *somewhat* impressive. Still, you are an amusing bunch, and I am short on amusements of late. What are you called, brave little Ebuouki man?"

"I am Two-Moons," he answered. "And you? You are andu'ai?"

"Yes!" A small hint of surprise laced the bi-tonal voice, followed by an eerie, musical laugh. "I'm half surprised you remember us so quickly. Your kind finds it so easy to forget. But you, little Ebuouki man, *you* might be worth the trouble after all."

Two-Moons was still in the process of deciding if he liked the sound of that when the andu'ai bent down toward him, and as its face came into view he found it difficult to restrain an instinctual flinch. He had never seen a living andu'ai this close before, but he had happened upon a tapestry once at the Citadel of Swords in Ishtin. It was more accurate than he had feared to believe at the time. Aside from its imposing height, the andu'ai had girth to match, though hidden in part by flowing silks of indigo and silver; and its face – gods, but that was enough to stop the beating of any heart. The smooth, hairless skin, a frosty blue-green in complexion, was broken by two prominent features: the eyes, cat-like saucers of amber centered on a black slivers of pupil, glowing like lanterns; and a hideous smile of needle-thin teeth spreading back across the sides of his face. Less than a foot from that jaw, Two-Moons had no doubt it could open to swallow him whole with the ease of a swamp python. He hardly noticed the thin, shallow nose and the tiny points of his ears.

"Have I startled you?" asked the giant with another snicker. Then his dark blue lips drew down over his predatory smile in a frown, and he said, "You must forgive me, little Two-Moons man, for my behavior. You are in no state for jests. I have been most uncivil. I must bring you back here and see to your health."

"Back?"

The cat eyes narrowed as the grin returned, though somewhat subdued this time, "You interest me, human. This, I will admit. But I don't venture to this side of the river myself without better reason than that."

As if by way of explanation, the figure rippled, and droplets of water dripped from its surface, increasing into rivulets as the face, body, and robes melted into a pool of water at Two-Moons' feet. Then the process reversed itself, and the pool reformed into the smiling andu'ai once more.

"A parlor trick, really, but useful. Water makes such an excellent conductive medium for simulacra, and it's so abundant here. But I forget myself again. It's high time we were leaving."

―⁂―

The explosion of light and sound shook Osrith to his knees. Kassakan helped him to his feet, staring out past the toppled columns and crumbling buildings around their camp toward the Dolset's far shore. The ruins about them obscured their view, but the glow from the miniature blue-white sun that hovered there reached out to pry away the shadows even here.

The full wonder of the city, for a few startling moments, was plain to see. It possessed all the things which made up any great city: domes sheathed in gold and silver, towers and mansions, a great plaza lined with statues and intricately fluted columns not a hundred yards away. And all of it on a scale near double the size of the same made by human hands. The destruction was on a grander scale as well, for this city had not simply been eaten at by time, it had been struck down, and its pieces were thrown and scattered on the floor and walls of the cavern where it had come to rest. Cooled streams of ancient lava ran like twisting, flowing causeways between buildings; towers lay like sheaves of discarded arrows; steam rose from the cracked golden dome of what looked like a cathedral; great fissures cracked the pavement for hundreds of feet in length, some more than twenty feet wide.

Then the darkness returned.

Kassakan made a series of clicks and hoots in her native speech, and dimmed her ball of light with a gesture. The moss globe still glowed next to Symmlrey, who slept oblivious if not peaceful, her shoulder re-set and bound, the shadows dancing playfully at the edge of its light. Silence returned as well, broken only by the rushing of the river.

Osrith whistled softly between his teeth.

"We may be in grave danger," whispered Kassakan.

"*Really?*" shot back Osrith.

"I mean beyond what we feared."

"When you're in a hole this deep, lizard, another few feet hardly makes a difference, now does it?" Despite his casual tone, Osrith began checking over his surviving arsenal of weaponry. "There's dead and there's dead, and when it happens it don't matter much what put you there."

"I'll remind you of that when the time comes," Kassakan said.

Osrith released the exasperated sigh he reserved for Kassakan alone. "*What* time, lizard?'

"When the andu'ai who cast that spell comes looking for *us*."

Osrith laughed. There was a point at which a situation became so hopeless or terrible or frightening, it passed from the realm of the real to the ridiculous. In Osrith's estimation, that point had come. He remembered in vivid detail his conversation with Two-Moons when they planned their expedition from within the walls of Castle Vae.

"Oh, yes," he said, "the main road to Dwynleigsh would be *far* too dangerous." He paused and nodded to himself, then continued with even more emphatic sarcasm. "Yes, let's take the secret route through the mountains, instead!"

"I suppose it's healthy to see humor in the situation."

"The *long* route under the mountain?" continued Osrith without pause. "No time for that! Take us through the ancient cursed city. That'll save us a ten-day, after all!"

"Osrith." Kassakan put her claw out to rest on his shoulder. "Enough. We need to leave this place as soon as possible. I would suggest *now*."

"And Two-Moons?" asked Osrith, collecting himself.

"I don't think there is anything we can do for him now. Just before that spell, there was a battle cry: *Waeuu ne N'Iuk*. It means *Song of Morning* in Ebuouki; it was the name of Two-Moons' wife." Osrith began to interrupt, but Kassakan shook her head to silence him, and continued softly, "It is their custom to shout the name of a loved one at the time of death, so that they may prepare a welcome in the greylands. He would not yell out her name unless he knew his death was certain. From the power of that spell, I fear he was right. He would not want us to join him."

"Damn." Osrith looked at Symmlrey, then back at Kassakan. "Let's get her back to the boat, then. You'll have to tow us. We don't have any paddles left in one piece."

The lizard nodded her head and patted Osrith's shoulder before removing her hand. "The worst of the river should be behind us. I don't think it will be a problem."

Despite their haste, it took longer than they hoped to break camp. Both were too tired, drained, and sore to move quickly, and Two-Moons' death had sapped any vestige of enthusiasm they had left. Fear motivated them, but it was a poor substitute, and ineffective at pushing them beyond their limit. There was no fire to douse, no tracks to hide, only Symmlrey and their packs to carry, but still time dragged on.

Osrith had seen many men die, and many friends, but he had always moved on. For someone he had hardly known, the weight of Two-Moons' death was oddly heavy on his heart. The old man was the type that invited death. An idealist. They always went first, drawn by their convictions and their honor into situations less driven people would avoid. Greed killed a lot of men, and generally they deserved it, but the biggest killer of all was faith. That was sad, he supposed, for he knew the world could afford to lose mercenaries like him in any number, and ill afford the loss of even one such as Two-Moons. He had tried faith himself, once, and it hadn't worked out too well. At least he'd found with greed his expectations were low enough to avoid disappointment.

"Osrith." Kassakan's tone was one of warning, and Osrith snapped his full attention to her immediately. Her nostrils were sniffing the sulfurous breeze. "The cave-manti are close – and in great numbers."

"How close and how many?"

"I think we should run," she answered with untoward calm, shifting Symmlrey on her shoulders.

Without another word, the pair broke into a dead sprint, running dangerously close to the edge of their light as they scrambled toward the river. Osrith had no wish to meet with a group of cave-manti. The kin held them in a category of healthy respect and avoided the creatures wherever possible, due mostly to their ravenous and unselective appetites. Generally reclusive, every so often the manti would come out of their holes and feed on anything in their path, much like locusts on the surface world. The primary difference being that locusts weren't ten feet tall, carnivorous, and capable of ripping a human in half with their mandibles. The kin told stories of livestock stripped of their flesh in moments by a horde in the midst of feeding, and common belief held that kin children, in particular, were a favorite treat. Aside perhaps for the Great Traitor Isulraad, the manti were thus the most feared of kin bogeymen.

It wasn't long before they were clambering down the remains of an oversized dwelling toward the stretch of sloped marble where they had moored the boat. With the river so close, Osrith almost felt they might make it. Then he saw that the boat was gone. They were trapped. There were no tracks visible on the smooth stone, but Osrith imagined it didn't take many of the manti to throw it back into the river. He cursed himself for his laziness. His mind had argued that they should take the boat with them to camp, but his weary body had refused to listen.

"Either we jump in or we make a stand," said Osrith, setting down his packs and taking his axe from his belt. He put his back to the river and looked sidelong at his friend. "I don't think I'd survive either, but you just might. Take the stone and go to Dwynleigsh, old friend. If anybody's going to paw my gold dragons, I want it to be you. And you're the only one of us in any shape to swim for it."

"I don't want the stone." Kassakan put Symmlrey down. "And I don't want your gold. Maybe there's a third option. They might listen to reason."

"Yeah, they might. But do you speak overgrown insect?"

"No," she admitted with a strange intensity in her gemstone eyes, "but they might recognize the universal language."

Kassakan's hands wove through the air with dancer's grace, and the lips on her snout moved in a silent recital. Osrith didn't bother to inquire further. Though not a great lover of magic, he recognized it quickly enough, and he wasn't about to protest in this case. Whether the soft clicking sounds and faint movement in the shadows were real or his imagination, he could feel their eyes on him, and they weren't far away. Then, like water bursting through a dam, light erupted from Kassakan's globe fivefold, and he could see the sounds and movement were not his imagination after all.

There were at least fifty of them, closing ranks in a semicircle, cordoning them off from all escape except the river behind them. The cave-manti were, in fact, quite similar to their surface cousins, not accounting for size. They stood erect, but centaur-like, using their lower four extremities for locomotion while their 'arms' were free to wield tools or, in this instance, weapons. And these were not the crude stone implements Osrith had expected. They carried spears, halberds, and glaives of exquisite craftsmanship, long and graceful, with metal hammered out to gleam and swirl like water at their ends. He didn't recall any stories regarding their skill in weapon-smithing, and then he remembered where they were.

This place must be littered with old andu'ai weapons, he realized.

One of the manti broke ranks. It advanced slowly with glaive raised, its mandibles clicking and scraping together rapidly, accompanied by a series of chirps from its throat. The sound reminded him of Kassakan's language somewhat, but it lacked the flute-like tones that made hosskanae so beautiful. Still, he reasoned, they hadn't killed them outright. They were trying to communicate. This was a good sign. At least, he was pretty sure it was a good sign.

The creature came closer, and Osrith steeled himself as it drew within striking distance. It towered over him, looking down with its eerie multifaceted eyes, and he tried not to grimace too noticeably at its pungent odor. Its carapace was a shiny black, almost reflective, and adorned with what appeared to be the scalps of its unfortunate prey. Some system of counting coup, he guessed. Osrith assumed this must be their leader because it had many more of the desiccated souvenirs than the rest.

"Can you understand *anything* it's saying?" Osrith asked Kassakan from the corner of his mouth.

"Not a click," she responded. "But those scalps are mostly dringli, perhaps they've heard of the axiom about the enemy of my enemy?"

"*Mostly* dringli," Osrith said. "What are the rest?"

"Kin, human – one smells vaguely of the aulden."

"That's not very encouraging," he muttered, "but if they wanted us dead, it looks like they had the opportunity."

The insectoid bent its head down toward Osrith, jabbed at his axe with its shining glaive, and issued another burst of staccato clicks. Osrith responded with a frown and tightened his grip. The next swipe of the glaive made contact with the axe, pushing it down and away. Osrith ground his teeth. He knew what it wanted, but the thought wasn't appealing.

"Kassakan?" he hissed, hoping she had another option.

"I don't think we have much choice," she said.

Osrith didn't break eye contact with the mantis leader as he crouched slowly to the ancient pavement. He laid his axe gingerly on the marble, and stood. One of the manti's four legs stepped over the weapon protectively even as it waved its glaive in the direction of Kassakan's light. There was a pause, and then darkness absolute as she extinguished her colorless fire.

Not long after that, sticky insect fingers were grabbing at him, pulling him along through the blackness as they chittered back and forth. Osrith could think of a lot of reasons they were still alive, and he hoped most of them were wrong.

Chapter Eighteen

Hunting Games

CALVRAIGN leaned against the polished ivory rail at the edge of his balcony. The suns had climbed past their summit at midday, beginning their slow, steady fall toward dusk. The clouds had thinned, allowing him an unobstructed view of the city from his vantage point on the face of the north tower. The immensity of the capital was just a flickering of soft orange lights and slender fingers of stone that pierced scattered clouds, reaching boldly from the earth to scratch at the underbelly of heaven. The glint of their alabaster finish was visible even from this distance, reflected like a phantom city in the viewing crystal of the Ciel Maer. Even in his most vivid daydream, Calvraign had not guessed at the beauty of this ancient city. It was remarkable to him that this place was the pride of the Seven Tribes when his own kind were yet clad in furs and hiding in caves, dancing on the edge of civilization.

Now things were different. It was the upstart humans in the gleaming city, their crude architectural additions like blemishes on the face of a masterpiece, and the aulden lurked in the shadows of their forests in contempt of their unwelcome usurpers. Not that Calvraign had so much as glimpsed any fae creature in his short years, nor heard such hatred directly from their lips. As most humans, he had only heard tales of their doings, some amusing, some frightening, most simply unnerving. Brohan always spoke of them as aloof but not necessarily unkind, though most folk did not share his light opinion of the ancient race. Magicians and meddlers, changelings, thieves of babes in the night: this was the common lore, and even Brohan agreed there was some truth to such rumors. But as terrified as Calvraign was of the fae, he was fascinated by their wisdom and power, intrigued by their mysteries, and now, upon seeing their ancient citadel, awed by their grace.

And here was he, a peasant barbarian from the hills, standing on the little island that served as home to Guillaume's fortress retreat. Not simply a guest, an *honored* guest, with servants to feed and clothe him and a wardrobe of fine warm garments that in themselves represented more money than he had ever hoped to call his own. He ran his fingers over the soft silk lining of his overshirt and chuckled to himself in barely restrained excitement. He only wished his mother could see him now.

The festivities at his arrival caught him off guard, but in the past few days, with Brohan's help, he'd learned the ways of court and how to interact with the nobles. In truth, he found it little different from playing with a spoiled child: avoid saying or doing anything that could provoke a tantrum, and treat individuals with a deference and courtesy that they believe is due them alone. Brohan had been pleased with his quick progress, if not a little chagrined. The bard feared he had created some sort of politicking monster, apparently.

Calvraign took another deep breath of the fresh, cold air. He closed his eyes, afraid to open them again and discover himself asleep on the slopes with his flock nowhere to be seen, victim of a daydream. But when his eyes opened, he was still here, on his balcony, in his room, at King's Keep.

"Your pardon, sir."

Calvraign turned from the balcony to see his young servant bowing at the entrance to his quarters. Seth was his name, but Calvraign hadn't been able to get much more out of him. He was a timid sort, and the *barbarian bard's* eminent status with the king probably unnerved him. But Calvraign was determined to work on the lad. He had little need for a servant, but great need for a companion who was not in the slightest concerned with the give and take of the court.

"Yes, Seth?" he said, trying to set the boy at ease with a smile.

The servant merely looked puzzled. "The Master Bard Brohan Madrharigal requests the honor of your presence, sir," he said with due formality.

It was all Calvraign could do to keep from laughing outright, but he restrained himself to prevent Seth from scurrying for a hole to hide in. This was certainly a humorous change in circumstance.

"By all means," said Calvraign with a smile, "show in the master bard."

Seth proffered another short bow and opened the door to the chamber, admitting a mildly perturbed Brohan.

Calvraign was quick to press the point on his teacher and mentor. "Ah, thank you, Seth. You may leave us now."

With obvious relief, the boy retreated from the main chamber to the small larder at the east end of the suite.

Calvraign turned a quizzical eye to the bard, pursing his lips. "Ah, Master Madrharigal," he sniffed. "I'm honored, of course, but I have so little time. Be quick about it, if you will."

Brohan nodded. "Yes, of course." He sat on the edge of the teak settee in the middle of the small receiving room and continued with good-natured sarcasm, "I realize you have," he searched for a seemingly elusive word, "*something* to do. A man of your station."

"Yes, I'm sure of it," responded Calvraign, still enjoying the theater of the moment. "I'll have to have my servant remind me exactly what that is."

"Well then, perhaps my news should wait," deferred Brohan. "I don't wish to inconvenience your schedule."

"That, I think, should be my decision, Master Bard. Out with your news!" Calvraign mimicked an impatient gesture he had noticed the Archbishop Renarre was quite fond of. "I haven't time for your games!"

Brohan could no longer maintain a straight face, or even, by any real degree, his composure. He broke into a fit of boisterous laughter at Calvraign's spontaneous impersonation, sliding down onto the seat of the settee with a soft creak.

"I would wager if the archbishop ever saw that, excommunication would be your only reward!" he said, recovering himself. "I would be sparing in its performance."

"That is one man I don't wish to even *notice* me," Calvraign agreed, joining the sitting bard.

"Well, too late for that, I'm afraid," mused Brohan as he gained some semblance of himself. "From the moment you entered that chamber, he was on edge. Mayhap even before you entered."

"I don't understand," Calvraign confessed. "What could I possibly have done to get his attention?"

"It's nothing that *you've* done, lad," surmised Brohan. "It's what the king has done that got his attention."

"To be fair, that got everyone's attention. Even *ours*."

"Sure enough," yielded Brohan, "sure enough. In fact, that still has my attention."

"Have you had a chance to speak with the king in private yet?"

"No," said Brohan. "He hasn't been out of the royal apartments since the reception. Too much carousing for his advanced age. Word has reached me that he will wish a private audience with you when he is able."

"Isn't that unusual? Even beyond the other night?" asked Calvraign.

It was uncommon perhaps, but not rare, for a brave warrior to be knighted for valor in service of his lord. It was not even odd for that title to be hereditary, or in some occasions even for land to be granted. General Kiev Vae, after innumerable campaigns defending the westernmost borders, was granted that same land along with his House status. That, of course, was quite rare. House status was a hard thing to come by other than birthright. None since had been so promoted into the ranks of the peerage.

"Yes it is," confirmed Brohan. "Admittedly, King Guillaume has always been generous in his support and curious about you and your progress. That much is old news to me. But his public display of affection, his mood, quite out of the ordinary. I underestimated his regard for your father."

"I still don't understand what this has to do with the archbishop."

"Who can tell, with that one?" Brohan threw his arms up in the air to underscore his exasperation. "If I were to hazard a guess, which I quite enjoy doing with politics – in private, of course – I would say he disapproves of your pagan upbringing. Not known for their devoutness to Illuné, the Cythe. He prefers keeping honors like this, how shall I say, *in the family.* Add to that the fact that Agrylon shares the king's enthusiasm, and he has every reason to hate you."

"*Hate* me?" croaked Calvraign, his eyes a-bulge in their sockets.

"Aye," said Brohan, "there is nothing on which they agree except their mutual hatred. If you are favored by one, you will be despised by the other."

"But he's a *priest!*"

"Oh, technically, yes," dismissed Brohan with a frown. "But at this point his duties regarding the Church are mostly political. Collecting tithes, persecuting heretics, blackmailing nobles, plotting to discredit his rivals, increasing his holdings and his influence on the king. Not to mention gathering his own private army of the Knights Lancer. There's very little proselytizing in his position anymore."

"But, that's just… *awful!*"

"Oh yes, but at this point all the branches of the Church are the same. Kazdann, Illuné, Irdik, it doesn't matter. Faith is a dying commodity."

"Artygalle…?"

Brohan smiled, patting Calvraign's shoulder in fatherly comfort, "Aye, Sir Artygalle is a good man. He has more genuine piety in his left foot than most of the court. Aside from a few like him, it's all lip service, I'm afraid."

"Even the king?" asked Calvraign, his hope dangling on the end of his tongue.

The bard shook his head. "Maybe once, long ago."

This made absolutely no sense to Calvraign. "Then *why* in the great wide world is the Church so powerful?"

"Because it's an institution now, boy – and *institutions* are powerful." He stood rather suddenly then, and stretched. "But this is neither here nor there. You've distracted me from my purpose, Cal. We have an invitation to accept!"

"An invitation?"

"Aye," said Brohan in a lowered voice, raising his eyebrows with a smile. "The Lady Aeolil has extended her cordial wish to have us join her and Prince Hiruld this afternoon for a ride."

Lady Aeolil, Calvraign groaned mentally, not thinking twice about the presence of the crown prince. Of course, it wasn't Hiruld he couldn't stop staring at. And, if it wasn't bad enough that he knew he was helpless in the throes of a desperate crush, having Brohan to delight in his misery only made matters worse.

"I look forward to it!" Calvraign lied with enthusiasm. He wasn't going to make this any easier for Brohan than it had to be.

&

Considering the ferocity of the winter that year in Providayne, the weather was more-or-less pleasant for the crown prince's riding party. The sky was clear and the suns bright, and the wind had quieted to a murmuring breeze. It was still cold, by all accounts, but beneath the layers of fur and cloth that the nobles had wrapped themselves in, it was comfortable enough for an afternoon ride.

Calvraign was no longer so intimidated by the men and women of title around him. They had accepted him into their own, pleasantly if not enthusiastically, and he found their ways pretentious but not unbearable. Brohan had helped the groom choose the right steed for Calvraign, who had only ridden once before in his life. She was an older mare, called Smoke for her coloring, with an even temperament but a grand look about her. In her day, she had been the groomsman's pride, and was clearly still his favorite in the ways that counted. She would shift this way or that with but the lightest touch on the reigns and never bent to search for a nibble while a rider was on her back. Neither Calvraign nor Brohan wanted him upon a mount that would appear any less stately than the rest of the party.

Shortly after this business was finished, however, Brohan drifted away toward Aeolil. Calvraign was about to reluctantly follow when he was approached by Calamyr Vespurial, perhaps the last person of the lively throng he had expected to greet him, astride a powerful roan gelding. Calamyr had the pale skin tone common to the aristocracy, and flashing blue eyes. His light blond hair was coifed about the nape of his neck, falling just over the collar of his thick winter garments. His doublet and cape were of forest green, trimmed in purest gold and touched with a prismatic glimmer of precious stones. A pendant hung about his neck in the shape of a diving eagle with outstretched claws.

"Good greetings to you, Sir Calvraign." His accent was as rich as his raiment. "I hope I am not intruding. If you would allow me, it would be my pleasure to accompany you this day. I fear my good name slightly tarnished by my unseemly behavior the other night."

Calvraign tried not to be too impressed with his casual eloquence and easy manner. Brohan had warned him that acting like a commoner would have him treated as such. "It was I who acted the buffoon, milord," replied Calvraign. "You should have no worries – but I would welcome your company."

"Excellent. A fresh start then," said Calamyr with a one-sided grin as his horse fell alongside Smoke. "Today will not be a good day for hawk or hunt – but for conversation, I think, it will do nicely."

The riding party was clattering through the bridge gate-house now, with a detachment of the royal guard and various retainers at either end and each side of the main group. The ponderous main gate was already open, and their way lay clear to the bridge that spanned the gap between Dwynleigsh and King's Keep over the Ciel Maer. The grey support columns that sank into the frosted lake were granite, as was most of the bridge itself, but some portions were of wood, ready to be torched into ash in the event of siege. No one had ever attempted such a siege, to Calvraign's knowledge, either by land or blockade, and he doubted very much if anyone ever would. In total, the bridge was the better part of an Imperial league in length. If he were a general, he would take the city and leave the king on his little island. Capturing a king was merely symbolic if all his holdings were in your thrall.

They rode on, engaged mostly in small talk, and to his surprise, Calvraign found Calamyr quite pleasant. Calvraign could sense his confidence like a static charge between them, reminding him that whatever character he might pretend to have, Calamyr already possessed by virtue of his high birth and noble upbringing. He wore a long sword at his side, sheathed in a jeweled scabbard and secured with a golden peace knot.

Calvraign felt the tug of the bare leather scabbard that held his father's sword and looked back across the water to hide his envy.

Calamyr told him of the wars, and his part in them, with somewhere between Brohan's theatrics and Artygalle's thoughtful reserve. As an heir to the vast House Vespurial, he had been granted his spurs as a right of heredity. As a captain in the cavalry, that right had been tested and proved in the heat and blood of battle. He was not much older than Calvraign, perhaps two or three years, but already he had felled a score of enemy knights and was respected by his peers in matters of war.

The crossing seemed to take no time at all, and Calvraign was so engrossed in Calamyr's recitation that he hardly noticed when they passed into the bustle and hum of Dwynleigsh itself through the Harbor Gate. There were a few ships hauled into dry dock for the length of winter, and even one Maeziir boat, unwilling to allow the dangers of the season to hinder their all-important commerce, putting sail into the ice-strewn lake. The docks themselves were walled off by several defensive partitions, the first jutting from the lake to enclose the small inner harbor, the second flush with the shore line, creating a sort of bailey between the lake wall and the city wall proper. Fishermen sat in small lean-tos on the thicker ice in the shallows closer to shore, their lines disappearing in the rough holes they cut in the lake's surface. All before them made way for the entourage, baring their heads and bowing as their crown prince made his way through their midst.

When Calvraign finally had the presence of mind to look about him, they were well within the city walls, riding down the wide main thoroughfare and almost to the crossroads in the center of the lower city. From there they would head to the West Gate and out into the country for their outing. The smells of roasted nuts, fried apples and fresh baked bread wafted from the vendors and the bakeries as they passed. Even in the cold of winter, the city was a hive of activity. Merchants and hucksters sold everything from foodstuffs to textiles, linens, jewelry, and the odd 'ancient fae trinket' or two.

Even more impressive than the variety of goods was the diversity of people. There were dozens and dozens of dusky-skinned Maeziir, mostly wealthy merchants and bankers; a scattering of the fairer folk of the Southlands, enjoying the peace of the traditional winter truce; and more than a few tall, bearded sailors bellowing and singing of some foreign shore. There were so many people in the crowds that soon individual faces melted away into a whirlpool of shifting expression, color and noise. Calvraign almost felt panic sneak in on his excitement as he tried to estimate how many times Craignuuwn and all its folk could fit inside this massive city. Then, piercing the crowds in a shimmering rainbow of swirling cloth, a small party of men made their way just ahead of them and off into Argys Yard. Their skin glinted like burnished copper in the sun. Their gait was steady and purposeful, even through the jostling of the crowd, and their bearing straight and regal.

Calvraign sifted through lessons in his mind even as they drifted out of sight. "Ishti'in?" he said, excited and uncertain, touching Calamyr's sleeve and pointing at the disappearing figures. "They were Ishti'in!" he said again, but this time with certainty.

Calamyr glanced and shrugged. "Yes, a delegation of some sort has been sent by their king, or *padrah*, or whatever it is they call him." He watched the milling crowd fill the empty spaces left by the Ishti'in like tide pools, as unconcerned and uninterested in their passing as he himself seemed. "The world is full of barbarians, Calvraign, and you'll see all sorts here. Soon enough, you won't even notice them."

Calvraign was still sensitive about the ease with which the wellborn bandied about that term, but with a look at Calamyr's face he realized no inference to his own heritage was intended, so he let the matter drop. But Gods Above, the last thing he wanted was *not* to notice them. The Ishti'in were from a land so far west that it didn't even appear on most maps. And these men he'd seen for but an instant were more vivid and real and mysterious than even his wildest fantasies had been. There were no people on Rahn so exotic or mysterious, save perhaps the Kaojinn. He wondered if Brohan had seen them.

"Still, 'tis a sight, this city, even for me," continued Calamyr. "You never *quite* become accustomed to it."

"Aye," sighed Calvraign, as they passed beneath a canopy of poplar and elm, green as if in the gay spring of Birthingmoon. Ahead of them, an archway flanked by two eagle-headed marble guardians loomed over the crossroads. "Even the stories don't do it justice. It's hard to understand why the aulden deserted such a work of beauty."

Calamyr placed a hand on the boy's shoulder, his grip hard but not painful. "They abandoned it because we *took* it from them, Calvraign. Surely Master Madrharigal taught you as much. Regardless, building a city that pleases the eye alone is of little worth to its occupants. Strength is more valuable than beauty. That is why we have added our own human touch, so we don't lose it as did they. Dwynleigsh is not likely to fall a second time."

Calvraign was slow to respond. In matters of history, he was inclined to believe the master bard over the nobleman, but his innate sense of courtesy made disputing him difficult. "*History always by the victor is writ,*" he quoted from Kiev Vae's *Ethics And War*.

Calamyr stopped short his own reply and smiled. He was not one to miss a diplomatic response. He nodded his approval of the boy's quick aplomb. "Well said, Sir Calvraign," he praised with discernible honesty.

"If you are as quick with a blade as you are in conversation, I'm glad our first encounter did not color our friendship."

Calvraign couldn't help but grin at the memory of that awkward attempt at honor. Looking back now, he could think of several methods wherein the same result could have been accomplished. Methods that did not involve knocking over two of the most important young lords at court. "Yes," he agreed aloud, but then, with a note of resignation, "A pity Lord Garath's pride is so great."

Calamyr rolled his eyes. "*Garath,*" he said in exasperation. "He acts a man half his age. Thank the bright moon he's not the heir. Ezriel has a head for it, but not poor Garath. His temper is hot as the hells and less forgiving. Don't worry yourself over the matter. Eventually I'll dissuade him from his aloofness, if the king doesn't first, and you'll see he's not so bad after all."

Calvraign shrugged. "All in time, I suppose."

Presently they were turning westward, and the smells of food were washed away by the thick scent of hot metal, sulfur and ozone. They passed through Smithy's Row without speaking, for the clamor of mallets pounding on steel drowned out any attempt. Business was always good for the smiths at tourney festivals, for aside from war, this was the venue for much of their trade. It was said that at the Winter Festival there were arms enough to put steel in the hands of every man, woman and child of Dwynleigsh. After seeing the gleam of countless blades as they passed, Calvraign no longer dismissed this as hyperbole.

Just as they drew near one of the city's great parks, now packed with merchants, their wares, and the tents of those with no luck at other accommodation, Calamyr tapped his arm. "Over there," he said, indicating a relatively small area devoid of activity. A large canvas was secured over what Calvraign guessed to be a statue. "This is the monument King Guillaume commissioned in honor of his son, Vingeaux. He will unveil it at the ceremony where he names the Winter Champion."

"Did you know him?"

"Yes, though not well. He would have made a good king. Bad piece of luck, that. We searched for the back-stabbing Macc whoreson who felled him for three weeks, but found not a trace." Calamyr sighed, shaking his head with a solemn sadness. "A foul way to die," he said. "He deserved better."

Calvraign was somewhat ashamed of his curiosity, but he couldn't help but pursue the matter. Scant news of the prince's death had reached Craignuuwn. "What do you mean? Was he dealt dishonor?"

Calamyr looked at him out of the corner of his eye. "Aye, he was dealt dishonor. We were on patrol just south of Paerytigel, and he strayed too far afield from the rest of us. Always in the van was Vingeaux, he and Alain and Grumwyr. An arrow found his horse from ambush, and trapped him under his mount. He was run through by some Calahyr dog before Alain could turn about in his saddle, and they feathered him next. If Bellivue hadn't charged in when he did, both their heads would be on some skull-bearer's lance in Callah Tur. The murderer had the gall to salute our ranks with his befouled blade before he fled." He scowled with deep revulsion. "The thing had been greased with a most noisome poison. The physics had no other means to describe the state of my good prince's body."

Calvraign felt his stomach tighten, partly in sympathy for the dead, and partly because he could still see, silhouetted against the sky by a flash of lightning, the shadowy knight on a hill, and the same again scant days ago at the North Gate. He shuddered, and the skin tingled and rose up in gooseflesh on his arms and neck. He could almost feel a voice whispering a cold breath of warning in his ear.

Just the wind, he told himself. *It's just the wind.* But he couldn't help noticing that the canvas didn't so much as stir in the midday air as they rode past the park and on to the West Gate beyond.

༄

King Guillaume watched the procession of young lords and ladies file through the Bridge House Gate from his window, his brown-speckled hand running through the coarse silver-grey of his unshaven face. There was a slight tremor in those hands this day, not from his age or infirmity but from the sleeplessness brought on by his dark memories, and dreams that were darker still. Images still danced in his thoughts of the shadow man with his pale, unforgiving face.

"Remember our bargain, my king."

Guillaume's lower lip trembled. Worse than simply being a fool was realizing it with every waking moment.

"Your son is mine."

"What's to be done, Agrylon?" he sobbed, leaving the window at his back. Unkingly tears spattered down the wrinkled cheeks of the face that not many days before had been so brightened by cheer. "Tell me what to do, old friend."

The wizard sat in the corner, his eyes poking out of the darkness like small jewels limned in gold. "There's naught to be done but what's been done already. Your worry now is more guilt than reason."

"Perhaps," whispered the king. "But then why does *he* pay me visitation again?"

"To serve as a reminder of your accord. I think you are in no danger, save for what you subject yourself in these sleepless nights and useless admonitions."

"Myself?" the king hissed, the tears now hot with rage. "You think it is for my *own* saggy skin I fear? You wretched creature! He has already taken my dear Vingeaux. I don't wish to surrender any more sons to his hand."

Agrylon was silent.

Guillaume paced his finely appointed bedchamber, his eyes oblivious to the riches surrounding him. His bare feet made no noise as they sank into the thick carpet, his ankle-length cotton nightshirt rustling softly against the skin of his legs. His hand continued to fidget in his whiskers, tugging and twisting at the hairs as if to wring an answer from them. He stopped in front of his advisor, looking down at him with an almost pleading cast to his weary face.

"Perhaps the time has come." His voice was expectant but uncertain.

"No," said Agrylon.

"But if *this* is what upsets him...?"

"I have told you before, I do not advise such forthrightness. It would be best if you kept your peace, for now. There will be time enough for all that later. Much later."

Guillaume pursed his lips, searching for a reply, but he could find none among his restless, worried thoughts. He finally nodded, shuffling over to his bed.

"Yes, later," he mumbled absently. "Later."

The king crawled under his expansive and elaborate quilt. His moistened eyes stared with a vacant, distant look at the carving of dragons and gryphons that crawled up his bedposts to the canopy above his head. Agrylon remained in the darkness, watching with unblinking eyes as Guillaume hovered on the verge of a fitful sleep.

"Better too late than too soon," said the wizard in his soft voice that was not quite a whisper. A log hissed and popped in the fireplace, spitting an ember out past the hearth to smolder listlessly on the edge of the carpet.

Guillaume blinked, then closed his eyes under the weight of sleep too long denied. His breath was ragged and unsure of itself, but it was more peace than he had known for days, regardless.

Aeolil looked behind her once more at the odd pairing of Calvraign and Calamyr. She kept the glance short so that it wouldn't be noticed by her gossipy companions. The last thing she wanted to start was yet another rumor about her *wayward affections*. The simple fact of the matter was that she felt a debt was owed the young knight at Vespurial's side, and had wanted a chance to express her thanks. Hiruld had been anxious to meet him too, whether of his own will or his father's she didn't know, and she thought Brohan might just be embarrassed about his pupil's absence from the prince's company. It was hard to tell from his face, or his voice, or even his manner. But she felt, somehow, that he was as uncomfortable as she with the situation.

"Heigh-ho!" yelled Hiruld as the wolfhounds began barking and sprinting ahead of them.

Fortunately, the prince didn't feel in the least snubbed, so intent was he on this lackluster hunt. Hiruld shot off at a full gallop, still in the company of his guard, wet clumps of snow flying out behind his horse as he waved his right hand in the air beside his head. They hadn't found so much as a stray hare this day, for which she was grateful in a way. In the Western Marches you hunted to eat, not to make sport, and she found little joy in it – especially this sort of hunt, all dogs and horses and running about to and fro. She absently scratched at her left wrist, where her hawk Swiftwing would perch on a *real* hunt.

"Well, off he goes," said Brohan. "Though I dare say he won't catch a cold today with the dogs running so close to two score horse. Everything this side of the woods went to ground half an hour ago."

"I doubt he much cares, really," said Aeolil. "As long as it serves to keep him out of the keep for the day." She checked herself from looking behind them once more, disguising the motion with a shrug.

"He'll be all right," comforted Brohan, not so easily fooled. "I was worried at first, too, but he's really quite capable. And Calamyr's not such a terribly bad sort."

Aeolil was glad he had brought it up. She didn't want to appear fussy or jealous or any of the other emotions men attributed to women if they showed concern. But concerned she was. "He's not a *bad* sort, necessarily," she admitted, "but he certainly doesn't do anything without purpose. The king has put your young friend in the midst of a hornet's nest, I'm afraid. Everyone is all atwitter about His Majesty's new favorite."

Brohan turned in his saddle and cocked an eyebrow at her. "He's not as young as all that, milady! Why, I believe he is your own age, if I'm not mistaken, within a year or two."

Aeolil flushed. "Yes, of course, but you take my meaning."

"Ah, yes," said the bard, "I do at that. And I hope I don't misread you, either, if I think you don't necessarily share his, um, *interest*, let's call it, which you have certainly noticed. I'm afraid his eyes sometimes betray his will." He tossed his hands in the air. "What can one expect, really? But still, the lad did you a service, and you wish to see that he is assured of your thanks without any misunderstandings. Yes?"

"Said truer than my own words, Master Bard. I don't wish to do him injury, yet neither-"

"Peace, milady, and have no worries. He fancies you, yes, but look at him. Too shy yet with women to take liberty *or* offense. I would hate to think he'd lose so valuable a friend for fear of misunderstanding or gossip."

"Thank you," she said with a great breath. "You have set me at ease."

"Hmm, well, that's a dangerous place to be," he said with a grin. "Perhaps you should take a step back. But since I have remained in your good graces, I would be obliged if you could grant me a small favor."

"Master Madrharigal, it would be my pleasure! Aside from your kindness before the feast, I feel I owe you for the privilege of your company."

"It's not for me, you understand," he began, with the faintest trace of unease, "but the good knight who made the journey with us from the north, Sir Artygalle of Tiriel. He lost his horse to the winter, crossing the mountains, and yet he is commanded by his liege to joust in the tourney. I would gladly reimburse you from my own chest, if you could see your way to providing him a mount from your stables. He saved Calvraign's life, and I feel I owe him the best."

Aeolil was quiet for a moment. She loved her horses better than she cared for most people, and life as a steed in battle was not an easy one. Even on loan for one tourney there were any number of ways a horse could be hurt, maimed or even killed. With the lists already closed and most of the premium horse flesh already accounted for, Aeolil could see the knight would be hard pressed to find a suitable steed. She knew it hadn't been easy for Brohan to ask for this, but that knowledge didn't make it any easier for her to answer.

"Yes, of course," she said, with as little reluctance as she could manage. "But let me meet him first. It would do me well to know what kind of person he is. I hope you don't think me ungrateful."

"Not at all, milady. But rest assured, if I was not certain of his character, I would not even make such a request. Meanwhile, our private chat appears to be over. Here thunders your prince."

Normally, Aeolil would have taken offense at the assumptions of such a remark, but from Brohan, she knew it to be only jest, and so responded with a chagrined smile. And then Hiruld was upon them, his face beaten red by the cold and his eyes watery from his hard ride. He was smiling as if he'd returned with the most spectacular prize, and yet was empty-handed for all his enthusiasm. He was a man with more heart for the chase than the kill. His horse snorted wearily.

"No luck, My Prince?" said Brohan in good cheer.

"Alas, no. All things with any sense have long since found shelter from this cold." Hiruld looked to the sky and the encroaching gloom of clouds from the west. "As should we, I suppose, though I hate to be the sensible one."

"Yes, I fear we've already played out our welcome with the daylight. Only another hour or so left," mentioned Aeolil with her own shrewd look to the sky. "Should we signal retirement?"

Hiruld nodded to his herald. "Sound the retreat, good Bellivue. We're off for home now."

The knight nodded. "As you wish, My Prince," he said, and blew three short followed by one long tone. The hunt slowed its less than hurried pace and turned, most with relief but a few with genuine disappointment, and headed back toward the awakening lights of Dwynleigsh.

Hiruld, with nothing to distract him on the return journey, began immediately to look about him. "Now where has that young Cythe knight got to all of the sudden? I was quite looking forward to making his better acquaintance."

"The young Lord Calamyr has been monopolizing him all day, I'm afraid," said Brohan. "No doubt filling his head with stories of his prowess – and maybe even a war story or two."

Hiruld chuckled. "You are irrepressible, Master Bard. I quite like that. But see here – Bells, go fetch them to me at once. I'll not let them escape my company the whole of the day."

"As you wish, My Prince," answered his herald, and rode off immediately to the oblivious young men, not more than a hundred feet away.

Aeolil watched Bellivue as he hailed them. He gave the impression of a humble attendant, but he was a powerful and experienced knight in his own right, and geas-bound to protect the life of the crown prince, even at the expense of his own. Vingeaux's herald, Alain, had met that bloody obligation in the end, as Bellivue was full aware. It was Bells that saved their corpses from the dark knight and his skull-bearers.

After a brief exchange, all three rode back at a canter.

"My Prince," said Calamyr with a bow, and then nodded in the direction of the Lady Vae and Brohan. Calvraign made his best approximation of Calamyr's introduction but avoided meeting Aeolil's eyes.

"Well met, both of you," Hiruld said. "I hope we haven't interrupted any great dissertations?"

"No, Sire," Calamyr answered. "Young Sir Calvraign was just finishing his lecture concerning politics. Very interesting, I must say. Master Madrharigal was busy this last ten-year."

The prince cocked his head. "Oh, and what insights did you provide for Lord Calamyr from your vantage point in the Crehr?"

"Nothing worth mention, Sire," mumbled Calvraign with an afflicted scowl at Calamyr.

"Nonsense," scoffed Calamyr. "He's feeling shy. I'll paraphrase him, with your permission?"

Hiruld waved him on.

"He thinks the peers bicker too much and that we've driven the king to distraction and despair. He further asserts that this is the cause of the lingering conflict in the south, and that we are, oh how did he put it – *leasing the war from the Maccs with our own blood as the tithe*. Quite poetic."

Hiruld turned slowly toward Calvraign, who was holding his chin up in defense of his words. A slow smile crept across the prince's face, and he reached out to punch Calvraign on the shoulder with his fist. "Straight words, sir knight, straight as an arrow. And don't be all in a piss with Calamyr. He knows my thoughts on such matters, even if he would disagree with us. He did no betrayal to you."

"No, Sire," replied Calvraign, mustering his good humor, "but he certainly enjoyed the sport of it."

"That I did!" confessed Vespurial with conviction. "A bastard I may sometimes be, but a liar am I never."

Aeolil watched as the three of them continued, testing each other's boundaries and pulling each other's strings, as men often seemed to enjoy. And, as far as she was concerned, acting like exceptionally loud idiots. She was content to ride behind the three jovial men and chat quietly with Brohan. It was refreshing to speak with a man who had no interest in impressing or wooing her. The conversation was never strained or halted, even when the subject matter drifted to areas deemed unsuitable for women. The master bard didn't seem to care, or to condescend, and this she found best of all his traits.

They both ceased worrying over Calvraign after the first hour of their ride home had passed them by. It was clear that Hiruld liked his open manner and probity. Aeolil noted the glances the prince exchanged with Calamyr behind the Cythe's back that showed his surprise and his affection with a smile, a nod and a wink. She felt the relief come over her like a strong draught of wine, washing away the tightness in her neck and her belly and allowing her to truly enjoy the rest of the outing. She hoped Brohan had found similar comfort in the approval of the crown prince for his apprentice, but he made no outward sign one way or the other.

As they broke through the thin veil of trees that shielded the blushing lights of Dwynleigsh like the shy rosy cheeks of a young bride, Aeolil was satisfied that the day had gone well after all.

Seth Briggin let out a great breath of air as he laid down his oversized bundle on the small larder table. He had come away with his needed supplies, but at the expense of Dar's long lasting enmity. He had no regrets, however. Keeping his new master happy was much more important to him than the esteem of the chief cook's assistant, even if that meant his own allotment of bread and meat might dwindle in quality as a result.

Seth unpacked his parcels and put the items away with care, making sure they were snugly wrapped in their protective cheesecloth. He had worked hard to gain the trust of the castellan for just such a posting as this, and he would not let a cranky kitchen despot rob him of his glory. When Burton had assigned him the duties of Sir Calvraign's personal attendant, it had been a welcome if not tremendous honor. But, since that first night, things had changed. Seth was no longer entrusted merely with picking up after some uncouth hill man whom it pleased the king to treat well; now he was attending a knight whom it was said the king favored above all but his own family. He had overheard Burton explaining to Sir Calvraign that there had been a mistake and that a new servant would be found immediately, one with more experience and standing as suited his position, but the offer had been flatly denied.

"Nonsense, he's the best servant I've ever had!" Calvraign had said. "Don't you agree, Master Madrharigal?"

And the King's Bard had indeed agreed, and the castellan had slunk out of the room with the grace of a scolded dog begging for scraps at the table. Later, Burton had made it clear that any complaints would be taken out of his tender skin with the help of a willow switch, with interest, and it would be the end of his days in the Keep. Seth didn't want to make any mistakes, not because of the punishment he would surely receive, but because he had always been taught to repay kindness shown with twofold kindness in return.

He certainly *would be* the best servant Sir Calvraign ever had!

Once the much coveted and dearly procured pastries were safely away in the cupboards, Seth turned his attention to the wine rack. Three half-gallon flagons sat upturned and clean beneath the wooden casket of fine Inzirii wine he had gotten from the king's cellar. All the best vintage was kept there, and he was sure to double check the wax seal about the spigot to ensure there'd been no unwelcome samplings. The vintner's purplish smear was unbroken, and with a satisfied smile, Seth left the closet-sized larder and began his inch-by-inch inspection of the quarters proper.

Seth picked over the furnishings piece by piece, his young eyes squinting in a solemn appraisal of their dust-chaste surfaces. He was armed with a rag soaked in berrin seed oil, which struck out at any lingering filth with a lightning-fast swipe of his arms. Its pleasant aroma filled the room as he made slow and careful progress into the bedchambers. The light outside the window was dim from the last retreating streaks of daylight, and he knew the hunt would be returning soon. Perhaps they would feast in the hall and drink until dawn, in which case his efforts here would likely go unnoticed; or maybe Sir Calvraign would retire here in the company of some lords or knights for a late dinner and song from the master bard.

Seth found himself over-attending the wardrobe with his cloth and left it with one more dutiful swipe to make a final examination of the bedding. The bedclothes were tucked tightly beneath the mattress, and the thick, colorful quilt that waited at the foot of the bed smelled fresh and clean with a faint hint of lavender. He fluffed the down pillows with an expert touch and went to put a log on the waning fire. Another storm was blowing in, and no doubt even a man of Calvraign's hardened experience would appreciate a warm chamber.

Seth sat in the rocking chair that faced the hearth with the poker resting on his lap, watching carefully to see that the new wood took flame. Sergeant Faeldor had told him all about the mysterious Calvraign and his many adventures, which were apparently already legend in the wild hill lands. It was hard at first to reconcile the image of the bloody warrior with Calvraign's seeming innocence and lighthearted manner, but Faeldor had explained that this was normal for the heroes of the Cythe, who fought under sway of a madness brought about by old spirits and pagan gods long forgotten in civilized lands.

"Just see you don't fire his wrath, lad," the grizzled guardsman had warned over his half empty wine skin. *"When his aspect's upon him, his eyes'll bulge out his head, and he'll froth at his mouth like a mad dog – and he won't stop a' killin' until his bloodlust is passed over him. Killed his first hundred men by the time he was half your age, he did!"*

Seth found he had been holding his breath at the memory. It certainly explained why the king saw fit to keep him in light spirits with the master bard's constant company.

The fire had taken to the log, licking up the sides in delight. He sighed, knowing he should retire to his small cot of a bed in his modest adjoining room to rest until he was needed. But the warmth of the happy fire penetrated his tired bones with gentle insistence, urging him to stay awhile by its side. He knew he shouldn't, but his own arguments were too imprecise to defy the quiet reasoning of the flames and the chair and his body's tired aches.

A click later, Seth Briggin slept in an exhausted sort of peace, telling himself even as he drifted off that it would just be for a moment.

Chapter Nineteen

Prey at Bedtime

CALVRAIGN had thought that, with the unassuming help of the ever-careful Smoke, the ride itself had been quite enjoyable. As the hooves of their mounts once again scrabbled on the cobblestones of Dwynleigsh, however, he realized that this was no longer true. He now had a very clear and painful sensation to give proper definition to the term *saddle sore*, which until now had only provided color to Brohan's stories of long and punishing rides. His buttocks were tender, his legs cramped and tired, and his lower back was tense and tight about his spine. He looked at the far-away shadow of King's Keep and tried to remember how long it had taken them to navigate the city earlier that day. There was still an active bustle around him, but now he took little notice, his curiosity enervated by his discomfort.

Hiruld and the others had drifted off slightly ahead of him, and he was thankful they were not here to see his changed mood. He felt that a good impression had been made, and he had no wish to undo his luck at this point. As if in spite of his relief, he heard the rhythmic clop of a horse fall in to his right. He steeled himself to make a good show of it. The ride would be done and he alone in his warm, soft bed soon enough.

Calvraign looked over to see Lady Aeolil riding primly at his side. With an effort, he kept from looking away, and did a fair job of calming his blush. He was thankful she was well covered for the wintry outing, sparing him the energy needed to keep his willful eyes from wandering.

"I was hoping to have the chance to thank you in person for your courtesy, Sir Calvraign," she remarked with a broad smile. "Better late than not at all, I suppose."

He reddened now, and was thankful for the excuse. "No need, milady. Brohan was more help than me, I think."

"Well, accept my good will anyway," she said, and Calvraign felt himself drawn in to the clearness of her deep blue gaze. "I insist on that. Anything less would be bad manners, and even the king's favorite must mind his manners."

"Yes, of course," he said quickly, then with a conscious effort to at least appear in control of himself, he added, "At your service, milady."

"Well, you have already learned to submit to my indomitable will. Brohan does not exaggerate – you are a quick study."

Calvraign grinned, pleased with the passing remark of Brohan's approval, and felt himself relaxing slowly into the conversation. It really wasn't too much different from speaking with Brohan or Calamyr, save that he had never admired the balance of their faces quite so much, been drawn into the beauty and clearness of their eyes, or wondered at the fullness of their red lips. He felt the tension threatening to return and decided perhaps this chain of thought was the root of the problem. He looked about for something to distract himself.

The fluttering pennants that flew from the roof timbers of Saint Kaissus Field caught his eye. "Who will be your champion for the tourney?"

Aeolil raised her eyebrows. "*My* champion?" she said innocently.

The blush on his cheeks grew darker. "I meant for House Vae," he said. "Do you have a personal champion as well?"

"I should hope I have no reason for one," she answered, "but the evening is young, and there are any number of ways one's honor can be tarnished."

Calvraign was relieved when she smiled, then, but slightly unsettled. He didn't remember there being many sarcastic noblewomen in the great stories and legends on which he'd been weaned. He had been intimidated enough by her beauty, now he found himself equally cowed by her wit.

"As for House Vae," she continued a moment later, "one of my personal entourage will be our champion." She pointed to one of the stern-faced sentries riding in the rear guard. "Right there, just to the left of Captal Malade, with the beard, that's Sir Chadwick. He's fair enough with a lance, but when it comes down to blades, I'm afraid he'll be rather outmatched by the likes of Grumwyr or even your new friend Calamyr."

Calvraign tried not to stare too long at the knight. He wasn't as large as Bleys – and he certainly remembered Bleys – and though his face was serious, it lacked a certain hardness such as the captal's possessed. "Why doesn't Bleys, um, Sir Malade, fight as champion?"

Aeolil rolled her eyes and shook her head. "He's convinced he must live in my shadow, I'm afraid. He thinks the moment he leaves my side I'll be murdered or kidnapped."

"Who would murder *you*?" Calvraign blurted out before he could stop himself. He felt his pulse hot in his ears again. "I mean, what possible reason…?"

Calvraign saw that her expression had changed. She was still amused, and he felt he could credit himself with that, unfortunately, but the shallowness of her smile hinted at melancholy. "My father and my brother were killed when I was younger," she explained, her voice still mild. "Bleys thinks I'm still in danger. He's wrong, of course, but I can't convince him otherwise."

"I'm sorry," Calvraign said, and for once had no difficulty in meeting her eyes.

"I know you understand," she replied, "having lost your own father, I mean. Thank you."

They were both quiet as they continued through the city, lost in their own thoughts and the continuing drumbeat of horse's hooves. The Harbor Gate loomed ahead, though still deceptively distant, when Calvraign finally spoke again.

"Does he blame himself?"

Aeolil looked puzzled for a moment, "Oh, you mean Bleys?" she said with a shake of her head. "No, not *himself*, though he's generous enough with it. He wasn't there, though I don't think it would have mattered. That was someone else, and he left us shortly after. It was a hard thing to bear."

"You must have been angry," Calvraign said. "I was too young when they brought my father's sword home to really understand. But since then, it's hard for me not to be angry."

"At first, yes," she confessed, "but not as much now. My mother needs me more than I need to be angry. And I can't change it, no matter how mad I get, so it seems a waste. Not that I don't still miss them. I'll always miss them, but I can't live for them anymore."

"I understand," said Calvraign, who was quite surprised that he did. Perhaps if nothing else, loss was blind to class or rank.

"I thought you might," she said, and her smile returned for only an instant before her face dried up into a more serious cast. "I think the king's favor is colored by such thoughts. And don't misunderstand me, I mean no disrespect to your father's memory or his deeds, but the king's affections seem oddly intense."

"What do you mean?" Calvraign wasn't sure if he was offended or not, but he wanted to hear more. He was still curious about the extent of his esteem in the king's eyes.

"You are without a father, and he is without one son – and for the former, he may also bear some pang of guilt. Perhaps he feels that if he adopts you as a sort of honorary son, you may fill the void in his heart left by Vingeaux's sad passing, and maybe he, likewise, might fill the empty spaces in your heart. At least, that is my thinking."

Calvraign thought about that for a moment. It did make a certain sort of sense. Brohan always mentioned that the king was interested in his progress and concerned for his welfare, so it was not implausible that it might become something more in the light of such a grievous absence.

"I hadn't thought of it that way," he admitted, "but you may be right."

"I don't like unsolved puzzles. It's one of my weaknesses."

"Not at all." Calvraign dismissed her self-deprecation with a vigorous shake of his head. He looked up to see the Harbor Gate only a stone's throw distant, and found himself wishing the day were not yet at a close. His saddle sores seemed a small inconvenience now, compared with the prospect of parting her company. He felt like more of a simpleton than ever before for avoiding her all day.

As they rode the final stretch across the bridge engaged in pleasant but less weighty talk, Calvraign found himself hoping for some excuse to speak with her again soon.

༄

"You're badly smitten, Cal, there's no use in denying it," stated Brohan again. "Not to worry, though. There are worse afflictions than love; not many, but there are worse."

"Must you do that?" fumed Calvraign none too quietly as they ascended the spiral stair that led to the Guest Hall.

"Do what?"

"Make light of everything all the time. I don't think this is funny at all."

"No reason the rest of us can't be amused," Brohan said without pause. "It's only fair you see what it's like on this side of infatuation."

"Now what's that supposed to mean?" growled Calvraign, whose humor was already strained to the limit. He marched down the hall toward his door at the far end, not favoring Brohan with more than a sidelong, irritated glance. The hanging tapestries fluttered after him as he passed.

"I think you know," countered the bard, his tone reproving but still mild. "Do you believe Callagh Breigh spent so much time running you down to practice hunting faeries?"

"Oh, *that*," Calvraign said with a grunting sigh. "That was different. She's just a girl." He stopped to put the key in the lock, but noticed with some surprise that the door opened slowly and lightly on its greased hinges. "Unlocked," he said quizzically.

Brohan held Calvraign back with a firm hand on his shoulder, and a concealed knife slid from his other sleeve. Calvraign was about to protest, but the severe look on his mentor's face was so out of character that he stood there, silent and unmoving, as Brohan stalked into the room. He returned less than a click later, the knife at home again in the loose sleeve of his doublet, his lopsided smile also back where it belonged.

"It seems good Mr. Seth has fallen asleep while tending your fire," he whispered. "Come and see."

They tiptoed into the bedchamber and found Seth still asleep on the rocking chair with the heavy iron poker at rest in his lap. His reddish brown hair was a tousled heap on top of his head, and his mouth was slack in the deepest of sleeps. Calvraign tried not to laugh, but succeeded only in disguising it as a quiet snicker.

"Should I wake him?" asked Brohan.

"No, leave him there," whispered back Calvraign. "No need embarrassing him now. I just want to get to sleep and I'm much too tired to reassure him that I won't tell that fat old castellan."

"As you wish," said Brohan. "Though I can't imagine he's your first choice for bedroom companionship."

"At least he'll leave me in peace," groaned Calvraign. "Go and drink yourself silly or charm some scullery girl or whatever it is you do all night."

Brohan opened his mouth to reply, then thought better of it and merely nodded on his way out of Calvraign's apartments with a perfunctory good night. Calvraign took one of his spare blankets and laid it over Seth's slumbering form with a curt half-smile. The home he had grown up in had not equaled the size of his suite here in King's Keep. And he couldn't help feeling guilty that his entire day passed without a single chore while others labored in his service. It was hard to begrudge the weary servant a sound night's sleep simply for the luxury of being alone.

He changed for bed without too much noise, not enough to wake up Seth, at any rate, and climbed into the welcoming comfort of his bed. It was early yet to sleep, for the riders had not been out long after dark, and most were feasting in the main hall somewhere below. But when he discovered Aeolil would not be joining the rest of the party for dinner, he quickly lost all energy and appetite, and he'd made his excuses shortly after. He stared at the dark stone of the ceiling, feeling an odd, queasy sort of loneliness.

Maybe Brohan is right. Maybe it is only fair.

Not long after, his heavy lids closed and brought down with them the welcoming peace of sleep.

◊

Seth awoke thinking at first that he had only been asleep for a few clicks, but the presence of the blanket laying over him quickly dispelled that illusion. He sat still, eyes open and horrified, staring at the remnants of his fire and wondering how he could be so blasted stupid. He had wanted so badly to do a good job! He felt the threat of tears, and growing tightness in his throat.

Many boys his age dreamed of being soldiers or adventurers or kings or nobles. Not Seth. All the young Briggin boy wanted was to one day take over the duties of Burton and be the castellan of King's Keep. He loved the commotion and the excitement of preparing the kitchen and the hall for a feast, or the rush to provide accommodations for surprise visitors of high rank, or organizing the cleaning and preparation for the festivals and holidays. He cared nothing for swords and armor and dashing about on horses like a madman, and he never had.

This certainly isn't the way to be about it, he scolded himself. He would apologize in the morning and hope that he didn't arouse Sir Calvraign's legendary temper. He was about to rise when he heard a soft scratch on the smooth polished stone floor behind him and to his left, from the direction of the bed.

Demons take me, I've woke him! He looked out of the corner of his eye, careful not to move his head and draw any attention to himself, and was immediately grateful for his caution.

Calvraign lay sleeping, oblivious and serene, but there was another man in the room: tall, garbed in black, lit only vaguely in the dying glow of firelight. The mysterious figure was reaching into his cloak, pulling out a small bag. Seth wasn't sure if it was just a trick of the flickering light, but it seemed the bag itself was moving. No! Something *in* the bag – *several* somethings.

Cold sweat beaded on Seth's brow. He knew he had no time to sit here mired in indecision. Whatever the intruder was doing, it certainly didn't look friendly, and he was the only one available to stop him. He felt the cold weight of the iron in his lap, and knew he had only one option. With a silent prayer to Kazdann for pure and simple strength, he leapt up off the chair with a loud yell, heaving the blanket toward the shadowed shape over the bed.

The man spun adroitly on one heel, the bag half-opened in his right hand as his left reached for something else within his flapping cloak. Before he could act further, the blanket sailed over his head like a net, blinding him and fouling his arms. Not a breath later, Seth had leaped on the bed and was delivering blow after blow to the man under the blanket.

Calvraign was stirring now, crying out some Cythe curse in his confusion as he sat up and scrambled away from the commotion. Seth's luckless victim had fallen like a sack of grain at his last blow, landing with a thud on the floor. Calvraign's mouth hung agape as he took in the scene before him.

"That man," panted Seth, "snuck in. With that bag."

"What? What are you talking about? What bag?"

"Here." Seth pointed at the bag that lay on the mattress, and the small shapes that moved about it with a barely audible clicking sound. "Stay back, I'll get a light."

Seth ran over toward the fireplace and lit a candle from the lip of the hearth. His face was sweaty and terrified in its feeble halo. They leaned over the bed together, still keeping their distance somewhat, as Seth brought the illuminating flame down to the writhing blotch of shapes on the mattress.

A dozen spiders, smaller than the tip of a finger, scurried about, in, and around the open bag. They were covered in short, shiny black fur with tiny red marks just behind their mandibles, which rattled together unceasingly to produce the clicking noise Seth had heard. Both onlookers were pale.

"What are they?" asked Calvraign, but from his tone Seth could tell he already knew.

"Hive spiders," whispered Seth, and not a moment later set fire to the fine linens and silks that had covered Calvraign in his sleep not long before. The fire hungrily devoured the bedding and the skittering spiders as they looked on, hearts pounding to the same rapid beat, until they were sure that the remnants of their nightmare were consumed completely in the flames.

Chapter Twenty

Paying Debts

AEOLIL rubbed the thick-bristled brush along the horse's back in long, firm strokes, leaning forward from the waist to put more of her weight into the work. Her hair was fastened haphazardly behind her neck in what resembled a lustrous auburn snarl more than a loose braid, a few odd stems of straw orphaned within the tangled mess. She was warm in her fur-lined riding leathers, and comfortable. She had always loved her horses, but here in King's Keep, the stables had the added appeal of allowing her a reprieve from the encumbrance of her formal attire. She quelled those thoughts quickly, hoping to avoid any more acute pains of homesickness.

A soft muzzle brushed her cheek, and she leaned into it, hugging the stallion's head with her left arm and scratching between his ears. He pawed the straw floor with one hoof and snorted. She smiled. Windthane was the most powerful and stately of all the steeds in the stable. She was biased somewhat, for she owned him, but she still felt the assessment was a fair one. He was tall, broad, and dapple-grey, with strength to bear a knight in arms, fully armored, and still shoulder the weight of his own barding without strain. And Windthane was fast, faster than many a horse bred solely for racing, and if she didn't know better, she would think he was the proudest horse she had ever laid eyes on. It had always been a girlish fancy of hers to think of her animals in human terms, one of the few girlish things she had not yet convinced herself to leave behind.

A rooster crowed from the pens, twenty yards beyond the back wall of the stable, and with its everyday cackle of delight, Aeolil sighed. She had no great love of waking before either sun had yet crested the horizon, but it was the sole way she could steal some time alone with the horses. If she waited until daybreak, Bleys would be on duty and unwilling to wait just beyond the stable doors. No, he saw fit to stand on guard outside the stall itself, scowling at the stable hands. With Chadwick and Stefan she had better luck; they would post themselves one outside each of the two stable entrances. They, at least, had some respect for her privacy.

Aeolil looked up at the knock on the stall door. A young man stood there, dressed in casual, if not poor, attire. A long brown cloak of wool hung from his shoulders, the hood thrown back, covering him from his neck to his well-worn boots. A glimpse of coarse fabric was visible beneath, but nothing more. From his stance and carriage, she judged him a soldier of some sort. His features were unassuming, neither handsome nor plain – a thoroughly average man.

"Your pardon, good lady," he said, his words tinged with the clipped syllables of a Northern accent. "May I trouble you for a moment?"

He was a stranger, she assumed. Not only from his accent, but because he failed to recognize her as a lady of rank. None would dare speak to a noblewoman in such an informal manner within King's Keep, where etiquette was like bread at mealtime – seldom noticed unless absent. Still, his tone was very polite for a soldier addressing a stable hand. *A messenger, maybe?* His eyes were steady as they held hers – not with the cold scrutiny of men like Bleys, or the lecherous hints of countless others. This was different. It was softer, but no less intent of purpose.

"That all depends," she said after her brief scrutiny, "on what sort of trouble you refer to."

He cocked his head at her, eyebrows lifting slightly. "Oh." A brief but genuine smile curved his lips for a moment; then he shrugged and continued. "I am Sir Artygalle. I am to meet Lady Aeolil in the stables at daybreak. Her men sent me through. Might you know where I can find her, please?"

This was Brohan's great knight? Aeolil tried to refrain from hasty judgments, but this man did not appear like any knight whom she had ever known. Even those less concerned with ceremony and pretense, which were common enough in her lands, carried themselves with a certain dignity – a confidence and bearing that were unmistakable. This man scarcely had the aplomb of a squire. Regardless, she could not help but admire the courtesy he extended a young woman who, to his eyes, was but a common serf. She thought this quality more admirable, and genuine, than the more courtly airs she had expected.

"I think that can be arranged," she said. She hung the horse brush from its wooden peg on the back wall, caught sight of her leathered arm, and smiled at the irony. She had been so taken aback by his appearance she hadn't even thought what he would think of her own. Should a lady really dress down like this, even to tend horse? Should she even *be* tending horse? Perhaps there was something in the well at King's Keep that induced aloofness. She was certain that five years gone, she wouldn't so much as blink at Sir Artygalle's apparent lack of decorum.

"I beg your pardon, sir knight," she started again, allowing her most charming smile to brighten her face, "but I am she, and you are most welcome here. I was expecting you, of course. I apologize for my appearance."

Artygalle's mild brown eyes widened a bit, and his smile returned to soften his surprise with amusement. "It is I who should apologize, milady," he said, bending to one knee and dipping his head. "I judged too quickly. I confess to being somewhat distracted by your horse. He is remarkable."

"That I won't argue," Aeolil extended her hand, palm upward. "But please get up, sir. There's no need for that here."

"As you wish." Artygalle stood, looking from her to the horse and then back again. "I owe you a great deal even for considering this. If my liege's charge was not so urgent, I would withdraw myself from the lists rather than beg for charity."

"Nonsense," quipped Aeolil. "I am in Master Madrharigal's debt, and he in yours. This is a fair and honorable transaction. If Windthane will have you, that is. He has a rather volatile temperament. Have you much experience?"

Artygalle had removed his wool-lined gauntlet and approached Windthane's muzzle with his bare hand outstretched. His manner answered her question better than any comforting words. He met the horse with the same frank and honest gaze that he had met her, and spoke in a lilting tongue she did not recognize. Each word was a sweet musical note that sang peace. Windthane shared her reaction, nuzzling and licking the outstretched hand like a grotesquely oversized dog.

Aeolil realized she had been holding her breath, and released it with a sigh. "That was beautiful," she breathed. "What was it?"

"Qeyniir," he replied. "I learned it while just a squire. My master," he paused, then shook his head, "my *former* master, was our ambassador to their people. I spent more than a few years in Bael Naerth. I spoke mostly nonsense, but I've learned animals find its tone quite soothing."

"Yes, it seems so."

"He is magnificent. Windthane, you say?" Artygalle ran his bare fingers down the animal's neck with a boyish smile. "Brohan did not overstate the matter in the least. Are you certain you'll allow me to rob your stables?"

"I will not squander my debts. In the tourney you won't need a riding horse, or a racer. You'll need a war-horse, and of those I have only one. Take care of him, but *do* take him. I can't say I thought well of it until now, but since I've met you, I believe it's the right thing. He's less trusting than I, and he has taken to you."

"Thank you, milady. I will honor your trust, and Windthane's."

Aeolil watched him continue his soothing whispers and gentle caress of Windthane's muzzle in silence, pretending to busy herself with an examination of the horse's rear flank. If there was one thing she had become adept at in the last few years, it was pretending to be at work on one thing while her mind was quite occupied with another. And her mind was truly busy this morning.

Agrylon said that to all things there was a pattern, much like a tapestry, and for those who cared to look it was easy enough to see. True power, true insight, came when one could see the individual threads before the design took shape, to know their place in it before it had been woven, to see the possibilities of what could be. And this was troublesome, because until the last fibers were twined together, the tapestry could be altered or even unraveled.

Still, of all Agrylon's teachings, this concept came most naturally to her. Without realizing it, she had always viewed the world around her in this way; seen these threads, analyzed them, manipulated them, initiated and implemented her own vision of how they should be. She had thought of it as no more than politics, but now she saw it was beyond those simple concepts of machination and counter-machination. She saw the grander application. The more powerful one, and the more dangerous.

The events of this year had the promise of being more than the sum of their parts. She could sense it in Agrylon; his moods and his dealings with Renarre were both more intense and more intricate than the routine of past years. And she could feel it in herself. Somewhere in her mind, lurking just out of conscious thought, she could almost see the pattern taking shape. She knew it was there, but she could not yet see how or why it might develop into the future.

She felt perhaps that Calvraign's appearance held some portent, after the reactions he stirred up in the king and court. What, exactly, that could be, she did not know. He was bright, and his intentions seemed pure. That he could influence the king was clear. If he could influence him *enough* remained to be seen. And this man Artygalle – what of him? Was he what he appeared? And what *did* he appear – this knight dressed as a peasant who charmed horses with pretty words? Was it so simple? Had he stumbled across Brohan and Calvraign in their time of need purely by chance, and then the master bard had likewise found her disadvantaged, and in so helping her gained a favor to pass along? Such things didn't sit well with her. They begged more questions than delivered answers, and those answers begat more questions of their own.

One of Agrylon's pet phrases seemed fitting: *Things do not happen by chance, but if they do it's for a reason.* She guessed that he enjoyed such turns of phrase more for the power he felt in confusing others than for entertainment or enlightenment. It was hard to tell exactly what Agrylon's intentions were, for anything or anyone. He treasured his secrets even more than his magic. He only trusted her with the latter.

Aeolil looked up past Artygalle, who had continued Windthane's grooming where she had left off, as the stable door was darkened by the looming figure of Bleys Malade. He was broad enough to fill the doorway, and bent his head to clear the frame. His jaw clenched when he eyed Artygalle. She steeled herself for the confrontation, surprised it had taken him this long to appear, and met his hard eyes without a blink of concern. She stepped forward to interpose herself between the two men, but Bleys had already closed the distance.

"Who is *this*, milady?" he snarled, as if Artygalle were incapable or unworthy of speech. "I gave strict orders you were not be left alone with anyone."

"I can't very well be alone *and* with someone at the same time, now can I?" she snapped back, irritated and embarrassed by his demeanor. "This is-"

"We've no time for *introductions*!" The color in his face darkened as he raised his voice and stepped closer. "Dismiss him and gather yourself. We're returning you to your chambers."

Aeolil was startled by his tone, and her pulse quickened. Bleys could be irritable and domineering, but she had never seen him so blatantly disrespectful. Not for a long time, anyway. "Bleys," she began, but the sound had scarcely cleared her throat when Artygalle spoke.

"Sir," he said, his voice calm and measured. "You will not insult this lady in my presence. Though she can doubtless deal with you herself, I don't intend to test her. Lower your voice and stand back, please."

Bleys lowered his eyes for a moment to the smaller man, but his expression remained unmoved. "This is none of your concern, boy. Tend the horse and shut your mouth. I'm in no mood to talk."

"I have no wish to cross blades with you, sir," Artygalle continued, "but I will draw steel if you do not stand back."

Bleys' expression changed slightly, and his hand crept over the hilt of his broad sword. "Stand away, milady," he said, caution edging out anger in his voice. "Who are you to bear arms within King's Keep, squire?"

"If you had allowed the lady to finish her introduction, you'd have discovered that in short order, sir. I am Sir Artygalle of Tiriel, a knight in the Order of Andulin, and at the service of Lady Vae." Artygalle pulled apart the folds of his cloak and indicated a small talisman hanging there from a thin chain. The winged sword of a knight of the Church was set against the backdrop of a golden shield, the symbol of his Order.

"A lancer, eh?" Bleys didn't disguise his contempt. "Don't expect *that* to impress me. Run back to Renarre and tell him to leave the lady alone. And leave that blade sheathed unless you want to lose an arm."

"I don't need or wish to impress, you, sir. Nor do I care of your opinion of the archbishop. But I will not tolerate an uncivil tongue wagged at Lady Aeolil."

Aeolil knew Bleys well enough to know he was not convinced of Artygalle's claims, let alone his intentions. She placed a hand on Artygalle's shoulder and squeezed herself in-between he and Bleys. "Enough, gentlemen. The knight is who he claims to be. I have it on good authority," she said, though she realized, in fact, she didn't. She had instructed Chadwick that he would be meeting her here, but beyond the fact that he *was* here, presumably with the knowledge of her guards, she had no idea if he was whom he claimed. She trusted him, however, even if Brohan hadn't mentioned he was a lancer. "Thank you both for your concern for my honor and safety. Consider the matter resolved." Artygalle nodded, but Bleys made no outward show of acknowledgment. She sighed. He wouldn't, of course. "Now, Captal Malade, what is amiss?"

"There was trouble last night," he explained, one eye on Artygalle, "in the Cythe's quarters."

Both Aeolil and Artygalle jumped at that, but she was first to voice surprise. "Calvraign? Is he all right? What happened, Bleys?"

"So far as I know, he's fine. Vanelorn has him sequestered somewhere with the Prince's Guard. Now," he motioned to the door, "may we leave, milady?"

Aeolil recognized his tone. Whenever Bleys moved on from belligerent to patient, it meant his temper was under a thin layer of restraint. He was not simply being paranoid, as was his usual wont, but worried and concerned. Whatever had happened to Calvraign, or perhaps the fact that anything had happened at all, had clearly changed his perspective on security within the Keep. As, in fact, it had for her. Perhaps she had been too hard on Bleys these past years.

"Yes, captal, we shall be going," she answered. "But I wish to see Sir Calvraign. I assume Master Madrharigal is with him? Arrange it with Vanelorn, please."

"Milady..." Bleys' veneer of patience cracked.

"There will be no argument," she stated evenly, "nor discussion, nor complaining. I understand your concerns, but I will have this done. Do you understand *me*, captal?"

Bleys paused, then straightened. "Yes, milady."

"May I accompany you, milady?" Artygalle asked. "I am not yet known here," he said, glancing at Bleys, "and I wish to cause no further confusion."

"Of course, sir."

Bleys chewed on his lip in aggravation. His eyes were hard, but his words were resigned. "As you wish, milady."

"We will await you here," Aeolil said. "Send in Stefan and Chadwick if you like."

"I will," he stated, glancing once more at the plain knight before turning to leave.

"And, Bleys," Aeolil added, the command in her voice replaced by sincerity. It still stopped him at the door. "Thank you."

"Of course, milady," he said, and left them, jaws clenched and shaking his head.

Chapter Twenty-One

Too Much Talk

THE hearth was ablaze in the prince's receiving chamber, warming the cool morning air but not Calvraign's mood. Hiruld had generously provided a breakfast of pastries, cold meats, and mulled cider, and even replaced the clothing damaged by the fire in Calvraign's bedchamber. Most importantly to Calvraign, however, were the men-at-arms that the prince had assigned him from the ranks of his Guard. He was only too aware that he owed his life to the alertness of a sleepy servant, and although he was grateful to Seth, he didn't want to rely on that happenstance in the future. Nor, he guessed, did young Mister Briggin.

The steward was even more shaken than Calvraign, and slept now only because the prince's personal physic had given him a powerful draught. Calvraign had been offered the same, but refused. He was in no mood to sleep, and moreover, the others involved him in their discussion little enough without him giving them further excuse. They sat around the oval marble table, the handsome meal all but ignored in favor of the warm cider and the debate, which was hotter still.

The words of Sir Tuoerval were the most contentious and biting. He was knight captain general of the lancers, a warrior-priest who commanded the respect of both the nobles and clergy. Like Vanelorn, he was of the old guard. His face showed lines of age and scars of battle, his old skull lined only with a thin fuzz of retreating grey hair. But his voice was still strong, and he spoke only harsh words this morning, "…and if Vanelorn cannot secure the safety of the Keep, then steps should be taken. His pride may blind him, but there's no need for us to be blinded by it as well. The Parade of the Lists is this very highsuns, My Prince. Are we to stand back and wait for this to happen again?"

"Oh, horse spit," a deep bass voice replied, not sparing sarcasm.

Calvraign's eyes shifted to the man called Inulf, the commander of Hiruld's personal guard. He was big, like Bleys or Grumwyr, but older, and his accent was thick and foreign. His beard was not the trimmed thing of the nobility, but a thick tangle of midnight black that matched the color of his long tresses and his eyes. His appearance was fierce, but this in itself did not startle Calvraign. Inulf reminded him of the wild hill people that lived in the Crehr, freemen beholding to none – barbarians even from his barbarian's reckoning. The commander's deep voice, combined with his strange accent, had a more unsettling effect.

"And I suppose you lancers be them for the job, huh? Eh? That will make you happy, old man?"

"Keep your tongue civil," scolded Tuoerval with a look of strained dignity. "Keeping the king and his guests safe shall make me happy enough."

"And the Fox, too, eh? He will be happy?"

"You *dare*!" exclaimed the captain general, rising to his feet as quickly as the blood rose in his cheeks. "I will have an apology for that, you pagan dog, or I will have satisfaction!"

Inulf smiled, exposing a mouth only partially filled with the convenience of teeth. "I speak what I feel. You like, you don't like, I don' care. Honest words. You talk like sugar on hemlock; taste sweet, but still kill you, eh?"

Tuoerval began to tug at the fingers of his gauntlet. "I will have your –"

"You will have your seat, Sir Tuoerval," said Hiruld dryly. "Don't allow this dirty barbarian to get the better of you." Calvraign noticed Inulf's smile broaden. "You are a civilized man and a Knight of the Lance – how would that look?"

"My Prince, this lout –"

"Your seat, sir," insisted Hiruld. "Perhaps you mistook that as a *request*."

Tuoerval sat down.

Hiruld drummed his fingers on the table and fidgeted in his chair. He didn't appear comfortable in the role of mediator or disciplinarian, but Calvraign noticed he was no less effective for his distaste. "Blame whom you wish later, gentlemen, but my concern is more in the why and the how of the matter. The lord high marshal selected all of us with good reason: myself, to represent my Royal Father's interests; Inulf to speak for the men under his command who now guard Calvraign; and Sir Tuoerval, for the Church. Brohan is here rather of his own insistence, but with my blessing. So, speak to your concerns, but please, for once in this gods-forsaken keep, leave your politics out of the discussion."

Calvraign's name was not mentioned as anything more than a topic, a fact that didn't escape his notice or his growing irritation. Even Brohan made no offer to allow him into their conversation. He knew they had more experience with things of this nature, but since it had been *his* life that was threatened, he felt eminently qualified to broach the subject. He gathered his frustration together, hoping he could use it to feign courage and speak his piece. But, even as he gathered himself up to approach the table, Brohan turned his head and motioned him to stay with a flick of his hand.

Calvraign slumped back in his seat, his thoughts again in disarray, and frowned into the fire as the debate at the table began anew. Why anybody wanted him dead, he could not begin to guess. Inulf insisted that it must have been someone already within the Keep itself, a case of mistaken identity or political motives. Brohan agreed, but Tuoerval and Hiruld were less taken with that notion. Foreign assassins were their guess, but that made even less sense to Calvraign. Could it all have been a mistake? There were many guests within the Keep for the tourney, and they *had* changed his quarters at the king's request after that first night.

The other detail that nagged at him was the method of the attempt. To die as the host meal of hive spiders was perhaps the worst fate one could imagine. It was certainly among the worst *he* could think up. If the infestation was discovered quickly, it was *sometimes* possible to amputate the blighted body part. Barring that, death came slowly. Only the most ruthless of assassins would employ such a weapon, and the risk of exposure drove up the cost. Who wanted him to die a horrific death, and was rich enough to afford it? He heard the same questions echoed at the table, each point dissected and examined, but with no more success.

There was a knock at the door, and it swung open to admit Sir Vanelorn. He marched in, his full shirt of mail rustling with each step, and threw a blackened chunk of metal on the table. It rattled across the polished stone surface and silenced the room like a gavel. Two guardsmen pulled the door shut behind him.

"My Prince," he said, "this was found on the assassin's corpse. He was too badly burned to identify, as were most of his belongings, but *it* survived intact."

"By the Swords," breathed Hiruld, staring at the smudged silver of the brooch.

"It's a badge of service," explained Vanelorn to the others, "for an officer of House Vespurial."

"Interesting," mused Tuoerval.

"Convenient," said Vanelorn, "but I will speak with Calamyr myself. The brooches are common enough among their soldiers, but the silver ones are rare."

Tuoerval rose and bowed to the prince. "I must take this news to His Holiness right away," he said. No one made an effort to stop him as he left.

"Juut," spat Inulf in his native tongue, watching the doors close behind the captain general. "He's fool old man. Run to Fox, tell the Fox, spy for Fox. He's not to think for himself, eh?"

"He's no fool, Inulf," Vanelorn spoke quietly, sagging beneath an invisible weight. "He's as pompous as you are crude, but that makes neither of you fools. He wouldn't concern me if he was."

Inulf shrugged. "He talks much but does little, yes? I say let him talk."

"This stinks of politics," Vanelorn said, plucking a piece of dried fruit from the table and rolling it between his fingers. "It's been more than thirty years since last I smelled such stink." He looked over at Calvraign, his eyes dull, his lips drawn down into a frown. "It saddens me you were such a target, sir. And it shames me that only a lad and his luck came between you and death. When the time comes, I will ask your forgiveness. Until then, I will ask only your patience."

Calvraign was startled by the old knight's supplicant tone. Seeing such humiliation in the eyes of the man who had fought next to his father at Vlue Macc made the blood heat in his face. He cleared his head of questions and got up from his chair by the fire. "Sir Vanelorn, you have no need to ask my forgiveness. This surprised all of us, I would guess. If you feel a need for amends, only see to it that Seth is rewarded for his courage. He did us both a great service with his bravery."

Vanelorn smiled faintly and put down the piece of dried fruit. "You are a generous young man, Sir Calvraign. I accept and thank you for your kindness, if not your absolution. And I have already spoken with Burton about the boy, rest assured. I must leave you all once more, I'm afraid; the king is in quite the rage this morning. Perhaps you could accompany me, My Prince, and soothe your father's mood."

"Of course," agreed Hiruld without pause.

"We shall take your leave then." Vanelorn nodded to Calvraign. "But expect the Lady Aeolil soon. She wished to see you immediately. If there is anyone worth your trust in this hornet's nest, it is she."

Calvraign paid the appropriate respects as they left, giving his best show of nonplussed calm. It would not do to let them know how shaken he was. But when the doors closed, leaving him in the company only of

Brohan, he couldn't help but channel his relief into a voluminous sigh. He felt safe with Brohan, even more than knowing three of the Prince's Guard stood outside his door. Brohan was an anchor, a familiar presence amidst all this chaos and speculation. Calvraign sat across from the master bard, picking up a piece of reddish cheese and popping it into his mouth. It was rather sharp, but not unpalatable, and the taste improved when washed down with the mulled cider.

Brohan was quiet. Odd enough in itself, but more pronounced due to the sour look on his face. Calvraign could tell it was more than anger and frustration that robbed the smile from his lips. Like Vanelorn, Brohan felt guilty for not protecting him – as if either of them should have suspected he would be attacked. The whole notion was ridiculous to Calvraign.

"Cal," Brohan said, dragging him out of speculation, "are you sure you didn't get at least a glimpse of him?"

"By the time I was awake, he was covered by a blanket," Calvraign answered with a shrug. "Even Seth didn't make him out too well. Just a *dark figure*, he said."

Brohan nodded, but his uncharacteristic grimace only deepened, his smooth face lined in thought. "Yes," he said to himself, "a dark figure."

"Brohan…" Calvraign hesitated, still unsure whether he should confess his hallucinations. He knew that it was nerves and imagination conspiring against his sanity, and he didn't want Brohan to think he took this matter lightly by worrying over such nonsense. Then again, after last night, perhaps it was not so nonsensical after all. "I think that man, whoever he was, I think he'd been following us."

"What?" Brohan's eyes shot wide open even as his brows knit above them. "What are you talking about?"

"I thought I saw a dark-cloaked man watching me a few times since we left Craignuuwn. I was sure I just imagined it. I couldn't believe anyone would want to follow *me*, after all. But now… ." He shook his head. "I know it sounds stupid, Brohan. I'm sorry. I just thought you should know."

Brohan brought his fist down on the stone table with a loud smack, and Calvraign flinched. "*What?* Why didn't you tell me?" His voice snapped like a whip. "By the gods, boy, how long has this gone on?"

"I, well, since…" Calvraign's lips fumbled over the words. "The storm, out on the plains, before we met Artygalle. Is it important?"

"*Important?*" mimicked Brohan, clenching one of his fists on the table. "Cal." He stopped, drew a deep breath, and continued in a less adversarial tone. "Cal, never keep something like that from me again. I don't care how laughable it may seem at the time. Do you understand?"

"Yes," Calvraign answered, though he wasn't so sure he did.

"I'm sorry to yell at you, Cal. It's not your fault. I should have told you why we left Craignuuwn on such short notice. You had no way of knowing."

"Knowing what?"

"Your mother had one of her visions. She saw you *threatened* by a dark figure, a man in a black cloak."

Calvraign sat a moment in silence, his temper building but under tight control. He had thought that at long last Brohan considered him a man rather than a boy. The realization that this was not true, that Brohan's confidence was not everything it had seemed, bit deep into his pride. "Dare I ask why you didn't tell me?" he said, the words bitten off just short of belligerence. "If you *had* told me, don't you think we could have avoided this?"

"I..." But Brohan couldn't finish his thought. He looked away before continuing, "Yes, you're right, I should have told you before. I'm sorry. I forget sometimes that you are not such a child anymore. If not in Craignuuwn, I should have realized the difference in you once we arrived here. You made your mark so quickly, came into your own, but I..." He pursed his lips. "I *am* sorry, Cal."

The bard's honesty and regret salved Calvraign's wounded self-regard. He recognized the change in himself to which Brohan referred – a growing confidence and a calm, perceptive directness he had not displayed before. It was as if all the training and instruction he had received in Craignuuwn lay dormant, waiting for the rich soil of King's Keep in which to plant its roots and bloom. He was, by no means *grown* – but he had built a strong foundation. He knew that, and he knew now that Brohan did as well.

"No matter," he said, reaching out to pat Brohan's clenched fist. "What's done is done. Whatever or whoever the man was, he's dead now."

Brohan looked up, but not with the relief Calvraign had expected. He shook his head slowly from side to side, his smile still buried in lines of doubt. "It's not that easy, I'm afraid."

"He's dead, Brohan. How much easier does that get?"

"Tell me about the figure you saw. Everything you can remember."

"I told you, he was covered in a blanket."

"No, Cal," said Brohan. "I mean the man in the cloak you thought was watching you. Tell me about *him*."

Calvraign considered a moment. He didn't remember much, now that he put his mind to it. "Well," he said, trying to distill his thoughts into words. "It was sort of like a dream, in a way, because it only seemed half-real. That first time, in the storm, I saw him in the distance, and when I moved toward him, he drew a sword, and then the lightning bolt struck. After that, I felt it a few more times, that something was watching me, but nothing so clear as that first time. It was just a shadow, always out of the corner of my eye, and a chill, and then a lingering unease. But it was never as if he was really *there*. I thought I was just imagining things."

"It seems not," Brohan said, a flicker of a grin returning to his face. "I suspect the apparition was real, if not physically present."

"And you say Mother dreamed about him?"

"I think so," Brohan answered slowly, "but I don't think the assassin and your shadowy interloper are one and the same."

Calvraign frowned. That wasn't particularly comforting. "Brohan, you obviously know more than you're telling. Don't make me guess at it."

"I believe I've learned my lesson in that regard." Brohan's smile finally conquered the warring emotion on his face, but his eyes were still wary. "You'll have to steel yourself, Cal, because my suspicions are of a nasty bent. I hope that I'm wrong, that I misunderstood your mother's vision, and that last night's business will be the end of it. I hope that, but I can't say as I believe it."

"Oh, just get on with it, for gods' sakes," Calvraign pleaded. "As bad as the news might be, the waiting has to be worse."

"I believe the man in your mother's vision was none other than the Pale Man, Cal. She saw him standing, well," Brohan licked his lips, "over your body, with blood all over his sword. You may understand now why I was hesitant."

Calvraign wasn't sure how long he sat with his mouth hanging open before he spoke, but he hoped it wasn't quite as long as it seemed. "Why would you think that, Brohan? How could that possibly be true? The Pale Man. I mean, is he even *real*?"

"Oh, yes," confirmed Brohan, scholarly once more. "He is real. And though I've not a clue why, the man with the sword that your mother described is almost certainly he. Hence my doubts that good Mr. Seth had the fortune of slaying him, and hence my concern about your dark apparition."

"I was wrong," Calvraign whispered, suppressing a tremble in his voice, "the waiting wasn't so bad."

Brohan poured some fresh cider into Calvraign's mug from the fine porcelain carafe between them. "Cal, as I told your mother, a vision isn't a literal foretelling of the future. The future can never really be told until it happens, even by the gods. But some events are more likely than others, and that is what your mother's vision is. It is *one* event, *one* possibility, and *only* one of many."

"You'll have to pardon my reluctance to take much comfort in that distinction."

"Of course. That's why we are *here*, after all. It's where your mother and I thought you safest. That it is only one possibility does not mean we should ignore it. We should work to avoid it at all costs."

"How do you propose we do that?"

"First, we need to discover what interest such as the Pale Man would have in you. He does not kill by accident or coincidence, so in some way you must pose a threat or inconvenience to him."

"But Brohan, this makes no sense at all," said Calvraign, getting up from the table to pace away his nervous energy. "If the figure I've been seeing is the Pale Man, why am I alive? Why send an assassin when he's been so close to me himself? Why toy with me at all? And anyway, what threat could I ever be to one of the Walking Gods? You have to be wrong."

"All good questions, but I'm not wrong, lad. I wish I were."

"How can you be so certain? Visions aren't usually so specific are they? Couldn't this just be some dramatic metaphor?"

"No." Brohan's blunt denial was without pause or doubt. "Seeing that sword in a dream is no metaphor. It is only what it is. The Pale Man wants you dead, now or in the future, but dead. You'll have to accept that if we're to eventually avoid it."

Calvraign closed his eyes and rubbed his temple with his fingertips. This was *insane*. "Blood and ruin, Brohan," he said, for lack of anything more insightful. He felt fear like a beast in his heart, tearing away at his confidence. It left him feeling naked and vulnerable, the sharp point of a sword a tangible sensation between his shoulder blades. He jumped when the doors opened, turning to put the fire to his back and reaching for a sword that wasn't there.

One of his new guards, Bouwain, he thought, gave a brief salute. "Sir Calvraign, the Lady Aeolil Vae wishes to see you, in company of Captal Malade and Sir Artygalle."

"Of course," he managed, disguising his panic with an exaggerated gesture of welcome. "Please send them in! Thank you."

Calvraign ceased his pacing with a conscious effort and turned to face the door with an illusion of calm. Aeolil entered impatiently, and Calvraign almost forgot his worries, distracted by her well-worn and form-fitting riding leathers. Everything he knew regarding court etiquette told him this was highly inappropriate; a quick look at the face of Bleys Malade, one step behind her, confirmed his suspicions. There was no need for a properly brought-up lady to wear pants of any kind, because any properly brought-up lady would only think of riding side-saddle. Apparently, the distinguished Lady Aeolil was not so well brought up, after all. Her attire didn't offend his barbarian sensibilities in the least, however. In fact, he found her more radiant than ever. Her beauty was complimented by the natural flush in her cheeks and the strands of hay mixed in with her tousled auburn hair. With an effort, he reminded himself not to stare.

"I'm glad to see you intact, Calvraign," she said, without the distance of formality. "This news was quite a shock."

Too Much Talk

"Yes, to me especially," he replied with a courteous bow.

"My friend," said Artygalle, also ignoring any formal niceties. He stepped in close, taking Calvraign's forearms in a firm grip. "Thank Illuné you are well. Know that your enemies are my enemies."

Calvraign smiled and nodded. He wasn't sure what the proper response was, but he knew it was no small thing for a knight to commit to such a matter of honor. He wondered if the assurance would have been so easily given had Artygalle known that amongst his enemies was the Pale Man. *Best not to mention that bit*, he decided.

"Please sit and join us for breakfast, all of you," he said with a welcoming wave toward the table.

The invitation to sit was accepted by all but Bleys, but none made a hasty grab at any of the food. It seemed all of Hiruld's careful provisioning would be for naught this morning. Brohan made his greetings in a brief but friendly manner and filled their cups with the last of the cider.

Aeolil smiled her thanks at the bard, but directed her question to Calvraign. "What happened? No one has been forthcoming with details."

"Apparently someone thought I was the ideal place to start a hive-spider nest," Calvraign said. "But, by Oghran's Luck, my personal steward and his fire iron convinced him this was not such a good idea."

"Hive-spiders?" repeated Artygalle with a shocked grimace. "Who would do such a thing?"

"Obviously someone who wanted this to seem an act of the gods rather than a murder," said Aeolil. "Had he succeeded, the assumption would be that you picked them up in the wilds."

Calvraign nodded in agreement, a little surprised by Aeolil's subdued reaction. Artygalle had flinched at the mere mention of hive-spiders, while she had only raised her eyebrows. He was more than a little impressed by her instantaneous grasp of the situation, and her analysis. During the entire debate at this very table, none had raised the possibility that this was designed to appear an accident. "Yes," he agreed, "but who would want me dead?" *Besides the Pale Man*, he added silently.

"The question should be who *doesn't* want you dead," said Aeolil.

"Excuse me?" Calvraign said, immediately wishing he could speak again, but about an octave lower.

"You know what a stir you've caused here, Calvraign," she said. "Think of all those who've had plans compromised or outright ruined by your presence at court."

"You mean like Renarre?"

"Well, he's certainly made his suspicions of you clear. The last thing he wants is King Guillaume to feel lively enough to start interfering with Church politics again. He's had almost a free hand this last year.

Yes, mark him among your obvious enemies. But the obvious is only the beginning.

"Take Prince Hiruld, for instance. He could resent the favor shown you by his father. Try as he might, he's not been able to lift the king's spirits after Vingeaux's death. Then you come along, and the king is all but skipping into court. Jealousy is a powerful motive."

"But I thought Hiruld liked me. We got on well enough at the hunt," protested Calvraign.

"Indeed you did," she agreed, "but what better way to cover his tracks? He might even be the first to say his fond farewells at your funeral. His father would think him your greatest friend and admirer."

"Hiruld's not the scheming sort," said Brohan. "I've known him longer even than you, Aeolil."

"No, he's not," she said, "and truthfully, I don't believe he would have anything to do with such a thing. But still, it's best to examine every possibility before dismissing it."

"True enough," conceded Brohan. "And who else would you add to this list?"

"Garath Malminnion certainly thinks of Calvraign as an enemy already. He might want to remove you before you become closer with the royals and a greater threat. He might also resent your growing friendship with Calamyr. And as for House Vespurial, they might not want the king's spirits and vigor renewed any more than Renarre. Their power has only grown during the king's disinterest and isolation. In fact, any of the Houses might want you removed for that reason alone. If you wish, you may add any number of knights from Vlue Macc, or their descendants, who may resent the memories of their failure that you dredged up. I could go on, if you like."

"I doubt that's necessary, Lady Aeolil," said Brohan. "Your point is taken. I gather you discount the possibility of a foreign attack?"

"No," she said, shaking her head slightly, "but I would say it is less likely. Infiltrating King's Keep would be no easy task without help from within unless the assassin was one of the Shrouded. And let us speak plain: had one of the Shrouded gained entry to his rooms with intent to kill, dead Calvraign and his servant would certainly be."

Brohan shook his head with a wry smile. "One might first convince me that the Shrouded *exist* before extolling their deadly efficiency. Such exploits are best left in the *Nine and Ninety Tales*."

"Let's look simply to motive then," she said without pause, though Calvraign thought there was a glint of defiance in her eyes. "Neither Aeyrdyn nor Mneyril have any need of a strong Providaynian monarch, but I doubt they would risk any such scheme on their own. The Maccs, if they could get in the Keep, would be better served to kill any number of nobles or knights before Calvraign. Also, news of his arrival can hardly have spread *that* fast amongst the realm's enemies."

"Have they discovered no clue of this villain's identity?" asked Artygalle.

"Vanelorn found a marking of House Vespurial among his remains," said Calvraign. "A silver brooch of some sort."

"You can all but remove Calamyr from your list, then," said Aeolil. "If House Vespurial were behind this, they would not be so careless."

"Rumor has it you have Agrylon's ear, milady," Brohan said with a sidelong glance in Aeolil's direction. "Is there perhaps any light he may shed on the subject for us?"

Aeolil stiffened, but the hard look she returned was softened at the edges by the glimmer of a smile. "His ear I may have," she said, "but the lord high chamberlain's lips remain tightly sealed. I have not seen him since last night, even if he were inclined to speak by some miracle. He does have plans for you, Calvraign." She turned her head to look at him directly. "I only wish I knew what they were."

"What is it about *me* that has people plotting and scheming?" Calvraign said, a little louder and more flustered than he'd intended. He had no problem taking politics and maneuvering into stride when he was an objective observer, but now that he was becoming the focus, he found it less palatable. "I have absolutely nothing to my name but my father's sword and Hiruld's clothing. The more you all talk about this, the more absurd the whole thing seems. Why should Agrylon or Renarre give two gryphs that a barbarian minstrel is at court? Was my father some long-lost Dacadian prince, or a Maccalite warlord? What? What could it possibly be?"

"Ibhraign was a warrior descended from warriors," said Brohan. "There was no royal blood in his veins." Then the master bard's eyes widened, and he thrust a finger up into the air. "But perhaps it's not your *father's* blood that interests Agrylon. Your mother has the Gift. That's no secret in your village. I never thought to ask you. Have you ever had a vision, Cal?"

Calvraign was momentarily heartened by Brohan's revelation, but had to dispel it with the honest truth. "No. Unless you count, well, *you know*."

Brohan shook his head. "No."

"Your mother is a seer?" Aeolil asked.

"Not as such, but she's had an occasional dream of foretelling. She said her mother had the same."

Aeolil rubbed her fist against her lips, kissing her knuckles in thought, and Calvraign watched her intently. He blinked his attention away, trying instead to focus on Artygalle, but the knight's face and mannerisms just weren't as interesting. He sat still and quiet, listening carefully but saying nothing. Artygalle caught Calvraign's eyes on him and returned a comforting smile.

"I'm sure if he had the Gift, it would have manifested years ago," said Brohan, "in his first years of manhood. By now, he is too far out of tune with the *iiyir* tides."

"Yes," said Aeolil, her voice muffled by her hand, "but he would pass it along to his children. Agrylon sees himself as a breeder and groomer of sorts. He constantly speaks of pairing this family with that or this person with the other – myself included. Calvraign might only be the first step in one such plan."

Brohan chuckled and picked up a long-cooled breakfast bun from its tray and pointed it at Calvraign. "I would take odds that Agrylon has been fueling the king's admiration for you, lad. A commoner may not marry into the aristocracy, but a knight – *that* is a different matter entirely. A knight may accumulate wealth and lands, maybe even respect and honor along the way, and eventually join the ranks of the peerage. Give him a couple of years, and he'll have you a lordling or better, Cal."

"Not if I'm dead," returned Calvraign sourly. The weight of the stress and lack of sleep bore down on his already dark mood. Each time the situation appeared to be within the grasp of his understanding, it expanded in his palm until it split the gaps of his fingers and spilled free. He was growing weary of stooping over to pick up the pieces all the time. As if in agreement with his thoughts, an unsightly yawn escaped his lips.

Artygalle rose from the table and bowed to Aeolil. "With all due respect, milady, I believe we have outstayed our welcome." Then, to Calvraign, "You have only to tell me if you need me, but I must away to prepare for the Parade of the Lists. By your leave?"

"Go, go! I'm sure you've wasted enough of your time with me," said Calvraign, extending his arm across the table to clasp hands with the knight. "I'm glad to call you a friend and ally, Sir Artygalle. Thank you."

Aeolil also rose, motioning to Bleys that they would depart. "I'll talk to Agrylon, but I can't guarantee that will do any good. With your safety now the concern of half the castle, you should sleep soundly. I know you have no reason to trust me more than any other, but I hope you know my concern and intent are sincere."

"I never doubted either, milady."

Aeolil smiled. "I will see you at the royal pavilion, then, for the parade," she said.

Brohan took a bite of his sweet bun as the door closed behind them. "Well," he said in mid-mouthful. "Lines are being drawn, lad, and many of them around you. I'd advise getting some rest before the Parade. We'll want to put on a good show."

Calvraign reclined on the settee, staring up at the wood rafters that stretched above his head. The flickering light of the fire and torches cast a legion of warring shadows on the stage of dark grey stone, and even as he imagined the outcome of their desperate battle, he lapsed into a restless slumber.

Chapter Twenty-Two

Another for the Lists

Sir Artygalle led Windthane across the open expanse of the bridge that linked King's Keep to Dwynleigsh, joining the gathering throng of knights, steeds, and squires that made their way to the city. He was without the convenience of a squire himself, but the tasks involved were familiar enough to him. When he left Tiriel a moon ago, those same tasks had been his own in the service of Sir Ghaerieal. But now that his master's task was *his*, there was no one to take up his old duties. He'd thought Illuné had delivered Calvraign to him for just that task, but once knighted by the king, it would have been an insult even to ask. The Goddess clearly had greater things in mind for that one. It made no real difference to Artygalle. As She willed, so he would follow.

Artygalle kept a careful pace, holding back the anxious horse at his side. The bridge was slick with a thin film of frost that the cloud-veiled suns were powerless to melt away. He had seen one knight run afoul of the ice already, falling with a clatter of mail and shield to the hard stone. He had stopped to offer assistance, but received a scowling rebuke for his kindness. His own armor rode on Windthane's back, carefully wrapped in oiled cloth and canvass to ward off the elements. It was plain compared to the extravagance of those around him, but they, he reminded himself, were the cream of the Providaynian peerage. Theirs were suits inlaid with precious gems and metals, some so elaborately etched as to resemble pieces of art rather than practical armor. The plumes that streamed from their helms in the strong winds were of silk or feathers from exotic birds, their coloring chosen carefully to match their Liege-House.

"Out of the way, squire! Make way for Sir Graeme of Bardyn-Oak!"

Artygalle moved aside at the sound of the booming voice, pulling Windthane to rest as well. A small entourage made its way past him, a knight in green enameled armor at its center. His shield bore the blazon of a sprawling ancient oak by a river with a gryphon sejant in sinister chief. A vassal of House adh Boighn, evidently, and of no small means, judging by his retainers and ornate gear.

"You'd best tell your master to hurry it along, squire," joked one of the nobleman's rear-guard, "or you'll have to do the fighting for him!"

Artygalle took the taunt in good humor, nodding respectfully to the man's back as they marched onward. Rather than cause a stir here on the bridge, let him see the error of his assumption on Saint Kaissus Field.

He waited for an opening to rejoin the procession and slid back unnoticed behind two stately knights and their squires. He recognized the golden eagle of House Vespurial, and his companion's banner bore the black wolf's head on blue and gold of House Malminnion. It was none other than Calamyr and Garath, of whom he'd heard so much of late. He remained in place behind them, at a discrete listening distance, and took full advantage of the Goddess' good graces.

Calamyr was speaking, his voice a venomous snarl. "...as if I would stoop to such a thing! I could have struck Vanelorn for suggesting it, I tell you. What nonsense!"

"I knew that hill-boy would cause trouble," Garath said in a rather smug tone. "Didn't I tell you so?"

"Oh, shut up," Calamyr snapped back. "As if it's his fault some idiot tried to have him killed. He bears you no ill will – I don't see why you can't let go of yours. If you keep nattering like that, Vanelorn will be pointing his finger at you next."

"Don't be ridiculous. He's *my* subject, after all. Why bother killing him?"

"He's not your subject anymore, Garath," Calamyr reminded him. "The king made him a knight in the Order Royal, and they answer to no man but the king. Or did you forget his hearty welcome?"

"I didn't forget," mumbled Garath like a chastised student. "What a disgrace."

"The only disgrace, my friend, is the way Vanelorn dragged my family name through the mud," responded Calamyr. "And all because of some trinket."

"The whole matter will be forgotten soon enough." Garath took a moment to steady his horse on the slick paving stones, and Artygalle admired his handling skill. "Vanelorn may be a senile old fool, but Willanel and Inulf won't let this go for long. At least you don't have Ezriel to worry about. I was beginning to hope he'd miss the festival entirely this year."

"I thought he was held up by the snows."

"Oghran would not be so kind. Tremayne and his outriders just came in this morning. The main party will arrive later today, tomorrow at the latest."

Artygalle wondered what the source of bad blood was between the two Malminnion brothers. From the way Garath spoke, it was more than sibling rivalry. Social concerns were really not his specialty, but he would have to become more familiar with such considerations in order to build support for Tiriel during the tourney. One brother might be ally, the other enemy, and he needed to discern such things readily. Ghaerieal had known the ways of Providaynian court and politics as well as sword and lance, and Artygalle felt stabbing remorse in his heart at the unbidden memories of his departed master. In all of his life, he had never felt more alone.

Palm open, he made the sign of the moon on his breast and bowed his head. *Illuné, You have my trust, my heart, and my way,* he prayed. *Give me Your strength and wisdom that I may do Your will and abide by Your grace, Amen.*

"Are you the one called Artygalle, from Tiriel?"

The voice had an officious ring to it, neither pleasant nor unfriendly, and Artygalle looked up to find the source. The horse caught his attention first, a magnificent white mare with her mane in braids. She was barded in lightweight chain with a silver-trimmed steel cap polished to mirror brightness covering her muzzle. On her back, sitting straight in the saddle, was a knight in the same shining armor. The helm was open, and a young face looked down on him from within. Etched into the right breast of his breastplate, a winged sword over a full moon: the Order of Illuné.

"I am he," answered Artygalle. "How may I be of service to you, Brother?"

The knight looked down without tilting his head. "On the morrow, before the Opening Melee, report to His Holiness the Archbishop at Saint Severun's Cathedral. He wishes to speak with you."

"I would consider it an honor," he agreed. The knight gathered in his reins and prepared to push on. "May I have your name before you're away, Brother?" asked Artygalle.

"*Your Grace* will do for now," was the curt response.

Artygalle watched the knight's back as he spurred off into the crowd, heedless of those around him. *Even within the Church, there are those for whom power and station is more important than faith,* Ghaerieal had warned him. It certainly seemed the case for that man, but Artygalle chastised himself for making assumptions. It was not for him to judge his Brothers. This was not Tiriel, and as he had just reminded himself moments ago, the intricate nature of politics in the Providaynian capital surely demanded different skills and mindset. He had almost convinced himself that such behavior might be appropriate when Calamyr's words voiced his original feeling.

"His Grace is an ass to everyone, Sir Artygalle," the young rake said, leading his horse on foot back through the concourse. If there were those that frowned on his casual obstruction to their progress across the bridge, none made it known. "Don't let it niggle at you."

Artygalle was confused and surprised at the nobleman's appearance, and his slack-jawed stare didn't hide the fact well. "Yes," he said as Calamyr arrived before him, "no offense was taken."

"I must admit, you startled me, Sir Artygalle," Calamyr went on, motioning that they should continue on their way. "I had thought it was a squire following us, not a knight, but well met in any case. Calvraign speaks quite highly of you."

Artygalle's shame blanched the color from his face. "I apologize, milord. I intended no affront."

Calamyr laughed. "Of course you didn't, sir. Listening is no affront, and I can't say I fault your reasoning. You do your friend honor. Regardless, I have nothing to hide."

Artygalle saw Garath, still on horseback, and their squires, waiting ahead. A sour expression curled the skin around the nobleman's neatly trimmed beard, and the lines already etched on his young face betrayed the constancy of this mood. It saddened Artygalle to see anyone with so little happiness, especially one of his station with so much to be thankful for. The scrutiny he gave Artygalle in return promised his disposition would not lighten on his account.

Artygalle looked to Calamyr's more friendly countenance. "Who was His Grace, milord, if you'll pardon my asking?"

"That was Derrigin Sinhd, Curate of Breakwater Gorge and Knight Commander in the Order of Illuné. Don't miss a title; he'll notice. If there's a man in this world more arrogant than I, it is he, but without my impeccable grace and humor. I don't think he was happy to play errand boy to a knight dressed as a squire. Somewhat beneath his dignity."

Artygalle gave his customary nod and remained silent.

"I've had my fill of this bridge," said Garath. "Let's be off it before the wind blows us off."

"Garath," said Calamyr as they proceeded, "may I introduce Sir Artygalle of Tiriel. He's a lancer, I hear, but the Northern variety doesn't appear so stuffy."

"At your service, milord," said Artygalle. He was already tired of these formal greetings, and the day was still young.

Garath saluted Artygalle with too much haste to be considered absolutely proper. "Well met," he said, eyeing Windthane. "That's quite a horse, but maybe you should have saved a gryph or two for some armor."

"You have a discerning eye, milord," replied Artygalle, "but I must confess that I ride at the Lady Aeolil's courtesy. Windthane is hers."

Garath and Calamyr shared a wide-eyed look. Artygalle couldn't help feeling some small satisfaction from their surprise.

Calamyr recovered first, flashing a confident smile. "I am impressed, sir knight. Rumor has it Lady Aeolil keeps her stables shuttered tightly."

Garath agreed with a quick nod. "Aye, what oil loosened *those* hinges? I only pray I'm the first to tell Ezriel."

The two noblemen laughed, leaving Artygalle to wonder at their private joke. He didn't care for the insinuation behind their words. He knew he should keep quiet, but the thought of anyone with less than the utmost respect for his kind patron irked him. "I hope there is no offense intended Lady Aeolil. She is a kind and honorable lady, and I would defend her good name with my life."

Calamyr sucked in his laugh with a quick breath and arched a curious brow at Artygalle. "At ease, sir, please. We often forget ourselves, Garath and I, but no offense was intended – at least not to Aeolil. And I certainly don't wish to cross blades until we reach the field. Isn't that so, Garath?"

Garath looked over at his friend with an uncertain frown. "I suppose." The lack of apology in his tone was made all the more blatant by the unmistakable challenge in his eyes. "But, you'll need thicker skin than that to survive long in Dwynleigsh."

Artygalle made ready to respond, but Calamyr's tongue was quicker. "Gods, must you always be so contrary?" he snapped. "Your own skin is no thicker than a silk kerchief. I have a mind to challenge you myself if it will shut you up."

"And risk dirtying your pretty ensemble on my account?" Garath countered, grinning reluctantly. "I doubt it. The ladies haven't even seen you yet."

"Point well taken," agreed Calamyr with a mock salute. "You'll have your turn soon enough."

Artygalle suppressed a sigh. Clearly they thought this normal and acceptable behavior, but in Tiriel such was not considered polite discussion. He walked on beside them as they bickered and joked back and forth, trying to avoid inclusion in their banter entirely.

Perhaps he should be more restrained with his indignant outcries, next time. If it was their custom to throw such veiled comments and insults around so freely, he could hardly go around challenging every member of the court in turn. And, he admitted to himself, his experiences in Tiriel were with the brothers of his Order, not the aristocracy. Amidst their own, those nobles might behave much the same.

They slowed to a stop at the gatehouse, trapped in a massive bottleneck as the parade attempted to sift through from the bridge into the city. The crowd gathered in the streets beyond made a low rumbling noise like a continuous roar of thunder. Artygalle had spent his days exploring the vast city, and was less intimidated by it than when he first arrived, but this turnout was unsettling. Thousands were waiting to watch the coming tourney. The greatest and most notorious knights from every realm in the East would be here to compete for the King's Lance under the auspices of the Winter Truce, and he would be there among them, doing battle. He swallowed the dry lump in his throat. If he had a choice, this would not be his first tournament. But here he was, and as far as choices went, he was severely lacking.

Calamyr remounted beside him, and Artygalle noticed all the knights and squires taking up positions in miniature formations all around him. His heart quickened in his chest. "I don't understand. I thought the Parade was to begin later, before the pavilions."

"Yes, the official Parade will," said Garath, straightening his tabard, "but it's customary to put on a show for the city on the way there. I assumed you knew."

"No," Artygalle said, even more quiet than normal. He had neither the time nor means to don his armor now, and he felt a slow churning begin in his stomach. This would not be an auspicious start as Lord Elvaeir's champion.

"You might as well mount up," said Calamyr. "You'll just have to make the best of it. You may ride between us if you wish."

"That is a kind offer, Lord Calamyr, but I suggest you go on ahead. I will be a moment, and you have your own appearances to maintain without worrying for mine."

"As you wish," said Calamyr. "Good day, then, sir."

"And good luck," added Garath with an uncharacteristic smile. Whether from sympathy or amusement, or a bit of each, Artygalle couldn't tell.

He didn't watch them as they took their places in the advancing queue; he had enough details to worry over without second-guessing himself. By the time he had rearranged his packs and taken the saddle, the procession of knights and nobles was thinning, and he had no trouble slipping through the Harbor Gate into Dwynleigsh.

The crowd still waited, cheering from windows, balconies and in a surging mass on the sides of the smooth-paved streets. Many had strips of cloth or miniature pennants with the colors of their favorite House or individual champion, waving them aloft with loud whoops and cheers of encouragement. He saw none with the scarlet and white of Tiriel, nor did he expect to. Lord Elvaeir had not sent a champion in four years, since his last dispute with House Jiraud, and no natives of his homeland had braved the howling snows to lend him support. But that was not important to him. Those watching the field were only as invested in his victory as much as their purses would allow or Oghran's spirit moved them. And he was not here to win fame or the crowd's adoration. His reasons were of much greater consequence.

The spectators didn't know this, however, nor did he think they would care if they had, but he attracted their notice just the same. At first, it was mostly surprised laughter that reached his ears. Then, muttered questions and whispered insults grew in both volume and candor, evolving finally into outright taunts. Artygalle kept his back straight and his eyes forward throughout, staring at the capes of those before him. It wasn't his personal pride that moved him to make a show of his inviolability, but the sense of honor Ghaerieal had instilled in him. He was a Knight Lancer in the Order of Andulin, and as long as he had Illuné's blessing, he could live without the shifting loyalties of mortals.

Not that it made their words sting any less.

"You missed Market Day, farm boy!" yelled a merchant from one side.

"I hope you polished your wooden sword!" from the other.

And then a lady's voice, with the overly enunciated accent of an Aerydii: "The Fool's Parade is on the morrow, boy!"

Artygalle continued to ride, eyes forward, ignoring the insults. They were brash to make any such comment to a knight, who by virtue of rank would be well within rights to exact any number of penalties upon them. Normally, he would expect the support of the peers who rode with him to Saint Kaissus Field. An insult to one of their number was an insult to all of that rank. But today, whether because they silently agreed with the crowd's opinion or because they thought it a strategic advantage to unnerve him, they remained silent. This only emboldened the crowd into more frequent and vociferous slurs.

Cowards like nothing better than easy sport, he thought, as if repeating the phrase would make the reality less painful.

"May as well give *me* the horse and sword," the latest voice called out. "At least I'll make a show of it."

Artygalle pulled in the reins and brought his horse to a halt. The affront in itself was no more bothersome than the others, but it provided him with an idea and opportunity to halt the annoying catcalls. Windthane shook his head and snorted a plume of fine mist as Artygalle turned in the saddle to face the direction of the taunt. He spotted the man towards the front row – a middle-aged man, a Maeziir by his dusky complexion, and a Guilder of some small affluence from the moderate finery of his dress. His face reddened somewhat as he noticed the knight's attention focus on him, and he attempted to slip deeper into the ranks of onlookers. The crowd was not accommodating. They sensed the chance of a fight, or at least a harsh dressing down, and they had no desire to let one of the parties escape before they had their fun. Especially a well-to-do foreigner.

Artygalle nudged Windthane up to the crowd's perimeter with a quick side shuffle, and looked down at the man. "What is your name, sir?" he asked.

"I beg your pardon?" the Guilder responded indignantly.

"I asked for your name," repeated Artygalle without even the hint of impatience or anger in his voice.

The man paused, looked around him, and then frowned. "I am Veipo of Abruosk. What business is it of yours?"

"I will need your name to add you to the List in my place," explained Artygalle, drawing his sword and offering it hilt first across his forearm in one terrified blink of Veipo's eyes. "Take the sword and the horse, as well as my lord's charge to win the King's Lance. I will vouch for you with the Master of the List."

Those in the front of the crowd began to chuckle and murmur, but this time at the Maeziiri's expense. Some of the laughter stopped when the more observant among them noticed the brooch that fastened the plain cloak at Artygalle's neck. The winged sword and shield was a rare token, but a familiar one. The merchant wet his lips, which he attempted to raise into a confident smile.

"Come, take it," prodded Artygalle, leaning down to bring the hilt even closer to the man.

"He's a lancer," someone whispered.

"That's the Order of Andulin," voiced another.

Veipo blanched further as similar comments multiplied around him. "No, no," he said. "Just a jest. A little jest, that's all."

Artygalle could have allowed him to squirm there for quite some time, but that was not his aim. "Ah, a jest!" he said with a smile. "Forgive me. Go with my blessing, then. And may Illuné chase the shadows from your doorstep."

Veipo exhaled and nodded, smiling like an idiot but obviously relieved. The Guilder knew the narrow ledge he had crossed, as did the crowd still surrounding him. Artygalle would have been well within his rights to insist some form of reparation from Veipo, including fines or imprisonment, and everyone knew it.

Artygalle started back down the road, now at the very back of the parade ranks. The merchants and low-level aristocrats were already thinning out, heading to Saint Kaissus Field for the Commencement. The cold glances they shot him spoke plainer than words what they thought of his display. Knights who took vows of poverty were troublesome enough to the rich, and Artygalle knew that his unintentional show of his meager assets only made them more uncomfortable. But, as he had hoped, his display of grace and lack of vindictiveness had curried the grudging respect and even favor of the commoners in the throng.

"What is your name, sir?" someone shouted. "For whom do you ride?"

"I am Artygalle of Tiriel," he answered, a bit of confidence seeping into him, "and I ride for my Lord Elvaeir and the Grace of Illuné."

He still heard the laughter and insults of some as he passed deeper into the city, but he rode on unconcerned. For now, amongst those same shouts of shame and ridicule, there were new cries to combat them. Not from the wealthy, and few from the middle-classed, but from the men, women and children who fleshed out their ranks, dressed not much different than he.

For every distasteful expletive from the higher born, there were ten more shouts of "Luck and Light be with you, sir!"

He knew it shouldn't matter, that their support or condemnation was all secondary to his goal, but he found their encouragement raised his spirits and his strength of will. He would bear his burdens alone if he must, but bolstered by their enthusiasm, he decided that it wasn't necessary. No one rode for them in the great tourneys. No one bore their colors of ragtag brown and coarse linen grey before them into battle. No one risked or gained anything for them. All these nobles fought for was reputation, pride and purse. But he would not, and while his goal was the charge of Elvaeir, his fight would be for *them*.

Artygalle raised his sword in salute to the crowd, turning once to each side with the same respect he would shortly show the king and court. Another cheer drowned out another chorus of disrespects, and the city came alive as he passed. The clouds were thinning, the suns warming, and to Artygalle, it was like a new start to the day.

Chapter Twenty-Three

Fire at the Gates

DIEAVAUL stood back to examine his work, checking over each of the inscriptions he had carved into the granite for blemish or careless error. There could be no inconsistencies – each sigil must be perfect. The stone gate that barred his way into the underkin's mountain stronghold was a secure one. It was ancient, bound by powerful magics, and well hidden. In fact, he had not known the place existed at all until what seemed the entire side of the mountain was loosed upon him and his force the night before. Only the power of *ilnymhorrim* had enabled him to escape unscathed, cutting through the Veil for a brief walk through Shadow to a point out of harm's way. Most of his retinue had not been so lucky. He had saved those few he could without wasting his *iiyir* or undue time, but in the end only six of fifty were left in useful condition.

If he could slip through the Veil in similar fashion to just beyond the door, his dilemma would be solved. But Dieavaul knew better than to take the prospect of a Shadow-walk so lightly. Without clear foreknowledge of his destination, most especially within such a huge mass of stone, he could just as easily return within a wall or floor or other solid object. That would rid the world of his presence in a heartbeat. And the kin were of Faerie just as the aulden – that way would be guarded, also.

Brute force, then, seemed his only option, and he had been far too tired after regaining the summit and discovering this cave. Since his escape through Shadow had taken them back down the mountain, to a place familiar enough to be relatively safe, they had been forced to traverse much of the same steep ground a second miserable time.

Almost a full day wasted.

It will only be wasted if I fail, he corrected himself.

Dieavaul stretched his arms wide, fingers splayed, his eyelids fluttering as he fell into a trance. The surviving hrumm backed against the far wall, their bestial yellow eyes reflecting a shared fear of their master and his dreaded power, their hackles rising as the air crackled with invisible energy. Dieavaul whipped the inner flames of his *iiyir* into a blazing inferno restrained by his will, focused by the complex gesticulations of his slender fingers as they danced fluid patterns in the air, and finally released by the word of power that issued from his taut lips. With its utterance, the Pale Man felt the familiar white-hot energy flood his senses, washing away all other sensation with its cleansing rage as swirling flames shot from his outstretched hands to strike at his target.

Orange-red fire licked at the obstinate stone, and the sigils came alive, glowing with hellish heat as they redoubled the energies Dieavaul had cast upon them, weakening the gate's formidable wards. Molten rock rolled sluggishly down to the cave floor, pooling and solidifying in a shiny mass at Dieavaul's feet.

Even as he watched the slag cool, he knew the spell had failed to breach the entrance. Dieavaul eyed the gate with a growing sense of resignation. It was clear that his own resources were not up to the task at hand. Given time, perhaps, and adequate rest, he could prepare a spell more tailored to the situation. He had neither, however, which only added more credence to the course he must now take, despite his reservations.

A century or so earlier, he would have thought little of tapping into the power of his sword, allowing the black unliving energies of its maker into his being and twisting it to serve his own designs. But with age came wisdom, and Dieavaul recognized the price he paid for such frequent, careless use of so great a power. For every instance he drew too deeply upon the artifact for strength or aid, a growing piece of his innermost being, his will, even his soul, became less and less his own and more the domain of the Dark God of which the weapon was irrevocably a part. *Deathbringer,* some human had called it. An apt appellation if not a little trite – for its wielder as well as its victims.

Dieavaul thought back to the *wilhorwhyr* he had slain, the boy called Jasper. The image of the boy's young, young soul writhing in the inside-out torture of *ilnymhorrim's* thrall gave him genuine pleasure. No mortal could conceive the level of suffering in his prisoner as, despite all that he ever held sacred in life, he was compelled to obey and assist in the betrayal of those same beliefs in his eternal death-within-death. Strong or weak when of the flesh, it mattered little once sent to dwell in the Bone Tower. Once within that small corner of the Dark God's twisted soul, enveloped in the celestial miasma of all that philosophers called evil, there was no sleep, no respite, no escape. Whether king, hero or peasant, hope perished swiftly.

Jasper had tried to resist, as they all did at first, under the false illusion of hope his preconceived notions of justice inspired. In the end he simply had no choice but to obey, just as all those who had fallen before him. The dead boy had vomited up his knowledge of this Two-Moons, his aulden bitch, and the soul-thief called Bloodhawk.

Dieavaul had never felt a *wilhorwhyr's* torment before, and it was like a draught of the finest vintage, so pure and noble his angst and so bitter the despair of his treachery. Many more long days of indulgence awaited with that one.

Dieavaul exhaled, shrugging off such thoughts and resigning himself to the inevitable. *Ilnymhorrim* would be hungry; it had not fed after the Shadow-walk. His gaze swept over the hrumm warriors pressed against the opposite wall of the cave. Not its meal of choice, but options were limited, and he had no intention of sacrificing any of his own life force for the deed.

Two should suffice.

"Shaa has need of a sacrifice," he said in a grave near-whisper. "He bids only warriors come. Which of you here will send your souls to his aid?"

Dieavaul watched as they stepped forward, eager for their place of honor in the Host of the Accursed. He acted with speed and certainty, selecting the two strongest of the survivors before they began killing each other for the privilege of sacrifice. He found himself amused at the irony. Where he sent them, there would be no god waiting for them, no glory, no war. They would have eternity to contemplate their mistake.

⁂

Captain Sul Vaujn looked over the men and women in his command with respect and genuine fondness. They were like family, out here on the fringes of the known world, hundreds of leagues from civilization and a mere hundred feet from the surface world. He took their care seriously.

Many of these same soldiers had fought with him under Captain Fruenh in the Deeping Wars. Of course, until that dringli arrow in Vurdann found its mark, he had been merely Lieutenant Vaujn, and damn happy about it. Command had its downfalls. He would lay down his life for them, as they would for him – and this day he might well have to ask it of them.

His company numbered twelve, himself included, which according to his arithmetic, didn't stack up well against the flame-spewing demigod blasting at their door. Fortunately, this stronghold had originally been built to fend off the andu'ai, back when their kind was troublesome, and so it could be dealt a fair number of blows, magical or otherwise.

Mother Chloe, his wife and the resident chaplain of Brecholt's Spur Outpost Number Nine, whistled through clenched teeth. She stared with fixed eyes into a water-filled marble basin. Rippling on the surface of the fluid, normally crystal clear as a mountain spring, was the figure of a pale warrior in dark garb, his hands gripped around blade and hilt of a sword of bone-like steel. The bloody remains of two hrumm warriors littered the floor of the cave at his feet. There was no sound, but it was clear he was speaking. Probably a spell, Vaujn knew, and evidently one that required a blood sacrifice. That made the captain of the watch uneasy.

"Chloe, what in the Pits is that bastard up to?" he said finally, deciding she wouldn't volunteer the information soon enough to suit him.

Mother Chloe shrugged, meeting her husband's gaze with honest candor. "If I read that spell right, and mind you I'm not sure with aulden magic, I reckon we have about fifteen clicks before he slags that whole door. He's binding a word of unmaking with words of shadow and fire. It might take two castings, and hopefully that would tire even *him* out, but he does have a couple extra hrumm back there."

Vaujn looked at the troops assembled in the temple behind them. They stared back with typical stolid gravity. They were soldiers of the Upper Watch, and they might be terrified by the power being unleashed at their door, but they wouldn't show it. That was not the kin way.

The kin way was to gripe about it, and gripe bitterly.

"What a mess," began Corporal Sturng Darrow in a tone that would've made his mother proud. "Damn *Shaddach Chi* was bound to come in and stir everything up. Didn't I tell you we should've played dead, Vaujn? But no, you had to have your fun and tumble the mountain on 'em."

There was a general grumbling of assent.

It wasn't kin custom to address superior officers by title; some members of court even got away with calling the king by his childhood nickname, *Ruuh*. But when a title was conferred on subordinates, that meant serious business, reminding them of their place. Which explained why Sturng shrunk back at his captain's retort.

"Shut up, *Corporal* ! If I asked for your lousy advice every time our backs were against the wall, we'd all be dead three times over by now!" Someone muttered something about it *only taking once* from the back ranks, but Vaujn ignored the remark and pressed on. "I didn't ask for this any more than you did, but damn our kind hearts, we'll just have to handle it. Chloe says that pasty aulden freak'll blast his way in here real soon, so we have to make a decision quick."

Vaujn paused to pass his eyes over the formation of sturdy kin and, in no small part, to figure out what he was going to say next. With a nod to himself, he continued. "Now, as I see it, we have two options. One: we stand our ground and fight like even the *Shaddach Chi* have never fought, and we burn our names into the slate of history with dignity and valor. A hundred hundred years from now, they will still sing of the courage of Outpost Number Nine!" There was a slight shuffling in the ranks as some of the veterans straightened their backs with pride, and the youthful eyes of the inexperienced lit up with the ignorant fire of the untested. "Or two: we run like hell and don't look back!"

There was a distinct silence.

Vaujn looked at the image of the dark magics being gathered still shimmering in the holy water at his left and exchanged a look with his wife. Her eyes chastised him silently. *I should've taken it easy on the slate of history bit,* he thought. He hadn't considered that there was the slimmest chance of firing up his troops for battle. It was obvious they were outmatched. Any sane kin could see that.

"Look at the power he wields! We have nothing to combat such magics!" he said. "There is no shame in retreat against such a foe!"

"Did Magliuk run from the wyrm at Dinnoch?" questioned the aging Sergeant Mueszner without so much as a quaver in his tone, the bushy grey hair crowning his eyes leaping like launching eagles as he raised his brows. He bore his hammer aloft over his head and roared in a strengthening basso rumble. "Did Birijohr run from Asharak? Did Hulgar flee from the Hordes of Uhlmon-zaar?"

"Yes, yes, your point is taken, old friend," he soothed. Vaujn felt he was losing control of the situation, but if he lost his temper with Mueszner, he would never regain them. Rumor had it he'd lived in Outpost Number Nine before it even bore that name. "But we're not the like of Birijohr. We are simple soldiers, and *he* is Guhddan-kinne!" He nodded pointedly at the image in the bowl.

"The kin have never run from great battles!" came a confident young voice.

"If we're going to die, I'd rather die with a sword in my breast than in my back!" yelled another.

Vaujn could see the situation was deteriorating rapidly. He somehow had to make them understand, and within the space of increasingly scant time. Then, just before he began to really lose his temper, Chloe stood from her place by the scrying pool and turned around so quickly that her beautiful chestnut warbraids whipped into his face. As he blinked away the sting, he hoped by all that was holy under the mountain that he was misunderstanding his wife's words.

"You are braver by half than any of those kin of legend!" she screamed in her best preaching voice. "Let your courage guide you!"

Vaujn stared wide-eyed as his wife continued to goad them toward suicide with words like *bravery* and *honor*. Not a click had passed, and already they were stomping their iron-shod feet on the floor and rapping their weapons against their shields. He felt a cold sweat break out on his palms as his beloved wife raised her voice once again above the motley din.

"Is our honor not worth the cost of pain?" she asked rhetorically.

"Pain before dishonor!" they replied with the typical response.

"Is our honor not worth our lives?" she yelled again.

"Death before dishonor!" they chanted.

"Is our honor not worth eternal damnation?" she exhorted feverishly.

"Damnation before…" Though a few of the younger voices finished the phrase, most of the kin were taken aback, and their mouths hung empty on the words. They were fairly certain that wasn't the way the verse progressed.

"What?" asked Mueszner in a tone that reflected their general confusion.

"*Damnation!*" raved Chloe. "The sword of the Guhddan-kinne does not simply send you beyond the Veil with a mortal blow! This blade cuts so deep it sunders the strings that hold your soul and binds you to ages of bloody torment at the service of the Dark God!" As a priest, she had somehow managed to spit all that out in one breath with the proper inflection. She took another deep breath, and continued, "Brave beyond words are those who so risk eternity! To your posts, then. He will be through before long now!"

This time it was Mother Chloe who was answered with silence. All eyes shifted to Vaujn. "Uh, Captain, what would you recommend, sir?" asked Mueszner hopefully.

Vaujn repressed the smile and wink he so desperately wanted to flash the stout woman next to him. He truly did love his wife. First he had to help them save face, give them an honorable way out of this situation. "Well, I know you're all eager for battle, but I must disagree with my, uh, with Mother Chloe. I think it best if we retreat under the mountain. We need to warn Osrith that the outpost has fallen. This could put him in

Fire at the Gates

great danger. Perhaps we will even be of some service to him. I can't have you risk so much to gain so little, I'm afraid."

"Yes," agreed Darrow, "Osrith is *Shaddach Chi*. We owe him that much!"

"Yes, to the *Shaddach Chi*! Warn the *Shaddach Chi*!" they quickly took up the chant.

"Right then," said Vaujn in his best command tone, "to the South Passage on Level Forty Two. We'll take the river. Double-time, now. He's just made a big dent. One more and the outer gate's done for!"

The column of guardsmen streamed out of the temple in the quick and orderly fashion with which they prided themselves. Slightly quicker than normal, perhaps, but still orderly. Vaujn and Chloe brought up the rear of the column.

"Thanks," he whispered in her ear, "I was in trouble there."

"Mmm," she agreed, her eyes skeptical, "I noticed you didn't mention that by following Osrith, we're going through Mordigul's Plunge, now did you?"

Vaujn shrugged, eyes forward. "No, I must've forgotten to mention that part." They marched on for another few clicks as he chewed on his mustache in silence. "They'll understand," he said finally. "I know they will."

"I hope you're trying to convince yourself," grumbled his wife as the boats drew into sight at the underground river dock. Packs of emergency gear were already being stowed as they approached. "Because it's not working for me."

☙

This time, when the smoke cleared, there was no more door. A billowing cloud of ash swept across Dieavaul and the one surviving hrumm warrior, revealing a ragged and uneven gap where before there had been a barricade of implacable rock. Not without cost was the use of magic, like any other tool, and Dieavaul slumped from the effort of casting three greater spells within the half of an hour.

The Pale Man regarded his newly made entrance with respect. The kin of old had mighty wards, and with the ages, their enchantment had seeped deep into the rock to its very source, no longer protecting but joining it. Seeping down into the very energy of the stone itself, they had become as one, *bonded*, and the *iiyir* within this native rock was ancient and powerful indeed. This was no simple matter of dispelling a charm of locking or a spell of binding. This was a test of his *il-iiyir*, his command of the *ur-iiyir*, and the strength of his connection to his own source.

Mormikar himself would have struggled to breach this gate, he thought in satisfaction. *Dmylriani, too. Or could she at all?* He reconsidered. *She was a sycophant, begging at the petty energies of nature to do her bidding.*

He often wondered how his mentor would react if she knew to what purpose he had devoted his knowledge and skill. How her milk-pure skin would flush over her high cheekbones at the betrayal of her trust and his oath to the Collegiate Arcana. How her Lyymiruian blood must boil at the concept of drawing power from the nether world of Shadow. But she had sailed away by then, across the Easerai, on her foolish little quest. Never to return. Never to witness her pupil's ascendency.

All the better. One less obstacle in my path, and she's saved me the effort of removing her.

Dieavaul shook his head, clearing it of such useless musing. What point in wondering what she would think? He drew himself up again, this time for a lesser spell. It was a relief casting this, a mere flirtation, really, with the bonesword in sheath and distant from his thoughts. A moment later he stepped through the smoking hole, avoiding the smoldering edges, and waited.

The craftsmanship of the kin betrayed them. They could not fashion their works without leaving a trace of themselves behind. The filaments of kin *iiyir* ran through the stone around him like veins of precious metals, humming back to tickle Dieavaul's skin in warning.

Once again it was hard to feign surprise. Traps everywhere, devious and complex. Too numerous to dispel with any reasonable magics, too dangerous to disarm by hand. This would be a challenge. The kin were notorious as engineers of devices mechanical. *And this is merely the outer entryway*, he reminded himself. He turned to the hrumm standing respectfully behind him.

"Come," he beckoned.

The hrumm moved forward, its huge meaty hands gripping its battle-axe in either eagerness or fear. "Master?" it asked, its strong jaws laboring over the odd human tongue. The tattoos near its eyes steamed eerily as its sweat met the brutal cold of the thin mountain air.

"They've gone to ground," said the Pale Man quietly. "Can you help me root them out?"

The hrumm must have understood that the question was rhetorical, but responded anyway. "Yes, *Gal Pakh*. I go first. Clear way for you. Yes?"

Dieavaul nodded.

Hesitantly, the hrumm moved into the long passageway, low to the ground and sniffing. Dieavaul's Host was experienced. This was not its first sortie into a kin-hold. Its eyes were faintly luminous in the dark as it scoured the floor, ceiling, and walls. After a painstaking search, it set its thick fingers to work in an unobtrusive niche on the west wall.

The hrumm grunted and bit on its tongue in concentration, eventually rewarded with a satisfying *click*.

It turned its head toward its master in triumph. A breath later, a slab of rock weighing tens of tons fell from its seamless perch in the roof. The hrumm had just enough time to look up before it was crushed, but not quite enough to scream. The echo of the impact rattled hollowly in the long corridor.

Dieavaul sighed, his lip twitching in irritation. It was to be expected that the miserable creature would fall afoul of the kin traps. That wasn't the issue. He found it annoying that it had fallen victim to the very *first* trap, however. It could take him hours to work his way through all of them. Though he could sense them with magic, the traps themselves were mostly mechanical, and he could not dispel them with a word and a gesture. He would have to use more complicated magics, spells of holding and slowing and the like.

This, then, was his limit. He would not storm a kin stronghold singlehanded, even if it meant an inopportune delay to securing the dreamstone. *Let Turlun hide in the Deeps*, he thought. Dieavaul knew Osrith's intended destination. He could afford patience. Finding him again was only a matter of waiting and watching for *when*.

The hilt of *ilnymhorrim* hummed against his waist.

"Yes?" he muttered, a faint smile coming to his lips. "You tire of this too."

Though the sword had no voice, it made its wants known – sometimes more insistently than others – but known nonetheless. And this time, at least, it seemed they agreed. The whisper of the sword's will scraped like ice and steel behind his ears.

Dieavaul turned away from the charred hole in the side of the mountain and swept his sword through the thin air of the cave. A slice appeared in mid-air, spreading like a parchment slowly burning under the heat of a candle, opening into a hole of swirling grey – hundreds of greys from light to dark and back to light again, but devoid of color or form. *Perhaps some good came of this after all*, he reflected as he stood before the howling gate of Shadow. If nothing else, he had inconvenienced them. *Delaying them may serve me just as well.*

The Pale Man stepped through, disappearing within the portal. The fringes of the doorway bent inwards in his wake as if he were a great wind, pulling the ragged edges of its sides together until they caught, meshed, and folded back into reality.

The wind howled through the lifeless cave, tugging at the flapping cloaks of its butchered occupants as if to rouse them from a deep slumber. But none stirred as the wailing of winter sang its cold and lonely dirge.

The dead slept on.

Chapter Twenty-Four

Casting Shadows

AEOLIL pounded on the ancient wooden door again, and the sound of her impatience echoed down the staircase behind her. She knew that the door was not really that thick, but she also knew from years as Agrylon's pupil that it would be more difficult to breach than the castle gate. This door had been here since the aulden called it home, and it was infused with more protective wards than even Agrylon could account. And, perhaps more significantly, it was still a part of the original wooden tower that lay smothered beneath the thick stones that Grand Duke Milo Jiraud had erected back in Providayne's provincial days. In the city, such thoughtless second-guessing of fae architecture had killed many of the songwood buildings, but here some unknown power kept the buried trees alive.

She shook her head at the door that refused to open. An *iiyir* convergence, Agrylon called it, a place where the ley lines were thick and abundant. He had been trying to tap into that same power for the majority of his lifetime, as he suspected the aulden once did, but with no real luck. He had only enough information to illuminate what the Ceearmyltu had been able to accomplish with such power, but all traces of *how* they accomplished it were either too well hidden or long vanished.

The door opened, and a purplish light spilled from the chamber within. Aeolil felt gooseflesh rising on her skin as she perceived the *iiyir* traces licking her awareness. She entered, and the door shut itself behind her. Aside from the colored light that spilled from the casting circle in the center of the floor the room was covered in a cloak of grey shadows. Within this darkness, hovering like ghosts in the dusky light at the edges of the chamber, were hundreds of books and arcane writings, scroll sheaves, charts, maps and a small collection of artifacts the wizard used in his more powerful incantations. There were no windows in the tower room, no other doors, no wall hangings or decorations. His treasure, if any, was his collected information and, she had no doubt, some array of things he deemed best to keep secret from even her.

Agrylon stood over the casting circle, passing his hand over the runes carved by song into the polished wooden floor by aulden mystics, ages past. They were all over the floor, a dizzying array of patterns and geometric shapes. Agrylon refused to speak of them, claiming such knowledge at her early stage in the Craft would be more dangerous than useful. There was a good chance that was the truth, but with Agrylon she was never sure. She read his lips as he mumbled the words of power in a quick chant.

"A divining?" she inquired after he was finished. She knew better than to distract him in mid-spell.

He only nodded, not turning to face her as she approached. He was still intent on the purple glow before him. The color deepened, then brightened, alternating in intensity around the form suspended in the eerie radiance. At first the figure was vague and incomplete, a shifting intimation of a man, but as her eyes adjusted she could see the features of the face coalesce into solid form, followed soon after by the rest of the body. There was no life to its shifting, translucent vapors, but the image was clear.

"Who is that?" she asked.

"That *was* our would-be assassin," he said. "Do you recognize him?"

"No. How did you…?"

Agrylon waved casually to the center of the divining circle, indicating a nondescript mass crumpled there. Aeolil saw the charred fringe of a cloak, the sole of a boot, and a long bone with dangling pieces of charred flesh ending in the grisly remnants of a hand. The corpse had been dumped there with little care or respect.

"Vanelorn was most cooperative, for a change," continued the wizard, "or most desperate. No matter his reason, it's less than I hoped to discover. He is rather well cooked, I'm afraid."

Aeolil nodded. Aside from blackened flesh and contorted limbs, there wasn't much to look at.

"Here." Agrylon made a fan-like gesture with the fingers of his left hand, and the glowing body disappeared below the neck. The disembodied head enlarged to twice its normal size, and the wizard pointed at the man's eyes. "There is some scarring on his brow. A sigil of some sort, but I have not been able to decipher it."

Aeolil guessed that one of the deadly blows from the fire iron had landed squarely on his temple, and obfuscated the marking with ruptured flesh and splintered skull. Whatever design the sigil had once represented, it was now but tendrils licking the edges of a gaping wound. "That servant's aim was too true," she muttered.

Agrylon's eyes darted to her for a moment, his face pinched in thought. "The tides are with me," he said, stroking his beard. "I believe I will call him back for a little chat."

Aeolil stifled a grimace at the thought. She'd seen him do it once before, call the dead back from the greylands for a parlay, and it was no small feat, even for a Wizard of the Eleventh Order, like Agryon. Tampering with Shadow had brought death, ruin or madness upon many who had undertaken the task capriciously.

"Agrylon..."

"Do you want to know what is afoot," he said, even as he brought a well-worn tome down from the shelf, "or sit and wait for the answers to come looking?"

"The *ur'iiyir* is on the ebb. At least wait for the tides so that –"

"Please don't presume to lecture me," Agrylon interrupted again, shaking his head as he leafed through his text to the appropriate passages. "The world-tides are receding, but my *iiyir* has not ebbed as yet. Now, fetch me some gaengrhe powder and *srhrilakiin* blood and leave the sorcery to me."

Aeolil took a deep breath. For such a major spell, common wisdom held that the *ur'iiyir* of the world-tide and the *il'iiyir* of the caster's own internal tides should both be at their peak. Agrylon, with hundreds of years' experience and a pedigree that extended back to the days of Empire, only heeded common wisdom when it suited his purpose. There was, in fact, little common about the man at all. She shook her head, restraining her irritation by concentrating on the task at hand. It was a mechanism of day-to-day survival as his underappreciated disciple, and she had nearly mastered it.

The gaengrhe powder was on the lower shelf of collected materials, with the crushed herbs. It was derived from the desiccated husks of the gaengrhe plant, dried and pounded to dust with a silver mortar and pestle, then left to age for a decade or more in the dark. It was vital that no natural light shone on the powder, or its ability to compel truth from the shadowborn would be negated. She opened the opaque jar and measured out an even spoonful into a clay bowl.

The blood was a tar-like ichor that stank of rotten vegetables. It hid behind the more common of the rarest ingredients on the top shelf, labeled in the inscrutable and dangerous calligraphy of *iilariish,* the runic inscriptions of the magi. She knew enough to read the magescript only in her peripheral vision. To read the writing directly would invite any number of unpleasant side effects, death not the least among them.

Agrylon took the components from her and set to work mixing them in the proper proportion, until there was a thick, pungent paste covering his fingers. He spread the mixture into the outline of one of the casting circles on the floor, chanting quietly. Aeolil stood back as he worked. Preparation for ritualized magic such as this required the caster's undivided attention. There could be no deviation from the parameters set forth in the spell. Even the slightest misstep could lessen the effectiveness of the summoning, or worse still, weaken or dispel the protective wards altogether.

Agrylon stood, raising his hands into the air as his chant increased in both speed and volume. Aeolil's heartbeat matched the rhythm of his words even as the crackle of gathering *iiyir* charged the air around her. Spectral flames of blackness flickered to life around the summoning circle, drawing light away from the purple glow surrounding the assassin's body and into their hungry sputtering shadows.

Aeolil knew that the spell was complete when there was nothing left but the blackness inside the circle. The purple hue of the divining was gone. In its place, the Dark. The flames were like faint chalk outlines amidst the blackness, bleeding from the inner ring of the casting circle, trickling one by one toward the form within until it was surrounded in a pool like pale moonlight. Agrylon spoke a final word of power, and the tendrils seeped into the burnt carcass – oozing into the eye sockets, ear canals, and the gaping breathless mouth. Where there was no such convenient entry, they soaked through the flesh like water into a sponge until the whole of the dead man glowed faintly in the non-light.

Agrylon faced the cardinal directions in turn, pausing long enough to offer each a separate gesture and calling upon the corresponding power of the elements. "By the Foundations of Earth, by the Firmament of the Skies, by the Consuming Flame and by the Restoring Waters of Life – I compel you to come forth, spirit," commanded Agrylon, his hands outstretched.

The husk of radiant flesh twitched.

"Between the Illumination of Light, that reveals all things, and the Obscuration of the Dark, that consumes revelation, I bring you forth from the Balance of Shadow, to speak truth. What is your name, spirit?"

There was a low, tortured moan, a sound of pure despair that crawled up Aeolil's spine. The dead man rose on the blackened sinew and muscle that clung to the scorched bone of its legs, drawn upward like a tattered marionette on the invisible strings of a sadistic puppeteer.

"*Corbhin*," the dead man spoke, his voice a rasping echo of the soul-splitting moan that heralded his re-entry into the realm of the living. "*I am... I was Corbhin of Vespa.*"

"You served Calamyr?"

"*I served the House Vespurial,*" he answered. "*Why do you bring me here? What do you want of me?*"

Aeolil had hardened her heart against sentiment. She'd had to in order to survive after the murder of her father and brother. Any bit of softness left exposed to the world had then sunk even deeper with the anchor of Kiev's horrible death not long after. Even so, the desperation in that voice struck her to the core. She almost felt pity for him – so palpable was his longing for release. She reminded herself what he had done to keep her sympathy at arm's length.

Agrylon exhibited no such conflict; his voice was stern and commanding. "Who ordered the death of Calvraign?"

"*I know no Calvraign. I know of no orders for his death. I was an honorable man. I... I don't know what you want of me, but...*" His dead mouth hung open in a rasping sigh. "*Please do not send me back. Not back to the Dark.*"

Agrylon's brow creased. "The Cythe barbarian. You attacked him before your death – who commanded you to attack the boy? What were you promised?"

"*I know nothing of this,*" the spirit answered. "*I was killed with my men, on patrol north of Vespa. We were taken. She took us to the Dark.*"

Aeolil looked to Agrylon's face for a sneer of disbelief or anger at the dead man's refusal to speak the truth. She hoped to find something other than the perplexed frown that met her gaze.

"*Please, before She hears you – before She comes for me. Please help me. Send me away! I would rather suffer Oblivion than the Dark.*"

Agrylon's momentary bewilderment evaporated into a look of realization and, if not fear, foreboding. "Impossible," he whispered.

"*Hurry! She comes. She comes!*"

Agrylon's hands spun through the air as he barked the word of dissolution. The black flames should have extinguished. The chalky form should have collapsed back to empty flesh. The spirit should have fled back to whence it came.

Nothing.

Then the flame erupted into a column that licked the ceiling, boiling along the living wood and the invisible barrier of the casting circle, demanding release. Agrylon stepped back with his right foot, as if bracing against a strong wind, his hands splayed palm up before him, his face a grimace as he strained against some unseen force.

"Aeolil," he barked. "To me! Quickly!"

Aeolil knew he didn't need her physical aid. She began reciting a spell of communion, forging a thread of *iiyir* into a ley line to link their tides and shore up his wavering hold on whatever lay beyond the flames.

Corbhin's body convulsed as his spirit emitted an inhuman shriek. Aeolil shuddered, her concentration wavering but not breaking. A bony arm punched out of Corbhin's stomach with a moist pop, then another from his left shoulder. *"She comes!"* he wailed, as another arm burst from his hip, shattering the bone with a loud crack. The talons at the end of the appendages flexed, dropping bits of discarded human tissue to the ground. *"She comes!"* His legs split in two, each falling away to reveal two chitin-plated limbs. The four legs sprouted from the beast's hips at angles from the emerging torso, two facing forward and two facing the rear. The appendages arched upward to barbed knees before bending backward to end in sharp spear-like points that clacked heavily on the floor.

Aeolil felt the ethereal tug on the ley line that signaled her spell's success, and Agrylon immediately drew on her energies. He siphoned the *iiyir* hungrily, and she allowed him to channel the power with reluctant trust. Such symbiosis was no small thing even amongst close friends, but Aeolil was without the convenience of choice, and she knew it.

Three more arms erupted from the flailing physical remains of Corbhin, accompanied by screams of increasing intensity and desperation. His ribs were jutting through his chest now, his skin tearing from his neck to his abdomen as the black-furred mass within sought to burst through.

Agrylon pressed his hands forward, his eyes like amber flames. He spoke words of power that Aeolil could not identify, but she fell to her knees, retching at the mere sound of them.

Words of Shadow.

Aeolil shuddered at the thought. She coughed, spittle dripping from her lips to join the vomit between her legs. She could feel the essence of those dark incantations resonating in the filaments of *iiyir* that joined them, like the spread of infection. She almost severed their connection, but she maintained the link, certain that in this case Agrylon was, at the very least, the lesser of two evils.

The blackness receded, sucked into the half-transfigured being that once had been the body of Corbhin of Vespa, and he burned again. The black flames burned, but they did not consume. Aeolil could see it on Agrylon's face, in the dimming of his angry eyes; sense it in the faltering connection of their ley line. He was losing the battle. Agrylon, Wizard of the Eleventh Order, a Black Robe of the Dacadian Legions, had not the strength to hold back this creature of the Dark. Even with the succor of his apprentice, the black fire began to creep from the tortured shell to once again test the confines of the casting circle.

Aeolil watched in growing fear as Agrylon's face contorted from exertion to desperation and finally to pain, and then in surprise, as he severed their bond abruptly.

Corbhin's spirit screams ceased, replaced by a quiet rasp. *"She's here."*

Without pause, the last remnants of his mortal self were ripped away by the hideous thing within. An oblong head emerged, crowned by three curved horns, each six inches long. There were two rows of thirteen yellow eyes, one spray of blinking orbs to each half of the horrid head. The mouth ran vertically from bearded chin to leathery brow, bisecting the creature's face, lined with rows of soiled ivory teeth that oozed glutinous saliva as its jaws flexed.

Even as the last bits of the once-human face dropped away, the fanged maw opened and uttered a word that split the air like a thunderclap. Agrylon was thrown backward, flung like a doll across the room from the impact of the word of power, his eyes and nose bleeding before he even struck the far wall. Even though she had not been in the direct path of the word, the aftershock sent Aeolil reeling back onto her elbows.

The thing struggled against the invisible walls of the protective enchantment, slowly breaking through into the world beyond Shadow. It clawed its way toward Agrylon, gnashing its teeth in anticipation of whatever fate it had in store for the wizard.

Aeolil's fear almost overwhelmed her. She lay still. Having not yet attracted its attention, she didn't wish to do so now. An image flashed in her mind: a memory from childhood, in the glades outside the castle walls where she lay trying to gather her skirts after being thrown by her pony. An unshaven man in officer's garb was dragging her from the sod by a fistful of her torn dress, his sword planted through a mountain viper's neck scant feet away. *"Survive first,"* he'd told her, and it was the first of many times. It was his mantra, and it had served him well.

Aeolil sucked in a shivering breath. She knew what was loose, and it was no mere spirit or shadowborn minion. This was a *Neva Seough*, a Demon of the Dark, a full-blooded beast of unfathomable evil with claw, fang and blackest of *iiyir* at its disposal. Such were the monsters of the ancient tales that did battle with saints, avatars and heroes. They were unspeakable, nightmares even for the likes of andu'ai and perhaps even dragonkind.

And Aeolil knew that she was all that stood between it and freedom. Not just the freedom to kill Agrylon, or her, but to break free into the realm of the living and wreak havoc unseen since the Devastations.

Survive first, Aeolil reminded herself, but she knew her limits. Defeating it was not within her power, not even with luck, surprise and Agrylon's war-staff.

The Staff! Aeolil spotted it across the room, not far from its fallen master. A Black Robe's war-staff was a potent weapon, bound with many spells and attuned to the *il'iiyir* of its wielder. If she could get it to Agrylon, if she could rouse him, perhaps he could turn the battle.

She scanned the room, trying to piece together a plan that could delay the Neva Seough's escape long enough for her to bring Agrylon back into the fray. She eyed a few key ingredients on the nearby shelf, assessed her own small inventory of spells, and decided upon her course. In her hasty analysis, it seemed the best chance of turning this Shadow back to the Dark, but she was uneasy with the key element of her plan: being the bait.

Aeolil eyed the demon's progress as her fingers slipped into the hidden pouches within the bodice of her dress, removing the components she would need for each of the spells she planned to cast. There would be no time to gather them after her plan was set into action; preparation and speed of execution were her only chance for survival.

One of the demon's claws pierced into the light, and the Dark erupted from the casting circle, breaking the confines of its wards and sundering Agrylon's spell of containment entirely. Shadow leaked like a grey cloud into the room from the puncture in the casting circle's wards, swallowing the light hungrily.

"Agrylon," the thing rumbled, its voice a thick basso rasp, repeating the name with each methodical, unrushed step, "Agryloooooon." All of its eyes were focused on the fallen wizard, its breath coming in heaving gasps. *"Long have I waited for this. Long have I hoped to repay you for your great treachery. But worry not. I will not kill you just yet. The Nameless One awaits your audience in Erkenàdun. She wishes to have a* word *with you."*

Aeolil rose up on one knee, drawing her trembling arms up into casting position, and set her plan in motion.

First, she sent a jar of silver shavings flying from the shelf with a quick gesture and minor nudge of *iiyir*. A more forceful application of the spell shattered the jar in mid-air, spraying its contents in the direction of the gloating demon. As the shards of glass and tiny silver shavings flew toward her target, she set her third spell into motion with a minor word of power. It was one of the first offensive spells most apprentices learned from their masters: infusing a mundane object with a small quantity of *iiyir* to energize it, and then binding that with directed kinesis to create a deadly projectile. For an unprotected human or animal, it could easily deal a mortal blow if the caster's aim was true. Aeolil harbored no such unrealistic expectation in this case, nor was that the intent of her plan.

The enchanted fragments flashed through the congealing gloom like lancets of captive lightning. The Neva Seough's dark flesh sizzled with each impact, penetrating and transforming several of its myriad eyes into vapor with a pop and hiss. The wounds glowed softly after each impact, bleeding pus and trailing noxious smoke.

There was no scream. No roar of pain. In fact, there was almost no reaction from it at all. But the attack had achieved its desired effect.

The Neva Seough turned on her.

Aeolil wasted no time celebrating her fate as the demon's new meal. One last thrust of kinesis toppled Agrylon's war-staff next to his limp hands.

"Whelp," spat the Neva Seough.

Survive first, she reminded herself again, clearing her mind and gathering her *il'iiyir* for one last spell. Aeolil watched as the tentacle that passed for the creature's tongue slipped out from behind its cage of teeth to taste the air like a snake.

"You are almost ripe!" it exclaimed. *"Two prizes in one visit: a Black Robe and a young breeder for the Pits."*

It feeds on your fear. It is goading you. Ignore it, she thought, drawing a short figure in the air with the thumb and index finger of her left hand. *Focus or die. This is your only chance.*

The demon's presence loomed before her, overpowering her senses with its size, smell, and the blackness of the *iiyir* that emanated from it. There were evil men in the world, and Aeolil had met some of them, but this was beyond that. This wasn't evil that resided within a human shell. It wasn't mere greed or amorality. This was evil distilled to its purest impure physical essence, and the black *iiyir* flowed through its veins like mortal's blood.

It's too close, she thought, even as she brought her right palm to her lips.

Its tentacle grabbed her wrist scant inches from her mouth. The appendage snaked around her fingers, sniffing at the powder in her palm. It laughed, drawing itself up before her like a mountain, a shadow blocking out a shadow.

"Oh," it mocked. *"Shall you put me to sleep with your powerful magic, little sorceress?"* Its laughter brought the fetid stench of old death hissing through its teeth. *"I should bend you over backward and suck your entrails out from your loins."*

Aeolil didn't waste her breath on banter. She blew out across her palm, scattering the small residuum of sand and sulfur into a thin plume that stretched out beyond the Neva Seough's shoulder. She whispered the one-word incantation that comprised this child's spell even as her arm was yanked violently behind her back, thrusting her chest out toward the maw of the beast.

It's done, she thought, but her relief was swallowed by sheer terror.

It laughed again, its tentacle-tongue snapping around her delicate neck as two of its arms pinned hers to her side. Warm urine trickled down her thigh, but considering her circumstance, she felt no shame. It pulled her head back as it squeezed her airway shut and whispered into her ear, saliva dripping down her shoulder. *"That was the best that the apprentice of mighty Agrylon could manage?"*

It turned toward Agrylon, bending her body backward violently as it dragged her behind. Aeolil choked out a gasp through its stranglehold. Her head swam. Her vision blurred. She knew consciousness was fleeting. Even as she fought the slide into oblivion, she felt the dizziness crowding out her thoughts. *Survive first!* she screamed at herself, but the demon seemed unaware of her flailing limbs and errant kicks as she struggled for freedom.

If the spell hadn't worked, if it hadn't been powerful enough to counteract Agrylon's battered unconsciousness, she dared not imagine what degradations awaited her in the Pits. Then she heard his voice.

"Myszdraelh!" Agrylon spat.

The Neva Seough dropped Aeolil immediately to the floor, and she rolled clear with what strength she had left. She sucked in a lungful of precious air, scowling at the hot stench but thankful for life. She scrambled backward on her elbows until she bumped into a bookshelf, shaking with fear and relief.

"*Myszdraelh!*" boomed Agrylon again, his voice gaining strength. The demon's eyes snapped wide open, and its limbs twitched limply at the utterance of the word. "I name thee, Myszdraelh of the Neva Seough. I name thee and I command thee. Into the circle, demon – and take your shadows with you!"

Myszdraelh convulsed across the floor, slack-jawed and writhing in spasms. The Dark that had enveloped the room oozed like thick oil back to whence it came, following in the wake of its liberator to cower behind the wards not long since shattered.

Agrylon stood over the failed casting circle, his robes the only shadow not retreating from the incandescent lightning licking his outstretched war-staff. "That's twice you've underestimated me," the wizard said, "and once for my apprentice."

"You will not bend me by name alone," Myszdraelh hissed.

"Won't I?" Agrylon challenged. "You appear well bent already."

"Your world is ending, wizard. Enjoy your moment while you may. Dine on me now, for I will sup on your shallow soul for eternity."

Agrylon's smile barely bent the curvature of his lips. "You are a guest in my world, Neva Seough. What do you know of its *end?*"

"By the time you realize the folly of your arrogance, we shall –"

Agrylon tapped the haft of his staff on the floor, and the constricting energies about the demon pulsed brightly. Myszdraelh hissed in pain, and Aeolil flinched as the residual energy charged the air between them. "Why do you seek the death of Calvraign the Cythe?"

"*Call him what you will, it is too late for him now,*" it screeched, its maw struggling against each word. "*You may compel my speech, but it is too late. Your nightmares are loose.*"

Agrylon lowered his staff toward the Neva Seough. Myszdraelh squirmed; its neck twisting as if caught in a tightening noose. Its eyes bulged in their sockets as Agrylon whispered fiercely between clenched teeth, "Speak plainly, Myszdraelh, I am not long on patience."

"He... He is your key," the demon snarled. "*Without your key, your way is locked. If your way is locked, then you fail – and your failure will be our victory. So the Nameless One has foreseen.*"

From past experience, Aeolil recognized the rasping sound coming from Agrylon's throat as a chuckle. She wasn't fond of the noise. It was disturbing, like the triumphant caw of a villain from a bard's tale. "I have a *ring* full of keys, demonspawn. But thank you for letting me know which the Nameless One thinks most important. I'll be sure to tuck it away."

Agrylon approached to the very perimeter of the restored circle, his back to Aeolil. "But, lest you think trifling in my affairs may go unpunished... ."

There was a pause, and then Aeolil heard a faint whisper. She could not make out the word that Agrylon spoke, but the Neva Seough was not so fortunate. Myszdraelh's eyes flickered and then burst into flashes of indigo flame. It let loose a howl, its jaws gnashing, as its steaming, empty sockets bubbled over with scalding pus.

Agrylon raised his staff over his head and uttered a final word of dissolution. The casting circle came to life one last time, a beacon of light that swallowed the shadows from floor to ceiling. The next moment, Myszdraelh was gone.

Aeolil sat in silence as Agrylon surveyed the blackened mess of the casting circle, leaning heavily on his staff. He shook his head, frowning. He was showing the strain of the encounter now that his adversary was vanquished, his posture stooped and his breath coming hard through his clenched teeth.

"That shouldn't have happened," he muttered, turning to look at her with a cocked eyebrow.

Aeolil stood, her legs still shaking, but her voice steady. "You opened a doorway to the Dark, Agrylon! To the very Dark itself. What shouldn't have happened was you *opening* the gods-bedamned door in the first place!"

"No," Agrylon replied, with a nonchalant shrug and a shake of his head. "The door was to Shadow, to the outskirts of Shadow, no less. The dead man was a conduit, and a bit of clever bait, too."

"Bait?"

"A worm, squirming on a hook. When we took a bite, the Dark came through him to get to us."

"The Dark can't just come through Shadow because you knocked."

"No, indeed," agreed Agrylon, "it simply should not have happened."

"But it did."

"Aye. It did." The wizard scratched at the dried blood that caked his silver mustache. "Tomorrow will be a busy day. You may go and clean yourself up. I will summon you if I need you."

Aeolil clenched her hands into fists at her side. "If you *need* me?" she mocked. "I just saved your life. I think you owe me an explanation – and now, not tomorrow, *if you need me*."

Agrylon tilted his chin upward and looked archly down on his pupil. "You did well, Aeolil, all things considered, but don't become enamored with yourself. As I recall, you didn't save anyone, but you did assist *me* in saving us both. You affirmed my choice of an apprentice, most assuredly."

"I affirmed-" Aeolil clamped down on her lower lip with her teeth, and then drew in a deep breath. There was only one way she could see around his self-satisfaction, and that was to skip straight to his secrets. "Why Calvraign, Agrylon?" she asked. "Which key is he on your ring? Which lock does he fit?"

The wizard turned away, walking over to one of his bookshelves and glancing over its contents. "There is much you do not know, Aeolil," he said, as if each word spoken was a bit of tedium dragged from his lips. "Much you do not need to know, and much you *should* not know."

Aeolil stared at his back, wondering if this were really the time to test him. Always she had been the attentive student, the obedient servant, and afforded him the respect his status deserved. But now, covered in her own piss and vomit, with the slaver of a demon still painting her breastbone and a fate of rape and death only a click behind her, she stared at his indifferent back and steeled herself for confrontation.

"I know enough. I know that you've been beside yourself ever since he arrived. I could tell you didn't expect it, or plan for it, but both you and Guillaume were pleased. I know you, and you aren't *pleased* by surprises, yet somehow this fit into your plans. Why? What does Calvraign have to offer you?"

Agrylon didn't acknowledge her. He continued perusing his texts, the blackened nail of his index finger tapping the spines of the books as he reviewed their titles, one by one.

Aeolil narrowed her eyes, feeling a dangerous thrill as she recalled her conversation with Calvraign. "Or is it his *children* you're after?"

She jumped back as Agrylon wheeled on her, his eyes literally glowing with rage. She thought for a moment that he might strike her, and backed away another step. But he made no further move, standing there with his hands clenched on his war-staff and the gold burning like fire in his eyes. "What do you know of it? Don't play games with *me*, girl! Did you speak to the king?"

"No," she replied, startled by his visceral reaction. "I know that his mother has the Gift. I can see how that would interest you. But what would Guillaume care of such things? Or have you bothered to let him in on the specifics of your little plot?"

Agrylon gathered himself, relaxing his tight muscles with a deep but quiet breath. "I don't much care for your tone," he informed her, "and my business with the king is my own. I see that you've taken a liking to the boy, but don't think for a moment that matters in the grand balance of things."

"I see," she said. "Then we shall soon discover if the king is as tight-lipped as you on the subject. Hiruld and I will be close enough to make some conversation at the royal pavilion this afternoon."

Agrylon didn't respond immediately. He watched her intently, and she could feel his eyes study her face, looking into and through her. "Tread softly, lest you wake the beast, Lady Aeolil."

"Oh, put your nursery rhymes away," she snapped. "I'm not a child anymore. At least show the backbone to threaten me outside of some stale metaphor! You're as melodramatic as the Neva Seough."

Aeolil shook her head, trying to calm her frustration and appeal to him with reason, or compassion – whichever might work. "Calvraign is a genuinely good man, Agrylon, and that is a rare enough thing that I will risk your enmity on his account if I must. Please. What do you have in store for him?"

"Very well," the wizard said, "I will tell you something of what I intend."

Aeolil suppressed a victorious smile. He would be evasive and vague, but with Agrylon even a table scrap should be considered healthy fare.

"The king and I have plans for him, yes. We always have," he admitted. "Do you think the likes of Brohan Madrharigal are dispatched to just any widow's son? No, we knew he would be something special from the beginning. You surmised it correctly enough, yourself. His mother has the Gift, as do many of those in her line. If he is paired appropriately, his progeny will be powerful indeed."

"And yours to mold," prompted Aeolil.

"Of course. And in the meantime, we have the makings of a fine general. Vanelorn can only stay fit and hale for so long. The king will need a new lord high marshal, and if the king at that time is Hiruld, he will need the likes of Calvraign to guide him."

"You certainly have a good deal of confidence in a shepherd not long from the hills. Don't you think a more seasoned knight would be suited for that task?"

"From Brohan's reports, the boy is no slouch with a blade. I'm sure he can hold his own for now. By the time the spring campaign comes around, he'll be a good sight better. The war will season him in quick order." Agrylon smiled, but that was seldom a comforting gesture from him. "Your shepherd will be a veteran knight within the year."

"A lord high marshal must be much more than a veteran knight, and you know it. He's a bit old to begin training at the War College. Or has Brohan been schooling him in strategy and tactics for the past ten years as well – grooming your little warlord for you?"

"As a matter of strict fact, yes. How many men can say they came within a move of beating Brohan Madrharigal in *Mylyr Gaeal*? Not the beginner's board, mind you, but all five tiers with the *iiyir* tides and all. Not a small feat for a young man about your age, eh, Lady Aeolil?"

"No," she said, stunned and a little disconcerted. *Calvraign* had almost beaten Brohan on the Grand Master's board? No one had come within eight moves of a victory over Brohan for longer than she had been at court, not even Agrylon or Renarre, who were the closest Providayne had to offer the bard in competition. She had heard once that some lord at Aeth'lyn Fann had achieved a stalemate, but even that had been hard fought. She tried to reconcile this with her perception of the young Cythe, but the mantle of master strategist didn't rest easily on his shoulders in her mind.

How many such plans did Agrylon yet have in the forge of his intrigues, she wondered, like embers at a slow burn waiting to be coaxed into open flame? How many like Calvraign that he waited patiently to temper and craft into instruments of his own liking? If what he said of him were even partly true, he would fit the needs of House Jiraud quite nicely.

"So, you raised him away from court, with Brohan providing a better education than most nobles would ever hope for and passing along his own personal loyalties to the king in the bargain. And of course he'll be ideal for garnering support from the Cythe for the wars. He'll have no ulterior motives, no other House loyalties to get in the way. Very convenient, all in all."

Agrylon turned away from her again, shuffling over to replace his war-staff. "I prefer to think of it as capitalizing on opportunity."

"Do you?" Aeolil saw one major flaw in his scheme. "Have you given much thought to what Calvraign will make of all this once he figures it out? That same sense of strategy you're so keen on will serve him just as well in dissecting your reasons and motivations. It might drive him to wonder exactly when your interest in him was piqued, whether before or after his father's untimely but very convenient death, for example. You'd best heed your own advice, Agrylon – *don't wake the beast.*"

Agrylon looked back at her for a moment, and something passed over his face, if for an instant. She couldn't be sure if it was amusement or anticipation, but it certainly wasn't the hint of fear she'd expected.

"I always tread softly," he said, looking back to his bookshelf. "It's my nature."

Chapter Twenty-Five

A Most Generous Host

OSRITH wasn't sure how long it had been since their capture at the river's edge, but he guessed they'd been carried for at least an hour through the ruined city. In the complete absence of light, it was impossible for Osrith to catch any further glimpse of the Sunken City or its fallen wonders. His sense of smell was also useless, numbed by the thick stench of the severed scalps that flapped rhythmically against his captor's carapace. His ears were his salvation, providing at least some method of reckoning their progress and surroundings.

The powerful roar of the river had faded, still present but subdued by distance. Osrith marked time by the steady staccato click of the manti appendages on the smooth marble, noting the softer, uneven tread when they crossed rougher, unhewn stone. He wondered how quickly the creatures could move on both sets of legs, trying to judge by the receding noise of the river how far they had traveled from their place of capture. From his position – bound, gagged, and strapped to the back of a mantis soldier – there was not much else to consider.

They halted, and the odd chirping and clicking of the manti language was the only sound that stirred the air. Then, just as suddenly, Osrith felt the pressure on the leather straps fastened around his waist tighten and dig into his abdomen. He winced in pain, grunting into his gag. His position shifted forward on the mantis' back, and he felt different muscle groups working beneath him as the creature walked. All six appendages were in use now, but they were not moving any faster. If anything, their progress had slowed. It took him a moment, but he identified the change.

They were climbing. Not up a staircase or a ladder, but scaling a cliff or wall of some sort. He could hear manti climbing to his left and to his right, as well as in front – above – them. They were making the ascent as a unit. Osrith was impressed by that maneuver. He wondered how the strong high walls of a surface keep would fare against even a small group of manti warriors.

Osrith calculated it was ten clicks before the mantis beneath him shifted back to a more horizontal posture, and he was relieved that the climb was over. The temperature was several degrees warmer here, and the air was laced with a sulfurous scent acrid enough to penetrate even the pungent aroma of his keeper.

The mantis settled down on its haunches, and Osrith relaxed, preparing for a brief rest. Instead, the pit of his stomach seemed to fall suddenly down to his ankles, and he felt, just for a moment, as if he weighed no more than a leaf on the wind. Numbly, he realized that the mantis had not been resting, but coiling like a spring. It had jumped, propelling them up and out over what he could only assume was a yawning chasm. Hot air rushed up at them as they flew across the gap, intensifying as they arced downward. He could imagine a river of lava running somewhere beneath. He even thought he heard the sound of its bubbling murmur, but there was no sign of it in the impenetrable artificial night.

The landing wasn't as rough as Osrith had expected; the experienced and flexible legs of the mantis warrior absorbed most of the shock. They waited for a short time, the silence occasionally punctuated by the thud of another landing. One such thud was much louder than the others, followed by a brief but thunderous clatter of flailing appendages. There was a series of rapid chirps immediately following the commotion, and a flurry of activity. Osrith chuckled at the apparent crash landing, guessing that his bulky reptilian friend had been a bit more a burden than even the cave-manti could handle easily. A growing tenor drone of what sounded like a dozen violins accompanied the tumult. Puzzled, Osrith stilled his own laughter to pinpoint the source of the music.

He was amazed to discover the manti themselves were making the noise. His own guard joined in the chorus, rubbing his right hind legs together to produce a beautiful rich hum that even the king's minstrels might envy. Osrith realized that the *demon feeders* of kin legend, the stealers of babes in the night, the scourge of the underworld, were laughing at one of their own for falling down. If he hadn't been convinced he was about to die a horrible death, he would have found it extremely funny. As it was, he managed to find it mildly amusing.

The music and brief rest were broken up in short order, and soon they were on their way, continuing in silence. Once again, Osrith heard the distinct sharp click of marble under mantis feet. They ascended four separate staircases, broad ones from the numbers on either side of him, but despite his best efforts he couldn't count how many steps to each one. So many clattering appendages confused things considerably. A sharp turn to the left, and a set of doors creaked open before them. Here it sounded as if most of the manti hung back. The noises of their progress echoed closely now, suggesting a hallway. Then through two more sets of doors, past the splash of water spilling into water to his left – perhaps a fountain or a well – and then finally the glimmer of light ahead. The outline of a broad double door was etched in soft gold light, like a beacon out of nowhere. The manti stopped before it and released their prisoners. Osrith stretched his sore limbs as his bindings were sliced away and hoped for some water to wash the taste of gag from his mouth. Without ceremony or explanation, the manti pushed their prisoners through into the welcome if temporarily painful light and slammed the door behind them.

Osrith's eyes adjusted slowly, his surroundings dissolving from pitch black to indistinct shadows and then finally to discernable shapes. He looked about him, trying to take in his newly revealed environs before the darkness returned. He would have described the place as a library, except that the scale was so vast, the word didn't seem to do it justice. He stood in the middle of an intersection from which four great halls stretched out to the very edge of his perception, each over forty feet in height and at least double that in length. Doors, like the one they had come through, were set between the halls.

From the floor to the ceiling, each wall was nothing but shelves, and each shelf was filled to its capacity with scroll cases of bone, metal or vellum. Chandeliers hung at regular intervals from the arched ceiling overhead, each holding an array of glowing orbs in place of conventional candles, spreading a diffuse and gentle light on the lines of chairs and narrow reading tables that bisected each hall.

Osrith scratched at his beard with his right hand, because the manti had stripped him of all the weapons with which he would normally fidget. Kassakan shifted Symmlrey from her great shoulders, laying her down on the round table in the middle of the intersection. Her tongue flicked out across her teeth in a nervous gesture of her own.

"We wait here, I guess," Osrith said.

"These are the Fourteen Halls," Kassakan whispered, though from her detached tone, Osrith wasn't even sure she was addressing him in particular, "the Great Library of Oszmagoth."

"*Fourteen?*" Osrith shook his head to avoid picturing this room and everything in it duplicated several times over.

"Aside from the library at Azgadaan, it is the greatest collection of knowledge the world has ever known. I thought it a myth."

"No myth, Hosskan," a familiar old voice said from behind them, "no more than I."

Osrith turned with a wry grin. "You're a tough old bastard, Two–" The name caught in his throat as he caught sight of his companion. The *wilhorwhyr* appeared to be uninjured, striding confidently toward them with a welcoming smile.

But his eyes...

His eyes stared into them like amber swords, unwavering and inhuman. The body was Two-Moons', but the eyes were something else entirely.

Kassakan's hard stare confirmed Osrith's own gut reaction. "What have you done to Two-Moons, Old One?" she asked. Her tone carried a cautious insistence Osrith had not heard in her before.

"Ah, the little Ebuouki man. He is *resting*. But don't worry yourself, Hosskan, I'm just borrowing this shell," he spread his arms wide and laughed, "to welcome you to my home!"

"Who are you?" asked Kassakan, and Osrith could hear her struggling to keep the edge out of her voice.

"I am Qal Jir'aatu," he said, "the Keeper of Scrolls."

"Qal Jir'aatu," Kassakan repeated, and Osrith saw the suspicion in her eyes, though her voice remained calm and steady. "Legend has it you perished defending the Halls from Seoughal and Aguohn."

"Really?" Two-Moons was within an arm's length of them now, those fierce eyes shifting between them. "Legend has it, eh? Well, well," he paused as if in reflection, "how terribly... *dramatic*. I didn't think anyone spoke of such things anymore. With all *these* running around," he pointed off-handedly at Osrith, "it's a wonder anything of importance is remembered at all. In any event, as you can see, they weren't entirely successful in doing away with me."

"What do you want with us?" Osrith demanded. Whatever that thing in Two-Moons was, he didn't care for it much. "Why did you bring us here?"

"Your human is speaking, hosskan, and it annoys me," Jir'aatu made no attempt to disguise his irritation. "Silence it."

Kassakan's swift hand stifled Osrith's insult behind her fingers. "He is not *my* human," she explained. "He is my companion."

"Don't quibble terms with me. I see his leash, plain as the tides."

Osrith had no idea what this Jir'aatu thing was talking about, but he didn't appreciate the implication. He reached up to push away Kassakan's silencing hand, but she held firm on his impatient mouth.

"It's not a leash," she said. "We are *j'iitai*."

Two-Moons' mouth twisted as if he'd eaten something sour. "Bound to a *human*?" he decried. "How sad for you."

"That is our business. Regardless, what he asks is valid – what *do* you want?"

Jir'aatu laughed. "An expansive question, that. Let us say only that I will help you, and you will help me."

Osrith succeeded in pushing away the lizard's hand. He made an effort not to sound too irritable. "You don't seem to be asking for our help so much as telling us we'll give it."

"Yes," agreed Jir'aatu.

"And how exactly have you decided we'll help each other?" Osrith asked.

"Your Ebuouki man and I have worked out all the details already. For my part, I can have you resting comfortably in Dwynleigsh by daybreak. For yours, well, the three of you have only to go on your way. I ask nothing of you."

"And Two-Moons?" said Kassakan. "You aren't borrowing him, as you said. You've taken him, haven't you?"

"We have our own arrangement."

Osrith resumed the scratching of his beard. He didn't like the sound of this deal Jir'aatu had struck up with Two-Moons, even if it did mean an unexpected shortening of the journey ahead. If this thing was an andu'ai, as it claimed, then it hàd power and deceit in equal proportion. He knew that, Kassakan knew that, and in all probability Two-Moons knew that, too. If there were any humans who still knew of the andu'ai, he would wager it was the *wilhorwhyr*.

"You expect us to just leave him behind with you?" he said.

"I expect you have no choice, human," said the interloper, and with a gesture Osrith felt cold invisible fingers clutch at his heart, squeezing it to a standstill. He fell down to his knees, his muscles frozen by the formless will that held him. "I could simply have taken this shell and done away with all of you," explained the Old One, "but I chose to be more civilized. If you prefer to ignore my good will, to be contentious and contrary, I will repay you in kind."

Osrith grimaced, clawing at the smooth floor, struggling to resist the spell. Kassakan had taught him how to combat this sort of magic, to fight it with every ounce of his stubborn will. Jir'aatu was simply using his control of the *iiyir* to circumvent and supplant Osrith's natural balance, and he fought to free his immobilized body from the usurping magics that held him. With a sharp pain, his heart beat once, twice, a feeble but defiant gesture against the iron grip that sought to still it. The dreamstone burned into his chest with every sickly little pump of his lifeblood, and he felt slow tendrils of control snake through him. He sucked in a shallow breath through his clenched jaws, his hand twitched. Then the shackles evaporated, and he fell forward onto his arms, trembling with every new breath.

"What's this?" Jir'aatu said, bemused, "a little human with an *iiyiraal*? Wherever did you come across that?" He knelt down and fished the dreamstone out from under Osrith's tunic, holding it between his thumb and forefinger. "Not many of these left lying around, I wouldn't imagine."

Osrith's hand grasped Two-Moons' wrist. "Leave it," he growled.

"What a waste," Jir'aatu sighed, releasing his grip and standing. He watched Osrith recover with a passing curiosity. Then he walked over to Symmlrey, tracing the line of her cheekbone with a finger and cocking his head to one side. His voice lost some of its manic edge, fading into a whisper. "Lovely, isn't she?"

Osrith's stomach twisted as he watched the possessed body of Symmlrey's friend and mentor caress her skin with such obvious lust. He struggled to his feet, even as Kassakan moved to stand protectively over the unconscious aulden.

"I doubt Two-Moons allowed you any liberty with her, Qal Jir'aatu," the lizard warned.

Two-Moons' eyes looked up sharply at the use of that name, and he raised his hand from its unwelcome passage over her contours. "No," he said, his voice was distant, "but I may change my mind shortly."

"You're a liar as well as a thief, then?" Osrith said. "Your word means nothing?"

"Once it meant everything, human. But now, well, I am not entirely *sane*, I suppose. After the first few hundred years flitting from shell to shell, living in the most horrid of conditions." He shook his head, looking back at Symmlrey. "That's certainly had the effect Seoughal hoped for. And I've not had a *shoungeighl* in quite a long time. She *pleases* me immensely." Sweat was beading on his brow.

"I don't know what you've done with Two-Moons while you're in there," Osrith said, "but I don't think any *pleasing* with her will sit well with him."

"I think you had best let our friend out for a while, Old One," said Kassakan. "You took an oath as a *qal*. You must not betray it."

"So long ago," muttered Jir'aatu. "That means little to me now."

"You gave up everything for that oath," Kassakan reasoned. "This whole city fell on the basis of that oath. You can't betray their memory after all this time. You fought to free the *shoungeighl* all those centuries ago, and now you would take her against her will? You would keep her trapped with you down here in the smothering dark? You know she would die from it. Could you be responsible for that?"

Jir'aatu wiped the perspiration from his face. "Your little Ebuouki man wants to come out now, for a bit. Perhaps you are right. Don't trust me. I don't trust myself. I'll let him back just for a moment… to recover myself."

Kassakan reached out to steady the old man as his body jerked suddenly. He blinked, and in that instant the eyes that looked out at them were tired, bloodshot, and unmistakably Two-Moons'.

"Ingryst help me," he said, quavering.

"Will it be back?" Osrith asked.

Two-Moons nodded. "Yes, and soon. I must take you to the Wellspring and send you on your way. There isn't much time."

Osrith grabbed his arm roughly. "You're not actually *staying* here?"

"I am," Two-Moons responded with confidence. "It's the only way."

"My friend," Kassakan interjected, "this is not wise. Jir'aatu only wants you as a shell, a comfortable house to dwell in. Even he admits he can't be completely trusted."

"Kassakan, I have no illusions about this. But I have seen Jir'aatu more clearly than you could ever hope to. He is just sane enough to know what has happened to his mind, and he needs a stable host to return him from the brink of madness. He saved my life and my soul – I owe him whatever I may give in return. It may destroy me in the process, but it may also be our salvation."

"What are you talking about?" Osrith saw the implacable determination in the old man's eyes, and it worried him.

"Don't either of you see? This is the *Fourteen Halls!*" His passion only made Osrith more nervous. "No other place on Rahn will offer me what is here. The cure to the Wasting, the secrets of the *iiyir* well… All of it is likely to be here. And Jir'aatu was the *qal* – with our minds bound together, he will lead me to the knowledge we seek in short order."

"If you aren't subsumed, first," Kassakan argued, but Osrith could see she was already being swayed by the possibility.

"There's no point discussing it. The decision is mine alone."

"If you want to play host to this damn thing, we can't stop you," Osrith conceded with a shrug. He didn't want to leave Two-Moons here, but they couldn't stand around arguing about it much longer. It was clear that reason wasn't going to get through to him, no matter what they said, so he decided a purely emotional appeal was worth a quick try. "But what about *her*?"

Two-Moons looked down at Symmlrey's sleeping form, his mouth tight and down-turned. "She'll have to make her own way." Two-Moons touched her cheek with a gentle, fatherly touch, and then put his palm to her forehead, muttering something under his breath. "Wake, child," he whispered after a moment, and her eyelids fluttered open.

She focused slowly, reaching up to rub the injury at her temple before settling on her shoulder. "Two-Moons?" she said, her speech still somewhat shaky. "Thank Ingryst. What happened? Where are we?"

"I'll explain it as we go," he soothed. "We don't have much time."

Captain Sul Vaujn wiped his broad sword on the dringli carcass and examined its edge to check for damage from the melee. The ruddy steel was keen and straight, with no sign of chip or fracture, and he smiled to himself. This sword had been good to him over the years, and he was pleased they had come out of one more battle together, both none the worse for wear.

"All accounted for, Captain," reported Sergeant Mueszner, returning from his survey of the trail downstream. "Sending the lead boat over the falls got their attention, all right. They never knew what hit 'em."

Vaujn clapped his friend and subordinate on the shoulder and grinned. "I thought it might. Good work, one and all, that was."

And he meant it, too. He'd been worried his squad might be rusty when it came to combat after their little hiatus at Outpost Number Nine, but the ambush had gone without a hitch. More than twice their number in dringli cut down without more than a scratch or two to show for their trouble. Not that it had been a fair fight, but Vaujn didn't care much about fair when it came to war. He wanted to come out of it with his squad intact and their goal complete, and he wasn't too particular about the details in between. If Mother Chloe could scry out enemy positions from halfway upstream, then, by Rondainaken, they'd take advantage of it. "How about the boats? Are we ready to make the portage down the Great Stair?"

"Any click now, sir," assured the sergeant.

"Good, let me know when we're ready to get started. I'm going to consult with Chloe one more time, see if she's found anything out yet."

Mueszner nodded and went back to the rest of the squad, who were still hard at work rearranging the boats and supplies for their trek down to the base of Mordigul's Plunge. Vaujn walked in the opposite direction, toward the back of the dringli lair. It was just a shallow cave in the rock face, scattered with hides and pelts and lightly provisioned. That meant their main base of operations was nearby, but Vaujn didn't plan on staying nearby for long. Chloe was in the back of the room, as far removed from the commotion and the river as she could be, peering down at her stone basin with a frown.

"Any luck?" he asked her.

"Something is blocking me out," she said, stirring the water in the bowl with her finger. "I can't even tell what."

"Damn place is still chock full of andu'ai magic, is all," reassured Vaujn with the casual confidence of complete ignorance. He wanted to keep moving and put the Sunken City and all its mythical dangers behind them.

"I don't think so," she contradicted. "It's an active effort to shield – wait, it's clearing up a little."

Vaujn remained quiet and still while she concentrated on the pool. A series of indistinct forms were swimming about, but he couldn't make anything out clearly. His wife continued staring for several clicks, heedless of his impatience to be on their way. He thought she was beautiful when she concentrated like that, the way her brow would knit and her left eye would squint more than the right. He squelched the sudden desire to stroke her braids.

"Not good," she said simply, looking up from her work.

"What?"

"It's not too clear. The interference is still there. It just seems... distracted. All I can tell is that there are shadowborn on the south bank and a horde of cave-manti on the north, along with whoever or whatever likes its privacy. *And –*" she looked up with an unhappy glower "*– our Shaddach Chi and his friends are in the city, too.*"

Vaujn rolled his eyes. "What? Are you sure?"

"I'm sure," she confirmed. "Maybe their boat sank and stranded them here, or the dringli injured them and they were forced to rest. Whatever the reason, I saw them."

Vaujn pinched the bridge of his nose. This wasn't good news. There was probably nothing they could do for Osrith and his companions, but he was bound by oath to help him in any way he could. And if that meant a doomed rescue attempt, it wouldn't be the first in kin history.

"Can you read the stones?" he asked.

"Not from here. We'll have to get down closer to the city. Once we're there, no amount of interference can keep me from communing with the mountain directly."

"Once we're there, that interference might be the least of our worries."

The Great Stair was a figurative term, Vaujn finally decided, carefully picking his way across another gaping crack in the granite. It wasn't an artificial construct, as he had always thought, but a slippery tumble of rocks that made a slightly less dangerous descent than the waterfall it paralleled. There were four kin to each of the two remaining boats, and four, including himself, Chloe and Mueszner, who were scouting ahead and keeping watch for hostiles.

"I think I see the end of it up ahead!" yelled out Sturng Darrow, the last of the four on guard and the furthest in front. "About a hundred hetahrs!"

Vaujn caught his breath and peered down past Darrow, and he, too, thought he saw the crumbling path smooth out into more stable ground. They were making good time down the treacherous expanse of rocks, but fatigue could wreak havoc even on the most sure-footed kin.

"Boats down!" he commanded. "We rest five counts, and then we finish it off. Rotate crews!"

The squad responded crisply, placing the boats perpendicular to the steep slope before stretching their tired muscles. Vaujn regretted the circumstances of their journey because, in all reality, this was a very beautiful place. The Dolset rushed over the cliff and splashed over the rocks in a furious abandon. It was a sight wasted on the likes of dringli, but the churning waters stirred his soul as they carved out their passage in the deep rock of this ancient mountain. Water was a sculptor that ran wild and free over its medium. Some thought it a battle between elements, but Vaujn liked to think it was more like a lover's caress that stroked and smoothed the roughness from the rock.

"Reminds me of Kabuhl Falls," Mueszner said from behind him.

"Wilder," Vaujn commented. "Freer."

"I'll be glad when we put it behind us," the sergeant added.

"Me too."

The respite was needed, but to the impatient kin it passed slower than they would have liked. The crews rotated, all but Mother Chloe, who couldn't carry a boat and concentrate on her divinations simultaneously. Vaujn took his turn, though, shouldering his portion of the burden without complaint. They ported the boats upside down with one stout set of shoulders to each of the crossbeams. Vaujn liked hard work. He always thought clearer when he sweated.

The rest of the unit was no slower than he to the task, and they were off again down the slope without delay. Vaujn was particularly pleased with the lack of protest from the squad. He'd thought they would revolt and throw him to the rockfishers when he first told them where Osrith had gone, and where they must follow. The legends spoke dread things of this place, and it was not a trifling matter to ignore such tales. But they had taken up the challenge with the stoic determination of true champions, deciding to look fate in its eye and face it down rather than balk at the possible dangers. Not that the Guhddan-kinne stalking them didn't provide some incentive.

"Watch your step," someone shouted from ahead of him, cutting through the roar of the falls.

Vaujn shifted his concentration from where they'd been to where he was walking. The footing had indeed become more treacherous. The rocks, more smoothed by the pummeling that the Dolset meted out at the base of the falls, were therefore slicker and more rounded, inviting a careless foot to wedge between them and crack. He felt his boots slip on more than one occasion as they struggled with the boats over the last bit of the Stair.

"Hold 'em up, sir," the same warning voice shouted as they reached more level ground.

Vaujn peeked out from under the boat frame to see which of his unit was addressing them, then gave the order when he recognized her. "All halt!" he barked. "What is it, Läzch?"

The young woman who had taken Sturng's place on point knelt with her crossbow readied, staring off to her left at the rock face. Her face shield was down, and only the wispy fringes of her blonde hair were visible from behind the helm's snarling caricature of her face. She was his youngest squad member, but his best in tracking and marksmanship. Sturng was capable enough, but Vaujn found himself grateful that the rotation had worked out the way it had.

"Cave-mantis," she said, tracking some spot high up on the wall with her weapon. "Just one. Up there."

Vaujn tried to follow her finger to the point on the wall where he imagined the thing was clinging, but mostly all he saw was the side of the boat. "What's it doing?"

"I think it's watching us, sir," she said. "I can put a bolt in it."

"Wait!" He ducked his head back under the boat, then out the other side, "Chloe?"

"What?"

"Can you hold it there? I don't want to kill it and get the whole horde after us, but we can't just let it go either. It might be close to feeding time."

A dozen kin feet shifted and scraped on the rock.

Mother Chloe didn't answer, but closed her eyes and knelt with one hand splayed on the ground. She beseeched the mountain with words mouthed rather than spoken, and reached her free hand up toward the watching mantis. The spirits within the rock awakened slowly to her *call*, for they had grown sluggish over the many years spent at the edge of the Sunken City's dire wards. But awaken they did, and the rock encircled the mantis in a solid and unbreakable embrace. Chloe continued her silent chant until the stone had seeped between the creature's mandibles, effectively silencing it, and then she took a deep breath and stood.

"An hour maybe," she warned, "but no more."

"What about the city? Can you scry anything yet?"

Chloe shot her husband an irritated glance. "Not without stopping, I can't. Besides, the closer we get, the clearer it will be."

"Let's move on," he ordered. He didn't much like the idea of being on top of whatever it was before they discovered its identity, but he knew Chloe well, and if she didn't think it was worth her time yet, it wasn't. "We'll stop up there where the ruins start in earnest. Keep a sharp eye, Läzch, no telling what's in there."

"Can't we just float the boats?" Darrow asked. "Why go through the city if we don't have to?"

Vaujn blew air noisily through his lips. He knew he'd have to tell them at some point; he was just hoping the time wouldn't come so soon. "We came down here to find Osrith," he said, "and that's where he's at."

"This just gets worse and worse," mumbled the corporal, almost under his breath. "Damn *Shaddach Chi*."

Chapter Twenty-Six

The Wellspring

Two-Moons led them out of the Fourteen Halls and down a wide and mostly intact staircase of an unknown green and black stone, once again following a glowing orb of Kassakan's crafting. Even so, most of the Sunken City was still in shadow.

"So you're saying this Jir'aatu was one of the good andu'ai? One of Jiliath's rebel mages?" Osrith's tone was doubtful. If Two-Moons and Kassakan were correct, and this *qal* was one of the nicer specimens of his race, he was alternately relieved and worried. "Doesn't *seem* real friendly."

"As I explained – he's quite mad," Two-Moons said. "When the city was destroyed, his physical form was destroyed also. Seoughal cursed him with a non-corporeal existence, and such has he lived for centuries."

Osrith shrugged. "Non-what?"

"He is in spirit form," explained Kassakan, "and must abide in the bodies of others. And his choice of accommodations here is obviously limited. I doubt any mortal could have withstood such an existence."

Osrith scowled over at the *wilhorwhyr*. "And he's in *you* now. I'm sorry. I don't like it."

"I'm not asking you to like it," returned Two-Moons, fixing Osrith with a glare of his own. "We all do what we must."

"If you fought him, you could free yourself," suggested Symmlrey. She walked by her own strength now, somewhat unsteady but unwilling to accept assistance. She, like Osrith, was not pleased with Two-Moons' plan. "I don't understand why you *must* do this at all."

Two-Moons' face softened as he looked to his young Initiate, but his resolve remained strong. "If the worst were to happen to me, and I ceased to be anything but a shell for the Old One, at least you would be in Dwynleigsh and our mission would not be foiled. And there is the prospect of so much more, my child. If I can help restore the sanity to Jir'aatu's mind, he will be a great ally for our cause." He reached for her shoulder then, and spoke to her with the love and firmness of a proud father to his child. "It is time for you to follow your own course, now – to go where Ingryst guides you. I release you from your training, and beseech you to continue in the wisdom of your own judgment. If I do not see you hence, know that you will always be in my heart and memory."

Symmlrey tightened her jaw and placed her hand over his. Her voice carried only a hint of her warring emotions. "And you, mine," she said.

Osrith looked away, irritated that one by one Two-Moons was gaining their blessing for his absurd strategy. They turned down a once-grand passageway lined with murals of exacting detail and vibrant color. The main figures were all andu'ai, but beyond that, Osrith didn't waste any time absorbing the details of the work. After what he estimated was two hundred feet or more, they passed under an archway into the room beyond.

It was an oval courtyard, about a hundred feet in length and fifty across at its widest point. In the center steamed a pool of shimmering water, lit from within by a deep blue light. The perimeter was a series of massive alternating gold and silver arches spanning the gaps between slender copper pillars. The apex of each fluted column was crowned with twisting characters from an alphabet Osrith didn't recognize, but assumed were andu'ai. Each was distinct from the others, but all were of the same bloodshot black stone. Their confiscated weapons and supplies already awaited them, stacked neatly just inside the doorway. Osrith started sorting through the pile immediately, easing his discomfort by degrees with each weapon he recovered.

"The Wellspring," said Two-Moons with an indicative wave. "We must wait a short while." He groaned and wavered on his feet. "Before I send… you… ."

Symmlrey had his arm in an instant, steadying him. "Are you all right?"

"Jir'aatu," he whispered, closing his eyes.

Osrith stepped over to Two-Moons and grabbed his face roughly in his hands. "You fight him, old man!" he ordered. "Fight him!"

"Yes," nodded the *wilhorwhyr*, "safe for now. Only a little longer."

Symmlrey herded Osrith away protectively, wiping a tear or bead of sweat from Two-Moons' pasty cheek. "Tell us about the Wellspring," she said gently. "Where will it bring us?"

Two-Moons made a weak effort at a smile. "Meyr ga'Glyleyn," he said. "King's Keep. There are a number of ley lines still intact from here, but that one should be most convenient for our purpose. The bonds are weak from disuse and the aftershocks of the Fall, so Jir'aatu thinks it best to wait until his *iiyir* tides are at their height."

"And how long will that be?" Osrith said, folding his arms across his chest.

"An hour, possibly more."

Osrith didn't much like the sound of that. "You sure he just doesn't want to wait until you're asleep again?"

"I don't think we have much choice," Kassakan said. "Two-Moons cannot open or control the Wellspring. For that, we will need Jir'aatu."

"Wonderful," Osrith grumbled. "Does this make anyone else nervous?"

"As I said, we haven't much choice," replied Kassakan, "but I suspect Two-Moons still retains enough control to ensure our safety, even when Qal Jir'aatu has use of his body."

"Yes," Two-Moons assured them, lowering himself to sit by the edge of the Wellspring. He looked across the water, eyes glazed, as if concentrating on something unseen on the opposite, artificial shore of the glowing water.

Osrith wondered if it were his imagination or paranoia that detected an unnatural yellowish gleam in that gaze. Symmlrey also stared away into the distance, but Osrith at least suspected the content of her silent thoughts. In an hour, she would leave behind more than simply a companion, and she would take on more than a simple burden. He couldn't guess at her age from her appearance – the fae didn't age much physically – but from her manner he judged she was young by their standards. He didn't envy her the responsibility she had inherited. He counted himself fortunate that within a day he would most likely be paid in full and drinking away his pains at the *Gimpy Wyrm*. That thought brought a slight smile to his face.

He couldn't wait to be rid of the damned stone hanging on his neck, however precious Jir'aatu seemed to think the thing. Times weren't going to be easy. He knew that. From everything the *wilhorwhyr* had discovered and the apparent strength of Malakuur, war was inevitable. But war he could deal with. He'd been in wars aplenty over his career as a sell-sword.

With the dreamstone on someone else's neck, and Dieavaul no longer after *his*, he could get back to what he knew best. No more magic rocks, no more andu'ai, no Sunken Cities. Perhaps after the spring thaws he would return to Vae. They would need all the steel and experience they could find to hold the Marches. Evynine would need him.

"Ah, little kinfolk running about in my city?" The glint in Two-Moons' eyes had intensified. Osrith no longer wondered if it was a product of his imagination. The reawakened Jir'aatu tapped his chin with a finger. "What to do? What to do?"

"What are you talking about?" snapped Osrith. Vaujn had said in no uncertain terms that there were no kin anywhere near this place.

"The little Ebuouki man insists that you know them," continued Jir'aatu, "but I can't abide their presence in my city. They bring back so many bad memories."

"His name is Two-Moons," said Symmlrey icily. "You are a part of each other now, and he deserves your respect."

The chuckle that passed Two-Moons' lips sounded nothing like him, both smug and mocking. "Ah, my lovely *shoungeighl*, you are awake. Come sit with me."

Symmlrey's perfect face distorted into an ugly mask of hatred. "We are not your *little children* anymore, Qal Jir'aatu," she said, "and I will not be a token for your amusement. Now, what of these kin you claim to see?"

"I suppose I should admire your spirit, as they say, but in truth I find it *most* annoying. I would watch the insolence in your tone, lest I tire overmuch of your presence. Your lives matter little to me other than as temporary amusement."

"Is that so?" Symmlrey knelt down to Jir'aatu, looking him square in his inhuman eyes. "Then burn me down with your ancient magics, Great *Qal*." Her sarcasm sent Osrith's hand to his axe haft instantly, and earned her a warning glance from both him and Kassakan. She didn't heed either. "Make me your mindless slave or loving servant, if you're able. I don't think you can. I think your little plan backfired on you, Old One. You're too weak to use him as you will, and every moment you share with him, he gains in strength. Your *little Ebuouki man* is going to heal you whether you truly intended it or not. If I err, then prove me wrong."

Two-Moons didn't blink. "You tempt fate," he said, "but more dangerously, you tempt *me*."

Osrith remembered the crushing grip of invisible hands on his body, silencing his heart and smothering his breath. He wasn't sure he shared Symmlrey's conviction concerning the impotence of the andu'ai's magic. "Why don't you two exchange threats later?" he said. "But for right now, you can tell us about these underkin."

"See for yourself," Jir'aatu said with a disdainful gesture of his hand.

The Wellspring

The air above the pool erupted into a scintillating tornado of color, the meandering rainbows lasting but an instant before rushing together into a translucent reflection of twelve kin, hovering above the still waters. Osrith blinked away tears after the momentary flash of brightness, taking in the small company and focusing, somewhat astonished, on their leader.

"Vaujn?" Osrith's mouth hung open in an unflattering gape. "What in the Pits?"

"Dieavaul must have chased them down here," said Kassakan, more concerned than surprised. "Possibly the same day we left, or the next. But it seems they are all intact."

"Keep your beasties away from them, Jir'aatu," said Osrith, his gape replaced quickly with a warning scowl. "They won't bother you if you don't bother them."

The *qal* had his own look of disgust. "I will not have their kind in my demesnes," he said flatly.

"Bring them here," said Symmlrey, "and we'll take them with us. We won't allow you to harm them. They saved our lives. *Your* life, as well."

"They have done nothing for me," snapped the andu'ai. "I can't repay every debt this little Ebuo– this *Two-Moons*, has accumulated. They shall leave or I shall destroy the lot of them."

"No, Jir'aatu, leave them be." Kassakan loomed over the old man, but her hand fell gently on his back. "You must save your strength for the Wellspring, and honor your bargain. You agreed to spare Two-Moons' friends, and these are his friends as sure as we. They will undoubtedly be the last to pass through here for quite some time."

Qal Jir'aatu stared at the image with lingering distaste, but his anger seemed abated by Kassakan's calm words. Osrith didn't know if it was her magic or her manner, but that gentle voice had soothed many an agitated temper over the course of their time together, including his own.

"One of you should be off to bring them here, then," said the human with the andu'ai eyes. "I will hasten the fashioning of the portal just to be rid of the traitorous little fiends."

"I'll go," volunteered Osrith, knowing there would be no objections. He was obviously best suited to deal with the kin, and as far as he was concerned, *they* were best suited to stay and watch over Jir'aatu. "How am I supposed to find them?"

"T'nkh't'chk will take you to them," said Jir'aatu, and a cave-mantis immediately appeared from one of the recessed archways to wait by the corridor for Osrith. It was at least as tall as the specimen that had brought them from the riverbank, but its carapace was adorned with even more scalps and other once-living trinkets of esteem.

Osrith palmed a moss globe and took a deep breath of the relatively fresh air within the courtyard. It would probably be his last for quite a while.

⁂

It took twenty clicks to find Vaujn and his kin, by Osrith's reckoning, but he supposed T'nkh't'chk could have covered the same distance in half that time. He had to jog to keep up, regardless, and was the subject of several impatient glances. He couldn't see any emotion within the honeycomb facets of the cave-manti's eyes, but he did notice that T'nkh't'chk rubbed its rear appendages together more rapidly whenever it was forced to wait. The resulting sound was not unlike the night-song of the crickets that used to sing every summer in his father's fields, but considerably louder and deeper in tone. Whatever the purpose of the impromptu tune, whether simple anxiety, agitation, or some cave-manti mating song, T'nkh't'chk ceased making it once the kin were near.

The kin marched in cadence, precise and orderly in their twin columns, crossbows at the ready and face shields down. Osrith had mixed feelings about seeing the kin soldiers here. First, he felt guilt, and no small measure of it, for he had brought Dieavaul, and evidently great destruction, to Outpost Number Nine. But also he felt relief, for they all lived and seemed no worse for their journey.

He shouted a quick greeting in kinspeak before showing himself, and even so kept his hands empty before him. He imagined the kin were at least as nervous and ill at ease in this place as he was, and didn't want to risk explaining his appearance to a hail of crossbow bolts. As it turned out, they didn't seem too surprised at his arrival.

Captain Vaujn shook his head and frowned. "There you are. I thought we were going to have to march to the heart of this damn place to find you."

Osrith saluted them, scanning the twelve wary sets of eyes that were fixed on him. "The day's not over yet," he said.

The kin weren't much pleased with his explanation, nor were they eager to put their trust in the scalp-covered mantis, T'nkh't'chk, or his andu'ai master. In the end, however, they knew that none of the choices afforded them were any more desirable. Like Osrith, they decided that they could overlook the questionable method of their escape for the chance to put this place behind them quickly. This didn't prevent them from muttering a few choice phrases as they trudged on towards the Wellspring.

The Wellspring

Vaujn kept pace with Osrith, just a few steps behind T'nkh't'chk, but well in the van of his own force. The captain took one last look over his shoulder to satisfy himself of their privacy before speaking to the *Shaddach Chi* beside him. "I hope you know what you're doing. I'm risking more than my good name by trusting you. The lives of my people, and my wife, are riding on this, too."

"I know that. You think *I'm* not worried? Between the Wellspring and Jir'aatu and these big bug people." He pointed at T'nkh't'chk's back. "I don't trust *any* of them. I don't even know how much I trust Two-Moons anymore. That's why we have to do this. We have to get away from here, far away, and as quickly as we can."

"I told you not to come this way," grumbled Vaujn.

"That you did," affirmed Osrith, "and next time I'll listen to you. You have my promise on that – my word as *Shaddach Chi*."

"Aye," Vaujn said, looking up at Osrith with a creeping grin, one eyebrow arched. "*Next* time. If it's all the same to you, I'd just as soon avoid a next time."

༄

Two-Moons couldn't decide if the sensation was more akin to soaring or floating. Watching as if a spectator through his own eyes as Qal Jir'aatu made the preparations to bring the Wellspring back to life, he felt connected but distant from the body he had called home for so many years, watching with a detached interest as his hands wove intricate symbols in the air. He faced each archway in turn, gesturing before the andu'ai characters of dark stone, surprised and fascinated that their meanings were now obvious to him. They were alive – flowing, beautiful glyphs rather than the static, two-dimensional runes of mortals. Congealing power spilled from them in rivulets of shimmering cerulean down the archways and into the luminous waters of the Wellspring itself.

This was but a mote in the corner of his newfound awareness. All of Oszmagoth lay before him, open to him, tied to him. The cave-manti, or the *ohk'tkh'chk*, as they called themselves, were as familiar to him as his own tribe, some like his children. He knew them: their language, their ways, and their unspoken communion. He could feel the shadowborn prowling in the darkened reaches of the far bank as if they were insects on his leg, bothersome but contained. They had hungered for his soul since the Great War.

No, not *his* soul – Jir'aatu's.

The dringli, hovering gnat-like in the rifts and caverns that spiraled from the Sunken City like the strands of a great web: they were less than insects to him. And there, the human and the underkin, coming up the broken steps of the Chancellery Hall where the traitors had ambushed and overcome the mighty Thuoringil. He could still see his city now, as it had been, astride the mountain peaks, glowing proudly by day and brooding quietly by night. *Yes.*

No, Two-Moons corrected himself, willing invisible walls around his thoughts. *Not the human, but Osrith; not my city, but Jir'aatu's. His thoughts, his madness – not mine.*

But it is yours, said another voice in his head. *Now it is all ours.*

Two-Moons flinched mentally. It was true, what the Old One said. They were a part of each other, integrating and intermingling more with every passing moment. He fought back a growing sense of panic. He would not lose himself to this odd union if he could control their joining. If he could preserve his sanity and identity, then it would go better for both of them. He could do it. He would. There was no other way for his plan to work. Jir'aatu's knowledge would be worth nothing without guidance and direction.

Don't fight, me, said the voice again. *I don't have the strength to do this alone. Help me.*

Yes, Two-Moons answered, letting his calm spread outward like a salve, ordering their thoughts. *I'm here.*

At that moment it became clear how fragile was their symbiosis. Anything less than measured control would bleed into and affect Jir'aatu's consciousness, with unpredictable but likely unpleasant or deadly results. Two-Moons couldn't explain his realization, but he could feel the fragile balance between them, the delicate interplay of their being. He didn't need any better reason than that to restrain any potentially dangerous thoughts. He put the future out of his mind, concentrating on the moment before him. He was still aware *right now*, and that was what mattered.

"They're here," Symmlrey whispered to him.

Osrith stood there with his battle squad of kin, their armor and faces awash in the blue light of the glyphs and the Wellspring. The *iiyiraal* around the mercenary's neck emitted its own soft glow, and Two-Moons felt his eyes drawn to it. Before he even asked the question consciously, he realized the answer was already there, waiting for him to notice.

Yes, Jir'aatu's mind whispered, *now you see.*

Two-Moons fought to control his lips, to move his sluggish flesh in warning and explanation, but when he spoke, the words were not his. "Hurry, you must all be ready to enter when I finalize the spell. Time is short."

Let me tell them! Two-Moons implored, keeping his thoughts ordered and calm with an effort. He couldn't afford to destabilize the mage in the midst of this spell and leave his companions stranded within the tenuous fabric of the Veil.

There is no time, Jir'aatu replied.

"I guess this is it," said Osrith with a nod. "I hope you know what you're doing, old man."

Kassakan lowered her head to Two-Moons in a half bow. "Peace and good fortune, friend."

She and Osrith stepped away to rejoin the kin, who were keeping a conspicuous distance, leaving only Symmlrey to stand with Two-Moons. He watched helplessly as his hands completed the gestures that focused and defined the energy at his command, the word that would unleash the magic ready at his lips. He stood there, frozen in concentration amidst the rushing power he held at bay, as Osrith, Kassakan, and the kin all lined up at the edge of the water.

"Ingryst keep you," Symmlrey said, and placed her hand on his heart before turning to join the others.

Take care, my child, he thought, even as Jir'aatu spoke the word that fully awakened the Wellspring.

The travelers shielded their eyes from the intensity of the light that erupted from the pool, hesitating at the brink of the open portal. A rumble like distant thunder shook the stones at their feet, and several of the glyphs ignited in sparkling amber flames.

"Go!" Two-Moons yelled, and this time it was his voice, at least in part.

Kassakan was the first to enter, diving in headfirst. She disappeared instantly and the intense glow of the water diminished slightly. Symmlrey followed suit, glancing once at Two-Moons before vanishing. Again the light dimmed.

"Hurry!" urged Two-Moons and Jir'aatu with one voice. "All of you must go now!"

Osrith and Captain Vaujn exchanged a telling look, and the next instant the whole of the remaining company took a running jump into the water. The Wellspring swallowed all of them, sucking them down with every last glimmer of light and power to sail through the in-between of reality.

Two-Moons collapsed and lay there, silent in the dark, and hoped they emerged on this side of Shadow. He shivered as a breeze cooled his sweat.

"Are you well, Master?" chirped T'nkh't'chk from his side.

"I'll be fine," assured Two-Moons, hardly noticing the ease with which he spoke their language. He dragged himself to his feet.

"And the soft-skins are away?"

"Yes, child," he said, leaning on his bodyguard's carapace. "They are away." *And gods help them*, he added to himself.

Jir'aatu was drained and resting, and though this put the burden of recuperation mostly on Two-Moons, he accepted that role as one of necessity. It would take weeks, if not months or years, for the healing to begin. And then, if that much were successful, at least as much time to find the answers he sought. He could waste little time with worry now; there was much to do, and his work had only begun.

Chapter Twenty-Seven

Shadows and Portents

P AKH THAOLL slept. It was not a peaceful rest, yet neither was it troubled. It was, if anything, *expectant*. Today, even as the glaring suns beat down on the day-walkers somewhere above its head, it slept and it waited – waited for its master to find it in the restless dreams of sleep.

Unbeknownst to the hrumm, it had been found already. Dieavaul watched it there for a moment, from his perch in the land of dreams. Thaoll hunted here in its un-waking world, guided and spurred in its chase by phantom scents of blood and fear. It was a pure predator, acting on instincts as old as time, its heart on fire with killing lust. The nameless human it pursued screeched in terror, but this only heightened the hunter's resolve. And there, in that windless world, under a canopy of blackest night, it fell upon the fleeing man. Its jaws worked, clenching, tearing and chewing at the nonexistent flesh of its imaginary prey. And with every bite, it knew peace.

Dieavaul smiled.

Pakh Thaoll was a good choice, he thought, allowing a rare hint of approval to cross his face. It was of *Pakh Ma* Dhoamag's *ruukmwr*, the closest equivalent the hrumm had to family. As hermaphrodites, their complex system of mating and reproduction left no easy correlation between their hereditary units and those of other mortals. He could simplify the whole matter by calling Thaoll the *son of* Dhoamag, but that would be as inaccurate as it was lazy. Thaoll didn't have two parents, it had ten or twenty of them, depending on how many of its *ruukmwr* had taken part in the mating rites. Only the strongest were selected by the *pakh ma*, chosen to indulge in a ritual that could last for days. Each hrumm would become pregnant with at least one child, and all involved would share lineage with the offspring. It was odd, and more than a little disgusting to Dieavaul, but it was an important aspect of their race and their culture. And understanding the hrumm as best he could is what led him to be their feared and esteemed *Gal Pakh*. Even Thar Duhlgma, the high priest of their horrible deity, showed Dieavaul the respect of that title.

"Thaoll," spoke the Pale Man, a translucent ghost in the primal forest of its dream.

"Yes, *Gal Pakh*," responded the hrumm, its visions fading as its Master's form solidified from the hazy mist. "How may I serve?"

"It is time. Gather your force and prepare for Lord Mejul."

"Yes, Master."

"Meet him at the West Gate. You will not recognize his human form, but he will reveal himself to you. With his help and your disguises, you should pass their sentries without incident."

"Yes, *Gal Pakh*. It will be done."

"Remember Thaoll, you are to do his bidding as if it were mine. Our success depends on your unquestioning obedience. Do not stop to weigh costs. There may be no return from this, once it has begun."

Thaoll didn't hesitate even a moment in response. "Then we will hunt with the Fallen in Kyztsaraak."

"You honor your *ruukmwr* and bring glory to Shaa, Pakh Thaoll," praised Dieavaul, his image and voice fading as he pulled himself back through the filmy half-world of the Veil to rejoin his abandoned flesh, leaving the hrumm alone again in its dream. Whether or not Shaa actually awarded Thaoll a place among the honored dead hardly mattered to the Pale Man. That its group of elite *graomwrnokk* were successful, at any cost, was all that concerned him.

Dieavaul stirred from his trance, blinking away the shadow world and standing to stretch his limbs. Physically, he still felt somewhat weak from his ordeal in the mountains, and his body needed some rest despite the relatively undiminished potency of his *iiyir*. He crossed the silk-carpeted floor of his meditation chamber to its solitary furnishing: a wine rack and serving shelf. He stopped and peered silently at his collection for a moment before deciding upon a sparkling strawberry wine of Symbian vintage. A bit cloying for his taste normally, but well crafted. He preferred the dry and robust reds of Inzirii making, on most occasions, but after spellcraft the sweeter draughts often tempted him.

Dieavaul swirled the rose-colored contents around in the crystal decanter, admiring the light as it was twisted and bent by finely chiseled facets, dancing on the austere walls. He poured some of the wine into a matching, thin-stemmed glass and sipped at it delicately. With the patience and understanding of a connoisseur, he rolled the fluid across his tongue before allowing it to dribble down his throat.

Perfection can never be rushed, he mused, *whether in wine or war*.

Dieavaul put the empty glass down, savoring the last fiery trace of its surrendered contents before turning back to his casting circle and the work still at hand. Perfection also accepted no delay, and he had taken enough rest from his last spell. He walked back to the center of the room and paused at the edge of the carpet, where it relinquished a five-foot circle to rune-carved obsidian, and gathered his thoughts. He formed the image of Mejul in his mind: his physical presence, his Shadow essence, the unmistakable sense of his *iiyir*, and even the human shell in which he currently dwelled. Then he sat, and began a slow monotone chant.

Dieavaul could feel his *iiyir* resonating with each word, forming the patterns of energy that would once more open a portal through the Veil. Unlike his dream-walks with Osrith, he had no need of *ilnymhorrim* to track down the subject of this spell. Mejul was known to him, and willing, and this required of him nothing more than some of his own *iiyir*.

His awareness departed his physical self, leaving it behind gladly to soar out over league upon league as if each was but a footstep. He was not truly within Shadow here, or truly in the waking world, but threading along somewhere within the Veil itself, in-between the in-between.

He found Mejul quickly enough, out in the city itself and far from the interfering ley lines of King's Keep, however dormant they might be. Dieavaul did not want Agrylon stumbling upon their link and eavesdropping, not when their subterfuge had existed undetected for so long right beneath his nose. The Shadowyn Lord's human host remained staring into nothingness out across the great northern plains from the city wall. It was unnecessary for Mejul to sleep to sense or speak with Dieavaul. Even in this mortal form, he existed partly of Shadow.

None of the passing guards could even guess at the wordless conversation that took place right in their midst, only half a world away. None would have reason to suspect the downfall of their kingdom and their world was being plotted behind the quiet, noble face that peered into the darkness next to them. And certainly none would think to disturb the quiet reverie of a knight cloaked in the blue and gold trappings of the Prince's Guard.

༄

Guillaume awoke with a start, his arthritic fingers clutching the rumpled bedclothes up about his chin. The shutters had blown open, and the wind now howled into his chamber, sucking away any warmth or comfort with its merciless chill. His breath caught in his lungs as his eyes quested the dark corners for any hint of lurking shadows. The afterimage of the recurring nightmare faded as the less threatening shapes of his furnishings were etched by the glowing moonlight. His panicked heartbeat slowed as he realized he'd left the wraith in the world of his dreams.

The knock at the door sent him upright and the covers flying. Cursing, he slipped his feet into the doeskin slippers at his bedside and shuffled over to the door. There weren't many who would pester his sleep, but the king had idea enough who it must be. The wizard seldom felt himself bound by court convention or even common human decency. He pulled the door open, his temper rising, ready to curb Agrylon's impertinence once and for all.

But the figure at his door wasn't Agrylon.

Guillaume backpedaled, tripping on his own feet and landing with a jolt on his backbone. His eyes and mouth were wide, but his cry of alarm was caught in the back of his throat. The cloaked shadow drifted past the limp bodies of the King's Guard and into the bedchamber as the king himself scrambled back on his elbows.

My king, the soundless voice whispered in his mind, a hint of mockery in its unspoken words.

"What do you want?" Guillaume managed to croak. He knew now the chill was not from the wind alone.

The doom of your House awaits on Ebhan-nuád.

"I have done what you asked! What more do you want of me?"

The familiar sunken face of grey bent down to Guillaume's with eyes the same ashen, lifeless hue. And again the ethereal voice spoke within his skull. *Remember Vingeaux,* it warned, *lest your entire line perish forthwith. Don't forget our bargain. Your son is* mine!

"No!" Guillaume cried out, a small fleck of spittle foaming at his quivering lips. "Be gone! Leave me in peace!"

You've had your peace, my king, said the wraith, dissolving into memory even as he watched. *Now leave me mine.*

"Agrylon!" screamed the king. "Agrylon!" But none stirred in the antechamber beyond his door. He crawled on his knees to the doorframe and rested his head on the coolness of a brass hinge, sobbing and trembling like a newborn babe. "Bring me Agrylon!"

The only answer was the creak of broken shutters in the wind.

༄

Aeolil wiped the rheum from the corners of her eyes and looked at Agrylon again, perplexed. She wasn't sure what amount of her comprehension yet lingered on her pillow, where until quite recently she had rested almost comfortably, but she guessed it to be nearly half. It was well enough that she had forgone the Feast of First Night and retired early, or she'd have had no sleep at all. She didn't yet know the details, but something had alarmed the king and then Agrylon in turn. The wizard still frowned out the window of his observation tower, as if the mere display of his ire would alter the lay of the sky and erase whatever evil he saw. She tried again to fathom the enormity of what he claimed, but her mind could not wrap itself around the impossibility of it.

She looked at the signs again herself, over his shoulder. She was not a seer, nor even by strict definition was Agrylon, but they both knew enough to see that something was wrong with the scattering of the stars and constellations. Frowning, she turned back to compare the sight with the tumble of charts on the desk. She rubbed at her temples, trying to chase away the clinging drowsiness that fogged her thinking. It was doubly – no, *triply* – wrong.

Illuné was out of phase, as was Ghaest, both a day or more advanced in their cycle. And there, blazing east to west across the cloudless sky, was the fiery trail of Kazdann, three years too early. But even these paled in comparison to the disarray apparent in the Dragonmeet. Normally Pyderion dominated the stars of the three dragons. It was the brightest and the focal point of the three arms of the constellation. But tonight it was but a flickering hint of light, barely distinguishable from its siblings. More worrisome still was the ascendance of Ewanbheir, the Black Star, sign and namesake of the Dark God. It swallowed the light of its neighbors greedily, shifting the balance of the three dragons.

All wrong, and impossible besides.

Celestial bodies moved along on set courses through the sky, their patterns preordained by the Unspoken Gods when they had set order to the universe. She bit at her lower lip, and Agrylon tugged on his white beard, which shone like luminous silver in the moonlight. They exchanged a worried glance as Agrylon turned his back on the window, evidently satisfied that the omens were there, regardless of his wishes.

"Damned Pits of Erkenàdun," he said, pulling at the hair on his chin. "It seems impossible, but the king is right to be worried. *Ebhan-nuád.*"

"I don't understand," confessed Aeolil. "The time is not right."

"Nor is it ever right," Agrylon replied tersely. "It matters not how it came to be. Or, at least, it matters little right *now*."

Aeolil had never seen worry on her mentor's face before, or fear, until their recent encounter with the Neva Seough. Tonight both were evident again. Neither spoke of the demon, or their brush with the Dark, but the very silence of it hung in the air between them. "Is this what pulls the tides out of phase? They've been erratic of late."

"Yes," sighed Agrylon, slumping as he crossed the short distance to the desk. Aeolil couldn't recall ever seeing him look so old. "That and much more, I fear. There is no worse omen, nothing more dreaded in all our lore. The barriers between our world and that of Shadow are at their weakest now. Even the dead may walk among us, given half a reason." He paused to rummage through his scrolls, seizing upon a particularly old and yellowed piece of parchment. "A game is in progress, Aeolil, and we've not even been *playing* our pieces, let alone defending against theirs. Now it may be too late."

"Is it the Neva Seough?"

Agrylon shoved the scroll into his voluminous, deep purple robes. "That Myszdraelh and her ilk enjoy the spectacle of our peril, I have no doubt. However, I cannot say for certain that this work is *of* the Dark. Would that they could so prevail upon our world." He shrugged. "But to work such magic as that through the Veil, no. I think not. Were such the case, odds are we would never have combated Myszdraelh to defeat. Or, indeed, that the demons would need such indirect means to attack us at all."

"Then who? And to what purpose?"

"There are not many who could work such magics. One might say our nexus has just been captured. The Old Ones once had such power." He pursed his lips, thinking. "Brohan told His Majesty stories of andu'ai in the northlands. Rumors, we thought. Perhaps I dismissed them too quickly."

Aeolil's heart skipped a beat. "The andu'ai?"

"I am reduced to guessing, but no fae or human since Miithrak has possessed such power."

"Then what can we do?" Her head was still spinning with the very thought of the Old Ones coming back for what once was theirs. As a child, she had believed an andu'ai lived in her wardrobe waiting to devour her, and had forced her father or her guardsmen to search it thoroughly each night before sleep. She wished now the fear was so easy to dispel. "If this magic is as powerful as you say, how can we counteract it?"

"We can't," stated Agrylon with resigned calm. "*Ebhan-nuád* will be upon us this Midride, the very night of the Feast of Illuné. There is naught we can do to stop that. But, we *can* prepare ourselves for it."

"Prepare for what?" asked Aeolil, unable to control a slight tremor in her voice. "We don't know what to defend against."

"Indeed." Agrylon put his hand on her shoulder in a rare show of comfort. "A tricky bit that will be. For now, we must report back to the king. I doubt he will be fond of what we tell him."

"We?" Aeolil's surprise nudged away her growing fears momentarily. Not even Guillaume knew the true nature of her apprenticeship to Agrylon.

"It's time for me to part with some of my secrets," he said, leading her towards the door. "You, I'm afraid, will have to be one of them."

As much as the prospect of entering his clandestine world of grand designs was intriguing and long overdue, her greatest hope was that the transformation of the skies surprised more than just Agrylon. If this was a product of nature rather than design, then none would have time or opportunity to take advantage of it. She hoped for that, but she couldn't say she really believed it. Such things did not happen by chance.

They found the king in his day chamber, his nightclothes covered by a thick ermine robe. A goblet was in his hand, and a half-empty flagon of wine rested on the table by the blazing hearth. A dozen of the King's Guard stood in full battle dress, their eyes wide and alert. The cheeriness of the room, with its airy design and bright decorations, was dampened by the late hour and their collective mood. The only person moving in the room was Willanel, the Captal of King's Keep, second only to Vanelorn in matters of security.

"I will have their spurs for this, Your Majesty, *that* I promise you." His words were angry, and his middle-aged face red from ill-concealed rage. "They are a disgrace, the lot of them – sleeping at post. I will not have this in the Royal Guard, Your Majesty, I will not indeed!"

"Stay your anger and leave us," Agrylon said, his soft voice cutting through Willanel's ranting. "I must speak with His Majesty alone."

The captal shook his head. "I don't think that is wise, Lord High Chamberlain."

"Leave us!" commanded Agrylon with a quick wave of his fingers.

Willanel and his men were on the other side of the door before they even realized they had obeyed. Aeolil remained in the wizard's shadow, watching the king as discreetly as she could manage. He did not look well. His face was drawn and haggard, and his beard clung like a grey haze to his chin. A dribble of red wine painted his lips a bloody red, and his eyes sought comfort in the design of the carpet at his feet.

"Well?" muttered Guillaume.

"The news is not good, Your Majesty," Agrylon said evenly. "*Ebhannuád* is indeed nigh."

The king's head sagged further to his breast. "Then we are truly lost."

"Not lost," corrected Agrylon. "Forewarned."

"He grows bolder and more powerful with every day," Guillaume said without lifting his head. "He's come out of my dreams to threaten me in the flesh. And he marched through your wards and my honor guard as if they weren't even there. So tell me, what hope is there that he may be stopped from his vengeance?"

Agrylon knelt before the king, taking his hand in a firm grip and looking him directly in his downcast eyes. "I can fashion stronger wards for you and yours, and we will double the guards about the royal family. We do not know if it is vengeance he seeks."

The king only continued to shake his head.

"And Aeolil," the wizard said with obvious reluctance, "Lady Aeolil is trained in the Craft by my own hand." Guillaume finally reacted, looking up at Aeolil as if just realizing she was there. "She has not the power or knowledge yet to cast the greater spells, but her *il-iiyir* is at its peak with the full moons. Together we will weave a most potent defense."

Aeolil wanted to add her own words of comfort, but in truth, she had none to offer. Despite Agrylon's assurances, she had more than a trifling doubt in their power to stop whatever it was that was unfolding around them. It was also obvious enough that they had a clearer picture of the danger they faced than she, but it was not the time to press that point. For now, it would be best to calm the king's nerves. The Winter Festival would continue in a few hours with the Opening Melee, and he must keep up appearances even in these times.

But later, she would drag more of the truth from Agrylon. He'd said himself that he needed her, and for her to be of help, he would be forced to relinquish more of his precious secrets.

She hoped she would be ready to hear them.

⁂

Jylkir brushed past Caethys without comment, ignoring the sentry's disapproving stare as she ascended the winding stairs inside the Guard Tree. Du'uwneyyl had been careful since the night of the *nyrul cayl* to have the *wilhorwhyr* under closer guard. Not a night passed that Jylkir did not regret her delay in attempting his release. Now all chance of escape was gone. At least he was still alive – that gave her some hope. With the news that there would be no opposition of the Priest Kings, she had feared he would be put to death. Had he been full-blooded human, dead he would have been, and without hesitation. But however diluted, his blood was still partially of the Elyrmirea, and Meimniyl would not spill that lightly.

Her worry now was that Meimniyl would not retain her power for much longer. The influence of Ryaleyr and Hlemyrae on the other *caylaeni* grew with each passing day, and with the arrival of the Macc prince and the Malakuuri ambassador, things seemed only to be growing worse.

She sang the words of opening without much thought, stepping into the *wilhorwhyr's* cell and sealing the entrance behind her. Bloodhawk sat at the far end of the small room, kneeling on the crude pallet that served as his bed. He didn't turn as she entered, staring intently out of the small window she sang for him on a previous visit. Somehow she had convinced Du'uwneyyl that it would be a harmless gesture.

"Welcome," the *wilhorwhyr* said, with but a trace of sarcasm in his voice.

"I brought you some nuts and flatbread," she said, reaching into her pouch for the items. It wasn't much, more in fact than the *cayl* allowed. They didn't intend him to regain his strength.

"Thank you," he said, but still didn't turn to look at her.

She set the food down next to his pallet, following his eyes as they gazed at the sky. The clouds hung like wispy curtains framing the stars and moons above. She frowned when she saw the comet streaking its way across the heavens.

"An ill omen, if you believe in such things," said Bloodhawk, mirroring her thoughts.

"What is it?"

The halfblood finally turned toward her then, leaving the spectacle above to his back. "Signs. Portents." He smiled wanly. "And none good, I'm afraid."

"I thought you held little stock in the lay of the stars and sky."

"Very little," he confirmed, "but I am wary of things that alter it out of hand. It is many years yet before we should see the Bringer of War again. And the moons, they rush through their phases. These things may not foretell our future, but they are certainly reflecting our present."

Jylkir looked past him into the night. She was not surprised to see that he was right. *It's all wrong,* she thought. The andu'ai had once aligned the stars to affect the outcomes of their greater spells. At one time her people had done the same. Such meddling was often as dangerous to the caster as the victims, however. *Who wields such forgotten powers now?*

"You don't think someone is trying to turn the tides?" she asked.

"It matters little what I think," he said dryly. "Look at what's before you. The Pale Man is about, there's an iiyir-well tapped in Malakuur, andu'ai are on the march, the winter is early and unduly harsh, an unstoppable plague is creeping across the Realms, and now the skies themselves turn traitor. Do you think all that coincidence?"

"Of course not," she said. "No more than I think this arranged truce with the Maccs and the Priest Kings is coincidence. But against such power, what am I to do? It is all I can manage to sneak you an extra piece of bread."

"More than I, at least," said Bloodhawk. "We must hope my friends were more successful in our plan. If Malakuur has agents amongst you, then most certainly it has them in Providayne. But I haven't given up hope just yet. I cannot believe that the Ceearmyltu will long be fooled by this pretense of friendship. Eventually some of your kind will see the error in this course and take steps to change it. Until then, we can only wait and plan for our opportunity." He popped a nut into his mouth and tore off a piece of flatbread. "Why don't you tell me about your new *friends*?"

Jylkir turned away from the window. It was easier to focus on the smaller aspects of their dilemma when she wasn't faced with the evidence of its enormity. "They have ever been a war-like people, the Maccs, but not evil. Not like these men who have come before us.

"Prince Ruoghen is young and arrogant, but he's taken his fair share of skulls in battle – warriors of note, Du'uwneyyl says – and he's walked Kazdann's Fire. His bloodlust has him at odds with his mother, the Iron Queen, but he has the loyalty of many in their clan."

"He's walked the fire?" asked Bloodhawk, leaning forward. "And how many has he taken? How many skulls?"

Jylkir thought for a moment, trying to remember the procession of his grand entrance. It had been a gruesome pageant. "Ten or twelve," she finally said. "There were two rows of skull-bearers, his honor guard, and they bore them along on pikes, with trailing banners."

"Thirteen would give him claim for a legitimate challenge," he mused. "That's the ancient measure of a chieftan: *bloodline of the clan lords, thirteen skulls and Kazdann's blessing*. You're sure it wasn't thirteen? He didn't wear a skull on his cuirass or helm?"

Jylkir shook her head. "Twelve, I think."

Bloodhawk hissed and frowned. "A man with ten skulls is not yet desperate for his last. A man with thirteen may have greater power, but he's more careful when he uses it, more predictable, because he fears losing it. A man with twelve is most dangerous, both desperate and eager. He can be unpredictable. What of the other, the Malakuuri?"

"Lombarde, he is named. He's a worse sort, I think. He has an air of calm about him, and intellect, and his words are full of reassuring eloquence. He has stirred many a sleeping heart with his pleas for justice, but I don't trust him. The *trees* don't trust him. I don't know why. He is more reasonable than Ruoughen, and more intelligent, but there is something about him. Something cold and... ." She shrugged. "I don't trust him."

"Wise enough. Do they bring terms?"

"They claim no quarrel with us, pretending to seek only their just revenge on Providayne."

"Probably true, for the moment," put in Bloodhawk. "You're far too valuable as allies for now."

"Yes," she agreed, "and despite Meimniyl's insistence on non-interference, I sense that Ryaleyr looks at the Maccs much as they look at her. Not so much a trusted ally as a useful, and ultimately disposable, tool. One or both sides will suffer for that, in the end."

"Ideally both, for the Priest Kings," Bloodhawk muttered. "And although my comrades may have warned Providayne of the trouble on their western front, none know of any threat from the south."

"But they are already at war with the Maccs," Jylkir said, puzzled. "Won't they be alert for trouble from the south?"

Bloodhawk shook his head. "No, not from this quarter. Throughout the wars between the northern and southern kingdoms, the battleground has always been the plains of Paerytm. The deep reaches of the Caerwood are thought filled with vengeful elves and black magics, and no sane general would take an army through it. With an alliance, the Maccs will come unhindered through your lands and attack the soft underbelly of Providayne. No one has ever thought such an alliance possible, myself included, so no one will be prepared for it."

"And if the humans over-commit to the west?"

"Aye, a nice trap." Bloodhawk crunched another nut between his teeth. "And who's to say this Macc Queen won't take advantage of her wayward son's attack and press in on the southeastern border? Whatever their dispute, she'd likely forget or forgive it for such an opportunity. And then Providayne will become a clear example of Ebiqitek's first maxim of warfare: *it's hard to win a battle with a front at your back.* It is a questionable pun, but a sound observation."

"What are we to do?" Jylkir felt an empty sense of hopelessness settling into her belly. "I am only a treesinger. I don't have skill at war, or powerful magic, or influence with the *cayl*. I don't see what chance we have to avert this war. It appears a flawless strategy."

"No," said Bloodhawk, his mouth full of bread. "If you'll forgive me quoting the Warmaster again, *every perfect plan has at least one flaw.* The weak link for this one lies in their supply lines. Conquest could quickly turn to retreat if their lines of communication and supply are cut off. I don't know how many Maccs this Ruoghen has to command, but the forces we spied to the west were too large to live off the land for any length of time."

"Yes, but locked in here, you aren't likely to warn anyone of the danger. And without warning... ." She saw no need to state the obvious.

"I've no clever words or quotes to answer that," Bloodhawk agreed. "Which leads us to the next matter. We must start planning our escape."

Jylkir didn't answer for a moment. She returned his gaze with an open-mouthed incredulity. "Escape?" she said, then more emphatically, "*We?*"

"I will need your help," he said evenly, "and I doubt you will be much welcome here after that. For a time, anyway."

"Bloodhawk." She sighed. She doubted she could be of any assistance. Not with Du'uwneyyl's watchful eyes always on her back. "You overestimate me."

"I think not," he said, still assured in both his speech and demeanor. "Perhaps you underestimate yourself?"

Jylkir closed her eyes. She wanted to help him, she truly did, but she couldn't see how. She could open the way out of the Guard Tree, but from there he would have to fight or sneak his way through the entire tribe. That would be no mean feat. And then there was the ever-present shadow of her sister. Du'uwneyyl was the finest warrior of the Eastern Tribes, a champion several times over at the Finn Gaeal in both bow and blade. And she could track any living thing to the ends of her forest.

"Do you even have the strength?" she asked.

"I believe I can manage," he said.

Jylkir closed her mouth into a puzzled frown, noting for the first time in her visit that his eyes were clear of fever and his skin no longer paled by sickness or fatigue. When had he recovered from the hrummish poison? On his meager diet, even with her clandestine supplements, he should still be weak. "How?" she said, puzzled.

"You are not the only one here who doesn't trust the new allies of the *cayl*, remember?" A grin tugged at the corner of his mouth. He caressed the smooth interior bark of the Guard Tree with the fingers of his right hand. "I have shared strength with your old friend, Llri."

Jylkir kept her mouth from falling open again with a conscious effort. She had heard of the *wilhorwhyr* before, allies that they were in the Blood Wars, but she had never met one before Bloodhawk. They were a people of the west, predominantly. Most of the Ceearmyltu, and the other Eastern Tribes, considered their mythical abilities just that, stories that had expanded over the centuries from mere exaggeration into accepted lore. It was not an easy thing for her people to accept that humans might have the aptitude to intrude in their ancient ways. The thought left even her apprehensive and skeptical.

"You have spoken to her?" she asked, but even as the question left her lips, it was answered by the warmth and peace that flowed up and into her from the wood at her feet.

Bloodhawk shook his head. "I had some small experience with the *ilyela* of the Elyrmirea, enough to know they are not the common trees of the wood. Yet I could not truly speak with her, not *sing* to her, at least not in the same fashion as you," he said. "But I am aware of her being, as she is of mine. That proved to be enough."

The humming of her precious Llri echoed the sincerity of his words. Any doubts she may have harbored, whether of her own ability or of Bloodhawk's veracity, fell away at that sweet silent song. The *ilyela* were displeased, their songs saddened or absent in the wake of these welcomed intruders. She and Ililysiun had discussed that very topic the previous night, though the *caylaeni* had expressed no optimism that these concerns would be taken seriously by the *lyaeyni* or the *cayl*.

The *ilyela* didn't wish to wait for the Ceearmyltu. They had come up with a strategy of their own.

"I will do what I can," she said, still not certain what that could be.

"Good," the *wilhorwhyr* responded, looking back out the window. "Then let's be about it."

Chapter Twenty-Eight

Shades of Memory

Aeolil hugged the white shawl about her shoulders and suppressed a shiver. The wool was somewhat natty around the edges, but it had served to keep her warm since she was fifteen, and it provided a familiar comfort along with simple warmth. At the moment, the former was far more valuable, if equally scarce. Sleep had been elusive after her meeting with Agrylon and the king, despite the overwhelming exhaustion that hung leaden on her limbs. The dreams of her childhood had come back to torment her, of andu'ai and shadow beasts gnawing on her bones, given new life by the events of the previous few hours.

Worst of all the nightmares, her father's horse, rider-less and foam-mouthed, pulling up grass before the walls of Castle Vae. That day had not haunted her memory so vividly for years. Possibly the conversation with Calvraign from a few nights past had sparked the recurrence of those ugly images, or possibly it was only a manifestation of more recent fears. Whatever the reason, she had given up on rest and dressed herself in her warmest garments for a visit to the garden. There she might find a chance at some peace.

Aeolil shooed away her bleary-eyed attendants who were awakened by the stir of her preparations. They were only too happy to return to their adjoining room and enjoy perhaps another hour of sleep. As she stepped into the hall, Chadwick was there immediately to greet her. Stefan stood a step or two behind his elder, both positioned conveniently to block her egress.

"For goodness' sake, milady," Sir Chadwick said, already exasperated in his first sentence. "What are you doing?"

"I cannot sleep," she said with just the right amount of early morning hauteur, "and I wish to visit the garden."

Chadwick and Stefan were not pleased, if she read their glances correctly. Bleys was not known for his forgiving tongue, and they had received more than enough verbal lashings in the past ten-day. Now, after the assassination attempt on Calvraign, the captal walked a fine line between wary and wrathful. Neither wished to be the cause of pushing him over that line, but of late Aeolil tread within a thin enough margin of her own.

"Captal Malade left very strict instructions regarding your safety, milady," said Chadwick. His words were cautious, but not hesitant. "I think it would go easier for all of us if we followed them."

"Am I to infer that he forbade you to allow me leave of my quarters?" she asked.

"The captal *requested* that you remain in your rooms until such time as he joins us. After the attempt on Sir Calvraign, he wishes you not to take liberty with your safety."

"Nevertheless," she said archly, "I am going to the garden." She knew this put them in an awkward spot, caught between the wishes of their liege-lady and their superior officer, and she regretted that. She knew the quiet young Stefan had already taken more than his share of the captal's anger, and would take more of the same without comment. She had known Chadwick for some years, and didn't wish to cause him any undue friction with Bleys. But neither would she allow herself to be confined against her will. "Unless you intend to restrain me?"

Chadwick shrugged at Stefan and spread his arms helplessly before Aeolil. "You know I will not, milady. But please, reconsider this."

"I appreciate your situation," she said, "and I apologize for putting you in it, but I am going whether it pleases Bleys or not."

"Very well." Chadwick sighed. "Off to the garden we go."

It was a few clicks before they were on their way. Chadwick had to make arrangements for the relief guards to take up position at her door to mask her absence, and leave a message for Captal Malade in the event he arrived before their return. Aeolil felt another pang of remorse for Chadwick. He was already sacrificing much-needed sleep and he would be fighting in the Champions' Melee in but two days' time. She doubted that this added stress would help his mental preparations. She wondered whom he had drawn as an opponent for the first round.

"I believe we're ready, milady," he said, almost forlornly.

She swallowed her guilt and nodded. "Very well. Let's be on our way."

There weren't many astir in the castle at this hour, save for the odd servant or two and the guards, who seemed both more numerous and more alert than normal. She tried putting the revelations of the past day or two in perspective. It was hard for her to account for so much happening in so little time. Just yesterday, she had learned of Calvraign's ordeal and at least some of Agrylon's plans for him, attended the Parade of the Lists and the Commencement Ceremony, and been awakened from a troubled sleep to learn she hadn't been nearly as troubled as she ought to have been. If events unfolded at this pace consistently, it could turn out to be the longest ten-day of her life.

Chadwick went on ahead as they walked the last few feet toward the garden door and motioned her to wait. She complied, containing her impatience to avoid yet another argument. The knight spent at least ten clicks in the garden before returning with a nod of approval. It seemed an unlikely place for trouble, but considering recent events, she thought better of second-guessing his caution.

Aeolil hurried down the steps into the garden, holding up the dancing hem of her skirts. The suns yet slept, but even in darkness this was a beautiful place. A beam of moonlight happened through the clouds, glimmering on the reflecting pool and the statues frozen in a stationary frolic around it. The tree leaves rustled in the lake breeze, whispering amongst themselves. She breathed in the thick scents around her and held the moment in her consciousness. When next she felt the whirlpool of fear and doubt, she would have this moment of uncomplicated peace to steady her.

She circled the pool, winding between the stone children, her eyes wandering across the fluid lines of inscriptions around the perimeter of the water. She wondered if this was a dialect with which Artygalle was familiar. He had spoken some of the aulden tongue. Perhaps he could read their script as well, and translate for her. She would love to know the origin and meaning of this place. From the innocence of the statues, to the choice and placement of the vegetation, to the golden stones that glittered beneath the water, such care was taken with its design, she found it hard to believe that it had always been simply a garden.

When she first discovered the garden, years ago, her entourage had discouraged her from frequenting it. The feeling of peace that she felt translated to unease for some, her fascination to disdain. The illusions that sometimes skipped across the surface of the water were not so much intriguing as terrifying to most of the court. The fact that it was considered forbidden fed her desire to spend time here, and over the years that childish want had evolved into a mature appreciation of its wonder. Here, all the complexities of her life, all the choices, seemed simpler.

Aeolil sat down in front of the pool and shut her eyes, trying to lose herself in that simplicity, to enjoy the luxury of thought and analysis without the distraction of worry or a preoccupation with consequence. This place had served her well in the past to contemplate the intricacies of politics and the ramifications of her marriage to this suitor or that, but now the strands she examined were of even broader significance. Calvraign, Agrylon and Myszdraelh, the onset of *Ebhan-nuád*, and the apparition that threatened the king. She searched for the connections and their relation to each other. It would all make sense when viewed in the proper light, or from the appropriate angle. All the pieces would fit together.

Aeolil felt a surge run through her, racing along her nerves from every extremity to meet like a whirlwind in her chest. She slumped onto her hands as the statues began to shift and spin around her.

"Milady?" Stefan approached from his post, a discreet distance from the pool.

She held up a hand to quiet his concern, but left the other on the ground for support. She adjusted to the shift in the *iiyir*, calming her body even as her mind reeled. What was going on? She had always felt it stirring here, like a self-contained current within the greater flow of the tides. But this was more akin to one of Agrylon's greater spells – a summoning or invocation of considerable power.

"Stefan," she said, recovering her breath. "Find Bleys or Vanelorn, and tell them something is amiss. Bring them quickly!" *No sense sending anyone for Agrylon*, she thought. She was certain he felt the disturbance already.

Stefan didn't pause to question her. "Yes, milady," he said, "right away." He left at a sprint, taking the stairs two at a time.

Chadwick knelt next to her. "What is it? What's wrong?"

"Get back," she said, regaining her feet.

Chadwick swallowed his protest as a bright golden light erupted like a captured sun from the reflecting pool. He tripped on his feet as he drew his sword, landing on his backside with his blade out before him.

Aeolil took a careful step backward, her hands already weaving the beginnings of a basic spell of warding. Standing there, silhouetted by the pillar of light that now lit the garden, she felt the futility of the gesture. She didn't have the means to combat whatever this was. If she could but hinder it long enough for Agrylon to arrive... .

Chadwick scrambled to his feet in front of Aeolil, the terror kept from his face by years of discipline. "Run!" he shouted, pushing her back with his free arm.

Aeolil struggled to maintain her concentration on the spell as Chadwick inadvertently disrupted her gestures and thus her focus of the *iiyir*. But it was too late. She could already feel control of the magic slipping away from her, even as the light before her grew to a blinding intensity. Just as she reached up to shield her eyes, a shadow sprang out from within the light – an inhuman shadow. She heard a loud thump as it landed not five feet from them, and the hiss of Chadwick's sword cutting through empty air. There was a grunt of pain and the clatter of steel on stone, and Aeolil began counting the last precious moments of her life. She blinked, trying to make sense of it all, squinting through her fingers. All she could see was the gigantic shadow holding Chadwick off the ground with one arm and another, considerably smaller shadow leaping out of the water to land in the garden with a cat's grace.

"Peace! Peace!" a throaty voice begged. "We mean you no harm!"

Something about the sound of that voice was familiar and calming, and the edge fell away from her burgeoning panic. Chadwick was gently lowered to the ground, and the light emanating from the pool dimmed. Color began to bleed back into the figures, and she realized with profound shock that the voice was indeed known to her.

Before she could say anything further, there were more forms appearing out of the pool's dwindling brilliance. But instead of diving from the water, they shot from the pool a yard or more into the air, feet first, and then fell back with a multitude of splashes. A shimmering vortex sucked the remaining light back into the pool with a resounding peal like a thunderclap. In the aftermath, the dim pre-dawn glow seemed dark as deepest midnight.

Aeolil stared wide-eyed at the reptilian figure that stood dripping a few feet in front of her, looking with concern on the unconscious Chadwick at her feet. "Kassakan?" she whispered, afraid she would wake herself from this odd dream.

"Oh dear," the lizard lamented, bending down to examine the fallen guard more closely. "I hadn't intended to knock him out."

"Kassakan?" repeated Aeolil, the questions of how or why buried beneath the shock and exultation of the *who*. She ignored the ribald curses hurled back and forth by the splashing figures in the reflecting pool and was only dimly aware of the woman behind the hosskan turning back to help them.

Kassakan looked up, cocking her head. "You know me?" she asked. "I'm afraid I don't recall you."

Aeolil smiled and reached out to touch the scales on the lizard's snout. The slick cool surface was real enough beneath her fingers. This was no illusion. "I have changed more than you over the years," she said.

Kassakan sat, cradling Chadwick's head in her lap, her double-lidded eyes blinking rapidly as she sniffed the young noblewoman. "Merciful Creator!" she said. "Aeolil!"

"Are you all right? How did you – no, *what* are you doing here?" Aeolil bit down on her quickly expanding list of questions. There would be time for all that later. She knelt down on the opposite side of her guard, facing Kassakan. "Chadwick... . Is he hurt?"

"Not badly," the lizard said, her claws both dexterous and delicate as they lifted his eyelids. "But he'd do well not to exert himself for a day or two. As for us," she indicated the woman, and the companions she was helping to pull from the water behind her, "we have news to impart. Can you take us to the king?"

"I don't think that will be a problem," Aeolil said. "Half the King's Guard shall be arriving here shortly. Things are rather on edge of late, and I didn't know what to think."

"A wise enough course," agreed Kassakan, "things being what they are."

"Your news is not good, then?"

Kassakan only shook her head. Aeolil began to pry further, but her eyes caught the movement of a dripping, muscular man approaching them from the reflecting pool. She blinked twice, in case her eyes had deceived her, but he did not disappear or take on another form. He only came closer.

Captal Turlun, she thought, her mouth going dry. *Osrith.*

Older, grayer, slightly less limber, perhaps, but it was certainly him. She supposed that made some sort of sense, considering Kassakan's presence, but it unsettled her. *What brought him from his self-imposed exile?* Certainly it was no trifling matter.

"Worry about him later, lizard," the familiar voice grumbled. "I want to get this over with. He'll be all-"

Osrith's sentence fell off his tongue as he caught sight of the young Lady Vae. Aeolil knew that he recognized her immediately. His eyes dropped, his lips curled downward, and the color drained from his face. After all these years, still the guilt held him in thrall. She could understand how it haunted him, to a degree. She wished that day had faded more into the haze of her own memory.

"Osrith," she said, her smile more melancholy than she would have liked. "It is good to see you again."

"Milady," the mercenary replied, his voice flat.

Aeolil reached out and grasped his hand firmly, squeezing it between both of hers. Then she heard the tramp of iron shod boots at the door and turned, prepared to ease any belligerence or suspicion. Vanelorn's harried visage came into view through the doorframe, taking in the whole scene with one efficient glance.

Aeolil gave Osrith's hand another reassuring squeeze, relieved that it hadn't been Bleys who'd come upon them first. *That reunion will be unpleasant, at the very best.* She straightened as the lord high marshal approached, gathering her wits to answer his coming barrage of questions. She didn't begin to know the answers just yet, but she knew that another piece of this elusive puzzle had just fallen into place.

༄

Calvraign threw away his down coverlet and sprang from bed in one violent motion, shouting something unintelligible even before fully awake. He wheeled uncertainly on his feet, his head heavy on his shoulders and his stomach knotted and uneasy. He fell against his dressing table and slid to the floor, trying to keep down the vomit that was creeping up his throat. The room spun around him, which wasn't much help, but he kept control with some careful breaths.

Too much wine, he thought to himself. He'd partaken of both ales and mead in generous portions on occasion, back in Craignuuwn, but he had no experience with the strong sweet wines served at King's Keep. Definitely not in the quantities available last evening at the Feast of First Night. As Aeolil had not been in attendance, he had fallen in first with Calamyr, then Prince Hiruld and finally, and with more disastrous consequence, Stuart adh Boighn.

Hiruld's young friend had strong opinions concerning each of the wines at the table, and shared both his feelings and the beverages in question with Calvraign first hand.

The events of the night rushed past his eyes in an incoherent jumble. Had he really danced the shepherd's jig with Stuart on the prince's table? He ran his tongue around the chalky interior of his mouth, trying to recall what else he had done. A particularly salacious bit of verse was running through his head, and Calvraign squinted away the memory of the drunken sing-a-long. There was always a chance the others would be too drunk to remember it. He groaned and crawled back toward his bed. If he slept late, he would only miss the bake-off of wintercakes and spice breads; the Opening Melee did not start until highsuns, or thereabouts.

A cold draft of air blew across his back and he hunched his shoulders in a miserable shiver. "Blood and ruin," he muttered, dragging himself up to his unsteady feet and stumbling toward the window. To his surprise, it was already tightly shuttered.

"*Calvraign.*"

The voice cut through his cloudy awareness like an icy dagger, sending another shiver through his bones. He turned slowly, knowing already that when he did, he would face the same dark apparition that had haunted his shadow in recent days. It had never spoken to Calvraign before, but still he knew. Even so, when he met the gaze of those expressionless black eyes, he leaned back heavily on the window ledge.

"I know who you are," he said, forcing each word from his fear-tightened throat.

"Beware the Ebhan-nuád," it said, grey robes flowing and tattered in an ethereal breeze, *"or share your father's fate."*

Calvraign swallowed. The mention of his father both angered and terrified him. "Then I would die a hero."

"You would die a fool," the empty voice corrected.

"Ibhraign was no fool, Pale Man," Calvraign spat, tensing his muscles and readying for what he guessed would be the last, and most idiotic, act of his life.

"Is that what you think?"

Its tone was so devoid of expression Calvraign couldn't tell if the remark intended surprise or mockery. Whether one or both, he didn't much care. He made a clumsy leap and sailed through the fading apparition, catching only a handful of air and a lingering chill. When he regained himself he was alone. The room was spinning again, and his stomach heaved. This time he didn't have the strength to fight it.

As he emptied his stomach's contents onto the edge of the carpet, Calvraign wondered why he was still alive. Either the Pale Man was powerless to harm him in that ghostly form, or he was being toyed with. Either way it didn't make any sense. If he couldn't harm him, why visit him, why *warn* him? More puzzling, if this creature were as powerful as both Brohan and legend described, why didn't it just kill him, if that's what it wanted? He would have to ask Brohan at his first opportunity, but another spasm brought his full attention back to his physical distress.

Calvraign wasn't sure how long he'd lain on his elbows, retching, before Seth arrived at his side. His steward grabbed him under his armpits and lifted him up and away from the stinking pool on the floor. The room was still tilting around him as he took a seat on the edge of his bed. A mug of water was pressed into his hand and he drank it, washing away some of the bitter taste in his mouth.

"I'll have someone in to take care of that straight away, sir," Seth was saying. "Come, lean on me."

Calvraign obeyed, leaning on the younger man as he was led out of his bedroom and through his chamber's small receiving room. Seth was nudging him toward the door to his small bath and privy in a fashion the shepherd should have been quick to recognize. Inside, Calvraign found the copper tub already brimming with steaming, scented, water. Seth moved aside the bucket he had used to ferry in the heated water from the fire and helped Calvraign out of his soiled garments.

"I need to speak with Brohan," Calvraign said, stepping over the rim of the tub. "Right away."

Seth nodded indulgently. "He said much the same about you. That's why you need to clean yourself up."

Calvraign accepted a thick bar of soap as he settled into the soothing warmth of the tub. The tension in his muscles lulled somewhat, and he settled his head against the padded headrest. He resisted a compelling desire to return to the oblivious peace of sleep, to some place, any place, where he could pretend his visitation was just the stuff of nightmare.

"Brohan said what?" he asked, feeling as if someone else were manipulating his lips. *No more wine for you tonight, young Askewneheur,* he added to himself.

"We've had a rather eventful morning, sir," Seth said as he stuffed Calvraign's soiled nightclothes into the empty bucket. "There was some commotion in the king's chambers last night, or so says Burton, and rumor has it a messenger arrived in the wee hours with some sort of dire news. Master Madrharigal has been in twice already to see if you'd recovered."

Calvraign rubbed his throbbing temple with the balls of his fingers. *How much could possibly go on in this damn castle within the space of a few days?* "The king? Is he well? Why didn't you wake me?" he snapped, none to graciously.

Seth's eyes widened a little, and he reined in the grin that had been growing on his perpetually serious face. "Yes sir, all's well, sir. And we did try, sir. Waking you, that is. Master Madrharigal suggested we let you sleep it off. So you would be more, um, co... co..."

"Coherent," provided Calvraign, just before submersing his head underwater. He rubbed his hands through his scalp vigorously, wishing he could stay in this sheltering warmth all day. He didn't think the extra sleep had done him much good. He came up for breath reluctantly, and then set about cleaning himself.

Seth came and went, taking away the bucket of clothes and returning with towels, some lilac oil for his hair, and fresh woolen undergarments. Calvraign didn't feel much better after his bath, but he did feel somewhat refreshed. The advantage to this was that he felt his thoughts were clearer and sharper. The disadvantage lay in the fact that he felt his discomfort a little more acutely as well. His eyes felt dry and swollen, his throat sore, and his stomach was still an unsettled mess.

When he returned to the sitting room, he found Seth awaiting him with the rest of his clothes and a small cup. Calvraign immediately refused the latter with a quick shake of his head. Even the thought of food and drink made him ill.

"You should try it," insisted Seth, holding up the cup once more. "Baeson swears by it."

"Who?" Calvraign frowned skeptically.

"Prince Hiruld's steward. He claims it will take the edge off."

Calvraign accepted the cup but peered at the clear liquid with obvious reluctance. Its odor was strong, reminiscent of charcoal and sulfur, and he wrinkled his nose in distaste. "This is supposed to help?"

"Baeson said it works best if you don't taste it," Seth handed him a pair of spearmint leaves. "Just drink it down quick and start chewing on these."

Calvraign closed his eyes and swallowed all of the drink in one mighty gulp. The spearmint helped, but even so he felt a cold sweat break out on his brow as he fought back a fresh wave of nausea. With an effort, he un-puckered his mouth and licked his lips. "Gods, that is a foul concoction!" he exclaimed.

"The trick, my lad," said Brohan from the doorway with a smirk, "is not to be so deep in your cups you need such a remedy to help you climb out."

"Your advice is about a day late," Calvraign answered, relieved to see the master bard.

"Yes, well I tried the same line on you last night, but you received it rather coldly. I believe you claimed there was not a cup you could not climb out of, and challenged me to a contest of dueling gwythirs."

"I said that?" moaned Calvraign.

"You did. And you lost a few bars into the duel, by the way. Not your best performance."

Calvraign winced, happy not to remember after all.

"You'd best be getting dressed," Brohan said, his tone more serious as he shut the door behind him. "We have an appointment with Lady Aeolil before we head to the royal pavilion."

"Is it about the king? What happened?" Calvraign asked, "And what about these messengers?"

"Now where could you have heard about all that?" Brohan looked sidelong at Seth, who was suddenly quite engrossed in smoothing Calvraign's chemise. "I don't remember mentioning all that much about specifics, earlier." He returned his full attention to Calvraign. "It's always good to have multiple sources of information in King's Keep. Be sure to reward as well as guard them. But, that is *not* what concerns you, my lad. She spoke with Agrylon about you, and wished to relay her information personally."

"What did she find out?"

"I haven't the faintest, lad," Brohan laughed. "She wouldn't tell me, regardless of my charm and persistence. As I said, she wants to tell you personally. But don't dally too long, other matters are quickly becoming a priority for her."

Calvraign fidgeted as Seth assembled the multiple layers of his formal garments, which earned him a disapproving frown from his young steward. It was hard for him to concentrate on Seth's irritation or his own appearance, however, with thoughts of the Pale Man running rampant through his slowly clearing head. He didn't think Brohan would receive the news well, and he wasn't entirely sure how he should bring up the subject.

"You haven't really experienced the Winter Festival until you've had fresh spice bread," Brohan was saying, taking a seat and stretching casually. "And not the ones they bring you at the pavilion. Oh no, you'll want the *real* ones, lad. I suggest the vendors along Saint Hedhrian's Way or Peddler's Row."

Calvraign stared through Brohan as he continued his impromptu dissertation on the quality of spice bread versus wintercakes. Normally he would find the topic fascinating, as he was fond of sweets, but this morning it simply wasn't enough to hold his attention. Brohan, having years of experience in lecturing Calvraign, wasn't fooled for long. The master bard stopped in mid-sentence and crossed his arms.

"Hello?" he mocked. "Is there anyone in the castle, or have you just left a light burning in the tower?"

"I'm sorry, Brohan," Calvraign lifted his neck so Seth could finish straightening the collar of his thick winter doublet. He found the raised collar of the garment very uncomfortable, but knew he would appreciate it once out in the cold. "I had a bit of a start myself, this morning."

"I shouldn't wonder," replied Brohan. "I told Seth to keep you away from the looking glass until after you'd bathed."

"I hate to ruin your good humor, but I don't think you'll find this amusing."

Brohan adopted a more serious expression, mirroring the concern on Calvraign's face. "Out with it, lad. I don't like waiting for bad news."

"All right, then," agreed Calvraign, with an extended breath. "I was paid another visit by our elusive phantom."

Brohan bolted out of his seat, his hand falling to his sword hilt. Seth jumped back a little and swallowed somewhat nervously, his eyes flicking back and forth between the other men. "What do you mean, Cal?"

"He came to me this morning, in my chambers, and issued some sort of cryptic warning. He was gone in the space of a few breaths. Good thing, too, for I was in no state to do him battle."

"You're certain it wasn't the wine that saw him?"

"Aye, I'm sure," Calvraign said. "If anything, he was *more* substantial than before, not less. He'd never spoken to me before, after all. I don't think I could've dreamt this up had I wanted."

"Nevertheless," Brohan mused, scratching his chin. "The Pale Man is a dream-walker. He may have come to you in your sleep, invaded your thoughts."

Calvraign shook his head. "I was awake, and surely so. I woke up screaming *before* he came. But I am less troubled by the how than the why, Brohan. I've been thinking on it all morning. I was at his mercy, by the gods, and not for the first time. If my mother's dream were true, I'd be dead now. He wants something else from me aside from simple death."

"That is certainly a possibility, Cal. What did he say, exactly, in this cryptic warning?"

"Excuse me, sirs," interjected Seth, looking not much better than Calvraign had fifteen clicks earlier. "But if you'll not be needing me further… ."

Calvraign and Brohan both looked at the young man as if just remembering he had been privy to their entire discussion. Brohan recovered first. "Of course. You may be on your way, Mister Briggin. You have our leave and our strictest confidence, I trust?"

Seth inclined his head, and his voice was not much more than a whisper. "Even if you didn't, I wouldn't speak such names openly."

"A wise enough course, Seth," agreed Brohan. "Wiser than us, no doubt."

"I didn't mean to upset you, Seth," added Calvraign, walking the steward to the door. "You know how we minstrels can be. More imagination than we know what to do with. Certainly more than will do us any good."

The door closed behind the shaken attendant.

"We should be more careful in the future," Brohan said. "I think Seth is trustworthy, from terror as well as honesty, but we really shouldn't be testing Oghran's good graces like that."

Calvraign agreed with a shallow nod.

"Now," Brohan continued, "you were about to tell me of this warning?"

Calvraign described the incident as best as he could manage. Though he'd been somewhat addled by the effects of sleep and drink, the shock of the encounter had left him with a vivid recollection. He took the opportunity to describe the apparition in great detail, as well as its speech and manner. Unlike the previous visits, this time Calvraign had seen it clearly, and he intended to use that to his best advantage. Knowledge alone wasn't power, but it was a strong foundation.

Brohan paced the room as Calvraign spoke, chewing at his well-manicured nails. Even when his apprentice had finished, he continued to pace in silence.

"Brohan?" Calvraign said, trying to provoke a response. He was met with a silencing finger and an irritated shake of the master bard's head.

Undoubtedly he was busy mentally reciting every piece of text, verse and rumor he had ever learned about the Pale Man.

When Brohan finally did speak, it took Calvraign by surprise. "We may take some small comfort in one thing, Cal," he said. "This thing you saw was not the Pale Man."

"But, Ma's dream," stuttered Calvraign.

"No," insisted Brohan. "Two different things. The figure in your mother's vision was most certainly the Pale Man. I have *no* doubts about that. But this shadow you've been seeing is not he. You described his skin as ashen and his cloak tattered. Neither are traits of the Pale Man. And the sword. In all the lore he darkens with his presence, in every vision or dream he has appeared, that sword is there with him. *Ilnymhorrim*. It is his token. I made a careless assumption."

"Then *what* is going on?"

"What indeed? The Pale Man still wishes you dead, or will in the future, but this other – this *Greycloak* we'll call him. About him, I can only guess."

"Please do," insisted Calvraign, taking a seat. "I'm beginning to wish I was still hung-over and dull-witted so this wouldn't frustrate me so."

"Well, whoever Greycloak is, be pleased at who he *isn't*. It's still quite possible he is one of the Pale Man's pawns, a shadowyn or dream-walker of some sort, but it is not the Walking God himself. Of that we should be thankful. And there is the other possibility that whoever he is, he means you no ill."

"Don't be daft, Brohan." Calvraign made no pretense of his irritation. "He may not be ready or able to kill me, but it doesn't mean he's *friendly*."

"No, it doesn't. But why the warning, then?" Brohan held up his finger. "Think on it. He said to beware the *Ebhan-nuád*, lest you die like your father. You, of course, retorted that it would do you proud to be butchered in the prime of your life in exchange for the nebulous honors of a martyr's heroism. To which Master Greycloak responded, quite accurately, that you would die a fool. Then, flustered by the assumed aspersion on your father's name, when in reality it was only *you* he insulted, you indignantly informed him that not only was Ibhraign no fool but then addressed this Greycloak as the Pale Man. And he said... ?"

Calvraign was familiar enough with Brohan's lecturing technique to respond without delay, "*Is that what you think?*"

"Which you took to mean?"

"He was mocking my father and the way he died."

"Or he was expressing surprise that you thought he was the Pale Man. You said his voice was emotionless, so no meaning can be conveyed through inflection. Since you believed his intentions hostile, that is how you interpreted his words – a warning and threat all in one. But, if his motive is *not* hostile, his intent might only be the former."

Calvraign's head was beginning to hurt again, and he doubted more of Baeson's potion would be much help, this time. "Why do you have to make everything so complicated, Brohan?"

"I'm not making it complicated, I'm just looking at it less simply."

"Another choice turn of phrase for the master bard," Calvraign said, grinning despite his headache.

"I'll be sure to write that one down," returned Brohan. "I rather like it."

"So, which is it? Friend or foe? What do I do?"

"I don't know. Maybe I shall visit the royal archives while you enjoy the tourney this afternoon. If I can steal a moment of Agrylon's time, that might also prove helpful. Whether the warning is benevolent or just accurate, we have some time, at least. *Ebhan-nuád* comes but once every forty years or so, and it's another few before it's due again."

Calvraign looped his sword belt around his waist and straightened the old scabbard that housed his father's sword. He took an extra moment to ensure that the braided silk cord of his peace-knot snugly secured hilt to scabbard, then looked back up at Brohan with a tired smile. "Aye," he said. "At least there's that."

Chapter Twenty-Nine

Whispers of Death

THE Undying King sat astride a beautiful roan destrier, gazing out past the twilit canyons and withered trees of the high desert that surrounded his hold on High Rock. Once, he had simply been Uaigh Malagch, the high king of Maccalah. But that was before he had made his desperate bargain, before ransoming his soul to the Dark for the gift of eternal flesh and a hope of revenge.

A gift not without price, the Pale Man considered as he kicked his nameless black courser up the rocky slope, feeling the weight of *ilnymhorrim's* scabbard against his thigh, *not unlike my own.*

Malagch looked off to the east, toward the Ridge, the shadows of approaching night reaching like fingers out across his wasted lands, harbingers of his will. Anger brimmed in those eyes, day or night, summer or winter. Anger fueled his will, nursed his vengeance, and as Dieavaul had only recently convinced him, anger had colored his judgment, obscured his strategies, and unhinged his patience. The Undying King still saw the world through his anger, but he was no longer blinded by it.

The gathered nobility of Malakuur watched the Pale Man warily as he approached. He found it ironic that they were liege-bound to a dead king, and yet somehow felt disquiet at his own presence. It had not been *he* that launched the war against the Empire, not *he* who had lost that war, not *he* who had lashed out in petty vengeance and lost the lands of their fathers and grandfathers in recompense. In fact, though he had served in the legions at the time, it had not even been he who had brought down the Great Devastations upon them. Still, intimidation and fear could be useful tools, especially with the highborn, and he cultivated it carefully.

Even so, *highborn* was a courteous term for the vanquished chieftains that passed for the noble houses of Malakuur. These were but the descended sons of the banished clan lords of Old Maccalah, those who had followed High King Gareath Malagch into defeat, and then repeated their folly when his son Uaigh sought his vengeance in the second of the Realmwars. It had won them only disgrace and exile at the hands of the Dacadian Legions.

The Great Hagh Mac had been sent to the fertile Southlands, the honorable Cal Calha, to the rocky hills south of Paertym in Callah Tur. But Emperor Lucian had saved banishment west of the Ridge for his most hated of enemies, and so the Clan Malagch was exiled beyond the East, to the unnamed and unknown lands now called Malakuur. Roughly translated from the old Dacadian tongue, *Malagch's paradise.*

Dieavaul ascended the slope toward the small mounted retinue. It was no accident that he must pass each lord in turn on his way to Malagch. The thar enjoyed reminding his loyal host who it was that acted as his right hand and with what dread weapon enforced his will. The reminder served the Pale Man just as well, reinforcing the fact that many and deft sworn swords protected Malagch from harm. Dieavaul admired that. Uaigh had his moments.

As if sensing his thoughts, Malagch turned briefly. His face was still smooth, sun-kissed copper, though carved from hard lines. His dark eyes still glittered in the waning evening light. His black hair fell in thick waves about his ears and neck, held back from his face only by the slim circlet of prismatic metal that crowned his brow. Indeed, there was little to show that he was dead, that he had been dead for more than a century. At least, not to the common eye.

Dieavaul didn't need his eyes for any such observation – his memory served just as well. The Black Robe Esmaedi had lived through Malagch's last fateful attack against the might of the Empire. That time, in defeat, there was no Dmylriani to counsel peace; there was no shared respect with any of the foe; there was only Agrylon and Gaious, and the rest of the Twelve. When the Devastations were released upon Malakuur, thousands upon thousands had perished in the indiscriminate fire of their retribution. The sky had fallen. The air had burned. The ground had risen up and crashed back upon them.

Malagch had burned with rage and taken the vows of a thar, a priest-king. Not to Oa or the Three Sisters, not even to bloody Kazdann, but to the Dark God, Ewanbheir.

These were the heirs to broken dreams and long lost promise, sworn to a banner that had led them to ruin. And here they stood, ready to follow again, poised to reclaim the lands once lost by their great-grandsires these hundreds of years gone.

Caedgh Mailéion was the first of the Malakuuri lords that Dieavaul rode past. His ice-blue eyes were steady, observant, and ever brooding beneath his pale brow and jet-black tumble of hair. In his dyed-black wolverine cloak, he bore a striking resemblance to the man whose conflicted loyalties had shamed his Clan and led them to exile. Doona Mailéion had refused to bend a knee with his clan lord, Kieyr adh Boighn, when Kieyr spurned the Maccs to swear fealty to the Imperial Crown. But Doona's loyalty to the Clans was also a betrayal of his liege-lord, and the family was forever tainted as oath breakers – even by those who had welcomed his steel and his war banner to their cause.

Honor is such a fickle thing, Dieavaul mused. *I trust young Caedgh to always do the right thing – even if it is the stupidest.*

But the young chieftain of Clan Mailéion commanded respect in the rank and file of the Malakuuri army. He had charisma, and therefore he was useful beyond whatever misguided sense of personal honor he might also bring with him into battle. And, whatever might be said of Dieavaul, he did not squander his resources.

"Caedgh," greeted the Pale Man, informally. It was not an accidental gesture of respect.

The Mailéion nodded in return. "M'lord."

"You keep your own counsel tonight?"

"Aye," he acknowledged. "This is the third night we've so gathered to gaze upon our armies." Caedgh shook his head. "I find no use in it."

"Even so, best not leave Thar Malagch in the unattended company of the Baign or he might march off to war prematurely."

A thin smile spread on Caedgh's lips. "Perhaps."

Dieavaul left him with that, moving on to the next tier of Malagch's liege-sworn. Ciarn adh Connla and Orden Fuar Laeig watched the Pale Man pass, lips drawn tight, eyes wary. Unlike Caedgh, they bore little resemblance to their ancient namesakes, in appearance or disposition. Ciarn was thin, face drawn and eyes hollow, and a less-than-remarkable warrior. Orden was stout enough, but he lacked the skill with Craft or blade that had made his great-great-grandsire the greatest of Macc wizards, and the most respected councilor of their kings.

All for the best, the Pale Man reflected. He had killed the first Orden Fuar Laeig during the Realmwars, and he'd been trouble enough. If this man were even a shadow of his progenitor, he'd prove more a rival than an ally. *Some lineages are best left to rot.*

Dieavaul wasted no breath on them, proceeding to the crest of the hill. First, past Eilis, Malagch's young concubine-of-the-moment, sitting a braided parade mare. She was at least five moons full with his child, eating a spice cake. He admired the strong line of her jaw and her wide, brown eyes. There was no concern in them at his presence, no fear that she sat here nibbling while the Undying King and his lieutenants planned their conquests.

She was a favorite of Malagch, and blinded by that favor, as her late predecessors had been. She wore a flowing velvet gown of midnight black with a jeweled brocade and lace trim. A tiara of diamonds and heart stones was centered upon her brow, and a necklace of threaded gold dangled from her neck. Her face was plump and flushed from her condition, her hair long and lustrous, her breasts swollen with mother's milk she would never need.

She was a fool to think this could last, more of a fool to want it to. *What lie had Malagch told her? That she would be his eternal queen? That the unnatural seed his ever-dying body had planted in her would one day be heir to the world?* He wondered how anyone could be so gullible, and gave her a charming smile.

Dyar adh Baign was the only clan lord at the summit, side-by-side with Malagch, a sign of the Undying King's respect, if not his trust.

He is showing his age, now, Dieavaul noticed. His hair was greyer, his skin wrinkled in deeper creases. Not that Dyar had ever been handsome. His face scarred by pox, his nose half-eaten by a wolf, his hair thinning on a reddened scalp – he was not pleasant to look upon. But it was not charm or beauty he offered the thars. As his men often joked around their cook fires: *Aye, his nose is half gone – but you should see the* wolf!

"What news?" asked the Undying King without turning from his reverie.

"The *wilhorwhyr* infiltrated your lines. Azgur was seen with the armies," Dieavaul stated, waving at the massed forces far below, "and Azgur and one of Shakah's priestesses were tracked back to the *iiyir* well. Mejul reports that all this news and the *iiyiraal* have been delivered to Agrylon. But-"

"So you failed," Malagch interrupted.

"Let's not quibble over failures, Uaigh," Dieavaul countered evenly. "What you lost, I could not bring back. Keep better track of your dreams, and I will keep better track of those who walk them, and we'll both be better served."

"What they know, they know," Dyar grated out before his words choked off into a strangled cough. He dabbed at his lips with a kerchief, adding one more crimson stain to the silk. "Knowing," he continued, when he recovered his breath, "will not be enough to save them."

"Perhaps not," conceded Dieavaul. "It might be enough to kill a few more of us along the way, however."

"And so it goes," scoffed Dyar. "It's a bloody war, not a gods-be-damned coronation ball."

Turlun, realized Dieavaul. *He reminds me of Osrith Turlun. No wonder I don't like him.*

"But...?" pressed Malagch.

"But they do not suspect Mejul, and *Pakh Ma* Thaoll and his *graomwrnokk* are already within the walls. Though they may benefit from this time to prepare for war, it is likely too late for them to save Hiruld. And there is no reason to believe they suspect any move against Meyr ga'Glyleyn."

"Balls!" spat the Baign. "Then what worry? Once Hiruld is dead and that mare-ga-whatsit is ours, the Darkening will be upon them. What use 're their armies 'gainst the will of the Dark God? We'll have our vengeance in a few days' time."

"Your confidence is somewhat bewildering," Dieavaul answered. "*Assuming* victory has not ended well for the clans in the past. When the Darkening comes, it will mean the doom of Providayne, but it may not mean victory for us."

Dyar adh Baign sent a bloody stream of spittle to the ground. "It wasn't your empire that won that war. It was the Devastations. This time, *we* will rain fire and darkness on our enemies."

"Really?" Dieavaul turned his attention from Dyar, nudging his horse closer to the king. "And what if the doom prophesied for Providayne is conquest at the hands of the Ceearmyltu? Would that be victory for us? How long will this alliance last if the likes of Ryaleyr regain Dwynleigsh and tap Meyr ga'Glyleyn? We will rue the day we gave her the means to wield such power.

"And what of Azgur and Seoughal? The double-edged nature of their allegiance should be obvious, even to the Baign. If the andu'ai gain advantage over us...." Dieavaul shook his head, letting that possibility fester in silence for a moment. "No. The defeat of Providayne and our *victory* are two very different things."

"All true," agreed Malagch, spreading his gauntleted hands before him, palms upward. "We have discussed your worries endlessly. You argued that chasing the dreamstone was folly, and now you are vexed that the chase was fruitless? What is your point?"

What is my point? wondered Dieavaul. *Do I fear victory or defeat?*

"It's done," Malagch continued. "Your caution against complacency is noted. But we must move forward. What of the aulden? Has your revenant turned them?"

"Soon," sighed Dieavaul. "While in the Sacred Grove, he must remain invisible to me, or we risk discovery. But the groundwork has been laid."

"Groundwork," mumbled Dyar, "I am sick to dying of *groundwork*. Spring your damned trap."

Ah, realized the Pale Man, *this is what I fear. Impatience. Idiocy. How many times has Clan Malagch been so close to unquestioned victory, only to spoil the hanging with a loose knot?*

"I know this is not your way," he said. "But unless they are set against each other, when we come through the pass they will stand together against *us*. They have their gods, too, Baign. Dark. Light. They will fight in their own way, but they will not hand us victory or defeat."

"You give them too much time," replied Dyar, unconvinced. "You just said as much. They know that we prepare for war, that we ride with the andu'ai."

Dieavaul shook his head. "Things they are told, and things they know – things they *believe* – are not the same. There's a truth there, yes – we cannot afford to tarry too long.

"But think on this: how do the Ebuouki bring down the mammoth of the plains? One spear? Two? No. They flank it, they bleed it with well-placed spears, and they run it until it drops. When it is helpless, they kill it."

"Some of the tribes just run them off a cliff. That seems to work, too."

"We've done enough running off the cliff," interjected Malagch. "We wait. Mejul and Thaoll will do their part, and we must be ready to do ours."

Dieavaul smiled, a thin thing on his face, but a deep feeling of satisfaction in the core of his being.

This time, it just may work.

Chapter Thirty

Wisdom, Honor & Valor

Saint Severun's Cathedral served not only as the place of worship for much of Dwynleigsh, but as the official seat of the archbishop and the Holy Quorum as well. It bore the name of the old Dacadian missionary who had taken the Word of the Swords to the wilderness in the brief span between the two Realmwars. It served as both monument and tomb for the ancient martyr. The grounds were austere, paved in cool white stone in the stead of trees or grass.

Like all churches of Illuné, the main chapel was a great dome, representing the moon that bore the name of the Goddess. Four paths led to its doors, one from each of the cardinal directions. This architectural gesture of welcome was somewhat lessened by the Border Knights who stood guard, two at each entrance, silent and motionless behind polished ceremonial armor. Though far from the frontiers which were the focus of their charter, Severun was the patron saint of their Order, and it was they who supplied the honor guard as a matter of deference.

There were satellite buildings in each quartered segment of the estate, all of the same somber argent and grey construction. The only hint to the purpose of each building was a small identifying crest crowning its doorframe: a book and quill for the library; a cot and two moons for the dormitory; a loaf of bread for the dinner hall; these and many more. The basilica as a whole covered the entirety of one of the city's many small hills, and dominated the southeastern quarter of the capital.

Artygalle walked on this holy ground in awe. Saint Severun's was the epicenter of the Holy Mother Church, and one of the oldest surviving human temples on all of Rahn. Even at this early hour, the place was alive with activity. Priests, acolytes and seminarians ran about on silent errands. Lancers in full regalia made ready to depart for Saint Kaissus Field, and servants and worshipers skittered about unnoticed between them.

None mistook him for a peasant today, he reflected, shifting under the weight of his mail coat. Riding now in tourney dress, replete in Ghaerieal's old tabard of snow-white cloth with the three scarlet bears of Tiriel, rampant, and his somewhat battered shield with its frowning owl's head on Windthane's right hind-quarter – it was hard to take him for anything but a knight. Artygalle felt an imposter in the raiment of his dead master, astride a borrowed horse and bearing an assumed burden. He tried to shove the doubt aside, but next to the lancers and their casual assurance, he felt nothing more than a squire.

He took a deep breath against the panic in his belly, and recited a passage from *Honorable Combat* with a small, soundless, movement of his lips:

Judge not your foe by the burnish of his mail or the gem of his cloak, but rather the intelligence in his eyes and the carriage of his person. Wealth may buy armor and sword, but it makes not a soldier. Rank may allow for genteel manners and civil discourse, but it makes not a soldier. So then do not first judge your foe, but do him battle and consider his capacity after. This makes your determination a true one.

The ancient words of Kiev Vae still rang true, bringing Artygalle some comfort. Even so, he had no idea where to go from here. The instructions of Curate Sinhd had not been elaborate. Artygalle cast around for a likely spot to tether Windthane, hoping that at some point in his stay in Dwynleigsh he would actually know what he was doing.

"Allow me, Sir Artygalle."

Artygalle looked down at the young boy whose hands reached eagerly for Windthane's reins. He was no more than twelve or thirteen summers, with skin black as midnight and a smooth, hairless scalp. His light-green almond-shaped eyes were all the more piercing staring from beneath that dark brow.

Artygalle knew the same stories regarding the Kaojinn and Ishti'in as everyone else, but had never thought to see a living example of either in his lifetime. Certainly not as a squire in Saint Severun's Cathedral, whichever of those races the boy might be. Still, odd though he was, he was a servant of the Goddess, just as himself, and that was good enough credential in Artygalle's mind. The foreigner's slim body was almost entirely enveloped by the voluminous surcoat that hung limply from his shoulders. The breast bore the device of the winged sword and shield. Artygalle recognized the outfit; he had worn one like it for many years.

Artygalle dismounted Windthane, but held on to the reins in his left hand as he eyed the boy. "Did His Holiness send you for me, squire?" He took special care to be civil. He'd been brushed aside by many an impatient knight, and it was not a pleasant feeling. He supposed it could easily be worse for this boy, given the nature of his heritage and the range of superstitions regarding his people.

"Yes sir," the boy answered. "I'm to be in your service, sir. Um, that is, if you like."

Artygalle wondered if that's how his own uncultivated confidence appeared to others. He hid a smile with a scratch of his cheek. "I would be honored," he said, relinquishing the reins. "What are you called?"

"Inoval, sir," he answered, taking Windthane with a tremor in his hands. The horse snorted and pawed at the smooth stone of the courtyard. "This way, sir."

Artygalle kept a reassuring palm on the side of Windthane's neck as Inoval led him toward the main temple dome. Inoval was an old Mneyrilen name, and the squire had no accent to speak of, which raised a whole new series of questions. How long had he been in Dwynleigsh? How had he come here at all? And how had he come to be in the service of the archbishop? Questions for later, he supposed, when there was time to spare.

Inoval waved down another boy, who wore the tanned leather trousers and wool shirt of a stable hand. They exchanged some brief words, and moments later Windthane was headed off with the new boy, hopefully on the way to a comfortable stable pen. Artygalle suppressed an anxious sigh and reminded himself that he shouldn't grow so close to a horse that was not even his.

They arrived outside the west doors of the sanctuary and halted before the crossed halberds of the Border Knights who stood guard. Inoval bowed deeply. "May I present Sir Artygalle of Tiriel, summoned this day before His Holiness the Archbishop Renarre."

The knights moved their weapons aside wordlessly, and Inoval preceded his master into the cathedral. As Artygalle drew even with the knights, one of them leaned a mailed shoulder into his chest, stopping him in the doorframe. Artygalle tensed, surprised and somewhat alarmed at the confrontation.

The guard's full-helm leaned in close as he whispered, "Watch your back, Brother. Your first challenge won't be in the tourney, today."

Then the way was clear again, and Artygalle joined his new squire in the entrance hall. He wasn't sure what to make of that warning. He knew there were some rivalries between the Orders of the Church, but he hadn't thought it to be anything worthy of such a whispered caution. Would anyone dare to scheme or pit Brother against Brother before the archbishop himself? He remembered the way Aeolil had spoken of Renarre the previous day in Calvraign's chambers. Although it was not a flattering portrait she painted, she had afforded equally dubious motives to most of the Houses of Providayne, including the crown prince. Laypeople often misinterpreted the motives of the Church, and likely this had been the case with Lady Aeolil. One couldn't become the Archbishop of the Holy Mother Church without wisdom, honor and valor. This left him no closer to understanding the guard's vague warning. He would have to be cautious and watchful, that was all.

Artygalle bowed his head as he entered the Outer Hall, which surrounded the Sanctuary in a concentric circle, and followed Inoval to their left, toward the northern half of the circular building. Though built on a much grander scale than the simple chapel that served his Order, the layout was familiar. They passed by two evenly spaced statues before stopping in front of a floor-length black velvet curtain. Beyond this thin barrier, access was restricted to the clergy or those on official business.

"Wait here, please, sir," Inoval said, and slipped through the curtain.

Artygalle looked over the life-sized statue of Saint Evmae that stood to his left, appreciating the sculptor's scrupulous attention to detail. Many times, and this was especially true with the historical saints, the artists took some liberties with the style of dress or armor of their subject. He had seen representations of saints like Hrethbarhe or Balthoervan in more recent garb, a mistake that was less obvious in the likeness of a modern-day saint like Andulin or Igaine. Then it occurred to him that this might not be recent work, but one of the cathedral's original statues. He was tempted to tour the rest of the Outer Hall and examine the other eleven saints in closer detail, but he knew this was no time to indulge his curiosity.

Inoval's head peeped through the velvet. "His Holiness will see you now, Sir Artygalle."

Artygalle followed Inoval through the curtains and then through a heavy door of silvered belwood to their right. He took a moment to catch his breath. The inner sanctum was more remarkable than he'd imagined.

From this vantage he could see every aspect of the cathedral's construction. To his right, row upon row of polished wooden pews, with enough seating for a thousand or more of Illuné's children. At the far southern end of the dome were the Grand Boxes, a balcony jutting without visible support some fifteen feet from the floor, which he guessed could seat close to a hundred of the rank-and-file nobility.

The Ecclesiastical Boxes extended in the same impossible fashion just on the southern half of the temple's midpoint, one on the eastern and western walls respectively, but only a third of the size and slightly higher than the Grand Boxes. Members of the Holy Quorum and others of high standing in the Church would worship there.

The Royal Boxes were identical to the Ecclesiastical pair for all intents and purposes, but were on the northern half of the center-point, the closest of all the flying boxes to the chantry and reserved for the royal family and their guests alone.

Artygalle followed Inoval off to his left, ascending the smooth, shallow steps that led from the main floor to the altar and the imposing thirty-five-foot statue of Illuné. The first tier of steps ended in a landing, where Artygalle dropped to one knee and made the circular sign of the moon on his breast. He prayed for a moment, his head slightly bowed, and then looked up again. Illuné looked down on him, Her hands crossed on the pommel of Her sword, which rested point down on the floor.

She was beautiful. He couldn't place what stone the statue was fashioned from. It was like nothing he'd seen before, a lustrous pale blue-green, taking in the light of the candelabra on the altar and redoubling its brilliance back into the rest of the church. The detail of the workmanship made Her seem so alive, especially in the serenity of Her placid face, and yet that same minutiae betrayed itself in the static nature of its portrayal.

With a twinge of disappointment, Artygalle saw the statue for what it was – a work of art. It was a symbol, and wonderfully wrought, perhaps the most beautiful thing he had ever seen, but it was no more She than the moon that bore Her name.

Don't confuse Her symbol with Her grace, he admonished himself.

Three priests, dressed in the robes of high ceremony, chanted the morning prayer as Archbishop Renarre placed the holy basin on the altar before the likeness of Illuné. He made the sign of the moon over the water within the silver bowl, speaking the words of the blessing in a soft but clear tone. When he had finished, he raised the basin above his head, as if offering it to the stone Goddess, and placed it in the center of the altar table.

Renarre stood, facing the three priests, the knight, squire, and the multitude of empty pews. He raised his arms, palms upward, and said, "Come and receive the blessing of Illuné, who gives us this gift as a sign of Her grace and power, and renew yourselves in Her service."

Each priest came forward in turn, kneeling before the archbishop as he anointed him with the holy water. "In Your Wisdom I trust, and in

Your Way I follow," each said, and were answered with, "Rise and serve, blessed servants of the Goddess."

The priests made a final bow before exiting. The archbishop remained on the upper level of the dais for another moment, and then descended to the landing. He smiled at Inoval with a paternal wink and nodded at the door. Inoval retreated the same way the priests had departed, leaving Artygalle and the archbishop alone within the church.

Renarre looked him over a moment in silence, and Artygalle returned the examination. The archbishop was in his later years, and his fine snow-white hair, trimmed just over his ears, showed traces of the fiery red that had earned him the addendum *the Fox* in his youth. His nose was hawk-like, and his lips severe, though upturned into a smile. His eyes were sharp, and his gaze uncompromising. Artygalle decided that the stories about his intimidating presence had not been exaggerated. His robes of office made him more so, as the voluminous folds of dark blue cloth lent him a girth he did not possess, judging from the slenderness of his wrists and fingers.

"Sir Artygalle," the archbishop said finally. His voice was smooth and welcoming, and he clasped the knight's hand in a firm gesture of welcome. "We are so pleased you were able to come before us."

Artygalle remained on one knee, and again made the sign of the moon on his chest. "It is my duty and my pleasure, Your Holiness."

"Ah, just so. Rise, sir knight, and speak with us for a moment. But let us continue in my chambers, I think we will find it more comfortable."

Artygalle stood. "As you wish, Your Holiness."

"You have traveled a long way from Tiriel," Renarre said, walking in long slow strides to the door. "What news from our Brothers in the cold north?"

"My Lord Elvaeir has prepared a message for you, Your Holiness. If I may?" Artygalle passed a vellum scroll case from his belt to the waiting hands of the archbishop. "You have afforded me a great honor to present it in person."

Renarre smiled, taking the case from Artygalle and examining the wax seals that guaranteed its confidentiality. "I recognize Lord Elvaeir's seal, but this other, the owl... . Is that your blazon, sir? It seems to ring a distant bell in my memory."

"No, Your Holiness," replied Artygalle, his throat tightening. "It was my departed master's seal. Sir Ghaerieal passed on his charge to me."

Renarre raised his brow, turning slightly as he walked through the door that Artygalle had entered earlier. "So, you were his companion?"

"No, Your Holiness, I was his squire. He had planned to knight me in the Ordination Ceremony after the Feast of Illuné. He was forced to confer my knighthood less formally, but I still have his letter of intent for Captain

General Tuoerval. By the custom of my Order, this is only a formality. I have already assumed my master's duties and his place in the lists."

"I see that you have." Renarre smiled, his arm resting on the young knight's shoulder like a shepherd's crook. "I will pass your letter of intent along to Sir Tuoerval before this afternoon, and we will make it official." He paused for a moment, coming to a halt and tilting his head to one side. "I remember Ghaerieal: headstrong, but brave, and a good man. We are saddened by his loss."

Artygalle nodded. He still found it difficult to speak of Ghaerieal in the past tense.

The archbishop turned to face a segment of blank wall and pressed his signet ring against it. The wall shifted somewhat, and the archbishop pushed it open. Artygalle had never seen such a well-concealed passage, and Renarre smiled at the puzzlement on his face.

"It's more of a cosmetic touch, these days, I'm afraid," he explained. "The secret got out long ago. This leads to my private library and offices, as well as those of Sir Tuoerval. On the east side, a similar passage leads down to storerooms and such. Shall we?"

Artygalle wasn't fool enough to think the archbishop was actually asking his opinion, and immediately stepped through the opening and started down the steep, narrow spiral stair. Renarre was a step behind. The walls pressed in close, and Artygalle was relieved when they emerged into a spacious hallway at the bottom of the stairs.

The archbishop once again took the lead, heading toward the door at the end of the candlelit hall. Artygalle looked, but he couldn't see where or how the smoke escaped to the surface. Even the smell here was pleasant, unlike the dank and musty under-levels of the monastery where he'd been raised.

The door was well polished and embossed with a silver moon, but otherwise plain. Within, the archbishop's office offered both a simple elegance and welcoming warmth. Facing the door was a great desk, its surface almost entirely camouflaged by several precise stacks of parchments and some leather bound books. A quill and inkwell rested to the left of the sole empty space on the desk, just in front of the chair. The wall behind the desk was a bookshelf, and it held row upon row of neatly ordered volumes. Ghaerieal had been adamant that he learn the ancient tongues, both the secular and religious dialects, and most were represented here. Artygalle marveled that some of these tomes dated back to Imperial days. Each shelf was organized chronologically and by author, progressing from the oldest tomes on the left to the most recent on the right.

Renarre walked around behind his desk and sat in a high-backed mahogany chair padded with velvet cushions. Though not a throne in any sense, it did add a more regal aspect to his already authoritative figure. "Please," the archbishop said, pointing at the door.

Artygalle closed it without comment. There were two other doors on that wall, one adjacent to each corner, and a series of framed charts and maps hung at eye level between them. From what he could tell, they depicted the size and disposition of the Church's holdings. The lands of each of the Great Houses were painted their own muted colors, and each of the cities and castles bore markings clarifying population as well as their natural resources and economic strengths. Artygalle's eyes drifted naturally to the north, where Tiriel was nestled in the eastern reaches of the High Ridge.

Renarre set the scroll case Artygalle had delivered on his desk and broke its seal with a fastidious flick of his nail. He spread out the parchments, examining the writing line by line with a puckered frown. Artygalle waited, still as a rock, while the archbishop read the message in its entirety.

"This is *disturbing* news," Renarre said, "albeit somewhat incredible. Are you quite certain His Lordship does not exaggerate his dilemma?"

"Quite certain, Your Holiness," responded Artygalle with conviction.

"I see." Renarre drummed his fingers in a methodical but unhurried fashion, humming quietly with each down stroke. His eyes were focused on some invisible point off to the left of Artygalle's head. "Elvaeir must be hard pressed, then."

"We fight bravely, Your Holiness, but bravery cannot win the day alone. We are sorely outnumbered."

"So says Elvaeir," agreed the archbishop, tapping the parchment on his desk, "but I'm afraid there is little the Church can do. The king's war with the Maccs has spread the Knights Lancer quite thin enough, according to Sir Tuoerval, and I am inclined to agree. But, rest assured, we will review the matter. What of Aeyrdyn and Mneyril? Have the dukes no aid to offer you?"

Artygalle shook his head slowly. "They are reluctant. My lord dispatched others to plead our case in their courts, but it is my understanding that they are here for the Winter Festival, in any case. My hope is to win the King's Lance, Your Holiness, and prove the worth of our cause and claim."

Renarre's eyebrows shot upward in a show of unrestrained surprise, and his words came out in a bit of a rush. "You intend to... ." He stopped himself, and with a few quick blinks, regained his composure. "That is an ambitious goal for such a young knight, Brother Artygalle. More so considering you weren't even the knight chosen for the task. It is honorable and right that you carry through on your master's charge, but in all practicality, perhaps you should rethink this strategy."

"I know the field is formidable, but circumstance has left me little alternative. I have faith that Illuné will recognize the righteousness of my fight. If I begin with Her as my only ally, it will be enough to win a hundred more by Endride."

"Your faith is commendable, but... ." The archbishop sighed. "Illuné has more than the fate of Tiriel to worry over. Yours may not be the only just cause to take the field."

"That is for Illuné to decide, Your Holiness. I can only do what I can do. In the end, it will be as She wills."

There was a brief silence before Renarre continued. "I can see Ghaerieal's trust was well placed," he said. "You are a man of rare faith."

"Thank you, Your Holiness." Artygalle felt both pride and sorrow, thinking of his master's understated smile of approval.

The archbishop rested his chin on thumb and forefinger, once again lost in thought. He looked at Artygalle again, and then closed his eyes as he inhaled a deep breath. When he exhaled, a moment later, he opened his eyes and smiled. "I think your presence here serves more than Elvaeir's needs, Brother Artygalle. I believe that Illuné, in Her Infinite Grace, has sent you to us for reasons two-fold."

Artygalle couldn't begin to think what he was talking about, but he was honored by the archbishop's trust, all the same. "Yes, Your Holiness?"

"You know this Sir Calvraign?" asked Renarre.

"I traveled with he and Master Madrharigal for a time, and I call him friend," stated Artygalle, his calm dissolving slightly into a guarded unease. Aeolil's words of the previous day and the temple guard's warning both lingered just on the other side of his innate trust for the leader of the Holy Church.

"What is your view on the young man?"

Artygalle spoke slowly, thinking carefully over each word. "He possesses intelligence and insight beyond my own, but he is foremost a good and caring man. I am both proud and glad to know him."

Renarre nodded. "So he appears."

"I beg your pardon, Holiness," interjected Artygalle, "but he is just as he seems. I would stake my honor and my life upon it."

The Holy Father did not raise his voice, but Artygalle sensed the warmth ebb from his tone. "I don't care to be interrupted," he stated, giving each syllable its due. "Do you presume to know my mind?"

"Of course not, Your Holiness." Artygalle's mouth dried up around his tongue and he swallowed with an effort. "I apologize for speaking out of turn."

The archbishop brushed at his desk as if physically removing the annoyance from his presence. "Sir Calvraign is *not* what he seems, despite your honor and your life. You may not know it, and he may not know it, but he is being used. There's no other explanation for all that's gone on around him. What it is he has to offer, I do not know, but follow the strings on the marionette back to the puppeteer and you will find Agrylon there, smiling back at you. *That* is something to stake your honor and your life on, Brother Artygalle."

"What interest would he have in Calvraign, Your Holiness?"

"If you are truly this young man's friend, that is what you need to discover."

"Me?" Artygalle shook his head, bewildered. "With all due respect, Your Holiness, I am not one for court intrigues. As you've seen here, I'm not skilled at concealing my thoughts or my beliefs."

"What is the Fifth Rule of Action in Saint Kaissus' *Treatise on War*?"

The words came out of Artygalle's mouth by rote: "When you may, choose your field of battle, but always prepare for the choice to be made for you."

Renarre inclined his head slightly. "Yes. Do you understand? This may not be the battle field to which you are accustomed, Brother, but of a certainty, it has chosen you."

"Then what should I do?"

"Watch him, and watch those around him. We must discover to what purpose they intend to put him." The archbishop leaned closer over his desk. "His life may depend on it."

Artygalle stiffened his back, clenching his fists into balls at his sides. The archbishop was right. The truest tests of faith came when life chose your battles and forced you to overcome them. He had not chosen the tourney, and he had not chosen this, but he would not fail at either effort.

"If that is what must be done, Your Holiness," said Artygalle, "then I will do it."

"I knew you would," the archbishop answered, smiling fondly at the knight. "I knew you would."

Chapter Thirty-One

Welcome to Wait

O SRITH ran his fingers through his newly trimmed beard, sending a few stray whiskers to litter Aeolil's rug. He tried to scatter the dark bits of hair with the toes of his new boots before they were noticed, but he'd hardly started his attempt when a servant coughed and glared pointedly in his direction. Osrith scowled in reply and then turned his back on the lady-in-waiting, crossing his arms as he peered expectantly at the door.

It was the best he'd felt since fleeing Gai's tower, and the cleanest, besides. He could have lingered in the bath for an hour or more, with a tankard or three of ale to complete his repose, but he still had business to settle. For Osrith, business came before everything else. He was beginning to wonder if the same ethic held true for Vaujn or Kassakan.

Both were late, by his reckoning, and he didn't fancy spending any time alone with Lady Aeolil when she arrived. Aside from their shared past, seeing the little girl he'd last known eight years ago as a mature young woman made him acutely aware of his years. Seeing how she had grown was the harshest measure of the time he had spent in the Deeps.

Osrith looked around the sitting room, seeing little evidence that a proper lady received her guests or spent her idle hours here. There was no loom, easel, or gwythir to pass the time. There were some books, and what looked like a year-mark and constellation chart by the window, but little else.

A grin threatened at the corners of his mouth, but he fought it back. Like her mother, Aeolil had always had some contrary notions of her place in court and society. He remembered taking her riding – long leisurely lopes across the hills, thundering gallops through the fields, even slow walks in the half-tamed woods. He wondered if she still refused to ride sidesaddle. He hoped so.

Vaujn's arrival spared him further reminiscence. Aeolil's lady-in-waiting saw him in with a disconcerted stare and excused herself from their presence with a nod. The kinsman had cleaned himself up, polished his armor, and even re-braided his beard as if for a full inspection. He carried his war-helm under the crook of his arm, its intricately worked and grimacing face a stylized mirror of the captain's own, albeit much more intimidating in its frozen, metallic battle rage. Osrith supposed his attention to decorum made sense. The kin of Outpost Number Nine were the first to contact the court of Providayne in quite a while, and Vaujn was their ranking officer. He was, in all respects that mattered, the acting ambassador of King Ruuhigan. He certainly looked the part: a paragon of underkin pride, all rigid backbone and glittering steel.

"What?" Vaujn said, rather sharp, returning Osrith's dubious look. "You think I overdid it?"

Osrith spread out his hands, indicating his own formal attire. "I can't say you look any more foolish than I do," he said. It had been a long while since he'd worn the blue and silver of House Vae, and though part of him felt at ease in the stately trappings of knighthood, it was a remote and distant corner of his mind.

Vaujn made a noncommittal grunt in the back of his throat, looking around his surroundings with interest. Osrith could see where his eyes were drawn. Not to the expensive trappings which dangled from the walls, or the furniture with all its gilt and polish, or even the books, charts and other intellectual paraphernalia. Instead, his eyes focused on the smooth joints of the wooden cross bars in the ceiling, the mortar that glued the stones of the wall, and the symmetry of the arched windows that looked out across the Ciel Maer at the city of Dwynleigsh.

His frown was telling.

"Not too impressed, are you?" Osrith tried to keep the amusement from his tone, but he wasn't sure if Vaujn would've noticed.

The kinsman shrugged. "Not exactly a work of art," he sighed, "but I suppose it's in no danger of collapse."

"Well, for us ignorant human folk, this place is considered pretty grand, so watch your mouth," Osrith warned. "We don't need to start any more wars on this visit than we have to."

Vaujn grunted again and peered out the window at the distant city. "Our records show that my people did some work in this city, a while back – some temples and such. You think I'll be able to take a peek while I'm here?"

"After I collect my silver, I'll hire out a whole school of historians to take you around all the sights. That's the least I can do for dragging you up here."

Vaujn agreed with a nod. "It's a start, anyway."

"How are the others adjusting?" Osrith said, joining Vaujn at the window.

"Well enough," the kinsman answered. "We were all a little worried by that initial reception, but it seems things have settled down some since you delivered that rock to the king. Speaking of which, any news yet?"

Osrith laughed. "Not for me. I'm a disgraced knight errant in Providayne, not an honored *Shaddach Chi*. I'll be lucky if they don't weasel out of paying me in full for my trouble. If it weren't for Lady Aeolil, I'd likely be awaiting their pleasure in the gaol instead of parading around in this get-up."

"With your charming personality? That's hard to imagine."

"Yeah, there's that to account for, too. I was never much for impressing the more genteel aristocracy."

"That explains why *we* like you so much," Vaujn said with a grin.

"It should also tell you how careful you're going to have to be," Osrith said, his tone turning serious. "Unlike King Ruuhigan's Hall, here in Providayne sarcasm isn't considered a courtly virtue. One quip too many might land you in a duel or at the wrong end of the hangman's noose. Humans consider words an affront to honor as much as actions."

"Well, that's pretty stupid," the kinsman scoffed.

"So you wouldn't be offended if I started introducing you as my little *dwarf* friend?"

Vaujn's face colored a dark, dangerous red. "No more offended than you would be with my sword up your -"

"I think I made my point," Osrith interrupted, "and you made yours. Just be careful what you say."

Vaujn stared back out the window, folding his arms across his broad chest as his complexion slowly returned to normal. Osrith suspected the kinsman's dour mood wouldn't last long. As much as the kin hated being referred to as dwarves, or gnomes, or other diminutives popularized in bards' tales, he hadn't actually *called* him by one of those names.

Besides, Osrith was the kin's best friend and ally amongst the humans of Dwynleigsh, and he was confident that Vaujn realized that as well as he.

"Where *is* Kassakan?" Osrith grumbled, distracting himself from Vaujn's ill temper with frustrations of his own. "It's not like her to be late."

"That sorcerer wanted her ear on something," Vaujn said. "She seems popular enough here despite the company she keeps."

"You know how pie-eyed people get around the hosskan," dismissed Osrith. "Vessels of wisdom, blessed by the gods, and all that. She couldn't fart without them taking it as a sign."

Vaujn's earlier anger was now deflated to a more pragmatic skepticism. "That old wizard didn't look particularly pie-eyed to me."

"No," admitted Osrith, "not that one. Maybe it's best if she's there to keep an eye on him, after all. I don't trust his type much."

"Yeah, but who's keeping an eye on *us*?"

"I guess we're on our own, for now," Osrith said, leafing through the constellation charts by the window. "At least until Lady Aeolil gets here. She'll look out for us."

"Are you sure we can trust her?"

Vaujn's tone was carefully neutral, but Osrith still felt his pulse rush at the suggestion. He took a calming breath. It was a fair question. "I'm sure," he answered evenly.

"It's been a while since you knew her," Vaujn persisted, "and you know as well as I do that trust doesn't age well."

"Look," said Osrith, beginning to lose his patience despite the validity of the kinsman's caution, "before I ever swore fealty to Old Ruuh, or fought with the *Shaddach Chi*, I served her family. She doesn't need to earn my trust; she *has* it. It's as simple as that."

Vaujn chuckled, and the last of his earlier annoyance dissolved from his features completely.

"What now?" Osrith said. He was glad that the captain's foul temper had obviously left him, but dubious that this good fortune was at his expense.

"Sounds a lot like me settling the matter of whether or not we should trust *you*, not too long ago. Shaddach Chi *doesn't need to earn our trust*, I said, *he has it already*." Vaujn slapped him roughly on the back. "So I guess that settles that. Good enough for you is well enough for me."

Osrith let the conversation lapse into silence, staring out quietly into the advancing light of morning. Vaujn seemed equally content with the view and the silence. Whatever thoughts drifted through their minds remained unspoken.

For Osrith, the thoughts weren't pleasant. The king's haggard face haunted his memory like the last ember of a stubborn pit fire, his hollow old eyes full of fear and uncertainty. Osrith had been expecting that, but not *before* he'd delivered the dreamstone and whatever message Gai had locked inside.

The wizard's reaction to the rock hadn't set him any more at ease. Surprise first, then perhaps a small touch of sorrow, and finally the gleam of something between expectation and excitement. *Not many of those still lying around*, Jir'aatu had said. An *iiyiraal*, he'd called it, whatever that was. Osrith didn't want to dwell too much on what significance the rock he'd hung on his neck for so long might have, but he couldn't help thinking it contained more than a simple warning. Not many words were exchanged in that brief meeting. There were no explanations or revelations from that tight-lipped pair, nothing more than the perfunctory formalities.

But Osrith read volumes in the mute testimony of their eyes. Something was amiss in Dwynleigsh. Aeolil had alluded to it in the garden, Vanelorn's manner had suggested it as he played escort and watchdog, but the king and his chamberlain had confirmed it by their conspicuous silence.

What all that meant for Providayne, he wasn't sure. In most ways, he didn't care, either. He wasn't a native of this kingdom, and he had no personal loyalty to Guillaume, but if the weakness in that old man was a reflection of the nation he ruled... .

Osrith shook the thought off. He couldn't concern himself with things on that grand a scale. He would take responsibility for himself, maybe a squad of good warriors, but beyond that he didn't concern himself with the politics of the moment. Even so, whatever befell Providayne would have repercussions on House Vae as well, and though he could abandon hundreds or thousands to his cynicism, Evynine and Aeolil, just those two, he could not.

He wondered if Symmlrey was still in her own bleak audience with Agrylon and the king. Vanelorn had ushered her in while seeing Osrith out. She'd appeared fairly composed, and he guessed she'd need to be. Unless things had changed completely in the last eight years, the aulden were greeted with guarded suspicion at best. Here in the courts of the East, *wilhorwhyr* weren't thought of much better. They didn't bend a knee to anyone or anything but their god, Ingryst, and that included kings and nobles. Her news would keep their interest, and its importance would keep her safe, but he doubted she'd see much in the way of open friendship here.

Osrith looked over at Vaujn. At least with the kin, there was some history of trust and cooperation, even if it was hundreds of years ago. While they were thought of as strange and different, they weren't seen as threatening. The human kingdoms had never warred with the kin, at least not that anyone remembered, and so they were thought of as the jolly little dwarves of legend who happily made toys and gadgets in their cozy mountain homes.

Both history and legend were less forgiving to the aulden. His own father had believed that every sick pig or blight on his crops was their work. Osrith had never been convinced they worked in such petty ways, but he didn't count himself among those few who thought of the aulden as noble and good, either. Behind the exaggeration of their reputation, he believed there was at least some truth. Ill will didn't spring up between the races just as a matter of course.

"I know I'm an underworlder and all," said Vaujn with a quick scratch at his nose, "so I won't pretend to know the customs of those hereabouts, but do you mind telling me how they plan on having a tourney in *that* kind of weather?"

The clouds were thickening into a dark shroud over the city, and snow had begun to fall in a lazy flurry outside. "Kaissus Field's got a roof," Osrith replied. "It's all made of some fae wood. Keeps out the rain and snow, blocks the wind, stays warm enough if you're dressed right. It's about the only thing left more or less untouched from the old city."

Vaujn's face brightened. "We don't have to sit outside?"

Osrith shook his head.

"I might like this place, after all," decided the kinsman.

"You might, at that," agreed Osrith, "but you may've picked a bad time to visit."

"A bad time," agreed an icy voice from the door, "and traitor's company."

Osrith saw him there from the corner of his eye, darkening the doorframe, clad in mail, eyes gleaming and lips snarling. Bleys hadn't changed much, perhaps a little grey speckling his mustache, but naught else. He'd looked much the same standing at the gatehouse the day Osrith took his leave of service from House Vae. It was as if he'd stood around sneering for eight years, waiting for Osrith to come find him again.

"Bleys. *Captal* Prentis mentioned you'd been stationed here," Osrith returned, his own tone not lacking in contempt. He hoped the words cut Bleys like the steel he was forbidden to draw here in King's Keep, but it was hard to tell through his existing glower if the barb had stuck him. "When you have time, we can settle accounts."

"A headsman would settle things fine," Bleys said, striding into the room. "Or a hanging. I've petitioned Vanelorn for both."

"As long as they don't settle it in that order," Osrith replied.

Vaujn coughed into his mailed sleeve. "Excuse me, sirs," he said, interposing himself between the two taller men. "I don't believe I've been introduced. I'm Captain Sul Vaujn, commander of a squad of His

Majesty's Watch currently on loan from the Crown to Sir Osrith Turlun. He is *Shaddach Chi*. We will die to the last bloody kin to protect him. Well met."

Bleys spared a glance down at the kin and quirked his lip. "I've dropped scat bigger than you," he said. "You're not in the Deeps anymore. I'll take you and your squad of ugly little trolls if you come between me and justice for Hestan ne Vae."

Vaujn sprang forward, but Osrith managed to grab his arm and hold him back. The kin was strong, but without better leverage he could not break Osrith's grip. And Vaujn was too disciplined a soldier to struggle against an officer, no matter how dented his pride. He eased off, but stood his ground.

Bleys looked back up at Osrith. "And justice for Hestan's son, Andrew. Funny how Kiev and Osrith both escaped, though, isn't it? Everyone always remarked how little Kiev resembled his father – *he favored his mother*, they said. I wonder. Maybe he did favor his father, but the chip had fallen from a different block?"

"You think you can bait me so easily?" Osrith pretended calm, but the rage was there, and it was no small effort to keep it bottled. "I've heard it before, and time passing hasn't made it any truer. I failed Hestan. I failed Andrew. I failed Evynine and Kiev and Aeolil and the whole damn House Vae, and I failed Kraye and Hardt that day the Pale Man sent them all to the Dark with Hestan. For that, I might deserve a noose or an axe or worse. But I won't die to satisfy your lies, Bleys, and I won't let Vanelorn ease it along for you. You want me done, you'll have to do the killing yourself."

"Good," approved Bleys. "I look forward to the day. You will have to convince Lady Aeolil to grant me leave – she forbade me to cross blades with you. Until then, I will be waiting and watching. I know why you must be here. But this time, I'll be here to stop you."

Osrith watched Bleys depart, his pulse pounding hot behind his eyes, and slapped Vaujn on the back. "Don't get any ideas. He's mine."

Vaujn stood clenching and unclenching his jaws, staring at the empty doorway. "Don't keep me waiting," he warned, "or that scurl might trip into a score of swords and roll over onto my spear."

"Yeah, funny how those things can happen," acknowledged Osrith. "And we'll probably have to watch our step, too. Accidents can happen to anybody – *especially* when they're well planned."

Chapter Thirty-Two

A Rhyme for All Reasons

AEOLIL thought the king's day chamber looked much less austere when cast by the light of day, even in the wan illumination of this dreary winter morn. The room comprised the entirety of the highest tower in the central keep, affording spectacular views from its four banks of long, high windows. The price of such a remarkable panorama was paid primarily in the cold drafts that infiltrated the room from the seeping boundaries between the glasswork and stonemasonry.

There were four hearths, one between each pair of windows, and they were fully stoked to abate the penetrating cold. The furniture was lavish, but the oval carpet in the center of the wood-tiled floor, which bore the elaborate crest of House Jiraud, was undoubtedly the centerpiece. The background was deepest cerulean, set with a roaring lion's head overlaying the blazing golden sun, holding the smaller silver sun in its jaws. The House motto was written in silver thread around the exterior – *Peace through Strength, Strength through Wisdom.*

A table with a dozen high-backed chairs stood atop the rug. Aeolil found that the chairs' detailed carvings tended to dig into her back, their purpose clearly for opulent show rather than comfort; she would stand for now. Around the room's exterior wall were several sitting benches and small tables, some set by the fireplaces, others by the windows, but designed with more of an eye for both comfort and style.

Dozens of swords hung on the walls from various fiefs, nations and individuals allegiant to Providayne, and shields with full coats-of-arms represented those allied but not liege-sworn to House Jiraud. A door was set to the left of each fireplace, each leading to a spiral stair and also to four small balcony gardens. At this time of year, all but the rock garden were bare and typically unvisited.

Guillaume stood by one of the hearths, one hand resting on the mantle, the other on his hip. He was dressed in his best winter finery, as they all were, with one of his lesser crowns on his brow and his ceremonial sword at his side. His freshly groomed mane of grey hair curled about his shoulders, and his bearded face, though wrinkled from time, appeared more wise than old. In everything but his tired eyes did he appear the perfect picture of a king.

Agrylon stood just to his side, in his traditional black-robed garb, and today his golden chain of office hung ponderously from his neck. His face was its typical mask of composure, but Aeolil had spent far too much time with the wizard to be fooled by that deception.

Vanelorn paced the length of the room, attempting no such illusion of calm. Within the privacy of this chamber his worry and frustration were plain to read on his scarred face. The lord high marshal bore the weight of his responsibility like a true warrior, but he was honest about the burden.

Kassakan stood to Aeolil's right, and the young noblewoman took comfort in the hosskan's presence. As a child, Kassakan had been both her friend and tutor. Long before Agrylon had seen her potential in the ways of the Craft, Kassakan had gently encouraged it. She had never doubted the hosskan's intent or motives. The day Kassakan left Castle Vae had been as heartbreaking as Osrith's departure earlier that same year.

Most mesmerizing and disturbing of all the room's occupants was the *wilhorwhyr*, Symmlrey. Aeolil had heard all the rumors about the aulden and their disarming beauty, but she'd never expected to witness it herself, let alone be influenced by it. She felt her gaze drawn back to those sapphire-violet eyes, embraced by them, fulfilled by them. To look away meant emptiness.

Aeolil was at a loss. She'd never been moved by anyone's beauty before, male or female. She did her best to ignore the *wilhorwhyr*, but the compulsion to admire the precision of her form and features was increasingly hard to restrain. She hoped they would get on to business soon, before she embarrassed herself like a gawking child.

"There's no sense in delay," Symmlrey said, her intent face still lovely even as she glared at Guillaume. "You know what must be done. Do it."

"Have a care how you address the king!" Vanelorn's voice was as raw as his temper, but he avoided eye contact with the *wilhorwhyr*.

"He's not my king," she answered, "and this isn't the time to mince words. There's too much at stake."

"She's right, Your Majesty," said Agrylon from Guillaume's shoulder. "We must not delay."

Guillaume sighed, staring into the fire. "My own dreams have been bad enough of late. I don't relish this."

"Osrith didn't drag that stone hundreds of leagues for you to wax poetic about your own problems, and I'm not waiting here for want of things to do. You're wasting time."

Aeolil marveled at Symmlrey's frankness. People who spoke like that to the king ended up in shackles or shallow graves, and judging from Vanelorn's expression, the *wilhorwhyr* was avoiding both those fates by the narrow margin these circumstances provided.

"Still your tongue!" Guillaume spat, turning on Symmlrey, fuming more than marveling at her brash tongue. "There is more at work here than you know."

"As is the case with us all, good king," Kassakan said, "until you read the stone."

The king's head sagged, but he nodded his head in resigned defeat. "Tell me again what I must do."

Agrylon lead the king to the nearest settee. "Recline here and clear your thoughts. I will place you in a trance, and Gai's message will be made known to you."

The king was at rest in short order, attended closely by Agrylon and Kassakan while Vanelorn looked on warily from a distance. According to Agrylon, the dreamstone was keyed to the king's *iiyir*, somehow, and would allow whatever message Gai had enclosed to be dreamt by proxy.

Symmlrey looked away, uninterested and unconcerned with the process. This was once a common method of communication between aulden bards, and her impatience was clear from her tense stance, the shuffling of her feet, and the crossing and re-crossing of her arms.

"Milady," Aeolil said, stepping closer to the aulden, her pulse quickening. "May I have a word?"

The aulden seemed surprised that someone was addressing her. "I have no honorific. Just Symmlrey will do. Your mother proved most kind to us in the Marches. I should be no less kind to her daughter."

"Yes, I suppose first I owe you thanks for all you did at Castle Vae. Kassakan told me your own journey has not been without sacrifice. My House is in debt to you and to the *wilhorwhyr*. Truly. Many lives were saved, including Osrith's. So – thank you."

"Most of that thanks is due my companions, not myself. I am but the last of us left to accept it."

"Well, I, regardless." Aeolil flushed. "I am glad you are here."

Symmlrey quirked an eyebrow, then frowned. "I am sorry," she explained, pricking her index finger on the edge of her thumbnail. A small bead of blood welled up, which she then dabbed on Aeolil's finger, muttering something in auldenish under her breath.

Aeolil felt a small charge, barely discernible, in the tides. "What…?"

"Take the blood like this," she said, putting her own finger to her mouth. "Freely given, it frees you from the glamour. I daren't undo the charm altogether. Not here in this place."

Aeolil put the blood to her lips and tasted it, uncertain. It was slightly sweet, as if tinged with sap rather than iron, and as soon as it touched her tongue a surge of heat flashed through her, head to toe. She blinked. Symmlrey might still be the most beautiful woman she had ever seen, but gone was the unnatural magnetism of her presence.

"I suppose those legends are true, at least," Aeolil said, swallowing hard. "Somewhat disarming to know you had me in your thrall."

Symmlrey's hard visage melted into a small snicker. "No, no. The glamour is only a small shift in *il'iiyir*. Those affected are merely brought into tune with my tide. Those who are strong with their own tides may be drawn to me, trust me more easily, but the charm would be short-lived. I cannot influence anyone of strong will to do much that they'd not normally do."

"So, of what use is it here, then? If you cannot use it to influence the king, or Vanelorn, why bother?"

"Have you ever tried to fight someone you cannot look at? Since most of your warriors are men-folk, it serves me well that they constantly avert their eyes. They feel the glamour, even if they do not understand it, so they fear it."

"But it affected me as well."

"Differently. With you it is fascination, for them something more like *infatuation*. There is a difference. But, no matter – my aulden charms weren't what you wished to speak with me about."

"No," Aeolil agreed. "It is the garden – the place you and the others arrived. It is said to be of aulden crafting. I've long been enchanted by it. What is it?"

"Meyr ga'Glyleyn," Symmlrey answered, her expression softening. "A most wonderful and sacred place."

"I sensed a sort of *peace* there," Aeolil explained, "but I couldn't discern its intent. I knew it was not simply a plot for flowers."

Symmlrey smiled. "There is nothing simple about Meyr ga'Glyleyn. It is an ancient and powerful source of *iiyir*, much like the place we traveled from in Oszmagoth. And it is a plot of sorts. A resting place."

Aeolil sensed she did not mean a place of *repose*. "What do you mean?"

"Long ago, when Dwynleigsh was yet the city of the Ceearmyltu, Meyr ga'Glyleyn had many uses. It is a convergence of *iiyir*, a rare meeting of ley lines, and so a place of great power. The *lyaeyni* of the Ceearmyltu decreed that the departed souls of the tribe's children be interred there, to imbue it with innocence and peace, and discourage the abuse of its power. A golden stone was committed to the pool for each so honored. Their spirits linger there even to this day. I sensed them from the moment we stepped out of the Wellspring."

Aeolil felt a little ill at ease. "It's a *cemetery*, then?"

"Not in the human sense. The Veil is not so uncompromising for my kind as it is for yours. At times, the spirits of our dead may bridge the small gap between our world and the next, but they are trapped completely in neither place."

"That's beautiful," Aeolil said. She thought back to the glittering illusions that danced across the water, knowing now what they must be. She felt a lump in the back of her throat. If there was only a place such as that where she could visit her father and brothers.

The torches fluttered as a sudden wind sprang from nowhere, and the flames of the hearth died away to the barest flicker. In the growing darkness, Aeolil double-checked each window to ensure it was closed. They all were. She shivered in the cold and dark that descended over them, pulling her woolen cape about her shoulders. She watched as her misty breath floated away from her lips only to be whipped away by the ever-increasing wind.

"It is time," Symmlrey said, her expression retreating to subdued neutrality as she nodded at the king.

Aeolil turned her own attention back to the reclining monarch, whose rest was now fitful. His lips were quivering, trying to form words, but only a faint whimper issued forth. The dreamstone was alive with the invisible fire of active *iiyir*, growing in strength with the mysterious wind, and Aeolil was alarmed at its intensity. A dreamstone was a rare enough thing, but it was not a talisman with this sort of power.

"Speak," whispered Agrylon into the king's ear, his right index finger tracing a pattern of command in the air.

The king's body shook, his arms and legs flailing in a spasmodic fit. The old eyes stared up at the wizard by his side, wide and bulging, but rolled up so far into the back of his head that only the whites were visible. Guillaume moaned, his lips drawn back across his face in a horrible grimace, the sound of his cries like an echo of the wind that howled through the room, low and mourning.

Aeolil felt bile in her throat, and her knees went weak. A strong arm held her steady, looping under her armpits as the world went spinning around her. The dreamstone was a hot coal in her awareness, diverting and swallowing the *iiyir* tides like a whirlpool and then expelling them again like a waterspout. Her abdomen cramped, and she sucked in a ragged breath.

Center, she told herself. *Find your center.*

"Where…?" The king's voice was distant and not his own, the veins on his neck and face swollen and blue across the flat pallor of his face. "*Where is this place?*"

Aeolil shuddered, trying to concentrate, redirecting her thoughts from the pain. As a woman, this time of the month was of the greatest bother and vexation – *unclean and unwelcome*, as the physics said. As a mage, it was also the peak of her power, the cresting of her personal *iiyir* tides. And this day, in near perfect conjunction with the world tides as well.

For a man the shifts were not so great, the adjustments not so dizzying. For him, the ebb and flow of the tides was steady, measured and constant. Ripples on a pond, each day the same as the next. For a woman, it was the raging crash of surf, building slowly and breaking with fury and abandon.

Center, she reminded herself yet again, frustrated with her lack of control. She was no little girl, flustered and helpless at the unwitting changes in her body, caught unawares. She could – she *would* – master it.

Aeolil disengaged herself from Symmlrey's supporting arm, unsteady but standing on her own. She found her focus and grabbed it. The spinning slowed, but didn't cease. The pain eased, but didn't vanish. She felt her body once more her domain rather than her prison. And even as she managed to compose herself, so the dreamstone calmed its own raging storm of *iiyir*.

Aeolil saw the king's shuddering body and sensed the rift, invisible though it was, as it stabilized around him: a tenuous connection between this world and the next. She realized what was happening with mingled awe and disbelief. This was no *dream* being filtered through Guillaume.

"Speak, and then to your rest," Agrylon said, his voice almost tender.

The king's face contorted, his head lolling one way and then the next, his hands clawing into the cushions. A voice not his own spoke from his throat. "*Agrylon*," it said, "*I'm not… long… for this world.*"

Agrylon smiled briefly, stroking the king's brow. "Do the best you can, Gaious."

The name was a familiar one to Aeolil, though she'd never met the man. She'd heard Agrylon mention Gaious many times, but mostly with an addendum such as *that old fool in the mountains.*

"*You… you're in it deep… Agrylon.*" Each syllable was its own separate struggle from his tortured lips. "*You and your king. The Prophecy of the Darkening.*"

"Tell me," Agrylon squeezed the words from his tight pressed lips. He drew a sigil in the air with his finger, and the rushing wind stopped, the king's convulsions stopped, Aeolil even feared for a moment that her heart had stopped.

"Tell me," he repeated, his words now charged with magic. "Tell me of the Darkening."

In the ensuing silence, the otherworldly voice seemed even more out of place. To Aeolil, Guillaume's body, limp in the aftermath of his hard fought struggle to speak, resembled nothing more than a talking corpse. That was fitting, she supposed.

"*No, Agrylon – dust off your own tomes, I've no time for the stale verse of prophecy. It is enough to know you are in its midst. Left to your own, this you would not have known until too late. If not too late already.*"

"What is your message, then?" Agrylon's tight lips belied his impatience.

"*Message?*" The word was a throaty rasp from the king's throat. "*You misunderstand. I've given you all the message I have to give – the Darkening is nigh. You must dispel it.*

"*This is no dreamstone meant to impart a vision. This* iiyiraal *is a gift, and a warning, and your hope and your doom. The Undying King and the Pale Man seek not simple conquest. Ewanbheir has sent them for the secret of the Fifth Devastation.*"

Agrylon paled. Aeolil looked to Symmlrey for explanation, but she merely shrugged. The Twelve had unleashed the Four Devastations upon Malakuur to end the Second Realmwar. Earth, Air, Fire, and Water – one Devastation for each of the Elements.

A Fifth, she wondered, *but what?*

She turned to Kassakan, but the lizard paid her no mind. Instead, in one swift step, she loomed over the king.

"Gaious, speak swift," Kassakan implored. "How can the dreamstone help us? How can we stop the Darkening?"

"*The irony, Blessed One,*" the voice in the king replied, "*is that the plain answer is hidden within the very artifice contrived for your protection. You will have to read the Prophecy, I'm afraid. And, well, you all know how Prophecy is writ – it will be fulfilled through one interpretation or another. Such vagueness is a handy way to tell the future – a shell game. Would that I could speak plainly.*"

The king grasped at Agrylon's black robes, clutching the fabric at the gold-trimmed cuff between his fingers. "*The glamour you crafted was a dense weave, Agrylon – and dangerous. I cannot defeat it. Were I to speak the truth of it, it would tumble as nonsense from my lips under ward of your stolen Word. You may live to regret your clever deceit. Myszdraelh will not be the last She sends to bring it home.*

"*So – I will say it as I must.*" The king's face slackened; his chest trembled. "*Tell the prince,*" he managed. "*Tell him, and give him the stone. Ebhan-nuád is but the start of it. The rest will be upon you to decipher from the Prophecy.*" His eyes closed, and then opened to focus on Agrylon once more. "*But you must tell the prince – or it will all be on your head.*"

Exhaling deeply, he unclenched his hand and dropped the dreamstone to the floor. Then Guillaume slept, his body slack with exhaustion, and the ethereal presence of Gaious was gone from him.

Aeolil almost stumbled as the power of the dreamstone left the room with a silent, invisible rush of *iiyir*. She drew a ragged breath.

"Go to your rest, now," said Agrylon, and Aeolil heard a note of brimming but controlled emotion as he continued in a strained whisper. "Be at peace."

Trembling, Aeolil moved beside the wizard, placing her hand on his shoulder. She realized she had never really *touched* the man before, in friendship or anger, despite the many years she had known him. "Was he your friend?" she asked.

"He was a Black Robe of Dacadia. The First among the Twelve." Agrylon clenched his jaws tightly and swallowed with an effort. "And he was my brother."

Aeolil was shocked. Before today she would never have guessed they were even on good terms. In fact, the last time Agrylon had visited the seer, he'd returned in the foulest of tempers, cursing his name from the Pits to the Heavens. She watched as he mutely retrieved the dreamstone from the floor, running his thumb and forefinger across its smooth surface.

"What was all that nonsense about?" demanded Vanelorn. All eyes went to the old warrior, who was approaching Guillaume like a physic approaching a plague bearer.

Agrylon barely tilted his head at the lord high marshal. "Nothing you would understand."

Vanelorn bristled, but didn't reply.

"The gist of it is clear enough, if not the specifics," the wizard continued, turning pointedly away from the knight. "It seems to support the accounts of both Turlun and our *wilhorwhyr*, here. We must explore the matter in more depth, but not here and not now. I must prepare the king for his appearance at the festival. Perhaps tonight we may study this prophecy at length."

"Waiting gains us nothing," said Symmlrey. "We must act now, if it's not to be in vain. Disrupting your tournament is a small price to pay."

Vanelorn glanced at her with disdain as he walked over to examine Guillaume. "He's not *your* king, remember? None of this is your concern."

"He's not my king, and this is not my land, but this *is* my concern. What happens here will affect East and West alike, without regard for the boundaries your kind are so fond of drawing on maps. My interests and my enemy are the same as yours."

Vanelorn nodded, accepting her reply with the same silence he had shown Agrylon. Aeolil saw the conflict in his eyes, and the fear. For thirty years he had been lord high marshal, and he had met the threats to this kingdom with a calm and guiding hand. Both Guillaume and his father had benefited from the experience of this wise and noble warrior. But this was no border dispute or treaty negotiation. This was something beyond his experience entirely. Worse yet, this situation forced him to defer to Agrylon. It was no secret that the wizard was tolerated rather than trusted by the rest of the Privy Council, and Vanelorn paramount among them. He was no fool, however. He might grumble at the indignity, but he would accept it.

"Your concerns are both real and reasonable," Agrylon said, "but we do not operate within reason alone, here at King's Keep. We have politics to consider, as well. If His Majesty were to be absent from the royal pavilion, there would be great unrest. There are those among the Council of Lords who would see the end of House Jiraud's rule. If we are to meet the threats of our foreign enemies, we must not add oil to these domestic fires."

Symmlrey made no pretense of hiding her contempt. "Foolishness. *Explain* it to them. The salvation of this kingdom is as much their concern as anyone else's, if not more."

"On the contrary," Agrylon warned, "we must tell no one of this prophecy. It will breed unrest. We will reveal what we must when the time is right."

"If I may suggest an alternative," Kassakan said, and both wizard and *wilhorwhyr* turned their attention to her. "I think we must do both. While it is a political necessity for the king and prince to attend the royal pavilion for the festival today, and while I'm certain Agrylon will wish to accompany them, I have no such obligation. In fact, I would much rather devote my energy to examining this prophecy more closely. If you give me your leave, I will avail myself of the considerable resources in the King's Library. When your duties at the tourney and the Feast of Prince's Bread are complete, and when you feel the circumstance otherwise appropriate, we may reconvene our council and review matters."

"Then I will help you with your research," Symmlrey said.

"I think it might be best if you were to attend the tourney as well," Kassakan suggested. "Unobtrusively, of course," she added quickly, seeing the disapproval taking shape in Agrylon's eyes. "You would serve our interests better, I think, if you were watching over the king and his heir apparent."

"*I* would be honored to help you, Kassakan," Aeolil said hopefully.

Agrylon doused that hope immediately. "No. You will represent House Vae at the pavilion. The prince is expecting you, as is Sir Calvraign, and you, too, have appearances to maintain."

"Then perhaps we might ask Master Madrharigal to help," Aeolil said, managing to put aside her disappointment. "His knowledge of lore is extensive enough in itself to be helpful, and he has always had the king's trust. Speed should be of the essence, considering the lay of the sky."

Agrylon considered the suggestion in silence, his face knotted in displeasure. "Very well. Haste breeds necessity, after all. I'll send word to the master bard." The wizard turned to address the rest of them. "If none here have yet seen the portents to which the lady refers, this very Midride *Ebhan-nuád* will be upon us."

"I sensed a shifting of the *ur'iiyir*," Kassakan said, "but that means… I thought the art of turning the tides long lost, even to the Old Ones."

"Evidently not," Symmlrey muttered.

The hosskan's tongue flicked out momentarily to polish the smooth ivory of her teeth. "Vanelorn, Inulf and Willanel should all speak with Osrith concerning the Pale Man. There's no telling exactly what his involvement in this will be, but they could stand to learn from his experience, however painful the memories might remain."

Agrylon studied her face for a moment. "Yes," he agreed. "Vanelorn, perhaps you should have Inulf and Willanel double the Royal Guard."

"Aye," agreed the lord marshal, grateful for something to do. "I'll see to it."

Symmlrey watched as the knight left the room. "They'll need more than a contingent of the palace guard to protect them from the Pale Man."

Aeolil knew as much from bitter experience. She tried not to think about that. The problems of the present were too demanding for her to be distracted by her past. Like Osrith, she would have to deal with the memories, regardless of the pain. "What *will* protect him?"

"A good question," said Agrylon, his attention on the dreamstone, holding it up to his eyes, as if it held some answer to their dilemma on its polished surface. "This may offer its wearer some limited defense from magical attack, but whatever else Gai meant, I don't yet know. But the morning grows late," he pronounced, "and I must prepare the king for the tourney. Let us consider this council adjourned."

Kassakan took Aeolil's slender arm and retreated from the receiving room without further delay, followed closely by Symmlrey. Aeolil relaxed and allowed herself to be led. It freed her mind to think about the situation with the attention it deserved, and with the hosskan, at least, she had no fear of being led astray.

Chapter Thirty-Three

Cutting it Fine

"Y OU may await Lady Aeolil within," the young guard said, admitting Calvraign and Brohan with a reserved but friendly smile. It was Stefan, if Calvraign remembered the name correctly, but he didn't recognize his counterpart.

Once inside, Calvraign hadn't time to notice his surroundings. His attention was drawn before all else to the shorter of the room's two occupants, who frowned back at him with a look that could generously be termed *unimpressed*. Calvraign stared, his feet rooted to the spot and his breath caught up in the back of his throat, until Brohan's gentle nudge pushed him forward and broke his trance. He was still wide-eyed and dumbstruck, but at least he'd regained control of his limbs.

"Don't mind him," said the taller one, who wasn't much more than an indistinct blur out of the corner of Calvraign's distracted eye. He rested a hand on the shoulder of his shorter companion. "His mother dropped him a lot as a child – but he likes the attention."

With an effort, Calvraign diverted his attention to the speaker, a powerfully built, bearded knight in the livery of House Vae. For just a moment, he looked somewhat like Bleys. But this man was older, not quite as tall, and leaner. There was a grin at the corner of his mouth, but nothing to suggest an easy humor in the glimmer of his eyes. Maybe it was in that cold-blooded appraisal that a similarity to Captal Malade could most easily be found.

Calvraign looked back at the underkin, increasingly aware that his silence was moving swiftly from merely embarrassing to outright rudeness. He sensed Brohan still standing behind him, but the master bard held his tongue. Calvraign found Brohan less and less inclined to defuse this sort of awkward situation.

Oh, gather up your wits, he told himself. Brohan was only treating him as he wanted himself to be treated – like a man. He forced himself to swallow. "*Mishtigge,*" he ventured, managing to keep his voice even.

The kinsman's frown faltered, and then fell away completely. "Well met, boy," he said, marching up to the young man and offering both a smile and hand in welcome.

Calvraign kneeled to bring their eyes level, or started to. A firm hand from Brohan held his tunic tightly, forcing him to remain standing, and Cal took the hint. "I am Calvraign Askewneheur," he said, grasping the kinsman's hand as firmly as he was able. The return grip was somewhat more powerful and a little uncomfortable, but not painful. He couldn't think of anything else to say, and he'd already used up most of his practical kin vocabulary with his greeting, so he settled for a simple and heartfelt, "I am honored to meet you, sir."

"I'm called Vaujn," the kin answered, releasing his grip, "captain in His Royal Majesty's Upper Watch, Outpost Number Nine."

Calvraign's head rushed with a hundred questions about the kin and the Deeps, all of which he decided to ignore. If he wanted to avoid seeming the gawking simpleton, or at least any *more* of one, he would have to put away his curiosity for a while. As the court's resident oddity for the past few days – the *enigmatic genteel barbarian* – he knew how irritating such inquisitiveness could be. In all likelihood, the kinsman just wanted to be treated with the same respect and deference as any other visitor with his rank.

Calvraign turned slightly toward Brohan. "And this is Master Madrharigal, the King's Bard."

Vaujn and Brohan exchanged a brief greeting before the kinsman introduced his companion. "And *that* is Sir Osrith Turlun of the *Shaddach Chi*. He's a few other things, too, but you'll figure that out for yourself soon enough."

"*Shaddach Chi?*" echoed Brohan.

The master bard voiced the surprise that lingered in Calvraign's own thoughts. If there was an elite cadre of warriors that had earned either the fear or respect of all the peoples and races of Rahn, it was they. To his knowledge there had never been a human, or any other race but the underkin themselves, in their ranks. He looked over the knight again, wondering why he was wearing Lady Aeolil's colors if he were a knight in service to the underkin king. Something about that irritated him, and he identified the jealousy quickly and with a twinge of self-reproach. He remembered Seth's excited gossip: *and rumor has it a messenger arrived in the wee hours with some sort of dire news.* Yes, that was probably it. Not that his awareness diluted his jealousy much.

"Sir Osrith was once the Captal of House Vae," explained Brohan, glancing at Calvraign, his eyes narrowing in a silent caution to his student. "About a ten-year ago, if I remember right."

The knight stiffened, and realization spread through Calvraign, salving his initial reaction. This was the man Aeolil had mentioned, the one responsible for the death of her father and brother, or at least responsible for not stopping it. Although she'd made it clear enough that she didn't blame him. Calvraign decided it wasn't his place to second-guess her. Besides, the man was *Shaddach Chi*, which had been enough to impress even the unflappable Master Madrharigal.

"Some things are best left in the past, Master Bard." Osrith's voice was raw, and he made no attempt to hide the warning in its tone.

"Aye," agreed Brohan. "*Mistakes I leave to rot with time, with lessons learned in present mind.* Or so says the Old Sage himself, eh?"

"Right," snapped Osrith, with little agreement or enthusiasm in his sarcasm.

Calvraign didn't think the philosophies of the Learned Corrison offered much in the way of comfort to the knight. Such phrases were mainstays of households both plain and noble, but a bit cloy when confronted with such a harsh example of adversity. If Brohan had a weakness, it was not knowing when to leave off teaching or lecturing, and perhaps more importantly, to *whom* he shouldn't teach or lecture. Calvraign decided it best to change the subject as quickly as possible. "When do you expect the Lady Aeolil?" he asked.

"At her convenience," said Osrith. "She's busy with matters of state, from what I gather." The once-captal paused, and Calvraign felt himself undressed and unarmed before his powerful scrutiny. "What business have *you* with Her Ladyship?"

"Perhaps it's more appropriate to ask what business she has with *us*, Sir Osrith," said Brohan, whose attention hadn't wavered from the knight for a moment. "We are here at her request. She and Sir Calvraign have matters to discuss."

That brought a chuckle from the dour lips of the *Shaddach Chi*. "Sir Calvraign, is it? I've seen youngsters in the lists before, but don't they usually have their whiskers before their spurs?"

Vaujn made a rather lame attempt to hide his laughter behind a fist, in guise of a cough, and Calvraign split his glare evenly between the two of them. He was still a little uncomfortable with his knighthood himself, and not much more secure in his girlishly smooth face. But he didn't want the wound to show. Once a wound was obvious, it became a target for repeated attack, and Calvraign had no wish to go over this territory more than once.

"I suppose I haven't really earned either, as yet," he said with as much calm as he could muster. "My father evidently had enough whiskers and bravery for the both of us." Calvraign ran a hand along his cheek with a wry smile. "I'm hoping I'll grow into it, though."

"Fair enough," Osrith said, but Vaujn still hid his mouth behind his fist.

"Excuse me," Stefan's voice interrupted from the cracked doorway. "Lady Aeolil requests that you all proceed to the Bridge House Gate. She has sent word that she will meet you there."

"Well," said Osrith, "let's not keep her waiting."

Calvraign couldn't help but agree. Aside from the prospect of seeing her again, which held considerable appeal, he didn't want to miss even a moment of the Opening Melee. Even if it meant he had to wait a little longer to hear Aeolil's news, whatever that was, he suspected that seeing the best knights of the realm engaged in mock battle would keep him suitably entertained. In fact, he decided, the distraction would do him good.

<hr />

"No, no, no!" screamed the Chief Steward, directly in Seth's left ear. "Not so *thin*, damnit! I said slice them fine and narrow, by the Fiery Pits, not bloody well transparent!" Seth stared down at the mess he'd made of some perfectly good potatoes and cringed. This was a poor choice of days to disappoint Markus, whose patience was already stretched to the limit by the demands of the Winter Festival's many feasts. "I'm sorry," he said, his voice breaking midway through the apology. "I was-"

"Shut up!" Markus railed, causing Seth to flinch. The Chief Steward's pale complexion was gaining color dangerously fast, and sweat beaded on his brow from the heat of the ovens roasting beef, mutton and fowl. The rest of the kitchen staff went about their work, too busy to take notice of someone else's misfortune.

"You gettin' a mite big in the britches, Mister Briggin? You forgotten what real work's all about, now that you order others around to do it for you? You'd think y' hadn't seen the kitchen in a ten-year!"

"N...no sir, I-"

"Shut up!" Markus repeated, with even greater volume. "Put down the knife before you make a bigger mess of things!"

Seth practically threw it down next to the thinly sliced potatoes. He didn't say a word, realizing that Markus had no desire to hear his voice for any reason. He waited meekly for whatever punishment he might receive. The sooner Markus told him, the sooner he could get to work at it and dig his way out of disfavor. Again.

"Burton needs your help upstairs," explained the Chief Steward, somewhat more calm of voice, but no less red of face, "and I suggest you put a little more concentration into it than you did down here. He's not as forgiving as I am."

Seth knew that to be true from painful personal experience, and decided not to test the castellan's patience as he'd unwittingly tested Markus. "Yes, sir."

"Right then. Go wash some of that grime off ye, so you're presentable, and get up to the Malminnion's apartments. *Baron* Ezriel is just recently in, and you know how exacting he can be. And don't dally any or I'll tan whatever hide Burton leaves over for me!"

Seth was off in a blink, running with reckless haste through the busy kitchen, dodging and weaving between the staff and narrowly avoiding several collisions on his way. Men and women balancing dishes, foodstuffs, and wood for the fire all called out after him to be more attentive, but Seth paid them no mind. He didn't want to keep Burton, and consequently Lord Malminnion, waiting any longer than necessary.

As he careered out the door leading to the pantry, and beyond to the spiral stair and escape, he ran headlong into the heavyset Dar. The chief cook's assistant stumbled, balancing an armful of dry goods, and shouted a particularly lewd insult as Seth darted past. He climbed up and away two steps at a time, skipping over the uneven trip-step hiding a third of the way up the flight without a second thought.

Seth passed the first landing without pause, and the second, finally slowing by the time he reached the third. He was ascending at a normal rate by the time he reached the fifth level, his breathing strained, and here he exited the stair. Directly ahead was the door to the central barracks, but they were still an hour or more from reveille, and he had no desire to disturb their hard earned slumber. He turned up the hall to his right, which led thirty feet to the northeast barracks. Their watch had started before dawn and he found it empty, as he'd expected. He ran around to his right toward the washbasin. There was some fresh water left in the granite bowl, and Seth began sponging himself off with a stray cloth.

The cold water helped him gain a little focus on the events of the morning. The words that Sir Calvraign and Master Madrharigal had so casually tossed around still troubled him, and he knew that distraction had cost him some of Markus' respect. He regretted that. Markus had always been fair with him, if more than a little stern. Normally Seth was very good at doing his job with a single-minded attention to detail. Knowing what was going on and allowing oneself to be distracted by it were two very different things. He'd not followed that rule today, and he resolved to better discipline himself in the future, or someone else surely would.

With that thought in mind, Seth quickly checked his reflection in the piece of polished steel that served the soldiers as a crude mirror. He was presentable, at least, but he couldn't say much more than that. His limited time allowed for nothing more thorough, however, and he backtracked to the stairs at a brisk pace.

The apartments of House Malminnion weren't in the Central Keep, but the smaller South Keep, and it took Seth at least ten clicks to make his way up to and across the thin catwalk that connected the towers. He wasn't overly fond of the Flying Bridge, an expanse of stone not more than three feet in width that spanned the sixty-foot gap between the keeps. There was no railing, only a guide rope that he clung to most insistently. In his mind it was not near enough insurance against the deadly plummet to the rocks over a hundred feet below. He felt the solid construction of the South Keep under his soles after quick but careful passage over the bridge, and breathed an audible sigh of relief. It wasn't so much that he was afraid of heights, but he was *acutely* aware of them.

The guards hardly blinked as he passed. There weren't many of the servants better known about King's Keep than Seth, and the guards on this side of the bridge paid him no more heed than the other. He made his way through the apartments of House Myrtma, then down a flight to those of House Malminnion. The House Guard pointed him in the direction of Burton, and three long hallways and a sharp left turn brought him to the door of Baron Ezriel's Master Bedroom and thus right to the base of the castellan's boot. There were four young girls carrying in supplies through the door, but they kept their eyes down at their feet. The servants of the Malminnion brothers weren't known for their independent spirit. Not for long, anyway.

"There you are!" The portly old castellan gave Seth a quick looking over, frowning unpleasantly all the while. "I was beginning to wonder if Markus was going to part with you before the New Year."

"He told me to –"

"Yes, yes, keep the excuses to yourself, Mister Briggin, we have work to do."

"Yes sir," said Seth, wondering if anyone would let him finish a sentence today.

"Lord Garath evidently overlooked mentioning that his esteemed brother would be joining us for the festival," explained Burton, "and his accommodation is far from ready. I can't waste any more time over here, I've things enough to occupy me back in the Central Keep. I leave it to you."

Seth's stomach fell through his shoes. "Excuse me, sir?"

The castellan's jaw hardened. "I said *I leave it to you*. I've no one else on staff available right now. Take care of it. And get to work, his servants are at your disposal, but I don't want to hear that you've been slacking off. Do you understand me, Mister Briggin?"

"Yes, sir. When will Lord Ezriel be arriving?"

Burton was already on his way out the door. "Arriving?" His laugh was decidedly unsympathetic. "He's here already! You have until after the tourney today to make ready. He's occupied with his brother for now. And remember, it's Lord *Malminnion* now. He's no lordling, he's the *baron*."

Seth's eyes widened as he looked about the room. There were no linens, no bed sheets, a fine layer of dust lay over everything, and the hearth was dead cold and empty. And that was just what he noticed straight away. He began making a list in his head, prioritizing the tasks he needed to complete and trying to calculate his chances of succeeding in the scant time allotted. He wondered if Burton much cared one way or another.

Seth cleared his head. *No sense worrying about that yet,* he thought. There was too much to do. "Ladies," he said, clapping his hands lightly to get their attention. They looked up like scolded dogs, all except the last one – she had some fire left in her eyes – and Seth felt a little guilty. "My name is Mister Briggin," he continued, softening his tone but making sure to retain an element of authority. "I'm afraid we don't have much time for introductions, so I'll learn your names as we go. First of all, one of you bring all that back into the hall. We need to do a thorough cleaning before we clutter up the room. I need another of you to go to the storeroom in the basement and ask the porter to bring up three loads of firewood. In the meantime, you other two can help me clean up. I'll get some hot water and berrin seed oil, and then we can get started."

"I'll go find the porter," the lively-eyed girl stated.

Seth watched after her as she left, struck silent by the casual confidence of her voice and her comportment. As she reached the hall, her head dropped, and her shoulders sagged, transforming her seamlessly into a meek servant girl once more. Seth grinned. *A fox in the hen house, eh?*

By the time Seth returned from fetching the supplies he required, Lord Malminnion's servants had cleared the chests of their master's belongings from the bedroom, and even began dusting. He joined them with a smile and a nod of approval, glad that they were neither trying to avoid the work nor waiting for his specific command to start it.

Seth delegated the workload as fairly as he could, avoiding the temptation to give himself the most demanding work. If there was one lesson he had learned from Burton, it was to keep some semblance of distance between the one giving orders and those taking them. He should work hard, but appropriately, so that his subordinates would appreciate his help without depending on him too much.

The elder brother Malminnion had been away from his quarters here for more than two years, and the work was slow going. The last two times he had visited the capital, Ezriel had stayed at Saint Severun's. As a knight lieutenant general in the Order of Irdik, he spent increasingly more time with his ecclesiastical brothers than with the aristocrats and politicians of King's Keep. Why he'd chosen to house himself here this time around wasn't really an issue that concerned Seth, other than the challenge it posed to arrange on such short notice. They made steady progress, and Seth encouraged them to talk as they worked, even managing to learn their names in the process.

Iaede and Braede were sisters, separated by only a year at fourteen and fifteen respectively. They had been in Ezriel's household since they were little girls, and were quick to follow orders. They spoke little at first, but warmed to Seth's amiable and unassuming presence. Deirdre was older, at sixteen, and quiet. She answered any and all questions in the briefest fashion possible, though always respectful, carefully measuring the cost of her syllables. Seth didn't invest much time in prying any more talk from her lips; conversation was incidental to the task at hand.

The door swung open with a bang, and Seth turned, alarmed at the noise. He was even more alarmed at what he saw next. The girl who'd gone for lumber had reappeared, an oversized load of firewood stacked in her arms. She was breathing hard, and sweating, but there was only the faintest tremble in her shoulders from the weight of her burden. Seth scrambled to help, flustered at seeing the young girl with such a heavy load, and directed her toward the iron bassinet next to the hearth. He knelt down and helped her unload the wood.

"Where's the porter, girl? I didn't mean for you to carry all this yourself!" Seth couldn't believe she'd taken it upon herself to bring the wood, let alone such a hefty load. He removed and stacked the logs as quickly as he could. "It's seven, no, *eight* flights from the basement!"

"Aye," she breathed, sticking out her lower lip and blowing a stray clump of her short brown hair from her sticky brow. "But I'd've more luck finding a unicorn than your porter, today. And if we don't get that fire started soon, we'll not warm this place afore evening."

Seth was transfixed by the frankness in her rich chestnut eyes as she spoke, wide and round on the doe-white skin of her face. He found her accent, though thicker than the other girls', to be strangely familiar. There was a lilting softness to her vowels, made all the more noticeable by the harshness with which she ground out her consonants.

"You're very beautiful," he blurted, the words spilling out before he could trap them safely in his throat. He really hadn't intended to speak his revelation aloud, and found the temperature in the frigid room suddenly much too warm. "For a porter," he added lamely, his voice breaking in mid-sentence. "You should let him do this kind of work."

The girl smiled at him with a questioning look, clearly amused and surprised at his words. "Shush now, or you'll make the others jealous," she teased in a whisper. She winked as she stood, brushing bits of wood from her plain servant's garb.

Seth found himself watching her a little too intently as she smoothed the cloth of the dress against her skin. It was fitted just slightly too snug for her figure, probably a hand-me-down of some sort, and his imagination began to take liberties with the rather flattering results. He started building up a fire to distract himself, arranging the kindling with unerring and well-practiced precision before laying the first layer of heavier wood.

"I'll go for the next load," she said, and headed for the door.

Seth's gaze lingered for a moment on the swaying of her slender, girlish hips as she left the room, then turned back to the beginnings of his fire. He took the flint and steel from his tunic pocket and struck them several times over the kindling, with a little more vigor than normal. It didn't take long for the sparks to catch, and he nursed it along patiently until the draft from the chimney caught hold and drew the flames upward.

He sat and watched the fire burn more steadily as the two sisters and Deirdre went about their business behind him, talking quietly amongst themselves. He didn't know if they had noticed his exchange with their companion, but that wasn't a great concern of his at the moment. *She* had heard it, and that was all that mattered. He'd developed a crush on the nameless girl and then made an ass of himself in the space of a click. It had been a while since his last crush, the obligatory pubescent infatuation with Lady Aeolil that all of his friends had gone through, and he thought he'd safely outgrown that stage.

Wrong again, Mister Briggin, he thought wryly to himself, *wrong again.*

Chapter Thirty-Four

The Price of Friendship

THE High Blade of the Ceearmyltu was not known for her easy humor, so there were no comments from the assembled *nyrul cayl* or their guests when she entered the Great Tree almost five fingers past highsuns. Prince Ruoughn wore a haughty look of impatience, but Lombarde's thin lips were close to his ear, whispering words of distraction or appeasement. Jylkir doubted if Du'uwneyyl cared which. If these humans had a dispute with the High Blade, her sister would welcome the chance to settle the account in blood.

Jylkir had seen the prince and the ambassador at practice with their blades the morning before. Ruoughn's sword was too big for him to use in a balanced stance, and he favored a high, arcing attack, which left him vulnerable to a quick thrust. Against Du'uwneyyl he might last two strokes. Lombarde, though more thoughtful in his strikes, had a predictable pattern of defense. He might last four.

Stop daydreaming, she chastised herself. As tempting as it would be to watch Du'uwneyyl do away with them, that was not how things were developing. Meimniyl saw a use for them, and Jylkir knew her sister wouldn't betray her duty by disputing the *lyaeyni's* will.

"Welcome, High Blade," Meimniyl said. "Please be seated, and we will commence our council."

Du'uwneyyl took the empty seat to the right of the *lyaeyni* without comment. The council room of the Great Tree had been sung into an oval shape, and the chair-like depressions in the bark all faced inward to the empty heart of the chamber. The *caylaeni* spread out from either side of the *lyaeyni's* seat in descending order of seniority, leaving the position directly opposite Meimniyl for their human guests. Jylkir stood off to the left of the humans, serving as a page for the council meeting, at Ililysiun's suggestion.

Feylobhar stood. As the eldest amongst them, it was her honor to call the meeting to order. Her face was still smooth, and her eyes still bright, but over the centuries her soft snow-white skin had gained the hint of copper that revealed her age. "Let us voice the knowledge of our minds and the truth in our hearts," she intoned. "Who will speak first?"

Meimniyl waved away her right to make the initial address to the *cayl*, and Ililysiun's voice entered the awaiting silence. "It was my understanding that we had agreed to leave the humans to themselves," she said. Her emotion was plain in the quaver of her speech, plainer still since she had spoken out of turn. The elder *caylaeni* looked in disapproval at their youngest member. Though not strictly forbidden, it was custom for age to precede youth.

Ililysiun met their stares with some degree of trepidation, but there was no apology in her eyes. Jylkir admired her for her strength and bravery, although she was alarmed by her lack of caution in such a delicate matter.

"You should understand your place in this council," shot back Hlemyrae, jabbing a finger like a nocked arrow across the room. "Keep your place!"

Niealihu shifted in her seat next to Du'uwneyyl, giving Hlemyrae a sharp look. "Her words were hasty, but she at least kept a civil tongue," she admonished. "And, I must admit, her question is valid. I, too, thought this matter decided. Let the humans do as they will. We owe nothing to either side."

Chastised, Hlemyrae remained silent, but Ryaleyr was quick to weigh in. "The question is not what we owe them, my sisters, but what they owe us. These humans," she said, indicating Lombarde and the Macc prince, "can help us reclaim that debt."

"What is this debt you speak of, Ryaleyr?" Ililysiun turned to the *caylaeni* at her left, gesturing with empty palms upturned. "What debt would be worth such a war?"

"Dwynleigsh," responded Ryaleyr calmly. "Dwynleigsh and Meyr ga'Glyleyn."

"They only took what we gave them!" Ililysiun's voice was filled with a rare fire. "Your shallow excuses reveal the depth of your ambitions, Ryaleyr. A war, even a victorious one, will not bring back the past."

"I don't care to re-live the past. I propose to take the present firmly in hand. Not just for ourselves, and not for my so-called ambition, but for the generations of Ceearmyltu to come."

"She speaks truth," agreed Hlemyrae. "We have a duty to the future of our tribe. If we do not stop the humans now, when we have the opportunity, we will cease to exist. Our traditions, our culture, our Sacred Grove – all of it gone into the pages of history, if any even care to remember us."

"Yes," mused Meimniyl, "but though there is some truth to your words, what of these humans? Why trust them any more than we trust the others?"

Ruoughn's face reddened. "How –?"

"If I may answer that, respected *Lyaeyni*," cut in Lombarde with a placating pat on the angered prince's shoulder. "I believe I may explain away your fears and suspicions."

The hair on the back of Jylkir's neck shivered to attention on her skin. Lombarde was a thin man, tall and bronze-skinned, with what passed for handsome traits on a human: angular features, intense dark eyes, and an even smile. Too even. Too controlled. She shared Ililysiun's feelings about this one: *his passion is intense, but his intents are passionless.*

"We come to you out of need, not out of strength," he said. Jylkir noted his legs shift almost imperceptibly. He wanted to stand for his speech, but he knew better than to rise before the *nyrul cayl*. "Malakuur and Maccalah do not have the means to conquer Providayne without you. How many times have we met defeat on the plains of Paerytm or between the steep granite walls of Ten Man Pass? Without your aid, it might well turn out the same. Don't trust us because we say you should, trust us because we need you more than you need us."

"Allies of the moment. Friends of opportunity." Feylobhar said the words with disgust. "These are not reasons to give our trust. What of the aftermath? You will not need us after your war. What's to prevent you from making us your enemy as suddenly as you now call us friend? Your masters in Malakuur have never been much for keeping their word before."

"I cannot answer for our past, respected *caylaeni*, only for our present. But let me remind you that as a nation, Malakuur has never made war upon the Ceearmyltu, only on your human neighbors. Can Providayne make the same claim? We want nothing more than what was taken from us, much like you.

"As I have said before, our animosity for Providayne does not stem from envy or greed, but simple justice. The lands north of the Caerwood were once those of Old Maccalah, of both our peoples –" Lombarde tightened his grip on Prince Ruoughn's shoulder in a show of unity "– just as Dwynleigsh and the northern wood were yours. Why not send these descendants of the Dacadian usurpers back to the coast from whence they came? Why not let things be as they once were?"

"As they once were?" scoffed Ililysiun. "How far in the past shall we go? Perhaps to the days when you cowered under the heel of the Old Foe? Or maybe to the days of Cachaillan and Lalc Malcha, when it was both your peoples who slowly ate away at our lands through treaty and trickery?"

"Be still, young one," said Hlemyrae with mocking sweetness. "You overstate your objections, as usual."

"No," disagreed Feylobhar with a slow shake of her head. "She *under*states it. I remember the exodus from Dwynleigsh, and the butchery of the Blood Wars, and the desperate treaties with the Maccs of old. The *ylohim* drank deep of your kinsmen's blood, but even this was not enough. Still you came. I remember turning even the *ilyela* to murder, and so deep were they in the lust of the bloodsong – may it remain forever unsung – that we near lost them to the Dark, forever. These were sad times. What reason have we to think it will be any different now?"

The bloodsong. Jylkir shuddered. *May it remain forever unsung*, she agreed.

Ryaleyr raised her thin arm, bowing slightly across the empty room at her elder. "With the greatest of respect, venerable one, I must point out that in the past we made war upon our sister tribes as well, while now this would be unthinkable. We must accept that change is possible, even for the likes of humans. Regardless, the monarchs of Providayne have given us no reason to show them any greater deference than these Maccs. If we must choose between our enemies, why not choose those best able to further our own needs?"

"Your words are not entirely unreasonable, Ryaleyr," said Niealihu, "but Ililysiun's concerns are not yet addressed. What do we gain from this alliance if we are victorious?"

"Yes, ambassador. What indeed?" asked Meimniyl.

Lombarde smiled, an action that caused Jylkir's muscles to tense. She knew what he would say even before his lips parted to seep the words. Like a well-executed feint, he would dangle a fruit impossible to resist, one so tempting that it would cloud their reason. It had to be… .

"The city of Dwynleigsh," he said, "will be yours, and the majority of the Caerwood. As the respected *caylaeni* mentioned earlier, it is a debt too long unpaid. We will need only a small portion of what you now call the thinwood for ourselves, and the lands north of the forest."

Jylkir watched the effect the words had on the *cayl*. Meimniyl, Eleulii and Feylobhar all were stunned into open-mouthed shock. Niealihu frowned, as if disbelieving the words she had just heard. Ililysiun's eyes were wide with terror, for she saw that all her flowery protests were now hidden behind the shadow of that one devastating word. Dwynleigsh. The High Blade was composed, as always. Jylkir noted the lack of response on the faces of Ryaleyr and Hlemyrae with great interest. The very absence of surprise told a story all its own.

"And why would you surrender us such a prize?" Niealihu still frowned at the humans, as if trying to sift through their unspoken thoughts.

Prince Ruoughn could hold his silence no longer. Brushing off the hand of the Malakuuri ambassador, he spoke. "Why would we want it? That place ne'er brought us anything but ill luck. We want you to take it. We'll be happy enough with Vespa and Leyh. If you want Dwynleigsh so awful terrible, then help us set them out!"

Jylkir almost found the barbarian's rough, uncouth manner refreshing following Lombarde's cloying display of sincerity. But with one look at the Malakuuri's face, still so composed next to the bluster of the prince, she stopped herself short.

Of course, she thought. *How better to seal the edges of their ruse?*

The humans had to know that Lombarde's smooth, diplomatic speeches would leave lingering suspicions. Ruoughn's outburst was counterpoint to Lombarde's well-measured words, more believable because of the perceived honesty in his rashness and ignorance, and thus doubly effective. By convincing the Ceearmyltu that their would-be allies had no interest in Dwynleigsh, it would allay their misgivings about the alliance itself.

"Your promises are empty," Du'uwneyyl said, breaking her long silence. Her cold voice sent a ripple through her fellows, drawing them back to reality. "You ask us to pay in blood for something that isn't yours to give."

"I must beg exception to your words, most respected High Blade," said Lombarde, turning in her direction without pause. "Though you are certainly correct that Dwynleigsh is not ours to give, I must point out that we never proposed to simply give it to you at all, but to reward you with it when we are victorious. I believe our offer is made in good faith. If we claim the day, the prize will be yours. If not, quite frankly, we would owe you no debt."

"We would demand a token of some sort regardless of the war's outcome," stated Ryaleyr. "As an assurance of your good faith."

Lombarde nodded. "You are a shrewd negotiator, respected *caylaeni*. We came prepared for such a request." He drew out a bundle of gold and green cloth from between his legs. "Their Holy Majesties, the Thars of Malakuur, offer you this in recompense for you alliance. Win or lose, it is yours."

"Jylkir," said Meimniyl, her curiosity clearly piqued, "bring it here."

The treesinger stepped over to the Malakuuri ambassador in two swift strides. She took the bundle, feeling its weight and thickness in her hands. It was a tome of some sort, and she could sense the faint disturbance of iiyir at her fingertips. She handed it over to the *lyaeyni* with a sinking dread.

What have these animals stumbled across?

Jylkir heard a startled gasp as the gift was unveiled, then realized with a detached surprise that it was her own. The dark burgundy of the book's leather bindings was etched with an intricate andu'ai glyph of silver-blue that seemed to dance in a swirling pattern before her eyes. A sudden wave of nausea wrenched at her, forcing her to look away. Not only was it a Book of Power, she had little doubt that it was one of the lost andu'ai codices.

"It is called the Lloiuan Codex, I believe," said Lombarde, confirming her fears. "Their Holy Majesties seemed to think it would appeal to you. Apparently it is all but useless to them."

Jylkir was no proper mage, but, like all the Ceearmyltu and probably all of the Seven Tribes, she could recite the legends about the codices from memory. Of all these tales, those surrounding the Lloiuan Codex figured most prominently. It was the greatest gift of mighty Thuoringil, the andu'ai *qal* who had taught the Seven Tribes the true depth and meaning of magic as well as the science of reading the iiyir tides. And this book, his legacy, lost hundreds of years gone even as their freedom from Anduoun was gained, held spells and secrets unknown and undisturbed for centuries. It alone was worth more than any war could possibly cost. Jylkir's blood raged, an icy thunder in her heart. This was a gift that could not be refused, and Lombarde and his masters knew it as well as she.

Meimniyl's fingers trembled as they caressed the Codex. "A worthy gift, ambassador. And while we thank you both for your presence, you'll understand if we ask some time to consider your offer. Alone."

"Of course," answered Lombarde. "We will await your decision with high hopes."

"Jylkir," commanded the *lyaeyni*, "please see them out."

The treesinger nodded. "As you wish."

What is your game, Malakuuri? thought Jylkir as she escorted the humans from the Great Tree. She knew they meant betrayal. There was no other motive that could explain their foolhardy generosity.

She was only left to wonder how.

Chapter Thirty-Five

Day for Knights

Captain Vaujn was pleasantly surprised by Saint Kaissus Field. The aulden had never been known as architects, certainly not of the same caliber as his own race. They were creatures of the wilderness, nurturers and caretakers rather than builders, and constructs of rigid stone and harvested lumber were anathema to them. But this place might be an exception to that rule. It took a moment to adjust to the fact that the structure was wood, and *living* wood, no less, but once he got past that, its engineering was fascinating.

At first glance, he almost mistook the walls and roof for fitted timbers of some sort, albeit seamlessly crafted. On closer examination, however, he could see no evidence of artificial fastenings whatsoever. There were no nails, screws, or socket-bolts, no support lattices or fitted joints, nothing but a graceful unblemished curve of natural wood.

Ilyela *trees*, he thought, *songwood*. Molded by the voices and spells of aulden treesingers to take almost any form imaginable, much the same as the rock of mountain could be coaxed to do the bidding of those kin blessed with the Gift, like Chloe. He'd heard stories of the old aulden tree cities, like Dwynleigsh itself had once been, but he'd never seen any piece of them.

At their base, each tree had a girth of about six hetahrs, or twenty *feet*, in that infuriatingly inconsistent human standard of measurement. As they reached skyward, they bent in a convex arc, narrowing and twisting together to form the leafy roof overhead. It looked as if several gigantic hands of wood were sprouting from the earth, palms inward, with fingers entwined. There were smaller branches weaving between each sister tree, bridging the invisible gaps in braidworks so tight that sunlight could only filter through the foliage high overhead. Any other material would have required a much different scheme of support to be viable, especially at this scale – he estimated the Field to be at least one hundred eighty hetahrs in length, and at least half that in width – but the *ilyela* provided more resilience than stone and considerably more strength than normal wood. Vaujn still preferred stone, aesthetically and structurally, but he could see that this *ilyela* definitely had its own practical application.

The effect of this living canopy was an odd combination of feeling both safely enclosed and exposed to the elements. He shuddered as he watched the ant-like figures that crawled through the overhanging latticework, tending to the dangling multicolored glowlamps scattered above. Symmlrey was up there somewhere, watching like a hawk from her nest. For his own part, he would've gladly stayed within the hollow halls that honeycombed the massive wall of trunks, except for the entertaining show of arms to be seen below.

The vantage point of the royal pavilion was, not surprisingly, the best of the venue. It was at the oval Field's midpoint, and raised several hetahrs to maximize the view. The canopy, chairs, tables and sideboards had all been sung directly from the walls by some long-vanished treesinger, along with passageways leading back to a sitting room where guests could retreat to escape the noisy spectacle below. He leaned against the railing, staring out as the turf was smoothed and groomed for the next bout by a team of eight groundskeepers.

"Sir Artygalle is up next," he heard Sir Calvraign mention from over his shoulder.

Vaujn had found the boy a good sort, capable of intelligent conversation, unassuming, and the only other person in the pavilion *not* invited to the heated and private conversation that occupied Osrith and the others. The king, his son Hiruld, the wizard, the Lady Aeolil and the grizzled old Vanelorn were all engaged in a muted but intense discussion. Vaujn doubted if any of them had watched more than a fleeting moment of the tourney so far. Aside from the guards, it was just him and the boy.

"Friend of yours, is he?" Vaujn asked.

"Yes. But not of the oddsmakers, by the looks of it."

Vaujn watched as several men made their way about the perimeter of the crowd, holding up placards with the odds for the match. If his reading of the human runes was up to snuff, it looked as if the knight in question was in the hole, ten to one against. Vaujn's right hand twitched toward his belt pouch, but he restrained the move. He knew his wife was scrying on him, and he didn't want to explain how he'd gambled away their meager traveling funds on a whim.

With a sigh of resignation, the kinsman turned toward the young man. "Are you betting on him, then?"

Calvraign nodded. "A bit."

"So he's quite the lancer I suppose, eh?"

"I don't really know," answered Calvraign. "I've never seen him joust before. But he is my friend, so I thought I should back him."

"At ten to one, he must be a *good* friend."

Calvraign laughed, a sound that came easily and often from the boy. "Good enough, I guess."

Artygalle and his opponent, Sir Guir of Praed, took their positions at opposite ends of the field. Vaujn could see straight away why the oddsmakers favored the latter knight. Though his appearance in the Opening Melee meant he was not one of the elite knights of the realm, he was definitely the beneficiary of a wealthy patron. His armor was ornate and well-worked by human standards, and his horse and person were decked out in well-tailored finery. Sir Guir's squire trotted before his mounted master, waving a pennant that mirrored the device on his tabard – three copper sea horses rampant on a field of light blue.

By contrast, Calvraign's friend was at the poorer end of things, not to mention a little worse for wear. His armor seemed well worn and sturdy, but ill fitted to his frame. His tabard, with its three scarlet bears, matched neither the owl device on his shield nor the pennant carried by his dark-skinned squire. Vaujn tried to make out some sort of design on the pennant but, as far as he could tell, it was just a long streamer of ratty brown cloth.

He looked over at Calvraign skeptically, but the boy just shrugged.

The marshal of the field approached the royal pavilion to formally announce the combatants. "At the eastern quarter, I present the honorable Sir Guir of Praed, appointed heir of House Réneuhl of the Grand Duchy of Aeyrdyn and formerly squire to that city's champion, Sir Mellieux."

A loud burst of applause erupted from the common seating around the Aerydii pavilion to their left, and the grand duke himself lifted a hand in salute to his vassal. The middle-aged ruler seemed interested but unconcerned with the match-up below.

There was a pause while the commotion died down. "And at the western quarter," continued the marshal of the field in an equally passionless tone, "Sir Artygalle of Tiriel, Knight Lancer in the Order of Andulin and formerly squire to His Departed Grace, Knight Lieutenant General Ghaerieal of the Order of Andulin."

Calvraign began whooping and clapping like a commoner, which seemed appropriate considering the only other welcome the knight received was a smattering of applause from the lowborn seating and the ecclesiastical pavilion across the way.

That's it, Vaujn decided. *I like this boy for certain sure, now.*

It took either bravery or stupidity to place friendship before the airs and affectations of others, especially those of such esteemed rank and prestige that were frowning at them from all sides, and Calvraign didn't strike the stout kinsman as stupid. *Naïve, perhaps – but not stupid.* Where the boy might be lacking worldliness, instead of sniping from a concealing cloak of cynicism or hiding behind the trappings of political discretion, he wore his innocence like a crown, for all to see. Therein lay his appeal.

Vaujn joined him in a full-bellied roar of support, shouting out a traditional kin battle cry, "Verklämme Artygalle! Verklämme im mahr!"

That got their attention! He chuckled to himself and grinned mischievously up at Calvraign, who looked almost as shocked as the rest of the pavilion's occupants. Vaujn looked across at the equally surprised grand duke and his courtiers and waved cheerily at their dumbfounded stares.

Both knights raised their lances to salute the royal pavilion, and then squared themselves for the coming charge. Vaujn sensed a looming presence behind him and tensed, then relaxed as he recognized the gruff voice.

"Did you forget our little talk in the keep already?" Osrith gritted out between his clenched teeth.

"Refresh my memory," answered Vaujn, his eyes never leaving the field. The marshal dropped his white flag, and the knights spurred their horses into a thundering charge. Vaujn had never seen jousting before today, and it amazed him. Just calculating the amount of force that each lance tip carried to its point of impact, factoring in the mass of the horse, knight and armor and the speed they hurtled at each other, it was a wonder there weren't more deaths, even with the blunted tips of this friendly tourney.

"Our talk about not drawing attention to yourself? About the differences between an underkin hall and the royal cour –"

The crash of impact cut off the rest of Osrith's sentence, and Vaujn whistled appreciatively. "Looks like the oddsmakers were wrong, after all."

"That was a solid strike," added Osrith. "Good grip with his knees, kept his balance steady, used the horse instead of his arm strength to deliver the blow. That's how it should be done."

Vaujn nudged Calvraign. "Even faint praise is hard earned from him, boy. Looks like your friend might be worth betting on again."

Calvraign opened his mouth to respond, but Osrith was quicker. "Don't be too impressed, now. This is the Opening Melee. Working your way through a bunch of green wood isn't like chopping down a stand of hardened oak."

At least half of the arena's occupants still looked on in a hushed silence, but Artygalle's scattered supporters were cheering enthusiastically. Sir Guir was picking himself up from the ground unsteadily, obviously still dizzy from the blow he'd absorbed. Artygalle brought his steed around to Guir's side of the list to offer assistance to his vanquished opponent.

"That's a first," commented Vaujn.

"He's a lancer," explained Calvraign, "a knight of the Holy Church."

"I'll try not to hold that against him," Osrith mumbled.

"Oh," Vaujn said, as if satisfied by Calvraign's answer. In reality, he was a little confused at how humans separated their religious life from their everyday existence. In the Underkingdom, one kin was as much a *knight of the church* as the next, because they all carried the spirit of Rondainaken in their hearts. Chaplains like Mother Chloe served as spiritual guides, but they weren't held to standards different from any other kin. He shrugged it off. *Humans will be humans*, as his grandfather used to say.

Artygalle made his way to each of the five major pavilions, saluting the lords and ladies within as was customary. Last and longest of the salutes was to the royal pavilion, but instead of returning to his quarter to face the next challenger, he raced Windthane around the perimeter of the stands at a full gallop, holding his lance out in a traditional salute. This was met with more cheers from the lowborn, and conspicuous silence from the nobles in their pavilions.

"What's he doing?" cried out Lady Aeolil.

Vaujn was surprised she'd even been paying attention, as engrossed as she'd been in her parlay with the king and wizard.

"Sir Artygalle just won his first round," said Calvraign, his voice still showing his excitement.

"Yes, I saw that," she said impatiently, "I mean what is he doing *now*?"

"Showing off," suggested Osrith.

"No," Calvraign protested, giving Osrith a frustrated glare, "he's not the sort. I think he's just hailing the crowd."

Aeolil frowned, watching the display with obvious displeasure. "He'd better not do any damage to my horse," she grumbled.

Something about that amused Osrith, and he broke out into a rare chuckle.

"I wouldn't worry," said Prince Hiruld, his attention following Aeolil's. "He's a fine rider, from the looks of it."

Vaujn didn't know anything about horses, much less riding them, but he took the prince's word on faith. No one else disagreed with Hiruld either, but Vaujn wasn't sure if that had more to do with rank than truth.

The hours passed, and the victors of each match rotated in round-robin fashion until only two of their number remained undefeated. By this final round, the whole of Saint Kaissus Field was alive with cheers and chants, from the typically reserved nobles and clergymen of the pavilions to the boisterous peasants and middle-classed in the common seats. Even the archbishop was on his feet, along with some of the bishops of the Holy Quorum, all beaming at one of the last two knights below them. Sir Artygalle had made an impressive and almost effortless show of unhorsing opponent after opponent, much to the great pleasure of Calvraign – and the substantial betterment of his purse.

The king's attention was also on the field. "What do you know of this Sir William, Agrylon?"

"Nothing at all, Your Majesty," the wizard admitted.

"Vanelorn?" the king persisted. "Hiruld?"

It was the lord high marshal who answered. "Sir William is the Sheriff of Bettleshire, a vassal of House Vespurial. He has always been a fine and loyal subject, but this is his first time in the lists, I believe."

"He seems fair enough with the lance. What odds do you give him against this boy of Renarre's?"

Vaujn could tell Calvraign didn't care for that characterization of Artygalle, but he had the good sense not to say anything to the king. Or maybe it was Osrith's good sense, he reconsidered, belatedly noticing the *Shaddach Chi's* hand on Calvraign's arm.

"I would say the oddsmakers have finally gotten it right, Your Majesty." Vanelorn pointed down at the placards as they were toted around the extent of the field. "They are evenly matched, or close enough. William, I think, has better shield work, but this Artygalle can *ride*, Your Majesty, like none I've seen in years – save perhaps Garath or Stuart."

The king made a musing grumble in his throat. "Well, let's hope he has Oghran's luck as well as good shield work, then."

Vaujn poked Osrith in the ribs. "So why are they so fired up about this? I gather the king has a grudge or some such with that archbishop over there."

"Yeah," agreed Osrith. "There's that. And this whole saluting the crowd business isn't sitting too well with the blue bloods either."

"What do they care if he salutes the crowd?"

Osrith scowled. "It's not *seemly*. Don't want the lesser folk to feel too important now, do we?"

"Why not?"

"That's just the way they like it. Keep the commoners common, and you don't get trouble like the Maeziir Kings had a while back."

Vaujn wondered if Osrith was stringing him along like this on purpose, or if he just didn't know how to have a normal conversation. "What trouble did the Maeziir Kings have?"

"Well, they don't have *any* troubles now, if you catch my meaning. I don't suppose you ever heard of the Merchant Revolution in the Underkingdom? Mazod's ruled by the Council of Regents now. No king. No nobles. Just merchants. Not like it works any better, from what I could tell."

Vaujn was glad when the marshal of the field began with his introductions for the final match of the day. He'd had his fill of bad human beer, strange human politics, and even the novelty of human mounted combat was wearing off. Besides, he was getting hungry, and the little trays of sweets and meat pies had long since been devoured.

The rustlings and rumblings of the spectators subsided into a reverent sort of silence as the knights squared and saluted each other. The light filtering through the leaves overhead had thinned as afternoon wore on, and massive fire pits now provided much of the arena's light, as well as heat. Overhead, the glowlamps glittered like stars.

There was the briefest of pauses as shields were readied and squires hurried away, and then the combatants kicked their mounts forward into a charge. The horses churned up the beaten turf in a thick spray of mud and clay behind them, the knights brought their lances to bear, and then there was the now familiar crash of shield and lance.

Artygalle lurched in the saddle, his body sliding off to the right as his left foot came free of the stirrup. The audience sprang to its collective feet regardless of station. Vaujn waited for the young knight to make the inevitable final fall from his horse, but the moment never came.

Artygalle discarded his shattered lance and clung precariously to Windthane's neck and saddle horn, his wayward left foot catching on the beast's rump to secure his balance. With a loud grunt, Artygalle righted himself and rode back to his quarter. He was slumped over, and obviously favoring his shield arm, but he had not lost his seat. Neither had William, and though his lance had also shattered, he looked to have sustained no injury.

"Does either party wish to concede the match?" asked the marshal of the field.

Sir William reared his horse and nosed it over to his squire, already waiting with a fresh lance. "I do not!" he yelled clearly.

Artygalle steadied himself on Windthane's proud neck with his good arm as his squire attempted to adjust his badly dented shield. The metal was bent inward just below the painted owl beak, and his squire seemed increasingly distressed as he worked to mend it. A low murmuring began when there was no immediate answer. After a few tense, silent moments, Artygalle motioned his squire to the lance rack.

"I will not yield!" he yelled.

Vaujn hoped the strength of his conviction was greater than that of his voice.

"Well, you were right about his riding, Vanelorn," said the king, with some relief, "but I think he's through, now."

"Aye," agreed the lord high marshal, "that shield is biting into his arm. Likely as not it's broken."

The crowd hushed again as the knights prepared for their second run.

"So, do you think he's had it, too, Osrith?" Vaujn whispered to the *Shaddach Chi*.

"Hardly. If that last blow didn't knock him on his ass I don't know what would. And Sir Willy there is a bit too impressed with himself. He'll choke."

"I never thought I'd hear *you* being optimistic," Aeolil said with a smile, "let alone cheer for a lancer. And now, both in one afternoon!"

Osrith's only response was a humorless glower. The flag dropped, and the charge began anew.

Calvraign clutched at the rail. "He can't even hold up his lance – he's done for!"

"He'll bring it to bear when he has to," Osrith said. "He's tired and hurt. He's just saving his strength."

Osrith's words were borne out a few ticks later, as Artygalle hoisted his lance into striking ready just before contact with Sir William. Artygalle's shield received another blast, and his arm flew back as he tried to absorb the blow. His own lance shattered on William's shield, which in turn slid up to strike a glancing blow to William's great helm. Artygalle gripped hard at Windthane's flanks with his knees, and he kept to the saddle.

Sir William's lance had fallen, and he rode on past the end of the low, long list, his head on his chin. As Sir William's horse slowed to a stop, the knight slumped over and slid from the saddle. He landed on his shoulder, and then crumpled over to lie motionless, face down in the mud.

"Out before he hit the ground," said Osrith.

There was no series of salutes or charging about the arena from Artygalle this time. He dismounted with the aid of his squire and fell to his knees, resting the remainder of his weight on his good arm. He made the sign of the moon on his breast, even as his devotees cheered him in victory, and waited for the physics to come take him away. He would have to receive his respects from a sick bed, from the looks of it.

Vaujn glanced over at Calvraign, cheering with the best of them, then across at the feral smile of triumph on the distant face of the archbishop. The mood behind him was somewhat less ecstatic.

"Now we have to feed this lot," Guillaume complained. "Are you ready, Hiruld?"

"Aye, father," answered the prince. Hiruld stood and stretched, then moved up to the railing. Osrith pulled Vaujn and Calvraign back as Inulf and the Prince's Guard flanked their charge. Hiruld cleared his throat, and then shouted, "All hail Sir Artygalle of Tiriel, Champion of the Opening Melee! We shall see him further test his mettle in the King's Joust. For now, let the Feast of Prince's Bread commence!"

Vaujn felt a stirring in his belly. He liked the sound of that.

Chapter Thirty-Six

Keeping Places

SETH wiped the gathering sweat from his forehead and paused for a moment from his work. They had made good progress for a half-day's worth of labor, but given what still lay ahead, it hardly seemed enough. He couldn't fault the girls, who had worked hard and without complaint, though he didn't expect the same consideration from Burton. There would be no excuses for anything less than perfect. Not for him. Seth felt unreasoning panic grabbing hold of him for the second time in the last ten clicks.

Just keep working, he told himself, polishing a dressing table as if it were the only thing in his world, enraptured by the depth and color brought to the faded and long-neglected wood by his oiled cloth.

Iaede and Braede were still busy putting away the belongings from Lord Malminnion's many trunks. It was clear they'd been through the ritual of packing and unpacking his things many times. They went through the motions unconsciously, moving a little slower than an hour before, and slower still than the hour before that, but it remained a steady pace. Deirdre was still occupied with the larder, securing as much in the way of potable water and fresh victuals as she could pilfer from the kitchens. Seth had decided she'd have better luck than he. Dar had a well-known weakness for pretty young girls, and what Seth couldn't obtain legitimately himself, he was sure Deirdre could flirt out of him.

As for the nameless girl, she had taken it upon herself to fill in for the errant porter, carrying in loads of coal and peat after the firewood had been sufficiently stocked, and then making several trips to the well for fresh water. She was off to the cellars now, to find a barrel of spiritless cider for the rather conservative tastes of the elder Malminnion. Unlike Garath, Ezriel was well known for his abstinence from worldly pleasures, whether of the flesh, the pipe, or the goblet.

Seth finished with the dressing table and took a walk through the suite to survey their progress. *Stop worrying*, he told himself. *Everything of any importance is done already. It's just the little things, now.*

Seth found a little peace in that revelation, but he still felt anxious. His thoughts kept drifting back to that girl. He even found the accumulating grit on her flushed cheeks attractive. Worse yet, he still didn't know her name. Why he couldn't bring himself to ask, he wasn't sure, other than nerves, but he felt his crush increasingly obvious when he called each of the other girls by name, while she remained only an ambiguous *you*.

A trumpet blast, high and clear, interrupted his thoughts.

"They're on their way back," Seth said with a calm he certainly didn't feel. "Let's do our best to finish up. We've twenty clicks, perhaps thirty, before they reach the Bridge House Gate."

Seth went to the window in the sitting room, which overlooked the bailey, to see if there was any evidence of the procession returning from Saint Kaissus Field. He knew it was early for any glimpse of them, but his frazzled nerves demanded that he look. Seth peered out the thin glass of the window that, like all of the fae glass left over from the aulden, never fogged, despite the weather.

He nearly gasped aloud in alarm.

Seth calmed himself an instant later, realizing the column of knights was not one of the royal or noble parties returning from the festivities. They were Border Knights, about two dozen of them by his count, led by someone in the livery of the Crown Prince's Guard. That stood to reason. One could never be too careful, especially not lately, and moving some of the Border Knights from Saint Severun's to King's Keep made sense to him. Most importantly, it meant he still had time to put the finishing touches on Lord Malminnion's quarters.

"Where should I put it?"

Seth whirled to see the nameless girl, somewhat bent over from the weight of the cider barrel balanced on her back, standing patiently in the doorway. Quite suddenly, he felt conspicuously empty-handed.

"In the larder, here," he said, leading the way at a brisker pace than he'd really intended. His body seemed intent on making up for his momentary distraction with or without his conscious consent. "Right here," he said, helping her set it down.

"Ach," moaned the girl, rubbing at her lower back and making a face somewhere between a grin and a grimace. "I'd never guess *one* man could need so much!"

Seth looked about with quick little motions of his head and brought his finger to his lips. "Hush, or you'll get yourself in a right lot of trouble. A sharp wit can be more dangerous than a sharp blade, or something of the like. That's what Burton's always saying. Best to keep your place, if you don't want to lose it."

"I might be on borrowed ground," she replied smugly, "but ma skin's ma skin and ma words are ma words."

Seth found her petulance a little disturbing. He'd seen more than a few with similarly smart mouths wear the scars of their punishment the rest of their lives. He had no wish to see her soft flesh all bloody and laid open at the whipping post, or her tongue split for gossip and insubordination. "Maybe so," he said quietly, adopting his most serious and concerned expression, "but the whip won't much care who *owns* your skin when they flay it off of you."

If that image disturbed her at all, she made no outward show of it. "I know what a beating feels like, if that's what's worrying you. Anyway, it's not what you say as much as who you say it to. Unless *you're* doling out the lashes."

"Of course not!" he protested. The other girls looked over from their work, but he sent them right back to it with an irritated glance. The blood was pounding hotly behind his cheeks. "Just watch your mouth. I wouldn't want to be at-"

"This one giving you trouble?"

Seth didn't recognize the voice, but the tone was a familiar one. He pivoted smartly on his heel and found, more to his dread than surprise, Lord Ezriel Malminnion standing in the doorway. *He must've come in with those knights, if not before*, thought Seth. It had been some time since Seth had seen him, but he was a memorable figure.

Ezriel's face was lean and distinctive rather than handsome, but the contrast between his blue eyes and his long shining locks of shock-white hair was striking. His thin-lipped mouth was a flat, stern line, surrounded by an immaculately groomed jet-black goatee. He wasn't in his house colors, but rather the black and silver of the Order of the Star, of which he was the knight lieutenant general, and thus its highest-ranking member. As Seth heard it, only the archbishop and Knight Captain General Tuoerval had more influence in the Holy Quorum. He'd heard even more stories of his exacting perfectionism, and the penalties for falling short of his expectations. His discipline might not be called cruel, but it was certainly severe.

Seth tried not to wither under that stark and demanding gaze and the punishments he imagined it promised, for himself *or* the nameless girl. "Your Grace," he said, bending deeply at the waist and holding his bow for a full three ticks. "No trouble at all, sir. Castellan Burton asked me to make arrangements for your stay. I hope everything will meet with your approval. I was not expecting you quite so early."

"I have little patience for feasts," dismissed Ezriel. He entered the chamber, examining it in what Seth thought a deceptively casual appraisal. The other servants stood well out of his way, heads bowed. He stopped just short of Seth, looking down on him with unmasked authority. "She is a stubborn girl, like all her kind. Obstinate. Prideful. I have warned her once already to mend her ways."

"She worked quite hard, Your Grace," insisted Seth, trying hard to sound disinterested rather than defensive. For her part, the girl was at least pretending to be well-heeled. He hoped she had the good sense to stay that way for a while. "They all did, sir. You run a very orderly household. It was a pleasure working with them."

Ezriel studied him for a long moment before turning away and proceeding into his private bedchamber. "I'll be sure to let the castellan know of your efforts," he said at the door, "and you will be held accountable, accordingly."

The door shut with a firm click, punctuating Lord Malminnion's promise. The casual manner of the statement was more disconcerting than the words, despite the potential grief from Burton they threatened. Ezriel could have been discussing a turn in the weather for all the emotion in his voice.

It was that very *lack* in his voice that made Seth further appreciate his role in the grand scheme of things. He was a mote of dust, drifting about the heels of those like Ezriel, trying to avoid a chance encounter with the heavy and merciless toe of his boot, however wayward that crushing tread might prove.

"Thank you," the girl whispered, as if they might be overheard even now. She squeezed his hand.

"I'd best get along, myself," Seth said, his palms sweating. "I have other duties to see to today."

"Aye," she said, and moved away, heading toward the sitting room where her fellow servants had already adjourned to await the beckons of their master.

"Wait," said Seth, and she stopped halfway there, twisting to look at him over her shoulder. He gathered his courage, and after a quick swallow, managed a quiet, "What's your name?"

She smiled again, and her eyes glittered darkly in the flickering firelight. "Callagh," she said, "Callagh Breigh."

Chapter Thirty-Seven

A Friendly Toast

CALVRAIGN could see that these dark under-levels of Saint Kaissus Field provided Captain Vaujn with some sort of comfort. The stiffness in the kinsman's neck had slackened, and his breathing was more even and steady. Every once in a while, Vaujn's nostrils would flare, sucking in scents that Calvraign would've thought better left alone. Even so, he appreciated the company of his new friend. He could count the hours he'd known the stocky fellow on the fingers of one hand, or close enough, but he felt a sort of trust growing between himself and Vaujn, and even, to a smaller extent, with the hardened Osrith.

The under-levels were still in quite a commotion. Squires and stable hands were now emptying the underground stables and staging area where knights had awaited their turn in the combat above. Thankfully, a light breeze blew through the corridors of packed dirt, keeping the stench of sweat, oil and horse manure from settling too thickly in the air. As in the construction above, the wood of the supports looked like it was part of a living tree, a dense network of roots bearing the weight of the surrounding dirt.

Vaujn grabbed the arm of a young page who was hurrying past. "Hey, where're the wounded at?" Though phrased as a question, there was no doubt in anyone's mind that this was a command.

The boy's eyes shot wide open, and it looked like he might bolt before he finally spoke. "Just down there, sir," he said somewhat weakly, "and take a right."

Vaujn nodded a silent thanks, and the boy scurried off.

They found the wounded right where the page had said, a half dozen men either immobilized by their injuries or without the luxury of a personal physic. Artygalle fell into both categories, and lay on a straw pallet in the back of the room. His squire sat nervously by his side, standing guard over his master's discarded armor and sword. Calvraign marched purposefully toward his friend, doing his best to ignore the soft moans of pain coming from the other nondescript inhabitants of the small room. Broken limbs seemed the most common casualty of the joust, along with a bandaged head or two, but it didn't appear that any of those here were in any life-threatening danger.

"How fares the champion of the day?" Calvraign said with a wide unabashed smile.

Artygalle looked up, surprised, and struggled to raise himself on his good arm. "Calvraign!" he said, but words failed him when he saw the kinsman at his side.

"This is Captain Vaujn," supplied Calvraign, "from the Underkingdoms."

"An honor, Captain," said Artygalle, immediately attempting to rise.

Vaujn shrugged and nodded with a tolerant half-smile, uncomfortable with the attention. "Don't get up, by the All-father," he chastised, and gently restrained the knight. "The honor's all mine, anyway. If I ever get up on a horse and hit someone with a pole, I'd want to do it like you. Well fought."

Artygalle cast his eyes downward, and his cheeks regained a little color. "As the Goddess wills."

"I think she'd be willing to share the credit, at least!" Calvraign laughed.

"Aye, after all, it's *your* arm in the sling, eh?" agreed Vaujn.

Artygalle proffered a weak smile in response, but said nothing.

"Have you seen the surgeon yet?" asked Calvraign, looking at the bandaged arm speculatively. There was some blood seeping through the dressing, presumably where the damaged shield had dug into his arm, but it didn't appear broken.

"Only a physic so far, and he said I could wait."

Vaujn looked around the room at the other injured men, then up at Calvraign pointedly. "I don't see that Guir fellow here, or Sir William, and they both took a walloping. Is this the sort of preference the champion of the day receives from the king?"

Calvraign shrugged, angry and confused. He expected such stupidity and nonsense from rival Houses, but not from Guillaume. "It must be a mistake," he said, trying to sound as if he believed it himself. "We'll get you to the King's Surgeon himself, straight away."

Calvraign and Vaujn bent down to help the knight up, but Artygalle waved them away. "And what about these men?" he asked. "Who will tend to them?"

Calvraign stopped, his lips working silently on an explanation that didn't come. Vaujn hardly paused, dragging Artygalle up into a sitting position by his good arm. "Nice sentiment there, sir, but *they* don't have to fight again anytime soon. We'll send somebody down to check on them, but they'll keep. Now get up."

Artygalle got up to his feet with a wince and steadied himself on Calvraign's ready shoulder. Vaujn was now preoccupied with the armor and shield next to the pallet, running his fingers over the metal in an expert caress.

"I think this armor's in worse shape than you," he decided.

"We'll both manage," said Artygalle, defensive but not quite angry.

Vaujn wasn't paying him any attention, however. "Bring this along," he told the waiting squire, pointing at the armor.

The squire looked to his master.

"It's all right, Inoval, do as he says," confirmed Artygalle, though he didn't seem all that certain himself.

They made their way up through the under-levels, moving at a relatively slow pace. Though putting up a noble show of it, Artygalle had lost a lot of blood, and anything more would have risked him passing out. Calvraign took most of the knight's weight on himself, and Vaujn had wrestled most of the armor from Inoval, shouldering the burden without much apparent bother.

Calvraign wondered how the kinsman made himself so at home in such an alien environment. Whatever adjustments he himself had made to life in Dwynleigsh, it had to be much harder for the kinsman. Language, environment, custom and appearance were all foreign here, not to mention the political make-up of the capital. Vaujn just seemed to slice through it all, and though he might raise eyebrows, it didn't appear that he had raised any hackles.

The surface of Saint Kaissus Field was mayhem, a din of roars and shouts and songs that, when taken as a whole, resembled nothing more than a great waterfall of incoherent noise crashing on the witless ears of those who dared listen. The glowlamps above and the fire pits all around cast flickering shadows with abandon, dancing with beings of actual flesh as if they were one and the same. Men and women were running to and fro amidst the mob, bearing trays of food and drink to the hundreds gathered around.

"It's worse than when we left it!" Vaujn complained to whoever would listen.

"It's barely started, sir," Inoval shouted. "The festivities will last much longer than the food and drink."

Vaujn grabbed a small roasted bird from a tray as it whisked by them. "And why do they go to all this bother, again?"

"Tradition," explained Calvraign. "During the Civil War, a famine threatened the Midwinter Feast. King Argys' son Malaín distributed food and drink from his personal stores. The practice persisted long after the war, and it's become a show of thanks of sorts for all of His Majesty's subjects."

"Sounds expensive," said Vaujn, halfway through his snack.

"I'm sure it is, but it's not as if they feed the whole city anymore. Brohan said the privilege is decided by lottery now." Calvraign ducked a flying bone. "Still, there're several hundred here, at least."

"You should all stay and have your share," suggested Artygalle. "I'm not so terribly hurt as you're making out. I can find my way back to Saint Severun's with Inoval's help."

"Don't be daft!" admonished Calvraign cheerily. "There'll be food aplenty at the keep. Besides which, we'll have the honor of dining with today's champion!"

"As you wish," relented Artygalle, his eyelids sagging even as he spoke. He was obviously too tired to argue.

"May I make a suggestion, sirs?"

All eyes turned to the nervous young squire.

"Of course, Inoval," Artygalle said, smiling. "What is it?"

"Once we're outside the Field, we could rent a carriage. It would take us at least as far as the Harbor Gate, and be much less tiring for my master."

Everyone considered that to be a splendid idea, and once they'd escaped the rapidly evolving chaos that was the Feast of Prince's Bread, they did just that. There was a large selection of carriages available, lined up along King's Boulevard in a row of polished wood and brass. Most of the nobles remained within, paying their token respects to the old tradition even while they waited for their own raucous party to follow at King's Keep. The carriage masters clambered down from their seats, in a race for the first highborn customers of the evening, all claiming to have the most luxurious coach at the most reasonable price.

Through all this clamor, one voice rose above the rest, distinguishing itself with the most attractive offer by far. "Here we are, noble sirs, here

A Friendly Toast

we are! Over here! No cost to the Champion of the Day. That's right, over here! Over here, noble sirs!"

They climbed aboard without further ado, and the red-faced old driver greeted them with a gap-toothed smile. "Aye, fine show, that, sir. Well done, indeed! Won a pretty penny, I did, wagerin' on you, sir! Be a crime to charge you a wooden mark, it would! To the Keep, eh? Right then, off we go!"

The carriage was comfortable enough, though the jostling didn't seem a great pleasure for Artygalle. He tried to keep the discomfort to himself, but from the pallor of his face and the squint of his eyes, it was clear enough that he was still in a good deal of pain. The ride was mercifully short, however, and they pulled up to the Harbor Gate without incident. The driver was surprised when, upon viewing the carriage's occupants, the guards waved them through to cross the bridge. This was a rare privilege, and the carriage master mumbled happily to himself the whole way across.

They unloaded at the Bridge House Gate, and after a heated but fruitless attempt to pay the driver, entered King's Keep.

"Shall I send for a litter, sir?" asked one of the guards.

Calvraign started to agree, but Artygalle would have none of that indignity. "I will walk, sir," he said, "but thank you for your kindness."

They crossed the open expanse of the lower bailey, cluttered as it was with the livestock for the upkeep of all the festival guests, and a noticeably larger contingent of knights and men-at-arms. The honor guard of each visiting House had staked out their own separate region of the bailey, some playing at cards or throwing dice with their counterparts, others eyeing the men of other Houses warily.

Calvraign noticed that most any activity stopped as they passed, as attention was abruptly shifted in their direction. Some looked on in friendly curiosity, a few even waved hellos or saluted them, but there were more than a few who watched them with unmasked suspicion.

Crossing through the gate into the middle bailey alleviated some of this attention. It was empty, save for a few stable hands exercising the horses. Artygalle's gaze was drawn to the horses, parading in circles on their tethers while the stable hands clicked and cooed encouragement. Calvraign guessed at the worry in his eyes.

"Aeolil took care of Windthane," he assured his injured friend. "Don't worry yourself."

Artygalle smiled. "So Inoval said. I hope she was not overly put out on my behalf."

Calvraign laughed. "I think it was more on her own behalf. You worried her silly out there. She was pretending not to notice, but I was watching her, and she was beside herself once or twice, at least, worried for her horse."

"Aye," agreed Vaujn, "and you were pretending not to notice her not noticing. That was almost as much fun as the fighting."

Calvraign blushed. "I... I don't know what you mean," he stammered.

"That's okay, I think the rest of us do," Vaujn said.

As the Upper Gate House drew near, a small group of figures came into view, awaiting their arrival. Calvraign knew the reception was for them because the three gathered outside the gatehouse were all underkin. Vaujn's step quickened noticeably.

"Welcome back, Captain," said the first of the kin, and Calvraign was surprised at the melodic timbre of her voice. "Mother Chloe said that you were bringing in injured and we should give you a hand. She'll take care of him upstairs. As for that," she said, pointing at the pile of armor Vaujn carried, and then nodded to her two companions, "Daính and Thruhm will take that off your hands. The forge is already stoked up."

"Thank you, Läzch," Vaujn said, surrendering his portion of Artygalle's armor to one of his waiting soldiers. "How're things here?"

The kinswoman scratched at her cheek. "Not much I know about that, sir. We're just trying to stay out of the way, for the most part."

"Good enough," he said. "Let's get Sir Artygalle here up to Chloe and see what she can do for him. Oh, and this is Calvraign, if Chloe didn't already tell you."

"She did," confirmed Läzch. "Pleased to meet you, sir."

Calvraign was amazed that all of the kin were fluent in Dacadh, and felt a little guilty that he couldn't display equal familiarity with their native language. "The honor is mine, milady," he replied, unsure of what title might be considered proper.

He immediately wished he hadn't attempted to guess, as all the kin broke out into loud fits of laughter.

"Ah, after you, *milady*," Vaujn said, shaking his head.

Calvraign slumped his shoulders and sighed. He had a feeling he wouldn't be forgetting that mistake for some time. He certainly didn't have the opportunity on the rest of the trip to the kin's guest quarters. Vaujn and Läzch made a point of it. Even Artygalle was coaxed into a quick laugh here and there, sending a pained glance of apology to Calvraign for every errant chuckle.

The kin were located several levels lower than Calvraign's own accommodation. It was a position of moderate honor, and probably the best that could be done on such short notice. Calvraign conjured an amusing if completely fictional incident wherein the previous occupant was forcibly relocated to less desirable surroundings in order to give the kin their due respects. If there really had been such an expulsion, it was more likely done with a good deal of grace, aplomb and understanding for the put-out host. But that was much less fun to imagine.

A Friendly Toast

Two kinsmen stood guard outside the chamber door, arms crossed on their armored breasts, necks stiff, and brows stern. They wore their helms, but their face shields were pulled back to glare menacingly at the innocent ceiling.

"Sir!" greeted one of the kin in a deep baritone.

Captain Vaujn nodded to the soldier. "Ouwd," he said, then to the other, "Hæschp. How goes it?"

"All's well, sir," replied the one called Hæschp, knocking a brief pattern on the door before opening it.

Calvraign smiled at the guards as he entered, but they made no indication of noticing. A group of kin was waiting within, playing at a game of cards, and their expressions were less irresolute. Calvraign noted that the room was carefully laid out and organized like a miniature barracks, everything neatly in its place. Vaujn made introductions so fast that Calvraign had to give his full attention to remembering the faces that went with the strange names.

"...Sergeant Mueszner here, my acting lieutenant," he was saying, "and the one scowling over there is Corporal Darrow. Náinh is the smiling one with the winning hand and the corporal's coin. She's Daính's sister – he's the one with Artygalle's armor, remember. And this is Daehl. She's a mean old crone, be careful." Vaujn ducked a flying object with a grin. "And Cuhrbern is the one there about to get me a drink."

Cuhrbern took the hint and moved toward a wooden keg in the small larder as Vaujn turned to the last occupant of the room. "And it is my pleasure, sirs, to introduce my lovely wife and squad chaplain, Mother Chloe."

Calvraign and Artygalle both bowed slightly at the waist, the latter with some support from the former. Inoval stuck to the background, his lips silent but his eyes alert. "It is our pleasure, Mother Chloe," said Calvraign, endeavoring not to repeat his embarrassing mistake with Läzch. "You show us a great kindness."

"Yes," Artygalle agreed. "Thank you for your considerations. I am in your debt."

"Mmm," was the chaplain's rather ambiguous response, but Calvraign could see her attention was not on the etiquette of introduction. She was already leading Artygalle over to a vacant bed. "Let's have a look at you, then."

Vaujn nudged Calvraign over to a long table, where Cuhrbern delivered the captain's requested beverage. "Care for an ale? This is the best excuse we could drag out of the cellars. I'm afraid we're no longer very popular with the wine steward. I think he called Daehl *insufferable* and *rude*. My fault for sending her, I suppose. She's got what you might call *particular* taste when it comes to hops and barley, and she's not shy about expressing herself."

"*I've* got particular taste?" Daehl shot back.

Vaujn waved off her protest. "Anyway," he dismissed, "I figure we've got some time to drain a few tankards while we wait for dinner. Will you join me?"

Calvraign had absolutely no desire for anything remotely alcoholic. Even with most of the day behind him, his body remembered the consequences of the previous night quite clearly. "I don't think... " he saw something in Vaujn's eyes somewhere just short of disappointment, "...one or two will hurt."

"Bring another, Cuhrbern – for our friend," announced Vaujn in triumph. When the drink was delivered, he went on. "So, tell me a bit of yourself."

Despite Vaujn's lackluster description of the beer, it was by far the best that had ever passed Calvraign's lips. He tried to pace himself, but found the liquid flowed almost of its own volition as he spoke, and he'd drained his first about the same time he finished his rather abbreviated and uneventful life story.

"Well, that explains a lot," said Vaujn, motioning for refills. "You've got poise without pretense. I like that."

"Thank you," Calvraign said, pleased with the compliment. But he was all too aware that he was drinking the strong brew much too fast, and that the more he talked, the more likely he would be to continue this pace. He decided to shift the pressure of speaking onto the kinsman, not only for his curiosity, but also to preserve his sobriety. "What of you? How did you and yours come to be in King's Keep?"

"That would be Osrith's doing, mostly," answered Vaujn.

"Damn *Shaddach Chi*," Corporal Darrow mumbled from behind his cards.

Vaujn glared in his direction, but when he spoke, it was to Calvraign. "Yeah. He had some trouble with one of the Guhddan-kinne on his way here. Needless to say, that kind of trouble has a tendency to spill over a little, and we ended up, um, *escorting* him the rest of the way." The captain ignored the sudden fits of coughing that broke out amidst his eavesdropping squad. "So here we are."

Calvraign took an extremely small sip of his beer. "Trouble with what?"

"Oh, Guhddan-kinne, it's um," Vaujn searched for the words.

"It's like a demigod," supplied Chloe from the other side of the room, not pausing from her work. "*Relative of the gods* would be the literal translation, I think."

"Thanks," Vaujn said.

Calvraign's eyes widened. "That sounds like a good story! Did you kill it?"

Vaujn shook his head. "Not from lack of trying, but no. This Pale God's not so easy to slay as that."

"Pale *Man*," corrected his wife.

"Right. Anyway, ask Osrith about it someday, if you want your head bitten off and the answer shouted down your bloody throat. He's run into him before."

Calvraign sat in silence as his heart pounded like ten thousand angry drums in his chest. He tipped his mug and drained it in one prodigious swallow while Vaujn went on about wild dringli and Sunken Cities, cave-manti, and ancient-magic-better-left-alone. Normally, any one of these would have sparked his interest. But he'd stopped caring so much at the mention of the Pale Man.

"Thirsty, are you?" Vaujn asked, smiling happily. "Cuhrbern, get up and bring him another. Me too, while you're at it. You might not have any hair on your face yet, Calvraign, but I'll wager you've got some on your chest."

Calvraign didn't pay the captain any attention. He took his refilled mug from Cuhrbern with shaky hands and brought it once more to his lips. In Craignuuwn time passed at a predictable and constant rate. Life was lived in seasons there, with specific chores and responsibilities for each one. In the capital, he was learning, things happened from moment to moment, moving on from one to the next without regard of those caught in between. And right now, he was feeling crushed between a multitude of moments. Knighthood, hive-spiders, Greycloak, the Pale Man.

"… damndest way to travel," Vaujn was saying, "but handy, I'll admit."

Calvraign set his empty mug back on the table with a hollow clang. Cuhrbern, having understood at last that he was the designated servant of the hour, brought him another.

"Why was the Pale Man after Osrith, anyway?" Calvraign asked, his wits bolstered by the hearty liquid in his belly. *What was it Brohan was always saying about the enemy?* he thought, *Oh yes: know him better than you know yourself.*

"Good question. Something about a magic stone, an ear-all or something he called it."

Chloe sighed. "*Iiyiraal.*"

Vaujn's smile was strained. "Yes, *thank you*, dear. An ee-year-all," he said, sounding out each syllable. "He was supposed to bring it to the king, from what I understand. Don't know what for, but it must've been important for all the trouble it's caused."

Calvraign had heard of *iiyiraals*. The aulden had used the smaller ones to record dreams, messages, and even stories or songs. They called those dreamstones. The andu'ai of old had used larger ones as focal points for the casting of incredible magic. Andulin had used one like that – the Eye of Miithrak – to destroy the Starless Pool. In legend, at least.

"It must have contained a message," Calvraign thought aloud. "Something the Pale Man didn't want anyone else to know."

"I suppose," Vaujn said, indifferent. "It's out of our hands now, thank the All-father. Take my advice, stuff like that is best left alone, if you have any choice in the matter."

But I don't. Calvraign felt a little dizzy as he returned the empty mug to the table yet again.

Cuhrbern started to get up again, and not happily, but Vaujn motioned him to sit back down. "You might want to slow down there," advised the captain. "What it lacks in taste, it makes up for in wallop, if you catch my meaning. A smart man knows his limits, right?"

"Limits?" Calvraign scoffed, looking Vaujn straight in the eye. "I'm beyond my limits by just about any measurement, I'm afraid. All of them."

Vaujn shrugged. "Okay, then," he said. "Drink up! Cuhrbern, two more if you please!" He knocked his empty mug on Calvraign's. "To limits!" he chortled.

"To limits!" said Calvraign, returning the salute.

They never consummated their toast, however. At that moment a loud and agonized scream split the air. Not a startled shriek of surprise, or a muffled curse of pain, but the unmistakable, desperate shriek of a man meeting his death.

Chapter Thirty-Eight

When Answers Come Looking...

BROHAN stifled a yawn. He didn't feel like sleep, but his eyes were tired from hours of ceaseless reading. The hosskan had it worse, from what he could tell, as there were no chairs in the King's Library suited to her massive reptilian bulk. Kassakan didn't complain, though, and neither did the master bard. Despite the circumstances, having the chance to sort through the volumes of research, history and arcana made available by Guillaume and Agrylon was a guilty pleasure for the both of them. The joy diminished somewhat as time passed with no answers forthcoming, but only somewhat.

They hadn't spoken much of their reasons for this work yet, but as intensity eroded into fatigue, a word here and there helped keep them refreshed. First it had been the introductions. They had both heard of each other, perhaps even met in some trivial sense at this court or another, but they'd never spoken at length. Then a bit of idle chatter regarding Osrith in his more infamous years as a sell-sword, a topic that much intrigued Brohan. In Mazod and the Iron Coast, there was even a ribald song or two about his exploits, though they weren't popular with the authorities.

Kassakan pushed a leather-bound volume across the mahogany table. "It is written in Askani, and a dialect I'm not familiar with. The diagram, however – I believe it details the lay of stars at *Ebhan-nuád*. From the logbook, it appears to be pre-Imperial, during the reign of King Peallus."

"Askani?" Brohan said, skeptically. "Not a scholarly tongue. I can't imagine who would have been writing in Askani, nor any augurs or seers from the time of Peallus, either."

Brohan opened the book with a light touch, pressing the pages between his fingers. "It's calf skin," he observed. "A fine vellum, actually. That's consistent with Peallusian custom, and these are certainly Askani runes." He traced over the dark blocks and lines of the dead language with his finger. "The author's name is Elden Second Son."

Brohan shrugged, looking over at the hosskan and tapping the page with his finger. "*Second Son.* That is a title of their priestly caste, and a notable one. The First Son led the church. But they did not worship the Swords or the Old Ones in Askan – they were a breed apart, the Askani. Unfortunately, what they worshipped, exactly, the church purged from all memory as apostasy. Even what little I know is considered heresy. Some suspect it was the andu'ai-"

"No," Kassakan interrupted, "it was not the andu'ai. The Atrevus lancers crushed Askan, and the Quorum erased all but the hint of their culture from memory. In the *East*. We remember their legacy, if not their language, among the hosskan."

"*A legacy of blood and ruin I leave you, sons of Askan*," Brohan recited in mock pomp. "Ah, Archbishop Atrevus. One of my favorite zealots. I hope it rankles his spirit that the dramatic proclamation of his victory has degenerated into a base curse. A minor bit of revenge for the Askani, I suppose."

"Dragons," Kassakan stated, eyes on the master bard. "They revered dragons in Askan."

Brohan looked up, the light of the candelabra dancing in his eyes as he met her gaze. "Dragons?" he repeated expectantly.

Kassakan continued, "The Askani religion was an old one, older than the Dacadian Holy Mother Church or even the legends of the Three Swords themselves. Truth be told, and you will have to promise not to tell the current archbishop I said so, but the Three Swords themselves were once the Three Scions of this older church, before they were deified. Illuné First Daughter, Irdik Second Son and Kazdann Third Son. The Dacadian Church was once but a heterodox cult within the old church of Askan, Master Bard. Atrevus' pogrom was a bit of theological matricide, I'm afraid."

Brohan remained silent, absorbing the statement that he would have laughed at from any other source. And yet there was a truth there. The

Empire had conquered many lands, absorbed many different beliefs – even lived side-by-side with pagans to achieve their political end. The purges under Atrevus had been a brief and bloody period of intolerance, eliminating some deviance to established canon. Little was known of the suspect dogma itself, save in rumor or purely academic debate.

Not simply culled, but erased, Brohan reflected. *The Askani Church must have been in some way related to the Dacadian Church, or why the fervor? Why destroy all evidence of such a thing, unless it somehow could threaten their own sacred doctrine – or their power? Family made bitter enemies, indeed. The Civil War had proved as much. Had the Church once been so splintered, but better mended their wounds, more efficiently hidden their scars?*

"I don't tell you this to test your devoutness," Kassakan explained. "I expect you to be less a church man and more a man of the tides, anyway. Yes?"

Brohan snorted and rolled his eyes. "I know the game, Kassakan. I know what the gods are, and more importantly, what we are to *them.* Whether we talk of the Old Ones or the Swords, they are all the same to me."

Kassakan nodded, her eyes still fixed on Brohan, searching him for some sort of response. Brohan was rarely uncomfortable under scrutiny, but the hosskan who so routinely calmed burgeoning tempers now set him on edge. Perhaps, after all her talk, she was wondering how far she could actually trust him.

"I have a good idea who you really are, Brohan Madrharigal," Kassakan said, as if addressing his thoughts. "And that admission makes my life forfeit, just as what I'm revealing to you forfeits yours. May we agree to understand each other, and be lax in our respective obligations in the interest of expediency?"

Brohan reacted to the news only with a small frown. After all, this wasn't an entirely unexpected revelation, coming from one such as her. Regardless, he had no intention or desire to try to kill a N'skil'ah Adept like Kassakan Vril, regardless of what she suspected.

"On the contrary," he assured her. "I am almost relieved. I am no threat to you, Kassakan, and I trust you are not sharing this with me just to kill me for it. We know what we know, and will keep it to ourselves. Agreed?"

"So," Kassakan said, her tone stating *that's settled,* "you are now wondering, no doubt, what relevance all of this exposition on ancient religions may have to the text we have yet to read. Perhaps you even wonder how I can know so much of Askan without being literate in their script?"

"I *am* wondering that, yes," admitted Brohan.

"It is more simple a truth than you might imagine, and therefore also a dangerous one. The Scions of Askan were an evolution of an even more ancient religion. *Religion*, in fact, is too strong a word. It is a belief. My belief. The belief of the hosskan."

Brohan bit down his questions, knowing that Kassakan was not done confusing him with answers.

"The city was once named Az Hozkan – literally, *of the Hosskan*. We had settled there before the Old Foe were vanquished, fomenting rebellion amongst the humans and aiding the young insurrection of the fae. Lazy tongues and sloppy mapmakers eventually corrupted the name to Azhokan, then Azhkan, and finally to its current form, Askan. Nomenclature aside, it is important to note that we lived there, together and at peace with the human populace. We shared our knowledge and philosophy, and what was to become the Church was born there, as well as the shift in human loyalties that would eventually help defeat Anduoun."

Brohan almost laughed, but there was no easy mirth in this discourse, even for him. "Thus, you are suggesting that it was the hosskan who instigated the overthrow of the andu'ai, rather than the Three Swords; that the Three Swords, in fact, served as leaders of what was later deemed a heretic cult; that therefore, the resultant human ascendance in civilization on this continent is based on a lie.

"It's a bit much to absorb, and again I'm left wondering why it all matters right this moment, all things considered, true or not."

"In terms of history, I have scratched away only a bit of rust from the truth." Kassakan tapped the scales between her eyes with a single extended claw. "Just enough to caution you. If we have found the prophecy of which Gaious spoke, and it is not simply within a forbidden text, but one written by the hand of an apostate, and uncovers truths that the church went to great and bloody lengths to obliterate... How long will either of us live with this knowledge?"

"That is an excellent point," Brohan conceded, and then realization hushed his words into a guarded whisper. "You believe that this *is* the prophecy, then?"

"I do. Before Atrevus razed the city, there was an *y'rtai* in Askan, a sacred pool. There is a means of reading the future, a forbidden magic known to the hosskan, using the power of the *y'rtai* as conduit. It would have been a reliable oracle, if the attending N'skil'ah had channeled its power for such a purpose. Without belaboring yet another point, let us just say that the book itself is thick with *iiyir*, and undoubtedly of my kind. The very words are infused with power. I cannot read the script, but I can *feel* it."

"The N'skil'ah left some of her *iiyir* in the book?"

"Not some of it," Kassakan clarified. "She gave herself to the purpose of this prophecy. Her *iiyir* and her life bind the truth to these pages."

"Like Gai?" Brohan asked. "She is present within the tome?"

"I am trying *not* to belabor the point." Kassakan looked down, her eyes fixed unblinking at the clutter on the table, out of focus. "In death, we do not pass through the greylands, as other mortals. We transcend the shadowrealms through our *y'rtai*, and we rest in the Light. This N'skil'ah, she gave herself instead to the prophecy, and to the tome. She will never transcend death, but always be captive by it. Do you understand now the weight I give this text?"

"The scales must balance," Brohan said. "There must have been a danger of equal proportion to the sacrifice, or she would not have committed to such an act."

Kassakan looked back up, her voice soft. "We may have to make a similar decision, after you translate the Prophecy."

"Entirely too many people have been imbuing their life force in this and that to save the world, it seems," Brohan acknowledged. "Let's endeavor to see that practice ended, on our account."

Kassakan's lips drew back over her teeth, and a soft hissing noise brewed in the back of her throat. Brohan turned the page, beginning his work under the assumption that she was either about to laugh or preparing to eat him. Either way, there was very little he could do to stop her.

"Agreed," Kassakan snickered – a deep baritone growl from her chest accompanied by an audible hiss from her nostrils.

Upon hearing that rather disturbing sound, Brohan wondered if he might not rather have been eaten.

The translation was only moderately challenging. He was fairly fluent in Askani, but had to work out pieces here and there that did not correspond to modern teaching of the old runes. Since it shared a root language with Old Dacadh, a language that he'd mastered, any such delay was not long. It was purely academic, and though he typically enjoyed such an exercise, he found each deciphered word only added to his unease. Kassakan sat unmoving, waiting and watching as he worked.

At least she stopped laughing.

"Well," he sighed finally, rubbing his eyes as he finished the last page. He hadn't bothered to transcribe it. All things considered, it seemed best to lock up the words in the safer vault of his memory than to chance any ink to page. "It isn't long. The majority of it describes the signs and portents that will warn us of the impending doom they have named *The Darkening,* most of which we have missed already, apparently. Don't come late to a coronation or a prophecy, if you want either to do you any good. There is but a page and a half that speaks of what Gai referred to, I think."

Kassakan waited, her silence pushing him on. With another sigh, a habit he was getting far too comfortable with, Brohan began his recitation.

Fail, these troubled mortal realms of flesh.
Their memory is too short,
conceits too lame,
to ford the broadness of their vanities.
Prideful, they from heavens' sight avert.
With same scorn, star and moon withhold the shelter of their light.

Under a baneful sky, tied by tide and astral night,
speaks the Mouth of Shadow,
turning gates and rending lattice.
Now lets loose the flaming brand of war, to rage and burn,
and sate Third's thirst.

Within such riven-time the darkest star,
in siege of daylight, Dark'ning.
Undying King and Deathless Queen contest to slip their boundary.
Anduoun's children wake, to feast,
as fae on poison victory sup.

Only the blood of the lion's line,
unseal immortal doom.
Perish the prince, falter the Light,
the bonesword brings the end of dreams.
In a Pale Hand wielded, tis the death of all things.

"At least its not in *rhyming* verse," Brohan said, as he finished. "I detest that nonsense of Sumadrat and his like – cheap theatrics. Bad enough they won't speak plainly, but to be so evasive yet so conscious of assonance is... asinine."

"What *do* you make of it, then?" Kassakan asked, stretching her arms high over her head.

"Well, to begin with, the poetry is just awful, but perhaps it loses something in translation. As for the rest, well..." Brohan cleared his throat and tapped the table, unconsciously mimicking the habit of one of his favorite lecturers at the Bard College.

"The first two lines, all that about vanity and the rather selective eyesight of the Star and the Moon – standard stuff, that. The gods are displeased, and we've all brought our fate on our own heads. You never hear a prophecy start with *the gods were in error*. If it's good, thank the gods – but if it's bad, it's your own damn fault! So that much is established.

"The second and third stanzas get more to the heart of the matter, if by roundabout means. The baneful sky... You said Gai mentioned *Ebhannuád*, specifically? It could be a reference to that."

Kassakan nodded.

Brohan flinched at her quick acceptance. Somehow Calvraign's fate was also tied to *Ebhan-nuád. Is he caught up in this prophecy? Was that Greycloak's purpose – to warn him of what's to come?*

"Mouth of Shadow," he mused, interrupting his own wandering thoughts. "That could be any number of –"

"An *iiyir* well," Kassakan supplied, "and a powerful one."

"Ah." Brohan blinked. "That would explain *turning gates and rending lattice*, then. It refers to the Gates of Light, Dark and Shadow, and the *lattice* must be the ley lines that connect them. Like *Mylyr Gaeal*."

Again, a nod from the hosskan. "Yes. Take the Nexus to turn the tides. The flaming brand of war could then refer to almost any resultant conflict, in general, save for the mention of *Third's thirst*."

"Third Son," Brohan agreed. "Kazdann. There is no doubt there, but I am puzzled by the reference. Where there is war, there is always Kazdann. The question is whether he is a part of it, whether he has allied himself to the enemy of his own."

"He has no need to ally himself to relish the outcome, but I agree – the reference is vague as to his role."

"The third stanza then, where it names the *riven-time* specifically as *the Darkening*. This acts as our list of dramatis personae.

"The Undying King is obviously Thar Malagch. He is known as such often enough. The Deathless Queen. I… I can only assume it refers to whom I hope it doesn't. *She of no name, the blight of dreams; in blackest tide of evernight; She, the Deathless Queen*."

"The Nameless One," Kassakan confirmed. "Neva Seough."

"I would just as soon let the Undying King *contest his boundary*. At least he was once mortal, as is his boundary. He seeks escape from Malakuur and conquest of the East, as he always has, to be sure. What seeks the Nameless One? Not a cup of tea, I'll wager."

Kassakan offered no answer, so Brohan went on. "It also confirms the return of the andu'ai, with little useful elaboration. I admit to being puzzled by the reference to the fae. What their victory will be, and how it will be poisoned, we can only guess. It does seem to indicate that while the Old Foe shall return, the fae will be hard pressed to lend aid against them.

"And this brings us to the final stanza." Brohan paused for a moment, reciting the prophecy mentally to find his place. Kassakan waited without comment.

"*The blood of the lion's line*," he scoffed. "A son of House Jiraud, of which only one survives. Prince Hiruld. We may as well call him *the Chosen One*. Only he can do this, and only he can do that. And then, of course, *perish the prince* – if he dies, the caution regarding the Pale Man and the rather ominous *death of all things*."

Brohan's voice trailed off. Calvraign's destiny was also tied up with the bearer of the bonesword. *There are too many links between the lad and this prophecy. He will play a part in it, and not a minor one.*

The thought did not reassure Brohan in the least. It was not hard to piece together a few possibilities. He knew Calvraign and his boyish infatuation with the heroic. The lad wouldn't hesitate to sacrifice his life for House Jiraud's sole surviving prince if he thought it would make a difference. Greycloak's words rattled in his head – *or share your father's fate.*

"This is all very depressing," he finally stated. Kassakan had become distracted by something at the far end of the room, high on a shelf and behind a case of scrolls. "Aside from throwing in a brood of slaoithe or a flight of dragons, what else could there be to bring our doom? This is the end of an age. Perhaps even the end of all ages, if that's not too dramatic."

"Ah!" Kassakan exclaimed, picking out a thin book that had been wedged behind the scroll case. The leather binding was blotched white with rot, and a musty stink followed her to the table. "Kieramnor's *Discourse on Shadow and Veil*," she said. "Another forbidden tome. I wonder if Guillaume knows how many illegal texts his lord high chamberlain has squirreled away up here."

"I would think he makes it his business *not* to know," replied Brohan. "And fortunate for us it is, too."

"I suppose you're right," she agreed. "I wonder though – do you think even this the true extent of Agrylon's library?"

Brohan watched the hosskan's huge claws turn another page with the delicacy of a midwife cradling a newborn. "I should think not. I've known Agrylon for years, and sometimes I think I know him not at all. He's a man of mixed motives, at best. In these times, our trust seems more thrust upon him than deserved."

Kassakan was bobbing her head in agreement absently, skimming through the pages of her book, searching out some small morsel of information within the feast of knowledge. "Here!" she proclaimed, tapping a page. "*Ebhan-nuád* is examined in great detail. This should prove quite helpful!"

"Yes," Brohan warned, "but Kieramnor's studies drove him insane, or so the legends say. So read slowly and carefully."

"I will have to be more careful than slow, if I'm to find anything useful before Midride."

"Midride?" Brohan yawned, somewhat indelicately. "I'd think we could skip the feasting for this."

Kassakan stopped reading, closing the book as gingerly as she'd opened it moments ago. "The urgency, Master Bard," she began, then shook her head. "Brohan, *Ebhan-nuád* is this coming Midride. The tides have already been turned. The Darkening is all but upon us."

Brohan felt the blood drain from his face so fast that he was almost dizzy. "What?"

Kassakan shook her great snout side to side. "I assumed that Agrylon had already told you."

"By the gods," whispered Brohan, his wide open eyes staring past the hosskan at an invisible but awful realization. "He relayed the need to uncover the prophecy, but he didn't elaborate."

Brohan covered his face in his hands, shutting out the light, the room, and his looming hosskan companion so he could think. It made so much sense, of course. Why else the cryptic ghostly warnings from Greycloak, if the doom he spoke of were so distant. Why else this rush of disparate but troubling events, each a tributary feeding into a torrent, then rushing on to violent conclusion like a river runs to the falls?

Calvraign, he thought. *Calvraign is in great danger* now. There was no more time to puzzle this all out by himself, no more time for secrets. It was much too late for that now. *Besides*, he reasoned, *if there's one person I can trust…*

"Kassakan," Brohan said, and he took a deep, steadying breath. "There's something you should know."

The master bard explained all he knew about the lurking presence of Greycloak and the visions of Calvraign's mother. He spared no details but wasted no time, relating the events as efficiently as possible. As a master storyteller, he could spin a tale of any length with clarity, and that experience served him well. The hosskan listened, quiet and intense. When Brohan had finished, she paused only to lick her teeth before responding.

"The Pale Man intends to be busy this Midride," she said. "But something isn't as it seems. What threat does your apprentice pose their plans?"

"I wish I knew," Brohan answered. "He's a remarkable young man in so many ways – intelligent, insightful, and compassionate. He has the makings of a fine warrior, too, if not the disposition. I've always wondered what was intended for him. I'm not so naïve that I believe my services were bought out of gratitude to Ibhraign alone.

"Lady Aeolil hinted that Agrylon might be maneuvering the boy for his own reasons, perhaps to mingle the obviously strong bloodline of Ibhraign and Oona with that of the Great Houses. His father's line is strong in war, his mother's with the Gift – it is a powerful birthright. It could be that, or any number of other things."

"Is that why you kept this whole business secret?"

"It wasn't my intention at first, but my audience with the king was postponed long enough for me to reconsider revealing Oona's premonition to him. It seems that Agrylon is everywhere Guillaume is these days, even more than normal, and if what Aeolil suggested is true, well, let's just say I wanted to discover the whole truth before I revealed it piecemeal to others."

"Perhaps you and I should have a serious discussion with Agrylon," Kassakan said. "You part with your secrets, and together we can convince him to part with his own. This is no time to be playing allies against each other, and even Agrylon, with all his mixed motives, should see that."

Brohan rubbed his chin, considering the suggestion silently.

"Meanwhile," the hosskan continued, "we should resume our research. We have but scratched the surface here, discovered what we need to devote our attention to. We may yet have time – the prophecy did not say that the world would fail on *Ebhan-nuád*. Only that it would *begin* to."

Brohan had no choice but to concur. His vocalization of that agreement never came, however. In its stead, from somewhere above the library wherein they sat, there came a loud, shrieking scream that was cut off with disturbing abruptness.

Chapter Thirty-Nine

...Questions Pursue

SETH couldn't believe his eyes or his bad luck.
The Prince's Guard! he thought in dismay, still struggling with the very notion of it.

His mind raced back over the last half hour, as if that would shed light on what he'd just witnessed. With his work in the Malminnion apartments complete, he'd reported back to Markus, wishing to recover some of the Chief Steward's respect. Although the Feast of Prince's Bread was under way, there was still the matter of the king's more private feast for the knights and nobility. There should be plenty of work yet to do.

Markus had no need of him, however, and showed no sign of being impressed with Seth's offer. "Go find Burton," he'd commanded. "He's all worked up over something or other. He's ranting about unwanted guests and self-important bastards, but he didn't stay around long enough to explain. All the better, 's far as I care. Now get going!"

So he had, running about from place to place, always one step behind the furious castellan, following in his maddened wake. Then, at last, he heard Burton's voice bellowing from the Suns-set Terrace, just ahead.

He'd slowed then to catch his breath, more than content to let Burton finish his scolding without deflecting any of the ire onto himself.

"...don't care *who* you are," the castellan was raving. "You cannot simply authorize this without going through the proper channels! I can't be expected to accommodate this sort of request without word from Vanelorn or Willanel!"

Curious, Seth had crept a little closer, peering through a small window to squint at the figures arguing on the Terrace outside. Normally a popular enough spot, especially among young courting couples, the Suns-set Terrace was closed due to the high winds of recent storms. Lord Belmont's daughter Meg and Sir Geoffrey Demaoul, her betrothed, had almost been swept off to an untimely and doubtless messy demise just a ten-day gone. Seth could see Burton clearly enough, but all that he saw of the person he was addressing was the occasional flap of a gold-trimmed blue cloak from around the corner of a damnably opaque support column.

"You won't need to concern yourself over it any longer," replied the other. The tone was cold, the accent educated, but the voice was not a familiar one to Mister Briggin.

"I will concern myself with what I wish, sir!" the castellan spat. "Now, where is Willanel? You expressly said that–"

Seth swallowed at that memory. A mailed hand struck out and grabbed Burton around the throat like a serpent, dragging him forward off his feet. That in itself had surprised Seth, because the castellan was not by any means a slender man. Then there was that scream. He could still hear it echoing in his memory, a shriek of mingled shock, fear and pain, a sound cut off almost before it had begun by a loud and chilling snap. Worse than the scream, in Seth's memory, was the gurgling rasp that came after.

He'd watched in disbelief as the figure stalked from the concealing bulk of the column, dragging the limp carcass of the castellan behind him. Seth couldn't have moved, or even breathed, even though he'd wanted to run screaming, calling for old Sergeant Faeldor and all his men. He was a statue, frozen in place as surely as the Sentinels of Rivers' Run, watching but unable to act as Burton's body was hurled from the rampart.

The Prince's Guard! he repeated to himself, his thoughts back in the present. That realization still alarmed and confused him, but the blue cloak with the prince's golden stag and lion crest was unmistakable. *But why? Why?*

How long his retrospective had taken, in actual clicks, Seth had no idea. In practical terms, it was evidently just long enough for the murderer to turn away from his crime and stride across the length of the empty terrace to the door, which was now opening just ten or fifteen feet from the hapless and suitably terrified servant. He was torn for an instant whether or not he should attempt to flee or remain, hoping to avoid notice.

The instant passed quickly, and he found himself fleeing back the way he had come, crying out desperately for help. He could feel the eyes of the murderer on his back, knew in his heart that he was but footsteps behind, but couldn't force himself to turn and look. If he looked, he might actually see the doom closing on him from behind, and Seth much preferred the ignorance of his blind panic to that possibility.

Seth reached the stairs he had only recently ascended and jumped down them two at a time, thinking only of escape. His shaking legs somehow managed to navigate the steps without incident but were unable to slow him before he ran headlong into a massive green shape halfway down the flight. Seth slammed into the hard scales of the hosskan and flew back against the unforgiving surface of the spiral staircase. Stars swam before his eyes as the air rushed from his lungs, stilling his screams for help. His lips worked uselessly, trying to form words as he gasped for air.

"Seth?" a familiar voice said from behind the towering lizard. "Gods Above, boy, is that you?"

"Ma ... Master ... Mad ... Madrharigal," Seth managed in between his halting breaths. "Huh ... help me!"

"What's going on?" Brohan asked, squeezing past Kassakan. "What's wrong?"

"Be ... *behind* me!" Seth cried, his eyes bulging out of their sockets. He could feel unbidden tears dribbling down the side of his cheek. "The Prince's Guard!"

Brohan and Kassakan exchanged a truly confused look. "Take a breath, lad," advised Brohan. "Gather your wits before you speak. You aren't making sense."

This doesn't make any sense anyway! Seth thought angrily. He took the bard's advice, however, breathing in slow and steady until he could speak in a complete sentence again. Their presence helped calm him down some, for despite the tall murderous knight somewhere behind him, Seth took comfort in the fact that the giant, scaly hosskan was on *his* side.

"Burton's dead," he said. "One of the Prince's Guard killed him."

The two stared at him in open disbelief. "The castellan?" asked Brohan.

"Yes. Back there at the Suns-set Terrace. Broke his neck, I think, and tossed him over. I saw it, and now he's after *me*."

"Well, he's not here now," said Kassakan, helping Seth to his feet. "Why don't you show us where this happened."

Seth rubbed his lower back, which felt like it had been split in two, giving the hosskan a dubious frown. "You want me to go back there?"

The lizard prodded him forward, nodding. "Yes, if we're to find out what happened."

Seth shook his head. "But I just *told* you what happened!"

"Show us," insisted Kassakan. "It's all right. You'll be safe with us."

Seth relaxed. Something about that calm, steady voice subdued his panic and soothed it into a sort of relieved excitement. He swallowed, his fear dissolving and leaving a sense of security in its place. *Safe*, he thought, *I'm safe, now.*

"Back up this way," he said, turning and leading them up the stairs. Though his fears had been somewhat abated, his nerves were still very much on edge. He wiped his sweaty hands on his breeches repeatedly. "It just doesn't make sense," he kept repeating, but neither the hosskan nor the master bard offered him any easy solution.

The wind blew strong and cold over the Terrace, and Seth hovered as close to the security of the door as possible while Brohan and Kassakan poked about for anything suspicious. The hosskan had become tense the moment they neared the door, sniffing the air intently. She was no more at ease on the Terrace, though Seth would be surprised if any scent but the lake's were on this powerful wind. Brohan stood at the very edge of the balcony, leaning his body over the railing and peering down toward Burton's doom below.

Burton is dead. The thought rang like a bell tolling midnight, unwelcome and persistent. *Burton is dead*.

Seth had always hated Burton at least as much as he'd respected him. He was domineering, unappreciative and quick to anger. Unlike Markus, who was severe because he had to be, Burton had always been cruel because he liked it. He tormented his underlings because he had the power to get away with it, and Seth had always resented that. But now, with the memory of that thick neck snapped like a chicken's, his body thrown off the Terrace like garbage into a refuse heap, all Seth felt was sorrow. He was shocked when the first racking sob hit his body, unaware that he'd cared enough for the castellan to mourn him. He crouched down by the doorframe, crying into his sleeve. Whatever Burton had deserved, it surely hadn't been this.

The door opened, and Seth startled with a yelp. Before he could consciously cry for help, Kassakan was there, covering the distance between them in a blur to block the doorway. Seth was amazed that anything that big could move so fast.

So was the guard.

"Gods!" he exclaimed, flinching as the hosskan appeared as if from nowhere to confront him. He composed himself quickly, straightening his back and lifting his chin, "What goes on here?"

"Murder," Kassakan answered, standing aside to admit the guardsman. "And worse is sure to follow."

Chapter Forty

An Unpleasant Duty

THE Graveyard was called thus not because it was a place of burial but rather because the *ilyela* of this grove had perished, victim of a terrible blight a thousand or more years ago. It was a place silent and empty of the life that infused the rest of the Ceearmyltu Sacred Grove. For this reason it was an area that most of the tribe avoided, finding it a sad and lonely place. Jylkir decided long ago that these same qualities brought her sister here when she sought time to be alone within herself.

Du'uwneyyl sat high in the branches of dead wood, facing north – toward the human kingdom of Providayne. She ran one of her slender digits down the length of the sword in her lap, catching a glimpse of her somber reflection in its subdued blue-green shine. This weapon had been passed down from one High Blade to the next since the Great War, and it had seen near every conflict in between, perhaps even some before. To count the number it had sent unbidden to the greylands would defy reason. It should not balk at one more battle.

Not to say that the sword had any awareness. Jylkir knew better than that. It could not think, or speak, for though it was most certainly magical, it was not with such a powerful enchantment as that. Its edge was ever sharp, quick and light, and it struck truer than most. It was impervious to flame, undaunted by cold, but always cool to the touch. It was, in particular, a bane to Shadow. Its light alone could burn away the dark essence of the lesser shadowborn. It was all that, and just one small thing more.

"*In battle, let its edge be your will,*" High Blade Q'thriel had advised Du'uwneyyl, a century past. Jylkir would never forget that moment, when her sister's predecessor had handed over both her blade and her duty. "*In peace, let its light be your guide.*"

It was, quite literally, her moral compass. And now its ever-bright surface was dimmed to a dull, somber, grey. Du'uwneyyl stared out into the crisp winter that penetrated the dead grove, her mood not much warmer than the ice that clung to the barren tree limbs. Jylkir was one of the very few in the Ceearmyltu who could discern the subtle changes in the stark expressions of Du'uwneyyl's face that identified her moods.

"Sister?" ventured Jylkir, looking up from the base of the tree.

Du'uwneyyl glanced downward, but didn't seem surprised at her sister's appearance. "Are you speaking to me again?" she asked dryly.

"Out of necessity," replied Jylkir with a spite she didn't truly feel. As much as she hated the High Blade's words, her actions, even her beliefs, she loved her sister more. "What happened? Will it be war?"

Du'uwneyyl blinked, which was the equivalent of an exasperated shrug on her perpetually expressionless face. "You saw the Codex. What do you think?"

"It is war, then," hissed Jylkir, doing her absolute best to restrain her volume if not her temper. "And I suppose you went along with them? You've got your war with the humans now. Isn't that what you've always wanted?"

The High Blade looked down at her sword-of-office, grey as granite across her lap. "Humans disgust me," she said, her measured tones almost masking her rancor. "Even the slaoithe I understand more than humans. Slaoithe are born to evil. From the moment of conception, their wills are bent to violence and death. Not to eat, not to survive, but because it *pleases* them. Humans are worse yet. They aren't born to evil, no divine curse twists their hearts or shapes their destiny – they *choose* it."

"And which choice do you think the Malakuuri made, Du'uwneyyl?" argued Jylkir. "You would choose them as allies?"

"That's not for me to decide," Du'uwneyyl answered. "I command our forces in battle, sister, but I don't decide when we go to war, or with whom. That's the ken of the *lyaeyni* and the *cayl* alone, and they have already decided their course. They passed the Codex around from one to the next, and each in turn agreed to it – all except Ililysiun, of course. She stormed from the chamber before so much as touching a page."

"And you?" persisted Jylkir. "Did you paw over their bait with the rest of them, while Lombarde and his deathless master laugh at your naïveté? They mean to betray us, Du'uwneyyl! You yourself said as much at council!"

"One human's the same as the next," dismissed the High Blade. "We start with them." She pointed to the north. "And we deal with the others when we can."

"I'll have no part in this!" Jylkir didn't share her sister's need to mask what she felt. Her rage blossomed on her face clearly and honestly. "And I am *not* alone! The *ilyela* wish no part in it, either, nor do most of the treesingers. But don't listen to us, Du'uwneyyl. Don't listen to anyone. Just look! Look at your sword, damn you, and tell me then that this war is just!"

The High Blade ignored her sister's command and continued to stare out into the emptiness of the Graveyard. "I know all about your plans, Jylkir," she said softly, "you and Ililysiun and your half-man. Llri is old and weak. Too weak to hide any secrets from me."

Jylkir's breath caught in her throat. She tried to speak, but she couldn't form words through her emotions. Fear, for herself and her friends. Sorrow, for poor old Llri and whatever she'd gone through to protect their secret. And hatred. A growing, burning, blinding hatred for the woman who sat serenely in the branches above, who was drowning in bitterness and taking the rest of them down with her.

"Don't worry, Jylkir, I didn't betray your foolishness to the *cayl*," continued Du'uwneyyl. "I don't want to see you cast out, or worse. It's a moot point now, anyway."

Jylkir found her voice, if barely. "What...? What do you mean?"

In her heart, she already knew, but she had to hear it for herself. Sweat trickled down her face, despite the cold, and she felt light headed and unsure of her feet. *So, this is panic*, she thought. She'd never had occasion to panic before. Not like this.

Du'uwneyyl sheathed her sword and descended from the heights. Standing expressionless, Jylkir felt her eyes lured in and caught by her sister's intense gaze, like a moth drawn to flame. "Your half-man is considered a danger to this alliance. He's been sentenced to death."

"No," protested Jylkir, her voice no more than a whisper. "No," she repeated, somewhat louder.

"Their decision is final."

Jylkir closed her eyes. She couldn't allow this to happen. She had to stop it, whatever the cost. Even if it meant her life – or her sister's. "I won't let you," she stated, the calm and assurance of her voice startling her.

"Don't be a fool," chided Du'uwneyyl. "Why do you think I lured you out to the Graveyard?"

Jylkir looked around herself, at the cemetery of dead wood that surrounded them, her realization turning from astonishment to fury. There was no living *ilyela* for her to call upon, to reach down and subdue Du'uwneyyl while she rescued Bloodhawk. She was too far away to warn Llri. And she was no match for her sister in hand-to-hand combat. They were both well aware of that.

She lured *me here?* Jylkir raged at herself. *Of course she did,* a calm, almost mocking part of her mind answered. *She knew you'd be curious about the outcome of the council meeting. She knew you'd seek her out here, in her most private place. She knew you'd try to stop her. She beat you, like she always does.*

Jylkir's next cry was unintelligible. She threw herself at Du'uwneyyl with all of her strength, striking out with her fists as best she knew how. But her sister was High Blade. Jylkir's blows were shunted aside with ease, and she screeched in pain as her arms were twisted behind her back, immobilized in a merciless, iron grip. The treesinger kept struggling, despite the pain and the obvious futility. She wouldn't give up – she couldn't.

"You have your duties, Jylkir," Du'uwneyyl said, her breath was hot in her sister's ear, "and I have mine."

Jylkir was thrown to the ground hard. A knee dug into the small of her back, holding her relatively still while a thin cord was secured about her wrists, then her ankles. Jylkir continued to fight her sister and her bonds, cursing and sobbing in her despair.

"Your *duty*," Jylkir scoffed. "And what is that? Murdering a defenseless man? Are you so sure of your *duty*, sister?"

Du'uwneyyl rolled her immobilized sister over onto her back and shoved a wadded piece of cloth into her mouth. Jylkir looked up, tears of rage dribbling from her eyes, as the High Blade gripped the hilt of her sword and drew it a quarter of the way from its sheath.

A gleaming blue-green light lit the severe features of her sister's face. Jylkir felt the last of her hope disintegrate.

"I'm sure," said the High Blade of the Ceearmyltu, leaving the bound form of her sister to weep in the silence of the dead grove.

Jylkir found it somewhat ironic that it was Du'uwneyyl's own perception that she was useless and weak that contributed to her escape. All her life, she'd been reminded again and again that she didn't measure up as a warrior. As a treesinger, there was no dispute. Jylkir's *iiyir* tides ran very close to the *ilyela*, and her skill at crafting was equal to those twice her age and experience. But she was only a passable shot with the bow, and a truly horrid fencer. Indeed, children routinely outfought her during exercises. A mere boy of fifty had very recently thrashed her soundly, much to her shame and Du'uwneyyl's embarrassment.

And so Jylkir found her restraints not quite tight enough, the knots hasty and simple. If she'd been a stranger, she might well have been hogtied or beaten unconscious. *Or even dead*, she thought with a chill.

Despite her luck, Du'uwneyyl had already been gone for some time. Jylkir tried to guess how long it would take her to catch up with the High Blade, even as she started sprinting toward Llri.

You're too late. Too late.

She ignored the mocking chant and ran, swift and silent, pushing everything else out of her mind except for her determination. It wasn't long before the Graveyard was behind her, and the refreshing scent and feel of life surrounded her. She could feel the chorus of unheard song from the *ilyela*, encouraging her to run.

Yes, she passed this way, they sang to her. *Run! Run to Llri!*

She slowed only enough to avoid attracting any undue attention as she penetrated deeper into the inner rings of *ilyela* in the Sacred Grove. As it was, there were precious few paying attention to anything about them. Word had spread quickly, and most of the tribe seemed engaged in the debate over the war. Jylkir was pleased that despite the exhortations of revenge and recompense, at least some of her kind were opposed to the coming bloodshed.

Then the Guard Tree loomed in front of her. Duybhir stood just inside the entryway, watching Jylkir's approach with a disapproving shake of her head.

"You're too late," she said, both chastising and irritated. "Du'uwneyyl already went-"

The song sprang from Jylkir's lips as she closed the distance between them, and the rest of Duybhir's sentence was smothered in living wood. The guard sank into the now yielding bark as if it were mud, until she was completely silent and immobile. Only her fingertips, nostrils, and the toes of her boots still protruded from the coagulating trunk of the *ilyela*. Jylkir didn't spare her a second thought. She sang the word of closing, shutting herself and the imprisoned Duybhir from sight, then sealed the door with a word of binding.

The treesinger sprinted up the stairs, silent and determined. There would be no easy escape for her sister this time. She and Llri would see to that. She could feel that Bloodhawk was still alive. His life force yet resonated through Llri. But her sense of Du'uwneyyl was indistinct and uncertain. The High Blade was no more treesinger than Jylkir was a warrior, but they did share the same bloodline, and she was attuned to the *ilyela* just enough to confuse things. But once in her line of sight... .

Jylkir realized too late that she could have sung a different door into the cell, and potentially taken her sister by surprise. But, as she had so recently reminded herself, the tactics of battle were not her specialty. Even as she breached the doorway, Du'uwneyyl's arm intercepted her neck, knocking her backwards and to the floor of the tree. Jylkir's vision shimmered, blacked out, and returned. She sat in a daze, choking for breath, too disconcerted to summon the help of Llri.

"Damn it, Jylkir!" spat Du'uwneyyl, all pretense of control gone from her face and her voice. "I didn't want you to see this!"

Bloodhawk was bound securely to the wall of the tree, standing spread-eagled and helpless. He was not gagged, but silent, staring with quiet intensity at the High Blade who stood with sword bared before him. The light from the blade was blinding, casting everyone in the room with an unnatural blue-green hue.

Jylkir was more familiar with the feeling of panic as it spread through her this time. She didn't have the vocal control to sing a spell, and though accomplished, she was not yet on a level with the ancients who could sing to the *ilyela* with thought alone. She just managed to speak a few sputtering words. "Don't. Don't do it," she rasped, her voice unrecognizable. "Please."

"Silence!" snarled Du'uwneyyl, "You know *nothing*!" She wheeled on the prisoner, her sword coming to rest on his breast. "We are allied to Malakuur. Your life was forfeit from that moment on."

"So I gathered when they prepared me for execution," stated Bloodhawk. Then, as calmly as he might decline a drink, "I won't beg."

"Please," Jylkir repeated, grabbing for her sister with what little strength she had.

Du'uwneyyl ignored her. "I have no love for you, half-man," she said with a conviction impossible to doubt, "but I have less than that for the likes of these Priest Kings."

The sword flashed, severing the bonds of first one arm, then the other.

Bloodhawk blinked, his implacable veneer chipped if not cracked. "Thank you."

"Be still," interrupted the High Blade. "There's no time. You must strike me a blow to feign a struggle." She slit the bindings on his legs with her sword. "And none too gent -"

Du'uwneyyl reeled backward as Bloodhawk landed a solid blow to her delicate face. Blood welled from her lips and tongue as she stumbled back against the wall. Her cheek was already swelling. "Good," she said, blinking away the resultant dizziness. "Now fly like the wind, half-man!"

Chapter Forty-One

The Inevitable by Surprise

AEOLIL sipped at her honeyed tea, hoping some innocent warmth might find a way under her skin. The temperature had dropped with suns-set, even as the winds had picked up, and the conditions outside had gone from uncomfortable to dangerous over the last hour or so. From her window, Aeolil watched the guards as they walked the walls outside. They were bundled in heavy overcoats, their faces swaddled in thick scarves, and most were happy to spend a little extra time examining each guard house that happened along their route. She supposed Vanelorn and Willanel would frown on that, but she'd seen winters like this in the Marches and knew the consequences of exposure first hand.

"I would excuse them from duty, were I able."

The voice surprised her, and though she recognized it instantly, she spun in alarm all the same, spilling some of her steaming tea to the floor. She recovered her composure as quickly as it had gone, and bent down in a deep curtsy. "My Prince," she said, "you startled me."

Hiruld smiled, and the uncommonly serious lines of his face softened. The sparkle in his blue eyes had dimmed to a tired gleam, his carefree nature strangled into something more appropriate for the Heir Apparent.

Aeolil had wished for this change for so long that she felt both guilty and relieved to see it finally take hold.

"I'm sorry," the prince said. "It wasn't my intent. I am... distracted, by obvious matters."

"Burton?"

"No, not that. Poor man. He was a bastard, I know, but I was accustomed to his nature, and it simply became what I expected of him. King's Keep won't be the same without him."

Hiruld walked over and sat at the window seat, inviting Aeolil to join him with a soft pat of the cushions. She did. She'd seen him like this once before, upon receiving the news of Vingeaux's death, and sensing he had more to say, remained silent.

"This morning, I thought I understood my place in the world." His eyes dipped to his hands, which were wrapped tightly around each other. "Now, I'm not so certain." Hiruld shifted his focus to some indiscernible point out the window, still refusing to meet Aeolil's eyes. "I've always known the realm had enemies. And I don't just mean the Maccs – their enmity is a given – I mean the clever ones, the quiet ones. The economic maneuvers of the Maeziir, the plots of the grand and arch dukes, even the small treasons of those within the kingdom, like the archbishop. I'm not blind to it as some believe."

Aeolil shook her head. "I'm sure that's not the -"

"Aeolil, *please*," the prince countered, catching her eye for just the briefest of moments. "Let's not play the court game. I know the gossip, and some of it is probably worse than gossip, because it's true. I'm not the charismatic general that my brother was, or even my father in his day, and that is simply the way it is. I don't dispute it. Regardless, I don't come here seeking your consolation, or courting your affections. I came here because, aside from Stuart, you are the only one in this blasted world I trust. Even my father is content to play his little games with Agrylon. But you..." The prince sighed, and finally looked her in the eyes. "*You* are my closest friend."

Aeolil had heard and deflected most every sickly sweet flattery she could imagine since entering womanhood, and some before that. But this was no cheap confection designed to woo her senses away from her heart and cover the less pleasant taste of insincerity. Perhaps that was why it touched her, so genuine was the feeling and intent of that simple statement. A rare glint of tears shimmered in her eyes but, almost to her disappointment, remained only a glint.

"And now," he continued, "I've need of friends more than anything else."

Aeolil put her tea down on the ledge beside her and covered Hiruld's hands with her own. His skin felt cold as ice under her warm touch. "That

I will always be. My family has always been loyal to the Crown, and I will always be loyal to you – as my prince and as my friend."

Hiruld exhaled as if he'd been holding his breath since entering her chambers. "Thank you," he said, opening his clasped hands to enfold hers. He clenched his jaws, fighting off a surge of emotion with visible effort. He blinked several times and drew another deep breath. "Father told me about the dreamstone and the prophecy, about the danger of *Ebhan-nuád* and the Darkening. Suddenly I find myself in a most awkward position. The world in peril and me its expected savior. Vingeaux would have cherished the role. I'm left to wonder at the sanity of it."

Aeolil wondered too. Agrylon had given her a brief and altogether jarring summation of Kassakan and Brohan's illuminating discovery. The end of the world could be nigh. Hiruld was the last who could avert it. *Hiruld.*

"I'm not sure what I'll do," he said.

"You'll do what must be done, Hiruld," Aeolil said, eschewing his title for more familiar comfort. "We all will."

"That's why I've come," said the prince, looking away again.

Aeolil knit her brow. "You know you have my support."

"I'm afraid I need more than your support, milady." His voice was uncharacteristically soft. "I have thought of this often, and under different circumstances, I assure you. I had wanted this to be a question of emotion rather than politics, but I cannot bide my time awaiting that day any longer." He took another deep breath. "I must consolidate my allies, and strengthen my hand before clenching it into a fist. I will need your backing, and that of your House, as more than just a trusted friend. I must make assurances for the sake of the kingdom. Security, stability. An heir."

Hiruld's hands tightened around hers. She knew what was coming before he said it. "I must take a wife, and that wife must be strong, and intelligent, and capable in matters of court. In you, I have that and much more. You already have my heart, Aeolil – which I'm sure you know – just as I know that I've not yet earned yours. But I ask you now to take my name and share my crown, if not for love of me, then for love of this kingdom and for love of peace. In this, you would do me a great honor."

Aeolil again felt close to tears. Not from love, though she wished that were so, but from sadness. *No,* she thought desperately, *I'm not ready! Not yet!* She was not prepared to relinquish her independence, to forbear her name and freedom. Marriage to a prince meant one thing – producing an heir, and quickly, then another for insurance. Her life would no longer be dictated by her own wishes. It would revolve around her husband, her children, and most demanding of all, the needs of the kingdom. And though her mind screamed at her to refuse, Aeolil knew her duty.

"Of course I accept," she said, and lowered herself to one knee. She took the prince's hand to her lips and kissed it. She imagined Agrylon grinning in triumph, his pairing come to pass at long last, if not by his own arts. "And not just for the kingdom, or for peace. For *you*, Hiruld. We will stand together, or not at all, from this day forward."

"You'd best get up, then." He pulled her up off the floor as he stood. He smiled at her, but the melancholic look in his eye marked him a man all too aware that the answer he'd received was not for the reasons he'd hoped. "I don't want or expect you to change on my account," he said. "We don't need a soft happy queen. I'll need you to be as headstrong and willful as the day we met. I couldn't bear to think your spirit chained. Let it be our asset rather than your loss."

Aeolil felt the barest trickle of relief ease down the tense muscles of her back. She had never seen Hiruld so intense, and she liked it. Maybe, over the course of the years, she would grow to love him as more than just a friend. Maybe. "In public, I will do what I must for the stability of the throne. In private," she said, striking his chest a solid blow, "you'll take the brunt of my wrath for each and every indignity my station imposes."

Hiruld's smile spread, easing away the lingering fragments of hurt and sadness from his face. "I would expect no less from you."

Aeolil didn't allow herself any further self-pity. From this day forward she would have to be strong. She didn't have a choice. She wondered if she ever had.

Chapter Forty-Two

Cold Truth

OSRITH huddled against the shelter of a broad pillar, holding his winter cloak tight about his frame as the wind scoured the exposed surface of the Suns-set Terrace. The sky was dark, the light of moons and stars swallowed by a thick blanket of clouds. It was snowing again, and not the flimsy offerings of earlier flurries, but the thicker flakes of a full-fledged storm. Osrith had spent eight years in the Deeps but thirty before that under the open sky, and he could still read the signs well enough. They would be digging their way out of the keep tomorrow.

But that was only a minor concern. More immediate was the murder of Castellan Burton, which not only occupied the undivided attention of Kassakan but further delayed his promised payment of silver as well. Osrith had delivered the dreamstone and fulfilled his contract, and even answered the endless questions of Vanelorn, Willanel and Inulf. His openness had been gratis, an attempt to speed along his reward with the ready oil of friendly cooperation.

But still the exchequer balked. The excuses were quick and well prepared: *The king is far too busy to approve the transaction as yet. Unavoidable. Perhaps after the festival.* Thoughts of the Gimpy Wyrm danced elusively in his head, of a blazing fire, mulled grog, and a rented harem of licentious women, but he was increasingly certain his long-awaited compensation might forever remain unrealized.

Osrith snorted in disgust. He'd decided long ago that there were two things you never mixed with good business: ideals, because they invariably clouded judgment; and credit, because often as not, the coin ended up in someone else's pocket. *Might as well work for free*, he grumbled mentally, watching Symmlrey pick over the Terrace's flagstones almost as thoroughly as the wind.

"What does she think she's going to find?" Osrith yelled at Kassakan. Though only an arm's length away, the wind made normal conversation impossible.

"She wouldn't be looking if there was nothing to see," the lizard yelled back.

Osrith considered snorting in disgust again, but settled for a frown. He used to think Kassakan made a game of speaking like that – saying something while saying nothing – but later concluded that it was simply the way that her mind worked. She couldn't look at anything straight on. She had to see it from this angle and that and then upside down and backwards. Sometimes, this delicate and careful analysis was very helpful, but most of the time it was just annoying.

Symmlrey ceased her examination and motioned for the door. Osrith was only too happy to leave the frigid air for the shelter of the tower. Though the temperature inside was best described as *almost* warm, that was many degrees better than the bone-numbing cold outside. The guards Willanel had posted scowled as some of that precious warmth hurried out the open door.

Osrith shook the snow loose from his cloak and stomped his boots. "Did you find anything out there other than frostbite?" he asked.

Symmlrey pushed the hood back from her face, which remained almost translucently pale despite the vigorous beating of the wind on her cheeks. Her platinum hair was whipped about her head, some of the errant strands highlighted in gold from the flickering glow of the torches. The guards stared at her, transfixed. "Not much at all," she said, unaware or unconcerned with their fascination, "which worries me."

"Don't tell me," Osrith mocked. "This wasn't an accident."

Symmlrey ignored Osrith and his sarcasm, turning to Kassakan. "The dead man was quite large. Even someone the size of Osrith, or larger, couldn't overpower, kill, and throw a body that size over the railing without leaving some scrapes or scuff marks. Especially if the servant's account is true. A struggle in full mail leaves marks, even on stone, marks that the wind cannot erase."

Osrith had to concede that point. Even Kassakan might have a hard time tossing around that portly castellan in the way that boy had described. And he'd seen the kind of marks she was talking about. Then again, there *were* ways around that. He knew from experience.

"Are you sure this servant's reliable, Kassakan?" he asked.

"I believe Seth's account is honest and accurate," she said, and not for the first time that evening. "Master Madrharigal and I arrived on the scene within a few clicks, and my suspicions were immediately aroused."

"What, you saw something?"

"I saw nothing, but I *smelled* something. Something... ." She paused, and then leaned in closer to Osrith and the *wilhorwhyr*, away from the ears of the guards. "*Wrong*."

Osrith's spine tightened. The last time she'd smelled something *wrong* had been in Oszmagoth, and he remembered all too well what that something had been. He bit the word off in his mouth, conscious of Kassakan's obvious reluctance to let this information slip to the guards. He doubted she was worried about their trustworthiness so much as she wished to avoid a panic. Gods knew he wouldn't receive word of *srhrilakiin* loose in the keep very well if he were in their shoes.

Symmlrey looked from Kassakan's face to Osrith's, and then back again. "Wrong?" she echoed. "What do you mean?"

"*Du'uhorrim*," supplied the hosskan in auldenish.

Osrith's grasp of the tongue was only passable, but that was one word with which he was all too familiar. The kin word for *srhrilakiin* was disturbingly similar, *dhûnorihm*, or 'living shadow.'

Symmlrey nodded, her eyes narrowing in thought. "Then the question becomes *why*," she said. "But perhaps we should ask it elsewhere."

༄

Elsewhere, as it turned out, was in the increasingly crowded quarters of Vaujn and his company of kin. Osrith felt this place offered them both the safety of friendly ears and the best potential for friendly advice. The kin had been fighting *srhrilakiin* back when humans were running around naked and hunting with sticks. And Osrith, though experienced, knew when to defer to the experts.

The scene, when they arrived, was confusing. Two priests from the Order of Saint Aerylan were yelling passionately about something or other, gesturing impatiently at the sleeping form of Sir Artygalle. Mother Chloe had interposed herself between the anxious healers and the subject of their pleas, her husband on her right, and Calvraign on her left. For the moment, the other kin in the room were content to let them argue, but as tempers flared, Osrith knew that wasn't going to last much longer.

"I don't care *who* said to move him," Chloe stated. From her tone, it was clear it wasn't the first time. "He's resting comfortably where he is."

Vaujn nodded in grim agreement, a glint of challenge in his eyes.

"I am a knight in the Order Royal!" Calvraign announced, his words limping from a mouth unaccustomed to giving orders. "And I demand you leave him be!"

One of the white-robed priests spared him a dismissive grin, and the other was about to repeat himself yet again, raising his finger indignantly in the air, when Osrith stepped in. "What's this all about?" the mercenary demanded.

The priest turned to confront Osrith, but fell to one knee when he spied Kassakan behind him in the doorway. "Blessed One," he murmured. "You honor us."

Osrith rolled his eyes as Kassakan pushed past him and bowed to the healers. Though it was common for humans to fawn all over the hosskan, the Order of Saint Aerylan held them in near saintly regard. How and when the hosskan had earned this sort of reverence was rooted in the legend of the First Battle, but Osrith didn't know or care much about the specifics. He thought it had something to do with teaching Saint Aerylan herself how to save Irdik after the andu'ai gods had wounded him. Whatever it was, and however foolish he thought it, such deference did come in handy sometimes.

"None of you do the man any service by yelling and carrying on," she chastised. "Now, explain what's going on. Quietly."

"Our apologies, Blessed One. Of course, you are correct," the priest said, and hurried on to explain. "His Holiness, the archbishop, has instructed us to bring Sir Artygalle to the infirmary at Saint Severun's without delay. He does not trust the physics of King's Keep to look on him without bias. These... *people* will not release him to us."

Chloe opened her mouth, but shut it again at a glance from the hosskan.

"He appears comfortable enough where he is," reasoned Kassakan, "and these kin have no bias for or against the Knights Lancer. Would he rest any quieter at Saint Severun's?"

"But the archbishop–"

"Do you serve the needs of your patient, or the needs of His Holiness?"

The healer hesitated. "But he was most insistent, Blessed One."

Kassakan said nothing, but stared complacently into the eyes of the priest. The healer dropped his gaze. "I will inform His Holiness that Sir Artygalle is safe in your hands. I ask only that you tell us when he is awake and able to be moved."

"I will," promised Kassakan as she walked them to the door. "And please express my regrets to the archbishop."

The priests bowed again and left.

"Thank you," Chloe said, visibly relieved. "You might want to look at him yourself. I think your arts are more advanced than mine. His arm's not broken, but it might be cracked a little, judging from all the swelling and discoloration. Also, he's lost a bit of blood."

Kassakan joined Mother Chloe at the bedside. "I'll have a look."

"You do that," said Osrith, his impatience bleeding through into his voice. He grabbed Vaujn's arm and guided him over to the long table. "*We've* got matters to discuss."

"Matters?"

"Yeah. I'm sure you've been told about the castellan's little accident. No one really thinks it was an accident, of course, but there are appearances to keep up. It all boils down to this, though: we might have a *dhûnorihm* on the loose in the keep." Osrith took a seat across from Vaujn, and Symmlrey hovered behind him. "Kassakan said that the dreamstone foretold some dire threat to the prince, amongst other things. We have to figure out what's going on and put an end to it."

"And they're paying you how much to do this?" Vaujn asked.

Osrith shifted in his seat uncomfortably. "Nothing, exactly," he grumbled. "But I'm never going to get paid if this mess isn't sorted out soon. Will you help me hunt this thing down and get rid of it?"

"By my beard, Osrith!" Vaujn shouted, slamming the table with his fist and upsetting a tankard or two in the process. "We'll kill the damn thing twice, if you'll let us."

"This one is not of the average breed," said Symmlrey, her reserved speech in decided contrast to the captain's enthusiasm.

At this point, Symmlrey had the attention of the entire room. Osrith saw the glint of purpose taking light in the eyes of the kin, interest in those of Kassakan, and something less cerebral in Calvraign's awed stare.

Damn it, he thought, *I forgot about the kid.*

"Hey, Calvraign," he said, waving the young knight over. It was too late to keep him from falling under Symmlrey's glamour, but he'd promised Aeolil that he'd watch out for him. It seemed the least he could do. If nothing else, he could wipe the drool from his gaping mouth every once in a while. "Take a seat and listen. This concerns your king, so it concerns you."

Calvraign took the offered seat, and gave Symmlrey his undivided and rapt attention.

"Go on," said Osrith. "What were you saying about this thing's breeding?"

"The *du'uhorrim* have great strength, in all their varieties, and some are shape shifters. But this one, according to Seth, spoke with Burton as if they were known to each other. This sort of deception points to something more than any lesser shadowborn is capable of. This killer is masquerading as a human knight of some standing, one of the Prince's Guard, and clever enough to conceal this murder as an accident or suicide. If it hadn't been for the fortuitous eavesdropping of a servant, we would have little reason to suspect treachery, and no reason to suspect one of Inulf's men. That portion of the tower was deserted and forbidden, and most everyone in the keep was far removed and otherwise involved in the preparations for all the feasts."

"Okay," agreed Vaujn, "that all makes sense. Your average *srhrilakiin* just wants to suck the life out of you and be on its merry way, and this thing seems to have more complex intent. And if it went to all this trouble to kill the castellan, it must've felt this man had compromised its plan."

"But what is it, then?" asked Osrith.

"A shadowyn, probably, and a powerful one to remain undetected for who knows how long. Perhaps even a lord of the Shadowyn Court." Symmlrey looked across the room at Kassakan. "Do you agree?"

"I'm afraid I do," the hosskan said reluctantly.

"Well that's not good," Vaujn said. "Not good at all. You're saying we have some sort of shadowyn, or *worse*, running amok within the palace under the assumed identity of a trusted guardsman. I know your reputation, Osrith, and I've heard legends about the *wilhorwhyr* from the old days – and I'm sure you're no slouch in battle either, Kassakan – but this won't be any easy task."

Vaujn scratched at his beard. "I suppose we could pin it down, if we caught it by surprise. Kinsteel will pierce flesh and Shadow, hold it still so Chloe can cast it into a gem. You've a gem, Chloe?"

She nodded. Her frown, however, was not encouraging.

"We've managed it before," Vaujn mused, as if convincing himself or his wife.

She arched an eyebrow.

"Well... ." He shook his head. "Maybe not a shadowyn *lord*. But we've taken down shadowyn, sure enough. Once or twice."

"Binding a soul to a gem is tricky business," Mother Chloe said. "The incantation is complicated. Any distraction, any disruption, and it could go awry. If we cannot subdue it quickly, it may prove a match for all of us."

Osrith wanted to disagree, but there was no fighting the logic. He would rate a shadowyn just below Dieavaul in terms of pure lethality. He tried to remember the words of the prophecy Kassakan had told him about, something concerning the doom of the king and his line and the *Ebhan-nuád*, just days from now, this very Midride.

"Kassakan," he said, "you should tell Agrylon straight away. If this thing has slipped into the keep undetected, his wards must have been compromised. He'll need to figure out how or where and fix it, and then you two can start working up some kind of defense.

"I'll go ask around about Burton. If I can find out what got him killed, that might help us track down which of the guardsmen this thing is, or what exactly it has planned. Symmlrey, I'll trust you and the kin to do whatever you must, but we should be discreet. We don't want it to suspect we know who or what it is. Public word is that this was an accident. We should make sure that remains the public word."

"What can I do?" asked Calvraign, looking hopefully at Symmlrey. "Can I be of any help?"

Osrith got up from the table and grabbed hold of Calvraign's tunic. "Why don't you come with me?" he said, physically dragging the young man to his feet. "I doubt they'll need you underfoot."

"But," protested Calvraign, stumbling in Osrith's wake.

Osrith pulled him through the door and pushed him down the hallway. "Just keep walking," he advised. "It'll wear off in a click or two, if you're lucky."

Chapter Forty-Three

Persuasions

Brohan found the king in his bedchambers, attired for sleep but evidently finding none. It seemed, in his zeal, that His Majesty had even asked considerable help from the wine cellars, though the evidence suggested the empty flagons discarded at his bedside had been stingy in their assistance. The master bard attempted an easy expression of mirth, but his wan smile was more a thing of pity than happiness.

"Your Majesty requires a lullaby?" he asked. It was hard to see Guillaume like this, after so many years of strength. Self-pity didn't suit him.

The king didn't seem to notice the slight affront. Agrylon, nearly invisible in his seat by the fire, did. "Your tone lacks a certain respect, Master Madrharigal."

Brohan considered denying it and smoothing the situation over with a few choice words. He could, and quite easily, mollifying the wizard and amusing the king all at once. He chose not to. There was a time for deferral and pleasantries, and then there was a time for honesty, brutal though it might be.

"Your keep is in uproar, your kingdom not far behind, and Your Majesty is *drunk*. Meanwhile, your lord high chamberlain sits warming his mystic toes by the fire, content to watch while his own pot boils – taking time out, of course, to chastise my ill-placed sarcasm. To whom should I address my respects, then? The aging dotard of a king who chains himself to his sorrows, or the manipulative bastard of a sorcerer with more secrets than sense?"

Guillaume's eyes widened, and he drew himself up onto his feet to confront the bard. He swayed a bit, misplaced a foot on the hem of his nightgown, and fell to the floor in a heap of indignity. Agrylon didn't move a muscle, save to stoke the pipe in his hand with some fragrant leaf.

"Is it yet Vingeaux you mourn?" Brohan asked, pressing past the shallowness of his anger and into the deeper extent of his concern. As a man, Guillaume had every right to his fear and his sorrow. But he was king. And the king had other things to worry about. "You must put aside your grief, Your Majesty. Hiruld is threatened, as are you, and by forces too powerful for us to waste time on tears. The enemy is afoot within the keep even as we speak."

"My son," moaned Guillaume. "I've damned him. I damned them all."

Brohan hesitated, not sure what to make of that.

Agrylon was quick to fill the silence. "As you said, Master Madrharigal, the king is drunk." The wizard looked over at Guillaume fiercely. "And perhaps he shouldn't discuss such delicate matters."

Delicate matters, Brohan wondered. *Damning his sons? What are they on about?* "What is amiss, Your Majesty? Surely you don't blame yourself for Vingeaux's death, or this threat to Hiruld. I don't understand."

"The mistake was mine," he murmured, "awful that it was, and I tried to make amends. I tried – you must believe me! But now I see. Now I see."

Brohan would have dismissed the king's words as senseless ranting, fueled mostly by alcohol, save for the tense stare of Agrylon from the fireside. Whatever the king was rambling about, there was some truth to it. Some truth Agrylon wished well hidden and unspoken.

"What do you see?" Brohan prodded.

"You can never escape the consequences, Brohan. They always find you. They haunt you until you're mad." The king rubbed at his eyes. "It's my fault. I've damned them."

"Don't trouble yourself, Your Majesty," Agrylon said, igniting a long, thin stick from the fireplace. He lit his pipe with a casual puff. "You should rest. We can discuss this tomorrow."

The king ignored him. He pushed himself up on his arms, then to his knees, leaning against the bed frame and facing the master bard. He tried to square his shoulders, but he still listed against the bed, weak and tired. "I can still rule," he said, but it sounded as if he were attempting to convince himself as much as the bard. "I must. But there's so much you don't know, my friend." There was no anger in his voice, only exhaustion, sadness, and a trace of resignation.

"Then tell me," Brohan pleaded, gripping the king's arm. "I don't wish to see you like this anymore! You're a shadow of your old self, Guillaume! A fading shadow!"

"I must mend what I've wrought," he said. "For my son's sake, if not my own."

"Your Majesty!" There was no pretense of mildness in Agrylon's voice now, only a cold warning.

"I have ever been your friend, Guillaume, and my counsel, though sparing, has always been genuine." Brohan could see the king's torment written on the dry parchment of his face, and recognized it now as guilt more than self-pity. What no foreign nation could ever have done – subvert his confidence and conquer his will – Guillaume had done for them. It ate at him from within like rot eating at the heart of a great tree, leaving it to stand a hollow shell and a bitter reminder of its past stature. And so Providayne would soon follow, if nothing were done. "Whatever secrets Agrylon has had you swallow are lodged in your throat. Spit them out, Your Majesty, or you'll choke on them."

"Yes," agreed the king. "Yes, it's finally time." Guillaume looked over at his chamberlain defiantly. "It's time, Agrylon."

The wizard blew out a long streamer of smoke, and pointed at Brohan with his pipe stem. "Don't let him goad you, Your Majesty. He has motives of his own." The pipe smoke snaked out lazily across the room. "He serves the interests of the Bard College, and that puppet master in Aeth'lyn Fann." The aromatic cloud settled about the king like a thin, nebulous fog. "You should rest before considering such things. *Rest.*"

Guillaume's head slumped against his mattress, and he slept, still sitting up, at Agrylon's cue. Brohan turned to confront the wizard, even as the smoke drifted across to him. He recognized the smell as it tickled his nostrils. He gritted his teeth, angry that he hadn't noticed that sickly sweet stench before. *Fenyl weed,* he thought in disgust. *The better to keep him agreeable. If that old wizard thinks I'll be so easily...*

Brohan paused in mid-thought, and reconsidered. As a young man, or less than a hundred years ago, at any rate, he'd been confronted by a black bear just north of the Bryr Moill. They had startled each other in a small clearing, and being young and foolish, Brohan hadn't the presence of mind to calm it with a gentle song or an enchanted word. Instead, he fell down and played dead, and after some curious sniffing and a poke or two, the bear left the corpse for more worthy pursuits.

With that in mind, Brohan smiled across at Agrylon, his expression relaxed and his eyes vacant. *Let the bear think me dead.*

"You are very inquisitive, master bard," Agrylon said, returning the pipe to his mouth for another puff. "Perhaps you shouldn't be concerning yourself with these matters."

"Perhaps not," answered Brohan, careful not to sound too agreeable too quickly. He wanted to play on Agrylon's overconfidence without tripping his suspicions, and he was familiar enough with the effects of fenyl weed to do just that. It was an old trick common to less reputable magicians and travelling fortunetellers. The plant's fumes softened resistance to suggestion, curbed skepticism, and often loosened even the tightest of purse strings. But Brohan's aulden blood, sparse though it was, provided some resistance to all but the weed's cloy stink.

"It is best to leave these matters to the king and his councilors," Agrylon was saying. "He has most capable councilors, don't you think? No need to second-guess their advice, or delve too deeply into their affairs."

"They *are* capable," agreed Brohan, his voice still carefully distant, "but I have so many questions." *Just a touch of friendly defiance*, he thought, *to draw Agrylon out of these generalities and into more helpful specifics.*

"You must leave them unasked, for now. The king must not be bothered with questions of secrets or scandals." Agrylon tapped out the ashes from the bowl of his pipe, content to leave Brohan sitting in expectant silence while he considered his next words. "And Calvraign," he added finally, his voice most reasonable and calm, as if this were a trivial matter that they would surely agree upon. "I don't think his name should be brought up overmuch, do you? There are so many painful memories for the king in that boy's face. We should leave that be, shouldn't we?"

Calvraign? How deep is the lad in these schemes? And how important, that Agrylon specifically singled out his name, of all names, to safeguard. Aeolil had suggested as much, even if she hadn't been forthcoming with the details. Brohan decided it might be time to challenge the bear. "So he *is* one of your secrets, after all?"

Agrylon's brows shot upward, pulling the skin of his temples up into a wrinkled façade above the bridge of his nose. "Calvraign?" he said, belatedly incredulous. "Of course not. I merely wish to spare the king the unkind remembrances of that day by Vlue Macc. He is in a fragile state."

Brohan cast a simple, silent spell with the wave of a hand, dispersing the smoke and aroma of fenyl weed from the room. All trace of amusement was gone from his smooth face. "What is your game, Agrylon?"

"I don't know what you mean," he said, the menace in his tone contrasting the innocence of the words.

"Do you paint me a fool? That boy is my apprentice, my friend, and almost like a son to me," Brohan said. "Do you really think your half-hearted denials will deter me? He is in danger, and I won't sit idly by while it grows greater simply for your benefit. Now, what is his part in your meddling?"

The wizard went calmly about his business, replacing his pipe in a small leather carrying pouch, his lips and jaw securely shut. The darkening color of his face was all that betrayed his anger. Brohan felt a rare, cold rage beating in his own heart. There were not many in Providayne who would stand before Agrylon so unperturbed but, of these few, he was one.

"I will have an answer," he insisted.

"You are well out of your depth, Master Bard," warned the wizard.

"No fear, sir," smiled Brohan. "I can tread water for a time."

"You had best be in the shallows when your arms grow tired, or the current will suck you down deeper than memory."

"Ah, how lyrical," quipped Brohan, undaunted, "but I know my depth, Agrylon, and I never stray far from shore. You, however, seem to be a strong and fearless swimmer – headed out to sea. No doubt you are buoyed somewhat by your hot air, but when did *you* last look to land?"

The hairs on Brohan's neck rose with a tingle as he sensed the working of a powerful spell. But Agrylon still sat, motionless.

"Gentlemen," said the unmistakable voice of Kassakan Vril from the empty air, and both Brohan and Agrylon jumped. "I believe this discussion has gone quite far enough. Not to mention the metaphor, I'm afraid."

The air shimmered between them as if a maddened swarm of fireflies had sprung suddenly into existence, and just as suddenly decided they would rather be an imposing seven-foot lizard. Brohan stood blinking and taken aback. Agrylon sprang to his feet, a spell dancing at his fingertips. If he hadn't been so inordinately surprised himself, Brohan would have found the implacable wizard's moment of panic quite humorous.

"Please, don't stand on my account," Kassakan told the wizard, motioning at his chair. "I suppose I should have let you two banter back and forth a while longer, but I'm afraid it doesn't serve our common purposes well."

"This is the king's own bedchamber!" Agrylon seethed, his face hard as stone, but he resumed his seat.

"Then I'm in the right place," Kassakan said. She noticed Guillaume crumpled against the bed. "Is he all right?" she asked.

"Agrylon helped him to sleep, but he should be fine," said Brohan.

"There is little time for explanation, and less for pointless posturing," the hosskan admonished. Brohan listened, curious, but Agrylon's attention, though intense, was less gracious. "I'll be right to the point of the matter. Burton's murderer is most likely a shadowyn."

If Kassakan noticed the change in expression on either Brohan's or Agrylon's face, she didn't so much as pause to acknowledge it. "It's likely that such a creature will be vastly more powerful on *Ebhan-nuád*, and I think it not a large leap in logic to assume it allied to Malakuur. Osrith and the kin are hunting for it even now, but its guise as one of Hiruld's guardsmen is an obvious and ominous sign that the crown prince is likely in immediate peril."

"That's impossible," Agrylon sneered. "My wards -"

"Have been compromised, I'm afraid," Kassakan finished. "Or didn't you just notice me traipsing around completely invisible? Your spells should guard against that, shouldn't they? Just as they should muddle the kin priestess' scrying pool and prevent me from hopping hither and yon through the Veil. They accomplished neither. The only places still secure are your study and Meyr ga'Glyleyn, where more ancient magic is at work."

"I don't see how that's possible," Agrylon persisted.

"I don't think it matters that you see how," said Brohan. "It matters that you see that it *is*."

Kassakan picked up the king's limp form with care and laid him out on the bed in a more comfortable position. Brohan sat at the foot of the bed, near the king's feet, heedless of convention. The hosskan was looking at him expectantly, and he remembered their conversation from earlier in the day. He didn't trust Agrylon, and he doubted he would get the whole truth in return for his own honesty, but he decided not to play that game. Kassakan had been right. This was no time to play allies against each other.

"I don't know your plans for Calvraign, Agrylon, and for the moment I won't ask. Hopefully, when you hear what I have to say, you will volunteer the information that I couldn't drag from you by force."

For the second time that day, Brohan found himself telling all he knew about the mysterious Greycloak and Oona's bloody vision of the Pale Man. Repeating it only increased his feeling of foreboding. The prophecy, the bonesword, the andu'ai... and now, a shadowyn. He thought back to Artygalle's fear of *arachaemyyhl* and wondered if that were so far-fetched after all.

Agrylon hid his distress well, but Brohan was an adept at reading human expression, and he could see the signs. Two of the wizard's long bony fingers rubbed against each other incessantly in his lap, and the very lack of expression on his face bespoke iron control that in itself betrayed his worries – why exert iron control unless there was something to hide, after all? Brohan had no doubt: the news both surprised and disturbed the wizard, even if he didn't care to show it.

He was less shy about expressing his irritation, however. "You should have come to me immediately!" he hissed.

Brohan couldn't help but laugh a little at that. "Yes, following your fine example."

Kassakan emitted a low sigh that was either a threat or a sign of her growing frustration, possibly both. "Before you two start slinging epithets again, please remember that time is of the essence. Is there any light you may shed on this matter involving Calvraign, Agrylon? I don't think it prudent to deny your interest or involvement in the boy any longer."

"I won't deny it, but I'm not about to spell it out for you, either. His usefulness would then be compromised, at best."

"By the gods, man!" Brohan spat, standing and gesticulating in barely restrained anger. "Haven't you been listening? There's no more time for your blasted plots! I brought him here to protect him, damn it, not to embroil him in your endless schemes. And he won't be useful to you at all if he's *dead*!" Brohan crossed over to the wizard in his chair, staring down at him, eyes brimming with challenge. "Or is that how you intend to use him? A martyr for House Jiraud like Ibhraign was before him?"

"I will say only this," relented Agrylon, returning Brohan's glare with a steady gaze. "Calvraign's father leaves him a powerful legacy, and one which is tied inexorably to the fate of Providayne, for good or ill. To say more would be dangerous."

"Dangerous for your plans, or for the kingdom, Agrylon?" Kassakan's voice was still mild, but there was unmistakable reproach in her words. "This game you always play, you treat the world as if it were your own private contest of *mylyr gaeal*, but the consequences are greater than little pieces of ebony and ivory. You risk the destruction of the Eastern Realms, and all those who live within."

"In victory, risk is unavoidable."

Brohan pondered beating the truth out of the wizard. But, even enraged, he was not stupid. Agrylon was a power to be reckoned with, and a mage far beyond Brohan's own ability. Besides, despite his infuriating arrogance and secrecy, he was still their ally. He had too much invested in Providayne and in the dynasty of House Jiraud to simply watch it die. Agrylon must be truly convinced that keeping his secrets was in the best interests of the kingdom – and thus himself – and however mistaken he might be, Brohan saw no way to convince him of his error.

Black Robes are a breed apart.

"Your mind is your own to decide, of course," said Kassakan, "and your conscience your own to live with."

Brohan turned from the wizard in disgust. "What conscience?"

"I must examine my wards, if they are indeed broken," said Agrylon, rising and brushing small bits of soot from his dark robes. "Can you sit with the king for a bit while I'm about it?"

Kassakan nodded.

Agrylon left, and Brohan took his seat by the fire. "If any harm comes to Calvraign because of him, Kassakan, I'll kill him. I swear it."

The hosskan nodded again, staring into the fire. "You should tell me more about your apprentice, Brohan. I'm most curious about him. Most curious, indeed."

Chapter Forty-Four

Salt and Cookies

C ALVRAIGN trailed behind Osrith like a bit of helpless flotsam in the wake of a raging storm. Thus he fared somewhat better than most of the servants they left behind. Osrith had interrupted, awakened, badgered, insulted and even physically manhandled all of Burton's closest staff over the last hour or two. The man seemed to trust no answers, no matter how plausible, as he backtracked the entirety of both Seth's and Burton's day.

It didn't seem to be doing any good, as they hadn't learned anything useful except that Burton had been mad and Seth was in a panic, neither of which was apparently unusual. For the most part, Calvraign kept quiet. His head hurt, his mouth was dry, and he had no idea where he was going, let alone whom he should talk to. Osrith seemed content to ignore him, leaving nothing for Calvraign but to smile apologetically in his shadow as the grizzled knight scowled his way through King's Keep.

They were in the kitchens now, waiting by a long stone side table for a moment with the chief steward, Markus. Servants bustled back and forth, carrying out food and bringing in spent and broken dishes, dancing with unconscious precision around and about each other. The king's festivities were well under way now, and even with the death of Burton, the Keep continued on without pause. There was no time to grieve, or celebrate, or even to consider it – there was work to be done, a king and his court to serve. Calvraign wondered if those drinking and carousing off in the great hall even knew that Burton had died, or if they cared.

A whole life underfoot, he thought, with some discomfort. *But for an odd quirk of fate and a heroic father, I would be on the wrong side of the noble tread.*

"You don't talk much for a bard," observed Osrith, leaning against the wall with his arms folded across his breast. He looked almost patient, save for the fingers drumming his bicep.

"Sorry," apologized Calvraign immediately, feeling at a loss. *Am I a bard now?* he wondered. "Did you... want a story?" he ventured.

Osrith barked out a brief laugh. "It wasn't a complaint. I like my bards quiet."

"Oh."

"You sober yet?"

Calvraign shook his head. "No."

"Better slap yourself out of it, quick-like. There's going to be blood, and soon. Best if it's not yours."

"I'm, uh, I've... not really had much occasion for swordplay. That's what encouraged my thirst, I think."

"Yeah, well, when the swords come out, there won't be any *play* about it, boy," Osrith snarled. "Dry up and stay close. Here comes our man, so just go on back to that quiet act."

Calvraign saw a stocky man he thought he remembered as Markus walking upstream through the current of servants circulating around them, parting them with a glower to match Osrith's. He limped a bit on his right leg, but just a bit, and he was dressed in surprisingly well-tailored clothes. He spread his meaty arms wide as he drew near.

"What, damnit?" His face was severe, his tone no less so. "I've got a hall full of the king's personal guests to look after. Every time I get back to work, someone *else* wants to come have a chat."

Osrith pushed himself off the wall, and in one swift step he was towering over the chief steward. A blink later, he lifted the man off the floor by a fistful of his pretty shirt. "Shut it," Osrith snapped. "I don't give a fig. A man's dead. A man who owed me *money*. Now you find a quiet place we can talk and bring in some brown loaf and a pot of hotblack, or I'll take the debt out of your hide here and now."

Osrith had been very consistent about his lie. A former mercenary tracking down a debt would be less likely to draw the attention of whomever they were seeking than investigating the killing itself.

"How about a nice cup of tea?" seethed Markus, himself seeming ready to boil over. "I've plenty on hand. Perhaps a civil drink will do you some good."

"Hot. Black." hissed Osrith. "Save the tea for your mother."

Markus, still dangling an inch or two aloft, turned to a nearby scullion. "Have a pot of hotblack brewed up, and bring it with some brown loaf and butter to the east green room. After that, I'm not to be disturbed until this filthy draough son is done with me."

"Yessir," stuttered the boy before skittering off.

Osrith put Markus back on his feet. "Lead on."

Markus brushed his shirt down his chest, shaking his head at the inconvenience, but appearing somehow not to have been bullied into submission. He led them down the hall and away from the heat of the kitchen without a glance to either side or behind. A few clicks later, he was turning a key in the thick iron lock of a nondescript door.

Osrith pushed him through as soon as the bolt turned, waited for Calvraign to enter, and then slammed it behind them. It was a small room, filled with herb beds along the walls and several windows of tinted fae glass that allowed in ample light but selfishly hoarded heat. It smelled of fresh greens and tilled soil. Markus was waiting beside a small table set with four stools.

Before the echo of the closing door had even faded, Osrith's scowl had quirked into a small, boyish, grin. "Cookie, cookie, cookie," he said. "What a damn mess. How are you?"

"*Cookie*, is it?" laughed Markus. "Been a real long time, Oz. Or should I be calling you Salty, then?"

Osrith clapped Markus about the shoulders in a brief hug. "Actually, I never minded *Salty* much. Usually I'm called worse."

"That's for damn sure," agreed Markus, motioning them to sit. His eyes lingered on Calvraign, but his attention was more curious than threatening. "The court darling and the, well… *you*. Did Vanelorn put you in his shadow?"

"No," Osrith said, his eyes crinkling in thought as he turned toward Calvraign. "Aeolil. He's not really why I'm here, though, he's just in tow for the hotblack. I need to know about Burton, and whatever else you can tell me about what's been going on around here."

"You know," Markus drawled, scratching his cheek, "I don't really work for you anymore. Do you have coin?"

"I'm flush," Osrith answered. "What do your people tell you?"

Markus continued to stare across at them in silence until Osrith fished out a silver gryphon and pushed the coin across the table.

"Burton was on his way to meet Inulf and Willanel. Some troops had come in, late as you like and unannounced, and Burton noticed his larders a bit lighter for it. He didn't care for that one bit."

"What troops?" Osrith asked.

"I don't know, and he didn't say. Showed up sometime before or during Prince's Bread, from what I could pick up. Knights, I think, for how he carried on about them."

There was a knock at the door, and Osrith immediately assumed a more threatening posture, standing and leaning over the table. Markus resumed his look of stately defiance. Calvraign, unsure of what was expected of him in their ruse, settled for appearing bored. An iron kettle, a plate of thick brown bread and a liberal chunk of butter were delivered, along with a trio of stone cups and a dull broad knife. The servant seemed anxious to leave, and Markus gave him no excuse to tarry.

Osrith resumed his seat when they were alone again. "What about Inulf and Willanel?" he asked, pouring the steaming black drink into their cups. He pushed one to Calvraign with a meaningful look. "Are they purchased goods?"

Calvraign sniffed at the beverage, frowning back at Osrith as he took a tentative sip. Although aromatic enough, the flavor was distinctly bitter and very unlike the teas he'd grown up with in Craignuuwn. Still, the taste cut through the staleness in his mouth almost instantly.

"Willanel? No. He leaves behind blue and gold in the privy. Loyalty isn't his weakness. Besides, he's accounted for when Burton went flying. Inulf? Well, I *would* have said the same, but... Bellivue was here in a panic looking for him just before you showed up. He's disappeared."

"Ah, bugger it," Osrith spat. "Inulf? That can't be good, either way you cut the deck."

Markus nodded, then leaned across the table. "What's going on, Oz? I normally spot the storms coming when they're a ways off, but this here's dumped a gale on my head before I saw a cloud in the sky." Markus made a point of looking over at Calvraign. "Was a bit of clear sky lightning started it off, I'd say."

Calvraign took another drink of his hotblack, waiting for Osrith to answer. But this time the knight said nothing. He stared back at Markus, sipping his own hotblack, his expression neutral.

"You purse pinching bastard," complained Markus. He glared at Osrith and clenched his teeth as he pushed the silver gryphon back across the table. "You know," he said to Calvraign, "we didn't call him *Salty* 'cause of his tastes. He lightened the salt stores of Regent Arx, sold them off to a local bandit, then a day later he raided the bandit camp and fenced the salt right back to the Regent. What made it worse, we were deputized constables of the Regent at the time. Of course, it didn't bother me then, because I was in on it. Now, it loses some of its charm."

"Ah." Calvraign grinned through the veil of steam rising from his cup. "So, why did they call you Cookie?"

"I was the cook," Markus answered, curtly. "Now let's have it, Oz. The moons aren't waiting to rise on our account."

Osrith rapped his knuckles on the table and stood. "There's an assassin in King's Keep, after the royals themselves. Get your hackles up – and watch for sorcery. Everything bad there ever was is waiting to claim the Eastern Realms, and I mean *everything*. Malagch has the Pale Man and andu'ai under his banner, and there's shadows in the keep, even now. Big shadows, Cookie. They came after *him* with hive-spiders." Osrith tilted his head at Calvraign. "They're coming after the crown prince on *Ebhan-nuád*. Tell your people."

Calvraign almost choked on his hotblack. *We were sworn to secrecy!* He flinched as the hot liquid made painful passage down his throat, but managed to drink it rather than spit it out. "Sir Osri–"

"Shut it!" Osrith's fist bounced off of the table and then up in front of Calvraign's startled face, one finger pointing directly at his wide eyes.

Calvraign sat silent, stunned.

"Tell your people, Cookie. These half-ass halfwits won't even be done *arguing* by the time the attack comes. *Ebhan-nuád*. Be ready."

"I wouldn't figure you one for faerie stories, Oz," sniggered Markus. "And it's a bit early for a New Year's prank."

Osrith stood. "Bull scat. I wouldn't sit around waiting for the laughs to come, Cookie. The Pale Man is about – and you should know better than most that I'm not like to jest about *that*. We've got to go check up Seth's story now. You can throw us out if you want, save some pride." Osrith spared a bit of his glare for Calvraign. "Drink up, you'll need it."

Calvraign managed to hurry down the rest of his beverage. True to Osrith's claim, the stuff had seemed to pick him out of his semi-drunken pall. He licked his teeth and tried to swallow away the aftertaste. He had to quickstep to catch up to Osrith as he reached the door.

"Oz!" Markus called after him. "Oz, wait!"

"What?"

"You're serious?" The steward's eyes still betrayed his incredulity, one a little too wide, the other a little too narrow.

"No, it's a all a cock," Osrith retorted. "Happy New Year, Cookie."

"You *are* serious," Markus said softly, "or moon-touched. I'm not sure which."

"No reason he can't be both," put in Calvraign with a sly smile.

Markus laughed.

Osrith's eyes darted to Calvraign for a moment, but didn't even linger to glare before fixing again on the chief steward. "Probably not far off the mark," he agreed, his tone so cold it sucked the warmth of any humor from Calvraign's jest. "Just keep your eyes open – *all* of them. And be ready."

"I'll spread word to my folk," he said, agreeing but still not sounding convinced, "and I'll get word to the Fat Lady. She'll be glad to know you're above dirt again, I'm sure."

"No need to mention my name," balked Osrith.

"On the contrary. But Oz... another thing you should know. I do a lot of dealings with the Church hereabout, through a second, of course, but his man has been asking a lot of questions about your pup there. Not friendly ones, either."

"Hmmm." Osrith considered. "Agrylon's prize hound is the Fox's cur. So?"

"I said I dealt with the Church, not the Fox. The archbishop may be the least of your worries there. And the same front has been checking up on Inulf a lot lately. Curious that he's disappeared."

Osrith tossed another silver gryphon to Markus. "Thank you."

"*That* bit I give you based on our mutual love of the Church, and for better times. No charge." He offered up the coin, smiling.

"Keep it," dismissed Osrith, turning his back. "I don't trust courtesy. Better even than beholden."

Markus shrugged. "Keep your reasons, and I'll keep your gryphs. Now," he said, raising his voice, "get the dirty flaming hells out of my kitchens! *Out!*"

Calvraign hurried out behind Osrith, who stalked away down the corridor without another glance. Markus raised his arms in a fairly offensive gesture at their backs. His face was blotted with angry red as he continued to shout.

"Out! And if you find your gold, I hope you choke on it. Miserable hrummsucker!"

Eventually, some distance and intervening stone swallowed up his screams. Whether their bit of drama was a diversion or simply an amusement, it was complete. Osrith marched on, his brow knit.

Calvraign sucked up his nerve before he spoke. If it hadn't been apparent before, it was *very* apparent now that conversation with Osrith was not the same sort of back-and-forth he enjoyed with Brohan. But, through different means, he was still being patronized, if not marginalized.

"If you tell me what you're doing ahead of time," Calvraign said, trying to keep his tone firm but devoid of rancor, "then you won't have to tell me to *shut it*."

"Hah," Osrith clapped Calvraign's shoulder. "You couldn't have played it better. Hide something if you want people to see the truth in it. Human nature. That rise I got outta you was the grout in my tile, and it held together nice. You couldn't have mummed your way through it, though. Not with Cookie. He'd have spotted that straight off."

"You mean you *planned* that?" Calvraign exclaimed, realizing too late the implication of his surprised statement.

Osrith didn't miss it. "Yeah. I may be an idiot, but that doesn't mean I don't know what I'm doing."

He's really not as simple as he makes himself out to be, Calvraign thought as they walked along, now climbing several flights of stairs. *He is a surly ass, for certain sure, but he plays on that to his advantage.*

"Right then," Calvraign said, after some consideration, "but why did you sell out to him? I thought you were a king's man."

"Not bloody likely," Osrith said. "Understand this, boy: they aren't paying me, so they don't own me or my loyalty. The only person in this keep has that is Aeolil, and betray *her* I did not – and would not. But to Guillaume, I owe nothing."

"We're not talking just loyalty to one throne or the other," Calvraign persisted. "You're playing with the fate of the Eastern Realms."

"Sure's so, boy. Sure's so. But I'm not the one hiding behind secrets while the fire's stoking under my arse. Your king is the one needs a lecture, not me, gods save me. Do you think the people of the Iron Coast or the Free Cities don't deserve a chance to stand and fight? Only the mighty Sons of Empire get a chance to save the world, eh? And conveniently, themselves."

"No, no, that's not... Of course not." Calvraign stumbled over his words, his thoughts not far behind. "That's not, I mean, I'm sure that-"

"If you were sure you wouldn't be stuttering. No matter. Aeolil trusts me with your life. You'll have to decide if that's enough for you to trust me."

"No," Calvraign said, almost to himself. "I would have to trust Aeolil."

Osrith stopped short before a narrow door, turning to Calvraign with a startled blink. It was the first time all day that Calvraign had seen him look at all surprised.

"Well, boy, just because you don't know what you're doing, I guess that doesn't make you an idiot, eh?"

Osrith chortled at his joke as he threw open the door and let the freezing wind in to whistle in the hallway. Snowflakes swirled and eddied about their feet and against the stone. A narrow stone bridge arched into a cloud before all but disappearing. Presumably, it led to the tower that flickered like a shadowplay through the racing clouds.

"Careful," Osrith advised, and stepped onto the bridge.

Calvraign followed, watching the way Osrith would wrap one hand around the icy guide rope and not disengage until his other hand had crossed over for a similar hold. He mimicked as best he could, and successfully, though he couldn't manage it at quite the same speed. The wind was not only cold; it buffeted him from left, right, front and back, trying to dislodge him from his slippery purchase.

By the time they had safely crossed the expanse, Calvraign was trying to stomp the numbness from his feet and shake it from his fingers.

Two guards eyed Osrith warily as they entered the South Tower's antechamber.

Osrith spoke before a word of challenge could even pass their lips. "Sir Osrith Turlun and Sir Calvraign." He paused for just a moment before continuing, slowing to a more formal cadence. "Son of Dragonheart. We're looking for the steward boy. Heard he was along to the Malminnion apartments."

"Seth?" responded the older of the two men. "Aye, he's been about. Back and forth, here and there. Not sure as he's there now, though."

"We'll just have a look, then. If you do see him, send him down."

Osrith strode past the guards and descended the spiral stair. Calvraign felt their eyes on them, but neither man moved to block them. He almost regretted the ease of their passage. The thought of visiting the less-than-admired ruling family of the Crher ne Og set him on edge.

When he saw who waited at the doorstep, it pushed him over.

Chapter Forty-Five

A Taste of Home

CALLAGH Breigh set the barrel of spiced cider down at the sound of footsteps approaching from behind. For all that she tried to blend in, some instincts simply would not be covered by homespun and manners. She missed the feel of leather and fur against her skin, and the tautness of a bowstring on her fingers. She missed the heart-pounding joy of the wild, and the hunt, and she missed whomever or whatever it was she now remembered as Old Bones.

For Callagh Breigh, recently indentured servant of Baron Ezriel Malminnion, there was no reason to look or to care who approached. For Callagh Breigh, a huntress of the Crehr ne Og and apparent favorite of old and mostly forgotten powers, there was no helping it. When she turned and saw who was there, instinct and reason both fled to a thrill of something again more powerful. She choked back an empty sob and the embarrassing brimming of tears.

Are you going to cry? she admonished herself. *Stupid, silly girl!*

In part to save herself the indignity of an undammed teardrop, and in part out of some impulse not quite under her control, she rushed past a bearded knight and flung herself into Calvraign's arms. A look of blank surprise drained any real expression from his face, but he enfolded her in a hug and held her tight.

Callagh found his lips and kissed him. He smelled faintly of lilacs and tasted of bitter hotblack. *When did Cal start drinking hotblack?* she wondered, drawing him in for a deeper kiss. She didn't mind the taste too much, even if it reminded her somewhat less romantically of her father. She knew he would pull away, all flustered and red-faced, so she was going to make the most of his disconcerted fluster.

Callagh ran a hand down his smooth cheek, tracing his jaw down to his neck and then the collar of his shirt. She hung her fingers there, against his warm skin, feeling his quickened pulse.

"Well," said the knight beside them, in a droll baritone, "looks like you're already familiar with the help."

Calvraign tensed against her and pulled away. She wasn't surprised, but she was done playing a coy second with him in their dance. She kissed him one last time, letting her teeth catch his bottom lip as they finally separated.

Calvraign coughed and swallowed, shaking his flushed head. "Callagh," he said. "Gods! What are you doing *here*?"

"Hunting after wee little boys who've run away from home," she quipped, looking him over with a more serious eye than her light tone might suggest. "You've done well. Tales abound of the young Cythe warrior-bard outsmarting the Duath on the one day and outfighting all sort of nonsense on the next. You're the *Terror of the Crehr ne Og*. Little mention of your shepherding."

"Callagh, I... You know I had *nothing* to do with that!" Calvraign protested. "These stories, I don't even know where they came from!"

"I don't *care*, Cal. I'm just glad I found you in time – that you're safe."

"What are you, his sister?" Osrith questioned, and then made a face, reconsidering. "Maybe a friendly cousin?"

"Is this *your* man?" Callagh asked, a little annoyed that her reunion was sullied by his sarcasm.

"No, no. He's, um, a knight. Sir Turlun. Sir Osrith Turlun. We're looking into Burton's murder, but... Never mind that. By the Swords, what are you *doing* here?"

"I told you," she replied, rather archly. "I came after you. Everyone is on about you being in *mortal peril*, and Brohan whisked you from Craignuuwn like some prize hog at a woodsmote." Some anger crept in on Callagh's relief and excitement. "And you didn't even wait so long as to say goodbye t'me." She punched him in the chest, hard – and she was more than a little gratified when he winced in discomfort. "I came back and found your mother gabbing like a loon about *dark visions* and *pale men* and all sorts of nonsense. What was I to think?"

"Callagh," Calvraign began, looking askance at a very hard expression developing on Sir Osrith's face. "It's all a lot to explain."

"Aye, and you'd better. But there's scarce time, and I've some explanations of my own. Where's Brohan?"

"Why don't you two pups cuddle up and have a chat?" Osrith suggested with casual sarcasm. "Catch up on old times. *I* need to talk to the servants who worked with Mister Briggin. Can you at least point me at them?"

Callagh glared up at the knight again. His dismissal was businesslike rather than arrogant, but no less annoying. "They won't talk to you. Even if they'd looked up to see what's goin' on around them, they've not the stones to speak. They're like scared little hares. I'm the only one pays any attention to comings and goings, so's if you want to know anything, it's *me* you should be talking to."

"You?" Calvraign blurted. "Callagh – what are you talking about?"

"Never seen a sheep in wolf's clothing?" she joked. "I'm in *his* service, so I could come here and find you, and it's bloody awful. I don't mind the work so much, but the *praying*. Gods! He's on his knees more than a bloody consort and twice as noisy."

Osrith chortled. "You've a mouth on you, girl. I'm amazed he hasn't whipped you bloody."

Callagh watched Osrith's tight expression slacken, and his aggressive forward posture eased off just the slightest bit. She found it a little curious that her sharp tongue *pacified* him where it put most others off.

"Aye, mostly I keep it shut," she said. "In fact, I'd best get back with this cider, or I'll catch it good. He has guests, and he's not much for patience to begin with."

"Guests?" Osrith pressed her.

"Yes, and they're on about the same business with Burton as you. Before they sent me out for more drink, seemed they were after someone named Inulf for it. The archbishop and his man, Sir Two Weevils, or summat-like, and the other name I didn't catch at all."

"Tuoerval," Osrith said, scratching at his beard and looking over at Calvraign. "Between him, Renarre and Ezriel, that's the killing edge of the Holy Quorum."

"Why would they care about Burton, though?" Calvraign asked.

Osrith spread his hands and smiled. "The Church cares about *everyone*, didn't you know?" He snorted, as if disgusted with his own joke, and pulled the door open with a heave. "Forget about the servant girls. Let's invite ourselves to vespers."

Callagh watched after him as he stormed past her into the vestibule, startling the lancers stationed on guard by the inner door, and then she turned back to Calvraign. "What a cockersnipe," she said, hefting the cider back to her shoulder. "I think I might like him."

"Aye," Calvraign agreed with a smile, rushing past her to keep up. "You would."

Adopting her meekest affect, Callagh followed and then pressed past them through the door to Lord Malminnion's receiving chamber. The guards offered Osrith and Calvraign a civil but wary challenge, holding them behind her with crossed halberds.

Ezriel's tastes were perhaps best described as *martial*. Aside from the collection of swords hanging about the perimeter of the room, there was no décor to speak of. The table was unremarkable: a long oval that could seat perhaps two-dozen men comfortably, although now it sat only four, all bunched at the near end. Each place setting was of polished black stone – a plate and a goblet – but there was no centerpiece save a pair of discarded gauntlets.

Ezriel looked up from his conversation with the others long enough to catch her with his ice-blue gaze, but his eyes were quickly drawn to the commotion behind her.

"What's amiss?" he demanded with quiet authority.

Callagh set the cider down and folded her hands in front of her waist. It was easy to act abashed under his scrutiny, but it still chafed her.

"Milord," she responded, eyes downcast. "There are knights to see you."

"I have no time for knights," he said, turning back to the other three men at the table. "Tap the cider. I have a thirst."

He's not even going to let them in, she realized. "M'Lord," she repeated, trying to make her voice shake just a bit, for effect. "Please, may I have leave to speak?"

Ezriel turned back again. His face remained calm, but his eyes were a threat of lightning amidst an ominous thunderhead. "Quickly," he said with a nod of assent. The other men frowned in impatience.

"Milord, I overheard them speaking of Castellan Burton, and hoping for guidance from the Holy Church. I only thought you should know, milord. Thank you." She curtsied and withdrew in one motion, backing to the side table to tap the cider barrel.

"Now they come groveling to Mother Church," the archbishop sneered. "We should let them stew a bit longer."

"Agreed. I prefer my stew when the meat falls off the bone," added Tuoerval. "No hurry."

"If helping them will help the prince, then help them we must," the last man said. "Bickering is pointless."

"I suppose you are right, Bellivue," Ezriel agreed, with some reluctance. "This isn't the time for old feuds to poison the well, Elgin. Whatever our concerns with Guillaume, and regardless what plots Agrylon has at work, we know that the enemy readies to strike, and we must resolve to stop it."

"It won't be so simple, Ezriel," cautioned Renarre. "Always, you think it so simple. But there is no simple now."

Ezriel held up a conciliatory hand. "I know. While I respect your judgment, this is my hall, and now the seat of House Malminnion in Dwynleigsh. I will grant them a brief audience." He turned to the door. "Guards. Admit them."

Callagh had poured some cider into a large flagon and then poured some into each goblet before setting it on the table and retreating. She watched Osrith and Calvraign enter with careful, surreptitious glances. Sir Osrith was imposing, and Calvraign struck a dashing figure in his knightly attire. Aside from affection, she felt some pride at how he carried himself, and a small bit of surprise as well.

Have we both grown up in the space of a ten-day? she thought.

"Your Grace," Osrith said with a dip of the chin to Ezriel, and then acknowledged the others at the table. "Your Holiness. Sirs." She could see in his eyes that such deference did not come easily to him.

Osrith's gaze lingered on the one called Bellivue with uncomfortable intensity. Silence answered him, and Callagh stood back to observe the range of reactions from the seated men. Most of it was less than positive.

"Osrith Turlun," Tuoerval said, low and menacing like a threat. "I thought the earth had swallowed you up for good. It deserves another chance."

"You're an odd one to send for guidance from the Church," said Renarre with less obvious venom, even if his look was more poisonous still. "Did Agrylon send you and his new pet just to stir up my bile?"

"But I've never even *met* Agrylon," protested Calvraign, his voice trailing off as he shook his head in frustration.

"Sheathe your tongues," Ezriel demanded with frozen calm, and stood abruptly. "These are knights, and my guests. We owe them courtesy if nothing else."

"Courtesy?" Tuoerval scoffed. "He showed me none at Vlue Macc. I was bound and gagged and very nearly-"

"I almost regret *not* letting Malgleish finish you off," Osrith interjected. "But it was all or nothing, and I *liked* Hestan ne Vae. That was a long time ago, and I'm not here to quibble which side I was on in every battle I've ever fought."

"Then why are you here?" inquired Ezriel.

"Same as you lot. Sir Calvraign and I were tracking down Mister Briggin's account of things. Little did we know that the Church was already about it, with the help of no less than the prince's own herald."

Osrith shook his head in mock chagrin. "Imagine how silly we feel. Late to the party and all."

"Let's play no games," sighed Bellivue, his shoulders hunched and his expression downcast. "I am not here at the prince's direction. I have come of my own will to Ezriel, whom I trust greatly, because I fear that Hiruld's interests are not best looked after by his father or the wizard. They are deep in their own plots. I promised Vingeaux I would look after Hiruld, wherever and however I was able."

"Touching," noted Osrith, equal parts sarcastic and bitter. "I'm sure Sir Calvraign knows a song or two about well-intentioned betrayals and such. Ask him how many end well."

"Actually, sirs," Calvraign said, stepping up shoulder to shoulder with Osrith, "we're here for much the same reason as Sir Bellivue. If he has breached some implicit trust of the prince by speaking to you here, then we now share that distinction."

Osrith rolled his eyes, but waited in silence as Calvraign continued. "Your Holiness, I'm not much for politics. I know only that I don't know *enough* and no amount of training substitutes for experience within the fray. So I will speak plain to you. I do not know what Agrylon wishes of me, or how that might trouble the Church. But on my father's tomb, spear and sword, I swear to you that I've no designs other than to serve the king and this kingdom."

It took everything in Callagh's power to keep a smile off of her face. Watching Calvraign speak so confidently and so quickly, and in such company, vindicated her faith in him and stirred her pride. At the same time, she fought off a flush of embarrassment with a wince. *He sounds so bloody pretentious,* she thought.

"*Touching,*" Renarre responded, taking a moment to smirk at Osrith before turning his attention back to Calvraign. "I suppose your master has had you practice that speech for years. You deliver it well, I'll admit. *At least* as well as you sing of gooseberries. Both carry the same weight for me, boy. Save your breath."

Sir Bellivue rose, gathering his gauntlets from the table. "I've been through this already, and I haven't the stomach to hear it again. I will make my recommendation to Vanelorn and Willanel. Perhaps at the very least we'll be working toward the same end, if through different means." He pressed past Osrith and Calvraign at a brisk walk. "Gods save us all," he added, but without vigor.

"Bellivue," Ezriel called after him, stopping him in mid-step at the door. "My thanks for trying. I will speak with you on the morrow."

The herald turned and smiled sadly. "On the morrow, then, my friend," he said, and left.

Ezriel turned back to Renarre, "You would damn a candle for faint flame even if it were the last light left in the world."

"Metaphor doesn't suit you any more than subtlety, Ezriel," dismissed Renarre. "Stick to what you know."

"I know the Law of Swords," persisted Ezriel, "and I should not need to remind you. *A blade drawn in honor shall so be honored until tainted. What the sword earns, words cannot take away.*

"The sword he carries has defended this realm, the lands of my House, and the old tribes of the Crehr before that. Tremayne mentioned the boy on the road, and spoke well of him and Ibhraign, his father. *That* is what I know, Your Holiness."

"Ah, the *Dragonheart.*" Renarre chuckled the name and dusted imaginary lint from his stately robes.

Callagh stomach lurched. Calvraign blinked away a tear of anger, and his mouth worked silently over words that would not come. For their entire life, the name of Ibhraign was synonymous with *hero* among the Cythe. To impugn that fundamental truth was unthinkable for her, and she imagined even more so for his only son.

"A convenient hero for an inconvenient war," continued the archbishop. "Give the barbarians a hero. Someone they can be proud of. Someone loyal to the king." He paused. "Someone to *bring them in line*. I can hear Agrylon whispering in the royal ear now."

"I'm afraid you've underestimated the worth of my father and me," Calvraign said, but his voice was flat and devoid of emotion. The surprise and the anger were gone from him, or at least well hidden. "A much wiser man than you once observed that it is the life of a man that makes him, not his end. Ibhraign Askewneheur was a good man long before he was called Dragonheart. If there was some political advantage taken in his death, or in the telling of his legend, it does not diminish my father or the value of his life.

"But it is rather ironic," Calvraign said, shaking his head with a sad smile, "that making such an implication diminishes *you*. I could call you out to a duel for such affront. Challenge you to settle our score with steel."

The archbishop took a deep breath and nodded. "That is your right, of course. Do what you feel you must, for your honor."

"I see." Calvraign approached the table, rubbing his chin in thought. "You insult me, the simple barbarian, probe my weakness by questioning my father and my family honor. My temper will get the best of me, and I'll issue a challenge as the heat of my blood boils away reason. You would defer the duel, of course, and appoint a champion. Yes?"

Renarre's expression hardened. "That is my right."

"Of course it is, Your Holiness. And you have quite the stock of knighthood to throw at me, don't you?"

Callagh could see the light in Calvraign's eyes as strategies raced through his head. She guessed where his maneuver likely led. From the confused expressions surrounding her, no one else seemed to.

Calvraign reached the archbishop's seat, standing perhaps a bit too close to be entirely respectful of his station. "There are any number of battle-tested lancers at your disposal, including both Sir Tuoerval and Lord Malminnion. One, too old to risk; the other, far too high of rank, and perhaps less likely to agree, on principle."

"You enjoy hearing yourself speak, don't you?" sniped Renarre.

Calvraign didn't acknowledge the slight. "But of course, you don't really know my experience, do you? Are the stories true? Are they half-true? Might I be a match for your best, as my father doubtless was?"

Renarre snorted.

"But you have a Light Ascendant hidden in your hand – a trump card waiting to be played. How might I react if it is not some faceless lancer you send my way, but a trusted, and wounded, friend? A friend here for his own cause, surely which is known to you as well as me. Do I sacrifice his noble goal for my selfish honor? Do I perhaps fight below my best to spare him further harm? Oh, the doubts alone would certainly affect the battle. And, perhaps more importantly, forever shape our friendship, whether in victory or defeat.

"You thought that rather ingenious, didn't you? I'm sorry to disappoint you, but I will not deliver myself into such a trap. In fact, I will save you the trouble of thinking any further on plotting such outcomes. Were I to challenge you, and were you to defer, I too would appoint a champion. Sir Osrith would fight my battle and defend my family honor."

Osrith straightened, blinking in surprise. Renarre flinched, as if he'd been pinched under the table, shifting in his seat and rearranging his robes.

"We both know he would accept such duty simply for the pleasure of inconveniencing you and embarrassing the Church. Would Artygalle be a match for him? Would Osrith even *blink* in concern over whose mission is most noble, or worry over tender mercies or friendships?

"Your words are only words. My father is a legend. We shall see what truth survives over time. For now, I will save you the embarrassment of watching it proven true by the Law of Swords before the gathered throngs of the festival. I issue no challenge."

"You are not half as clever as you think," protested the archbishop.

Callagh saw the fear and doubt in the Fox's expression, however – drawn and blanched like bleached parchment over his face. *Oh, you did underestimate, him,* she thought. *But now he's tipped his hand, and you won't be so foolish again. Ah, Cal, ever in a rush for the nexus.*

"Well, I don't know how clever he thinks he is," Osrith stated. "But he's about twice as clever as *I* thought."

"Doubtless you are clever," Ezriel put in. "I fail to see the point of this discussion, however."

"The point, Lord Malminnion, is that I've no wish to make of myself an enemy, or take advantage of you. Since I've been here, I feel either over my head or on top of the world, but in neither instance with any ill intent. Can we not help each other find Burton's killer? Can we not help save the prince, and put aside other matters, other disagreements, for later?"

"You have an odd way of trying to gain our trust," objected Tuoerval.

Calvraign thought for a moment. "You judge Sir Osrith based on his past acts. You consider him untrustworthy now for whatever dishonor you imagine then. So what of me? You fought at Vlue Macc, as did my father. Did he fight with honor?"

Tuoerval chewed on his lip, looking away from the archbishop before grunting, "He did."

"Why is it your bitterness follows Sir Osrith to the present, but your respect does not follow my father's memory?"

Tuoerval only shook his head, staring down at the table.

"You speak of honor, and eloquently," Ezriel said to Calvraign. "I hope you prove as true as your words, young knight. So, what I know I will tell you, just as I told Bellivue. If you were our enemy, what we know would already be known to you and of little consequence.

"We have long watched Inulf. Some make little secret of that distrust." He indicated Tuoerval with a fleeting look. "Of late, his acts have been more and more suspicious. He has disappeared for some odd stretches of time, dismissed knights from the Prince's Guard with nary an explanation. And one such disappearance was at the time of Burton's murder, and he has yet to be found, despite our best efforts as well as Sir Bellivue's.

"In truth, I dislike Inulf, and I always have. He is gods-less and profane. But I have never had occasion to question his *loyalty*, and I do not do so now in light spirit. There is a shadow fallen across this keep, and he is either a part of it or victim of it."

"Fair enough," said Osrith. "So what do you suggest, then?"

"The captain of the Prince's Guard cannot be trusted with the prince's life, and as we can rule none of them out, his men are also suspect. There is only one sane course."

"Replace the Prince's Guard," surmised Calvraign.

"With lancers, no doubt," added Osrith.

"Willanel has suggested the same course, with his men, I'm sure," defended Ezriel. "As perhaps would Inulf, were he attendant to the prince and not gone astray. What did you suggest to Lady Evynine after Hestan and Andrew were slain, Sir Turlun?"

Callagh did not know to what Ezriel referred, but the ghosts that haunted Osrith's face showed he did. Calvraign looked away, too. *What does he know about it?*

"Bellivue has suspected a traitor in the guard since Vingeaux's death," pressed Ezriel, not waiting for a response. "That ambush was no accident, and most of the surviving knights now protect Hiruld. As much as it may seem self-serving, a guard made up of lancers, sworn to the Church above all and not to any rival House, would seem prudent."

"If you see an alternative, of course," Renarre said, almost taunting, "a House with suitable knights trained to the task, not beholden to personal or political interest and ready to relieve the Prince's Guard, you may suggest it. We only want what is best for the prince. We discussed with Bellivue at great length, and even he agreed – we did not see any other option."

Calvraign and Osrith looked up as one, sharing a subdued smile.

"Yeah," Osrith said, tapping his right hand to his midriff, parallel to the floor. "Well, maybe you weren't looking low enough."

Chapter Forty-Six

Out on a Limb

BLOODHAWK watched in silence.

It was not safe in the Ceearmyltu Grove. Half-aulden and a *wilhorwhyr*, he still knew his limits. Although the treesingers and the *ilyela* were his allies, and apparently the High Blade, he took nothing else for granted. Even with his lore and Jylkir's assistance, he could not hide long amongst an aulden tribe mobilizing for war.

The Macc encampment proved less a test of skill, however. The Ceearmyltu had relegated Ruoughn, Lombarde, and their soldiers well outside the Grove, and the eyes of the human sentries were not so keen. The Macc warriors stood leaning on their spears, relaxed and joking. They were celebrating and confident in their new alliance, even as he crept, inch by inch, deeper into their midst.

He'd appreciated Du'uwneyyl's advice but not heeded it. He could no more fly away from his duty than she could shirk hers. And though, at the moment, he did not know what that might entail precisely, the Macc camp was a logical and convenient first step. If he could not watch the Ceearmyltu directly, he would watch their new allies.

Prince Ruoughn and his men numbered about fifty. Not a large battle contingent, and certainly not enough to threaten the Ceearmyltu, but it was a respectable honor guard and enough to dissuade attack. The Malakuuri ambassador was less guarded, with only a dozen knights in his retinue. But one thing of both camps was evident: these were hardened men of battle, not an honor guard of prestige and rank, but blooded warriors all.

The prince and the ambassador had recently returned from the Grove, to much fanfare. The soldiers beat their shields and pumped their spears in the air with loud battle cries. Bloodhawk had not quite gotten close enough to hear whatever announcement brought forth their martial display, but it was clear that they were preparing for battle.

Part of the fir tree seemed to flinch beside him, and Jylkir settled next to him on a parallel branch. The needles of the fir were still thick, and concealed them from the distracted foe beneath.

"She's near," whispered Jylkir.

Bloodhawk nodded and pointed to an adjacent tree, where the limbs dipped close. A pair of tree-napes were grooming each other, their dexterous paws combing through molting fur and discarding the dun coat of autumn for the smooth white of winter. Their oddly human expressions were unconcerned with the commotion beneath the boughs, or with the graceful shape that flitted behind them.

"That's impressive," Jylkir admitted.

Bloodhawk didn't answer. He liked Jylkir, and he trusted her, but he saw no gain in revealing how he could expand and extend his senses, or from where he could draw assistance, if needed. Secrecy, silence and mystique had their uses.

One of the napes made a squeak like a giggle as it found a particularly large bug in its mate's mane, and then sucked the insect into its small, sharp teeth with a crunch.

Thank you, he said silently, touching the bright light of the tree-napes' minds. In response to his unspoken words, they skittered into the safety of the higher branches, clutching armfuls of collected fur that would soon line their nest.

Du'uwneyyl alighted on the branch above him without stirring so much as a needle. She crouched with her hands between her feet, ready to spring.

"You're in a hurry," commented Bloodhawk.

"I'm not trusted, half-man," she hissed, glaring at him from her bruised and swollen face. "And I don't know who to trust. Even my Blades..." She finished her thought only with a scowl. "I could not risk sending word by root – the treesingers are under too close a watch. I'm here under pretense of spying on our new friends, so I haven't long."

"They are girding for battle," Bloodhawk prompted.

"They are preparing to strike the humans in Dwynleigsh during some gathering on midweek day. Tomorrow."

"The Feast of Illuné," said Bloodhawk. "It is a holy day in their church. But *this* Midride? It is several days to Dwynleigsh yet from here, even at a brisk pace."

The High Blade arched an eyebrow. "Not through rainbows."

"But the Ways are closed to such a long journey," protested Bloodhawk. "The Sundering–"

"The codex *conveniently* contains a spell that will open a way-gate," explained Du'uwneyyl. "Briefly, but long enough."

"Nothing so suspicious as a convenient gift," Bloodhawk agreed. "The thars played that hand well."

"Burn me," cursed Jylkir. "There will be no means to warn them in time."

"I go first, with a vanguard of our best warriors. Ililysiun and the main host will follow. Ruoughn will take an honor guard of *men* through the Way. *Men*," Du'uwneyyl repeated in disgust. "If they don't rot Faerie as they pass, Ryaleyr will take through one final cadre after them."

"Ililysiun will lead…?" Jylkir almost choked on the word. "But she–"

"Precisely," said Du'uwneyyl. "She cannot refuse, or she will be cast out. If she lives, she will be broken by her deeds and useless, or so they hope. If she dies, no matter to them."

"And you?" asked Bloodhawk.

"I will have to trust that some of my Blades remain loyal to me above this twisted *cayl* we now follow. Still – like as not I will die on the morrow."

"No," Jylkir cried. "No. Then *do not go*."

"I am High Blade. I lead the tribe in battle."

"But–"

"Jylkir," rebuked Du'uwneyyl. "Do you think I have not considered this?" She tapped the hilt of her sword. "I am guided on this course. I freed the half-man, but I am not free myself. I go to war, for whatever purpose."

"That you must *go* may be clear," Bloodhawk said. "As to warring, perhaps somewhat less?"

Du'uwneyyl nodded. "Perhaps. I must go now. If you choose to follow, wait until tomorrow at dusk. The watch will be light and the tribe distracted to a one. Come through the Graveyard."

The High Blade reached out, cupping her sister's cheek, her lips drawing tight. Then, in a blink, she was gone the way she came, a phantom of the wood.

"I love you, too," whispered Jylkir.

Bloodhawk watched the treesinger for a moment before turning back to the Macc camp.

"We'd better sleep while we're able," he said.

"I don't suppose that War Master you're always quoting has any useful advice?"

Bloodhawk fished out a small pouch of nuts and dried vegetables from his belt. Now that he knew the timetable of the attack, rationing was the least of his concerns. He chewed for a moment before answering.

"Don't go to war on an empty stomach."

Chapter Forty-Seven

A Moment Alone

CALLAGH sat across the table from Calvraign, her cheek cradled in her hand. She'd left her third cup of mulled wine steaming untouched in front of her, the first two cups having brought a rosy bloom to her cheeks already. For Calvraign's part, he'd avoided the wine and stuck with hotblack.

Seth had invented some undisclosed matter of general upkeep, and Lord Malminnion had granted him leave to borrow Callagh for a short time. It was difficult to refuse such a request, considering the help Seth had rendered Ezriel's household. But there was no real work to be done, of course. Seth had delivered her to Calvraign, served them drinks, and left them alone. They had taken advantage of the chance to recount their rather memorable journeys to Dwynleigsh.

Calvraign watched the candlelight play across Callagh's face, gleaming with a strange sort of mischief in her eyes. Hers was not a beauty sung by bards or writ in histories, but in those dark eyes there had always been some spark that set her apart. She was his closest friend, closer than any of the boys in Craignuuwn or even Brohan had been. She knew him better than anyone could ever hope to know anyone. He *did* love her. As he looked upon her, he knew that he did and that he always would.

But then there was Aeolil. Even the thought of her made his heart race and his gut wrench. His infatuation burned bright with raw emotion, if fouled with lingering guilt.

I could just about write this song, he thought, *and it will end on a sour note in minor key.*

Vaelyhn had chosen death rather than choose between her two loves. In Calvraign's case, there were no warring faerie realms or magic phials of gods-light to complicate matters, and truthfully – he didn't know if Aeolil felt anything for him other than kind affection. Regardless, love, like fording a river, was most treacherous where two powerful currents met. And, if it wasn't enough that Calvraign felt carried away in the confluence of such waters, he suspected his boat was leaking.

"You've gotten quiet," accused Callagh. "I'll be summoned back to chambers, and you'll not have said another word. Of course, *talking* isn't the only thing we could be doing."

"Callagh," admonished Calvraign. "We aren't playing Lords and Ladies in Padhrag's strawbed. We're at King's Keep now!"

"Well, I'm sure they have a stable, if that's what's worrying you," she said lightly. "And I thought maybe tonight we could get beyond the *playing*."

Calvraign rolled his eyes, making a good show of dismissing her playful invitation, despite its appeal. "Oh, do you think that's what your spirit guide meant when he said *keep to the old ways*? Things aren't that simple."

"I think it's pretty simple," she countered, taking another sip of wine. "The parts *are* made to fit together, you know."

Calvraign could only shake his head. His throat constricted, suddenly very dry, and perspiration beaded wet on his brow. He forced himself to breathe and tried not to remember how good her embrace had felt.

Calvraign had been putting this moment off for years. He wondered why. If he loved her as he'd admitted to himself, there'd been abundant chance to take advantage of such opportunity over the years. It was no lack of desire on his part. In fact, if anything, his recent surrenders to her had only stoked that flame. So what was it? Was she too much like a sister for him, where Aeolil was a convenient, beautiful and unattainable fantasy?

Do you just think too damned much, perhaps? he scolded himself.

Callagh's fingers closed over his hand, and she brought his knuckles to her lips, kissing them with a soft, warm touch. "I have waited for you, Cal," she said. "Gods know I've been patient with you. Bevan once proposed to me, did you know? Two years gone, he come to Da' with an offer, and made good terms."

Calvraign flushed now with a different emotion, a different conflict. *That fat, lazy bastard Bevan?* The thought of the furrier's son pawing over her had his blood pounding. Bevan was dull and crude, with a pig nose and squinty eyes. *Jealousy is not the same as love,* he reasoned, but reason did nothing to still his anger.

"You said *no*, I suppose," he said, but with less of the light mirth he'd intended. He could hear the cold envy in his own voice, chilling away any warmth.

"Aye, Cal. I said no." She grinned, unaware or unconcerned with his darkening mood. "Aside from a game of *show me, show you* with Donagh Luhn, I've ever only courted one man, Cal – and you know it. You've *always* known it. I only trifled with Donagh on account of you taking such a shine to Bonnie-Leigh that summer. All these years, I've been in your pocket. It's made you a bit lazy, I think."

Donagh? Calvraign's jaw clenched. Donagh was from a proud line, a huntsman, tall and strong and a skilled shot. He was a good match for her. Yet the thought of them playing even some innocent adolescent peek-and-blush made him furious. The image of him holding her, laughing with her, even the idea of her looking at that fire-headed lout as she now looked at him, was maddening.

"Did he have an offer for you as well?" This time, there was no mistaking his tone, or the resentment that filled it.

"Ach, if Donagh had offered, I just might've said *yes*," she teased, with a squeeze of his hands and a dismissive laugh. "Donagh's done enough bedding, he's not fit for wedding, I'm afraid. Not for a chaste young thing like me."

"You're playing with me," Calvraign complained, pulling back his hands. He stood and turned from the table, walking over to open the shuttered doors to his balcony. The cold air felt good on his face. *Gods, wasn't I just sparring with an archbishop this very eve, only to mope like a petulant boy with a village girl?*

Callagh walked past him out onto the balcony, leaning over the railing to peer into the night. Glowlamps bobbed like fireflies on the distant shore of the city. She looked over her shoulder at him, her grin eaten at the edges by melancholy.

"I'm not a fine lady," she said. "I'm no prize, and..." She paused, and there was a little fire in her words as she continued. "... I'm no *baronette*."

Calvraign's chest swelled, an emanation from his heart that filled him but choked him like a weed, even as it seemed to sink down to his stomach. His fingers tingled, and his head swam. He'd never quite felt anything like it before. It was as if he'd filled up with a rush of love and been drained of any peace at the same time. *Is this what they mean by your heart sinking? Gods. What an accurate little cliché.*

Calvraign couldn't speak, and Callagh filled the silence as she looked back out at the city.

"Ezriel's girls may not talk, Cal, but there's ample trade in gossip just about everywhere else in this place. I've been everywhere I can manage to be, and heard everything I could manage to hear. Aside from conquering beasts and tricking faeries, you've had your way with all the ladies, didn't you know? Of it all, it's the talk of Lady Vae that rings true. She lends horses and mercenaries on your account, after all. She's pretty, I'll not argue. But she's not *me*."

Calvraign chewed at his lower lip. He remembered the summer that he'd flirted with Bonnie-Leigh, and he remembered how Callagh had lashed out. Not at *her*. To the contrary, if anything she'd been more civil to Bonnie than she'd ever been. She didn't cut down her competition; she rose above it – eyes always on her target. Calvraign had been tackled, punched, wrestled and tongue-lashed for a moon of Lucendays.

"I'm followed around by some dread apparition, soon to be fodder for the Pale Man, and dancing here and there through court politics," he said. "*You've* been wandering the wilderness talking to corpses and ravens and indenturing yourself as a housemaid because the spirits moved you to." Calvraign threw his arms up in the air. "And *this* is the best way you think we should be using our time? Everyone else is out trying to save the world, and we're talking of kisses and fancies."

Callagh shrugged. "Like as not, we'll be dead in a day's time, or swallowed by some unfathomable Dark. I don't need a crown of mistletoe or promise rings, but before you're all taken up in new rank and new acquaintance, I want the memory of you. And I want you to have the memory of me. I want to know you as a woman knows her man. I'll not hold you to a handfasting, Cal. But what if it all ends on *Ebhan-nuád*?"

Calvraign put an arm around her. She nestled comfortably into him, and her own arm circled his waist. "It's no lack of feeling," he said, unsure if he lied. There were definitely *feelings*, even if he wasn't certain what those feelings were, exactly. "But–"

Callagh turned into him, tightening her embrace and pressing close. There wasn't any place to escape unless he dove from his balcony, and not as much as a hair between them. His body betrayed any ruse of disinterest.

Calvraign's resolve faltered, and the image of Aeolil flickered and dimmed in his mind's light. Callagh's lips brushed his as she spoke, and her words were laced with the fragrant hint of mulling spices.

"You don't know what's good for you, Calvraign Askewneheur."

She pushed away from him and sauntered inside.

"Let me know when your head catches up with the rest of you," she shouted back to him. "But I'm not of a mind to wait much longer, Cal."

The chamber door clicked shut behind her, and Calvraign turned back to stare into the night. He was both relieved and disconcerted to be alone. *Love's not a river,* he thought. *It's a bloody quagmire, and I'm chasing bog-lights.*

Calvraign moved to the door, ready for the warmth of the hearth and peace of his coverlet, but a shadow detached itself from the wall, blocking retreat. Calvraign blinked, surprised, despite the shade's familiarity.

Greycloak.

The specter raised a hand, and a blast of air like ice hit Calvraign in the chest, knocking him back against the railing.

"*It is time,*" rasped its voice without sound.

Calvraign's head swam, and he felt his body crumble, boneless, against the balustrade, his balance faltering. The world lurched at him from far below as he slipped.

"Blood and ruin," he spat, and then his world went dark as he fell.

Chapter Forty-Eight

The Bitter Cup

AEOLIL winced, cradling her abdomen with one hand while the other was busy muddling raspberry leaf with orange blossoms and dried bilberries in the bottom of her teacup. The steam carried the fragrance to her nose with but a hint of the relief she hoped it would provide her cramping belly. Here in the plains of the midlands, crampbark was the more popular remedy, but Aeolil clung to this familiar tea to ease her monthly pains, despite the danger of staining her teeth. At this point, blue teeth were not her biggest worry.

Leave out the raspberry, and the tea she brewed was also a favorite to soothe the ills of women with child. Her mother had often joked of sending her father out to harvest bilberries. Blackhearts, the farmers called them – she assumed for their deep midnight-blue color. They grew in abundance north of the castle, where the soil was too acidic for much else but gorse or broom. Custom in the Marches protected the right of every man or woman to pick them, regardless of property right.

Even barons could pick them, her mother would jest with a sly wink. *I'm oft surprised you weren't born blue.*

There was a knock at her door, and Aeolil abandoned the memory.

"My lady," Stefan said, opening the door but a crack. "Sir Osrith is here."

"Show him in."

Osrith pushed past Stefan with his customary glower. He was dressed in a loose black shirt and matching breeches, his only adornment that of scabbard and broadsword. He came before her, dipping his head in an impatient bow, his eyes alert but still red from interrupted slumber.

"Milady," he acknowledged.

"I'm sorry for the late hour," she apologized. "But I have questions for you – and a favor."

Osrith spread his arms in surrender. "Here I am."

Aeolil nodded. She sipped at her tea, providing a moment to gather her thoughts.

"I need to call upon your allegiance to House Vae."

"You know you have it, for what it's worth."

That's what makes it more difficult to ask. "I hope it is worth the life of Sir Calvraign. I would like you to forswear your oath to Vae, and enter service as *his* man. Not as a mercenary – as a sworn-sword, and all that this implies. Just as you once did for my father."

Osrith shrugged, shaking his head. "I told you I'd keep an eye on him. Isn't that enough? I can watch out for him without oaths. I've only ever sworn *one* like *that*, and I intend it to be the last."

"I'm asking you to. If you honor the oath you swore to my House, you'll honor this request to serve another with the same steadfast loyalty."

"To honor your House I should forsake it?" He folded his arms across his breast, the cords of his muscles taut. "This smells like politics. That doesn't mean scat to me."

"It's not. Truly. I wouldn't ever ask you such a thing for politics," she said, wondering if even that much were true. "It is for Calvraign's sake, and perhaps for much more than that."

"Aeolil." Osrith's tone was respectful but edged with command, as if she were still the young girl hiding from imaginary hrumm under the hem of his cape. "What exactly are you talking about?"

A particularly severe cramp struck, and she doubled over, her head swimming with a strange hum. It was not from the moons-cycle; it was the tides. Her head cleared, but her body shivered with the echo. When she looked up again, Osrith was kneeling in front of her, picking up the pieces of her teacup.

Did I drop that?

"Lily?" Osrith's voice was oddly gentle, and he eyed her with concern. "Are you well?"

Lily. Aeolil smiled. She'd almost forgotten his pet name for her. He had rarely used it, and even so, she'd never let anyone else get away with it. She didn't even *like* lilies, after all. Although Osrith was more like a dear uncle or an old friend now, back then she had wanted nothing less than to marry him. She'd always tried so hard to impress him: the knight-errant, the un-mannered mercenary, the hardened soldier with the mysterious past. He was a hard man to resist for a young maid just short of a ten-year.

Strangely, she was bolstered by the memory of her childhood infatuation. He had been there for her when she needed him before, and he had been there for her family, even if not without loss. They had both come a long way, but inherently this was a man she trusted.

"I'm fine," she said, adjusting to the shifting tide. "Well, there's nothing to be done about it, at any rate. Your little Lily never had to worry about the red linens, did she?"

Osrith frowned, setting the broken pieces of porcelain on the nearby table. "I thought I smelled blackheart tea. Your mother used to send us out for that, you know – your father and I."

"I remember," she said. "I was just thinking about it before you came in. I'm sorry. It's not polite discussion."

"I'm not polite company," observed Osrith.

"No, you're not. But this is why I trust you with Calvraign, Osrith. He has never squired, not properly, and Agrylon has designs on him. Left to his own, he will be led down a path not of his choosing, and perhaps not to his benefit. You can look out for him as no one else can."

Osrith cleared his throat and shook his head again, not masking his reservations. "I like the boy fine, but he already has a master bard watching over him, and not the type who excels only in singing, mind you."

"He's been knighted. He will be at the king's command, and he shall be tethered to the court and Agrylon's interests. I've no doubt about that at all. They may call Brohan the *King's* Bard, but he is still beholden to a different master and may be called away at any time.

"No, Osrith. It must be you, and it must be a full-fledged oath of the sword-sworn, sanctified and bound by whatever gods you don't curse. I know you will always have our interests at heart, but you must keep his close to mind. Agrylon guards his secret with such vigor, its purpose – *Calvraign's* purpose – must be of great import. Please. Keep him safe, and teach him to *survive*, not simply to live."

"You were always a wordy child," Osrith complained. "Spent too much time with Kassakan, no doubt."

"You will do it, then?" she pressed.

"No," he answered. "Not of my free will. My place is by your side, and your mother's. War is coming."

"There is no place for you by my side, Osrith," Aeolil said, and the words saddened her even as she spoke them, for they were true. "Bleys is here, by mother's order. Prentis guards her and the castle. I must command you to accept Calvraign as your liege and release you from our service. If that is how it must be done, then so must it be. This I speak for House Vae."

"All bloody formal," muttered Osrith. "I suppose I've no choice, then, if my word to Hestan has any value at all. Whatever words I say, and whatever pledge I take, I will have an eye on you and your mother. I will do what I can for the boy, but that's the best I can promise. Why you'd trust *me* with him… ." He exhaled, clenching his teeth.

"And," Aeolil said, the words reluctant on her lips, "that brings us to the next matter."

Osrith spread his arms again. "Out with it, then."

"I need to know what happened that day, Osrith – how you and Kiev survived. Brohan told Agrylon that Calvraign is threatened by no less than the Pale Man. A *credible foretelling*, he called it. It's why I need your help, specifically. So that this time we will be prepared."

Color filled Osrith's cheeks and his eyes narrowed to hard slits. "Gods-be-buggered!" he shouted, his manners burned off by the heat of his anger. "What is *that* supposed to mean? Have you forgotten he butchered your father and brother last time we met, and nearly me and Kiev with them? Get some sense!"

"Yes, I remember that," Aeolil countered, biting the words off in an angry growl despite herself. She'd thought she could remain composed, but it was a raw wound for both of them, and she could not keep the edge from her own voice. "And I remember you brought Kiev home. Safe. You hate yourself for what you failed to do, but even in *that* you succeeded as none other I've heard. I wish you'd saved *all* of them, Osrith, with all my heart. You couldn't – but you did save *one*. Perhaps you can save one more."

"For all the good it did," Osrith muttered, turning his back on her to stalk to the other end of the room. "Who's to say Kiev was marked for killing at all?" he said, without turning. "Maybe it was just Andrew and Hestan he wanted."

"I don't believe that. Kassakan will not say much on the matter, but she says the Pale Man still intended pursuit until she arrived."

"Yeah. All the more reason to see I can't do what you ask. I'd already bled a cask by the time she showed. I was so close to grey, I could see the stitching in Death's knickers."

"Do you think I've not considered this?" exclaimed Aeolil. Her face was hot: from the moons-cycle, the tugging tides, and her boiling anger. "Do you think I secreted myself into Agrylon's service for thrills alone? On a dare? There's certainly no political advantage to sorcery in these times. It is *power*, Osrith. Power and knowledge.

"The Pale Man and his magic took my brother and my father, and taking them took *you* also. He shred my very world. Kassakan may have kept quiet, but Agrylon's library has given me ample to study over the years, and I have availed myself of that knowledge, Osrith. He has a power over you now – that is true. He is tuned to your tides. He may walk in your dreams, torment you, use you like a lodestone. I know all this, and a good sight more.

"But, Osrith," Aeolil felt the rage seething through her teeth in her angry whisper, "you have tasted the arcane Dark of that sword, and swallowed it, and *lived*. You, Osrith, may also have power over *him*."

"Bull scat."

"No! Listen to me, captal! He senses when you are near, but do you not also sense *him*?"

Osrith ran a hand over the old scar. "Aye," he agreed, in a whisper. "Like a twisting knife."

Aeolil nodded. "He *cannot* surprise you. You will know when he comes. His power is *our* power, too."

Osrith finally turned again to face her. "And how will I ward against his sorcery? He walks where he will through Shadow."

"You won't," she replied. "Kassakan will. She has already agreed to help us."

"Of course she has," he said, resigned.

"This is why we need to know – *I* need to know – what happened. What *exactly* happened that day? You did not defeat him in battle, and yet you defeated him by surviving. How?"

"That's no great mystery," he explained. "I don't like talking about it; doesn't mean I *can't*. I suppose I owe you as much. You were too young when it happened. Though I warn you the hearing of it won't be pleasant."

"I know," said Aeolil. "I don't relish it."

Osrith pinched his face into a scowl, his eyes looking past Aeolil and at something distant and far away, but all too vivid in his memory.

"Dieavaul ambushed us in a little gully down south of the mainway, but east of the Daemeyr. Baited us in with a ruse of some hrumm looting a wagon, then sprung a trap on Hestan and my men when they drew near. Hestan had ordered me to stay back with the boys. I guess he was at least a little suspicious, because usually it was Hardt who drew that duty. Mostly, Hestan liked me guarding his flank in battle. I suppose that saved me their fate, them that charged.

"I don't know if it was fire or lightning he hit them with, but it charred most of the company straight off, and his own hrumm, too. That's when Lynx died. I can't tell you how many nooses that boy'd slipped out of. *Chivalry from a distance*, he called it. And he died charging headlong into the fray like some damned heroic Knight of the Lance..." Osrith's voice trailed off.

Aeolil remembered Lynx. He was the youngest of Osrith's mercenaries, a sharp-witted man just past his second ten-year, a footpad with a deadly bow and a reputation for narrow escapes with a laugh.

"Kraye knew some spell-craft," continued Osrith. "Not enough to matter against a war mage like Dieavaul, but just enough to see a glimmer of what we were up against. He signaled retreat, like the smart soldier he was, but Dieavaul stepped through Shadow, and they were blade to blade in a heartbeat. Kraye didn't have time for any of his magic tricks, and Dieavaul took his head right off in less than a wink. I'd never seen anyone move that fast – like he was still a shadow."

Kraye had been handsome and self-confident. Dark-skinned, with piercing eyes edged in gleaming gold. His armor had been of ancient style, and his speech was accented with the formal tones of the Gold Coast. Her mother called him *the gentleman mercenary*. She remembered he and Osrith quarreling often and loudly, but lightly.

"He always claimed to be the last of some ancient and proud line," Osrith mused. "Said he could trace it back to the old families of Dachadaie itself. And that was it for him, gone in a bloody tick along with his proud lineage, whatever it was."

Osrith shrugged, but Aeolil saw it as a gesture of defeat rather than indifference. "Hardt had it worse. There were only a few of the guard left, and they rallied, for what that was worth. I was trying to send off the boys, but Andrew didn't want to leave your father."

"He wouldn't," whispered Aeolil in a fond melancholy.

"By the time I'd started them on their way back to the castle, Dieavaul had unleashed another of his spells. I don't know what it was called. They all have a name, you know – the Greater Spells. If I had to guess, I'd mark it as either the Black Wind or the Flaying Death. Staples of the old legions. I don't know. Not had occasion to survive many such spells in person. Magic like that – there's no wonder some don't weep much for your fallen empire.

"Whatever it was, it ate them up like a storm of razors, man and horse alike, all them that were left. All except Hardt and Hestan, and Hardt was done for. Just a pile of shredded bloody bits left of him, still trying to push your father back, but he was dead on his feet. He was just too stubborn to realize it as fast as the others."

Osrith took a deep breath and looked around the room with an impatient scowl. "Do you have anything stronger than tea in here?"

"There's some brandy in the decanter there on the sideboard." Aeolil pointed. "And goblets. Pour me one, too."

Osrith shuffled over and popped open the decanter, giving the contents a sniff. With a grunt of approval, he poured out two goblets, full to the brim.

"I'd known Hardt the longest. He'd bought me outta the gaol when I was about a ten-year, to serve in Ferus Whyr's Company. We'd been together since. He was a big, stupid, greedy oaf – and a mean bastard, besides – but he died a braver death than most. Funny, that."

"He always scared me," Aeolil admitted, and accepted the brimming glass of brandy. "Of all your men, he was the one that seemed the most like a killer."

Osrith snorted and quaffed a considerable measure of his drink. "Ah, Lily – we were *all* killers. Lynx was charming. Kraye was well-mannered. Blood was still on their hands, and on mine. A lot of blood. Hardt, well," he paused to wipe his mouth on his sleeve. "I suppose he was different. We were all good at it, numb to it a bit, but he *liked* it. He was still the closest I had to family.

"No matter. He was gone. I'd seen this pale, lanky faeling kill a dozen men along with my lieutenants in less time than I could wet myself. Only Hestan was left, and his time seemed short. I spurred on Blackdog to charge. I hoped maybe I could last a bit longer, give Hestan or the boys some time."

Osrith stopped talking and just stared, chewing his lip. Aeolil could sense with an impending dread what would come next. She steeled herself for it. *This is how my father died.*

"Hestan's horse had spooked and thrown him. All that blood, or the magic, or the bonesword – I don't know what did it, but it bolted for home. He was there on the ground, his leg broken or close enough, and Dieavaul laid him open – split him chest to groin, and he was done just like that.

"That was hard enough to see, but when I heard Andrew shouting, heard him closing behind me, charging at full gallop, I knew a different kind of fear. *Dread*, I suppose you'd call it."

"Oh, Andrew." Aeolil strangled a sob in her throat. *Damn you, you stupid brave boy! Damn you! Why didn't you run?*

"He was proud," said Osrith, as if answering her thoughts. "And naïve. And he loved his father. I tried to beat that garbage out of all of you, but Andrew... No. He charged, and then Kiev came after him."

Osrith finished his drink and slammed the goblet on the sideboard. "I tried to put myself between them, but he opened a bag of hell in our face. Shadowfire. I was close enough to see his eyes. He wasn't paying me much mind. He was following the path of the black flames, looking past me and straight at your brother, admiring his work. He smiled when the screaming started, but it didn't last long. I knew Andrew was gone then, too.

"He turned to me next, and Blackdog finally balked, so I hit the turf and rolled. Came up in perfect position. Struck him a killing blow right through the chest. Funny thing was, the sword didn't strike true, somehow. He was there, but not there, just kind of *in between,* and I didn't have any magic, no tricks, no way my mortal blade could touch him. And he knew it. I was left there wagging steel in the breeze."

"Did he suffer?" asked Aeolil, her thoughts frozen on Andrew's fate. For some reason, she needed him to tell her what she already knew.

"Aye," answered Osrith. "Shadowfire burns you fast, but not fast enough. He suffered. If the stories are true, he *still* suffers. You'd know more about that than I, I'd guess."

Yes, she thought. "But Kiev escaped, then?"

"I suppose the sight of Andrew burning black was a bit much even for blind courage. While I was up in Dieavaul's face, he got some sense and turned about. Not that I'd any time to wonder at the fortune."

"Go on," she prompted. " How did you escape?" *The worst is over,* she thought. *There's no one left to die, now.*

"He came at me high and fast, but I knew he was just drawing me off balance and out of position for a heart thrust. I also knew he was *too* fast, and untouchable besides. I couldn't kill him. I couldn't go toe-to-toe parrying and riposting. So," he exhaled, as if still wondering at his own actions. "I let him slip inside my guard, a smug smile on his face as he brought his sword in for the kill. I dropped my blade, and I grabbed the crossbar of his hilt in mid-strike, and I ran *myself* through on that damn bloody sword. Coldest thing I ever felt. It burned me with cold all the way through and out the other side.

"That surprised the bastard, sure enough. I figured if I was going to get stuck with the thing, better get stuck on *my terms*. I jabbed it through where it wouldn't kill me right off, and I held it there, and him with it. Turns out, that sword lives on both sides of the Veil, and so long as I held it, I was on both sides, too. I may have been a stuck pig, but he couldn't hide from me anymore – I was right there with him.

"So I grabbed his turkey neck in my other hand, and I gave it my all. Tried to choke the life right outta him. Had him worried, too, for a bit. He was tangled up with me, off balance, no leverage, and he couldn't use his magic – couldn't utter a word. I could feel his throat crushing under my fingers."

Osrith's eyes were glassy, distant in the realm of his recollection, his right hand clutched tight in a fist, knuckles white. Aeolil watched him there, studying him. She had always admired him and thought him both brave and capable. But now, she was in nothing short of awe. Tears rolled down her cheeks, tears of mourning and pride, and maybe vindication. If there had ever been a doubt that festered in her, it dissolved now. He'd done all he could for them, even if he didn't seem to believe it. All he could, and a little more.

"That's when Kassakan rode in on a rainbow, and Dieavaul managed to twist and push me off. I'd lost a lot of blood, and my strength was waning. I couldn't put up much more fight. I managed to fall away from him and the door he opened up in Shadow. I didn't want to *follow* him, wherever he was going, for damn sure.

"I don't know if he didn't have time to finish me, or if he was just dazed enough not to think of it, or maybe he was rightfully scared of the angry lizard bearing down on him all lit up with magic, but he made his escape and left me there bleeding to grey. The rest you know already."

Aeolil got up and crossed to him, wrapping her arms around him and burying her face in his broad chest. He smelled like oiled leather and stale sweat, and she could feel the angry pounding of his heart.

"Thank you, Osrith," she said. "Thank you for saving Kiev. For... for everything you've done."

"It's what I couldn't do that worries me – that what I couldn't do *then* will become what I can't do *now*. I barely escaped him."

Aeolil smiled up at him through her tears. "I'm not so certain that it wasn't him escaping *you*. Every day you live is a reminder of *his* failure, Osrith, not yours."

"No." He shook his head. "I got lucky, and you can't count on luck."

"Perhaps not," she agreed, hugging him tight, "but I *will* count on you, Captal Turlun. That, I surely will."

Chapter Forty-Nine

In Dreams Alive

PANIC.
I'm going to die.
Calvraign hung from his balcony ledge, his fingernails scraping across the ice-slick stone. He tried not to breathe, but even so, breath came, and each breath like a bellows echoing in a forge hall.
A dream – wake up before you fall!
There was a presence above him. Dark, but empty, it hung like a shroud over his quarters, enveloping them. His eyes were closed, pressed against the granite. Or was it marble? He couldn't remember, and he daren't open his eyes to check.
Slipping.
Wake up!
A thunder of blood pounded in his ears, his heartbeat like a hammer on the door to waking.
"Let go." Another voice. Dry, like crackling leaves. Familiar.
Wake up, he warned himself. *If you fall in your dream, if you die – then you die in the waking world!*
"Let go," the voice repeated. *"You must fall for me to catch you."*

Does that even make sense? Calvraign wondered. *Am I talking to myself?*

"Look down," the voice commanded.

Calvraign tilted his head down, cracking an eye open to peer down past his dangling legs to the reaches below. Instead of flagstones meeting the base of the tower, or waves meeting the lake-wall, shadows broke on blackness, the insubstantial meeting nothingness.

Oh, that's inviting.

"Ès cal en magh con gòn."

Upon hearing that phrase, Calvraign released his grip and fell, his eyelids pressed shut and the words following him down to the unknown. It was an old saying of the Cythe: *a son is a son until he becomes a man.* Marshal Bowen had recited the very same words when handing down his father's sword, at Ibhraign's interment.

When Calvraign opened his eyes again, he was no longer dangling, or falling, but standing on a hill. *That's settled, then,* he thought. *I'm definitely dreaming, or close enough. A sight better than the alternative, I suppose.*

There were trees all around, but there was no color. It was a forest of grey, like a shadow of his homeland. A castle rose from the mists at the crest of a nearby hill, pennants streaming in a wind he could not feel, capping an outcropping of stone that pointed to the far-away plains like granite fingers.

Or is that limestone?

"Yes, you know this place," the voice confirmed. "In a fashion."

Calvraign followed the trail toward the castle. It bore the same dull transparency as everything else around him, but here, it was not a crumble of forgotten rocks and moldering woodwork. It towered above him, each stone in place, mortar sound, timbers untouched by rot. It was formidable, as he'd always imagined it once had been.

"Car-an-Cythe," said the voice, still as if a whisper, though not quiet in its speaking. A man walked next to Calvraign. He wore armor and a long fluttering cloak, but his face was featureless and shifting, as if running from human sight. "It has cast a shadow longer and stronger than its source. Did the bard ever tell you its name?"

"No," Calvraign admitted, surprised at how easy conversation came. He was puzzled, but not afraid, which was a conundrum all its own. "I suppose he hinted at it, though. I didn't much care to put a name to that mystery, truth be told."

"Some mysteries we choose. Some are thrust upon us."

"I was wrong, before," Calvraign admitted. "You are not the Pale Man. We call you Greycloak, for lack of anything better."

"As good as any name to call the nameless."

"Who are you, then? What do you want of me? Why have you- ?"

"You are full of questions," interjected Greycloak, *"but I have only one answer."*

"Might I know it?"

"You might." Greycloak stopped at the massive gates. *"If you ask the right question. But the hearing and the knowing are not the same – you will forget the answer upon waking. The Wards are weak, but not broken outright. There is much I cannot say. Better that I help you answer your own questions."*

"But you do say *more* than you ever have," Calvraign said. "And you have brought me *here* to say it. You are no longer content to linger in my shadow. What has changed?"

"You know the answer to that."

"Ebhan-nuád," Calvraign breathed, remembering the verse that Brohan had just taught him:

"On Ebhan-nuád, from evernight,
the Dark will shroud the realm of Light.
Where perilous thin 'tween death and men,
and the Wards of Ghaest in ruin.

When Dead may walk and Life chagrin,
under light of the baleful moon.
In dreams alive, in sleeping wake,
the Hand of Death your soul to take.

On Ebhan-nuád, from evernight,
the Dark will shroud the realm of Light."

"There is much truth hidden in the old rhymes."

"Brohan always said that riddles were the way to cheat the wards, and rhymes the way to remember them."

"Yes," agreed Greycloak, entering the ghost of Car-an-Cythe and beckoning Calvraign to join him across the threshold.

"This isn't symbolic of anything, is it?" Calvraign asked, eyeing the darkened portal with some trepidation.

"Everything here is symbolic," dismissed the wraith. *"How you act defines what it symbolizes."*

"That's circular reasoning," said Calvraign, unconvinced, but he entered, regardless.

"Life and death are a circle. Sometimes reasoning follows suit."

"You're certainly taking advantage of your chance at conversation," Calvraign commented as they climbed a spiral stair into the heights of a tower. "You'd better hope this is a long dream."

"I've waited a long time for the chance, and likely I'll not have another. I'll take what I can while I may."

Calvraign watched the back of the apparition that led him through his dream. Knowing now that he was not the Pale Man, that he indeed seemed an ally rather than a foe, his identity was yet more intriguing. For now, he kept silent, watching and hoping for any further clue. He tried to stem a growing hope for fear of disappointment.

They entered the keep's great hall, and Calvraign was surprised to see that they were not alone. In fact, were the occupants not for all appearances merely the cast-off shadows of missing lords and ladies, he could easily have been in a feasting hall at King's Keep.

"This is an odd dream," he remarked.

"Dreams are doors to otherworld. Most only linger in the archway. We have passed through."

Calvraign stopped, looking around, eyes wide and apprehension creeping in to crowd out his curiosity. *If this is not my dream... .*

"Am I dead, then? Did I really fall? Is this the greylands?"

"You sleep, but you do not dream. There are many shades between Light and Dark, Calvraign. The naming of the greylands is no accident in its plurality. We now inhabit that which I call home, not so far removed from your own, and yet a world apart."

"Does everyone here talk like this?" Calvraign said, wondering now for the first time how he might escape this dream, or vision, or whatever trance he was in. *Not knowing where I am, it's hard to get where I'm going.*

"You only hear me as the wards permit, regardless of what I might say. It is by design, though I do not know its purpose."

"Aggravation of the living?" ventured Calvraign under his breath.

Greycloak had led him through the great room, and they now ascended another spiral stair. If his memory were true, a tower had stood thereabout in the living world, though the one he recalled had long ago fallen. A moment later, his recollection was vindicated when they entered a many-windowed room at the apex of the tall watchtower.

"I did not bring you here to discuss the wards or the rationale of my lord. Even here, I will not be safe for long."

"*You* will not be safe?" Calvraign said, bewildered. "What about me?"

Greycloak turned to him, and Calvraign was drawn into the shadows that lurked and spun within the cowl of his hood. He could hear the sounds of battle: swords clashing, cries of death and victory, the sound of flesh ripping and blood spilling.

A last rasp of rattled breath.

"I died a warrior," Greycloak said. *"But as I drew my last and looked into the eyes of Pheydryr for her judgment, I knew only bitterness. Peace was stolen from me by betrayal. I struck a bargain then with Pheydryr and Her Lord."*

Greycloak paused, and though the sounds of death and battle had faded away, it left a lingering disquiet. *"I made that bargain for you, to protect you; and I am at odds with my lord now for the same reason. Alas, Calvraign – there is no place you will be safe. Never again safe. Even now the threads unravel, exposing the truths that lurk in the hidden weave. But I will guard you from whatever I can."*

Realization spread from Calvraign's gut. As unsettling as were Greycloak's words, an excitement grew in him that he could not deter. Did not want to deter. A hope...

"Are you... ?" Calvraign faltered. "Are you my father's shade?" he finished, searching the swirling absence that was its face for any sign.

"No," answered Greycloak.

No, Calvraign repeated. That simple syllable of denial was a dagger thrust to his burgeoning hope and childish fantasy. For one beautiful moment, it had all made sense. Ibhraign had cheated death for his son, to watch over him and protect him when he needed it the most. Saved him on the plains, warned him at King's Keep, brought him here to see him one last time and pledge his protection. But this was no tale of Brohan's, waiting for its happy ending to arrive.

"I fought with your father at Vlue Macc," continued Greycloak, *"and you are closer to my heart than ever you may know. It is your mother's memory I honor in defense of you, not his. If I were capable of sorrow, I would offer it."*

"They must have left you out of the legend," Calvraign said in a forced levity, struggling against tears.

"Legends leave out many things. The truth, mostly."

"Was this why you brought me here? So that I could learn this about you? To know I could trust you?"

"I don't know. I only knew that at last I could, and I did. But that is as good a reason as any."

"Are you the same spirit that talks to Callagh? Old Bones, she calls him."

"No. Though we serve the same lord, this Old Bones and I. The girl is taken as a tool of broader purpose than I put myself on your account. Your fate means little to them, but everything to me. And the reverse is true, for her."

"It cannot be chance that we are both so favored as pawns," Calvraign said. "So to what –?"

Greycloak interrupted with a wave of his hand, his hood tilted as if the invisible head inside listened for something. *"Our time has run out. They have found me, and I must go if I am to be any further use to you. You must take your leave of my world, but I will return to yours on* Ebhan-nuád, *and I will be the sword in your shadow."*

"How do I –?"

"The same way you came," answered Greycloak before Calvraign finished asking. He raised his hand, and with an icy blast of air, Calvraign tumbled down into the night, the sound of howling wolves echoing in his ears.

Chapter Fifty

A Short Order

VAUJN stared up at the roiling clouds and caught a snowflake on his outstretched tongue. It had been a dark night, the moons cloaked in grey. The muted colors of dawn looked little different as they seeped through the haze. Shadows jumped in sputtering torch flames across the masonry walls that embraced the small courtyard. Vaujn let the snowmelt dribble down his throat and stuck his tongue out for another.

"If you're thirsty, there's a cistern around here somewhere," teased Mother Chloe. She stood at his left, the rest of the squad at attention in the rear. "Hunting this *dhûnorihm* isn't boring you, I trust?"

"Hardly," he scoffed, in earnest. "I'm surprised how good it feels. We were rotting away at Number Nine."

"Yes," she said, but there was no agreement in her affirmation. "Rotting *safely* away."

Vaujn gave his wife a sidelong glance, but then turned back to his vigil over the courtyard. "Is it the hunt that has you on edge, or my attitude?"

"Neither," she said. "And both."

"I know I've led us to danger, and I don't believe in destiny, but the deeper we get into this mess of Osrith's, the more right it feels."

"I know," she agreed, deflated. "That's what worries me."

"Still nothing?" Vaujn said, pointing at the scrying bowl in her hands. Sometimes he found comfort in stating the obvious.

"Just the undercurrent – invisible, but waiting to pull us under. The wards of this place have been bent more than broken, and masterfully so. It knows what it's doing. I'm wondering what we'll do if we find it."

Kill it, Vaujn thought, but kept it to himself. He knew that wasn't what she meant.

"I suppose now it won't be a matter of *finding it,* anymore," he said.

"This is a big risk you're taking," observed Chloe. "Osrith is gambling more than his honor, or yours, or ours – he's putting Ruuh's honor up for the taking. If we fail… ."

"We won't. Besides, it's not like we have a choice. The word of a *Shaddach Chi* bears the authority of the king his grand self. I'm going to say *no* when asked?"

"You could have complained more."

"There's always time for that," he pointed out with a smile, wrapping his arm around his wife's shoulder in a congenial hug.

Symmlrey's slender form loped toward them in long strides from the far end of the courtyard, and Vaujn withdrew from the casual embrace with Chloe to receive her news. He felt a kinship of strangers with Symmlrey here in this human land, but she was only the third aulden he'd ever met, so it was all a matter of degrees. Long before written histories were kept by either kin or aulden, before the Sundering, both their people had come here from Faerie. Once, like siblings. Now, perhaps distant cousins.

"Captain," the *wilhorwhyr* said with a deferential nod, and then again to Chloe. "Mother."

Vaujn wasted no pleasantries. "Any trace?"

"Faint," she admitted. "Too faint. There is a powerful masking at work, and beyond my skill to penetrate."

"I've had no more luck," admitted Chloe. "A *duaurnhuun* could sniff it out but I haven't the nose for it."

"Will your squad be ready if it sniffs *us* out, first?" Symmlrey asked. "If I understand things, that's the new plan, more or less."

"That's the plan," confirmed Vaujn. "We're just waiting on some wax and parchment to make it all binding and official."

"Blood makes things official," mused Symmlrey. "*liyir* makes things permanent. Crushed wood and melted wax… ?" She shook her head.

"Well," Vaujn shrugged. "Whatever. Anyway, that's what they're doing. We're waiting for Prince Hiruld to come inspect us and accept our appointment as his Guard. And you?"

"Dismissing the Prince's Guard and holding most of them at the wizard's tower is sure to be a pebble in the pond. I will watch for ripples."

A SHORT ORDER

"All righty," Vaujn said. He thought for a moment, trying to find an equally compelling metaphor, but when nothing came to mind, he settled for a traditional saying of the Upper Watch. "Sharp eye and sharp edge," he wished her.

Symmlrey disappeared as quickly and quietly as she had come. Color bled into the courtyard as more daylight penetrated the cloud cover. Vaujn hoped it wouldn't get too bright.

"I think we're the pebble," said Chloe, dipping her finger into the scrying bowl. "I only hope she doesn't stand and watch us sink to the bottom."

"Vershtig!" cursed Vaujn. "How do you do that? *We are the pebble.*" He shook his head and made a grating sort of growl in his throat.

Chloe rumpled her brow. "Are you worried about being *witty*?" she chided. "Sometimes I wonder if the All-father wasn't up to his eyes in a cask of ale when he breathed your soulfire."

"Everyone else is bantering and quoting like I'd missed rehearsal," he groused.

"Never mind. Here's our new charge, and it looks like he's got his parchment. Stick with the strong, silent soldier bit and worry a little less about being profound and poetic."

The prince arrived in the courtyard with a moderate entourage, including his herald knight Bellivue, Agrylon, Brohan and Calvraign. Osrith and Kassakan brought up the rear of the quiet procession. Vaujn wondered for a moment why Osrith had discarded the blue and silver of House Vae for nondescript and unadorned greys and blacks. But only for a moment.

Vaujn and the kin raised their swords as a unit and then brought blade to shield in three staccato blows.

"Prince Hiruld of Providayne," intoned Vaujn formally. "We offer shields to ward and swords to battle. Verklämme!"

Hiruld placed his hand on his breast. "Your swords and shields are a great gift, and honor me. Let the soldiers of King Ruuhigan of the Underkingdom be welcome, but let them also be feared. Sir Bellivue." He nodded to his herald, who approached Vaujn with a bundle of blue cloth trimmed in gold. "Captain Vaujn, I present you with the colors of my House, to wear in your defense of my person. House Jiraud offers thanks to you and to your esteemed king, and gladly accepts your service."

Vaujn accepted the tabards with a bow, and then handed them to Mother Chloe. "We will wear your colors with honor," he said.

Hiruld and Vaujn faced each other in awkward silence for a moment. Bellivue smiled and clapped Hiruld on the back. "That's the extent of it My Prince," he said. "This is your Guard now. It is official."

Vaujn exhaled. The prince seemed equally relieved. He held out his hand to his new captain, a broad smile on his face. "I truly am honored," he said. "But I was worried I wouldn't get the words right."

Vaujn clasped Hiruld's hand and returned the smile. "Aye, looks as we both made it through, Your Highness."

Mueszner took care of the details behind them, barking out orders to bring the disciplined kin squad into formation. From this moment on, they would not eat, drink or sleep without their first concern being the prince and his welfare. That was just fine with Vaujn except, maybe, for the *drinking* part.

"Why isn't he locked up with the others?" asked Vaujn, pointing at Bellivue. "No offense meant, but I thought we weren't taking chances."

"He's under geas," Agrylon explained. "He cannot do harm; he cannot be used to do harm. He is inviolate."

Hiruld laughed from deep in his belly and knocked Bellivue on the back so hard that the herald stumbled forward. "Bells has been my friend since I was knee-high to my brother, and he's watched over us both. If he'd meant my end, he'd have had it. With or without the spells upon him, I would sooner die than even suspect such betrayal by his hand."

Vaujn frowned back at the prince and tugged on a war braid. "Hrmph," he grunted. "Even so. Better off sticking him in the tower with the rest."

"No," Hiruld protested immediately, but he turned in surprise when Bellivue's hand touched his shoulder.

"Yes, My Prince," the herald said. "It is the wisest course. He is the captain of your guard – he must take no chances. I would do the same."

"Bells… ." Hiruld shrugged the comforting hand away. "First Inulf – now you? You're the only one left I *trust*."

"That is why you mustn't." Bellivue counseled with a calm smile. "I will go."

"But the geas," persisted Hiruld.

"My Prince," advised Brohan, "even Agrylon's wards have been muddied. Who's to say the geas has not somehow been weakened, also? Listen to your captain in this."

Agrylon glowered at Brohan, but nodded. "It is sound council."

Hiruld clenched his fists. "It's not right. I feel safer *with* his sword at my back, not having it locked in a tower."

"Prince Hiruld?" Calvraign stepped forward. "Captain Vaujn *must* be suspicious of all your guard. One of them is not what he seems. If you keep Sir Bellivue at your side, then time will be wasted guarding against an innocent man when we should be watching for the assassin. It doesn't besmirch his name.

"And," he continued, coming one step closer, standing shoulder to shoulder with the prince, "if there is any attack, he will be suspect as much as ally. He may be harmed. It is the best way for Bellivue to protect you – and for you to protect *him*."

Hiruld kicked at the dirt, clenching his jaw. In that moment, Vaujn thought he looked more like a petulant child than a prince. But he didn't judge him. Parting with familiar trust was never easy, for children or princes.

"Very well," Hiruld agreed, challenge lingering in his voice. "But we will escort you there ourselves, *in honor*."

"Let's get on with it, then," said Osrith. "We've only got a day to prepare and a lot to work out."

"You heard him," Vaujn barked. "Form up. Sir Bellivue – you have the Guard. Lead us on, sir – the honor is yours."

Chapter Fifty-One

Sacred Hours

ARTYGALLE practiced the Sacred Forms and recited the Laud of Dawn, both his voice and his swordwork in careful, measured cadence. His sword swept in graceful arcs through the chill air, tracing the smooth ovals of Hirundal's Butterflies in the dissipating mist of morning. The archer's yard was empty, and he recited the prayer aloud, each word and each swing bringing him closer to the peace before battle.

> *"This day, as each, from dawning to dusk,*
> *to the Swords I offer my oath.*
> *My blade, in aid of the weak – to strike, as they may not.*
> *My shield, to shelter the helpless – to defend, where they cannot.*
> *My faith, a Light through Dark and through Shadow,*
> *in battle, peace or parley,*
> *in wisdom, honor and valor,*
> *now and always, in Your way I follow."*

The Laud had been the daily affirmation of his Order since the time of Andulin. It anchored Artygalle's covenant with the Three Swords, centering his soul on his purpose and his duty. The routine of the prayers was a danger, for too easily it could devolve into unthinking habit. But Artygalle thought of each Sacred Hour and its accompanying devotion as a challenge to be a vessel of Illuné's Will, rather than an instrument of his own.

After completing the prayer, he continued with the Discipline of Steel. It, too, was an ancient chant, a regimen as old as Mother Church, or older. For where the Laud might feed his soul, the Discipline honed his skill to the precise and careful action that was necessary for victory in battle.

Artygalle shifted his feet, feeling his connection to the earth, the tread of his boots in the dust. "As the Dragon, firm of stance and right of balance."

He closed his eyes, inhaling, picturing the patterns and principles of attack, defense and counter-attack, that Ghaerieal had passed down to him. "As the Eagle, keen of sight and sound of judgment."

Artygalle's long sword flashed in a high inside strike. "As the Mountain Cat, swift and true of aim."

He returned to his base stance, and then concentrated on his shield work, alternating between high, middle and low guard, hiding a grimace under his helm. The arm was still sore, but serviceable. The armor and shield itself had been repaired and refitted, and Artygalle felt their comforting weight without encumbrance of movement. Daính and Thruhm had delivered the gleaming plate and chain to Inoval before heading to their own rendezvous with the rest of the kin. Vaujn's accompanying note had wished him the best of luck, noting that they had taken *extra care* with it, and he expected no payment save *a victory to make the oddsmakers weep*.

"As the Gryphon, bold of heart and without fear," he concluded.

Artygalle lowered his weapon for a moment, watching as Inoval led a small group of men to the edge of the yard, and then transitioned without pause into the Form of Eongés. It was a basic exercise, but it suited his purpose. Better to remain a bit guarded with one's full measure of skill on an open field the day before a tourney, after all.

The leader of the waiting men was dressed in a fine linen shirt of pure white with a velvet doublet trimmed in silver nape fur. He paced the very edge of Artygalle's range, despite Inoval's hesitant protests, close enough to demonstrate to the knight and his squire that he wished the exercise to end immediately. Artygalle recognized the man with little affection, and ignored him and his affront until the last of Eongés' prescribed motions was satisfied.

Although tempted to launch an aggressive display of Xhidar's Triangles just to see if Curate Sinhd would flinch, Artygalle resisted. Practicing one of the Sacred Forms out of spite closed the mind to learning, and if one was not intent on learning, what point in practice? He sheathed his weapon, reminding himself that humility and deference to those of higher office within Mother Church were an integral part of his vows. He owed it to himself, and to Inoval, to honor his oath to the letter.

"Your Grace," he acknowledged, removing his helm and enjoying the cold air on his hot brow. "I am at your service. How may I-"

"The *dragon*," Derrigin sniffed, wrinkling his nose as if he'd come upon something sour. "Is that the provincial version of the Discipline? The proper anchor for your stance is *the Bear – fortitude and strength*. There is no dragon."

He wastes no time launching an attack, mused Artygalle. *His own version of the Triangles – quick, hard words to thwart balance.*

"My Order has always recited it thus," he answered, after a calming breath, "since the time of Andulin."

"Yes? Well... We are generations past the reign of Cathellion and his sainted champion, aren't we? I'd thought such heresies were quelled along with Thunyr and his traitors; it's small wonder that bits and pieces escaped the purge. Are you Reformers, then, up in Tiriel?"

A parry, and a thrust.

"Of course not, Your Grace. His name is not even spoken, let alone his teachings. The Order of Andulin has always been set apart; perhaps some of our customs are out of touch with Mother Church. I apologize if I offended you. I will submit it to the archbishop's judgment."

"No matter," dismissed Derrigin, kicking a pebble with the toe of his boot. "I'd as soon keep your customs and your Order in antiquity, where they belong. I am not here to school you on orthodoxy."

Authority is his crutch, not his strength, noted Artygalle, pleased with the revelation of his successful feint. *What he readily wields over others, he fears himself.*

"His Holiness remains disappointed that he could not accommodate you at Saint Severun's, and he is concerned that your care here may have suffered from inattention, *at best*," Derrigin said, his hauteur returning without pause. "Will you be ready for the morrow?"

Artygalle flexed his fingers and rolled his left shoulder to demonstrate his mobility. "I'm fine, Your Grace," he answered. "My shoulder and my shield have both been mended well enough, as you can see."

"His Holiness hopes your new friendships continue to be so valuable – *for you*. The Cythe has shown somewhat less than due deference to the offices of Mother Church. You, I'm afraid, may be all that stands between Sir Calvraign and the influence of our enemies."

"Your Grace?"

"While you were resting under their tender care, your merry little band of dwarfs managed to insinuate themselves into royal service, displacing the Prince's Guard." Derrigin stepped in close, his powdered nose within a hair of Artygalle's sweaty cheek. "All at Sir Calvraign's suggestion, and at the expense of a company of loyal lancers, handpicked by the archbishop for that honor."

Artygalle wondered if the curate intended subtlety, for he certainly detected none. "You must have been disappointed. I am sure you worked hard for that honor, Your Grace."

"I care little for my own disappointment," discounted Derrigin, tilting his chin upward. "It is for the prince that I fear. And for your friend, which is the point of my visit. He has taken none other than Sir Osrith Turlun as his Master-at-Arms."

Artygalle thought perhaps the curate's own displeasure was somewhat understated, but there was no mistaking the vitriol when he spoke of the knight. "I do not know that name," he admitted, "but the kin seem of honorable intent. They have been kind to me. I am certain they will serve the prince well, though why -."

"No!" interjected Derrigin, spittle flying from his lips as he turned on Artygalle like a feral animal. "Still your tongue and stuff your simple platitudes. The Goddess does not follow in the wake of your humble tread, making things right with the world. Your head is up your arse! Worse, it's up *Andulin's* arse, and yet you think there's nary a stink. So *listen* when I speak, sir knight, and speak not another happy word without my leave. If you are to know your duty, and carry it out, you must know your enemy."

Artygalle pressed his lips together in a thin line, jaw clenched tight, and listened.

"The kin are under Turlun's thumb. Neither he nor they are to be trusted. Do you think it coincidence that you were held a comfortable hostage while *they* solidified their position at court?

"And this boy of the Cythe, your *friend*. What is the foundation of his faith? The training of a *bard*. Mother Church is tolerated by the barbarians, more than revered, and the bards are no better. Let us hope it is not too late for you to mend any damage."

The curate paused only long enough to breathe. Artygalle concentrated on measuring his own breath, listening quietly and offering no comment.

"*You* do not know him?" mocked Derrigin. "Mother Church knows him. *I* know him. *Sir* Osrith." The envenomed honorific betrayed his contempt for the title, as well as for the man. "He is a murderer and liar, and possibly worse. He was a promissory, once, meant for the Order of Myrvoerval. That was before he burned the monastery, and most of the sleeping brothers, to ash. They jailed him, but coin sprang him before the rope could stretch him. Such is the justice of the Iron Coast.

"The surviving brothers and the abbot did not live out a ten-year. He murdered and mutilated them to a bloody man. Even you must have heard the stories of the *Bane of Rhiém*."

"I have," confirmed Artygalle, the words tentative on his lips. He'd never given the legend of that scourge much credence. A whole priory hunted down to the last? It seemed more a dramatic and convenient fiction than a true accounting of fact. It would not be the first parable to inspire fear and increased vigilance in squires and acolytes who might be shirking their vows. "You believe it is this knight, Sir Osrith. That *he* was the murderer? Then why hasn't Mother Church brought him to justice?"

"My *belief* and His Holiness signing a writ of sanction are two very different things. I presented a case to the Holy Tribunal, but the Knights Justiciar ruled against vengeance, even on behalf of their own fallen brothers." Derrigin took a deep breath. "Such is the justice of Myrvoerval," he grated through clenched teeth. His eyes darted to the men behind him, and he licked his narrow lips into a forced smile. "I suppose I am a man of emotion and not so well governed by such stoic logic. My uncle was the abbot, you see."

"I'm sorry. You must have been very young when he died," consoled Artygalle. "But you do retain the right of challenge, Your Grace. Call this knight out and settle your account, and both your honor and my friend will be spared the taint of this man."

Derrigin was a pale man, but even so what little color that pricked his cheeks drained away. "When and if we meet on the field tomorrow, you will see I am no slouch with blade or lance, Sir Artygalle, but Osrith Turlun is no easy prey.

"When I was a boy, I watched as the rogue who murdered my uncle paraded through Saint Kaissus Field, tilting the King's Lance at the royal pavilion in victory. The Fourth Lance had fallen to him at Vlue Macc, and they'd scarcely been ransomed back before Sir Tuoerval fell to him again in tourney. He'd vanquished the best of Guillaume's peers for the second time in a ten-moon."

"He sounds formidable," admitted Artygalle.

"Formidable?" Derrigin scoffed. "There is a taint on him. He crossed blades with the Pale Man and lived to tell it. It's *unnatural*. Either he is in league with the Dark, or he survived what no man ever should. Either way, I will not deliver myself as a willing lamb into his arms."

"Am I to be your lamb, then?" asked Artygalle, calm but frank. "I am willing, if called upon, but I wish you might tell me what you actually want, Your Grace."

"My wants are irrelevant. It is the archbishop's desire that I warn you. He thinks you no lamb. On the contrary, His Holiness believes you may be the last best hope of countering those who have poisoned the king against the church."

"I have no standing with the king."

"Sir Calvraign has standing with the king, and you with Sir Calvraign. A scant hope, in my view, offering a nudge where a pummeling is due, but His Holiness wishes to keep these battles in the realm of ideas rather than blood and steel."

Watch your back, brother.

The words of that anonymous knight tugged at Artygalle's memory. One whisper. One warning. It had dogged him with a doubt that lamed his trust, supplanting it with a hesitance that made him suspicious and uncomfortable. He supposed that's what it was intended to do. Either the intent was pure and it truly served as a warning, or, if the intent proved more sinister, to distance him from allies and hinder his mission. In any case, the effect was the same.

"I am a sworn Knight of the Lance," he said carefully. "I will uphold my vows, and I will do all within my power to help Sir Calvraign live in the same example. Beyond that, I am not sure what I can promise."

Derrigin's upper lip curled. "Oh, what more could we possibly ask, sir?"

Ghaerieal had always taught that reciting the names of the Three Swords helped to curb a tongue that might strike out too quickly in anger. Artygalle did it twice. He held the slighter man's stare, trying to penetrate the mask of contempt and arrogance he wore, but to no effect.

"Your Grace," he said at last. "You are *determined* to offend me. What cause have I given you? Or is this some test of my restraint?"

"Restraint is but a civilized word for cowardice," goaded Derrigin. "Perhaps you are failing the test?"

At this point, any doubt Artygalle may have harbored about Derrigin's intentions vanished. The curate was hoping for nothing less than a violent response of some sort. Throwing about references to cowardice, whether veiled or not, could only have one purpose. Why he would wish to do such a thing remained a mystery, but Artygalle had no qualms about how he would respond.

"You are at leisure to decide that, Your Grace – it is, after all, *your* test. If I may beg your leave, I have a tourney to prepare for."

"Of course," conceded Derrigin with an overstated bow. "One last thing," he added, withdrawing a glistening brooch from his doublet. "Your talisman."

Artygalle eyed the small winged sword and shield, and his breath caught in a muted gasp. "Thank you," he said, his voice strangled as both joy and regret stole the wind from his words.

"Blessed and ordained by the archbishop and Captain General Tuoerval themselves. You are now officially recognized and registered in the lists of the Lance. No more prancing about in your Master's boots. Quite an honor. Do not waste it."

"I will not," Artygalle assured him.

"You may pass along your old one to the inkblot, here," added Derrigin with a disdainful nod at Inoval. "He is forthwith and permanently transferred to your service as a squire of your order. The lists have been so amended."

Derrigin turned from the field without another word, but given the sneer on his face, words were unnecessary to register his disgust.

Artygalle smiled. "He does not like you, either," he said, turning to the boy and meeting his bright gaze. He pinned the talisman to the squire's homespun shirt. "I suppose I am in good company, then."

Inoval took a knee and lowered his head. "I will serve you truly, sir."

"I've no doubt," declared Artygalle. "Now, rise and draw your sword. It is time you learned the Discipline of Steel."

"But I know the –"

"You are in the Order of Andulin, now," interjected Artygalle, without raising his voice. "Our customs are sometimes *out of touch* with Mother Church. But – they are *our* customs, and you must learn them."

Inoval nodded.

"Now, assume first position and repeat after me: *as the Dragon, firm of stance and right of balance...*"

Chapter Fifty-Two

Fitting Proposals

THE evening settled into night, a cloak of gloom trimmed in frost that concealed the omens hanging dread and unforgiving in the sky. But Guillaume knew they were there, and that knowledge weighed on him. It was his fault. All of it. He had done this to them – to his sons.

Ah, Vingeaux, he reflected. *You would have been a mighty king. I should have been there for you when it mattered. They came before we were ready. Agrylon assured me...* Guillaume looked across the room at the wizard, who stood arguing with Brohan by the fire. *You brought us to the edge, you old fool. Your brother was right. We should have left it alone.*

The chamber was dark, lit with fitful inconsistency by the fires struggling in the hearth and the torches sputtering along the walls. It was an odd assemblage gathered here: the familiar faces of Willanel and Vanelorn offset by a very solemn Aeolil Vae and a somewhat reserved Calvraign at her elbow, looking tired and troubled. Bleys Malade and Osrith Turlun stood on either side of their respective charges, trying to deal death with poisonous glares.

At least they *are human,* Guillaume thought, glancing around the room at the underkin honor guard that now wore his son's livery. He kept the frown from his face with a lifetime of practice. *Insanity.*

The king brought his crystal goblet of watered wine to his lips, but the liquid slipped over his tongue without taste. They were talking in circles, and had been for hours. The truth was that they had no idea what to defend against, or even where or how an attack might come. The end could come at any time, from anywhere, and the best his councilors had come up with was a troupe of stunted dwarves to guard his son from doom.

"Father? Are you well?"

Guillaume looked up into Hiruld's concerned eyes, so blue and vibrant, yet so lacking in command. The prince knew *how* to command, of course, but he still lacked the charisma that had been Vingeaux's hallmark – that dangerous depth of gaze that drew men in and made them *want* to follow. For all that Hiruld had, he did not have that.

He is a pretty one, the king thought. *He would have made a fancy bit of bride bait. That was the best I hoped of the boy.*

"Father?" persisted Hiruld.

"Stop fussing," reprimanded the king. "It's unbecoming. Why do you let everyone natter on like that? Take charge. Be a prince. Be a *king,* damn it. Do something."

Hiruld's concern retreated into puzzled injury. "But it is your council, Father. I-"

"Bah! You can't always wait for me to step in for you. Vingeaux didn't wait in the wings on my whims, now, did he?"

Hiruld's countenance darkened.

That's it, encouraged Guillaume, *get angry with me. Don't let me chastise you. Put this doddering old man in his place.*

"As you wish, father," Hiruld said, his lips tight about the words.

Guillaume watched in disappointment as his son walked away. *Weak,* he lamented. *My beautiful, laughing, wonderful boy has always been weak. And it will be the death of him, and perhaps the death of us all.*

Hiruld pounded his fist on the table, rattling the silver trimmed tableware and toppling a candelabrum. A servant swept in from her station to right the candles. Hiruld cleared his throat.

"The king has brought us here to agree upon our course and set it in motion. When he feels inclined, he may lead that conversation. It will be nice to know what the old man is doing about anything for a change, other than whispering with other old men and tripping on each other's robes."

The outburst quieted all conversation among the gathered peers, and Guillaume almost feared even to think in such profound silence, lest his very thoughts be overheard in the stillness.

Guillaume straightened and gritted his teeth. *Losing your temper is not command,* he fumed. *Vent your anger with me, man to man, prince to king. Not like this. Stupid and weak. What worse could I bring to the throne than this?*

"A poor time for jests, Hiruld," he scolded with detached hauteur, hoping to dispel the edge of his son's words with indifference.

Hiruld didn't acknowledge the effort at abeyance, save perhaps to raise his voice further. "I cannot replace my brother. He was a better man, a better prince, and a better *son* than I will ever be. But," he said, nodding to Guillaume, "I can and will replace my father. Times being what they are, I will need an heir of my own to replace me, and to that end I have chosen a wife."

Guillaume stopped in mid-step, his irritation at the veiled insult consumed by surprise at this revelation. The object of Hiruld's heart was no mystery, but the king had made it clear she was not to be pursued for marriage.

He couldn't be so –

"The House of Vae has consented to release the hand of its proud daughter, Aeolil, to mine. The kingdom needs happy news. I shall provide it tomorrow at Saint Kaissus Field, and announce our union before the peers, the commonage, and the Holy Mother Church."

– bloody stupid.

Guillaume tried to hide any sign of approval or disapproval. He avoided even a glance at Agrylon. The king's tired eyes watched the beautiful young lady as she transformed her own surprise into an understandable blush of excitement or embarrassment, sidling up to Hiruld with a radiant smile.

She is capable enough, Guillaume observed, *but her House is already a close ally. Tianel would have better suited us, or Jocelin of Mneyr, or even Xhidraxes' pouty little princess-in-exile. What is he thinking?* Guillaume noted Aeolil's blossoming figure and her penetrating blue eyes. *Perhaps the problem is what he's thinking* with.

"The kingdom also needs an heir, as does the *Lion's Line*," Hiruld continued. "If the prophecy is to be believed, we are running short of lions. The quicker this is remedied, the better for all of us."

"Not too quickly, for the lady's sake," Brohan quipped, abandoning his heated discussion with Agrylon to offer congratulations to Hiruld with a firm and far-too-familiar pat on the crown prince's back. "Gods bless your chosen bride and your union."

Hiruld was taken somewhat aback by the gesture, but smiled in appreciation of the sentiment. "Thank you, Master Bard."

What's he playing at? Guillaume had known Brohan since he himself was crown prince. He did not breach the protocols of court lightly. The king searched the room with a quick glance. Everyone was surprised, but most were smiling or laughing at the news. Most. But not all.

Calvraign. The boy stared in shock at the back of Aeolil's head, his mouth pursed and his face just a shade pale as he watched her stand with Hiruld. *Yes – she is a good match for you. Better for her. Better for you.* Guillaume clenched his jaw as he turned back to Hiruld. *Better for House Jiraud.*

"Your Majesty," called the King's Herald, tapping his staff. "Kassakan Vril and the *wilhorwhyr* have returned. In their company, may it please you, the Baron Ezriel Malminnion and High Vizier Rel Aevmiir of Mneyr."

"Yes, yes, let them all in." Guillaume waved dismissively. "See yourself and the servants out, Yauncey. Thank you. We are not to be disturbed."

The herald bowed. "And if the archduke answers your summons, Sire?"

"Rian?" Guillaume blew a noisy puff of air through his lips. "Not likely. He'd skip his own coronation if it were I who invited him. We've what we need here already, for all the good it'll do us."

Ezriel entered with a bow. "Your Majesty," he acknowledged, respectful as always. Ezriel was competent, driven, and had shown unswerving loyalty to the Crown along with his devotion to Mother Church. He was a vast improvement over Haoil and certainly preferable to the glowering, petulant Garath.

Guillaume hated him, all the same.

A pity he missed Hiruld's news. I'm almost tempted to rehash that business just to see him squirm.

The hosskan and the vizier came next, making slight but tolerable deference to the king. Though thin, Rel Aevmiir was near six feet tall, with a shaved pate and shorn brows and bright golden eyes that surpassed even Agrylon's in intensity. She was so pale that the blue tracery of her veins was unnaturally prominent. He would have to be careful what he said. Having the duke's pet wizard here was akin to having Curisinian himself loafing amiably in a chair.

The *wilhorwhyr* came last of all, her half-nod half too little. Guillaume frowned but let it pass, sure to avert his eyes from her beguiling gaze. *The sooner we're done with her, the better.* There were entirely too many of the fae about these days.

Guillaume cleared his throat, wresting any lingering attention from the new arrivals or Hiruld and his announcement. "It's good you've joined us. We are a hasty council," he said, "and we must make hasty plans."

"Perhaps a hasty *explanation* would be in order," Rel said, her voice low and cold. She looked past Guillaume, locking eyes with Agrylon. She then glanced at the king. "At Your Majesty's pleasure."

Agrylon didn't wait for permission to respond. "The Tides have turned, and a shadowyn is loose. It means to kill the crown prince."

The pair of wizards regarded each other in silence for a moment. Guillaume repressed a shiver. He preferred thinking of *their* time as one past and better forgotten. *Tales of wizardry are better than wizardry itself.*

"You've been well and truly occupied," Rel said. Neither her voice nor her eyes wavered as she spoke. "I was wondering why your chair was empty at Ahtur-Dan. Perl thought mayhap you'd joined your brother in the mountains, or chased after Dmylriani. I see you've just been busy weaving our doom."

"It is always good to see you, Rel," Agrylon answered, though his sharp tone indicated otherwise. "Whatever my actions bring, at least I am *acting*. Sitting and waiting and whiling away brings nothing. That is the greater doom."

Rel shook her head. "I remember you and Gaious making the same argument about the Devastations. I wonder if the Maccs agree that the worst we can do is *nothing*."

"Victory came at a price," agreed Agrylon. "But it was victory."

"If you might forgive me pointing it out," interjected Calvraign, fixing Agrylon with a fiercer look than Guillaume anticipated, "that victory brought down the Empire. If the cost of victory is defeat by another name, perhaps it's not victory at all."

"Enough," the king said simply, though in truth he didn't mind seeing Agrylon squirm on the hook. That it was Calvraign doing the baiting only made the squirming a bit sweeter. *How surprised is the puppeteer when his playthings pull back on the strings?* "You've all got in your barbs – let's leave it at that. We've a real enemy to fight without wasting time quarreling with each other. We've wizards and *wilhorwhyr* and bards enough to talk till dawn, but let's not be that long about it."

"What is left to discuss, Sire?" questioned Willanel with a frown. "This shade from netherwhere will strike at Hiruld on the morrow. We must remain between it and the prince, with swords at the ready."

"Swords?" Symmlrey almost laughed the word, but her tone was too dark to be called laughter. "Is your sword of mage-metal, or bonded, or forged with silver and moons-light? Or perhaps you've a sung-sword of ebonwood in your armory? Do you think steel or iron will pierce its skin?"

"What? I…" Willanel's voice trailed off into a flustered grumble.

"Do any of you possess such weapons?" asked Symmlrey. "Aside from the wizards and kin, have any of you even *seen* a shadowyn, let alone fought one?"

Vanelorn raised one hand, the fingers of his other tapping the hilt of his sword. "Aye, we've such weapons. A few. And the archbishop will consecrate the day with the Three Swords themselves. They will be ensconced at the royal pavilion. We should be ready to use them. Even this shadowyn you speak of should fear the divine swords, yes?

"As for experience, well, it's a fair assumption that none of the knights in this room has ever crossed paths or swords with such a thing." The old warrior gave Symmlrey a frank appraisal. "You have," he said. His eyes met hers without flinching, honest, and with not a hint of beglamoured fawning. "If you can help us, we are indebted to you and your order."

Symmlrey shrugged. "Weapons are only the beginning. We've little sense how it will attack, or where, and only a notion of who and when based on scraps of parchment and prophecy. It has been among you for days or weeks – possibly months or years – but only strikes *now* – on *Ebhan-nuád*. It must yet be vulnerable in human form and waits for its power to peak."

"No," Calvraign mused, almost to himself.

The aulden quirked an eyebrow at him, and he cleared his throat. The king waited in rapt attention. Calvraign had remained mostly silent. Guillaume had begun to wonder if Brohan had overstated the boy's strategic acumen.

"Killing a prince is not such a difficult task as that," Calvraign clarified. "No offense to Your Majesty intended. If this thing has been masquerading as the prince's own guardsman, the hard work has been done, and a dagger to the back would suffice. Why wait until it is in the most danger to strike – when it is surrounded by not only the most powerful wizards and warriors of the realm, but with the Three Swords at hand to strike it down? There is a deeper plan at work here. There must be. Put the prophecy out of mind, for a moment. Its divination of the future may be blinding us to more immediate concerns."

"You think we should *ignore* this prophecy?" exclaimed Willanel. "If the saints send us warning, we should raise our shields, by the Swords, or we are fools!"

"Not ignore it, no," soothed Calvraign. "But I have great hope that not *all* prophecies and foretellings come precisely true. There are wards that guard such things and hide truth, and sometimes the doom of words is more subtle."

"You sound like a wizard. Are you Agrylon's apprentice or Brohan's?" Willanel strode across to the prince. "You can sit and talk and mince words and truths. I will guard the prince."

"Sir, you sell the boy short," said Brohan. "He makes a valid point. I have spent my life studying stories and prophecies and the muddy places where they mingle. If you'll entertain a very brief example?"

The knight shrugged, his deference only slightly more obvious than his indifference.

"In the Far West, in the lands of Ish, they tell a story of a sword-dancer named Ulmuadeh Z'yuul. She was a rogue and an assassin, but a champion of the downtrodden against the depravities of Jildi'im, the infamous

Golden Padrah. In one of her final exploits, Z'yuul was captured by the padrah and faced with what the cruel despot hoped would be an impossible choice. Z'yuul couldn't be killed outright, you see, for she had safeguarded her soul in a ruby and flown it to the far shores of wasted Anduoun on the back of the dragon queen Orhm herself."

Brohan paused. "Which is *also* a good story. Perhaps later we can tell some of the *Nine and Ninety Tales* in their fullness -"

"Brohan," Guillaume warned. "Get on with your little parable, if you must, but make it quick. We're here to a purpose."

"Yes," the bard agreed with some reluctance. "So, where was I? Yes: the impossible choice. You see, Z'yuul had a somewhat forbidden fondness for the padrah's own daughter, Riazel. She had, in fact, wooed the princess' affection away from her father and his tyrant rule. In addition, his Counselor Spirits had warned Jildi'im *only by the sword of Ulmuadeh Z'yuul could he perish*. He was desperate to reconcile with his daughter and defeat his nemesis once and for all, so he summoned a pair of Arbiter Spirits and sealed a pact with her.

"Z'yuul agreed never to do harm to the padrah again, to leave his lands and never return during his rule, and to never again court or seek the affections of the Princess Riazel. The Spirits consecrated the oath, and Z'yuul was now trapped by her words. Or so thought the Golden Padrah.

"Z'yuul handed her sword to Riazel, who killed her father with the magic blade right where he stood. They lived happily every after. Well, until the nine and ninetieth tale, at any rate."

"So, she lied her way out of death." Willanel struggled with his temper. "She wouldn't be the first. The Ishti'in have no honor. I don't see how this makes a bit of difference to us."

"No, *you* don't," agreed Brohan. "But Sir Calvraign *does*. You see there was no lie in her words. The lie was in Jildi'im's *ears*. He listened carefully, but only heard the meaning he expected. The prophecy said that he would die by her sword, and her oath promised that she would never woo the Princess Riazel, and both came to pass just as promised. The sword of Z'yuul *did* kill the Golden Padrah, if by another hand. And upon his death, Riazel became paladirha – *queen*. She was no longer a princess, you see."

"Bah!" Willanel snorted.

"No," Osrith said. "He's long-winded, but he's right. Once you spell it all out, you can't see around it anymore. Like a dog worrying a wound – sometimes it just makes it worse. We take the warning for what it's worth. Leave the rest."

"And what does that mean?" asked Ezriel. There was more confusion than confrontation in his words. "What's it *worth* to us?"

"It's worth knowing that every kin here has fought shadowborn," Vaujn said. "We're equipped for it, we're ready for it, and Hiruld won't be out of our sight or in front of our lines. I don't know if the All-father put us here to this purpose, but we *are* well-suited for it."

The king scratched at his face to hide the hint of scowl curling his lips. "Yet you ran from the Pale Man. We're warned against him as well. What if he comes along? Will you run again?"

To his credit, the kin soldier shrugged off the question without any sign of offense. "I would retreat with the prince, yes. I've already been over this with Osrith, and that seems the safest course."

"Perhaps I should stay with the prince, My King," Willanel offered, and not for the first time, looking down at Vaujn with some distaste. "I will not run."

"I'd rather find a roundabout way to victory than go straight to defeat," Osrith countered, with the affront Guillaume expected from the kin brimming in the mercenary's face instead.

"You paraphrase *Retreat to Conquest* from *The Stands of Kiev Vae*," Ezriel said, surprised.

Guillaume recognized the pensive look transforming the knight captain general's features, and the king steeled himself. *He's going to quote some sacred truth, the pious bastard.*

Ezriel closed his eyes and spoke with reverence: "*The road traveled to victory oft wanders, yet the course to defeat may be a road both straight and smooth, paved with easy temptation.* That tactic won him the Western March. The Stands were five years of retreat."

Osrith rolled his eyes. Guillaume joined him in spirit, but managed an appreciative nod at the Baron Malminnion.

"Blood and ruin!" Calvraign's execration took the room by surprise, and Ezriel's look darkened. Calvraign continued, oblivious. "Fools we are, one and all! Fools!"

Silence.

Realization spread across Calvraign's face in an awkward smile. "My apologies, but, I'm afraid we've been missing the point."

"Explain," Guillaume said, both encouraging the boy and stilling any protest from the others.

Calvraign nodded, looking around the room. His gaze fell on a decorative game board of *Mylyr Gaeal*, and he hurried over to it. He took a moment to arrange the pieces, then looked up, eyes bright.

"Look here- " he pointed to the middle of the boards "-the Dark has taken the nexus on the *Rahn* tier, and it threatens the regent from here, and here. But the next move is *not* to take the regent. Too direct. Potentially too costly. There are too many pieces left to defend him, and nine out of ten players will start focusing on protecting the regent to distraction, because losing the regent could be an immediate and disastrous end to the game. But that is *not* how the game will be won."

Fitting Proposals

Guillaume didn't play much *Mylyr Gaeal* – real war had taken him from such leisurely pursuits in his youth – but Vingeaux had made a spectacle of it in court for several years, and so the king was familiar with it. He stilled his impatience, hoping that Calvraign could deliver some substance with his enthusiasm. Brohan and Agrylon were bobbing their heads in rare agreement. He took that as an encouraging sign.

"No, the proper stratagem is *diversion*." Calvraign placed the pieces in a fictional move and counter-move. "Not a simple feint, or a single sacrifice, but a gradual repositioning of pieces on all five tiers. One that appears intent on the regent, but in truth only serves to slip pieces into place for a grander and more patient strategy. The regent may be doomed for any number of reasons, but his doom does not have to come *first*. Indeed, often it's the regent left scurrying from tier to tier at the end of a game, clinging to life and relevance as his opponent claims tiles and pieces and even whole tiers around him."

Calvraign threw his hands into the air, turning to address Guillaume directly. "But we've already *lost* this round of the game, Your Majesty. They are hoping we'll tail around our regent to the exclusion of all else, when in truth I fear it is *all else* that they intend to take first."

"You refer to the force massing across the High Ridge?" Guillaume glanced at Symmlrey, then back to Calvraign. "Even assuming such a large force is ready to invade, the Marches would not fall quickly or easily."

"No, Your Majesty. That threat is real, and I've no doubt it's immediate for the Marches, but I refer to something right here in King's Keep. I think the shadowyn is here for some other purpose than Hiruld."

Guillaume stilled a bubbling murmur of dissent with a sharp look, allowing Calvraign to explain.

"It was Lord Malminnion's quotation that sparked the thought: *a road paved with easy temptation*. It made me think of Rivers' Run and the Sentinels. We're rushing down the road, but I think the enemy is preparing to circle in from behind. We will crow in victory for a moment, but when we turn around, we'll find we're surrounded, our Regent in a corner with no escape."

"Sir Calvraign," said Vanelorn, "and I mean this with the utmost of respect – having a head for *Mylyr Gaeal* and having a grip on war in the world of blood and steel are two different things. Mastering a game and mastering life…" The old knight turned to the king. "Your Majesty, the fact is that forces beyond our control and understanding wish to bring us down. We know this. If we believe this prophecy, which I do with some reluctance, we know that the crown prince is a target, and must ensure his protection without trying to decipher grander strategies that may or may not prove true."

Rel laughed, a soft sound like rustling leaves, but it crept up Guillaume's spine like ice. "Vanelorn, you have long guided this realm true," she said. "But here, you are wrong.

"It's apt that you mentioned Rivers' Run." Rel stepped to the game board, next to Calvraign, and smiled down at his game in progress. The king wouldn't have been surprised if the intensity of her gaze melted the pieces. "The Ceearmyltu played a version of *Mylyr Gaeal* called *iyanliyanu* – siege." She looked up, locking eyes with Calvraign. "If the besieged player loses her nexus, the sieging player gains a strength of arms from within the defender's ranks. It's called *raising the sentinels*."

Agrylon stepped forward, frowning at Rel and exchanging a knowing, if cautious, look. "Meyr ga'Glyleyn," he muttered.

She smiled. "When *all* the pieces protect one thing, it tends to leave others undefended."

Agrylon pursed his lips in thought for a moment. "Your Majesty," he said, with some reluctance, "she is not wrong. If somehow the magic within Meyr ga'Glyleyn is tapped, our footing would change. There are great magics that could be unleashed upon the city, and we would have little defense. It is a remote possibility that anyone could unlock the aulden wards, but a shadowyn... ."

Guillaume read the implication in the unspoken word.

"Then stay and defend it," said Hiruld, his voice firm in the silence. "I have many and more swords at my call, and one of my own. Any attack on my person at Saint Kaissus Field would be folly, and easily overcome. But if there is magic here that must be defended, I say stay and defend it."

"An admirable sentiment," Guillaume said, somewhat surprised that he meant it. "And a brave one – but not an advisable strategy, I think."

Guillaume held up a finger, again silencing the burgeoning arguments around him. He wanted time to think, and more nattering would simply fray his nerves. *Two threats*. The symmetry of it actually calmed him. *Two fronts*.

"We split our forces," Guillaume decided. "Sir Calvraign, as you brought the threat to light, you shall lead a small force to defend the aulden garden. You will have Sir Osrith and his experience at your disposal, as well as some men-at-arms, as you might require. The rest of us shall defend Prince Hiruld at the festival."

"I..." Calvraign paused, blinking in honest surprise. His eyes darted from the master bard to the mercenary at his side, then back to the king's. "As you wish, Your Majesty."

Vanelorn sighed, and his shoulders sagged. "Your Majesty, if he's right, and there really is a shadowyn here within the keep, I'm afraid he's damned by his own perception. Even with experienced knights at his side..." His voice trailed off, and he cast a sympathetic look at Calvraign.

Brohan stepped forward. "I will-"

"No," Guillaume interrupted. "*You* will be at the festival, in the royal pavilion. Agrylon as well."

Brohan was stricken to silence. Guillaume pressed his rare advantage before the bard found his tongue. "We are guarding against possibility, not planning for eventuality. Calvraign is our rear-guard. The rest of us here, *the vanguard*."

"I will stay here," said Kassakan Vril. "It is my place."

Guillaume considered the hosskan for a moment, and then nodded. She would do as she wished regardless if he granted her permission; therefore, he gave it freely. "So be it."

"Take this," Agrylon said, offering the dreamstone to Calvraign. "Its purpose is fulfilled, but it may offer you some protection if you encounter any shadowborn."

Guillaume hoped the wizard was right. It was a risk leaving Calvraign behind. It meant fewer swords to defend Hiruld against the shadowyn. And, if by Oghran's darkest whim the boy was right, and the danger was here at King's Keep...

Calvraign tied the leather thong about his neck and tucked the stone under his shirt. "Thank you," he said.

Osrith made a noncommittal grunt.

"And so your tier is set, King Guillaume," Rel said. "Agrylon and I had best be about preparing ours. Swords will win you only part of this battle."

"Do as you will. But you must keep this to yourself, Rel."

"Must I?" she replied archly. "The Black Robes answer only to the Emperor of Dacadia."

"The Black Robes died out with the Empire," dismissed the king.

Rel smiled, her lambent eyes fixed on Agrylon while she spoke. "Sleeping is not the same as death, Your Majesty."

Guillaume suppressed a shiver. If there was one thing on which he and the grand dukes agreed, it was that the Black Robes must never rise to power again.

"Yes, it's a good thing, too," said Brohan, melting the cold pall that had fallen on the room with Rel's words. He stepped in to usher the king away from the wizards. "Or there'd be a lot less napping, all around."

Guillaume let an honest chuckle escape his tight control and shook his head. He put a fond arm around the bard's shoulders as they left the room and the wizards behind. "I have missed you, Brohan. That I have."

"Well, then, let's the two of us share a cup of wine. I've a very special vintage in mind, but... it's best enjoyed before the end of the world."

"Ha!" Guillaume laughed again, and felt some tension leaking from his tired bones. "Then I suppose we'd best start drinking."

Chapter Fifty-Three

A Moment Too Soon

DARKNESS fell in upon Callagh. She didn't know where she was or where she was going. The path behind held nothing for her. *That,* she knew. She pushed forward, waving her hand in front of her face, but she could only imagine the outline of her fingers. She heard the flutter of low flame, but saw not even a hint of its light. She shivered, the muscles of her shoulders bunching into a painful knot at the base of her neck, yet she felt no chill.

Caw.

Callagh heard the raven croak, somewhere ahead. She dragged her sluggish feet onwards, her soles scraping along with an effort.

Caw.

She tried to speak – to call out in response – but her throat was tight, and no sound came. The ground gave beneath her feet, not crumbling away like a rockslide, but softening and congealing, thick mud sucking at her ankles, pulling her down like bogsand.

Caw.

The mud crept into Callagh's mouth: tasteless, textureless ooze seeping between her teeth, clogging her tongue, filling her throat. She thrashed, kicked, sank further. Her eyes bulged and lungs burned as she fought for breath.

You can't fight your way outta bogsand, she warned, like she was shouting at herself across a great chasm. Her own voice seemed distant to her ears, but she mustered calm.

Like sighting down an arrow, she thought, the hammering of her heart steadying as she imagined the string taut against her cheek and goose-feather fletching brushing her skin.

Caw.

Callagh reached up, stretching her fingers, straining upward toward the sound, toward the raven, the ferrier of souls, the *roibhe ahn cranaoght*.

Callagh sat upright in bed, kicking her blanket off with a scream, not so much waking from her dream as being *thrown* from it.

Iaede and Braede were already awake and sitting on either side of the bed they shared with her, eyes wide, skin pale and lips trembling.

Iaede reached out to brush Callagh's sleeve with a gentle but uncertain touch. "Are you all right?" she whispered.

Callagh rested her elbows on her knees and her sweaty brow in her palms, sucking in a welcome breath of air. Her nightclothes were also damp, steaming, and she trembled as the chill in the air cooled the fabric against her skin.

"Just a wee bit of the terrors," she answered, peeking over her fingers at the younger girl.

"It's not the raven?" Iaede asked, face ashen. "My ma said ravens were messengers for the spirits."

Callagh brought her gaze out of her hands to meet Iaede's eyes. "Did you hear it, too?"

Iaede nodded.

Is she in my dreams? Callagh wondered.

Iaede pointed behind Callagh. "It's been there for a bit, now."

Callagh turned to find an enormous raven perched by the washbasin, staring back at her.

Oh, she thought.

"Caw," it said.

"Blood and ruin," groaned Callagh. "I'd still prefer a bloody unicorn."

Braede had turned over and returned to sleep, the quilt up over her head. Iaede still propped herself up in heavy-eyed consternation. "What?"

"Ach, it's nothin'," dismissed Callagh. "An old jest. Go back to sleep, I'll take the damned thing out."

"Don't," Iaede breathed. "Don't go."

Callagh was already lacing her boots. She spared a quick grin for the younger girl. "Don't be daft," she teased gently. "I'll only be a moment."

"Fiogna..." Iaede struggled through a lump in her throat. "Fiogna said the same, and the spirits took her that very night."

Callagh grabbed her cloak from its hook and fastened it with the brooch she'd bequeathed herself from Old Bones. It felt warm to the touch. *Wonderful.* "I thought you said she just *ran off?*"

"Aye. She just ran off – followed some vision o' hers in the middle of the night – and *then* the spirits took her."

"Well, no spirits or visions here." The words came with ready confidence, but it was a shallow reassurance considering Callagh was confident it was indeed one or both. She knew better than Iaede the full extent of Fiogna's unfortunate and fiery end, if not exactly how it came to pass. "Just a wee birdie lost his way, is all."

Lost his way into a locked room with shuttered windows, you mean, she thought.

"Saints defend you, then."

Callagh smiled at the girl, but shook her head. "They're not *my* saints," she said. "Or yours." She poked a finger at the master's door. "They're *his.*"

The raven punctuated her remark with a timely cackle, and took wing to flee the room as soon as Callagh opened the door. She followed it close, she and the bird together barely gaining a distracted glance from the sentries as they passed.

∻

Seth hesitated at the darkened entrance to the cellar, but a nudge from Faeldor sent him through into the dark, a step ahead of the wan nimbus of torchlight.

"Ha. A'feard summin gonna eat ya?" the old soldier guffawed. "Get on, then, and get out. I'm a mind to sleep now, hear it? No bellar' achin'."

"Stop it, Faeldor," begged Seth, his legs all but buckling beneath him. "It's not funny. Give me the torch or come closer. I've not had a good run of luck lately."

Faeldor whistled, and his eyes bulged from his scraggly grey brow in mock fear . "Ha. Is'n a *drauogh* in dar, munchin' on bones? Ha, ha! I'd say yous luck ain't so much bad, now is it? Should be dead twice, as I count. But mays be tha' Lady Luck smiles a bit brighter on yous 'n the rest of us souls?"

"I'd just as soon have a nice bright torch, thank you," implored Seth.

Faeldor chuckled but stepped closer. Seth wondered why the torches in the cellar had been allowed to go out at all. Although the church called this the Day of Respite, that was a misnomer for the servants of King's Keep. There was no jousting or games or formal feasts, but the lords and ladies still required food, drink, and fresh linens for their repose. Repose could be hard work.

The pitch boys had best be dead already to leave the cellars dark the night before the Feast of Illuné, he thought, *or Markus will kill them.* He'd certainly never dared when he'd done his turn as pitch boy, years ago.

"Huh," puzzled Faeldor, pointing his torch at an empty bracket in the wall, his grizzled cheeks scrunched into a scowl. "No torch here neither. They take up all them torches every night, them boys?"

"No," answered Seth, pinching his lower lip between his teeth. "They don't. At least, not without leaving fresh ones behind."

"Early bit o' prank, then. Thems like to prank on yous. Always have."

Seth nodded. They might be lying in wait, ready for their chance to jump out of the shadows and give him a wet-fright. Or they could be lurking with the torches, hoping he would run to tell Markus, only to return with him and find nothing amiss. He'd suffered most every humiliation at the hands of his fellows, and saw little sign that such unwelcome attentions would ebb.

"Maybe," he agreed aloud, *but this is a mighty dangerous time to be pranking.* He could still hear the crunch of Burton's neck, still see the blue-and-gold-clad knight throwing him from the balcony like last night's rubbish. *It could be something else entirely,* he thought as an anxious quease festered in his belly. "Let's just be quick about it."

Calvraign and Brohan had been back and forth and in and out with the prince, the lord high chamberlain, Lady Aeolil, the young lancer, Artygalle – and just about every other captain and commander of the keep. They had all become increasingly intense as the day wore on, and tempers had stretched and thinned. Although Calvraign seemed almost comforted by whatever had happened in his quarters the night before, and excited by his recent royal appointment, the same had served to set everyone else on edge, most especially his new man-at-arms, Osrith.

Seth shook himself and drew in a deep breath. *Best to get on with it.*

Seth led Faeldor past neatly ordered casks of oak, labeled, tagged and sealed by the royal vintner; past rows of painted clay amphoras, stacked and waiting at attention like troops in reserve; on past the tidy racks of magnums and full, half and quarter bottles from every region of Rahn; back to the far end of the room, down a small open stair to the sunken chill-chambers where the rarest and most delicate of vintages were cellared.

"Wilderwine," he grumbled. Master Madrharigal had been very specific. He could still hear the ridiculous words in his head: *from the vineyard at Astin Meh Leyr, and nothing but.*

Seth had laughed off the request at first, thinking it a jest. Wilderwine was a bit of clever fancy, a convenient plot device for morality plays to ply bit players into compromising positions, or for trapping unsuspecting travelers in Faerie when daring to sup with the fair folk on the wrong side of the Veil. *And from Astin Meh Leyr, no less.* There was no vineyard at Astin Meh Leyr – only standing stones, and haunted ones, at that. But his laughter had died on uncertain lips under the unwavering and somber gaze of the master bard.

"Well, if there's any to be found, it'll be here," he assured himself.

"Wilderwine, eh?" The accent was foreign, but the voice familiar – deep enough to resonate in Seth's chest with each word. "What a boy like you need with such strong spirits, huh? Eh?"

Seth froze. The shadows loitering at the edge of Faeldor's torch fled before the massive man who loomed forward, a mountain of scale armor sprouting a thicket of tangled beard and crowned with fierce eyes glinting fire.

"Inulf!" spat Faeldor, his sword sliding from its scabbard with a well-oiled hiss. "Damns me foul bloody bad luck findin' *you*. Get'n you back, Seth boy. Back behind me."

Inulf smiled his broad, gap-toothed smile, spreading empty hands before him. "If it's dead I want you, dead you be, eh? Why waste words on dead men? Hmm? But best for you to stay back, sergeant, or my mind may be changing after all."

Seth had not moved, save to empty his bladder. Faeldor stood his ground, but did not advance. Inulf leaned forward, his eyes splitting attention between Seth and Faeldor's bared sword.

"Can you feel the Dark in your bones, boy?" His breath stank of *hemma* root, stale and sour. Seth struggled to keep his bile down as the warm odor washed over him. "Did you see its power on the terrace? Eh? I saw *you*."

Seth tried to speak, but his throat had seized shut.

"Go get it, then," prodded Inulf, drawing back to the very edge of the torchlight.

Seth forced himself forward, his breeches clinging wet and cold to his thighs. He searched the racks in silence.

Inulf chuckled. "I knew that bloody black bard would be after his vintage soon. But you'll need more than tree sap and aulden blood, now, boy. Tell him that. Tell him I said they wait too long. All of them. Chewing on secrets. Now…" He shook his head and spit over his shoulder. "Now they wait for death."

Seth paused in his search when he came upon a silver label on the lowest row of the rack. It was etched with a stylized tree and a circle of uncapped dolmens. *Astin Meh Leyr,* he marveled. He pulled a wooden bottle from the rack, turning it over in his hands, puzzled. There was no cork, no stopper – only one solid piece of smooth polished wood.

"Aye, that's it, boy – bottled and aged in songwood. What else it be, huh? Eh?"

Seth took a tentative step back with the bottle, closer to Faeldor and whatever protection he might provide. Very little, he guessed.

"Right then," drawled Inulf. "You got your wine, huh?" He stepped forward, hand outstretched. "Now give it here."

Since the only other option seemed to be *dying* for it, Seth handed the bottle to Inulf. Brohan hadn't mentioned that he should guard it with his life, so he made no hasty assumptions.

"Damnit, boy!" hissed Faeldor, but he made no move to fight.

Inulf brought the bottle to his lips and whispered something over the tapered end where a cork would normally sit. The wood opened, and he quaffed a measure with a loud gulp.

"Tell Brohan that I liked his wine." Inulf held out the bottle, once again whole, and Seth's quivering hand accepted it. "And tell him I'll see 'im in hell. Now run along, boy," he said, retreating into the shadows until only his haunting bass voice remained. "Run along."

* * *

The raven flew on ahead of Callagh in short bursts. Following quarry that wanted to be caught was no strain on her skills. Instead, she directed her attention to marking her way, noting the landmarks as she passed them and filing them away with a hunter's diligence. Callagh had once insisted to her father that she could never be lost, only *out of place*. He hadn't been impressed with the distinction, but then he was a man rarely impressed.

They wound down the stairs and left the tower, crossing the empty yard to arrive at the Temple of Swords and the bier of the deceased castellan. Callagh wasn't surprised. Not much of the counsel she'd received of late had come from the living. The raven paced along the wooden framework that supported the corpse for its customary viewing period. Burton had not been a man of the sword, or of nobility, but none-the-less he was an important man in his own way, and respects were due. Wrapped in oiled linen and sprinkled with fragrant herbs, the mostly frozen remains were not yet offensive to sight or smell.

The bird finally settled on the cadaver's head. It pecked at the wrappings on Burton's mouth, rending the fabric with the delicacy of a surgeon until the blue lips were free to snarl naked at the night.

"At least this one's not on fire," muttered Callagh.

Air hissed from Burton's mouth, and Callagh wrinkled her nose at the stench of rot.

"*Aldhal hag dé, ahn cranaoght,*" greeted a thin familiar voice from the dead man's lips.

Callagh looked around slowly, but there was no sign of life in the temple. She kept her voice low just to be safe. "A bit formal, don't you think?"

"It's only proper to show respects on such an occasion. It has been a generation since we have appointed a new warrior to the ranks of the *madhwr-rwn*."

Callagh's wit fled and left her with pursed lips and crumpled brow. "Calvraign?" she ventured.

"No," it answered. "He does not honor the old ways."

Keep to the old ways.

"Oh, bollocks!"

"You are the first to accept the honor *just* so, little ghost."

Callagh could hear the scolding in those words, even in a voice bereft of inflection. There was no greater honor than serving the Cythe as *madhwr-rwn* – and no greater responsibility.

"You can't be serious!" She forced a laugh, but it died a quick, quiet death even as it began. Talking with corpses was taking the fun out of conversation. They had little motivation to joke, she realized, let alone the desire. "You know the words," prompted Old Bones.

"I do."

"Say them."

"What? Like in the stories?"

"Where do you think stories come from, *ahn cranaoght*? Say them."

"Ach. This is daft. Did Cachaillan feel this bloody ridiculous?"

"No," it answered. "He said the words. As did we all. As will you."

Callagh rolled her eyes. "I will, will I?" *Of course I will.* "*You* said them? Who were *you*, then?" she said, mostly to delay the inevitable.

"One of many," it dismissed. "Say the words, now. Time is short. Say the words and make your oath."

Callagh drew her belt dagger and sliced her palm with a subdued wince. A thin line of blood followed the blade as it tracked across her flesh.

"Deeper," rasped the voice on Burton's lips. "The oath's as binding as what you give over to it. And swear it upon my talisman, for your own sake, mayhap I can ease your way."

Callagh hesitated. For a symbolic blood oath, a few drops freely given would suffice. If he wanted more than that, more than just symbolic fealty to the Macc-an-Cythe, and sworn upon his token…

Not just any *blood oath,* she reconsidered, with some concern, *it's blood magic.*

She licked her lips. It made sense. Joining the *madhwr-rwn* was not a pledge of friendship or exchange of goods at a woodsmote. Her da' always joked that the *madhwr-rwn* only met in secret circles as an excuse to drink undisturbed. He never believed in the mystique. But then, he didn't believe in much. She herself might have scoffed at the suggestion of some magical bonding ceremony not long ago, but her life had taken a decided turn toward widdershins, of late.

So, there it is, then, she decided.

Callagh cut again, pressing the edge hard to slice deep. She closed her eyes, gripping the brooch in her bloody hand, and recited the lines that Old Bones himself had taught her through his endless tales. It was the same oath spoken by the like of Cyhlt or Cuaihln from the age of heroes, or the somewhat less legendary *madhwr-rwn* of her own time: Faille and Gabhougn. And Ibhraign.

"On my blood I swear my heart and bind my soul,
To the will of Father Earth and Mother Suns of Sky"

Callagh shivered, a chill emanating from *within* her bones, and a burning heat from the trinket in her palm. Blood dripped in a steady *pit pat* on the veined marble floor. She took a knee, suddenly lightheaded. Air sighed from Burton's dead lips but Callagh couldn't make out if he said anything. She drew her bloody palm across her face, dabbing crimson on each cheek and her brow, and then finally down her lips and chin.

"With painted face I greet the dawn,
as the gods' own edge, the madhwr-rwn."

The cold deepened. Callagh blinked away an afterimage of shifting shadows, a phantom audience that filled the small chapel in grey, surrounding her. It was so fleeting, she wondered if it were her imagination. She certainly *hoped* it was.

"You *were* listening," said Old Bones, with a long creaking exhalation that approximated a chuckle. "Your oath so sworn, how long shall it abide, Callagh Breigh?"

"Until the suns fall from the sky, until the Deeps open up and swallow me, until the seas arise and drown me, you have my oath."

"It's done. Your blood is spilled. Your words are spoken. The Old Gods bless you. The old ways keep you."

Callagh stood, her legs still trembling, releasing the brooch and squeezing her bleeding hand tight into a fist. "What about my great deed?" she asked. "Aren't I s'posed to slay some beast or defeat a demon army or some such thing?"

"In your case, *ahn cranaoght*, the cart is put before the horse. You are young and untried, but needs be you're bonded to the *madhwr-rwn* before you can earn your place."

"It *needs be*, does it? How *needs it be*, exactly?"

"On *Ebhan-nuád*," it said, "there will be Shadows within shadows."

"Is that another bloody metaphor?" Callagh cocked her fists on her hips. "Can't you just *talk* to me now? Did I have to chop my whole damn hand off to get a straight answer? It's no wonder the world's gonna end –"

"*Don't. Be. Petulant.*"

The voice was not Old Bones. It was not louder, but it was stronger, commanding, and it whispered in her head without the need to move dead lips. Callagh's breath caught in her throat, and her heart stilled in her chest for just an instant. The blood roared in her ears, the surf of her pulse crashing impotently for release. And then heartbeat and breath returned, and she sucked in a grateful, slightly terrified breath.

"I am ever your friend, little ghost," Old Bones said. "But do not test Her patience. I am not the only one peeking through the crack in the door."

Callagh swallowed an angry response, narrowing her eyes at the corpse and screwing up her face into a scowl. *Her.* She did not need Old Bones to tell her to whom he referred. She knew the patron of the *madhwr-rwn*. Pheydryr. The Grey Lady. Death Herself. Callagh wondered if she had just gained purpose and power through the brief ritual, or if she'd fastened a leash around her neck. Either way, she knew how to avoid a beating. Her Da' had taught her that much.

I'm not a broken thing, she thought, steeling her nerve.

"Tell me, then. What am I to do about these shadows upon shadows?"

"Find Calvraign."

Callagh stiffened. *I'll not hurt Cal,* she resolved. *Not for the Grey Lady, or Old Bones, or anyone else.*

"Calvraign's no shadow," she stated with firm assurance.

"No," it agreed, "but he *casts* one."

"He... What does *that* mean?"

An empty rattle of breath answered her.

I'll have to get my bow, she thought. She'd made careful note of where Tremayne's quartermaster had stashed it in the baron's armory. *His Grace'll not be much happy with that, t'be sure.*

The raven cawed, and hopped onto her shoulder.

"Ah, look what I find? Two birds on one gravestone, eh? Ha!"

Callagh stiffened at the sound of the man's voice. His accent was thick, and his laugh low and menacing. She turned to see a dark shape at the door. Steel glittered in the torchlight.

Inulf.

"The spirits are bold tonight, eh? Shadows and ravens and little painted girls, huh? They let loose the things that *eat* them things as go bump in the night. Ha ha. But I think, little lass, I *think*... ." Inulf stepped forward, his dirty, bearded face leaning in from the shadows. "I think that this time, the spirits – they wait too long."

"They say you were taken by a shadowyn," Callagh said, keeping the bier between them as he advanced. A handful of men joined Inulf from the courtyard, swords drawn, armor partly concealed by thick winter cloaks. Blue cloaks trimmed in gold. "Renarre says you're possessed."

"Does he now? Me? Juut! The Fox say much, but know little. So busy with rabbits, misses hounds on his tracks." Inulf's smile contracted to a fierce grimace. "I never waste time on rabbits."

Callagh held her blood-wet dagger in front of her face, and Old Bones' talisman warmed at her breast.

"Hah! Silly pup." Inulf smiled again, his dark gaze locking with Callagh. "None o' that, eh? Hmm? Say hullo t' me loyal best – the *disappeared*." He waved his arms at his men. "*We* be the last you've time to trust."

Chapter Fifty-Four

A Pan for Frying

CALVRAIGN chafed against the unfamiliar weight of the mail shirt, but he supposed it served as counterweight to the surprising lightness of his heart. He turned from the parapet as the mists swallowed the king's procession at the far side of the bridge to Dwynleigsh. The towers of King's Keep now loomed above him, grey and wet in the morning.

Herein is the beast, he thought. *I feel it in my bones.*

"Are you drunk again?"

Calvraign jumped and blinked in surprise as Osrith appeared at the door, frowning.

"What? No! Of course not."

"You'd best wipe that fool grin off your face, then. This isn't some back-country nape hunt."

"I know you've more experience," Calvraign said, trying to sound firm, "but the king did leave *me* in command. Some small pretense of respect might-"

"I'm here to watch your back, not wipe your... ." Osrith stopped himself, and then smiled sweet as a nursemaid. "Not hold your hand," he amended. "Sir."

Calvraign stared at the older man in silence. *Words aren't going to impress him.* "Aye," he said. "So let's get at it, then. Did Lady Kassakan make it safely away?"

"She did. She'll be back at the garden with help or she'll not be back at all. Things being what they are, I'm wondering if it's not best to leave well enough alone and hope for the latter."

Osrith continued to make no secret of his distaste for this aspect of the stratagem. Calvraign continued to ignore it. *Kassakan agreed with me,* he thought, reassuring himself. This was no time to leave pieces on the board. It was all or nothing. "And the men are making their sweep?"

"Aye. Cleared the bridge house, the kennels, the stables and the other out-buildings. Sergeant Faeldor is heading through the South Keep now, and Sergeant Foss is ready for us at the Central Keep."

Calvraign nodded and settled his open-faced helm on his head. With one last look at the empty bridge, he followed Osrith down from the bridge house tower. Foss was waiting with two dozen men. He pounded a fist on his chest as Calvraign arrived.

Calvraign returned the salute. He'd been saluting so much this morning that it was almost natural. "Sergeant," he said, "lead on."

Foss was a barrel-chested man, and his deep voice carried in the still cold air of the empty baily as he barked out orders. The men selected for Calvraign's first command were efficient, if not especially excited about the mission, and they were swift and precise in response.

A chill touched Calvraign's spine, and he turned to peer behind him. He expected to see Greycloak lingering in his wake, but the shade had yet to appear. Instead, it was the bridge that again drew his attention. A Border Knight crossed the parapet of the bridge house, ever watchful.

"Osrith?"

"Hmm?"

"How is the bridge garrison deployed?"

"On the *bridge*?" Osrith scratched at his beard. "Well, they've got at least a dozen men on station at each gatehouse, and a few towers along the way, at the pylons. I think, at the least, Willanel leaves a pair on watch with a signal fire. Why?" he added, sarcasm seeping in to his voice now. "Are we going to search the bridge next?"

Foss snorted in wry appreciation, but Calvraign ignored the small affront. "No," he said, "but if we find this thing, we may need all the help we can get."

Foss and Osrith shared a quiet smirk.

"If we find this thing, we'll be in more trouble than an extra squad of men will fix," Osrith predicted. "No one expects us to find it. They just want us out of the way. If we *do* find it, we'd better hope Kassakan can hop back through a rainbow before it rips us all to bloody shreds."

Calvraign noted there was no amused snort from the sergeant this time. "We're going to find it," he said with a certainty he couldn't quite explain. "Or it'll find us."

Osrith grunted. "Don't be in such a hurry for Pheydryr's kiss, boy. She'll take a fancy to us soon enough without your help."

The ground floor of the central keep revealed an angry Markus and a busy kitchen, but it held no secrets. Calvraign found much to learn about the soldiers from their search, however. They were professional, methodical, and quick to obey if not always eager to please. Foss wasted no words, and his men wasted no time.

I might tell them what to do, but it's the sergeant that leads them, he noted.

The search of the second, third and fourth floors revealed nothing. The exercise was devolving into a chore. The soldiers remained thorough, but grew less guarded with each empty room they left behind.

Sergeant Foss' curse changed all of that.

"Demons Above!" he screamed, sending a dozen swords singing from their scabbards in a heartbeat. "On your guard, one and all!"

Osrith shouldered closer to Calvraign, his blade bared. Most of the squad was in the long hall on the fourth level, but Foss and a few others had just ascended the stairs to begin the search of the central barracks above. The sergeant appeared at the base of the steps, his face pale and drawn.

"Sir Calvraign," he reported. "Looks as you were right. They're all dead, sir. The whole watch killed in their sleep. Bloody mess."

"They're all dead?" Calvraign repeated. "How?"

"Throats slit, mostly. Some guts torn out here and there – those that woke up, maybe."

"Tighten up!" Osrith barked. "Something's here. Or *was*. Let's not let it catch *us* sleeping."

"Mullen's going on up to check the other barracks. Could be it got the morning watch before they woke and the night watch coming back for sleep."

Osrith tugged at Calvraign's elbow and brushed past Foss to head up the spiral stair. A soldier Calvraign assumed was Mullen met them at the landing, his face ashen.

"All dead," he choked out.

Osrith ignored the shaken soldier, examining the carnage in the barracks. Calvraign put his fist to his nose, trying to ward off the smell, and clenched his teeth. Everything was strangely in place, showing little sign of a struggle, but blood and viscera painted the floor and walls and soaked the mattresses.

"Don't fight it," Osrith advised, pacing down between the row of bunks and checking the wounds on the corpses. "Give it a good heave and save your energy for fighting."

Calvraign shook his head, though he thought he could smell that Foss' men may have had less luck keeping down breakfast. He felt light-headed, slipped as he turned, and fell to the floor inches from a lifeless body and the stench of blood and bowel. He twisted away, but his resolve fled, and he retched.

Osrith sighed. "Damn," he said, strangely calm to Calvraign's ears. "Got the lot of 'em. This ain't no shadow beast, either. Prints in the blood look like boots, and more than one tread."

Calvraign spit out the foul residue on his tongue and wiped his lips on the corner of his tunic, then regained his feet. His stomach was still sour and his legs a bit shaky. He saw the smeared tracks, and tried to make sense of the comings and goings.

"Does Inulf have a battle party of some sort within the keep?" he asked.

Foss entered behind them. His men kept a wary guard on the stairwell and the doors. "But that, that's impossible," he stammered.

"Yeah," Osrith growled, "it's a pisser when the *impossible* grabs your goolies and gives 'em a good yank, huh? Them being dead is just half the problem."

"Half?"

"If they killed all of the guards," he explained, "who was it out there on watch, exactly?"

"Blood and ruin!" Calvraign's eyes shot wide open as the icy itch between his shoulders returned, and it all made sense. "The bridge!" he yelled. "All of you to the bridge, *now*."

They descended two floors before a tremor shuddered through the stone and timber of the keep, scattering some to the floor and a few down the steps with a loud clamor. Strange battle cries rang out from below. Calvraign felt fear seep into his certitude even before he heard the man at the window shout, "The bridge, sir. They've fired the bridge!"

"Bloody hells," Osrith growled. "Now we've stepped in it."

Calvraign edged to an arrow slit and saw black smoke billowing into the sky and a growing blaze at the bridge house tower. Knights were running through the bailey. Screams and clashing blades echoed up the spiral stair from the kitchen, and a rush of panicked servants tried to flee to the upper floors, tangling with the guards as they pushed past.

"Find a door and lock it!" Osrith yelled after them.

"They're in the kitchen!" Foss bellowed at his men. "Get in there and push 'em back!"

"Watch the rear," Osrith advised. "They'll try to pinch us from top and bottom if they can."

"We need to regroup with Sergeant Faeldor," Foss said. "If we've any chance at all, it's with numbers."

"No, sergeant," Calvraign said. "We need to fight through to the garden. We can lose the keep, but we can't lose *that* – if we do, we lose the city as well."

Foss gave him a long look, but nodded.

They found Markus and Dar in the kitchens, barricading the door to the bailey. Calvraign counted three servants dead and one of his own men, with one knight in armor lying headless and spewing thick, dark blood from its gaping neck. It was the head that caught Calvraign's attention. Knocked from its helm by the deathblow, it had rolled close to the fire pit, and it snarled at them in defiance, mouth agape.

It wasn't human.

Hrumm! Calvraign realized.

A low throaty howl reverberated from the upper floors, followed by the sound of armored feet on stone, descending fast. Another howl answered from behind the blocked door, punctuated by relentless pounding.

"Well," Osrith said, rolling his shoulders and shifting the grip on his axe, "first things first."

༄

Seth pushed Iaede through the concealed door after Braede, and then followed through into the scurryway himself. Seth and the sisters were crowded between the narrow walls of the accessway that connected the baron's bedchamber, his sitting room and the outer hall. It wasn't a secret passage so much as an unobtrusive way to deliver wood to the ceramic heating stoves, but Seth hoped that whoever these knights were butchering the baron's men, they wouldn't know of the ways *between* the walls.

The sounds of pitched battle echoed beyond, drawing ever closer. Deirdre was still behind him, and Seth waited for her with the door cracked. A man screamed, and there was a clank of something heavy hitting the floor. An orphaned sword clattered through the doorway.

Deirdre stopped running and stood frozen for a moment, staring at Seth in terror, still halfway across the room from safety. Heavy footsteps approached, and she waved him away, turning to slide under the edge of a trailing coverlet on the bed.

Seth closed the door with a muted click, but winced at even that slight noise. There was no more screaming to hide the sounds of their escape. He didn't want to move – he barely dared breathe at all. He was scared even to look through the small peephole in the wall for fear the sound of his eyes moving in their sockets might bring their pursuers down on them.

Not for the first time, he hoped that Callagh was safe, wherever she'd gotten to. No one had seen her since the middle of the night, from what the sisters said. With any luck, she was visiting Calvraign where someone like Osrith could protect her.

Seth wasn't sure exactly how he stayed still, or quiet, or conscious, in the aftermath of the attack. Perhaps the fact that the girls maintained some semblance of composure lent him strength, or shamed him into stoic bravado. Likely as not, he decided, it was just paralysis from fear. He was becoming well acquainted with that condition.

Seth dared a glimpse through the peephole into Baron Ezriel's quarters. The bedchamber was still empty, but the sound of heavy footfalls echoed from the adjoining room. He could hear voices too, but couldn't recognize individual words – or even the language, he realized.

"Did they see us?" whispered Iaede.

Seth turned back to hush her with a finger to his lips. Her expression reflected his fear and uncertainty. A crash from the room beyond snapped his attention back to the peephole.

One of the killers was in the doorway, but he may as well have been an army for all Seth was concerned. The interloper advanced into the room, the torchlight a ruddy glow like blood on his breastplate and full helm. The sword in his hand was wet with a less metaphorical stain. Seth had seen at least three of the household guard cut down and assumed the fourth had fallen as well. He wondered whose blood adorned that blade: Tierry or Filchen or Makomber or some nameless face he'd seen but never met.

The knight cocked his head, as if listening intently.

A bead of sweat trickled from Seth's brow.

The knight twisted his head around again, taking a step forward. Seth started to ease the wooden plug into place over the peephole when the knight ripped the full helm from his head and threw it with a ringing clatter against the stone floor. Seth froze in place, unblinking. He stood transfixed by the creature's horrible tattooed visage, as if trapped in a nightmare from which he couldn't wake.

Is that a hrumm? he marveled. He could not even imagine how such a thing could gain access to the city, and to King's Keep, even dressed up in the garb of a Border Knight. *This isn't possible.* He was proud, at least, that this time he hadn't wet himself.

The hrumm sniffed the air, nostrils flaring as it sucked in the scents of the room. Its eyes were inhuman, like a mountain cat's, and Seth was sure it could see straight through the hidden door panel to find its prey.

But it didn't charge. The hrumm prowled across the floor, sniffing, sword at the ready, closer by inches, slow but certain of the scent.

It smells us.

A Pan for Frying

Seth's heart pounded as he realized there was nowhere to run. The slightest movement, the barest hint of noise, anything could bring it straight to them – anything at all. He was afraid even to replace the peephole cover.

The hrumm was mere feet away – and it was worse by far than any of the stories.

Deirdre sprang from her hiding place, running for the door. Seth didn't know if she meant to distract it, or to escape herself, but Iaede and Braede ran then, too, sprinting down the scurryway for the exit at the main hall, and he followed. The hrumm barely looked in Deirdre's direction. Instead, it leapt forward, crashing through the thin sliding door in a shower of splinters.

Iaede was directly in its path. She shrieked as it fell upon her. Its sword drove through her chest, chipping the stone behind her. A small sound popped from her throat, and a tear ran down her cheek, and then the sword was through and through once more. Seth fell to his knees as Iaede crumpled at the hrumm's feet. He watched the light and life fade from her eyes. A tiny, sad mewling passed her lips before her breath escaped forever, and the girl was still.

It was the second time he'd stood by and watched someone's murder. Seth felt a sick helplessness in his bones. The monster turned away from him, to chase down Braede, but it stumbled backward. A glittering point of steel poked through its shoulder blade. Then another ripped through its neck, spraying blood in its wake. The hrumm careened off the wall and fell face first a few feet from Seth, clawing at the floor as thick blood pumped from its opened throat.

The sound of battle again drifted from the baron's rooms, but this time the voices, and the language, were familiar. Seth looked through the shattered door in a daze. Another hrumm lay dead in the bedchamber, and a king's man slumped against the door clutching his gut, looking grey. Deirdre was there, too, her broken body splayed on the floor. Her throat was a mangled mess of flesh. Her glassy eyes gazed unseeing at the rafters.

"Seth!"

Seth turned at the sound of his name, surprised to see Callagh Breigh, bow in hand and her face smeared in blood, crouching in the scurryway in front of him.

"Ca… Callagh?" he sobbed, ashamed of his fear but unable to hide it.

"I brought help," she explained, her voice as gentle as her countenance was fierce. "You're safe for now."

Seth shook his head. "Deirdre," he moaned. "Iaede."

"I know," she said. The steel in Callagh's eyes flickered for a moment, but she blinked away the sentiment as fast as it came upon her. "None of that matters now. All that matters is Calvraign. Where can I find him, Seth? Where's Cal?"

Seth stuttered nonsense, trying to collect his thoughts in vain.

"Ah, bloody hells," said Callagh, squinting at Seth. "I'll just have to take ye' with me."

And she dragged him, protesting, out into the hall.

Chapter Fifty-Five

The King's Lance

AEOLIL assessed the champions with a wary eye. Suspecting attack, but not knowing from whom or whence it might come, the knights provided her little comfort. The pale fire of a hundred glow lamps shimmered in the gilt of their armor as they saluted the king and the royal pavilion. Even Artygalle was resplendent in his reworked mail. The kin had somehow repaired and refashioned his kit, and though it was not ornate, its craftsmanship was undeniable and beautiful to behold.

Artygalle was the only new face in the Champion's Melee. House Tirea had not sent a champion in the past few years, and ironically, Artygalle was here officially only as the champion of the Opening Melee, rather than Elvaeir's chosen man. Semantics aside, all knew he stood for Tiriel, win or lose.

The other Houses sent familiar faces. Chadwick represented her own family, and her eldest cousin Niklhas, for the House of adh Boighn. Calamyr and Grumwyr tilted for their respective Houses, Nevanne a'Cwille for Myrtma, and Ashgar Tremayne for Malminnion. The duchies each sent a champion, Mellieux for Aeyrdyn, as always; and the archduke's own daughter Jocelin stood for Mneyril. Lastly, Derrigin Sinhd represented Holy Mother Church and the lancers. As tradition warranted, the House Royal sent no champion to its own tourney.

With a rustle of heavy robes, Archbishop Renarre rose to his feet behind her. The dour mood of the pavilion had not improved on account of his presence. He crossed the short distance from their seats to the edge of the pavilion's balcony and faced the assemblage. Three acolytes were seated under the lip of the railing, hidden from those below. Each young boy cradled a scabbard and sword in his lap.

"Behold!" Renarre commanded, and the droning susurration of a thousand voices quieted to expectant silence. Aeolil was always astounded that somehow, within the cavernous confines of this living tree, a word spoken from any of the scattered pavilions could be heard clear and strong by the multitudes, no matter their seat or station.

Renarre reached for the first offered hilt and drew a shining sword of deep orange-red steel. Its length rippled in waves of subdued light like captured dawn. He extended the bare blade toward the knights and commenced the Consecration of Battle.

"*Calàthiél Nahaviir*," he intoned in Old Dacadh, officious and even, waving the weapon in a slow arc from left to right, "you are the edge of dawn's awakening, the Light that sunders Dark. It was with you that Irdik smote Gulgazamoun and severed the chains of the Ivory Throne. May you bring us the Wisdom of Irdik, this day."

Aeolil felt her lips moving in the appropriate response, efficient if thoughtless after years of rote training. The arena reverberated as thousands joined her.

"Irdik, First Sword among us, may your Wisdom guide us."

Renarre sank the sword point-first in its place behind the ceremonial kite shield that served as coat-of-arms and centerpiece of the royal pavilion. The shield was mounted on the outside edge of the balcony, and the sword crossed it from the top right quarter to the lower left. Once sheathed in the display, the only portion of the weapon still visible to the honored occupants was the protruding pommel.

Renarre withdrew a slender, silver long sword next, again extending and waving the blade left to right. It had a simple design and crossbar, but where Calàthiél smoldered, this blade *shone*. A pure silver light illuminated the somber expression on the archbishop's face as he continued the ancient ritual.

"*Elèndere*," he said, "you are the bright moonlight that assuages Shadow. It was with you that Illuné revealed and dispelled the Accursed. May you bring us the Honor of Illuné, this day."

Renarre sheathed Elèndere in similar fashion to Calàthiél, but crossing from left to right, as the throng responded in unison, "Illuné, Second Sword among us, may your Honor enlighten us."

When he hefted the last of them, a two-handed great sword, Aeolil could see the strain on his face. It was large enough that even a man the size of Grumwyr might have trouble wielding it effectively in battle, but the archbishop managed to hold it steady for the blessing, at least.

"*Gliyhtmuong,*" he said, lingering on the final *g* with a theatric and somewhat sinister intonation. Unlike its siblings, the steel did not glow or shine, but as its name was spoken, flames erupted on its blackened blade, licking from hand guard to point and burning with a heat Aeolil could feel even from her seat. The archbishop grimaced as sweat broke out on his brow, but finished the chant without interruption. "You are the fire that burns. It was with you that Kazdann brought the High Towers blazing to earth. May you bring us the Valor of Kazdann, this day."

"Kazdann, Third Sword among us, may your Valor swell in our hearts."

"Let those who do battle here today follow in the Wisdom, Honor and Valor of the Three Swords. If victory does not find the strongest among you, let the strongest among you find victory!"

"Victory!" responded the crowd.

Gliyhtmuong's fire extinguished as Renarre plunged it home in its resting place in the center of the hanging shield. With the last of the swords in place and the proceedings thus sanctified by Holy Mother Church, a huge roar erupted from the crowd in anticipation of the coming contest.

Aeolil did not share in the exuberance. She did not like sitting idly, and she found feats of arms fairly routine. Instead, doubt gnawed at her. They were fighting blind, and for all Agrylon's assurance that both the keep and the prince were defended from the shadowyn, whomever or however the creature might strike, the image of the Neva Seough sending the arrogant wizard flying bloody and broken in his tower hung persistent in her mind.

She watched Artygalle draw his lots and take his place with Windthane on the outs, waiting his turn. The marshal of the field and his scurrying minions combed the dirt of the list one last time, and the oddsmakers trekked around the field, placards in hand.

Artygalle has drawn Grumwyr, she realized with a pitying cringe. Winning on points was the only way to beat the Bear. He hadn't been unhorsed in recent memory. Points were not easy to come by, either. Avoiding his blows would deduct points from the tilt, and taking the blows had left many a knight littered upon the hard turf with little sense left rattling in his head. Mellieux had proved his only consistent challenge over the last few years.

The archbishop made his perfunctory graces to the king and prince, and retreated with haste to his own pavilion prior to the first joust. Aeolil thought perhaps he spared a bit of extra glower for the kin bodyguard around the crown prince, but she couldn't be certain. For their part, Vaujn and his cohort betrayed no sign of emotion through the intricate glares crafted into the faceplates of their helms. The *war face,* Vaujn called it, as she remembered.

"Agrylon cast an active warding," a voice whispered into her ear. "If this thing is about, we will know it."

Aeolil smiled and nodded at the master bard as he took a seat next to her. "And if it eludes this ward, as it apparently has those at the keep? Then what?"

"Ah. Well, those were *passive* wards, mind you. But if it can elude an *active* ward of a Black Robe, then it is far too powerful for any of us to even hope at victory. So we can rest easy. If we have any chance to stop it, then we will know when it comes. If we have *no* chance, it will pounce on us unawares and spare us a lot of fretting before we die."

"Don't jest," Aeolil scolded, watching Chadwick as he waited in parade rest for the signal to charge. He was up against Niklhas adh Boighn, who sat at the other end of the list chatting with his squire. Niklhas was confident and, given their comparative skill and stature, deserved to be.

"Sadly, I'm not joking," Brohan assured her.

Aeolil turned to the bard, searching his expression for a hint of levity, but his smile was a sad and uninspired one. He looked out past her, past the field, perhaps out past the Veil for all she could tell. Even a lowly sensitive, just barely touched with the barest sympathy for the *iiyir* tides, could feel the change in their flow. And Aeolil guessed that Brohan had more than simple sympathy.

The sound of hard contact brought her attention back to the field in time to see her cousin lurch out of his saddle, the victim of a stellar first blow from Chadwick. Her surprise evaporated into a moment of honest cheer at her guardsman's good fortune. Chadwick was tenacious and loyal and dutiful beyond compare, but if he was oft noticed by Oghran, it was only in her foulest moods.

The rounds came and went in a blur. Derrigin fell on points to the precise strikes of Jocelin, and Calamyr's youth and strength fell prey to the wile and skill of old Mellieux in a close match-up decided by a difference of but one contentious point. Nevanne won his tilt against Tremayne with surprising ease, but then the wolf captain was not known as a tourney-fighter. No one took him lightly on the field of battle, however.

When Grumwyr took to his massive warhorse and raised his lance high over his head, he received the loudest of cheers yet. He was a powerful knight with an explosive temper, and a crowd favorite.

They enjoy a little blood, don't they? When he knocks some lord on his arse or breaks his arm, it's a healthy reminder that we all may bleed.

Aeolil was surprised that Artygalle received a hearty welcome as well, including a full salute from the lancers across the field. She supposed, with Derrigin out of the hunt, he was the last of Mother Church's disciples still in the fray for the King's Lance. And, even if his mail was now polished, he *did* still bear that tattered banner of sackcloth.

"Do you *see* the tides, Aeolil?" Brohan's voice was distant, almost unrecognizable in its languor.

"I've not yet graduated the *iiyiraath*. Soon, perhaps," she sighed, "given the chance. I do feel the pull and flux."

His head bobbed in a slow nod. "If you are feeling what I am seeing, you must know that the tipping of scales is well under way."

"Yes," she agreed, a bit startled that Brohan, master bard though he was, had completed the tests of wizardry.

Artygalle and Grumwyr made their final salutes and kicked their steeds into a gallop. Aeolil counted the moments to impact with a trace of anxiety. She could spare only a little of her fear for a joust, but she pitied anyone struck by the Bear, man or horse – and in this case, either or both.

When their lances shattered without any unhorsing, Aeolil was slightly ashamed that she had never considered the possibility that Artygalle would keep his seat. Mostly, she was hoping he'd pull through with bruises rather than broken bones. But, to her amazement and that of the crowd, both riders discarded their splintered poles and circled the list to prepare for a second tilt.

The marshal held up his point tally, scoring even at three points apiece for solid blows to the shield. Grumwyr was looking over his shoulder, his visor raised to display a face with wide eyes and an open mouth. The drum of stomping feet and call of cheers was deafening. Even those in Grumwyr's quarter knew a good fight when they saw one.

"Well, this proves more a distraction than I'd thought," she muttered. The pavilion behind her was atwitter with discussion of the unexpected turn.

"Pair a knight and rider of Artygalle's skill with armor worked and bonded by the underkin, and you have a foe not easily dropped," remarked Brohan with a distracted air.

"Bonded? You mean enchanted? Faerie armor? He could be disqual–"

"No. The marshal wouldn't be so sloppy as that," dismissed Brohan. "Bonding is not enchantment so much as a *seduction* of steel. As the aulden once wrought this place with song, so can a skilled kinsmith bend rock, ore and metal to his will. Sir Artygalle's armor is not just mended; it is brought into its most perfect state. Good thing, too."

"Yes, good thing," echoed Aeolil.

"Chance would even dictate there are more than a few such suits among the wealthy and storied families here, and we may need them. But none of them are so *fresh*, I'll wager."

Artygalle's second charge left another lance shattered, even as he turned the point of Grumwyr's tip on the edge of his shield, deflecting the thrust harmlessly away. Aeolil couldn't recall the last time Grumwyr had failed to smash his lance.

"Is he *drunk*?" carped the king. "If he falls to this boy, Mellieux will be prancing around Praed with my lance for the next year, and I'll never hear the end of it from Rian."

"He'll unhorse the boy," insisted Hiruld. "He's taken by surprise, that's all. It's *Grumwyr*."

"With strength his only strength, his weakness shows," counseled Brohan over his shoulder.

"Strength his only strength," scoffed Guillaume. "Don't be daft. When we begin taking advice on battle from a bard, we shall know the kingdom is truly lost."

The horses charged, and Artygalle's lance shattered a third time on Grumwyr's shield. Grumwyr swept his lance in hard on Artygalle, but skewed high, taking him on the side of his helmet and knocking him off of his horse. The smaller knight fell into the list fence and spun to the ground with a metallic crash.

Both cheers and hisses greeted the strike, and there was great commotion in the common seating. Inoval sprinted toward Artygalle, who staggered to his feet, dazed. Grumwyr spurred his mount over to his fallen foe and dismounted to offer a steadying hand. Aeolil knew he would be disqualified for an illegal blow before the marshal even raised the red flag, and she suspected Grumwyr knew it, too. Though a brutish oaf, he was an honorable brutish oaf, she supposed.

The crowd was finally sated when the official declaration was made. "Sir Artygalle advances!"

Brohan shared a sly wink with Aeolil. "Desperation makes for carelessness. A lesson well learned."

Aeolil nodded. Artygalle and Grumwyr exchanged their knightly pleasantries and departed the field. Less pleasant discourse had erupted behind her, but she was not in the mood to join their spirited verbal quarrels. Brohan seemed to share that inclination.

The marshal paired the two lowest scoring knights to even the ranks for the second round, and Jocelin defeated Nevanne for the first time in their rivalry. She moved on to face Chadwick, and Artygalle was paired with Mellieux, and the final match-up seemed a foregone conclusion. As it turned out, the second round bore its fair share of surprise, as well.

When Artygalle dispatched Mellieux on their second tilt, sending the old veteran to the dirt, she could not feign astonishment. For all that he was relatively unknown, he had survived the brutal rigors of the Opening Melee and just unseated a perennial champion of the tourney. But when Chadwick, of all people, managed a startling blow that knocked Jocelin to dreams, Aeolil was truly shocked.

"I'd no idea your guardsman was such a fine jouster," commented Brohan. "He seems to have put you in quite a dilemma. Your House or your horse? Which will it be?"

Aeolil managed a grin. *Windthane, of course,* she thought, but only gave the bard a coy wink in response.

The marshal was announcing the final round and recounting the victories of the last knights standing as the oddsmakers were tallying up the wagers. Aeolil looked back at the royals and Agrylon. The former were exchanging hopes that Chadwick, as improbable as it may seem, might provide some hope of keeping the King's Lance from the gauntlets of one of Renarre's lancers.

As for the wizard, he only stared across at Rel Aevmiir, his counterpart in the Mneyr pavilion, leaning on his staff. From this distance, Duke Curisinian's vizier looked all but identical to Agrylon but for the vermillion and silver hue of her robes. She caught an expression flickering across their features, and wondered what thought might have crossed their minds, or *between* them, when she felt it, too.

The rush of *iiyir* was the most powerful yet, but she buffeted the surge with little reaction. It would have sent her to the floor but a day gone. She had at least become inured to the effects of the phenomena.

Brohan rubbed his forehead. "This is giving me an awful headache," he muttered.

Aeolil dabbed at the sweat beading on her own brow with a silk kerchief. "How long will it be like this?"

"Not much longer. It's but the crash of strong surf as the new tide comes in. Waves break, and the surf roars – we are but caught in the spray for a time. When the storm lessens and the flow steadies, it will settle to the ordinary routine, if a bit backward by our experience."

"Brohan," Aeolil whispered, bringing hand to lips to shield her words. "How did this enemy turn the tides in the first place, without anyone noticing? Agrylon pretends it of no consequence, but… ." She bit at her upper lip.

"Those that watch for such things did not watch carefully enough, milady."

"That's not much better an answer than Agrylon's. Was it *he* that missed the signs?"

"Yes," Brohan agreed in a tired sigh. "Him, too."

Trumpets interrupted their quiet exchange, and there was one last roar of expectation from the crowd. The knights saluted the honored pavilions in turn and took their places, awaiting the drop of the marshal's white flag.

"Perhaps lost in the glare of grand designs," reflected the bard, "but I suspect something else was at work. Some great magic was worked to shield the *greater* magic."

Artygalle tapped Windthane's flanks, and the horse launched down the list. Light sparkled in the mail of the charging knights, and Aeolil blinked, trying to clear her field of vision as motes of red, orange and yellow glittered in the very air before her eyes. She shook her head to clear the sudden dizziness as green and blue swirled into the color storm.

"Gods!" hissed Brohan, launching to his feet.

It's so wonderful, she thought, fascinated. Indigo and violet now joined the increasingly vivid tempest of lights.

A low humming buzzed inside her head. Her insides lurched. *Magic,* she realized. She reached out, trying to touch the shimmering sparks, even as a distant voice insisted not to look. A memory of sweet sap sparkled on her tongue, turned bitter, and she blinked.

Faerie glamour, she concluded as her thoughts cleared. She averted her eyes. *And something more. Something much more.*

There was no impact of lance on shield. A blinding light swallowed the list, and a roar like a thousand waterfalls exploded through the air. Aeolil brought her hands up, fingers interlaced in a ward, but the spell was interrupted when Brohan grabbed her by the bodice of her dress and lifted her from her seat.

Aeolil cried out in surprise.

Bleys drew his broad sword and ran toward her from his post, but the bard was quicker. Brohan was at the edge of the balcony in the space of a hummingbird's heartbeat, his eyes wide and wild, his lips drawn back and jaw clenched. His bright eyes seemed but shadows beneath his dark brow.

And without another word, he hefted her over the railing and threw her from the pavilion.

Chapter Fifty-Six

Now, Into the Fire

CALLAGH peered from the shadowed arch of the door, watching the rear guard that blocked the way across the flying bridge. Having discarded most of its armor, the hrumm crouched in unencumbered ease out in the middle of the narrow span. Its topknot whipped around its head, snapping in the wind. Its eyes were feral and alert.

"Just one?" Seth's whisper was so soft that it was almost inaudible above the howl of the temperamental gale. "That's good, right?"

"*None* would be better," she answered, and held out her bow. "Hold this. Follow quickly. If it doesn't rip me throat out."

Seth put his hands up to decline the weapon. "But why not...?"

"In *that* bloody wind?"

"Oh." Seth sighed the word, deflated, and licked his lips.

Callagh drew the long sword Inulf had given her. She wasn't much for sword work, certainly not with a long blade such as this, but she'd need the reach of the weapon out on the bridge.

"Shouldn't we wait for Inulf and Faeldor?" pleaded Seth.

Callagh shook her head. She still wasn't sure she should trust Inulf, let alone wait for him. "No. But I'll be quick about it," she said, and then smiled at Seth with a wink. "One way or the other."

The hrumm watched her emerge into the light with a disturbing lack of surprise.

"At least take a shield!" Seth yelled.

Callagh waved him off. The sword would be enough to manage. A heavy shield would throw off her balance, and there was little room for a misstep on the precarious finger of stone spanning the keeps.

A shadow soared past her shoulder with a thick croak, gliding on the powerful wind in a wide circle over the sentry. *Aye, thanks for the bloody help*, she thought sourly. *I can find me own way from here.*

The hrumm tapped the end of its sword on the bridge, as if beckoning her to come, and then raised it in challenge. Callagh resisted the urge to rush in. It had size and strength and the reach of her. One misstep and it would rip her head off or toss her from the bridge. She was a hunter, not a warrior, and in this case she had no doubt that between the two of them *she* was the prey.

The hrumm growled and bared its teeth, echoing her thought.

Callagh stepped forward, swinging to the edge of her reach to test its defenses. The hrumm surprised her with a full counterattack. It sprang forward, deflecting her tentative blade and launching a backstroke at her exposed face. It was all she could do to dance away without losing her balance, parrying awkwardly. She backpedalled, tripped over her feet and fell on her side. She swung her legs out over empty air, just avoiding the hrumm's sword as it chipped the stone less than an inch from her boot.

Callagh made an underpowered and desperate thrust at its exposed groin but the hrumm pivoted away and slashed down at her. She deflected the stroke, but the impact shook her from wrist to shoulder, and the clash of steel carried a discordant undertone as her blade broke off at the cross guard.

The hrumm bared its teeth and raised its sword for the killing blow. She threw the hilt at its snarling face and left a lucky trail of fresh blood from cheek to brow, marring its intricate tattoo with a jagged tear of flesh.

It howled, blinking blood out of its eye.

Callagh grabbed the slack guide rope in her fists and pulled it taut, launching herself up at the hrumm and entangling its raised sword-arm before it could recover and strike. It fell back one step, close to the edge and teetering on its back heel, but it did not fall – it hung there on the verge, glaring at her as it sought purchase, and reached for her throat with its free hand.

Callagh prepared to bite the outstretched claws as a last defense, but a sudden flutter of ebon wings came between her and the hrumm. The raven's furious quork rang in her ears and the hrumm swung wildly at the interloper. The shift in balance was too much, too fast, and it toppled from the bridge, flailing at empty wind as it fell.

Callagh shook with relief, her breath coming in shallow gasps of frigid air. The raven landed on the far side of the bridge, its black eyes fixing her with a midnight stare.

"Right, then," she decided. "Who needs a bloody unicorn?"

"Hah!"

Callagh felt heat stinging through the fabric at her neck and reached for her brooch, stroking the warm metal absently. *Inulf.*

"Can't be having a birdie fight all your battles for ye, eh? Huh?" He strode toward her, his smile wide and his eyes dark, blood soaking his gauntlets up to his elbows and painting his mail in a reckless spatter. "Faeldor holds the South Keep. It's for us to do what's to be done here. These hrumm have surprise mor'n numbers."

Callagh glanced at the three men that followed Inulf, two of them injured, and then at Seth, cowering behind them.

"An' we've got neither," she observed.

Inulf laughed and offered her his hand. "Don't be a'feard a dyin' now, girl. Be a'feard we be *too late*."

⁂

The timbers of the doors groaned, flexing inward with each successive blow. Calvraign wasn't sure which door would buckle first, whether death would come from the bailey or from the stairway to the great hall, only that either way they were trapped in between.

"Steady!" called Foss.

The sergeant had positioned his six crossbowmen behind overturned tables in the middle of the kitchen, three men facing each threatened door. The rest of the squad had formed up in a makeshift shield wall, ready to pivot toward the enemy from whichever direction they came, or split into two units if they came from both doors at once.

The rest of the furniture, cooking implements, half-prepared slabs of meat, and baskets of fruits and vegetables had been tossed to the side with the corpses. Osrith and Markus were wrestling a large cauldron of boiling fat off the fire. They hoisted it between them with the incongruous armor of oven mitts over their gauntlets, grimacing at the weight and the stench of the bubbling lard sloshing within.

"Stay behind me," Osrith grunted to Calvraign. "And get that torch ready."

Calvraign nodded, and lit a brand in the brazier to his right.

The door to the bailey shuddered one last time before shattering into a spray of wood chunks and flinders. The iron door handle clanged across the stone floor to settle at Calvraign's feet. Osrith and Markus charged and heaved the cauldron of hot oil onto the remains of the door. The greasy mess splattered across the timbers and the first hrumm to enter the breach.

It screamed as the boiling liquid washed over it, and Calvraign tossed the torch onto the floor in front of the hrumm. Flames erupted up the creature's legs, igniting it, and then spread along the floor and walls to nibble at the door fragments. Thick smoke billowed out, rolling into the room on the cold wind from the door.

There was a bark in hrummish, and then a leaf-headed spear point erupted from the blazing vanguard's chest, purchasing silence at the price of a gurgle and a shower of heart blood. The body and the spear were shoved out of the churning black cloud, clearing the bloody debris from the breach.

"They'll be up at us in a tick," warned Osrith, nudging Calvraign. "Watch the flanks. They'll try to power through and come at us from the sides. We need to keep them bottled up as long as we can."

"How long will that be?" Calvraign asked.

"Well, that all depends on how many of the bastards there are. Now stop talking and get in guard position."

Calvraign raised his shield and drew his father's blade, facing the door with a dry mouth and racing pulse.

"Bah!" Markus reached for his own sword, waving his off-hand in front of his face, scowling. "What a stink."

"All your cooking smells the same to me," said Osrith, his eyes shining bright from his soot-smeared face. He discarded the kitchen gloves and hefted his long axe in a loose two-handed grip.

The two veterans moved back in the ranks as Foss sent half his men to hold the entrance. With a shout, the soldiers engaged the hrumm at the smoking door. Calvraign looked into the smoldering eye sockets of the dead hrumm, a charred corpse in a bloody pool, still sizzling like a pig on a spit, and tightened the grip on his sword hilt to settle his nerve.

"Just hold your ground," Osrith advised over his shoulder, as if sensing Calvraign's unease, "and don't try any fancy tricks." He raised his voice over the clamor of swords on shields, never turning. "Hrumm are strong and quick – sometimes too quick. Take the advantage if they give it to you, but don't press for more – you'll just tire yourself out. Survive first."

"Hold that door!" yelled Foss. "Push the brutes back!"

The soldiers swung and parried in methodical cadence, well-practiced if not well-used skill keeping the onslaught at bay. Then one of the men went down, a sword stroke catching him in the neck just over the rim of his shield. The next in file moved to fill the hole, slipping on the oil and blood-wet stones, and a hrumm pushed forward a few short steps into the room behind its dented infantry shield, but the line held.

At the same time, a moaning crack of wood announced the demise of the door to the stairway. Calvraign turned as hrummish boots kicked the stubborn planks of wood free of the frame. Foss signaled his crossbowmen and sent half a dozen quarrels through the gaps. There was a sharp ringing retort as steel pierced steel and thumped into the flesh underneath, followed by a howl of pain. After the briefest pause, the rest of the door came smashing down.

Three hrumm overwhelmed the formation of defenders at the stairs in a bloody rush. There was no fire or smoke to hinder them, and they collapsed the left flank and streamed through to engage the second rank. Osrith took a half step forward.

So, this is battle, Calvraign thought. He was more scared than he imagined he'd be, but tried to draw strength from the steady calm of his men. He parried a high attack, responded with a low counter and lost himself in the rhythm of the fight.

Calvraign ducked in and out of the melee, his shield and sword flashing, defense and attack but separate steps in a larger dance of whirling steel. Men and hrumm struck and parried and fell around him as Foss barked orders to reform the line. He couldn't distinguish much of the larger fight. The screams and shouts and grunts and horrible gasps of death from friend and foe were a distant buzz in his ears.

Another hrumm bore down on him in a flurry of swift, strong strikes. Its eyes ate into him with a dreadful intensity as it attacked, and Calvraign's vision narrowed until the snarling grey-skinned beast was all he could see. It beat him back step by step, leveraging its size to dominate the exchange. Calvraign fought a measured defense, matching blows until he could find an advantage.

There, he thought, seeing his chance as he blinked sweat from his eyes. The hrumm's weakness lay in sloppy footwork – it planted awkwardly with each crossing down-stroke and overextended its balance. *That's it.*

Calvraign feinted to draw a strike, and then slipped in under the high swing and drove his sword through the hrumm's exposed armpit. The point of the sword split chain and cut through leather into flesh, penetrating deep into its chest and opening its heart.

Calvraign withdrew the blade, and blood pumped in thick gouts from the open wound. The hrumm fell to its knees, eyes rolling up into its head, and plummeted face-first into the ground. He stared at the corpse, triumph and revulsion warring in his head as hot pinpricks danced on his numb cheeks.

"Watch your left!"

Osrith's warning startled Calvraign from his momentary fugue. In a panic, he brought his sword and shield back into guard position and turned to face the attack, but he was too slow to block the sword scything down at him.

Osrith threw himself in front of Calvraign and in the path of the blow. The hook of the mercenary's long axe intercepted the stroke and turned the hrumm's swing to strike the floor in a shower of sparks. Osrith let the haft of the axe slide through his fingers and put the momentum of the deflection into a backswing that sent the hrumm's head half off its neck.

"Hells, boy! It's not *fencing*," barked the master-at-arms. He kicked the lifeless, bloody body back into the doorway, choking further ingress. "The fighting's *all around you*, not just in front of your fool face." He pointed at his eyes. "What you *don't* see kills you!"

Calvraign didn't waste the breath to answer. The line of battle had reformed, but the hrumm had gained ground and were pressing them in – forcing them back inch-by-inch toward the middle of the room. The crossbowmen had taken up swords for the close melee, and dragged what wounded they could back to the makeshift fortifications. From what little Calvraign could ascertain as he fought for his life, despite an initial advantage in numbers, there were precious few of his first command left alive.

Osrith fought with crazed precision. With every swing of his long axe, he drew blood or forced distance, never wasting a motion as he maneuvered and struck amongst the foe. He kicked a table into two advancing hrumm, catching them in their midriffs and stalling their rush. He pivoted and dealt with the flanking hrumm in an economy of movement that belied the ferocity of his attacks. The master-at-arms moved with such sureness and fought with such brutal certainty, Calvraign almost believed that he alone might bring victory.

But soon enough Osrith's brief surge transformed to a defensive struggle. The grizzled mercenary might be the last to fall, but Calvraign saw that without a change in fortune, they would not prevail against the hrumm. The thought of failing the king, failing the kingdom, delivering the world into some living hell prophesied before his birth, filled him with anger.

I will die like my father, he thought, taking a staggering blow to his shield. *But I won't even win the battle first.*

Calvraign's sword was heavier in his hands with every passing moment, his attacks landing with less and less force. The hrumm glaring down at him was tiring also, but its next swing drove him to his knees all the same. Calvraign lunged at its leg and stabbed into the meat of its thigh, but it barely flinched from the shallow wound, leaving Calvraign overextended and vulnerable. The hrumm reared back for a killing blow, but the death-stroke never fell. Its howl of victory died in its throat, punctuated by the whistle and thump of an arrow.

The mighty hrumm dropped.

Calvraign rolled to avoid the falling corpse as more arrows and a fresh battle cry filled the kitchen.

"*Luadh má Ciaerhán!*"

Calvraign looked up in surprise at the familiar oath; only to find Callagh Breigh standing in the doorway, bow in hand, loosing another shaft into a hrummish back. Swordsmen rushed past from the hall, but Calvraign could only stare at her.

Callagh's features were partially concealed by a mask of black face paint – or blood – applied in a traditional Cythe pattern over her eyes, nose, and cheeks. He wasn't sure, but he thought it was the mark of the *ravenswohde* – a mark that should be reserved for the likes of the *madhwrrwn* alone. She looked fierce indeed, regardless of the totem.

Osrith kicked him. "Get up and get moving! That drove 'em back to the bailey – but they're not done with us yet. You can blow her a kiss later."

"Ach, don't look so surprised," teased Callagh with a grin, lowering her bow. "Yer not even the first boy I've rescued today." She extended a hand to help him up. "Oh, and just you wait t'see who's behind me."

Chapter Fifty-Seven

Rainbows at Dusk

ARTYGALLE winced into the fading scintillation of lights, his helm ringing, his body rolling, tangled in the arms of a flailing assailant. As they spun through the dirt, Artygalle lashed out with his forearm, catching the blurry phantasm in the neck with a satisfying wet gurgle. It sprawled backward, and Artygalle gained a knee, straddled the body, and drew his long sword.

There must be some mistake, he thought, confused. *Some trick.*

The beautiful aulden face snarled back at him as she tried to push him off. Her blue-green chain armor glistened with the reflections of a hundred rainbows. Artygalle impaled her through the chest, instinct denying reason any chance to kill him with misplaced conjecture. She convulsed, but pushed back on the crossbar of his hilt, trying to extricate the blade.

The creatures of Faerie do not die as mortals do, Ghaerieal had once cautioned, even as they had been sent to make peace with the Qeyniir, years ago. *The killing of an aulden is brutal butchery, indeed.*

Artygalle leaned hard on the blade with his right arm, keeping her pinned beneath him, and raised his shield high above his head with his left. "*Ieylulki*," he whispered, and cleaved her head in two with a vicious blow from the edge of his round shield. Her struggle ceased.

Screams rent the air around him as he rose and turned, pulling his sword and shield from the corpse at his feet. He almost tripped on Sir Chadwick's headless body. A thick ooze of dark blood seeped from the stump of his neck, soaking into the hoof-churned soil. His head lay at an odd angle not far from the body, eyes still staring in wonder.

The aulden. Gods. It's come to this?

He spoke their tongue, and though he could not place the dialect, he could fully understand the shouts, commands and war cries of the fae as they ran amok through the ranks of knights, nobles, churchmen and spectators. In the initial attack, most fell without even raising a blade in defense.

Inoval ran toward him through the chaos, leading Windthane with one hand and pointing with the other. "Master, look out!"

Artygalle pivoted and ducked under his shield as an aulden sword lashed toward his neck. The force of the impact parted the aulden wraith from her blade and she stumbled back a half step, blinking in surprise, before bending light to dart away to safety.

"Inoval!" he yelled, nudging the fallen faerie sword with his boot. "Take this, and move quickly! Don't look at them straight on – they are moving through the Veil."

Artygalle hefted himself into the saddle. "Squire! *Run!* Go and spread the word – look away to strike true! Look away! They mean to have the king himself!"

Artygalle hoped the boy would make it, at least for a little while, but he could spare no more time here. He kicked Windthane in the flanks and headed at full gallop toward the unraveling rainbow converging on the royal pavilion.

The warhorse plunged into the tumult, shouldering aside human and aulden alike at a deft touch from Artygalle's knees. Battle was not new to the knight, and he did not flinch from killing simply because his opponents were of the fae. Their beautiful wonderful faces fell away from him bloodied, wounded or dead, and he pressed on. He would pause to grieve the slain after the battle. For now, he fed Pheydryr her due without remorse, repeating the Discipline of Steel in his head as he fought.

As the dragon, firm of stance and right of balance,
As the eagle, keen of sight and sound of judgment,
As the mountain cat, swift and true of aim,
As the gryphon, bold of heart and without fear.

The royal pavilion drew near, aflame but not burning in a magical firestorm the like of which Artygalle had never seen. Agrylon stood in the midst of the expanding fulguration, one hand on his war-staff and another raised high into the air as if calling down lightning.

Close enough, he thought, whirling Windthane in a tight turn. A golden-helmed aulden avoided the horse's striking forehooves only to be struck down by Artygalle's blade. She fell to the ground, twisting and clawing at the gaping wound splitting her chest, her sword landing well out of her reach. A boy stumbled away, turning to look up at Artygalle, his eyes wide and glassy.

"Run!" Artygalle commanded.

"We *were* running," the boy responded, hoarse and weak, and stood there, shaking.

Artygalle noted the corpses around him: two grown women, a girl, and a portly man with the heavy chain of a master smith hanging on his thick neck. They'd been cut down as they ran. A trail of bodies led back to the common seating just left of the royal pavilion. The swords of Faerie flashed among them still, unopposed.

Artygalle looked back at the pavilion. He could make out Vaujn and his kin guardsmen surrounding Prince Hiruld, and Vanelorn and the knights in attendance formed a wall of swords and shields around the king and the wizard. Behind him, he saw the Knights Lancer formed a similar defense about the personages of the Holy Quorum and the archbishop.

He heard the cries of the knights and the soldiers, calling on their brethren to defend the king or the church, but his eyes were drawn back to the slaughter of innocents, and he felt a strange peace in the midst of the battle – a certainty that cleansed any doubt from the mire of his conflicted loyalties.

Artygalle made the sign of the moon on his breast. *In Your wisdom I trust, and in Your way I follow.* "Pick up her sword and follow me," Artygalle told the smith's son. "And by the Grace of Illuné, we will not die running."

Artygalle veered to the right and tapped Windthane with his heels, vaulting the balustrade into the lower stands.

--- ᴄ⁄ᴏ ---

Vaujn stood transfixed and stunned for only a moment. Planning for an engagement required deep reflection, examination and consideration. Surviving an engagement required instinct and reflexes. And certainly a ravaging band of aulden attacking from a rift in the Veil had *not* been a part of his careful planning, so instinct and reflex would have to do.

"*Sturhntihr!*" he yelled, and the Prince's Guard formed up into the defensive rockfisher formation, their shields a kinsteel barrier around the prince.

"It's wonderful!" Hiruld sighed, motionless and transfixed by the approaching lights.

Vaujn punched him in the testicles, and the wonder rushed out of Hiruld's face with a groan as he doubled over.

"Get down, My Prince," Vaujn commanded. "And stay down. We need to get off this pavilion and outta this tree, or we're buggered sideways."

"This," gasped the prince, "this is the shadowyn?"

Vaujn pulled the lever on his crossbow, and with a click the string was drawn and the first bolt ready to fire. Three more bolts waited in the spring-loaded mechanism common to kin design, giving the relatively small squad a much-needed advantage.

"No," grunted the captain. *This may be worse.* "It's aulden and high magic."

Vaujn trained the weapon on the shimmering wave closing in on them, marching backward in unison with his squad. He held the left flank of the formation, where he could keep an eye on Hiruld and the approaching enemy.

"Aulden? Why would they…? Wait – what about my father?" Color crept back into Hiruld's face, and he lifted his head to peer out over the shield wall. "What of my father? Aeolil?"

Vaujn kicked Hiruld in the shin, and the prince's head snapped back immediately. "Stay down, you idiot! Your father and the rest will have to find their own way. *You're* supposed to save the damn world, remember?"

The ripples of *iiyir* from the bridge through the Veil were fading, as were the prismatic effects, but some of the aulden still walked on the other side, or blinked back and forth. Humans were dropping in bloody heaps everywhere. They were surprised, glamoured and overwhelmed, besides being largely unequipped to fight their ethereal foe.

Vaujn could make out a half-dozen aulden in the first wave that flowed toward them. The leader wielded a *wohrbrund*, a sooth-sword, so he marked her as High Blade. The black night of her eyes pierced through the ambient translucent hues, and Vaujn gritted his teeth.

We can't engage, he told himself, trying to dissolve any leftover bits of their former strategy into a useful tactic for retreat. But he was certain they'd be overtaken before reaching the relative safety of the exit to the under levels.

"Chloe," he yelled, "*Scmohg, scmohg!*"

He exchanged a gilded glance with his wife, catching just the hint of her eyes through her lowered visor. She nodded acknowledgment and muttered a charm under her breath as she tossed a handful of round stones from the pouch at her belt. They scattered and exploded into an obscuring wall of smoke to cover their retreat. As the cloud thickened, Vaujn barked out another command, and the formation moved right two steps at double time, angling for the same exit but from a different approach. This was a standard maneuver, but Vaujn was assuming that the aulden hadn't seen any kin tricks for at least as long as he he'd seen any of theirs.

Vaujn allowed himself no relief as the rear of the formation crossed the threshold into shelter. The aulden would not be stalled long by a wall of smoke, enchanted or not. They had already gained more time than he'd anticipated.

"'Ware!" Chloe screamed in rare panic.

The High Blade slipped in from the Veil, and Vaujn pivoted to face her down. Her sword sang through the air as it knocked away his well-aimed bolt, but she stepped back instead of pressing the attack.

"*Mishtigge*," she whispered. "I have bought you time. Get to bedrock. I will sing the way shut behind you."

Vaujn watched the glow of the *wohrbrund* confirm the honesty of her words and wasted no time questioning fortune. The High Blade sang a short, simple tune. It seemed awkward on her lips, but the branches of the *ilyela* responded, creaking stiff and slow to reach in and block the opening of the door in a tangled web of reawakened leaf and limbs.

Behind the aulden, Chloe's smoke was beginning to dissipate, and Vaujn could make out the forms of the High Blade's fallen sisters sprawled motionless on the ground.

By her own hand.

Vaujn tried to imagine a circumstance that could pit him against his own squad, and his stomach turned at the very thought.

"*Miiyeal*," he said, thinking it fitting to say his thanks in her own tongue.

The dark look in her eyes did nothing to hide the conflict in her thoughts, but she accepted his gesture with the traditional response before slipping back through the Veil. "*Aiea Lii.*"

Vaujn didn't tarry. He turned his attention back to his own. "Down deep and down fast," he said. "Let's put some rock between us and them."

Hurtling headfirst toward the ground, Aeolil extended her arms to break the fall and hoped the impact wouldn't snap her neck. She knew of a slowing spell, but couldn't recall it. She'd spent too much of her studies crafting fire and lightning, hoping to harness the deeper ways of power, often at the expense of more basic spellcraft. She'd wanted to avoid helplessness at all costs.

A few feet short of thus meeting such an ironic end, Aeolil was both puzzled and relieved that her descent slowed. The air around her thickened, like water, and buoyed her to a moderate tumble by the time her palms hit hard earth. She rolled, which was an awkward maneuver in her formal dress, but at least she had worn her least encumbering gown in the event of any trouble.

Two black boots settled with a soft step by her head.

"Call up your wards!" Brohan urged her, standing over her with sword drawn and glowing with cool light. "These are aulden – Ceearmyltu. They are here in numbers."

Aulden?

This revelation confused Aeolil as much as it relieved her that Brohan had *not* just tried to throw her to her death a few moments ago. Sources of *iiyir* bristled through the filaments, streams of power from a hundred nodes fading and growing and fading again.

Aeolil called up her strongest ward, drawing deep on the world tides, tainted though they were, to shore up her defense. As the *ur'iiyir* entered her, a new tapestry of patterns, colors and lights enveloped the world, overwhelming her senses with vision that transcended physical sight.

The haze of the rainbow bridge and the aulden glamour burned away like fog under the rays of morning suns-rise. The light of *iiyir* itself seemed to illuminate the world, a fire like the suns where the high magic opened the Veil; and lesser fires where each aulden tread, trailing sparks behind like orphaned motes from a beacon fire.

Beside her, Brohan was illuminated from within in blue-white radiance, his skin a translucent shell, his eyes alight like white-hot coals, his sword aglow in an opalescent sheen. Above her, from the royal pavilion, a star of red and orange pulsed like a heartbeat and near blinded her, matched only by a star of yellow fire across the field in the Mneyr pavilion and some lesser emanations of varying hues from the pavilion of Mother Church.

In a blink, the sensitivity dimmed, and the more familiar bounds of reality returned with but a hint of her brief glimpse into the shining world of Veil and Tide.

"Stay with me," Brohan directed. "We must sever the Way from its source."

"But Hiruld-"

"That's for Vaujn to deal with. Agrylon and Rel will be distraction enough for a time, but this is left for us."

Aeolil shadowed Brohan's footsteps as he danced lithely through the melee. The master bard engaged but little in combat, turning blades aside and slipping between foes rather than challenging them outright. The aulden, for their part, seemed to share his reluctance, and Aeolil enjoyed a convenience of proximity.

"There." Brohan pointed to an indistinct bit of shimmer near the center of the list. "That's the way-gate."

Aeolil drew her dagger. She'd laid an enchantment on the blade, expecting a shadowyn, but she supposed it would suffice to penetrate aulden defenses just as well. She ran her fingers down the blade to wake the fire in the steel with a word. The *iiyir* was sluggish at her call, but it flowed through her and into the metal, a faint glow spreading to the edges.

Brohan led her, one step ahead of chaos, through the melee. The bodies and activity thinned as they neared the center of the list, where a headless corpse marked the epicenter of the aulden gate spell. The battle had spread out from here and remained on the perimeter.

The eye of the storm, she thought.

A gleaming sword streaked out of nowhere at her neck, but Brohan's own sword knocked the blow aside. Aeolil finally recognized the sword that saved her life, like a brand of captive moonfire, and could not quite restrain a cry of surprise.

"Elèndere!"

Brohan and the aulden both shifted into guard stance, neither making any further move to attack. "Seemed a shame to waste a magic sword," the bard said, never looking away from the aulden sentry. "I left twice as many as I took."

The aulden said something beautiful, her brilliant indigo eyes like pinpoints of fire under her helm, darting back and forth between them.

Brohan shook his head, "I do not want to kill you, sister. The Ceearmyltu are not my enemy, and I am certainly not yours."

Aeolil looked around at the fighting that enveloped the pavilions and the stands. There was fire and blood aplenty consuming Saint Kaissus Field, and she could feel through the thread of *iiyir* that still connected her to Agrylon that though he still lived, he and Rel must be sorely taxed.

"There will be no more killing," Brohan assured, his voice sincere, soothing. "I will send you back through the Way. Back home. Just stand aside."

The aulden shook her head, but her sword lowered, just slightly.

"Don't break the long peace," Brohan pleaded. "You must not mar the honor of your tribe with this treachery."

She raised her sword again, and spat a stream of angry words at him. Beautiful, seductive, angry words. Aeolil dropped to her knees, feigning fatigue, and whispered a spell under her breath as they argued.

"Yes," Brohan persisted, his voice earnest. "But their deceit does not justify yours."

Aeolil imbued the newly summoned energy of the spell into her still smoldering dagger, and it came to life, pulling against her hands as Swiftwing might pull on his hawking tether. She gritted her teeth and held it still, adjusting her aim with a careful eye.

The aulden's lips moved to speak, but Aeolil did not wait for her words. She found her aim and released the dagger. It launched from her hands like the bolt from a crossbow, the glowing metal painting a white-hot afterimage in the air as it struck the aulden under the chin of her helm and into the delicate flesh beneath.

The aulden lurched backward, her sword flying. She threw her helm away, spinning to the ground, limbs flailing as she clutched at her opened neck and the burning metal lodged in her head. The sound of her screams drowned in the blood filling her throat, leaving only a sputtering, humming gurgle. She didn't stop struggling until the flames inside her skull melted her beautiful eyes and burned hungrily through the empty sockets.

Aeolil shook.

"She would have listened!" Brohan screamed, his voice both plaintive and angry.

It sounded like he was yelling at her from a distant tower. The look on his face was almost as hard to confront as the spectacle of the smoking corpse. Anger. Disappointment.

Betrayal.

"No time," she said, swallowing her emotions down deep, and the sad whisper of her first words fell away into a strength of certainty as she continued. "There was no time, Brohan. We survive. We survive, *first*."

Brohan nodded, but his expression did not soften. "Keep your wards strong. They may be back before I can break this gateway, even with Elèndere as a source." He paused, his eyes sad or admonishing, or both. "The next aulden we meet will not let her guard down."

Chapter Fifty-Eight

Dangerous Ways

JYLKIR clung to the branch of the *ylohim,* her cheek pressed against the smooth bark, watching Bloodhawk pick his way through the trees below her. He slipped through the Macc lines at a brisk pace, but slowed to a more careful, measured step once among her sisters. Du'uwneyyl and the Blades had entered the Way first, followed closely by Ililysiun and the first wave of the attack. The *lyaeyni* and the elder *caylaeni* stood at the entrance to the shining portal through the Veil, eyes open but unseeing the mortal world as they channeled and controlled the spell, locked together in communion. Ryaleyr and her cadre of warriors waited just within the threshold of the way-gate, impatient for the humans to cross through.

He's doomed, of course.

Jylkir did not doubt Bloodhawk's skill, or that he could overcome at least a few of her sisters before succumbing to their numbers, but he would not escape alive. However, with any luck at all, he could at least achieve the most important goal of their hasty plan by disrupting the spell and perhaps even destroying the codex.

But it will trap them, she thought, her eyes dry only because she had already emptied her tears. *They will be left to the mercies of the humans.*

Bloodhawk was very close now, his long knife at the ready. Jylkir could only make out his silhouette as he closed the remaining distance to his prey. She did not envy him the task of slaying a *lyaeyni*, striking her down unawares like an assassin. Bloodhawk deserved better than to be remembered as a common murderer.

Jylkir waited, but the *wilhorwhyr* had paused as Prince Ruoughn and Lombarde passed near. *Perhaps he can deal with one or both of them as well*, she hoped. Disquiet followed in the ambassador's wake, each quiet step a wound in the life around him. Her subtle unease at his presence was now an undeniable revulsion. The Maccs approached the rainbow bridge, singing out a boisterous battle hymn, and the Ceearmyltu readied themselves at the gateway. Bloodhawk coiled at the edge of his cover, ready to spring at his prey in the small clearing where the Way was opened. Jylkir saw his fingers tense about the hilt, and then...

Meimniyl's head sailed from her shoulders, the suns-light catching a glint of guilty steel amidst the fountain of her lifeblood. Her body stood motionless for a moment, arms upraised over the codex, before falling over its gilded pages. Jylkir blinked, disbelief and confusion mingling in her gut.

Bloodhawk hadn't moved.

Lombarde's curved blade returned for another stroke, opening Niealihu across the back of her shoulders as her eyes opened in alarm. Ruoghen strode hard into the fray. His bastard sword took Eleulii as she stirred from trance, and two of his skull-bearers butchered Hlemyrae before she could even draw steel. Feylobhar, her reflexes still sharp despite her age, had just enough warning to slide between their swords. The humans' blades whistled through empty air, but her own songwood knives slid silent from their scabbards and felled her would-be assassins in a blur.

The main force of the Maccs plowed into the rear of the Ceearmyltu formation. Those that did not die at the invisible doorstep of the way-gate were forced through and into the Veil. Ryaleyr's call to arms was cut off as the magical portal collapsed in a rush of air and a clap of thunder, leaving her and her host adrift in the shifting lights of Faerie.

Feylobhar screamed into the sudden stillness, and Jylkir could feel the elder's rage rushing through the Grove, spreading through root and limb, calling on the heart of the forest itself for aid. Aside from a rustling of leaves, the spirit of the woods gave no response. Even the *ylohim* were sluggish to the call. Jylkir could feel the blood thirst, but the ward trees did not, or could not, act.

Jylkir watched Feylobhar battling below her, faster and stronger than any human, but too old and slow and tired to last for long against such numbers. She could not see or feel Bloodhawk's presence. Her lips brushed the bark of the tree limb as she mouthed the Song of the First Tree tunelessly under her breath, hoping at least to help Feylobhar wake the spirits.

The irony of the Macc's betrayal wasn't lost on Jylkir. They had done what she and Bloodhawk had planned to do. Kill the *lyaeyni*. Close the gate. Trap her sisters somewhere in the mystic vortices of the Veil or within the walls of Dwynleigsh. The Macc strategy, in hindsight, seemed obvious. All of the warfaring aulden were dead or gone. Those left were what Du'uwneyyl called the *tenders and menders.*

Like me, she thought.

The Grove, and the Caerwood, was theirs for the taking.

Feylobhar had slain three more before the first Macc sword found its mark, cutting her from shoulder to hip. She stumbled, and another sword stabbed into her back. She killed another before they backed off, letting her bleed. She spat at them.

Where is Bloodhawk? she wondered, both anxious and hopeful. She looked with eyes both open and closed, but could find him with neither sight nor senses.

Two more swords cut into Feylobhar, one slicing open her thigh, the other stabbing deep into her chest. The latter swordsman fell back screaming, leaving his sword – and his sword hand – in the elder *caylaeni's* breast. She laughed, wild and mocking, choking back the blood welling in her throat.

"You," Feylobhar said in the old Macc tongue, pointing at Ruoughn. Blood painted her lips with every word. "You're... no... worthy... prince."

"Hah!" scoffed Ruoughn, pushing his way into the circle of men. He kept a length and a half of his bastard sword between him and Feylobhar, for all his thin bravado. "I will take your head back to my hall, and I will drink the first toast of my coronation from your gilded skull: *to the last of the Ceearmyltu.*" The prince took one more careful step closer, flushed and grinning. "As for your *other* parts, I can guarantee no such honor."

Jylkir saw a shadow shifting in the clearing, moving from corpse to corpse, silent as the dead. *Bloodhawk!* A slim hope blossomed in her then, and she tried again to join with the world tides and wake the slumbering Caerwood. The faint tickle of root and limb prickled under her skin, and the Grove called out to her, its voice far away but growing stronger.

"Coronation?" Feylobhar spat again. "You – a *king?*" She dropped heavily to one knee, wheezing. Her eyes were distant. "That will never be. Keep cowering, and you prove it so. Come closer, and I'll guarantee it."

Lombarde sighed. "End her, Ruoughn. Now."

Bloodhawk crept to the center of the clearing and nestled into the headless body of Meimniyl. *So close, now,* Jylkir thought, her heartbeat echoing through the wood of the *ylohim*. Her awareness seeped into the trees, firm but maddeningly slow. She could feel it now in the chaotic eddies and undercurrents of *iiyir*, and she clung to the ghost of it. The waves of the shattered way-gate still muddied the tides and drowned any hope of escape through bending light, but she nurtured the connection with the Song of the First Tree.

"We've feared the trees of the old forest," Ruoughn said, addressing his victorious men now rather than the bleeding ancient at his feet. "We've feared the Ceearmyltu." He hefted his sword high. "No more!" The stroke of the long, heavy blade brought the sharp crack of splitting bone and the softer, wetter sound of shearing flesh.

And with that, proud Feylobhar fell, split from shoulder to waist. She landed at Ruoughn's feet, her torso spilling squirming ropes of viscera onto the forest floor.

Jylkir didn't simply *see* her death – she felt it, smelled it, tasted it – Feylobhar's blood soaking into the soil, the end of her life as well as the nourishment left by her passing, her spirit fleeing the mortal realms... and a faint trace of *iiyir* surging into the sluggish tides of the grove. Jylkir followed the passage of Feylobhar's *il-iiyir*, like flecks of spume sucked along by a river current.

The river leads to the sea.

Jylkir was alone. The *lyaeyni* and the *cayl* and her sisters were dead or trapped in the Veil. Bloodhawk was gone, vanished back into the trees. But now, threaded to the needle of Feylobhar's spirit, weaving herself into the tapestry around her, she could sense the *wilhorwhyr's* familiar life shining in her expanding sight. And with him was a familiar power – a fire of both dark and light.

The codex, she realized, numb rather than angry. *He never meant to rescue her.*

"It's done!" Ruoghen laughed, and swung his sword into the nearest tree trunk. Jylkir flinched at the sympathetic pinch in her side. "It... is... done!"

The Maccs raised a cheer.

Lombard looked about, dour and wary, with his sword at the ready. "No," he said. "*Not* done."

Ruoughn surveyed the bloody remnants of his betrayal, bemused. His laughter retreated begrudgingly to a satisfied smirk. "As good as," he assured the ambassador. He retrieved his sword from the tree trunk and addressed his men with the steel held on high. "The dark mysterious elves of the wood are *dead*. Take what you want." He paused to pick up one of Feylobhar's knives. "Then light the torches. Give Kazdann his due!"

Jylkir shuddered. Her fear and anger flowed through her and into the Caerwood: smoke, fire, burning – she felt the memory of it coursing back into her from the wakening Grove, of flames licking along bark, crisping leaves, charring wood, *consuming* her. She bore the pain, even reveled in it, because it meant that finally, through the miasma of *iiyir* that had sundered the sources, the Grove was answering her song.

The humans grabbed skins of oil from a small handcart and emptied the contents all around them. When the dead aulden and the living foliage were glistening with the foul-smelling substance, one of them finally screamed, "*Burn the bastards out!*"

And the torches flew.

The first tongues of fire sprang to life all around her, hungry tendrils licking along the perimeters of her awareness, intruding on her expanding consciousness with searing pain. The men called to each other and lit more fires, laughing.

Jylkir dove deep into the tides, losing herself within the coursing energies, and she sang to the Grove. The human faces dissolved into the glow of their fires as she swam through the *iiyir*, their laughter and voices distorted to a buzz, their very presence reduced to that of troublesome gnats skittering across her skin.

Jylkir twitched her arm to swat at one of the insects. Her attack was careless and awkward, like a child swinging a heavy axe in a crowd. She could no longer see with her mortal eyes, she could not control the chaos she unleashed, but she felt the forest surge, and she tasted hot blood through her roots. An old anger intruded on her thoughts, bolstering and growing her infant rage. Much as Llri's song could calm her, set her drifting like a leaf on a stream, the notes of the *ylohim's* bloodsong enveloped her in an incoherent fury, pulling her deeper into the torrent.

Noises spilled from the men as they scattered.

Some ran. Some tried to hide. A few of them stung her, poking and hacking at her ancient bark or slicing at her vines. She crushed them, too, tore their flesh and drank deep.

Kill them all! the forest sang, in voices like stormclouds.

Jylkir tried to distance herself from the thunder, but the rage reverberated through her, and it ripped at her sanity as a gale might scatter autumn leaves.

Death walks among us, the forest cried. *Empty steps full of death.*

A hollow chill crept up her back. An entreaty of nothingness pulling at her soulstring. She felt it through the forest, a warning of something unseen and unknown. She recognized the sensation that sickened the forest, for that ethereal unease had sickened her before.

Lombarde, she realized, *is no mere servant of the Dark. He is* of *the Dark, itself.*

A pod of tree-napes scampered toward her, away from the fire and the feeding of the forest, but she let them come. While all else fled her wrath, from fox to bird to worm, the napes came. They were of the wood. Their lives beat with the forest's heart. They were warmth in the cold dark of her angry song.

The rest will die. All the men. All the firebringers and ironwielders. All of them.

"Bloodhawk," she protested, trying to find the *wilhorwhyr* again, either through his own life or the trailing ember of the codex he carried, but the bloodsong now overwhelmed her completely. She could no more hold back the dread will of the *ylohim* than she could topple the sky.

And the sky is everywhere, she thought, despairing.

All of them, the voices repeated in her head. *All of them,* they droned, over and again until each word pounded like a mallet on her bones. *All of them.*

Jylkir recoiled from the murder she had unleashed. For one moment, the power of the ancients had filled her, power unseen and unsung for centuries. But she could not contain it. She was too young, too inexperienced, and her grasp of the bloodsong was but an understanding of a single note within a layered and complex composition. The music had left her behind much as the growing conflagration enveloping the Grove had moved beyond the torches that now sputtered in the frost dusted dirt, spent and smoking.

Memories flooded her: Du'uwneyyl throwing her down at the base of the Guard Tree; pinning her in the Graveyard, helpless and bound; subduing her again in Bloodhawk's cell; reconciling with her sister, only to watch, helpless again, as the High Blade went to war. *It's all the same,* she realized. But this time, it was the *ylohim* and the ancient will of the Grove holding her down, useless.

Always the timid shadow, she scolded herself. She saw her life as a breeze murmuring through leaf and limb, rustling without disturbing. She was a wisp – a bright light in the forest that led nowhere. Insubstantial. Unimportant. She almost raised her own angry song, one full of darkness and rage, to turn it against the rebellious wood and tear a hole in the smothering sky. But even as the low, growling tone built in her throat, a hint of soft melody tickled behind her ears.

The bright lilt dissolved the clinging shadows clutching her heart, familiar and welcome as the first sweet breath of morning.

Llri.

In one interval of notes Jylkir understood. It was a simple progression, she realized, starting with a jump from the root note to the third branch and a run up to the fifth before returning to the root and repeating the pattern. She recognized the framework of the *shaping song* and added her voice to the silent *ilyela* chorus that resonated between the trees. She understood. *Death will feed only death.* Her anger would only further enrage the *ylohim*; it would spread as surely as throwing more oil on a fire. The way to end it was not with more death – it was with *life*.

The *ilyela* choir lifted her through the song until she could find her own way and lead them in turn. Although the songwood trees knew the ways of shaping, they could not shape themselves. That was left for the treesinger. For *her*.

Jylkir infiltrated the charging wrath of the bloodsong, singing in subversive counterpoint, weaving her line of melody through the sour undertones and pulling them into unexpected harmony. With the *ilyela* lending their strength, the bloodsong faltered.

Jylkir felt the ebb of the killing rage as the thrum of growth and life overcame the droning dirge, one note, one beat, at a time. She felt an exultation, an unknown triumph as she and Llri and the *ilyela* soothed the Grove back from the brink of the Dark. The madness faded to whispers, an age-old simmering vengeance, and the *iiyir* washed back into the flow of the world tides.

But there was no comforting peace in the absence of the bloodsong's ire. Jylkir opened her eyes, blinking away smoke and coughing. There was *pain*. The forest burned all around her. Waves of dry heat buffeted her skin, and she cringed at the smells of charring wood and boiling sap in her nostrils.

Jylkir tried to rise, but she could barely lift her head. She had left her strength in the singing of the songs. She had perhaps saved the Grove from the Dark, but she would not save it, or herself, from the fire. The world spun around her, and she felt consciousness slipping, but through the shifting grey and black haze around her, the napes began landing on the upper limbs of her tree, and she wondered… .

There was a grunt from below her, and a hand grasped the branch where she sprawled. The gloved fingers struggled to find purchase, and for a moment she dared hope, she dared to believe that the *wilhorwhyr* had come with the napes to rescue her from burning to ash.

But the man who pulled himself up was not Bloodhawk. He was not salvation.

Lombarde stood, wavering and bloodied, the left side of his face swollen and purple. He stepped carefully toward her, drawing his blade, watching her, gauging her. The napes issued a shrill warning from behind her, but she waited, helpless, unable even to kick his legs from under him.

Lombarde said nothing, but Jylkir saw her fate in his dark eyes.

Death walks among us.

"Give me the codex," he said, blood leaking from a mouth of broken teeth. He seemed oblivious to the pain. "Give it to me, and I'll give you a quick death."

Jylkir tried to smile, but her lip barely twitched. She tried to curse him, but only a moan escaped her lips.

Lombarde moved another wary step closer. "Give it to me, or I will have to take you back to him." His eyes followed some movement in the trees above and behind her. "Believe me, death is the merciful option."

The ambassador flinched as a nut bounced off of his injured cheek, and a tree-nape shrieked with pleasure. More nuts and more shrieks followed, but he withstood the assault with a sigh. "And call off your cat-monkeys. Unless they are throwing magic acorns."

A feathered shaft struck him in the chest with a crack and a deep thump, knocking the breath from his lungs. He staggered back, and another arrow seemed to sprout next to the first, pinning him to the tree trunk. He sagged and dropped his sword, his head lolling to one side.

Bloodhawk alighted on the branch between Jylkir and the dying Malakuuri, dropping from some position she assumed was within the pod of napes. Another arrow was nocked and drawn to his cheek.

Jylkir stared up at him, still motionless. *Thank you*, she thought. Bright, curious eyes met hers, and an elder nape, its furry face as white as its drooping moustache, reached out to comfort her, stroking her long hair as it might a napeling that had fallen from a tree.

"Well… played," whispered Lombarde, straining to lift his head. "I knew… cat-monkeys… ." He coughed. "Something not right. Now I know. Won't… won't fool me again."

Jylkir could only guess that somehow Bloodhawk had disguised himself within the pod of napes, both physically and within the tides, though she had never heard of such a thing. Another trick of the *wilhorwhyr*, no doubt.

"It only needed to fool you once," Bloodhawk answered, and loosed the third arrow.

"Not," hissed Lombarde, as the last of life drained from him, "so… simple."

As he expired, his face wavered for a moment. She would have assumed that the effect was a by-product of the waves of heat rising from the fires, muddying the air, but there was a darkness, too. A shadow passed before her eyes, and a chill ran the length of her body. She shivered, shoulders hunched against the cold, even as the inferno blazed about her.

Whether she blinked or passed out she couldn't say, but when next her eyes opened, Bloodhawk was lowering her by a thin cord of rope into a trampled space between the raging flames. There she joined another prone body, a large man burned, bloody and broken, his breath coming in labored rasps. Bloodhawk joined them there in an instant, surrounded by the pod of napes dancing and waving their arms at the fire.

"I'm sorry," he said. "Sorry that I was so late to your aid. I had to save *him*, first."

Bloodhawk brought a skin to her lips, and sweet nectar cleansed her tongue and brought fire to her belly. She recognized the healing draught as jujoehbe juice. She wondered idly which corpse he had taken it from.

Jylkir was able to nod, though her legs shook when she tried to stand, and she fell back to her knees. She gazed at the crumpled body, too exhausted to be surprised by the revelation that her life had come second to Prince Ruoughn's.

"Why?" she croaked, not quite exhausted enough not to at least be curious.

"Because," explained the *wilhorwhyr*, helping Jylkir to her feet, "if we manage to escape this fire, he'll have quite a tale to tell his mother. And I intend he gets that chance."

Chapter Fifty-Nine

Victims of Truth

GUILLAUME had not flinched from the faerie lights, to his great pride. It had all unfolded so quickly, and not at all as he'd expected. There was no shadowyn assassin hiding in their midst, ready to plunge a dagger into Hiruld's back. No traitor lurked in their ranks.

Poor Bells locked away and my son in the hands of cowardly underkin, the king thought, sparing a glance after the retreating column of the Prince's Guard. *That's what you get for trusting wizards and bards and little, stunted men from the bowels of the earth.*

Willanel called the knights to order, his blank face pale but stoic, and Vanelorn helped shore them up into ranks. Shimmering rainbows sprang from the blinding light in the field below, and all about them – above, below, between and behind – materializing into armored warriors. They were graceful, and wondrous, and alien. The steel of their weapons and armor reflected light in subtle hues of blue and green.

Aulden.

As the fae invaded their midst, Agrylon looked across Saint Kaissus Field to the Mneyr pavilion, one eyebrow crooked upward in what the king recognized as an expression of alarm. The wizard barked an unintelligible word, eyelids fluttering, and a dome of bluish light coalesced around them. The air crackled, enveloping the pavilion in a cloudless storm.

Guillaume was amazed at the speed with which the wizened man transformed from stately lord high chamberlain into a fearsome Black Robe. The man was ancient. He'd lived through battles that were already history by the time Guillaume was born. He'd survived the great civil war, and orchestrated the greatest destruction ever unleashed by mortal hands. Though perhaps taken aback, the wizard was not daunted for long by the unexpected arrival of the faerie host.

And even then, Guillaume had been first in the pavilion to draw his sword – not Vanelorn, not Willanel, and none of the young pups staring gape-mouthed at the aulden onslaught. No matter how old or dead he felt in court, his heart still pumped life into his old bones for battle. If this fight would be his last, he would ensure it was also his *best*, a death fit for songs and fables.

Despite the pride in his reflexes, Guillaume was quick to recognize both his peril and the providence of the planned defense against attack from Shadow. *Aulden*, he thought with a wry grin. *Agrylon never foresaw this. He's more old fool than he lets on. Just like me.*

Fortunately, whatever sorcery the fae had used to penetrate Saint Kaissus Field, they did not pierce Agrylon's wards so easily. The pavilion was alive with magic of its own, and it slowed the aulden and rooted them in the mortal realms. *Aulden or shadowyn,* he thought, his grin thinning to a grimace, *they're all the same.*

Below the pavilion, his subjects were less fortunate. The aulden winked in and out of existence like fireflies, here, there and gone again, blood and death in their wake. It was impossible to judge the enemy's number. *Are they forty or four hundred?* He couldn't tell. It was irrelevant. Whatever their force of arms, the result was a massacre. But he could no more help those dying below than he could his son, or the man next to him. It was all he could do to fend for himself.

Another of his royal guard fell before him, and the king slashed at the aulden woman who stepped over the corpse. He dealt her only a glancing blow, and she showed no sign of slowing her attack. He barely managed to turn aside her thrust.

A flash of lightning sent her backwards, stunned and smoking. Agrylon's war-staff effused a trail of crackling white light as the wizard spun it protectively about his liege.

At least, between wizards and bards, the former stay to fight, Guillaume thought.

"The swords," Agrylon yelled, his voice reverberating even through the clamor of battle. He pointed with the tip of his war-staff, which crackled in waves of blue fire, indicating the swords thrust into the pavilion's crest. "I have released the wards! Take them!"

The king noted with some confusion that Elèndere was already missing, but was relieved to see that Vanelorn had drawn Calàthiél. Malade, Aeolil's towering guardsman, wielded the ungainly bulk of Gliyhtmuong. Another aulden vaulted to the attack, however, and he turned his attention to deflecting her well-aimed strike. The impact knocked the breath from him, as well as any further thought of the missing blade.

"Willanel," Vanelorn cried, but Guillaume had lost sight of him in the melee. "Your flank!"

The captal was on Guillaume's left, in what used to be the second rank, but was now well into the third and perilously close to the king. Willanel's cross guard was locked up with the thin fae blade of his attacker. He tried to push her back with brute strength, where he had the advantage of her, but she held him there, exposed, just long enough for one of her fae sisters to run him through with a leaf-headed spear. He convulsed on the wooden shaft, useless and quivering, his spine severed. His killer shouted something in her native tongue and pressed toward Guillaume. The king saw a similar fate awaiting him if he couldn't gain a breath of space between him and his own assailant.

Agrylon leaned on his staff, breathing hard, his lips moving in a spell that might take a moment too long to craft. Sweat glistened on the creased skin of his aged face.

They're fast, the king thought with a grimace. *Too fast for old men.*

Vanelorn grabbed Willanel's body and pushed it down the spear to the haft, saddling the spearwoman with his now-sagging dead weight and stalling her advance. It slowed her for a heartbeat, and the grey knight wasted no time in running her through. The smoldering orange-red blade of Calàthiél parted the metal scales of her armor with a hiss and a scrape and emerged bloodied from her back. She dropped the spear and reached for a hilt at her belt, but Vanelorn twisted the blade as he withdrew it, and she fell, weeping blood from her split chest.

It proved just enough time for Agrylon to finish his enchantment and raise a wall of wind around them with a deafening roar. Vanelorn was with them in the eye of the conjured storm, but the rest were pushed back with the aulden.

Agrylon's eyelids fluttered, and he stumbled to one knee.

So very familiar, the king thought. All his defenders dead or dying around him, an unassailable foe pressing in, just him and Vanelorn left. This time there was no Dragonheart – no man skipping between shadows to strike like shifting winds on all sides of the assailed king.

How the Calahyr feared him, he remembered, laboring to catch his breath in the lull of battle. Guillaume had never believed the stories told about the Cythe and their painted warriors, whatever they called them in that maddening barbarous tongue of theirs. But that day the stories proved true, and Guillaume swore to never doubt such tales again – and also, never to speak of it. *Still loyal, that one. Loyal to the death even after he knew.*

The aulden rushed them. Guillaume braced himself, but the raging air keened in protest and threw its attackers back like an angry spirit.

"To the king," a deep voice bellowed, like an echo of his memory. Then again, "To the king!"

Guillaume could only make out faint shapes through the blurring whirlwind, but he could see the silhouette of Gliyhtmuong, limned in blood-red flame, burning through the shadows. The rallying cry brought some spirit back to the defenders, and the flaming sword ignited hope as the fae fell back.

"Burn them!" exhorted Guillaume. "Burn them one and all!"

Agrylon's eyes narrowed, and a frown pinched the corners of his mouth.

The cyclone faltered.

Vanelorn edged closer to the king until they stood back-to-back. They turned in a slow circle, surveying the blasted ruin of the royal pavilion, and the veterans realized that their exultation had been premature. The aulden retreat had drawn off the guard, and the three men stood alone as the main battle now raged two dozen feet away.

Into the empty space danced a graceful figure in blue-green mail, her sword aglow with an inner fire. It traced an incandescent after-image in the air as she darted past the wild swing of Agrylon's staff and out of Guillaume's field of vision.

Although he could not see the fight, he could feel Vanelorn's muscles laboring hard. Guillaume spun to fight side-by-side with his old friend and protector, only to find the aulden already vanished – and a long sagging rent in the lord high marshal's mail. Calàthiél dangled loose in Vanelorn's grip, and his knees buckled. Too late, Guillaume saw that hastening to aid the embattled knight had in fact left his back undefended. The aulden drew Agrylon out with a feint and spun back, striking Vanelorn across his back with a hard backswing that sliced through armor, flesh and bone. The old knight fell flat and lay still. Blood spread from his inert body, pooling on the ancient wood as his breath grew shallow.

Guillaume marveled that the aulden had woven her attack between them in such a way that Agrylon could not unleash his spells for fear of killing the king or the marshal. He had no doubt that she could kill him, and that she would. He could see the trajectory of her line of attack, and he was between her and the wizard.

Agrylon called out and gestured at Vanelorn, and his limp body flew like a discarded ragdoll into the aulden's approach. It slammed into her, knocking her to the side with a wet thump and a gasp of pain from the dying knight.

It spared Guillaume death for a moment, and he took full advantage of his reprieve. He turned to run, but came up short at the aulden rushing toward him, her swords drawn. *Another one!* He almost cried out, but clenched his jaw shut and raised his blade in a belated, desperate parry. She rushed past him, shouting in the aulden tongue, swords a blur of motion, and it was Guillaume's turn, at long last, to stand agape.

The wilhorwhyr, he thought in confused relief.

Guillaume had been a warrior since the time he could lift a sword. He had killed his first man when nary a bit of stubble darkened his chin. He was no stranger to combat. But he had never seen a display like that of the two aulden before him. They were a whirl of shining steel and twisting limbs, and it was a beautiful, terrifying sight to behold.

They are not mortal, he reminded himself. With every impossible movement, every sword stroke, every parry, the reality of it settled in. *They are not like us.*

"Agrylon," he said, in a hoarse whisper. He knew in the core of his being what must be done.

The Black Robe turned.

"Bring down your fire," he commanded. "Burn them both to ash."

⁂

Brohan studied the way-gate with a careful eye. The spell had threaded the essence of the mortal realm into a dense knot, and then expanded the weave to hold open a doorway through the Veil. A corresponding knot had created a similar opening from the world of Faerie. These two knots were then interwoven and joined at this singular point, creating a way-bridge between the two worlds. It was a Greater Spell, there was no doubt of that, the like of which Brohan had not seen in a score of years, but simple magic could undo complexity as easily as a plain, sharp blade could slice through the most complicated weavework of a fine tapestry. Destruction was less work than creation, requiring more force than control, but in this case there was a significant risk in the endeavour. Undoing the spell quickly, *cutting* the fabric of the worlds, meant discharging those bound energies in a sudden hemorrhage rather than a controlled bleed.

The master bard deconstructed the binding magic of the way-gate one thread at a time, first one from the mortal edge, then from Faerie. As the *iiyir* shot from the constraints of the spell, Brohan channeled it into the waiting, thirsty well of Elèndere. A more powerful wizard might have done so with less effort, or with less pain, but the channeling of such power left him sweating, tense and hissing curses under his breath.

"Almost," he said to Aeolil as he paused to recover his strength. The turn of the tides had thrown a fine silt of Shadow into the *ur'iiyir*, and the taint both tired and pained him. "Almost have it."

"Are there more coming?" she asked.

"Yes," he answered, peering into the distorted haze of the Way. He could see the faerie host through the shifting colors and mists, and he judged that whatever had prompted Meimniyl to lead the Ceearmyltu to war, this was no feint or half-hearted attack – it was the opening salvo of conquest. And they would be arriving at this side of the way-bridge very soon, indeed.

He looked around Saint Kaissus Field in apprehension. Although the pavilions seemed to be repelling the attack, or at least holding their own with the help of the Black Robes, elsewhere things were considerably more grim. If any more aulden came through the way-gate, even a handful, it might very well tip the balance beyond what Rel and Agrylon could compensate.

"If I can't close the Way soon…" Brohan's voice trailed off as an unexpected surge in the tides drew his attention back to the way-gate. The aulden within were now in disarray, their formation scattering as a seething ball of white-hot fire erupted from all sides around them. It was no spell that he recognized, and in fact, it seemed more like a wild discharge of *iiyir*, a chaotic storm front moving through the Veil, than an intentional, coherent casting of any sort.

It almost looks like…

"Aeolil," he said, dull with a sudden realization. "The gate is collapsing."

Aeolil's young face slackened with relief. "Goo–"

"No." He turned to her and squeezed her shoulder gently. For the panic that was welling up in him, his words were surprisingly calm. "It's *not* good. Not at all. First, there will be a Minor Devastation worth of wildfire blowing through the way-gate. And I can't close it in time." He sighed. That wasn't entirely true. "Not from this side."

"Not from *this* side?" Aeolil repeated, her brow furrowing.

"I won't need this anymore," he said, handing Elèndere to Aeolil. Her short-lived look of relief had now transformed to a tight expression of fear. Before she could utter any protest, Brohan stepped through the gate. "If Inulf lives when this is all done, tell him I enjoyed the elder vintage. He'll understand."

"Brohan!"

"Bring down your wards. All of them. This is going to hurt less if you are divested from the tides."

"Let me help you," she pleaded, taking a tentative step toward the gate.

Brohan smiled. "I think not," he said, even as the heat of angry lightning singed the back of his neck. His fingers described a series of complicated patterns in the air as he spoke, and he felt the tides bend to his summons. "With any luck at all, this will be but an end to one movement and not the end of my song. I have rather a long one planned out. I do hate an unresolved chord." He grimaced as the nimbus of the firestorm washed over him. "Tell Cal to be careful," he shouted as the conflagration enveloped him, and the edges of the way-gate stitched themselves together. "Keep an eye –"

The portal closed, and he finished his sentence with an agonized scream.

The tides exploded around him, filling the way-bridge with flames and screams and scattered bodies.

And darkness followed the fire.

༺༻

Artygalle had been killed several times, by his count, or should have been if not for the kin-wrought armor he wore. He was battered and bruised, tired and sore, and his ears were ringing from a glancing blow to his helm – but alive, he somehow still remained. The fae were even falling back from him now when he charged, and it seemed that perhaps he and his band of motley commoners might turn the tide in their corner of the battlefield. But then the battlefield itself turned traitor, and that hope dissolved as the living *ilyela* came to life around them.

Panic ran through the ranks as the haunting song began and the limbs stretched out to grab and trip and hold the humans.

Treesingers! Artygalle looked about wildly, trying to find the source of the song. *Only one voice,* he thought with some small relief. *Only one.*

Artygalle saw her, not two yards away, just as Windthane fell prey to the snarled grasp of wooden fingers closing around his hooves. Curling vines snaked up his rear legs, closing tight around his hocks. The horse kicked and wheeled, but could not break free, and the *ilyela* dragged him down. Artygalle escaped the saddle and stumbled away before the horse could roll on top of him. He kicked his way through tangling roots and cut at the reaching limbs and whipping vines. The old tree had been sleeping for hundreds of years, but once fully awake and at the call of such a powerful singer, Artygalle knew it would all be over for them soon. He had to reach the treesinger. He had to kill her before that could happen.

The aulden took full advantage of the turning tide in the battle, and Artygalle watched in horror as their shining swords poised like shards of rainbow to slay his now captive host. "No!" he screamed, still too far to strike and end the song. "No!"

The treesinger followed Artygalle's hopeless gaze, and the words of her song trailed off, sticking in her throat. "Na'a!" she shouted, instead.

Artygalle pushed quickly through the flaccid *ilyela*, wondering why she called the attack to a halt. He was mere steps from her, his sword raised.

"Na'a!" she repeated, and the look of despair on her face stopped Artygalle's charge. Tears streaked her blood-spattered cheeks. He stood poised, but a sword-length away. "Na'a!" she cried again.

The fae warriors finally heeded her command and lowered their weapons, some even dropping them at their feet.

Artygalle held his sword steady at her throat. A ring of holly and *ilyela* blossoms hung from her neck. *She's of the* cayl, he realized. "Yield," he said, almost pleading. "*He alei'ih*," he repeated in aulden. "*Ieylulki.*"

Her voice was like a sad song, melodic but without joy. "I end it. I end it, now," she said. "*He alei'ih! He alei'ih, Ceearmyltu ne!*"

Artygalle blinked, stunned by her surrender. She, who could have unleashed the whole of the massive grove that men called Saint Kaissus Field upon them, and brought death to hundreds in but a hand's span – she had ended the attack as suddenly as it began. She'd meant the song to end the fighting, but not in the way he'd expected.

Artygalle opened his mouth to thank her, but before he could speak, she thrust herself forward onto his sword. The point pierced her throat just above the collarbone and exited out the back of her neck. She looked up at Artygalle, the sadness in her eyes draining to a vacant stare as the light of life left her. He stood there, transfixed by the sight. He took his shaking hands from the hilt. Her corpse fell over. He would have screamed, but his legs failed him, and he dropped next to the dead *caylaeni*.

There came a peal of thunder from the middle of the list, where not long ago he had tilted for the King's Lance. Artygalle flinched from the noise and blinked at the bright light, but he was surprised to see the aulden falling in paroxysmal fits of pain, some even passing out, in the wake of the blast.

In the stillness that followed, Artygalle half expected it to rain.
Rain would be nice.
He closed his eyes, numb and nauseous. Exhausted.

Artygalle removed his helm. The air was pungent with the smells of battle. Blood, bowel, and iron. A nicker drew his attention to Windthane, who was struggling to stand. Artygalle wanted to sit, and rest, and be sick about the death and dying around him, but he moved over to his mount instead. He whispered soothing words, quieting the spooked horse as he freed it from the remains of the *ilyela* root.

When he looked up again, a group of knights sifted through the bodies. Ezriel Malminnion led them, his black and silver surcoat sprayed in red. He surveyed the scene with a critical eye. "You did well, Sir Artygalle," he said. "Fought bravely."

"She surrendered, Your Grace," Artygalle explained.

"A sword to the throat will take the fight out of most anyone," quipped a familiar voice. Calamyr walked over from Ezriel's left, holding a stained cloak to an injured arm. His smile was tense, and his face pale. "You made good terms."

Garath was not far behind his friend. Though unhurt, his mood was not so light. "We should finish the rest of them while we can," he said.

"Murder does not befit a warrior," chastised Ezriel. He frowned at his brother and shook his head with a sigh. "Regardless, their fate is not in your hands."

"She surrendered," repeated Artygalle. "You do not slay an enemy that yields."

"Just so," agreed Ezriel. "Come, Sir Artygalle. Many good men died this day, and we will pay them all our respects. But first we must tend to the living. We must see to the king."

Artygalle looked up at the royal pavilion. The king was just now being rejoined with his guard. He thought he recognized Symmlrey, unsteady on her feet, blade shaking in her hand, as the Royal Guard converged on her. One of the knights struck at her from behind.

"Hold!" Artygalle yelled, setting off at a run. "Hold!"

It was no longer the king he was worried about.

Chapter Sixty

Retreat to Conquest

"Turn back!" Hiruld's shock and confusion had transformed to anger. His face was crimson, his hands balled into fists. "Why have we run to ground?"

Vaujn pressed him forward. "Surviving the day is our victory, my prince."

Hiruld whirled, trying to push back against the flow of his underkin guards. "I can fight! By the Swords, I can *fight*."

Vaujn kept a firm hand on the prince's midsection, preventing his attempt to break ranks. "We can all fight. No question. What you can't do is *die*. Right? That's the rub. Best way to keep you alive is not to fight. Not now."

"It's not right," Hiruld fumed, his voice a growling whisper.

"Maybe not," agreed Vaujn, trying to give the prince a sympathetic frown as he prodded him forward again, "but it *is* best."

The undertunnels shook from the noise of combat above – indiscernible sounds, rumblings, and an occasional crack like thunder ran through the earth. Dirt sifted loose from the root-woven ceiling, sprinkling their helms and cloaks with a fine layer of grimy dust. Vaujn kept on, trying not to think too much about what transpired above. They had to get the prince to safety. Who they had left behind to die would be a question for another time.

"Left at fifty hetahrs," he instructed, but it was for the prince's benefit more than his squad. They'd seen maps. They knew the tunnels. "Then straight on."

No aulden had come underground, and there were no humans in the royal passageways. But Vaujn was anxious to exit the quiet, deserted areas for the bustle and panic of the main underlevels. If the aulden intended assassination then they would know where to intercept the squad's retreat. They had sung this tree in ages gone. There would be no secrets from them here. If the kin could reach the stables, however, just beyond there was a well – and the well reached down below the giant *ilyela* grove's root system, down beyond the influence and memory of the aulden, down to the comforting stone tunnels of the aquifer.

"Empty," reported Läzch from up ahead. "Nothing here."

"Take it slow anyway," grumbled Mueszner. "Slow, and keep your eyes open for *shimmer*. They can pop in from rainbows."

"Damn aulden," muttered Darrow.

Hiruld looked over his shoulder, working up another protest.

"I know," Vaujn said, and nudged the prince around the corner.

The smell of stale straw and fresh manure wafted down the passage. Along with the stench came the cool, wet hint of deep air from the well house. There were screams of panic, both human and equine, but the sounds were comforting. It meant they were closer. That much closer...

Then there was a crash, a distinct sound of a sword screeching against armor.

"No!" a voice yelled from the corner of the next intersection, still thirty hetahrs shy of the stable entrance. "A trap! 'Tis a trap!"

Vaujn and his squad raised their crossbows. There was more yelling, more din of battle, and an aulden body fell into the passage ahead. Her ruined chain shirt framed a bloody wound from chin to pelvis. A human knight backed into view, his blue cloak whirling, engaged with another aulden swordswoman. The knight was covered in blood, and his chain was torn across his chest and arms, but he fought hard and fast, and after trading strokes, he found his mark and sent his second attacker to the dirt.

When he turned, Vaujn recognized the blue and gold cloak and the face beneath the iron cap, but Hiruld was the first to voice it.

"Bells!" The prince jumped, his face alight with joy and relief. "Thank the gods! I should never have let them-"

"Steady there," Vaujn interrupted, stepping in front of the prince.

"What?" Hiruld gave the kin a dangerous look.

"*Sjhtojr,*" Vaujn ordered. The squad formed up into the stinger formation in two ranks, the first on its knees, all crossbows aimed at Bellivue. The knight halted.

"My Prince," Bellivue said, breathing hard. "You are betrayed. The aulden were awaiting you here."

"So were you, apparently," said Vaujn.

Chloe and Hæschp set down their crossbows. Chloe removed her scrying bowl, and Hæschp filled it with water from his skin before retrieving his weapon and returning to his place in formation. Chloe waved her hand over the bowl, chanting softly.

Hiruld pushed forward, but Vaujn held firm. "Just a moment, My Prince."

Chloe dropped a small onyx chip into the bowl and studied the ripples.

"Why aren't you in the tower?" Vaujn asked. "How did you get here?"

Bellivue sagged, shaking his head. "We've no more time for questioning loyalties, sir. Inulf is loose in the castle, and I'm afraid most of the guard have perished. I'm under geas by Agrylon's own hand. The bond is very strong. It called me here to his aid – led me to him."

"I'll bet it did." Vaujn spared a glance at Chloe, but her attention was still strictly on the bowl.

"We've little time left, Hiruld," Bellivue said, approaching.

"Don't come any closer," Vaujn warned.

"He just slew the aulden," Hiruld argued, struggling against Vaujn's staying hand. "Damn it all, I've known him longer than you. Release me, *dwarf!*"

Bellivue sheathed his blade. "The kin do you great service. But-"

Chloe looked up from her bowl. Vaujn saw the answer in her eyes before she uttered the word.

"*Dhûnorihm,*" she said.

Vaujn didn't have to issue the command to fire. Mother Chloe's proclamation was enough. A dozen bolts of kinsteel were loosed with a resonant twang, and Bellivue was struck with no less than eight. The impact drove him backward, and he stumbled. He cried out, but one of the bolts had entered his cheek and shattered his jaw, and he couldn't form actual words.

"No!" shouted Hiruld, "Bells! No!"

Another volley struck the prone body of the Prince's Herald. He twitched once more and then lay very still.

"What have you done?" raved the prince, and this time he pushed past Vaujn and his guard. "Bells!"

Läzch tackled him, and he kicked at her, trying to break free.

"Have you all gone mad?" Hiruld yelled. He had almost gained his feet when Mueszner put a heavy boot on his ankle.

"Stay down, you blessed fool," Vaujn snapped. "Who knows how long Bellivue's been dead, or possessed, or whatever. *That's* the shadowyn. And it might look dead, but right now it's just inconvenienced, so don't... get... any... *closer.*"

"Impossi–"

"He is still bleeding traces of Shadow, My Prince," Chloe explained, her tone more patient than Vaujn could hope to muster. "He shadow-walked right to your person. Just like the aulden walk through rainbows. He's not of the mortal world."

"I knew it," Vaujn said, nodding. "Osrith was right: *put them all in the tower and kill whoever shows up to help.* Best friend of the prince, an inviolate knight under geas, pure and noble and all that – even Agrylon comes to his defense. Then here he is, nice and convenient, *saving* the prince. Had to be him."

"You're very cynical," remarked Chloe.

"He looks nothing more than a dead man to me," Hiruld said, the defiance gone from his tone, replaced by something more resigned. "A dead friend."

Vaujn shuffled his feet. "You're *sure*, right, Chloe?"

She nodded. "He's waiting for someone to go check his body, preferably the prince himself. Then he'll pop up and unleash some horrible shadowfire on him. Remember Dathliil?"

Vaujn grunted. Taantun had lost half his squad to that one.

"This, at least, I prepared for." Chloe reached into her satchel and withdrew a large, pale gemstone. "I can inter it," she said, rubbing the stone with her thumb and then dropping it into her scrying bowl, "but the spell takes time, and it might get tired of waiting. If it gets up, keep killing it until I'm finished."

༄

Seth stumbled again, and then scrabbled his way back to his feet. The fighting was not far behind, but desperation proved effective fuel. He ran to the next intersection and waited, panting, for the others to catch up to him.

You know the way best, Calvraign had said. *Take us to the faerie garden.*

"I know the way best," he repeated aloud, as if to convince himself, catching his breath.

It was the only thing he could contribute to their survival. He couldn't swing a sword or heft a bow, not with the intent of hitting anything. More often than not he froze in terror at sight of the hrumm, and Inulf and Osrith terrified him only slightly less.

A door slammed shut behind him, and a bar clanged into its bracket. "That'll hold the bloody bastards," Foss was saying.

"Not for long," Osrith added, as the voices drew nearer.

Seth bit his lip, waiting as they came into sight at the end of the hallway and ran in his direction: Foss, with a few of his surviving men; Inulf and his; Osrith, Markus, Calvraign, and Callagh Breigh. The sight of her – sweaty, blood-stained, and glaring her ferocious glare – quickened his heart. Indeed, she scared him most of all, but for mostly different reasons.

"Down straight here, through Black Mirror Hall and up to Aventus Terrace. The door to the haunted garden is there, sirs."

The guardsmen made warding signs, and even Foss balked aloud. "Black Mirror Hall." He said the words as if simply speaking them was explanation for his concern. "Why not go out and around along Atrevus Terrace – it meets up with Aventus, too, don't it?"

"The hall is quickest, and there are two doors to bar behind us that way." Seth shrugged, puzzled by Foss' demeanor. *It's the haunted garden he should be worried about.*

The pounding on the door behind them produced a sharp crack.

"I go through there every Celanday," Seth insisted.

"All right," Foss acquiesced reluctantly. He turned to his men. "Straight through. Don't look at nothin'. Don't touch nothin'. Old magic in that hall. Black magic. Look in a black mirror, and it'll take your soul right out o' your body."

Seth swallowed. *Black magic?* "Well, um, the mirrors are all boarded up. I've never, um, it seemed safe."

Inulf laughed. "Old it be, and black – but just the *glass*, eh? Not the magic." He laughed again. "But never *safe*."

"I'd worry less about the hallway, and more about what's waiting for us at the other end." Osrith motioned them on. "Move."

Seth ran down the steps, passing between the double doors and beneath the great stone archway into Black Mirror Hall. On the surface, there was nothing remarkable about it. Most of it, in fact, was hidden in the shadows thrown by the scant torchlight. Inulf closed the doors behind them, and his men dropped a heavy black bar across its width, settling into brass brackets with a satisfying *thunk*.

A hand fell on his shoulder, and Seth jumped. He was relieved to find Calvraign's apologetic, if strained, smile at the other end of the clasping hand.

"Lead on, Seth," he said.

"Of course," Seth agreed, recognized the underlying order hidden in his master's gentle encouragement. Calvraign's eyes still had softness in them, and his voice still held kindness, but there was a hardness forming at the edges, caked in the blood of his friends and enemies. "Sorry."

Somehow, this time it seemed a sinister and foreboding place. The nondescript black velvet curtains that covered the mirrors, six to each side of the hall, rustled as they passed, revealing glimpses of the carved shutters beneath. He saw or imagined details in the intricate designs that he'd never noticed before – twining dragons, flying gryphons, a winged skull spitting fire. The shadowplay gave them all an unsettling illusion of movement.

"What was this place?" whispered Callagh, stopping in front of one of the mirrors. She parted the curtain, and traced a pair of squinting emerald eyes inlaid above the snarling snout of some horrid hellhound.

"I don't know," Osrith said. "If Kassakan were here, she'd give you some wonderful story about it. Keep moving."

Despite Foss' misgivings, and his newfound nervousness, or even Callagh daring to touch one of the mirror coverings, the hall proved as uneventful as any other time Seth had passed through, and he was thankful for that. Sometimes it seemed as if the moment someone noticed something, even when it had been around him without incident his whole life, it suddenly became a horrible and present danger.

Seth climbed the broad steps leading up out of the hall, glad to put it behind him. He waited by the door.

"Thank you, Seth," Calvraign said, just as the pounding began at the other entrance. "You've been very brave. Now…. Is there a place you can hide?"

"Hide?"

Calvraign pushed the doors open. Cold wind greeted them, and the scent of smoke. "The hrumm behind us will break through soon enough, but the last place you need to be is inside the garden."

"Yeah, and this would be the second to last," Osrith observed, looking around the manicured hedges and tarp-covered trees as they entered the terrace. "You could climb up there and hide under the canvas, maybe, and hope they don't smell you out."

"It's a little smoky," agreed Markus with a half-hearted smile.

"Good luck, boy. I wish you that. You be needing luck today." Inulf laughed and moved past them all to the garden door.

He laughs a lot, thought Seth with some irritation.

They couldn't bar the door from the outside, but it seemed the hrumm were making slow progress with the thicker doors and stronger bracket at the other end of Black Mirror Hall. They filed past, one by one, giving him a pat on the back or nod of thanks, but their minds were already on the battle ahead. Callagh came last of all, and Seth watched after her, a lump forming in his throat. She turned back, meeting his awkward stare with a wry smile.

"Ach," she said, walking back to him and leaning in close.

Seth thought she might give him a quick kiss on the cheek, and was surprised to find her dry lips pressing against his, firm and sure. She lingered long enough that when she broke the kiss, it was with a moist pop. He felt a little light-headed.

"I know you've been wonderin', poor thing," she said, tilting her head with an innocent look. "An' I thought it a shame if you were to die a-wonderin'."

Seth stared after her again as she joined the others. Calvraign had blushed, and split a glare between Callagh and Seth. Seth licked his tingling lips, and smiled. *You should not be smiling right now,* he told himself, but to no avail.

"What?" Callagh snapped, tapping Calvraign's chest with the tip of her bow. "D'you have a claim to make? No? Besides," she said with a wink, "when you're facing down death, it's nice to have something to live for."

"The scurryway!" Seth exclaimed. He would have to climb over the balustrade and lower himself to the roof of the grounds house, but from there it was not a long drop to the Summer Gardens. "I'll hide in the scuryway!"

The soldiers didn't appear to notice his revelation. They waited as Inulf cracked the door and peered into the garden. Calvraign still stood staring at Seth, however. He wondered if he might not pay a dear price for Callagh's recent show of affection. He backed slowly to the edge of the terrace.

"Hrumm," Inulf said, wiggling his fingers around his eyes. "*Graomwrnokk.*"

"How many?" asked Foss.

Inulf held up three fingers, but shook his head. "I'm sure more be sneakin' and hidin', yes? Hmm?"

"Aye, that'll be the way of it," agreed Osrith. "Coming down that stair, there won't be any sneaking or hiding for us."

"No, there won't," Calvraign said. "Not on the stair. Seth!"

Seth waited at the railing as Calvraign ran at him with Callagh, and Reime, the smallest of Foss' crossbowmen, trailed not far behind.

"As it happens," Calvraign said, "we're coming with you."

Chapter Sixty-One

Meyr ga'Glyleyn

THE scurryway was a narrow passage hidden behind a delicate facade of polished wood, carved in intricate twisting vines and leaves, backed with a thin lining of grey porous cloth. From a distance it was opaque, but with her eye pressed against it Callagh could see out into the garden courtyard. They were downwind of the *graomwrnokk*, although the whirling winds inside the small courtyard made this an uncertain enough thing.

Calvraign and Reime stood ready at the door with sword and crossbow. Seth had the sense to hide, and was huddled near the entrance of the scurryway. Callagh expected Osrith and the others would attack very soon, before the hrumm dogging their retreat caught them from behind. She kept her body still and breath quiet, as if stalking prey in the Ad Craign Uhl.

A familiar black shape settled onto a redberry tree, oily black wings folding in as it found its perch. She felt a chill in her bones, and her amulet burned, like when she'd sealed her oath, and not for the first time since her induction into the *madhwr-rwn*. When Inulf appeared, when she'd rescued Calvraign, when they'd passed through Black Mirror Hall.

The raven cocked its head.

She thought, for a moment, that a man stood with them in the crowded enclosure, but in a blink he was gone.

The raven quorked.

Yes, the voice said, like an itch tickling the inside of her ear. It wasn't Old Bones. It was the voice behind the shadows of the *madhwr-rwn.* The *other* voice. *Her* voice. *See him,* she commanded. *See my wayward son.*

The wound on Callagh's hand throbbed. A trickle of blood escaped her makeshift bandage.

The apparition swirled into being like smoke from a dying fire, coiling into the shape of a man, standing in the lee of Calvraign's shadow. Reime didn't appear to notice the specter, and this only confirmed the suspicion growing in her gut. He stood – half man, half shadow – like the ethereal patrons of the court that had presided over her blood pact with Old Bones.

This is Greycloak, she thought. *Calvraign's shadow. He's* madhwr-rwn?

Yes, hissed the quiet voice in her head. The amulet pulsed against her breast, in time with her pulse. *He of the Cythe. My knight. My promised. My very Hand. Bring him home to me, Callagh Breigh. Bring him home.*

Greycloak turned toward her. His face was one of welcome, a distant recollection darkened by shades of clinging grey, a shrouded warmth like the midday suns obscured by clouds. Callagh's mind reeled at the familiar memory that stood before her. Not her memory, exactly – she'd been too young when he'd left Craignuuwn to recognize him. But *they* told her. They whispered his name to her, over and again, memories not her own echoing in her thoughts.

Ibhraign!

"What?" The word was little more than a sigh.

Reime looked at her curiously. Calvraign was intent on what lay ahead.

The stairway door burst open, and Inulf led his men down into the courtyard, swords and shields at the ready, Osrith at the rear. As the hrumm jumped to defend themselves, Foss and his crossbowmen took position on the landing, taking aim at the charging enemy.

He must fulfill his oath. He is promised to me.

The voice filled Callagh's head. She watched herself slack the tension in her bowstring as if a spectator to her own actions. She drew the razor tip of an arrow across her wrist once. Twice. Bright red lines of blood glimmered on her pale flesh.

Claim him. Say the words to bring him home. Say the words.

Fresh blood welled, and she clasped the medallion, mumbling, as if another voice spoke through her, "On your blood you swore your heart and bound your soul."

Ibhraign looked at her, *through* her eyes to wherever it was she hovered, away from herself. A twinge of pain in her forearm startled her – the vague sensation of her own heartbeat returned to her, of breath, and voice.

"To…" She faltered.

Take him back.

"To the will of Father Earth," she continued, words forming despite herself, like muddy puddles sucking at her boot, "and… and Mother Suns of Sky."

Calvraign had stormed from the scurryway with a shout, and Reime followed, stepping out and to the left with the stock of his crossbow raised to his shoulder. Greycloak strained to join them. She could feel him pulling against her like a fish on a line, each word she spoke another twist of the hook.

"Please," Ibhraign said. His voice was plaintive, distant, and hollow, but it struck her as infinitely more human than the whispers skittering through her head, pulling the strings of her will. "I swore an oath before all others. For him. For his mother."

The raven spread its wings, preparing for flight.

There can be no oath before me, the voice raged. *Not to place or thing or even a wife.*

"With painted face to greet the dawn," Callagh regurgitated the words, heaving. Pain traveled up her arm, spreading to her shoulder, her heart. Ibhraign faltered, and strength coursed into her, filling her. His strength. His essence and his power – *hers.*

Mine, reminded the dread voice, and a jolt from the medallion scalded like burning oil through her nerves. *He cannot ungive what's been freely given. He is mine, and mine alone. Bring him home, Callagh Breigh, and you will be first among mortals in the* madhwr-rwn.

Ecstatic fire burned deep in Callagh's center. She wanted it, needed it, hungered for it, even as she felt it devouring her in agony. But as the hot life permeated her, so did her anger.

No, she railed at the invisible presence. *It is Ibhraign!*

Ibhraign is dead. This is my Hand. Return him to me.

Callagh narrowed her eyes. "The gods' own edge, the *madh-*" She bit down hard, slicing deep into her tongue as she cut the word in mid-syllable. She spat a mouthful of blood, and she shook as a choking rage from netherwhere drove her to her knees. The pain consumed her. The world spun, her head reeled, her chest heaved, but she dragged herself back to her feet, and she forced a smile. It was a practiced thing, a show of defiance rather than humor, and one until now she had reserved only for her father.

I am not a broken thing, she thought.

"*Luadh má Ciaerhán!*" she growled, the blood running out of her mouth like a feral animal. "*Eahr macc-an-Cythe!*"

And she followed Ibhraign the Dragonheart into battle.

⁓

"Keep your distance," Vaujn ordered, mostly for the benefit of Prince Hiruld. No one else seemed at all interested in approaching the well-feathered corpse.

The glaring warface of Chloe's helmet, discarded at her side, stared up at her as she sat deep in trance, her own eyes closed to the world around her. The gem in her bowl glowed in faint, sporadic pulses. She stopped chanting and now hummed and held a single note instead.

She's close, Vaujn thought. He didn't know much about his wife's magic, even after so many years of marriage and squad life, but he knew that when she settled on her key note, she'd found what she needed within the gem's lattice.

"I can't abide this," Hiruld said, his voice calm. "I truly cannot."

Vaujn was disturbed by the prince's shift in demeanor. The raging of emotion had its dangers, but he feared the peace of certainty all the more. *He's made up his mind about it.* "A moment more, and she'll draw it out. A moment more."

Bellivue twitched. The temperature in the hall dropped to that of a chill-house.

Chloe spoke, but not in any mortal tongue – this was the language of the earth. Of rock. Of stone. Of mountain hearts beating deep in the breast of creation. Her eyes opened wide, rolling back into her head. Water boiled around the pulsating gem. She muttered the incomprehensible again, her empty, white stare fixed on Bellivue.

Vaujn grabbed the prince's arm. "This is it."

Bellivue quaked. His body shook in stiff tremors.

Hiruld let out a strangled cry. His proud face paled.

Blackness seeped from the pores of Bellivue's skin, pooling around him. A low wheeze sputtered from his throat. His arm quivered, reaching up, hand grasping at air.

Hiruld dropped to his knees.

The gemstone flared, illuminating the concentric ripples that oscillated in the scrying bowl in Chloe's lap – out to the edge and then back to the center, collapsing and reforming, circles in a circular dance.

Bellivue's eyes opened. Black. Seeping tears like oil.

Hiruld's eyes closed. His hand trembled as he drew his sword from its scabbard.

Chloe's teeth ground together.

Vaujn stayed the prince's hand, sword half-drawn. "Patience, Your Highness. We've everything well in hand," he reassured, but Chloe's struggle and the resistance of the shadowborn troubled him. "Kill it again," he ordered. Another volley of bolts pierced the convulsing shadowyn.

"Back!" Hiruld yelled and pushed Vaujn away, freeing his blade and standing. "Stay back from me," he snarled. He looked down with eyes streaked in black. His voice was husky and strained. "Well and truly back."

"*Ver… vershtig,*" Vaujn sputtered, stumbling back from the force of the prince's shove. Shadowyn could move between mortal forms, given time and ritual magic, like shadow-walking *into* a soul, displacing it. But to leap into another body without preparation, *and* while the host was stuck full of kinsteel – Vaujn had never seen anything like it. *A lot of surprises, today.* "*Hetz ullak, Mueszner! Hetz ullak!*"

The sergeant spun, and the prince's sword scratched along the surface of his warface, scarring the grimacing likeness from cheek to cheek as he recoiled from the attack. "*Sjart!*" he cursed.

Vaujn took aim at Hiruld's leg. "Bring him down, but don't kill him, by the All-father. *Don't kill him!*"

The prince stumbled when Vaujn's bolt shattered his knee with a bloody pop, but his momentum carried him to his target: *Chloe.* Vaujn's stomach lurched. He scrabbled to his feet, pulled back the arming lever and loosed another bolt. This time his hasty aim proved wide.

The prince's blade split the air with a whistle.

Mueszner caught the downswing of the sword on the lath of his bow. It cracked, almost splitting in two. Hiruld bullied in close, while the old veteran was tangled in the remains of his weapon and off balance. The prince's sword scraped through the seam of the sergeant's faceplate, and one thrust ended him. One thrust, and Mueszner was limp and lifeless, bright crimson streaming over the gilt beard of his warface, bleeding out in the dirt.

"Blades!" Vaujn barked. "On the prince! Bring him down!"

The kin discarded their crossbows and advanced on the prodigal prince, melee weapons in hand. Hiruld stepped over Mueszner, kicking his corpse back into the chaplain. Water sloshed over the sides of her scrying bowl, and bright golden flame spiraled up from the lambent gemstone. Chloe's eyes popped open in alarm.

"No," she muttered, snatching the burning gem with a wince. Flames leaked from the cracks of her fingers, coiling around her fist like serpents. She rolled to the side, away from her attacker. Läzch, the fastest of the squad, raced to interpose herself between the prince and the chaplain, an axe in each hand.

From the corner of his eye, Vaujn saw a black shadow loom, arms outstretched. He turned. Bellivue was standing – or what *used to be* Bellivue. Any resemblance to its shed human skin had been consumed by the black *iiyir* of the being that stood there now. It was the size of a large man, its face empty and featureless but for eyes of smoke and a mouth of smoldering embers.

Impossible.

"The shadowyn!" he screamed. "'Ware the shadowyn! The bloody thing's in *both* of them!"

A blast of frigid air roared down the passageway, leaving a dusting of hoarfrost in its wake. Most of the squad was warily surrounding Hiruld, but Ouwd and Hæschp were the rearmost in formation, closest to the shadowyn, and as the wind blasted across them, they slowed to a stop. Ice formed around them, between them, freezing their limbs as well as their expressions of terror, under an *etahr* of clear blue rime.

The shadowyn's talons plucked a kinsteel bolt from its chest and flicked it toward Hæschp with a gesture and a word. The bolt sped to its mark, and Hæschp shattered into a blizzard of bloody sleet and frozen flesh.

"Chloe!" Vaujn yelled, turning to face the shadowborn. He didn't verbalize anything else. As his wife, and as his squad chaplain, she knew the subtext of that one cry. *Now what?*

Ouwd was next. With a crack like a mountain glacier sloughing a sheet of ice, the quartermaster burst into fragments, his prodigious bulk falling into a handful of frozen slabs. Vaujn avoided the chunks that rolled toward him, trying to keep his breath and temper even. It had been a long time since they'd suffered any losses in battle, and that interval had made it easy to forget how quickly it could all go to the Pits.

"The geas!" Chloe shouted, spreading her fingers into the packed dirt of the tunnel and then tracing runes that burned black at her touch. "It's pulling Hiruld's strings like a damn puppet," she explained. The shadowyn advanced, extracting another bolt from its torso. It sent the projectile flying, but the shaft disintegrated in mid-air over Chloe's hasty inscription, showering her faceplate with a fine mist of dust. "This ward won't last long," she added, and as if to accentuate her statement, another bolt exploded in front of her. The pieces that skittered across her helmet were larger this time, and carried more momentum through the barrier. "I can still trap him, but he disrupted the spell and severed the ley line. I don't have much left to give." Chloe raised her glowing fist. "If I'm to bind him to the lattice, I have to *touch* him."

Vaujn was glad that his warface did not mirror his actual expression. "Who makes up these rules?" he muttered under his breath.

The possessed prince had been dragged down by half of his own guard. He fought wildly, and with more strength than Vaujn thought purely natural, but Daehl drove her blade through the tendon of his right leg and, supernatural strength or no, it hobbled him. Daính and Náinh sat on his arms. The shadowyn hung back, discarding the inconvenient kinsteel bolts one by one but avoiding close combat with the battle-hardened kin.

"We can't wait for it," Vaujn worried aloud. "Once the last pin is out of the cushion, we're only in for worse."

"Did Magliuk run from the wyrm at Dinnoch?" Chloe asked, her innocent tone a thin veil for her sarcasm.

"Right," agreed Vaujn with a hollow laugh. *Suicide and glory it is, then.* "Squad, after me. Hildil, *hildil dhûnorihm!*"

Leaving the prince to squirm and flail behind them, the kin charged the shadowborn in a tight wedge.

"*Verklämme!*" Vaujn cried.

"*Verklämme im mahr!*" the squad answered.

They all knew what to expect from such a frontal assault. It wasn't the first time the kin of Outpost Number Nine had engaged a creature of the Dark. Chances were that half the squad would die before even reaching the shadowyn. Those that remained would have to hope that they could put enough kinsteel into its ethereal heart to prove lethal, and do it quickly, with minimal support from Mother Chloe. It made the reality of it no less difficult to bear.

The shadowyn spoke, but like Chloe, not in any mortal tongue. The word was not even one that Vaujn could *hear*. He felt it, reverberating through his limbs like a bubbling lake of magma poised to erupt, but there was no comprehending it. The shadowyn blazed in dark fire and met the first rank without flinching.

Náinh screamed as its talons tore through the metal of her helm and ripped through the flesh and bone of her head. She stumbled and collapsed, writhing as the black flames spread from her mauled half-face down her neck and then to her torso. She screamed while she could, which wasn't long.

Darrow tried to attack from the shrouding smoke of Náinh's body, but the shadowyn twisted away and swatted the blade, and the corporal, aside. He hit the tunnel wall head first, and wobbled to his knees. Daính went for its throat. It launched him into the ceiling in similar fashion, but when he fell back to the floor, he didn't move.

Läzch delivered a glancing blow with one of her axes, but had to shift her momentum to avoid a gout of black fire and lost much of the force behind the blow. She tumbled off to the side. Cuhrbern proved not as quick, and the shadowyn caught him square in the chest. The shadowfire melted through his breastplate and consumed him from within.

Vaujn could feel the cold heat of Cuhrbern's demise as he slipped in low under the shadowyn's guard. He drove his sword in hilt deep, up through its crotch and deep into its innards. The shadowyn roared, its maw opening like a forge stove, and Vaujn's face blistered in the heat, even under his helm. It clawed at him, clasping about his midsection, wrenching him and his sword away. Vaujn tried to bury the blade in its chest, but it twisted him until his bones crunched and snapped in its grip. Fire hotter than the shadowyn's magic seared up his spine, burned in his head, robbed him of breath.

Chloe screamed.

I should have let go of the sword, Vaujn thought as it threw him to the dirt. He crashed against the wall, legs over his head, upside down, staring back at the melee. *Should have left it in him.*

Vaujn's left arm sprouted at an acute angle in front of his face, bent backward at the elbow. Oddly, aside from the million piercing needles that burned in his skull, he didn't feel pain. He didn't feel anything.

That should really hurt, he thought as the world spun away from him. The pain was fading slowly to numbness.

Chloe collided with the shadowyn. A fury of golden fire erupted in the corridor, swallowing the blackness like dawn subduing the night. Black flames and golden fire entwined. A blast of air, heat, and force knocked down anything still afoot, and the rumble of the explosion shook dirt loose from the walls and ceiling. Pebbles danced in front of Vaujn's nose, hopping back and forth through the growing cloud of dirt that billowed around them.

Darrow crawled toward him, his helmet discarded, nose broken. Blood clotted the corporal's beard. "Captain?" he groaned. "Captain Vaujn?"

Vaujn couldn't move his head, but his eyes searched wildly for any sign of his wife as the dust settled around them. He could see Daehl and Läzch, still on their feet.

"It's gone," someone said. He thought it might be Thruhm. "The prince, too."

"I think she killed it," confirmed Läzch. She coughed.

"It may have returned the favor," the other voice answered. "She's in a bad way."

Vaujn couldn't cry. He couldn't utter a sound. He couldn't so much as draw a breath. His faceplate pivoted open, and a concerned face filled his view, even as his field of vision collapsed slowly into oblivion.

Chloe.

A hand touched his cheek, felt under his nose and lips for the passing of breath.

"Still alive," Darrow declared, relieved. "He's still alive."

"Not by much," assessed Daehl, kneeling next to the corporal. "Maybe not for long."

Their faces faded to darkness. The sound of their voices lasted a few moments longer, as if he were listening to their conversation from the bottom of a well. *Don't worry about me. Chloe. Save Chloe.*

Daehl wasted no time taking command, her voice raw but steady. "Läzch, go scout things out – see what's going on at the field and make sure there're no more surprises between us and the well house. Corporal, Thruhm – check on the wounded. I'll stay with the captain."

"Check on the dead, more like."

"Just get to it."

Vaujn heard a scuffling in the dirt.

"Damn shadowyn," grumbled Darrow.

And then cold and dark, and a singular thought, a clinging hope the sole light flickering in the blackness.

Chloe.

༄

Numbness crept from Osrith's arms to his shoulders, a dull ache that throbbed with every impact of axe on sword. Pain lurked beneath, like a fire struggling to burn a sodden log. Osrith kept his focus on footing, balance and timing. His breathing was even and strong. He kept time with the beat of his pounding pulse, like a drum-sergeant's cadence measuring each step, each swing, each parry. When skill could win a contest quickly, all the better – but Osrith never relied on that. Stamina and patience won the day more often than not, and though the hrumm had strength and stamina to spare, in battle they lacked patience.

Satisfied that he had provoked the beast's rage, Osrith stepped back, and then back again, feigning retreat, drawing it from the shelter of the redberry trees and the shrouds of streaming dragonmist. Another step back. He felt suns-light warming his neck. Osrith caught a swing on his axe haft, kneeling as he absorbed the force of the blow to clear the line of sight to the crossbowmen on the steps.

The graomwrnokk emerged from the shaded canopy of foliage. It hadn't taken two steps before a quarrel struck it high in the breast. It lurched, and Osrith sprang, splitting its skull with a powerful downstroke.

Osrith searched the trees for Calvraign, anxious to bring the boy back under his wing. Despite the lad's inexperience, he'd proved both his skill with a blade and his head for strategy. Still too quick to leap and too slow to dodge, but that was evidence of youth more than ability. Osrith had never seen the boy's father fight, but he'd been on the battlefield at Vlue Macc, and heard the stories the Calahyr told of the fated last stand of the Cythe stalwart, Ibhraign.

The Painted Man,
he danced in shadows.
Something, something…

Osrith forgot the rest. Reciting poetry had never been his strong suit.

He surveyed the battlefield, glancing past the flailing guardsmen and the snarling hrumm. The violence seemed out of place in the careful symmetry of the aulden garden. Blossoms fell from the redberry trees, gentle flurries of pink and white fluff curling through the air like snow. Inulf grimaced as he grappled with a hrumm, hand-to-hand. Both tumbled into the stillness of the reflecting pool, splashing in the shallow waters under the serene stares of aulden statuary.

There he is.

Calvraign and Callagh and Foss' man, Reime, had found the *graomwrnokk's pakh ma*, a huge brute with more ink than flesh on his exposed face. The boy was fighting hard, finding a rhythm, using the cover of the trees to his advantage, but he was avoiding Pheydreyr's embrace by a hair's breadth, and likely not for much longer. The hrumm fended off Calvraign's blows on a sturdy kite shield that bristled with three feathered shafts. One arrow hung loosely in the weave of its chain mail. Callagh was poised to loose another, looking for an opening.

Osrith stormed forward at a hard sprint. The *pakh ma* wielded a bastard sword one-handed, a feat of strength, to be sure, a show of what the hrumm called *fhaogk*, proof of might. Dominance. But for all its brawn, the balance of the blade was not meant for such a stance, and its speed and leverage suffered. It was a mistake that served to Calvraign's advantage, and Osrith hoped would serve to keep the boy alive a few moments longer.

"Oz!" Markus called from the steps.

Osrith only spared a glance over his shoulder. The erstwhile cook was cranking his crossbow and blowing a drop of sweat off of his upper lip. He was kneeling on the stairway with Foss and what was left of the crossbowmen.

"They're knockin' on the back door!" he shouted.

"Well, hold fast," Osrith yelled back, irritated. "I can't fly up there to help."

Markus muttered something under his breath, but Osrith didn't waste further thought on Cookie or his unpleasant commentary. He was a few long strides from delivering his own lesson on *fhaogk* to the hrummish war-chieftan, and he had no time or attention to spare. Reime was down, holding in his guts, and Calvraign's sword was caught on the *pakh ma's* shield. The giant hrumm aimed the deadly length of its blade at the boy's chest for a killing thrust. Osrith realized, just footsteps away, just an axe-length from saving him, that he would be too late.

Too late.

He *should* have been too late. But the bastard sword skewed off, parried into thin air, and Calvraign landed a riposte to its abdomen, drawing blood and a disconcerted howl. Osrith blinked. It almost seemed that just as he was turning his attention toward Calvraign and away from Markus, it was *almost* as if there were *two* of him fighting the hrumm.

But then Osrith was there in the melee himself, and he worried nothing for shadows or tricks of the light. The hrumm turned, bracing against the charge, but Osrith only feinted a cleaving strike, instead hooking its shield, pulling it out and away. As the hrumm lurched forward, Osrith stabbed it under the chin with the razor tip of his pointed axe haft. An arrow screamed into the *pakh ma's* chest, and Calvraign struck twice – *impossibly fast*, Osrith noted – one thrust to the sword arm and one to the chest.

Markus half-ran, half-fell, down the stairs to the garden, his crossbow tumbling before him. Hrumm had reached and overwhelmed the landing. Foss was trying to hold them, but he was the last man standing, and that was not likely to be for much longer.

A raven squawked, taking wing from the tree at Callagh's back.

Osrith's lungs burned, but he heaved his long axe back for one last blow.

Thunder rumbled in the enclosure of the garden. There was no sharp crack of lightning preceding it, only the deep booming peal of the aftershock. Osrith saw the *pakh ma's* eyes widen an instant before a gale of blistering air threw them both from their feet. The blast flattened him to the turf and his axe flew from his grip.

Osrith spat out a mouthful of dirt.

That would be the shadowyn, then, he thought. *A big one. That's Kassakan's cue.*

Osrith watched as black flames coalesced into a shape that was vaguely man-like, but writhing with more than its share of appendages. It dominated the steps of the reflecting pool, casting its limbs out, a strange chant on its unseen lips. A body dropped from its slithering arms into the water. Osrith recognized the inert form with a muttered curse.

Hiruld. That means the kin...

"Kassakan!" he screamed, regaining his feet.

The *pakh ma* also rose, blood streaming from its wounds, staggering but still hefting its sword with menacing purpose. Calvraign was on one knee, shaking his head and trying to stand. Callagh was face-first in the dirt next to Reime, rising slowly. Osrith drew his sword and took position between them and the hrumm. He was reluctant to turn a blind eye to the shadowyn, but the *pakh ma* was too close to ignore.

Kassakan was supposed to be here if the shadowyn showed up. Her... and help, besides.

But there was no sign of her. Osrith feared for the first time that perhaps she hadn't succeeded in her mission. The truth of it was, until this moment, he had hoped that she would fail. Now, he was hoping that she came through with the lesser of two evils. Soon.

"Hah! You *hungry*, huh? Eh?" Inulf's taunt gave Osrith some consolation that his back wasn't left completely exposed. "Come take a bite, skarl!"

That's a few more drips of the water clock, Osrith thought. *Where are you, lizard?*

Osrith closed the distance with the *pakh ma* faster than he thought entirely wise, but he needed to create more space for Calvraign and Callagh, or it would be on *them* first. It fell back, parrying, but Osrith was inside its guard and his sword hilt deep in its chest before it could counter.

It was a mortal blow, but the hrumm appeared in no hurry to accept its fate. It didn't scream. It didn't shout out any last heroic battle cry. It seized Osrith by the neck, claws scraping against mail, and threw him to the ground. It landed on top of him, crushing him into the dirt, knocking the breath from him. It smashed his head against a decorative marble treenape that lurked in frozen frolic beneath the trees. Osrith twisted, deflecting the blow on the crown of his helm. It lifted him up and pounded his head down again, this time striking the side of his face on the garden ornament.

The crack of Osrith's cheekbone fracturing echoed between his ears like the splitting of a great belwood. His vision blurred. He lashed out with his leg, kicking the hrumm in the gut. The *pakh ma* fell back, staggering. Osrith pulled on the blood-wet head of the marble nape, freeing it from the dirt with a lurch. The hrumm pounced again, one claw slicing a gash across Osrith's temple while the other snagged in the tight links of his kin-made mail, missing his throat by a claw's breadth. Osrith hit the hrumm across the side of its head with the statue, and then again, and once more. It reeled, eyes losing focus, and Osrith pushed it over. For good measure, he brought the heavy chunk of stone down on the hrumm's head with all his remaining strength. Then twice more until its skull cracked. With a wet thud its face caved in and its tenuous grip on life was finally severed.

"Kassakan!" Osrith struggled to one knee, wavering, breathing hard. Blood streamed into his left eye, but he could make out Callagh, still on the ground, not far away. Calvraign was on his feet, approaching the shadowyn. Osrith blinked his eye clear. He thought another warrior joined the boy, but in another blink the fleeting image was gone. Osrith's hand groped in the grass for his axe, and his fingers closed around the haft with a measure of relief.

"Back to the Pits with you!" Inulf's sword was wedged into the shadowyn's torso. It wrapped him in a flurry of tentacles. He continued to rip at it with his bare hands, trying to pull apart its shadowy maw. "I'll drag ye back. Drag ye back to grey." The appendages constricted, stealing his breath. "Back," he grunted, lips curling to reveal his stained teeth, his muscles like corded steel. "Back to the Pits."

The shadowyn responded only by continuing its dirge, the alien words and dissonant tone grating on their ears. Its serpentine limbs constricted tighter, *tighter*. Inulf was silent now, every breath a snarl of defiance, no time for words, struggling against the shadowborn's embrace, struggling until there was a sickening, hollow snap. Inulf slipped into the pool with a quiet splash.

Osrith stood. The garden spun around him. He stumbled forward, dragging his axe behind. He grit his teeth, trying to bring the world into focus, but two images danced a dizzying dance in his eyes. In one, Calvraign attacked alone. In the other, his shadow joined him, a blur of nothing following his footsteps.

"Kassakan!" Osrith screamed again, his voice cracking and hoarse. He started to run, but his head swam and he stumbled. He fell to one knee.

Calvraign's sword was a flash against the dark of the shadowyn – his strokes measured but sure. The shadowyn lashed back, striking fast, but its limbs curled away just shy of landing a blow, as if burned by fire.

Not now, you old fool. Get up. Get up or he's done.

Osrith saw Hestan torn in two all over again. He watched Andrew burn. He could smell it, taste the acrid stench on his tongue. He staggered forward, but despite all the assurance of bards, determination alone could not heal wounds or win battles. He couldn't make it there. Not in time to help. Gathering his remaining strength, he heaved his axe back over his head in both hands. He took what steps he could, as fast as he could, and brought his arms forward, snapping them as they cleared his head, launching the axe end over end in a throw that would surely have won a ribbon at the Harvest Festival.

The axe hummed through the air and struck the shadowyn in the middle of its incongruous mass. It made a sound that Osrith hoped was a scream. It wavered. Callagh loosed an arrow into it, and it flinched again, to Osrith's surprise. Usually only kinsteel or bonded weapons could pierce a creature from the other side of the Veil. Such had always been his experience.

Osrith didn't frown on Oghran's fortune, however. If a girl wearing a bloodmask could harm the demons, so much the better. Callagh stood back, straddling Reime's corpse, a bloody arrow nocked at her cheek. Calvraign and his ghostly protector converged, forcing the shadowyn deeper into the pool and away from the motionless prince.

Osrith prepared to yell Kassakan's name one final time when the courtyard came to life in dancing lights and shimmering rainbow fire. He blinked into the light, searching for his friend. She was there, a silhouette of light dispelling the blackness that engulfed the pool.

And, for better or for worse, she was not alone.

Chapter Sixty-Two

Succession

CALLAGH lifted herself up on her elbows and tried to shake the buzzing rising behind her ears. It was not one voice calling to her now, or a dozen, but hundreds of them. She recognized them, somehow. The voices of the dead. The *madhwr-rwn*. The drone swelled into a crescendo, skittering through her thoughts like the screaming trees of a cicada summer, pushing at her, pulling at her, prying at her will.

Reime lay next to her, lifeless, still clutching the mess of his guts in his pale fingers. Calvraign rose unsteadily to his feet. Osrith yelled for Kassakan and rammed into the hrummish *pakh ma* in a careless crash of steel and flesh. They tumbled in the dirt. A dozen ravens clutched the tree limbs around her, eyes empty and black, staring. The largest cocked its head at her, waiting... Waiting for her.

To do what? she wondered.

"Ahn cranaoght," Reime whispered, eyes still blank in death.

"Ach," Callagh said. "I've not time for a pithy li'l talk, now."

"I've time for us both. Just enough."

"Bollocks."

"You showed me a kindness once. More than I deserved, and more than I give back, but this is my kindness to you: let her have him. Give the Grey Lady her due. The *madhwr-rwn* are the strength of those who've come before. We are less without him. *You* are less."

"Less o' me's more than enough," Callagh growled, scrabbling in the dirt for her bow.

"No, *ahn cranaoght*," said Old Bones. "Not for this."

Osrith had pummeled the life from the *pakh ma*, and Calvraign was heading for the battle at the reflecting pool. Inulf's raging had ceased, rather suddenly, and Callagh felt a darkness encroaching that she couldn't truly see, like the air thickening before a storm. She pulled an arrow from the cracked quiver at her feet. She jabbed it deep into her thigh and yanked it out with a grimace. More than blood spilled from that wound. She let the heat of life leave her, too, a measured bit, giving it over to the barbed steel of the arrow just as she'd surrendered a piece of herself to the amulet.

Not so hard, she thought. She stood, her injured leg bleeding but firm, and drew the bowstring to her cheek.

"Shush, now," she whispered with a tap of her toe to the corpse's head, and waited for a clear shot. Calvraign stabbed and sliced at the shadowyn. Ibhraign swatted away its counter-attacks. Osrith staggered forward, still calling for Kassakan, bloodied and dizzy. Callagh waited for her moment. The buzzing in her head screamed *bring him home,* but her aim on the shadowyn never wavered.

Osrith threw his axe, and it flew into the creature's mid-section. The shadowyn writhed in response, mouth agape, and Callagh loosed her arrow into the open maw. It screamed again when the shaft struck true, and her heart thrilled. Her elation was momentary, as neither Osrith's axe nor her well-placed arrow brought it down.

"You would empty yourself to slay this Darkness, and this is not the darkest yet you must face. Not if you wish to save our people."

Callagh took another arrow, hesitating. *As binding as what you give over.* If she needed to give herself over, *all of her*, she'd need more than a pin-prick, but something slower than a heart thrust. She'd need time to take aim and loose the arrow, at least.

"All of you to kill this shadowyn and save your boy. Only a bit of you to bring Ibhraign home and save the Cythe," Old Bones reasoned. "Then, together, you – *we* – the *madhwr-rwn*, may fight the coming Dark. But *only* with the strength of all who've come before."

"I'll save 'em both and the bloody world besides."

"Bold talk. Empty words. To slay the Dark would take what's left of you, and some of us besides. The price is too dear."

The dead man's words scratched at the gilt of her bravado. "I'll pay any price," she said, hiding her doubt behind her defiance. *What will you give up for him?* she asked herself.

"Ahh," sighed Old Bones. "Doomed by a little girl's heart where I thought a woman's will resided. I'm disappointed, *ahn cranaoght*. I thought better of you. But I am spent. The choices worth making are never easy ones, and I leave you to yours. Be quick, or She will make it for you."

So make your choice, then, she chastised herself. Calvraign fought without fail before her, sparing not a glance in her direction as he edged closer to the discarded body of the prince. *He's made his. He made it long ago.*

A brilliance erupted from the pool, and the Darkness shrank back, leaving her in shadow. The ravens took flight, launching into the air like a cloud of midnight. The droning of voices ebbed to a soft prickling behind her ears until only one remained.

Do what must be done, Callagh Breigh.

A tight ache squeezed her chest, followed by a familiar shortness of breath.

I can't force you to act, but I can keep you from acting. Do My will, or you'll do no one's.

"I'll not let Cal die," she hissed. "And I'll not betray his da' – not for you or anyone. That's not my way." *Keep to the old ways,* ahn cranaoght. The words repeated in her head as she sought an answer. *A bargain. The Old Gods love to make a bargain... a trade.* She steeled herself, a plan sputtering from her lips before she'd even thought it through to conclusion. "But... but I *can* take his place. I'll be your bloody Hand. Do you hear me? Take me for him."

You can't take back what's freely given, Callagh Breigh. You'll be bound by blood and deed.

"Aye, I will," Callagh nodded. "And so'll you. Release your claim on him, and I'll go willingly."

Reime's corpse twitched, jaw working over empty words. The amulet burned in warning. *Don't approve now, do ya? Leave me to it, Old Bones. Leave me to my choice.* Callagh grasped the talisman tighter, even as it felt that her hand was consumed by fire.

Life for life. Soul for soul. Duty for duty.

Callagh cut carefully through skin and vein but spared her tendon. She would need the tendon. Hot tears streaked down her blood-daubed cheeks as fresh blood flowed down her arm, warm and wet, but her heart beat cold and empty in her breast. Colder and emptier with every breath.

"Life for life. Soul for soul. Duty for duty."

Dazed and empty inside, she let the crimson shaft fly.

Two-Moons paused in the rainbow of the Wellspring's passage.

Never leap into battle, little Ebuouki man, when you may come quietly to victory at a walk. If time moves too fast, then slow it down. Slow...

Two-Moons concentrated on halting his momentum, bringing himself sailing to a gentle stop at the way-gate's edge while Kassakan came through before him. The hosskan had bound several spells together in Oszmagoth, before they entered the Wellspring, and she unleashed the first of them immediately. Lightning was a nice choice, he thought, as it both illuminated and burned things of the Dark. The shadowyn recoiled. Had the world tides not been turned, perhaps she might even defeat it without assistance.

He allowed T'nkh't'chk and a dozen of his *k'th't* egress from the Way. There were hrumm milling about still, and it would be best to silence any distractions.

A curious assortment of mortals, he thought, though he recognized only the hosskan's bond-slave from the Sunken City, laying about half-dead.

Two-Moons pulled at the wandering thoughts of his other self. "Osrith," he said aloud, in a whisper that echoed in the torn fabric of the Veil that surrounded them.

A prince, a Death-kiss'd girl, a be-shadowed boy, and the shade itself. The makings of a song, yes?

Two-Moons kept his gaze – *their* gaze – on the shadowyn itself.

"What is that? *There*. The bright sliver within the Dark?"

Jir'aatu's thoughts seeped together with his, the answer coming as an answer already known almost before he asked the question.

"The prince's... soul?"

No. Not so simple. Look carefully. They are within each other now, much as we, but not by choice.

"We must save it – save *him*. He's the reason we've come. Kassakan said-"

We must destroy it to destroy the shadowyn. It is weak – near death, but there is no time for sharp knives and steady hands. As a hammer we strike – swift and sure and with no escape.

"But..."

Decisions can only be made on the choices at hand.

"He is chosen. Last of the lion's line. Marked by prophecy."

Their prophecy cannot rule our action. The shadowyn will open the Gate, bring through the Pale Man, awaken the Sentinels. The Darkening you so fear will come, and swiftly. To secure their prophecy would ensure our doom. We crush it now, and sift through the dust.

Two-Moons closed his eyes. The truth of their agreement did not ease his discomfort.

"Worse than murder," he said. He could reconcile the killing of a man for such stakes. But rending a soul, extinguishing the immortal spark of a man's being... *Oblivion.*

We will live with it. We together can do this. We apart cannot. Together, we are strong, little Ebuouki man.

Two-Moons and Jir'aatu, of mind and body together, unleashed the Light.

~

When Calvraign first conceived his plan, it had seemed simple enough. Broad strategy had the luxury of not being mired in tactical detail. A powerful, legendary being had sent Osrith and the kin though a magical gateway – why not send for help by the same means? If an opponent was putting its deadliest piece into play, why not summon his own?

In theory, it seemed a simple choice. *Yes, why not pit a half-dead, half-crazy andu'ai qal against an abomination from the greylands,* he thought. Moving an avatar from the Light tier to challenge an avatar from the Dark tier was but a matter of getting the pieces to the right places at the right time. A quick maneuver. A well-played turn.

Life, as Vanelorn had pointed out, was not mastered like a game of *Mylyr Gaeal.* Despite the convenient metaphors one might derive from it, in a game, moving pieces into play meant just that – placing a piece of ivory or silver or polished wood onto a square of a game board to challenge another piece of ivory or silver or polished wood. Accounts were settled by rule or with the roll of a die.

As Greycloak warded off yet another attack from the shadowyn, the counterpoint to reality was all too obvious. Calvraign ducked a flailing appendage, edging ever closer to the prone form of the crown prince. He knew he was overmatched – without Greycloak's aid, he would be joining Inulf in the greylands – but his goal was not victory in battle. His goal was simply *victory*. It meant to use the magic of the aulden pool – and Hiruld's death seemed integral to that design.

One step closer.

The shadowyn was increasingly amorphous, less and less like the man it had resembled upon arrival, its form shifting as a shadow in flickering light. It struck at Calvraign, menacing him with the talons at the end of its remaining arms, and Greycloak deflected them as Cal dodged backward. It moved inexorably toward the prince. Calvraign matched its movement.

An axe flew into the shadowyn, and an arrow followed a moment later. It lurched away with an inhuman scream, and Calvraign redoubled his assault, pushing the shadowyn back from the prince another few precious steps. It reeled, arms poised like snakes.

And then the world exploded.

At first, when the light blossomed around him, Calvraign assumed it was the end of his strategy as well as his life. Death had come, or possibly something worse. But then the cave-manti swarmed into the garden – a more terrifying sight than he'd imagined – followed by Kassakan Vril, rising from the water in a nimbus of white fire. His plan was working.

Lightning flashed.

A murder of crows took wing.

Calvraign ran to the prince, hoping to drag him clear while Ibhraign guarded his flank. The shadowyn fell back, leaving smoking tendrils of itself behind, on the defensive from the hosskanae magic. An arrow streaked into the fray, just missing Calvraign. He grabbed the prince's tunic, but watched out of the corner of his eye as Greycloak clutched at a black-fletched shaft where it sprouted in his breast. He reached out, as if pleading, and then the shade dispersed, blown away like shifting mists on a mercurial breeze.

Greycloak was gone.

Calvraign looked back, thinking to find a hrummish archer to blame for the killing strike, but instead he watched in horror as Callagh lowered her bow. She was gravely wounded, pale and bloody, her eyes distant but remorseless. Calvraign's gut twisted. He wanted to scream at the sky, but he had no time, not even to wonder *why*. Without Greycloak's warding blade to stand between them, the shadowyn turned from Kassakan to Calvraign and the prince, its grey eyes like gathering storm clouds on a starless night.

Calvraign dragged Hiruld one-handed through the water toward the edge of the pool. It was not far, but the prince was not an easy burden. He was almost to the smooth lip of marble when the shadowyn overtook him. It poured over him, enveloped him, smothered him in darkness. No sword or claw pierced him, but Calvraign felt his life seeping out of his body, a warm current feeding a cold, depthless lake. He fought blind, lashing out with stubborn anger at the slow death that surrounded him. His sword-arm was leaden, his blows weak and clumsy. Tentacles encircled his legs and brought him splashing down into the shallow water, still clutching Hiruld's thick collar. The many arms crept up his torso like eels, a slithering cold that burned even through his garments and armor. Calvraign's breath sputtered, trying to suck in air, but none came.

You are mine, now, said the voiceless Dark, scratching at the underside of his flesh.

Calvraign could see nothing, feel nothing but the sense of falling away and the Dark collapsing in on him like an avalanche. It was everywhere. Enervating. Frigid. Suffocating. It was *in* him. *Becoming* him.

Just as it took Bellivue, Calvraign realized. The memory of that day filled him as if it was his own, but in broken flashes, as if he were viewing it through the pieces of a fragmented mirror. Suns-light streaming through the forest leaves; ambushing Vingeaux and Alain, rending them flesh and soul; Bellivue charging in to the rescue. It had taken him then, unawares. Slipped inside the herald knight and ate him from within, bit by bit, a quiet evil behind a noble face, biding its time. *Here all along. Waiting. Vaujn was right.*

The Dark pressed in further, crowding him out, pushing him into a corner of his soul as he became something *else*. The other would soon consume him entirely. It etched like acid, eating away the old as it prepared for the new.

Thoughts invaded him. Thoughts not his own. Memories.

Mejul. It was more than a name, it was an *identity* and all that came with it. Desires and depredations. Stratagems and betrayals. Desolation. Death. Lust. Most of all, it was lust. Not lust for power or pleasure, but for *life*. Life in the light. Under the suns. Escape from the Shadowyn King and the shackles that held him thrall in undernland. Calvraign felt the desperation as if it were his own. *Mejul, Shadowyn Lord of Sliithe Mhat. I am no mortal's thrall. I will live. I will bring the Darkening and I will live again in you.*

Calvraign fought to keep some vestige of himself alive as his very soul came under siege. He pictured his mother's face, recalled the sweet spice of Callagh's kiss, remembered the ride through Dwynleigsh with Lady Aeolil. Mejul swept it all away like scurrying insects before a fire. He tried reciting his histories, from Lucian to Erigor, Lalc Malcha to Cal Calha, the Blood Wars to the *Song of Andulin*, but the words drifted off, unthought and unsaid. Calvraign visualized the complex fingerings of Spring Suite on the frets of his gwythir, trying to form the patterns of the phrases, build them into sections and movements, to see the line of melody as it sang through chordal changes, but it all collapsed into confused and meandering fragments.

And so good Sir Gullimer, Gullimer Sir, was stuffed in dough and baked today.

The tongue-tripping verse came naturally, its nonsense defying dissolution, persevering against Mejul's incursion. Calvraign felt the barest tingle of sensation, a warmth like the glowing peat bricks of a hearth fire. He clung for a moment more to the life that the darkness thieved away.

I command this flesh, Mejul's presence insisted, not deafening or angry, but calm, inevitable, like the cold of a moonless night. *Mine*. The Dark ripped a new piece from Calvraign, tearing and then twisting in the open wound, and then ripped more still. *Mine*, it demanded again, a hint of anger like the threat of dawn.

Oh, good Sir, good, good, Gullimer Sir, with gooseberries and a goose, they say.

The dreamstone hung heavy about his neck, dragging him down, beating in place of his silenced heart. Where Calvraign had striven to rise above the bogsand of the Dark, it pulled him down through the deepest mire of the Dark and out the other side. The comforting heat spread, diffuse but expanding. He huddled in the glow, and felt a sting in his fingertips, then his arms, his feet, and on to his legs.

In good Sir Gullimer's Pie, they say, good, good Sir Gullimer's Pie!

The pain, for all that it hurt, was still *sensation*, and Calvraign clung to it. The more sensation that burned through his nerves, the warmer the comforting fire, the brighter the kindling light, the stronger his failing spirit. Dim flickers returned to his vision, a roaring filled his ears, and the dreamstone pulsed with a fiery drumbeat on his chest.

Good sir, good, good, good, Sir Gullimer... ,

Calvraign knew he wasn't going to defeat the shadowyn with a song, but the longer he could forestall his demise, the better his chances of finding survival. Or more likely, of survival finding him.

... good Gullimer Sir, good Gullimer, Gullimer... .

Mejul flinched from a flash of lightning, and its grip on Calvraign melted away with the fading rumble of thunder. The darkness retreated, and warmth and life returned. Calvraign collapsed, breathless. Kassakan sagged. Behind the hosskan, steam rose from the surface of the water, taking shape in a monstrous form twice the size of any human. Gaping mouth. Needle teeth. Lambent oval eyes marred by the thinnest sliver of pupil.

Qal Jir'aatu.

In his wildest daydreams, even as they formed into his wildest *plans*, Calvraign had never imagined that he would be relieved to witness the arrival of an andu'ai on the battlefield, but relieved he certainly was. Jir'aatu raised his arms to the sky, and sang a note like two voices at once, hovering somewhere, atonally, in the vicinity of a dominant fifth. White-hot fire blossomed between his hands, pulsing whiter and hotter with each word.

Mejul wrenched Hiruld from Calvraign's grasp. It roared – a deafening wail – and ripped open the chest of the crown prince. It discarded the corpse with a splash, and dark clouds of blood billowed into the water from the ragged wound. The twitching organ erupted in black fire in the shadowyn's hand. The flames spread down the length of its arm and writhing body to ignite the aulden pool in cold-burning darkness.

Jir'aatu brought his arms down like an executioner swinging a heavy blade, and the Light met the Dark in a violent explosion.

Calvraign screamed as the blackfire burned around him, but the dreamstone was aglow in pearlescent light, and its thin sheen stood between him and the Dark. It could not spare him the pain, but it did spare him gruesome death. He was thankful to Agrylon for that, if nothing else. Calvraign rose, struggling forward as the undertow dragged at his legs, clutching his sword with both hands.

Hiruld's heart was pumping in the dark fist of the shadowyn, and the darkness blackened with every pulse, pushing back against the falling sky of Jir'aatu's magic.

Calvraign dragged himself forward one more step. One more. He raised his sword.

An arrow whistled past his shoulder, close enough that he felt the wind of its passing on his cheek.

"For Ibhraign!" Callagh shouted. "And for the bloody *madhwr-rwn!*"

The arrow struck the flaming heart, and it tumbled from the shadowyn's grasp, a dead blackened thing. The white fire pressed down on the faltering black flames. Mejul shrank bank. Calvraign sprang forward, driving his blade into the grey shifting eyes of the shadowborn with all the strength he could muster.

An aurora of light and fire consumed the garden.

It was still in the courtyard. And all was quiet.

Calvraign floated in the aulden pool, senseless, trying to blink away the blooming flowers of color that flickered in his vision.

"Well, now," Osrith said, wading out to him and wincing with every step. The right side of his face was swelling like a summerfruit, and blood still streamed from the lacerations on his temple. His obvious pain did little to temper his sarcasm. "That didn't go too badly, after all."

"Is it over?" Calvraign moaned.

"No," Kassakan replied, smoke still curling from her blackened scales. She cocked her head, sniffing the air. Her eyes enveloped him in soothing blue-green. "I'm afraid that it's only just beginning."

Osrith helped Calvraign to his feet, and together they stumbled out of the pool and onto one of the nearby benches. Calvraign looked around at the devastation of the once-placid garden as Osrith examined him for serious injury. One of Inulf's blue-cloaked men survived. Two of Foss' squad, and Foss himself, holding his face together with one hand, tended by Markus. The cave-manti were skittering across the ground and crawling up the walls. One of them was scalping the fallen *pakh ma*.

"You'll really want to watch those open-ended questions," Osrith was saying. "She'll jump in with a platitude or some profound sounding piece of nonsense any chance she gets. *It is only the beginning,*" he mocked. "Who else can say that and not sound like a damn fool?"

"Brohan," whispered Calvraign. Saying the master bard's name helped burn the fog from his thoughts. *Brohan is safe at the tourney-field. And Aeolil.* He blinked. *And the king,* he added belatedly. *Gods. We really did do it.* As the world came back into sharper focus he held up his hand to catch Osrith's in a firm but gentle grip.

But Hiruld is dead, he reminded himself, staring at the ripples traversing the bloody pool. *The cost of present victory may be our ultimate defeat.*

"I'm fine," Calvraign assured his man-at-arms. Osrith's right eye had swollen shut, his left was half-red from burst blood vessels, and his face had progressed beyond the realm of summerfruit and well into the domain of a buttercup squash. "You... *You* might be dead. Gods Between, man. If Seth sees your face he may put it in a pie and bake it."

Osrith coughed out a wet chuckle that languished into a groan. "Fire might feel nice. I'll sit here and wait for him."

Calvraign shivered. He had to agree. The cold wind was hard at work freezing his waterlogged garments. He needed to get to shelter, or he feared he might freeze along with them, but he wanted, he *needed*, to find Callagh Breigh. First, to hold her and feel the warmth of her, alive and well. Safe. And then, to answer the question of why.

Why did you kill him?

The sick wrench of that betrayal marred the joy and relief of victory. Part of him wanted to believe that he'd misunderstood the sequence of events, confused as he was in the fog of battle. Or that she'd had a reason, *some* reason that made sense to her. Some reason, in the midst of the shadowyn's attack, to destroy the one person that had kept him alive through the fighting.

She wasn't under the redberry tree, where last he'd seen her standing, bowstring still humming its deadly tune. "Callagh!" he shouted.

Her eyes, he remembered. *Her eyes were certain sure. Whatever moved her, it was no mistake.*

Calvraign searched her out near Reime's grey corpse, giving wide berth to the gargantuan insect gathering its trophy an arm-length away. Its companions were claiming similar tokens all around the courtyard. He tried his best to ignore the grisly work.

"Callagh!" he called out, but there was no answer. "Callagh!" he repeated.

A massive raven quorked, hopping between the branches of a tree, scattering blossoms in its wake. Calvraign watched the odd bird for a moment, and it emitted a series of loud shrieking calls the like of which he'd never heard in all his life. He approached, curious what would evoke such behavior, and stopped short when he saw the trail of blood and the body sitting there, propped against the tree trunk.

"Callagh!" Calvraign yelled again, but this time in desperation. *"Callagh!"*

Her head lolled toward him, pale as the snow. "Cal," she said, exhaling the word and then closing her eyes.

Calvraign stooped to her side, looking for the sword-stroke or the arrow that had laid her low. His fingers were cold and clumsy, and fumbled with the stiff fabric of her clothes.

"Ach," she said, her voice weak, "a little... late for that. Had yer chance."

"Where are you hurt, Callagh?"

She lifted her left arm, just a trifling bit. "Nice an' clean, " she said. "Saved 'im, though. Saved the both o' yous."

Calvraign pulled up her sleeve and stared at the long incision. She'd done her work too well.

"Kassakan!" Calvraign didn't recognize his own voice. He kept screaming until she arrived.

"Move aside," the hosskan said with a gentle nudge. "She's not left us, yet."

Calvraign moved back.

Kassakan placed one claw on Callagh's forehead, and one on her chest. The lizard growled from somewhere deep in her throat, an odd gargling warble, not quite melodic.

"No, don't," Callagh protested. "You can't."

"I *can*," assured Kassakan, confident rather than confrontational. The wound ceased weeping. The skin puckered together, pink and whole, as if it had been stitched by the king's surgeon.

"I gave my oath," Callagh was muttering under breath, as if in a fever, her head rolling from side to side. "Life for life. Soul for soul." Then she cried out, "I kept to the old ways! I *bloody* did."

"Her oath? To who?" Calvraign stared, blank and confused. "What's she on about?"

Kassakan ignored him, stroking Callagh's cheek as the pallor surrendered to reticent blooms of shy pink. "Aye," she soothed, nodding. "I can see the bindings in your tides. *Her* mark. You promised your life, Callagh Breigh, but that price cannot be paid until you die. And you aren't dead yet."

Callagh fell into a sleep, still murmuring, her chest rising in shallow but steady rhythm.

"Rest now. Be at peace," assured Kassakan. "If She wanted you, She'd have taken you."

Calvraign swallowed the congealing thickness in his throat. "I don't understand."

"You will have an abundance of time to work it all out, I'm afraid. We are alone on this island, wounded and tired and left with a ruin of burned and blackened wood floating where the bridge used to be. The smoke from the fires should alert the city, but with the ice flows, well, it may take a day or two to reach us in any numbers. If the keeps have not burned down, we should at least be sheltered and well provisioned. Although, I have it on good authority that the cave-manti are voracious eaters, so you may need Qal Jir'aatu to bring them home. Yes, there will be time. Time enough time for us to work out everyone's secrets."

Calvraign stared at his sleeping friend, incredulous. "She really is... Callagh is *madhwr-rwn*?"

"Yes, that's part of it, for her," agreed Kassakan. "She has made her pact, and she will bear the consequence of it. I am more intrigued with *you*."

"With me?"

"Aye, Sir Calvraign. With you. The sorcery Agrylon wove was both subtle and sublime, but it is unraveling, thread by thread, and slipping from the loom. Be it the turning of the tides or the shadowyn's dark magic, his subterfuge is undone. For me, at least, I begin to see..." Her nostrils flared as she sniffed the air between them. "Or perhaps, to *sense*, his hidden truths. I may also understand, perhaps, why they remained so well hidden."

Calvraign sighed. "Blood and ruin," he said, and then in growing irritation, "*What?* What does that bloody wizard want with me, by all the Gods Between?"

"He will want you to save him, of course. To save all of us." Kassakan's opalescent gaze fell onto him, comforting him, even as she terrified him more with every word. "Calvraign, I believe that with the death of Prince Hiruld..." She paused and rested a comforting claw on his shoulder. "Your Highness, I'm afraid that *you* are the last of the lion's line."

POSTLUDE

Dieavaul drank deep from the Symbian vintage. It was dry, like his mood, a robust barrel-aged red with a smoky finish. That seemed fitting, he supposed. He set down his goblet and tapped one finger against the half-empty decanter, his eyes distant and his thoughts wandering.

Disappointing, he thought. The Ceearmyltu broken. The humans of Dwynleigsh reeling. The crown prince dead. *So very close to perfect.* But Mejul faltered at Meyr ga'Glyleyn, and the Darkening languished, underfed, only a flicker of its potential flame spoiling the sacred waters. *And Lombarde. Lombarde lost the Codex.*

The audience hall was empty but for himself and the Undying King. It was dark, as Malagch preferred, and uncomfortably cold. Dieavaul pondered the triangular obsidian table and the likeness of the continent mapped out on its shiny surface. He watched as his breath plumed in the cold air and then spread like an ominous fog over the figurines that represented the deployment of generals and armies on the fields of battle.

"Very disappointing," he said aloud. "But I will take a disappointing victory over an accomplished defeat."

"You will *have* to," Malagch said. "As will we all."

The Pale Man considered the statement as he sipped his wine. "If it were so easy to orchestrate the conquest of the eastern realms, you'd have done it already."

Malagch nodded. "So you never tire of reminding me."

"It's a good start to a war. A nice beginning to their end." Dieavaul swirled the wine in his goblet. "Let's not distract ourselves over every lost opportunity. On balance, we gained much and lost little."

"Mejul," reminded Malagch. "The Codex."

"Mejul's failure is more lamentable than his destruction." Dieavaul shrugged. "But the codex," he said, his smooth porcelain skin wrinkling in a scowl, "is not an easy loss to suffer. Lombarde will answer for that."

"Punishing the already-dead cannot accomplish much."

"You have reason enough to hope so," countered Dieavaul. "But I find ways to motivate my thralls. Death is no easy escape from me."

Dieavaul raised a hand and opened the great double doors of the chamber with a nudge of well-placed kinesis. A *graomwrnokk* waited there, and turned to acknowledge its master. It entered the audience hall, dragging a thin, naked woman across the polished black floor. She didn't struggle. It threw her at the foot of the table and departed.

"Mercy, lords," she pleaded. "Mercy!"

The woman was half-starved, pale and sickly, her face drawn and gaunt. Dieavaul remembered her when she'd been beautiful, perhaps two years gone. Proud and fierce – defiant. Her hair, once a flow of fiery red that reached half-way down her back, shorn now to bloody stubble on her scalp. Her lips, once full and red and quick to pinch a suggestive smile, were blistered and broken. She was bruised and scraped from head to toe, from beatings and worse than simple beatings. That light in her eyes was gone now. Gone for a year, at least, replaced only by desperation. One by one, she had done every thing she had sworn she would never do. That and more, to please her tormentor. Not for a promise of gold, or freedom, or restoring her to her once proud station. Simply for the hope of a quick death. To end her own suffering.

She wanted to know about power. Dieavaul smiled. He had enjoyed breaking her, and keeping her broken. *She had learned.*

He would miss her.

The Pale Man stood and drew *ilnymhorrim*.

"M… Master," she stuttered, eyeing the bonesword warily.

"At last, my sweet – your reward."

She shook. Not from fear, but from hope. Hope that he would end it, finally. He had played this game with her many times before. She had nothing left to lose but her soul, and she was so mad now that even that she would give to end her suffering. Dieavaul hated for it to end. And to end in this way – with release instead of subjugation.

The scales must balance, he thought, resigned, and he carved the first sigil on the flesh between her breasts. She screamed as the sword both cut and burned her. Dieavaul couldn't spare the attention to enjoy her pain. He focused on the inscriptions, forging the new soul-chains with perfect lines of *iilariish*. She endured, her eyes brimming with tears.

When he'd finished, she lay sobbing and quivering at his feet, blood pooling on the polished black floor from her elegant wounds. Dieavaul tilted her chin upward with the tip of his sword to meet his smiling gaze.

"What good will he do you in that sad husk of a creature?" Malagch asked. "Why not another warrior? I've plenty of those."

POSTLUDE

"Sometimes you pit strength against strength." Dieavaul lowered the point to her neck, just above the breastbone. "Sometimes you pit strength against weakness." He pressed the razor tip into her flesh until a fresh bead of blood dribbled down her emaciated torso. "Rarely, you may even pit weakness against strength to great effect."

"Please," she whispered.

"I am giving you death," the Pale Man assured her. "But even in death, this flesh will serve me. By dying now, you will destroy everything you ever loved. But ..." He took a deep breath, searching out the strangled essence of Lombarde where he writhed in the Bone Tower, calling it back to the sword which had once taken his life. "... I *will* spare you. If you but ask, I will spare you, and the doom of the world will not be your doing."

"Please..."

The sound she made could have been a shuddering sigh, or a wracking sob, or some combination of those things. It was hard for Dieavaul to label that noise of absolute disgust and desperation, of surrender and cowardice, when all the ideals and dreams of a once-kind heart burned away to ash. But hearing that illusive sound filled him with satisfaction. It was the ultimate testament to his power over her and, one day, the world. *What a sound that will make.*

"Kill me, Master."

Dieavaul drove the sword home, slaying her instantly, freeing her soul with the knowledge that she chose that fate, without regard to the fate of the world. As he withdrew *ilnymhorrim* from her still-warm corpse, he spoke the word of unlife.

She convulsed, flailing in the mire of her own blood, and then a shadow passed over her, into her, and she was still. The magescript glowed a deep crimson, like hot coals under her skin. She took a shuddering breath.

"Master," the revenant croaked, even as the Dark seeped into her, closing her wounds slowly, painfully. Her eyes flickered and opened. "How may I serve?"

"You may serve me by recovering what you carelessly lost," Dieavaul said evenly. "But *first*, you may serve the Baign and his men in any way that they'll have you, until you understand the cost of your failure. The cost of failing me."

Lombarde's shaking hands felt at the contours of his new body, head bowed. "Master, I... Please..."

Dieavaul called in the guards and wiped his blade on the scruff of Lombarde's new scalp before sheathing it. He returned to the table and poured himself another cup of wine.

"Clean her up and give her to the Baign. He'll find some use for her." Dieavaul sat at the table. "And summon Azgur and the other thars."

Now, he thought. *Now, we go to war.*

❦

End of Book One

Acknowledgments

Thank you to my family, both immediate and extended, for your love and support and for the unceasing encouragement of my writing since the notion of telling stories first took hold of me.

To my wife Sigrid, who has indeed suffered long and hard through the glacial pace of this novel's progress. She has supported me, believed in me, been appropriately frustrated at me when I am a doofus, and occasionally allowed me to stay on as her shiftless *kept man* – I love you! **To my daughters Iliana and Sabine**, I love you too, more than you will ever know, and *even more* than I embarrass you. Really.

To Mom and Dad, for instilling in me a love of reading and writing and all things fantastic. Dad sat us on his lap and read *The Hobbit* and *The Lord of the Rings*, complete with pipe and smoke rings. Mom, although pipe-less, introduced us to *Narnia* and *The Hardy Boys* and many other lunch-time reads too numerous to mention.

To my brother Stephen, my partner in imagination. His hand-me-down books and encyclopedic knowledge of everything he's ever read filled in the foundations of my science fiction and fantasy lexicon. He introduced me to *Thomas Covenant the Unbeliever* and *The Many-Colored Land*, among others, and explained the intricacies of both the Marvel and DC universes. Especially *Batman*. Lots and lots of *Batman*.

To all my teachers, especially Mr. Patterson from the Dundalk Grammar School; Mrs. Sharon from Sutton Park in Dublin; and Mrs. Caron, Mrs. Lasky and Mrs. Skillman from Beechcroft. They taught the craft of writing, above and beyond the established curriculum.

To Ireland and the town of Dún Dealgan, for being my home for three green and misty years, and being so full of crumbling forts and round towers and words with too many consonants. I spent three years of my life nestled in the Mourne Mountains, and everyone told me how special the experience would be. I rolled my eyes at the time. Damn if they weren't right about it, though.

To my friends, co-workers and bosses who helped keep me somewhat sane in the modern workplace and may or may not have lived with me and played lots of video games. Also, to the less-than-ethical bosses and executives I've worked with and reported to – you made it easy to imagine life under aristocratic systems of government, and to one guy in particular – thanks for demonstrating the nature of betrayal so personally and explicitly. You suck, but that really helped.

Thank you **to Nicolas Lee and Aaron Thacker**, my beta readers, for your valuable input and taking the time to read and opine about this monster. It is appreciated more than you can know (although I'm hoping that mentioning it in the Acknowledgments pages will supply some credible evidence of this thanks). And to **Pat Burris and Todd Creamer**, my alpha readers. Todd rampaged through the earliest versions of the manuscript, butchering adverbs and passive voice like a killing wind.

To music in general, and to **RUSH** specifically.

To Mike Nash for the amazing cover. I hope people *do* actually judge the book by it.

Lastly, but not leastly, to my editor, Thomas Weaver, who would never have let me include something like *"lastly, but not leastly"* in the actual text of the novel. Thank you. Your help in keeping me straight on grammar and punctuation, as well as general story-crafting and continuity, were invaluable. The banter was fun, too. See you at the next manuscript!

Made in the USA
Lexington, KY
05 June 2014